OBLIQUE JOURNEYS

TOM CORBETT

"All in all, this book surpassed my expectations with exceptional characterization, a moving and perfectly paced plot, and also evoking emotions and covering topics that we have ignored.

—Nela

"An awe-inspiring read. 5 out of 5 stars."
—Jilantin

"Very compelling read about a tumultuous time in our history. I really enjoyed the character development and style of writing."

—DL

Reader reviews of the previous release of *A Clueless Rebel*:
*Amazon reader reviewers gave this work
an aggregate rating of 4.9 out of 5 stars!*

"His book screams of honesty, wit, and candor. The book made me chuckle many times and was highly entertaining and an easy read. I have read several of Tom Corbett's books and have enjoyed them all."

—Laura

"Tom Corbett is a gifted storyteller. He pours raw honesty and cleverness into his writings that amuses and inspires you."

—Jengel 106

"Corbett does an excellent job of weaving his tale in a way that both inspires and amuses, heartens, and saddens."

—Arcadia

"Tom Corbett has perfect comedic timing. He knows when to drop a strong, hilarious punchline. Throughout the read, I laughed and simply smiled at Corbett's sense of humor."

—Jacque Izzo

"I absolutely love this book… like spending a week listening to my favorite uncle talk about life."

—Meg

"Never a dull moment and I found it hard to put down."

—CQuinn

"Very enjoyable read that keeps you turning the pages for more."

—Margaret Holley

"…a hilarious trip down memory lane but at the same time emotionally raw and brutally honest."

—DL

Selected Praise for the Author's Non-Fiction Works

"A wonderful first-person account of the ground-level of welfare reform in recent times. It was a momentous time for reform of the nation's welfare system and Corbett was in the thick of it. He relates what happened with a wry, self-deprecating of humor, but there are serious lessons to be learned…"

—Robert Moffitt, Ph.D.,
Professor of Economics, Johns Hopkins U.

"Tom Corbett exposes the reader to the raw reality of confronting our most difficult social issues in this engaging, compelling, yet witty book. He brings the doing of policy alive, going beyond the dry numbers to reveal the human side of the equation."

—Dennis Dresang, Ph.D.,
Professor of Public Policy, U. of Wisconsin

"…I found "Ouch. Now I Remember" to be a witty yet edifying read, riddled with some funny moments… with many of them making me laugh out loud. I enjoy his writing style, it was comforting yet candid, like listening to a respected relative recount their own life with unabashed honesty."

—Pacific Book Review

"…throughout the memoir, Corbett's prose remains engaging, consistently mixing insight with the familiar jokes that one would from a close friend. A thoughtful memoir about life and politics told in a (n} … endearing style."

—Kirkus Review

"…the emergence of Corbett's humanistic world view…gives Ouch, Now I Remember intellectual gravitas. Corbett imparts an enormous amount of wisdom and humanity."

—Clarion Review

"If you genuinely want to understand how public policy works, read this book. Corbett's descriptions about how laws and programs are developed gives readers a real take away—genuine insight into the discipline of public policy."

—Mary Fairchild, Senior Fellow
National Conference of State Legislatures

"Corbett's stories from the front lines of policymaking, like All Quiet on the Western Front or The Things They Tarried, provide great insight into the way the world actually works, not what the generals or policy planners think is happening."

—Matt Stagner, Ph.D. Policy Fellow
Mathematica Policy Research, Inc.

"*The Boat Captain's Conundrum* is a winning performance."

—Forward Clarion Book Review

"Corbett takes a topic often shrouded in numbers and dense writing and turns it into an intellectual, yet conversational memoir."

—U.S. Review of Books

"Corbett's reflections, woven together with great insight and humor, transform public policy from a class that is boring and mundane to a career that can be engaging and germane."

—Karen Bogenschneider Ph.D., U. of Wisconsin

"I enjoy his writing style, it was comfortable yet candid, like listening to a respected relative recount their own life with unabashed honesty."

—Pacific Book Review

Reader Reviews For The Author's
Earlier Fictional Works

"Reading Tom Corbett's work will have you impressed and awed by his superb literary skills . . . the book is so engaging and captivating that one can only wish to read more from this author. *Ordinary Obsessions* will have you engrossed . . . as the plot is perfectly executed, and the story line flows well."

—Aaron

"The author honestly does a wonderful job of making the reader relate to each character and fall absolutely head over heels for each one and their journey through the book! With politics, power, religion, family drama, romance, and cultural struggle, this book exceeds expectations. I look forward to more by this author and cannot wait for the next gem he writes."

—Veronica White

"Fast moving political drama that will keep you turning the pages. I do not read a lot of political drama novels, but I could not put this one down. Ordinary Obsessions by Tom Corbett is engaging . . . it pulls you in with the emotions of the characters."

—Karen A.

"The author's writing style flows naturally and . . . the story develops with perfect pace. There is not one thing I would change about it."

—M.C.

"This book is inspirational as it relates to knowing ourselves better, understanding the world we want, and more so the things that most of us would love to do in life. Corbett's polished writing style alone will get you hooked but his sense of humor and passion for writing will keep you reading."

—Trizah Kelvin

"The author's writing style is so unique that I love to read his works. I get lost among the pages so easily."

—Carleen Makivich

"I . . . have always been impressed with his talents . . . and found myself drawn into each character's struggles and triumphs."

—Stacy E. Vance

"An awesome read! Five out of five stars!"

—J. Lantin

"An utterly compelling narrative of two disparate families separated by culture and experiences who come together by circumstances and serendipity."

—Amazon Customer

"It is easy to understand why this book comes so highly acclaimed. And the author's background as a professor of social sciences really comes into play . . . he has masterly shared the plight of two families who could not look more different."

—Erin P

"Tom Corbett's *Palpable Passions* is the perfect combination of fact and fiction as it educates its readers about current events in our world today."

—Lillie S

"*Palpable Passions* is truly a great read that will leave you feeling empowered and determined to make a difference in the world in your own way. *Highly recommend* everyone pick this up."

—Kimmy 4077

"I highly recommend (Felicitous Fates) if you love a book that keeps you guessing and questioning throughout."

—Hayley Branna

"(Felicitous Fates) will keep you riveted ... to the end. Thought provoking and unbelievable."

—G. F. Bard

"(Felicitous Fates is not a light read; you will really have to think. It kept me in the dark throughout."

—Amazon Customer

<h1 style="text-align:center">Other Books by the Author[1]</h1>

A Clueless Rebel (Revised edition, Papertown Press, 2022)[2]

A Wayward Academic: Reflections from the policy trenches (Revised edition, Papertown Press, 2021)[3]

Evidence-Based Policymaking: Envisioning a New Era of Theory, Research and Practice (2nd Ed.) with Karen Bogenschneider (Routledge Press, 2021)

Felicitous Fates (Papertown Press, 2021)

It Seemed Like a Good Idea at the Time (Revised edition, Papertown Press, 2020)[4]

Confessions of an Accidental Scholar (Revised edition, Papertown Press, 2020)[5]

Ordinary Obsessions (Papertown Press, 2019)

Palpable Passions (Papertown Press, 2017)

---

1   *Choices* was originally published as *Tenuous Tendrils* in 2016 by Xlibris Press.

2   Originally published as *Ouch, Now I Remember* in 2015 by Xlibris Press and rereleased under the current title by Hancock Press in 2018.

3   Originally published as *Browsing through My Candy Store* in 2014 by Xlibris Press and rereleased under the current title by Hancock Press in 2018.

4   Originally Published by Hancock Press in 2020.

5   Originally published as *The Boat Captain's Conundrum* in 2016 by Xlibris Press and rereleased under the current title by Hancock press in 2018.

Return to the Other Side of the World with Mary Jo Clark, Michael Simmonds, Katherine Sohn, and Hayward Turrentine (Strategic Press, 2013)

The Other Side of the World with Mary Jo Cark, Michael Simonds, and Hayward Turrentine (Strategic Press, 2011)

Evidence Based Policymaking: Insights from Policy-Minded Researchers and Research- Minded Policymakers. With Karen Bogenschneider (Routledge Press, 2010)

Policy into Action. With Mary Clare Lennon (Urban Institute Press, 2003)

OBLIQUE JOURNEYS

ACKNOWLEDGMENTS

I want to thank Matt Lancaster from Papertown Press and Mike Middleton, formerly from Hancock Press, for their encouragement and support along with Zoe Ryans for her technical help.

I also want to thank Ed Heinzelman, David Schoengold, Hilla Zerbst, Ann Schroeder, and Margaret Holley for looking over early drafts and still encouraging me to continue.

A DEDICATION

When my father passed in 1987, I went through his effects. I found a newspaper article on him from the 1930s. It was about the high school basketball team on which he played. When asked what he wanted to do as an adult, his dream was to become a journalist. Of course, as a poor Irish kid whose own father had been institutionalized with a mental disorder, college was out of the question. He did factory and janitorial work in the real world, at least after a youth spent close to the wild side of life. But he was a wonderful storyteller with a quintessential Irish wit. He bequeathed such blessings to me, though he was likely unaware of his generosity. Little did he realize that these were gifts I would value far beyond any material treasures he might have passed on, had he managed to accumulate such things. Bequests of the soul are the most unforgettable currency of all.

My unexpressed dream as a young urchin was to be a writer, which is reasonably close to journalism. Thus, I credit my dad for this long-hidden passion. As a small kid in the immediate post–World War II era, I was raised in a relatively disadvantaged, working-class neighborhood. My friends wanted to be cowboys or athletes or maybe astronauts, perhaps with the occasional would-be gangster in the lot. I, on the other hand, wanted to write great works of literature or at least something others might want to read. I did not share this dream with the other kids since that would have led to much derision and perhaps a whipping or two. Later, during my two years of heat and isolation as a Peace Corps Volunteer in rural India, I wrote a novel. I think my first effort was quite good, but it remained stuffed in drawers under a pile of underwear while I went about the adult tasks of making a living as an academic and policy wonk at a top research university, a vocation I enjoyed immensely. Eventually, this literary masterpiece was lost, perhaps discarded with soiled boxer shorts. My academic and policy careers, however, helped me achieve one sacrosanct childhood goal … avoiding all adult work that involved any heavy lifting whatsoever. Some dreams do come true.

Unlike my dad, I was fortunate enough to go to college. It was easier by the 1960s as opposed to his youth. It turned out that I enjoyed this intellectual environment so much that that I pretty much remained hidden within the bosom of the academy for the remainder of my adult life, with only some brief lapses. I majored in psychology as an undergraduate since that was the strongest department at Clark University, where I enrolled after a brief try for sainthood in a Catholic seminary. I had no idea at all what I wanted to do in life other than pursue a vocational path that did not demand real work. That lack of direction did not matter. What did, however, was the fact that my mind and imagination exploded within the intense cauldron of ideas that was Clark University in the tumultuous sixties. It was an unforgettable era and some of that feel has found a way into the subsequent pages.

While my secret ambition of being an author remained buried, it never died; Our early aspirations can be tenacious. As an undergraduate, I recall running into my English literature professor at the lunch counter one day. I confessed my Walter Mitty dream of becoming an author to him, something I rarely revealed for fear of the jocularity that was bound to follow. He was kind enough not to laugh out loud, though I'm certain he did roll his eyes a bit. He then asked me a question I've never forgotten. *Could I tell a good story?* I didn't have an answer at the time, so stood mute. According to him, that was the one and only key to the kingdom. Over the subsequent years I wrote many reports, journal articles, book chapters, and a few academic books and memoirs. But his query never left me, can I create a good story, one that others might want to read? When I sat down a few years ago to compose my first fictional work (second if you count that manuscript lost amidst soiled underwear), I felt it was time to answer that question at last. If I failed, no problem. I now was way too old to care much if people laughed. In any case, I already had escaped a career of real work, so my life had turned out fine. Besides, we write for ourselves, not others. I do at least.

In the pages that follow, I give you an updated version of my first novel, *Choices*. It is written for my dad, who bequeathed to me the precious gift of Celtic blarney. It would have been nice had he included his good looks and thick, dark hair but there it is.

These are the times that try men's souls. The summer soldier and the sunshine patriot will, in this crisis, shrink from service of their country, but he that stands by it now, deserves the love and thanks of man and woman. Tyranny, Your purpose in life harder the conflict the more glorious the triumph. What we obtain too cheap, we esteem too lightly; it is dearness only that gives everything its value. Heaven knows how to put a proper price upon its goods.
— Thomas Paine, The American Crisis,
December 23, 1776

We would rather be ruined than changed
We would rather die in our dread
Than climb the cross of the moment
And let our illusions die.

—W. H. Auden

Your purpose in life is to find your purpose and give your whole heart and soul to it.

—Buddha

CONTENTS

Prologue I

Chapter 1: Day 1 – VANCOUVER (4 decades later). 1

Chapter 2: Day 1 - Daybreak 22

Chapter 3: Day 1- Connie... 41

Chapter 4: Day 1- Late Afternoon............................... 54

Chapter 5: Day 2 – Glimpses Of A Life 67

Chapter 6: Day 2 – The Dinner 81

Chapter 7: Day 3 - Morning 93

Chapter 8: Day 3 - Victoria...................................... 127

Chapter 9: Day 3 - Evening 161

Chapter 10: Day 4 – Morning Musings 190

Chapter 11: Day 4 – The Family Gathers..................... 214

Chapter 12: Day 4 - Evening 243

Chapter 13: Day 5 - Morning 263

Chapter 14: Day 5 – Retirement Surprise 284

Chapter 15: Day 5 – Reflections.. 300

Chapter 16: Day 5 – Connecting... 317

Chapter 17: Day 5 – Shadows Of A Revolution 331

Chapter 18: Day 6 – Early Morning 351

Chapter 19: Day 6 – The Road To Whistler................................ 380

Chapter 20: Day 6 – Whistler 400

Chapter 21: Day 7 – Before Dawn 426

Chapter 22: Day 7 – Daybreak 439

Chapter 23: Day 7 - Denouement... 463

Epilogue 491

About The Author 501

PROLOGUE

A young man, clearly of college age, drove cautiously through dark and empty streets. It was a raw, November morning, typical of late fall in New England. The sharp, biting air presaged a winter season about to arrive. Was it here already? So soon? Though a brief episode of unexpected icy rain had ceased, its quick passing had not eased the traveller's concerns about the journey he now contemplated. Large snowflakes were emerging from the blackness above, not a good omen. The going would be slow, impeded both by inclement weather and his own doubts. He should have paid more attention to the weather forecast. The temperature clearly was falling, as was his sense of conviction.

An inconvenient cold front had swept into the area, likely from Canada. Why had that surprised him? He had lived here all his life. He knew the ancient aphorism … don't like the weather here, wait an hour. On this morning, however, it did not bring a smile to his lips. Nothing did. *Would the snow accumulate? That would make it even tougher,* he thought. Perhaps he should wait for a more propitious moment. After all, what was so important about today. Would not tomorrow do, or next week, or some unspecified moment in an indefinite future? Then he laughed at himself. *So typical, so pathetically typical.* Besides, you could never predict the weather here. This impending storm had come out of nowhere, which often occurred in New England. All just might be fine in an hour or two, as Bostonians eternally hoped.

He peered ahead. A faint hint of light suggested itself on the eastern horizon, or was that merely the illumination from a nearby town? He needed a moment to think, just to make sure. *Did he want to do this? More critically, could he do this?* Touching the brake, the car barely slowed as it slid seamlessly over the slick surface before stopping when it bumped against the curb. His tires did not have much tread, that would make the trip an iffy undertaking in this weather. He had meant to replace them, but money was tight, and he needed all that he could save for his escape.

Yes, it was an escape, was it not? Suddenly, he felt claustrophobic, strangled by indecision. He opened his window to the bitter air that slapped him with abrasive indifference, an assault he barely noticed. The cold acted as a sense of sobriety, forcing him to calculate the immensity of what lie before him just one more time. There he sat, looking within. In that moment, he detached himself from all surrounding sensations, from all that the elements that wished to intrude upon his private moment.

It seemed just yesterday that he and a small band of true believers sat around a student apartment, the kind adorned with the omnipresent poster of Che Guevara watching over them. As usual, they argued the same points they had done so for week after week, month after month. These rebellious youth discoursed and debated on war, racism, social injustice, poverty, and mostly about the need for a revolutionary moment. These were the universal calls in an age where utopian dreams seemed palpable and substantive change possible. Hope survived among this small group of believers against all erosions of belief that inexorably emerged out of their daily experiences. In their eyes, the news was bleak and unforgiving … war and social conflict and minorities being lynched while their churches were torched, their futures violated.

For his small group, the Archibald MacLeish poem was prescient, *all was flying apart, the center could not hold.* The American dream felt like a cruel hoax, a delusion held closely in the plebeian dreams of conventional men and women, at least those they had appointed as ordinary and devoid of any perceptible imagination. Josh wondered if the Gods were being kind to his friends by not permitting this tiny collection of idealists to peer too far into the future. Were that possible, they might see themselves being swept into some final abyss by their own hubris and unexamined zeal. Even absent an apocalyptic revelation, an ominous foreboding hung in the air.

One of them, a wiry young man named Morris Greenstein, broke through the separate conversations and usual banter common to the gathering. Known as Mo to all, he was a natural leader whose permanently intense visage was framed by a crown of frizzy, brown hair. He spoke with an intensity that commanded attention and gave his words an aura of gravitas and authority. Those in his presence typically listened.

"Do you know what I heard from a guy who works for Senator Morse?"

"Of course not, we're not fucking clairvoyant." The insult came from an equally thin, though striking young woman with long, dark hair, sharp facial features, and ferocious eyes.

"Always the sweet words, Carla, no wonder all the guys are lined up to do you," the frizzy-haired one responded.

"Screw you." She muttered under her breath, cursing herself for letting him get to her once again. Yet, she waited with the others to hear what he had to say.

"He told me that Johnson had a recorded conversation with Senators Fulbright and Russell about the escalation in Nam. Get this, our esteemed President admitted that he knew that sending more American boys was a mistake, a huge one, but he feared that the Republicans would have his balls if he didn't do it. There you go, thousands of Americans and probably hundreds of thousands of Asians will perish because the toughest guy in Washington does not have the balls to say no, not even to the opposition no less. What is wrong with this country? Doesn't anyone have the *cojones* to stand up for what is so totally obvious to anyone who does not have shit-for-brains? Kennedy never would have allowed this to happen, but they took him out before he could set things right."

Jeremiah Joshua Connelly, universally known as Josh, sat on the opposite side of the circle. He watched his friend closely. They were unlike each other in many ways. The leader of this group was aesthetic and intense, invariably coiled while ready to explode with ideas and energy. Morris had a brittle intelligence out of which a cornucopia of ideas and emotions flowed with abandon. He could paint Picassos or Rembrandts with the medium of words, not colors, and elicit passions from others with his aura of commitment. He had little need for explicit exhortations and commands. His eyes bore into you when you came into his view, usually rendering any object of his attentions mute and compliant. This moment, however, might be different.

In contrast, Josh was tall and handsome with a physical presence honed on many an athletic field. He was blessed with those dark Irish good looks that women found seductive, if not irresistible. He also had a pair of pale blue eyes that further enhanced his prospects with the distaff side, all packaged in an easy demeaner that put others at ease. He was more thoughtful than his peers, considering ideas and causes with greater care than most of the impetuous youth about him. What mostly attracted others, though, was his easy manner and a lopsided smile. People were comfortable around him; They found his attitude reassuring and his words soothing. Even as he questioned their arguments or positions, he did so with a dollop of charm and a touch of wit, and of course that crooked smile of his. Yet, something often bubbled within, a core capable of eruption with the proper incentives. Those who looked closely enough sensed a deepness not evident to casual observation.

He spoke up in his calm voice. "Why are you surprised, Mo? We know the Democrats are paralyzed on the Commie question. They haven't recovered from McCarthy yet. If one puts an ism on the end of any word, the good American public will crap in their pants. Shit, we probably should change our national motto from '*in God we trust*' to '*in fear we cower.*' Piece of advice to all of you, invest in a toilet paper company like I did. In six months, I should have enough for my yacht." The crowd snickered at his words, less the meaning than the easy manner of expression. They always smiled no matter what he said.

Mo sighed. He tried not to show his irritation when his good friend undercut his purpose, as he sometimes did. He liked Josh, perhaps feeling a pinch of jealousy at the gifts that life had bestowed on his friend. In fact, he admired this glib Irishman even as he occasionally found his humor and easy manner off putting. "Fine, leave 'em laughing like always. Sometimes, though, you have got to suck it up and do the right thing, even if no one else understands. Jokes no longer will do the job."

"I get that, Mo." Josh backed off.

"Do you? We are trying to speak truth to those on the edge of insanity. Just think about that. During the worst moments of the Cuban missile crisis, every member of the Joint Chiefs argued for invasion, some for a pre-emptive nuclear strike. Every goddamn one of them wanted to escalate. How Kafkaesque is that? They virtually called Kennedy a traitor for holding out. That fat pig who headed the Air Force was the worst—he barely could contain his vitriol toward Kennedy."

"Lemay," Josh added.

"What?" Mo was thrown off by the interruption.

"General Curtis Lemay." That's the fat pig your thinking of."

"Right ... thanks. He wanted to nuke Russia pre-emptively and drop the goddamn A bomb in Nam to bail out the French in 54 when they were about to lose their colony there. My God, these so-called adults running the country would long ago have reduced our world to a cinder in an instant. And for what? Do they really think they are the mature ones? What a laugh. They are adults only in terms of age. That's it! Otherwise, they are like kids playing war in a sandbox except we all share that same sandbox. Letting them play their games might be fine but not when we're the collateral damage."

"Damn right," someone uttered.

"Kennedy didn't give in, though, and just may have saved mankind for what that's worth." The speaker's eyes came alive. "I'm so tired of talking. It is time to do something. We have become the real adults in the room, in the country, the ones who see things as they really are … without illusions. It is time to strap on a pair."

"And do what, for Christ's sake, blow up the Pentagon?"

The wiry one looked around the circle with his typical intensity. "Perhaps … someday. But tonight, tonight, I only ask for one thing. I want each of us to pledge our trust and fidelity to one another."

"Mo is right," added the intense young woman named Carla, already dismissing his insult to her. "Change does not happen just by asking. Take women's suffrage! That didn't come about by asking politely. Female activists had been asking for decades, since the mid-1800s. They got nowhere. Then Alice Paul stepped up. She disrupted Wilson's inauguration in 1916 as scores of her followers were beaten and arrested. But she kept the pressure on until it just became too hard for Woodrow to hide behind the war that he got us into. It was only then that women finally got the vote. Not by being nice, but by accepting nothing less than victory … by being total pains in the asses. They went out and took it."

Mo picked up the argument. "Carla's right this time!"

"*This time?*" She thought but let him continue.

"We need to go beyond being irritating students. I'm tired of being ignored. No, time to do much more … create some real waves. So, I'm asking each of you to join me." With that, he put his hand out in front of him and looked about the room. "If you're prepared to escalate, to up our game, put your hand on mine. If not, just leave. I'll understand, we all will understand. What I'm asking is great, and not everyone can or should go there. Joining me now means breaking the law, risking your futures and your freedom. I can't say how exactly, just trust me. If you stay in this room, you will be part of history. The trajectory of your life will be altered, maybe for the better, maybe not. I offer no guarantees other than the opportunity to fight for a better world." He paused to look directly at each person about him. "Again, I do not expect this commitment from all of you. This is big and personally dangerous. If you choose to leave, all I ask is that you forget about this night."

"How can we commit if we don't know what you're talking about?" someone queried.

Mo looked surprised at the question, as if he had not expected it. "Commitment is everything, the details are incidental. Remember that. If you need specifics, you are not ready. You must believe in what we want to achieve. This is a choice about your conscience, your dedication to building a future we can embrace fully … whatever that means and whatever it takes. It is a huge undertaking, perhaps the biggest of our lives. Without question the biggest! But never forget that Chinese proverb that Kennedy favored … a journey of a thousand miles starts with the first step. Time for our first step … a pledge to one another. Then we can plan, but only among the committed."

An athletic-looking young man with a square face, stocky body, and short reddish-brown hair stirred. All looked in his direction as he stared directly at Josh for several moments, as if a question begged to be released and advice sought. Then, it was as if he realized that this choice was his alone. Without a further word, he slowly rose, murmured *"sorry,"* and exited the room with an expression etched to his face that none could quite explain. Was it contempt, sadness, anger, regret? It would be a matter of debate in future days.

"Peter, no!" Josh issued so softly no one heard. Then, for a moment, he rocked as if he meant to join him. A kind of inertia kept him rooted in his spot, however, and he settled back into his position. He looked about furtively to see if anyone had noticed his tiny movement. One after another, they shuffled forward to put a hand on the growing number of symbolic commitments. Only Josh held back. He looked intently at the wiry leader. They had been together so long, but this was a watershed moment. He just knew it. It was as if playtime was over, childhood complete. In this moment, you were crossing over into the unknown. He felt all eyes on him as he hesitated until his body seemed ready to explode from the tensions within. Then, slowly inching forward, his hand found the top of the pile. He hoped no one noticed the imperceptible tremor in his fingers.

Now, these many weeks later, on a cold morning in the inky void, Jeremiah Joshua Connelly realized that further dialogue was useless, both the endless discussions with others and, more critically, the continuous debate within his head. There was no easy answer. He had been thinking about what he should do ever since that night when he pledged himself to this group. In the weeks that followed, the early pranks and peaceful protests had turned into stronger actions that had crossed over the line to outright felonies. Things were escalating quickly, getting beyond his control. It was only a matter of time before the law caught up with them or, worse, someone died. In his own mind, he could accept his own demise, some nights that outcome seemed comforting in a way. The thought of taking another's life, however, was beyond his comprehension. Every soul has its boundary. *C'est tout finis,* he mused.

Time was running out for him on that cold wintry morning, or so it felt. He would either escape or submit fully no matter the cost. Half-measures were no longer acceptable, not even to himself, especially to himself. There was a problem, though. There was no analytical method for making such a choice. By disposition, he was a rational man. Here, and now, reason appeared useless. Feelings of loyalty, outrage, and principle swirled through his head. This conundrum was beyond conventional calculation. There were no acceptable metrics for comparing relative magnitudes among abstract dimensions like emotions, values, principles, and normative dispositions that waged an endless war in his mind and heart. How do you assess the comparative pulls of loyalty to friends against the specter of blood-letting violence or a cherished cause against a likely prison term? What price can be put on a destroyed life, his and others? He wanted to scream but bolted from the car instead.

He stood in the cold searching the faces from that not long-ago night. While they had gone over to the darker side only weeks ago, everything that had happened since seemed like suspended moments belonging to a previous life. Who were those leading him to the abyss?

The visage of Mo, their natural leader, appeared before him. This young man had a charisma that attracted others, a trait emerging from his ancestral pedigree. His grandfather was a revolutionary leader among the Bolsheviks during the October Revolution, which he always reminded people took place in November. His father's dad was principled, however. He stayed true to the original Communist tenets and to Trotsky, even after Lenin died and the self-serving Stalin bullied and murdered his way to absolute power. His grandfather came to realize he had backed the wrong horse and fled, eventually settling in America where his son and Mo's father worked in the steel mills but mostly focused on organizing unions and giving the bosses a hard time. Fleeing Russia had proved a wise move. Stalin had virtually all the original revolutionaries killed off, even those handpicked by Lenin himself. After Stalin had Trotsky murdered in Mexico City, Mo's grandfather feared he would be next for a long time. Until Stalin passed in 1953, he slept with a pistol under his pillow. He himself passed later in that decade as the word Communism was firmly entrenched as the *bete noire* of American politics.

Then, other spectral images swirled before Josh that bitter morning as more snow emerged from a black, infinite sky. Carla Shapiro was the daughter of a rabbi. As an only child, she had been raised as if she might somehow become a Rabbinical scholar herself. But she was not permitted to pursue her dream by her conservative father, so she substituted traditional academic studies instead. What she embraced from her religious upbringing was a sense of purpose, and a great deal of guilt. To her, life was pursuing something greater than herself … for seeking some vision of the good. From her traditional studies, she came to understand how the world worked. She instinctively sought to destroy the dystopian reality about her and seek a utopian alternative while her inbred guilt kept pushing her toward the unattainable. Social justice replaced Yahweh as her new God. Erecting a new utopia on earth became her new religion.

Bob Wilson, a pleasant and likable kid, had come to this group of crypto revolutionaries via a circuitous route. He had given the Catholic seminary a shot, studying for the priesthood for two years before enrolling at this decidedly secular college where his ideals drew him to the left-wing crowd. The switch in direction was semi-intentional, happening when his Catholic school of choice told him they did not take mid-year applicants. That bump in the road transformed his life. Soon, his passion for finding God quickly mutated from the transcendental to the political. If one could not achieve perfection outside of this world, then why not within it? After the fact, Bob came to realize his pursuit of the priesthood had been a misguided search for meaning in life. Josh had liked this quiet young man from day one, they had much in common.

Helen Mueller was a late addition to his circle. She was from a wealthy, Lutheran family but found her privilege a burden. She grew ashamed with having so much while others had so little. Yet, she always sensed that she never fit in no matter where she was. Though pleasant of appearance, she could not match her two sisters who dazzled with their beauty and poise. Helen had a roundish face and a body that leaned toward the chunky side. While her family glided through society with ease and the familiarity of those born to position, Helen struggled. Everything was conscious effort for her, and she grew tired of the perpetual pretence. It was as if no one had given her the proper lines to read during her life. She buried this overwhelming sense of unease, even failure, in an anger that burned below a conventional exterior. At times, Josh wondered if she had gravitated toward this new life out of simple spite for her family and her elite tribe.

James Daley, Jimmie to the group, was a follower. He wanted to belong. Unlike Josh, he did not have the athletic skills to compete in ways that might gain him any local notoriety. To compensate, he became a classic hanger-on, the guy who internalized the aura of others and did their bidding without question, sometimes in an annoying, obsequious manner. Josh always looked upon him as a slightly comical figure destined for either tragedy or anonymity, most likely the latter. Josh instinctively reached out to this underdog, sometimes speculating whether Jimmie might be better off seeking a life of quiet desperation as an accountant with a wife and 2.5 children. If only he had been fortunate enough to fall in with a different crowd. More than once, Josh verged on taking Jimmie aside to suggest he leave this group, perhaps finding his way in life with others less dangerous or at least less obsessed. But he never did, fearing that the lad would take this as another rejection. He did not want to hurt him further. Josh never wanted to hurt others.

Then, there was Katherine "Kit" Olson, the outsider. She was a blond beauty who followed Josh like an adoring puppy, even to the point of mouthing revolutionary slogans and pretending the requisite fervor. Josh could never quite respond to her; Her tendency to fall back on the usual feminine charms put him off. She fluttered her eyes at him once, and he almost laughed in her face. Perhaps his resistance to her charms is why she kept after him. Most of the males in her orbit made passes at her, virtually always in futility. Josh was different in her eyes. *Women were funny that way,* he had mused more than once, *they are indifferent, even cold, until they fall 'in love.' Then, they become obsessive. For them, love appears to be a crippling affliction, like a fatal virus.* Still, he doubted her attraction to him could sustain her faux commitment to leftist causes as the group drifted toward a scary cliff. She did not really belong. Funny, he mused, how we evolve and mutate into something new, shedding old skins as we transform in newer and seemingly chaotic directions. Life really is not a constant, but not all can accept such flux and uncertainty.

Josh had met Peter Favulli, his one other pre-college friend in this cabal besides Morris, through high school athletics. It was an odd connection. They attended different schools and he did not know any Italians from his own neighborhood. They were from a different tribe and lived in separate ethnic ghettoes. Early on, Peter grew up in the traditional Italian enclave of the North End, what had been the center of Boston in revolutionary times. Josh initially appreciated his skills on the playing fields and struck up a friendship as fellow athletes sometimes do. Their bond deepened as each appreciated the qualities of the other, a connection that went well beyond playing-field prowess. Besides, each was Catholic, ethnic, and working class, that was close enough.

When he visited Peter's home, he was struck by the sense of religious devotion that pervaded everything. It seemed to carry an aura from a different time with icons to saints and pictures of ancestors adorning the walls. Two of Peter's sisters would become nuns though one uncle and a couple of cousins were mobbed-up wise guys. Peter also had been drawn into the religious life and almost entered the seminary after high school. His devotion to God never quite got off the ground but, like Carla and Bob Wilson, he brought forward a conscience burdened with guilt and a sense of responsibility to do good. When Peter had risen that night and walked out the door, Josh had almost followed him ... almost. Why had he not? He wanted to. An answer came to him. It was easier not to do so. It all came down to a lack of courage and, perhaps, seeking an easier path in that moment. Had it been easier? Not likely! Nevertheless, he despised that insight into his possible motivations, despised himself.

There were, of course, others from his past who were long absent from Josh's college circle. They mostly were the neighborhood Irish toughs destined for lives of mediocre aspirations and modest outcomes. They all hung out in one another's homes until Josh began to think for himself and drift off in a different direction. The break was in slow motion. First, there were more silences. The jokes flew back and forth with less celerity and frequency. Then there were fewer excuses to get together, and finally the actual arguments started. The others remained trapped within their culture as Josh struggled to break away from his. They could not comprehend his emerging opinions and values while he thought them mired in a kind of encrusted cultural coffin.

There was one friendship from the old neighborhood circle that remained stubbornly tenacious. Terry Mahoney had been a defensive end on Josh's high school team, the one other player on his team clearly destined for a top-flight Division I college career. As expected, Terry secured a scholarship to Boston College and was touted as a possible All-American by his junior year. He was also a member of ROTC and committed to serving in Viet Nam if needed. For Mahoney, it was country first, football next, then family and tribal allegiances. Occasionally in their college careers, they would meet up for beers, but the bonds of friendship were strained by the separate paths being followed in life. Increasingly, their connection was eroded by political disputes and separate visions. They never stopped liking each other but found the communication gap too daunting. Disparate choices were followed by the inevitable unreconcilable passions.

His new circle had long been evolving, shedding old inhibitions as they became more focused and committed to stopping this war. They had connected at the teach-ins, the marches, and the never-ending debates of issues and evidence that had long ceased to sate a growing rage and sense of futility. Many had joined this crystallizing group only to fall away after a bit as the rhetoric became more frightening. Feeding off one another, those that remained hardened their commitment. Mo's call for doing something dramatic seemed natural and inevitable by the time he uttered sentiments that appeared to wed all of them to ever more extreme acts. Josh had wavered at each step: He always wavered. His life seemed to be caught up in some transformative struggle between what was right and what was expedient. Circumstances were cruel on occasion, not permitting extensive consideration and paralytic indecision. They compelled one to make a choice. He had long concluded that life was a series of binary choices, one way or the other. How to decide, that was the question? It was as if he were forever cast in the role of Macbeth ... to do or not to do. Why were his life's choices so hard? They appeared easier for others.

Josh revisited a common internal dialogue. The world must be so easy for those who see it in the harsh contrasts of black and white. Certitude is a calming anaesthetic that rubs off most confusion and doubt. What if you could just live out a given role, the words and actions set down for you. Then you would not be required to confront deeper, more existential choices. You could simply approach life with confidence and certitude, no deviations from the allotted script and few questions about the direction taken. Others seemed to live that way, debating little in their lives. He, however, had drawn the short straw. He was not to be so fortunate. Most days, he felt like a weak vine, weaving this way and that, looking for some tendril through which to attach its wandering path to something solid and permanent. Often, he saw himself grasping for something solid, seeking an anchor, but it was never there. Perhaps it was, but he could not see it. Certainty appeared an illusion that only others enjoyed. For him, only endless doubt and discontent lay ahead.

"Damn it!" he yelled into the darkness on that cold November morning. Then he walked to a nearby lamplight as he dug for a quarter in his pocket. How long had he been daydreaming? Already, a layer of snow was accumulating as larger flakes enveloped him with greater purpose. He stared at the coin for several moments. *Heads I go, tails I stay.* Then, he flipped it toward the sky, watching it tumble through the frigid air. Endlessly, it flipped over and over. He was mesmerized by the sight, willing somehow that it might continue an upward journey into infinity. Alas, the law of gravity held once again, as expected, bringing the coin and his fate back to earth. Upon landing, the 25-cent piece struck a jagged piece of concrete and bounced away from the sidewalk into the surrounding shadows. For a moment, he could not see how it had landed. On moving closer, he saw that it had settled into the accumulating puffy snow, the face obscured. *Even now*, he thought, *the Gods are screwing with me.* He kneeled beside the coin … trying to decide if he really wanted to see the result.

Nope, my choice, God, not yours. Besides, it's not like this is forever. He left the coin in the snow, unseen. For once, he would assume control of his life.

He returned to the car. One final time, he hesitated. Two images forced themselves into his head … Rachel and Eleni. These were the two others in his world who meant all to him … his dear sister and his one passionate love. He could lose them, but for how long … forever? That would … kill him. With supreme effort, he pushed their faces aside and started off again. Perhaps he would slide off the road and kill himself. *Not a bad outcome,* he said to himself, *but God is not that kind.* That thought chilled him more than the inclement weather. No way he had the courage for that ending. When he reached the highway, he paused only slightly before turning on to the west-bound ramp. For a couple of hours, Josh drove through occasional snow squalls and the haze of early morning. It was light when he exited Massachusetts and entered New York. Eventually, he slid into a northbound lane when he reached the interstate near Albany. Hours later, he stopped near a sign that said Welcome to Canada and *Bienvenu au Canada.* He made a sign of the cross before catching himself. He recalled seeing basketball players doing that before taking a foul shot, as if God would give a damn about the outcome of a high school athletic contest. Perhaps God did care about life-changing choices, or perhaps not. Who knew? In the end, God's wishes did not matter, only his own. He took one last deep breath before starting out again.

A border official asked his purpose for visiting Canada, as he casually eyed Josh's passport, an act Josh could not recall being done on prior visits up north. Were the rules changing? Did he look guilty, like someone running away from something or. worse, himself? The young man considered honesty before smiling and choosing to lie, "just visiting some friends for a bit."

"Is that right?" the border official asked with a hint of doubt.

For the first time, other than several skids on the slick roads, Josh became concerned. What had been a trickle of young men heading north to escape the draft was turning into a noticeable stream. Were they cracking down on this emigration trend? Perhaps the Canadians were afraid of antagonizing their American neighbors. He hadn't considered that. Frantically, Josh reached for some plausible story if he were pushed further to explain himself. Why hadn't he prepared better. Instead, all he managed to get out was "Yes, been too long. After all, you never want to lose touch with those that mean a lot to you."

After another pause, seemingly eternal to Josh, the official muttered "Have a nice visit … with your friends." He then handed his passport back with a smirk across his face.

"Nice Visit?" Josh mused.

All he could think about was nothing could ever be the same again.

CHAPTER 1

DAY 1 – VANCOUVER
(4 decades later)

"Do you know what a tendril is?"

"A root? A young root, I think," responded Rachel, breathlessly. "I'm sure, though, you're about to set me straight, oh omniscient one."

She had rushed from the house to catch up to her brother after spending a restless night thinking through all she wanted to say to him. Her mind's eye had played out numerous versions of a similar dialogue in which she penetrated his defenses with her incisive insights and deft verbal parries. Unfortunately, each imaginary conversation left her unsatisfied until it dawned on her. It had been some 45 years since they had enjoyed a close or intimate exchange. She barely knew him or the psychological defenses he might exercise. She no longer had any idea what might work or what evasive tactics he might employ.

When they had met over the years, infrequent as it was, their interactions were perfunctory, ritualized. It was if each had been handed a script. She hated that but never could escape the roles they instinctively fell back on. Perhaps real communication was no longer possible, a prospect she willed herself to reject. Tears had formed in her eyes as she slipped into a shallow, dream filled, sleep the night before, a restlessness finally interrupted when his voice reached out to her. Was he really calling to her? Was he ready to talk to her, be open at last? Could that be?

No! He was calling his dog in that peculiar voice all pet owners use. She bolted upright. He was slipping out of the house even before the first hint of dawn. She had recalled him saying that he always walked Morris, his beloved pug, before sunrise. It was then that solitude could be guaranteed, something he said he needed before the start of each day. That, and the fact that Morris, being a small dog, had an insufficient bladder.

"Close." Josh smiled. "It is a threadlike organ found in climbing plants like vines. They typically encircle both the plant and some other structure. They don't flower or anything like that. But they do perform an essential function—they grasp onto these other structures to keep the thing from falling over … from dying. Rather amazing. Okay, not amazing but interesting, at least to me."

Rachel Elizabeth Connelly tried to reprise the stirring speeches she practiced the night before as sleep eluded her. But they were gone now. Perhaps she should have gotten up to prepare notes. Her words were so stirring in her mind's eye, so full of truth, honesty, and passion, Now, they were lost in the penumbra of most nocturnal musings.

Instead, this came out. "So, this is what you think about before the damn sun is up. Okay, so just what's the point here, that I'm rootless or that I like clutching to things?"

"Hell, Rach, you've got to get past thinking everything is about you. I'm talking botany here."

She threw her head back and forced a harsh chuckle. "You really are a piece of work. We've hardly seen one another since I was in high school. One day, seemingly on a whim, you get in your VW Bug and just take off for parts unknown."

"Please, Rach, not this again," he responded weakly.

"Yes again!" She was angry, either at her brother or at the fact that she had lost her eloquent reasoning from the night before. "Damn, we had no freaking idea where you had gone, or what the hell even happened to you. Boom, you disappear. I thought you were dead for a long time. Did that ever cross your mind? Did you ever think about my feelings, what I might be going through?"

"More than you know." He tried.

"Well, you had one fantastic way of showing it."

"No … but I knew you would get over it." Immediately, he knew this was weak and certainly not persuasive. "Besides, we've been around this track before."

"Get over it? Really? Inside your head I suppose but that, my dear, never happened in mine." Her voice shivered in the morning dampness. "You don't *get over* some hurts. It's not a common cold."

"I can see that now," he whispered so softly he feared she hadn't heard what he considered an apology. Then louder. "That wasn't cool."

Rachel forced out a guttural response. "Not cool, not cool. Now there's an understatement for the ages. Jeremiah Joshua Connelly, you broke my heart and all you can say is that it wasn't cool."

The depth of her anger was reaching him. She never used his real first name. "I…. I"

"Shut up and listen." Her words cut through the morning silence. "For the longest time I thought you were dead, for crying out loud. Can you imagine what that did to me? Just imagine, you sit night after night wondering if the person you loved more than anyone else is gone … forever. You want a definition of Hell, that's it." She looked at her brother but, even in the dark, could see his eyes directed straight ahead. Instinctively, she knew she risked losing him again in that place he went to avoid the world in general and particularly conflict. She suddenly recalled that about him. He disliked conflict. She pulled in her anger. "Okay, here I commit to making your retirement from the academy into my first vacation in like forever and how do we start off? I get a botany lesson from the guy who struggled with all the high school sciences."

"Hell, I wasn't that bad, in science that is. The thing was that everyone paled in school next to you. You were the star in that department. Hell, you aced everything. I was jealous."

Rachel issued a grunt. "Don't butter me up. It won't work."

Josh then slowed his pace to look at his younger sister. "Why did you come? Just to yell at me since that's all you have done so far. I mean, my retirement isn't such a big deal, and you must realize that academics never retire, not really. We just find a way to avoid those pesky students. I could never understand why the University administration let the little buggers back in every fall semester."

"Humor is not going to cut it, not this time." She said absent emotion.

"Damn, that's all I got." He tried a weak smile.

The comely woman walking at his side did not return his gaze. She knew he would have that crooked smile on his face that never failed to touch her. She went inside herself instead, looking for some way to get to where she needed to be. After some moments looking for the proper response, she decided on honesty. "I was hoping for a rapprochement."

"A rapprochement?" Josh emitted a tiny chuckle. "I didn't think physicians were so literate."

"I'm warning you, don't joke when I'm about to pound you into a puddle of goo." Her expression went cold. "First, you do your usual dance so that we only exchange meaningless pleasantries when I finally get here … after a trip from hell I might add. Two postponed flights and then a screaming baby next to me on the plane. And then, you go to bed early claiming to be so tired. Exhausted from what? Hell, I did the travelling and the extra work to clear my clinical schedule. Then, I hear you escaping from me in the middle of the night, in the middle of the damn night. It was like you couldn't wait to get away from me."

"Hey, cut me some slack," Josh protested, "this is his usual time, Mo's time that is."

"Well, it looks like the night to me." She hesitated, recalling to her slight dismay that he had told her about his schedule with Morris. "No matter, I sprain a damn toe stumbling around in the dark to get some clothes on just so I can race to this rocky beach to find you. And what do I get? A botany lesson from the kid who couldn't tell a weed from a flower, at least he couldn't when I last knew him … really knew him, that is." Her voice caught a bit. She hated herself for losing control.

This was not turning out at all like she had pictured it in her mind. She felt herself sliding toward disaster.

"Morris!" Josh was looking down to the squat rumples of fur ambling happily alongside his feet. "How many times have we talked about women, what pains in the asses they are?" The dog slowed his waddle to look up at the human he adored. This was different, his canine companion must have thought. The morning walks were usually just the two of them, accomplished in silence where man and canine could meditate while focusing on their private issues of the moment. "Really now, how many times have you told me that broads are nothing but freaking trouble? Do I listen to you? No, I don't. And much to my own detriment, I might add. Consider this, my faithful companion. I've spent my whole life in school and you not a single day, except for that ill-fated obedience training disaster." He bent over to scratch behind his dog's ear. "I apologize for putting you through that, buddy. But at least they gave you a social promotion for being cute. No matter, there is no question that you remain the wise one while I continue to be the dumb ass. When will I learn? You may look a bit slow, but you carry in that ugly head of yours the wisdom and insight of Solomon himself."

Rachel knelt over to the pug next to her sibling as she recovered her composure. "Oh, sweetie, let me take you away from this hell you are in. My evil brother is such a bad influence on you. I would just love you to bits." She ran her hands over his wrinkled coat as he squirmed in delight at the attention. Morris was in his element; he loved attention. "Oh see, he loves me." Rachel was glad for this diversion. It was an opportunity to regain the upper hand. Why did she let him get to her?

"Hah, so much you know. Mo would love the Ripper if Jack scratched his ears."

"No matter, he is the only living thing in your house capable of any affection." Rachel grimaced at her own words.

"No argument here." Josh looked out over the inlet. The beach he walked most mornings ran eastward from the north end of the university campus, stretching along the southern edge of Burrard Inlet leading into English Bay and the city of Vancouver. Directly across the water, the mountains, still crowned with a topping of snow, were just beginning to emerge. They appeared to rise directly out of the water. To the right lay central Vancouver, shimmering in the receding blackness. He never tired of this view even though he walked along the beach most mornings since he had adopted the pug from a colleague who found the dog an inconvenience once his children were off to college. He found his canine companion great company, particularly now that he was not traveling as much. The two enjoyed ambling along this shoreline just as the ink of night yielded to the suggestive light of a new day. Random thoughts would overtake Josh until he realized that the world was in transition. What had been blackness pricked with tiny spots of light melted to a hazy grey. Another pause and then the grey fused with a hint of light blue punctured by the outline of tall buildings and immutable mountain peaks to the left of the city's silhouette. Yes, this metamorphosis never failed to capture him. This was his go-to place, not other people, but this inanimate place at this time of day. Perhaps his personal isolation really had left him lonelier than he had imagined. He sighed inaudibly.

Throughout the slow evolution of dawn each morning, his restless mind would flit from thought to thought, image to image, topic to topic. Work, women, the day's expectations, a long and tempestuous life—such things crowded his head, seeking attention. But nothing seemed to stay there long. Maybe he had been cursed with an attention deficit disorder, he often mused. Then he would dismiss that thought, choosing a different truth. He was blessed with a fertile mind and a fecund imagination. There were times, though, when he would entertain a dialogue within himself, pursuing a thought that intruded unbidden into his consciousness. At the conclusion of his imaginary exchange, he would consider how erudite he had been, oft wondering if there were some way to record his early morn musings. *That surely would end any of my remaining pretensions to brilliance*, he laughed to himself.

Morris squatted to do his business. He was late this morning, the break in the usual pattern must have put him off schedule. After Josh picked up the delicacies, his attention focused on the panoramic view and then his interior space—the long view and the most intimate apprehension. With each shift in focus, the world would have changed right on the edge of awareness, becoming more comprehensible. As the landscape gradually defined itself, it became familiar and comfortable, having been part of his world for decades now. How could that be? He thought Canada would be a temporary refuge, a place to hide from events and from himself until the world had righted itself or he had thought things through. But that rebalancing never happened or it had eluded his razor-sharp capacity for obfuscation and self-delusion. Here he was, about to retire from the faculty of the University of British Columbia. It seemed like yesterday that he had arrived in town not long after getting his doctorate from the University of Toronto. What happened to the decades? How long had he been here, well over three decades in this city, over four in Canada? Just where had this life gone, his vision of a life worth living?

"Mo," cooed Rachel, "want to run away with me? I would treat you much better than this bozo. You are just so cute. Ugly as sin but cute as the dickens, just like I remember your owner when he was a kid. Maybe that's the connection, why you ended up with this loser as your master, and no other. You see him as a twin brother."

"Really, how would you know? You were still in diapers when I graduated out of the toddler stage."

"I know." Rachel said with confidence.

"You do realize that Mo only communicates with me."

"Just because he has no choice. And, if you need to know, I saw your baby pictures. You were ugly as sin, big ears, but somehow managed to turn out okay." She then decided to try an indirect approach. "But what's with the name ... Mo? Really, Mo? And by the way, I haven't heard him say a word to you, not one growl."

"Mo and I communicate without the need for sound." Josh said as he looked at his sister. She had never lost her natural beauty, sandy blond hair in a stylish short cut. Unlike his more rugged and masculine look, she had a slim face with a classic composition that drew people to her. Most felt her looks were rather elegant though Josh had always thought her features a bit on the angular side. At times, her facial composition reminded him of the cubist visage he had seen in some museum. Yet all imperfections, if any really existed, were swept away by her eyes. He could never figure out their true color, pulsating between hazel and blue, depending on light and mood. But they were always inviting, taking you in with an implied transparency and sometimes an impish humor. Above all, they betrayed a quick wit and deep intelligence.

"No! We have our way of communicating through touch and looks."

"I bet," Rachel huffed with obvious incredulity while admitting to herself that so much communication does, in fact, happen that way. "But his name. Where did you come up with that?"

Josh smiled. "Surely you remember Mo, well Morris, from high school and later college when you visited. I even brought him around the house."

"Oh yeah, the skinny Jewish kid. But all I recall is that dad didn't like him, so he wasn't around much. Where is he now?"

Josh looked toward the Vancouver skyline, which had now sprung into a tentative existence. "Well, that is a really long story, one that's difficult to answer." Then he lapsed back into silence, looking afar at where the mountains were a mere hint in the receding darkness.

Suddenly, Rachel turned on him as her anger flared anew. "Here we go. You are going to shut me out again. I just know it. It's what you always do?"

"What are you talking about," his protest, while lacking conviction, now carried a tinge of anger.

Rachel realized that she was stirring up his Irish temper. Nevertheless, she continued. "Oh yeah, like your act is a big mystery. We string together two or three normal sentences and then you throw up this goddamn wall."

"Not fair," he tried even as he knew she was correct.

"Just listen to me for once." She yelled. "First, I lose you when I needed you most. You were gone, just gone. Poof, in college one day and then a disappearing act … a Houdini act. Okay, that I now understand. Wait, no I don't, not really. But let's get past that for the moment. After you graciously let us know you were alive, you never came back. You stayed an exile. You were not there when I graduated from high school, or college, or medical school, or got married, or when I had my daughter. You were nowhere to be found when my marriage collapsed, when mom and dad passed, or when I won any of my professional accolades or … "

"There were too many of those." He tried to slow her growing anger.

"What?" She was incredulous but pleased she was getting her feelings out at last.

"You got way too many of those awards. I'd be on a plane every other week" He tried.

She pulled on his arm so that he was forced to face her. "Aargh, you weren't there for anything, you cretin, nothing! Bad times, good times, it didn't matter. You just shut me down, as if I had bubonic plague or something. Hell, you shut us all down. Sure, Dad was furious, and Mom sort of disappeared, but they needed you. I needed you." Her throat was caught up with emotion. "I was so stupid that I never stopped loving you."

"I know." He tried once more.

"You did? In God's name, how could you possibly know? I kept writing. I can't count how many letters I sent and got nothing back."

"Wait, that's unfair. I wrote."

"Are you kidding? What…an occasional post card. 'Dear Rachel, I am alive. Thanks for your interest in my well-being and have a nice life.' I got more endearing notes from my butcher at Christmas. Did you ever meet me halfway, any way at all? No! Then, later, when we did finally connect, did we get close again? Did we become family? No! You could not wait for my visit to be over, as if it was a torture session. So, what was up with that?" He was startled by her anger, the passion.

She was not his kid sister anymore, that little girl who looked upon him with adoration.

For a moment, he struggled for a response, "well … it was difficult … you see …"

She cut him off, starting-in again. "Well, buddy, I'm here for a whole week, maybe longer … no matter how long it takes. I am going to be in your face until I get inside that head of yours even if it kills me, or you, or both of us. Got that!" Even in the first suggestion of light, he could see the flush on her face, the hard edge to be found in her eyes.

Josh looked at her closely, perhaps for the first time since she had arrived. *She did have their dad's Irish temper.* Where did that come from? He always thought she was like their mother—not only in looks but in temperament as well. The origins of Ora Maki Connelly were shrouded in apocryphal speculation. She had never talked openly about her family or background though they knew she had been born amid great conflict in a year that never had been revealed to anyone's satisfaction … the year changed in various versions. Her maiden name was Finnish, but there were suggestions that she had adopted that from an early marriage, more speculation of doubtful provenance. Her family were from Lithuania, or perhaps northwest Russia, or there was even an unsubstantiated rumor about the Ukraine. One fact seemed certain. Her family did live near St. Petersburg when the civil war between Reds and Whites erupted in the years after the October Revolution. That bloody conflict eventually drove the family survivors to Finland.

Whatever the truth, Josh mused, his mother had been forged of stern stuff, quiet and disciplined and resourceful. She never seemed to lose her composure unlike her husband, the father of Josh and Rachel. James Thomas Connelly, a classic son of the Emerald Isle, attacked life with bold abandon. He was a man of endless stories but absent much direction or purpose except for the cause of Irish freedom and bringing their exiled Catholic brothers from the north of that tortured island back into the tribal fold.

"Yeah, Rach, I got it. You want me to a real brother?" Then he smiled. "Can you give me an example of the Christmas notes your butcher writes."

"Don't even try to be cute, hear me? Your so-called Irish charm won't bail you out this time so don't even bother going there! And not wants by the way … demands." She fought back a tear. "I mean if it is not too much to ask. You know, if it is not an inconvenience or anything."

"Oh well, you can always ask." He slid into his wry smile that was his go-to default attitude. Immediately, he realized his error.

With lightning quickness, she punched him in the stomach. "Ouch!" he exhaled. "That really hurt."

"Good!" she fumed. It now was light enough for him to see her face flush with real anger.

"Alright, I give, I give." He managed to say through some real pain. "Just give me a moment." He took a couple of deep breaths. "I'll tell you why I have been … what's the word I'm looking for?"

"Try *an asshole*," Rachel spit out, her anger yet on the surface.

"Okay, I admit to being just a bit…distant."

"A bit," she scoffed, "Pluto is a bit distant. The other side of the Milky Way is a bit distant. You're not even in our own galaxy, emotionally that is."

"True, but even you have to admit that," he paused for effect as if deciding how to finish his thought, "you were kind of a real pain in the ass when we were growing up."

"What?" This caught her off guard.

"Now, hear me out before you destroy the family jewels." He instinctively shielded his genitals for a moment. "Remember those times in high school. I would bring a girl home when the folks were out and would work my way up to make my patented move."

"Wait," she almost smiled as if she recognized that resisting his charm might be useless, "those were your best moves. No wonder you couldn't get laid."

"Shush, my turn. You would waltz in and bust out with something like *'Oh, Josh, the public health people called a while back. They want a list of all your sexual victims over the past six months. Must be important because they sounded panicky like it was a crisis or something. In any case, they need to warn these girls of something dreadful.'*" He waited for another blow that did not come. "Remember that?"

Rachel could not repress a quick grin. "Oh yeah, fun days."

"Or there was the one about the child support people calling asking about when you were going to *'start supporting all your damn kids.'* Now he stepped back in anticipation of another strike from her. "You know, I pretty much never got a second date."

Rachel softened a bit at the memories. "Hah, that wasn't my fault. You should not have been such a hopeless putz."

"Nope, the real problem was that you were just a royal pain." For some inexplicable reason, Josh Connelly had relaxed a fraction and let his wit emerge again. He realized his mistake when her arm shot out again. This time, he bent over with a cry of pain while Mo growled. "Damn it, I give. Where the hell did you learn to hit like that?"

"Self-defense class." Rachel eyed him suspiciously, searching for any sign of disingenuousness or irony. But she only saw pain in his face. "Any more crap from you and I'll have you on your knees begging for mercy."

"Got it," he managed.

"Sure, I teased you back then but that was because I worshipped you. God knows why, but I would do anything to get your attention, even for a moment or two." Rachel wondered why she admitted this.

"Shit, you got my attention now."

Rachel sighed, interlocking her arm with his. "Sorry, I think I brought a lot of anger with me."

"No shit," he managed after several breathless gasps. "Where do you want to start? Wait, I've a suggestion on that one, maybe we can start with why the coroner will think I was a POW when they do my autopsy. How will you explain all my internal injuries?"

They continued to walk in silence for a while. By now, his face was visible in the morning's subdued light, the mountains now were defined against the hint of a blue sky and the Vancouver skyline was visible in all its detail, augmented by the faintest beat of a waking, pulsating city. Rachel fondly recalled teasing her older sibling. Yeah, she thought, it was immature, quite out of character for her. But she was desperate for his attention, that was so true. He seemed so worldly to her ... intelligent and passionate with the same wry, even cynical, view on the world he inherited from his dad. She would follow him around, looking for any sign of attention from him. Whatever she was seeking in him was never fully satisfied. She always wanted more.

"Rach, to be honest I've no good explanation for being such an ass. The best I can do is admit to being totally embarrassed."

"What?" she prompted when his words appeared to end.

"I've no explanation for letting you down. I just felt bad about things, I felt like such a failure, letting Dad down, my friends, all those who had such hopes for me. If it helps, you were the one I thought about every day. Once you start running, though, it is hard to stop. Running from you ... was something I cannot accept. I just ... cannot. Hard to talk about. It is easier to keep things inside, unsaid. So damn Irish I guess."

They walked in silence some more, she thought about where to go next. His apparent honesty disarmed her. "Josh, I get it. I do. We were still kids when we let things go south, or north in your case. So, I have a proposition. Let's start over, clean slate. How about I ask a few questions. Right, a Q. and A. That should work. Okay, so bear with me, with some questions I have. This won't take more than four to six weeks."

"Funny." Josh exhaled.

"Just relax. Let me start with something easy, not from way back when but with something more recent but which has always confused me. What about your marriage to Usha? That's a puzzler. Without warning, you sent a letter saying you were married—married! I mean, what the hell. You were always moaning about marriage being hell on earth. Then, no warning, this woman comes out of the blue. Nary a word about her and then just a letter. *'Dear Rachel, I had to take the dog to the vet for worms and, by the way, I got married last week.'* So, I trek up here to meet her. What happens, I get treated as an inconvenience. I never felt welcome, not really. In truth, she was quite nice, but you seemed to put up your usual wall. But It was more than that, something I still can't get. It was like there was no feeling, no intimacy, no … love between this woman and you. It was like you were simply good friends. Then, after several years, it was over. No build up, no apparent reason. It struck me that you tired of the current model or, more likely, she got tired of living with a freaking robot. Okay, what's the story with that? Shit, do you have any idea at all how badly I wanted us to be a family again? When I heard you were getting married, that excited me. I thought you might be joining the rest of humanity, that I might get to know what the hell was going on in your life."

Josh realized she had finished. "Yeah, I didn't handle that very well."

"You didn't handle it at all," she whispered.

"Well, it's a bit embarrassing to talk about."

"What happened to the toughest kid on the block that I knew way back when. Then, you never backed down."

"Well, that only involved physical pain." He murmured the words in so slight a voice she almost missed it.

She responded with an even voice, as if now she were in command of her emotions. "Not a problem, take your time! But remember this. I'll outwait you. I swear, I will stay in your face until you open-up or pigs fly. I'm deadly serious about that. So, if you don't want me to quit my job and move in permanently, you damn well better give me more than a few jokes."

He looked at her for several moments, finding her expression resolute. "Alright, I'll try at least." As usual, he found his insides knotted tightly. Could he get this out? Maybe there was some escape. The earth might open-up and swallow them whole. Maybe he would have a coronary that would spare him from thinking about these private things that pained him so. No, one look and he realized she would not relent nor would there be any miraculous rescue. He sighed. "Here's the thing. You nailed it. We were just friends. You see, it…it wasn't exactly a marriage, a real marriage."

He felt her eyes boring into him. "And that means?"

"How to say this, it was like an arrangement. Try to understand, Usha and I had been close for some time, we could talk and share and laugh, and there was little chance it would get serious. It was just comfortable. And by the way, despite my rhetoric back then it is not true that I wanted to nail every woman that crossed my path … just 80 percent of them." He caught himself, covering his stomach in anticipation of a blow from his sibling. She glared but did not strike, so he continued. "Right, no more jokes, I promise. Here's the thing, at some point, we realized how close we had become. We went to dinner, movies, museums, concerts, and even travelled together. It was weird, I guess. Everyone thought we were a great couple. I even met some of her family, she had several siblings. Then it hit us. Even though we never shared a place, we had become this public couple. No one asked me or her to an event or dinner party, they asked us over even though we were not committed in any legal sense, just companions. To me, she was the perfect woman."

"Wait," Rachel was confused. "You must explain that one.

"Easy, she would never fall in love with me."

"Oh god," Rachel moaned softly. "Just keep going."

"Then one day she seemed off … too quiet. By this time, I was pretty much on to her moods, not bad for a guy, I must say." After a quick peak to see if she were about to strike, he determined all was safe. "After prodding and pushing a bit, she came out with the worst kept secret in the world. She preferred women."

"I just knew it." She stopped there.

"That explained why I liked her so much. She was safe. Still, I asked her about the secrecy? Everyone was out, weren't they? She went on about her family, from India as you know. Not just that but they were very conservative. They would take her sexual preference quite badly as in freak out. Not her siblings so much as those of her parent's generation. Already, they were quite upset that she was obviously with this guy, me, and not married. Still, if we didn't live together in sin, it might be something that could be ignored. Probably not for long, though. She was way past the age when she should have been married, like by a decade or so. And how were they going to find a suitable mate now that she clearly was spoiled goods."

"And they would find you suitable? Amazing!" She cracked a tiny smile.

"Hah, hah! The thing is that the courting process is such a transactional negotiation in that culture, at least for the older folk. Her parents were ratcheting up the pressure. The big thing for her was whether she could face coming out of the closet. That would have been beyond the pale in her mind. She would be shunned by many, an outcast. When she started to cry, I realized just how much pain she was in all the time. She was stuck, emotionally and culturally. She couldn't admit publicly who she was and was finding it harder and harder to play at being my girlfriend absent at least the appearance of marriage. I remember listening that day, and it just came out. *No problem*, I blurted out, *we'll just get married*."

Rachel stopped in her tracks. She was not prepared for the openness and needed a moment to process what he was saying. "Wait, you just casually proposed marriage, just to be a nice guy, without expecting any sex? Do I have that right?"

"Not quite true. We were doing it, often enough at least. Oddly enough, she never refused me that, not that I pushed the issue. I could sense something missing there, for her at least, so we just settled into our comfortable routine. I was happy to know she preferred women. Early on, I thought maybe I was losing my touch in the satisfying women department." Rachel grimaced but let it pass. "Besides, I did get a lot out of it, the relationship, not so much the sex but even that was okay, for me at least. Guess you're right, though, it was a casual choice, not one well thought out."

"Unbelievable!" She emitted. "My only sibling is a crazy man."

Morris suddenly turned around and started back down the beach toward Langara Avenue, pulling at his chain with some urgency. He had long satisfied the purpose of the journey and knew food awaited his return home. Besides, they had passed the usual turning point, and Morris was, as they say, a creature of habit. Josh continued. "She turned me down, of course, making all the sensible arguments that she could not possibly ask me to sacrifice so much for her, she could never be a real woman for me, that I might have to accommodate her female lovers on occasion, and blah, blah, blah. She relented after a bit. After all, this was perfect in a way. We liked each other's company, and we could be the great cover for each other. I would make her family happy and not expect her to be a real wife. She would nominally be my partner in the eyes of the world. Each of us could pursue other relationships, presumably casual, without fuss or recriminations. We still had to be discrete of course."

"And you found this acceptable?"

"Acceptable? Hell, I thought it grand. What is the big problem with women, from the male perspective, that is?"

"Oh, I'm not going to like this." Rachel managed.

"They get attached. You need to be nice to reel them in, and then you can't get rid of them, at least not easily. When you try for an exit, there are the tears and all that emotional nonsense." *Whoops*, he thought to himself, *Rachel was right, she won't like all this.* But he was in too deep. "Well, you know what I mean. I would now have a built-in excuse for other women as to why I could never be serious. You know … make a commitment. I could tell some gal I had lucked out with that, while I liked her a lot and that what we had was special, I was in this committed relationship. If only we had met earlier. Besides, some women preferred that, really, and for the same reason I did, though probably not all that many. I'll admit there probably are some pissed-off females out there."

"Thanks for the lesson in female psychology, Doctor Ruth. By the way, you better start guarding those family jewels now, they are a most endangered species at this moment."

Josh edged away from her but continued. "In my defense, I always, well mostly, told women going in that commitment was off the table. I was an honest bastard." Realizing how stupid that sounded, he continued quickly. "Back to Usha, it took me a while, but I finally convinced her. I find I can be quite persuasive. We got married. It wasn't lavish but enough to give her cover with her family. Of course, then the questions about children started. We never anticipated that one. Silly, when I think about that now. Of course, her family would expect children, her biological clock was ticking. Besides needing to deflect her parents about having kids, all was great. Later I realized I never even asked if she wanted children. I just assumed she wouldn't."

"Typical man," Rachel grunted, "only thinking of himself."

"Fair enough. Still, we really got along quite well and, by the way, it turned out she agreed with me on the kid's thing. I figured out at one point that not being emotionally invested makes any relationship a lot easier. Hmm, I should write a scholarly paper on that. And she really could whip up a whole number of badass curries. I just love Indian food. Got hooked when I consulted there for a bit. The big cost was a couple of extra inches on my waist. We actually were happier than most conventionally married couples we knew."

"You are nuts, but that's not news." After more thought, Rachel added. "In the end, it obviously didn't last. What went wrong?"

"No," he replied thoughtfully, "it didn't last, but not on my account. After a while, I imagined this just might go the distance. I was content for sure. Then I started noticing changes, the kind of incremental differences that a nimrod like me might miss for a while, but not forever. Eventually, I sucked it up and asked. Someone had come into her life, a woman she thought she loved, had a crush on at least. It was some legal scholar she met at a professional conference. They started collaborating, and the intellectual connection became physical. Well, as fond as she was of me, she knew the difference between liking some clown and really being emotionally taken with someone. I could never compete with that. For her, it was time. She would just face her family and the world. I supported her as much as I could, but these are things you face alone in the end. I think that is one of the immutable truths in life, we all face the important things by ourselves. Some choices invite pain. I do love her in my own way, and she loves me."

"So, you are still friends?"

"Of course, that will never end. We care for one another. I helped her through the transition, and we stay in touch. She is at the University of Toronto now with her partner. It wasn't easy but her family came around eventually. They had grown to like me. They listened to me; Can you believe that?"

They walked in silence for a few minutes before Rachel broke the quiet. "Let me ask one of the big questions. Have you ever been in love with anyone … aside from yourself of course?"

"You think I love myself? That's delightful. I suppose someone might believe that since I am quite lovable. After all, it is hard to improve on perfection." More silence followed as he thought on that question but, to his increasing discomfort, he now worried that another blow might come his way.

It was apparent that Rachel was willing to wait for as long as it took. She had learned one thing from training her own pet dogs. You give the command once and then wait. No need to repeat; the animal knows. Of course, Rachel considered that maybe her brother wasn't as trainable as pets. That disturbing possibility hung in her head, so she decided on a prompt, breaking her training rule.

"And so, have you ever been in love?" She asked firmly. "That's not a trick question."

"Aside from you?"

"Shit, that doesn't count. Romantic love." She sounded exasperated.

His body seemed to shudder. "Her name was Eleni." His words barely rose to the level of a whisper.

"Eleni? I don't remember her. Do I know her?"

"You two never met, she was from my college days, but I never brought her home. But she is long out of the picture." Her brother's nonresponse caught her by surprise. Rachel suddenly thought of the old Apostle's Creed she learned as a child. There was the part where *"born to the Virgin Mary"* was followed by *"suffered under Pontius Pilate."* It was as if all the important stuff, Christ's teachings were irrelevant, all reduced to that single comma which separated the two phrases. To Rachel's ear, his words came across as *'I loved her,'* and *'she was gone.'* The things unsaid often are what a story is all about.

"Want to talk more about her?" Rachel asked almost timidly.

"Not now," he said too quickly. "Besides, Mo and I talk about women all the time."

"Really? I'd love to be a fly on the wall for those discussions." Rachel went to a lighter tone, signalling that she would not push him on this now.

"Like Mo and I discuss all the time, women are nothing but trouble, even where it should be easy like in the sack. You get some of these women going, and then it takes forever to get them over the top. Shit, you start foreplay in January and they finally come in April. You're too pooped by then to get off yourself." Josh was still chuckling at his obvious attempt at a witty deflection when her fist slammed into his stomach once again. He had let his guard down one time too many. "Damn, that really does hurt," he expelled through the pain. "I'm not going to survive this week."

"Well, you're disgusting … you deserve a little pain."

"Nonsense," he gasped, "I have written testimonials from scores of women saying I'm really quite good." As he said the words, he inched his way beyond her reach.

"You can't evade, deflect, and somehow misdirect your life from me anymore. Before I assault you to the point where they will need to put a toe tag on your cold remains, I'm going to find out who you have become, for better or worse. To do that, I am taking you apart, limb by limb, secret by secret, disgusting habit by disgusting habit. Do you understand, mister? Do you?"

The sun was up fully now. It glistened off the snow that capped the mountains across the water. After a few minutes, he had fully recovered and pointed toward the distant peaks. "You know, Rachel, you can ski in the morning here and swim in the afternoon." He had told many visitors that over the years. What made him such a chamber of commerce spokesperson? He didn't ski, ever, and seldom swam except in heated pools. "Not evading. Just sharing something special with you. I never meant to spend my life here, you know. It is another thing that just kind of happened, one of those choices that was not quite a decision or is it the opposite, a decision that's not quite a choice."

"It is lovely." She offered distractedly, obviously thinking deeper thoughts while ignoring his conundrum.

"Rachel," he drew out her name as if he were still considering how to end his thought, "I need to ask one more time. Why are you here now? What is so important after all this time."

"I think," she said as if she had not heard his words, "that I want to find out if there is any of that boy still inside you … that boy I loved so."

"Me too," he whispered as he stopped to look out over the water, taking her hand in his.

"Good." She felt calm for the first time that morning.

"One request, then"

"Which is?

He smiled. "Don't kill me before you get your answer."

"Tough bargain, but okay. It's a deal."

"I can admit to loving one thing, besides Mo." He sighed. "I do love this place."

"What's not to love." She moved next to him and took his hand. "But even you must admit, it is not another human being. It is lovely but it's not alive."

The two of them watched as a new day broke behind the Vancouver skyline.

CHAPTER 2

DAY 1 - DAYBREAK

A passer-by walking his dog did a double-take. The new day now had sufficient light to permit recognition of others even at a distance. Yes, the dog-walker said to himself, that was Professor Connelly with his dog Morris. He saw them often in the morning, but the third figure confused him. Who was the female? That indeed was different. The Professor was known as friendly but pretty much a loner, someone who preferred his own company or so all his neighbors had concluded. He was always polite enough, quick to share a joke. Yet, he was private, as if revealing himself invited some danger best kept at a distance. Perfunctory greetings and brief sessions of small talk were all they exchanged even after several years of crossing paths on their morning ritual. Should he initiate a conversation today? No, the man concluded. Though today was different, he dared not intrude absent some form of permission.

The vigil of the three figures, two humans and a pet, was not to be interrupted. They stood as statues standing guard over the bay, the city, and the mountains for some time. Rachel's presence at his side pushed Joshua Connelly to places within his head he typically tried hard to avoid. The anguish of his youthful *hegira* had never quite left him as he felt compelled to flee his country for Canada some four plus decades earlier. After all, it defined him in so many ways. Still, he could never quite pull together the threads of those moments when his former life seemed to evaporate without substantial consideration or even thought. How could that be?

He did recall certain emotions … they were yet clear to him. The pressures that had built up inside him had been real, that lost feeling of events sweeping him along in ways that contradicted who he was. In that other life, an existence so remote and foreign that it did not feel authentic, he felt himself evolving into a person that seemed alien, that he had trouble recognizing and which frightened him on occasion. After all, he had walked away from football simply because he was wracked with guilt over injuring another player. And now, two years into college, he had inched toward the cusp of something much worse, leaning toward spasms of violence he did not understand and feared he might not be able to control.

He recalled isolated snippets of his late-night college dialogues. Does man really have free will or are we merely pawns responding to greater and unseen forces? What is a purposeful life, one worth the effort and pain? Do the ends ever justify the means? Are there evils in the world that cannot be ignored, that demand a personal response if you are not to violate your moral compass or worse, forfeit your soul? Can we see into the future with any clarity, or be clever enough to appreciate the consequences of our present actions, intended and unintended, to embrace what we do today? Why, in God's name, are we here? That last plea inevitably stumped him no matter how many times he revisited his conundrums.

"You seem far away." It was Rachel's voice.

"I am" he responded distractedly.

"That's okay." She put her head on his shoulder, her earlier anger spent. There would be time to get where she wanted to be, she could be patient. She would not be returning to Wisconsin in anger, not yet.

Inside his head, Josh effortlessly segued back to those days of rage and confusion. While so much was lost after a long and eventful life, one set of feelings remained to him with a bitter clarity. He had been torn in so many ways back then, agonizing between visions of right and wrong. He was ripped asunder amidst conflicting loyalties among friends and family, driven by a matrix of competing theories about how to make sense of what was going on in the world about him. He was cursed, that was his problem then and probably now. From birth, he had been cursed with a mind capable of nuanced thinking and a conscience crippled by competing sentiments. In the end, he never made an actual decision, a real choice. If he had been capable of that, he might have been able to diminish his pain and resolve his conflicts. He merely acted to ease the immediate hurt, to find some relief.

One long-ago day, almost on impulse, he began to pack some belongings in his VW bug, gassed it up, emptied his bank account, and then drove around aimlessly, mostly visiting local sites that meant much to him. Eventually, he found an all-night diner. There he sat until the night staff began to eye him with suspicion. Compelled to act, or so he surmised, he got back in his vehicle and again drove aimlessly until he drifted to the curb as the streets slickened with that unexpected sleet and then snow. No matter how hard he tried, he could no longer retrieve any memory of making a deliberate choice. How can that possibly be? He must have but now he could not retrieve it, nor the process for arriving at any conclusion. So much of that period of his life appeared lost in the penumbra of mishappen memories and distorted images.

Josh forced himself back to the present. "I've never gotten tired of this and yet I'm not sure I know how I got here," he murmured.

Rachel was not certain his words were for her. Still, she was caught in his apparent contemplative spirit as a sense of peace washed over her. She surrendered to this aura of serenity, even as she realized its fleeting character. "I get that," she quietly responded even though she was not certain a response was necessary. "But I'll theorize that you originally got here on a plane."

Josh said nothing in return, though he appreciated her soft witticism. Nor did he make any movement that might spoil the moment. How many times had he paused at this very spot to witness and acknowledge the daily ritual of morning renewal? He loved both his adopted city, and the city of Victoria across the Georgian channel. When he first visited decades ago, he recalled reading that there were more restaurants per capita in Vancouver, including more ethnic restaurants, than any other city in North America. He usually doubted the veracity of such claims, attributing such to overexuberant assertions by the chamber of commerce, but it seemed credible at first glance. Then he noticed something. He would pass Indian, Chinese, Indonesian, Vietnamese, and even African restaurants that were mostly empty and then would come across a McDonald's that was packed. Oh well.

He slowly realized that physical beauty or even a cornucopia of culinary delights are not what make this place special. *It was the people,* he thought to himself. A mosaic of tribes from what had been the British empire crowded into this part of the world yet seemed to sustain a sense of harmony and civility. You step off a curb, and cars would screech to a halt to let you cross. In the Boston area, where he grew up, it was different. Step off the curb, and motorists would aim for you. Then, they would back up over your body one more time for the inconvenience you had caused them in the first instance. He had read recently that the worst drivers in the United States could be found in Beantown while the second worst were found just down the road in Worcester, Massachusetts where he had gone to college. There were no doubts in Josh's mind as to the veracity of these honors. He remembered with total clarity that the drivers back there were crazy. He should know. He had been one of them.

"I'm glad you're here," he whispered. "I really am."

Rachel was not sure she heard him correctly but decided not to seek clarification. She liked what she thought she had heard. In that quiet moment between them, she wondered what he might be thinking about. She chuckled inside. Isn't this what females always do, try to figure out what the men in their lives are thinking about. *What a waste of time,* she mused. In her experience, males had few deeper thoughts worth exploring, focusing mostly on food or sex or sports or things so insubstantial as to bore her to tears. And yet she could not help herself. He had been such a huge part of her early life until he wasn't.

She forced herself back to those troubled days when she was in high school and he off to college. She missed him terribly, his dry humor, his teasing, his stimulating commentary on issues large and small. What she loved most, had always loved most, was his patience with her. She could ask anything, and he would come up with an answer. He made up many of his so-called insights, but she loved the fact that he tried. And there were times when she did marvel at his thoughts and insights. He really had been that rare male worthy of her attention.

The high school boys she knew were useless, leering at her as she developed and trying to *cop a feel* as they would say. Their attempts to get her attention were juvenile beyond calculation. But there was her brother, taking her to the library or the museum in Boston. He instinctively knew of her loneliness when he left for college. He recognized that her chronological peers were beneath and behind her. They were not as intelligent and, more importantly, far less inquisitive. He thus worked hard to keep in touch. They typically met on neutral grounds, away from home and parents, to avoid the unavoidable family conflict. She felt as if they were Bonnie and Clyde, on the run from the authorities who were bent on bringing them to justice.

Often, he would take her to his campus, introduce her to his friends. Over time, the cast of characters in his orbit evolved, becoming more serious and even hard edged. They laughed less and discussed deeper political topics more. It bothered and fascinated her at the same time since she had no context in her normal life to put what she was hearing during these brief visits into any perspective. She could sense the world changing, evolving into a more threatening milieu. That injected divided emotions into her daily contemplation of life. On the one hand, she felt superior to the schoolgirls around her who blabbered on about boys and makeup and all things lacking substance or merit. She was now pondering larger issues, even if they were borrowed from her sibling's world. She recalled being thrilled by that adult like world and repelled as well. Inside, she knew that innocence would soon be lost to her.

Suddenly, a brusque breeze off the bay hit Rachel, disrupting her reverie. Part of her wanted to break the spell, but the better part of her hated losing this sense of intimacy between them. She did not want that to end. She uttered one word. "Beautiful." He did not respond.

Then her thoughts drifted to that long-ago cold November day. He was supposed to meet her at a pizza place they used as a rendezvous site. He had stopped coming home altogether by then, the fights had escalated to a breaking point. She had concluded that is what happened to love that had been lost. There appears no middle ground. You go from adoration straight past dislike to rage. The betrayal of expectations is too present, too real. So, with the wider family bonds broken, she treasured her occasional meetings with him so that Josh could remain her older brother, her mentor, her hero, her rock and faux parent. But he never showed that fateful day. She waited for a long time. Worse, he never even called or sent some message. She knew something had been bothering him, but he would never reveal what. Now, he was gone, had disappeared. She had been left with conjecture, unsatisfying speculation.

Puzzlement evolved into frustration which turned to concern which quickly mutated into anger. Where was he? As the days passed with no word, her anger became fear and then dread. He was dead, she was sure of it. Something about his new friends had concerned her and now the worst had come to pass, or so she surmised. She knew about his anti-war feelings, that was no secret. She shared them, at first because of his conviction and later because of her own. At the same time, she also knew he was keeping things from her, to spare her from the darker hues of his life. She tracked a couple of them down on campus, but they knew nothing about his whereabouts or fate.

His new and private world was the source of the family conflict, along with giving up football. He thought of her as a little girl, not ready to share his burdens. In her head she was far from that. He was her life and she wanted them to share everything, good and bad. Perhaps he had gone from protest to something worse. No matter, that would be okay, she trusted his judgment. He probably was afraid for her, reluctant to get her involved in whatever was going on. What else could explain his secrecy, his silence? In her desperation, she ultimately decided he was in jail somewhere and no one was telling her. Irish families would keep secrets, even from each other. That was it. He was in jail. That must be it. She clung to that illusion for some time.

"You never got in touch at the beginning." It struck her that she was being obtuse, throwing out a non sequitur. Still, she knew he would understand. How could he not?

Rachel waited for him to say something. He did, but it came as an orthogonal response. "Rach, did I ever tell you how much you remind me of Mom?"

It struck her that he had responded with a non sequitur to her non sequitur. "The ice maiden ... thanks a lot." Frustrated again with what she saw as another transparent evasion on his part, she suppressed a strong desire to hit him again in the stomach.

"Well, not so much that, but maybe you've got something there. The image of ice maiden does work. She was remote, untouchable in a way, and you ..." He chuckled but sucked in his tummy, anticipating another blow that never came. "Seriously, I was thinking of the physical similarity. You have the same light hair, the same delicate facial features, the bluish eyes that are not quite blue. And you are slim like her, you probably never had an extra pound."

"Nice save. You're not as dumb as you look." She eyed him suspiciously.

"Then again, I was thinking that mom was discipline and focus and purpose, everything dad was not. She kept us together and made sure we never went astray. Not that she had to worry about you. I still recall, night after night, you sitting diligently at the kitchen table buried in books while I was out marauding the neighborhood with my friends. She was contemplative and thoughtful, like you."

"Bull, you were not that different from me," she retorted, realizing to her dismay that she inexplicitly had let a compliment escape. "I saw you reading a lot, and I know you thought about stuff, about all kinds of stuff that I thought important at the time."

"No, not in the same way. It wasn't the same at all. I buried myself in history, biographies, and a bit of fiction when I wasn't checking out the dirty mags in my room. But you were serious. You loved math and science and the tough subjects. I escaped into the past and other people's lives. You were already thinking of the future, what you wanted to be and accomplish. I had no freaking idea what I wanted in life. Even then I was escaping through the vicarious offerings of other people's lives, mostly people no longer alive. You were always so … intense. No, serious. Hmm, as I think back, I never heard you talk about boys, never saw you date. Did you ever do that back then?"

"Oh, a bit," she retorted weakly. "But they were all so useless, just horny little shits."

"No argument from me. Why do you think all dads want to lock up their daughters? They know how boys are since they were one once. Hell, if I had a daughter, I would fit her out with a chastity belt at thirteen, make that twelve. They still make those, I hope?" He noticed that Rachel smiled, which relaxed him. "But my point is that I was always so proud of you. You were what I was not. I was a dreamer, someone who easily got lost within a fantasy world that could be conjured up by my fertile imagination. I did have that." He paused as if reaching further back. "I remember Mom looking at you as you studied, your eyes furrowed in such concentration. I knew what she was thinking, at least I think I did. You were going to be what she never had a chance at achieving. You were her hope. She was so proud of you. I could see that."

With that, Morris pulled on his leash. He was not a dog to be ignored. They obeyed and crossed over Marine Drive. "I never knew what she thought, about me most of all. She never said a word." Rachel kept her head down while Josh tried to decipher whether his sister could have missed what was so obvious to him. Could she really have missed their mother's adoration of her? Then he got his answer. "Why didn't she say something? Why didn't anyone say something. I felt so…different, like a freak. I never felt I fit in…to anything around me. How strange that we can't see what's right in front of us."

"I doubt she knew how to express love or anything positive—she had been scarred by so much stuff early in life. Damn, I wish I had said something back then. Maybe if you hadn't been so busy screwing with my lame attempts to seduce the young lasses, I would have told you just how special you were. I must have done that, at least on occasion."

"Well ….?"

"Sure, make me feel like shit. Hell, I do know I was more than a bit jealous. Now that is sad, to be jealous of your bratty little sister. Early on, though, you talked about becoming a doctor. Did you know that mom would somehow get that into conversations with her friends? Come to think of it, did she have friends? She was so distant, remote. Let's say her acquaintances. Anyway, she would go on about her daughter being so smart. *'She is going to be a doctor, you know.'* And everyone would nod because they knew it was likely to be true even though success for a girl in our neighborhood was not getting knocked-up by age sixteen."

"She never said that to me, not to my face."

Josh looked at her, noticing the moisture in her eyes. "Damn, they were damaged. I would expect dad to be a shit. Daughters were irrelevant … it was the boys who counted. Girls were destined to be good wives. But boys could carry on the family name and pride. Even when I was around, I could not figure him out all the time. He was so dominant and yet so … vulnerable, I guess. In his mind, he had failed … I sensed he felt that. What always puzzled me was how someone so robust on the outside be so delicate inside. He looked to me for some validation of his life, and you know what I did. I broke his heart."

"Dad loved you, and he did show it." she tried to sound confident, but it came out forced.

"Yeah, I know, until he didn't anymore. Better never to have seen love at all."

She thought there might be more, but he remained silent. "Want to know something funny, sad maybe. I never knew how you felt, you never ever said …" Her voice caught, she paused. "We were such a pair, so typically Irish. Neither of us would admit to a weakness or emotion if it whacked us upside the head."

"Hey, my excuse is that I was a guy … just a young stupid shit."

"And now?" she asked.

"Now I'm an old stupid shit."

Rachel stopped to look at him, her eyes full of moisture. "I adored you. To me, you understood the world. You had passion and conviction and a sense of what was right that, I don't know, inspired me. I was motivated to do good from listening and watching you."

"Really?" Josh managed to genuine surprise.

"Yes, really," she was frustrated with what she suspected was false modesty. "That's what made what happened all so tragic, why it hurt so damn much. I almost fell apart. I did for a while, fall apart that is. For weeks I felt paralyzed." When she looked at him, there was nothing false in his expression.

"But you didn't, did you? Not really and surely not for long. You must know that I never stopped following you and what you were accomplishing. First it was through friends and more recently through the internet. I followed you in med school at Johns Hopkins, the Boston Children's Hospital internship, the Chicago residency, all top spots. I would brag to my friends up here about my brainy sister, the one who had to make my parents proud because I was such a screwup."

"You weren't. Just stop that." Her temper was rising. "Damn, you are an academic star. Just how many of those came from our neighborhood?"

"I was a screw-up, at least in what mattered," he said absent emotion. "Never forget, I was the one that was supposed to make Dad's world okay. He couldn't do it for himself, and Mom never let him forget that. But he had this son that would right all wrongs and correct all shortcomings. His son would go to Boston College, maybe even Notre Dame, on a football scholarship. After that, there would be no limits. Perhaps he would see his son play ball on Sundays. You know that was his dream. I never cared about that, at least not after I realized there were more important things. But it was his dream for sure, and that's what the Irish have in abundance … ridiculous dreams."

Rachel sensed his pain. She felt a real tear slipping down her cheek. "But then the football stopped. And you and Dad, well, it just got worse. I never really understood, but I could see your pain. I suppose that spurred me on in some way. I felt I had to do better to make up for those things that sent the family into a spiral. Some things I never fully understood but could feel. Of course, it was not hard to figure out there was a problem at home when the screaming and the banging of doors would go on night after night. God, how many times I cried myself to sleep."

"Listen, Rach, giving up football was a lot more than leaving the game behind. I had to escape this life being pushed on me. It was never my choice, not really. Okay, at first it was. I liked the adulation. Who wouldn't? Toward the end, though, I kept having these doubts. Dad kept pumping me up. *'Practice harder, hit harder, you can do it, son. Hey, kiddo, scouts will be at the game. This is it, time to man up and show them just how tough you are. No weakness and no quarter.'* His voice, his desperation, never left my head."

"He could be relentless." Rachel concurred.

"I so remember that night." He paused as if waiting for the images to stop buffering in his mind.

"Wait, which night?" Then Rachel kicked herself for asking a question with such an obvious answer.

"The night football ended for me. We were beating the crap out of St. Peter's High—they were not particularly good in any case."

"Josh," Rachel tugged her brother closer. "You don't have to go there."

"No, I do. I still have nightmares about this. After all these years, I still …" He hesitated. "Who would have cared if they had scored one crummy touchdown? We were up by over forty points by then. I was out of the game; it was a laugher. Then they got down to our goal line against our third stringers. I just ran out to our huddle during a time out and told my substitute to get the hell off the field. Those bastards were not going to score on my watch. I never really thought about it, just did it. I think I remember the coach yelling at me but can't recall what. I could only see his lips moving. No matter, I saw this undersized halfback circle the right side of their line toward the end zone. I was the only one fast enough to catch him. Shit, I could've just taken him down so easily, probably blown the kid over with a big breath. It would have been so simple. But no, I had to drive him into the ground, show the scouts what a badass I was. No quarter, right! I had to prove I was worthy of wearing the Irish blue and gold. My ticket to Catholic heaven, Notre Dame, and Dad's affections were on the line. They weren't, of course. Hell, the scouts probably had left by then, probably already had seen enough since I was no longer supposed to be in the game. The college scouts weren't the issue. What really was on the line was his love, or so I thought. I had to show him how tough I was. So, I dug deep and sprung at this poor shit with everything I had. Almost from the first impact, I heard some sickening cry. Maybe I always just imagined this, but I sensed his body go limp. That's what comes to me at night ... what I heard and felt in that moment. The kid was just lying there, whimpering."

"Josh, please."

"Let me finish. Somewhere, I knew instantaneously what had happened, but I pushed it away, refused to look. I jumped up all proud and juiced, looking at the stands for dad. I think the silence all around jarred me back to reality. When I looked down at this kid, his helmet was off. The look on his face was ... something I've never been able to erase. It was if he already knew his life was over. I just stared. I had crippled him. At that moment I knew it ... I just knew it was over." Then he stopped.

"Really? You knew his life was over? How could you have known then and there." Rachel asked softly.

"No, not that. What I knew was that football was over for me. They would all say that the hit was clean or whatever. What BS. Most of them never looked into his eyes at that moment, never saw what I saw. I've never been able to get his face out of my head."

"Josh..." Rachel tried to take control.

He would not let go. "What was I doing out there? What was I becoming? Standing on that field, it just hit me. Enough … just enough! Maybe it was that silence, it was deafening. It was never silent on a football field. It was at that moment, though. The kid said nothing, the fans did not make a sound, my teammates looked away. The other team looked at me in such a way, I can't describe it. Whatever, it just hit me in that instant. I had become someone I loathed. What I never told anyone is that there were two cripples on the field that day, that poor son-of-a-bitch and me. I walked off that field and never put pads on again."

Rachel took him into her arms and clenched him tightly. He could sense the salty tears against his neck. "It's okay. It's okay." That was all she could think to say.

"Hey, Rach, what's with all these biblical names—Rachel and Elizabeth and Joshua and Jeremiah. Really, what's up with that crap? I mean, what Catholic family even reads the damn Bible?"

"Nice try, bozo," she said, wiping away a tear. "Are we just a bit panicky that you might have to deal with a few tears? But thank you."

"For what?"

She kissed him on the cheek. "For opening up about that night. You never did back then, you know."

"Really?" He was genuinely surprised, searching his memory for evidence that might refute her but came up with nothing.

"Not when I was around. I kept waiting. I wanted to ask about the football thing, about all kinds of stuff, but seldom could work up the courage … to get into the hard issues. Intellectual questions were fine, the harder the better. Personal ones seemed taboo." Then she remembered one time when he did talk about it, briefly. She decided not to back track, though.

"Wow, I was wounded more than I realized."

Rachel did a quick calculation, deciding that it might be best not to dig into things too quickly. "Okay, you've been good so I should reward such behavior. You do realize I'm quite good at shaping behavior, having trained more than one dog myself. While canines usually are more trainable than males, the same techniques apply. So, I will tell you the secret behind our names."

"What? Are you saying that you know why we're stuck with biblical names unless, that is, you're using my old trick?"

"Trick?" She grinned.

"Yes, feigning omniscience while buying some time to gin up some BS explanation. That's my trick, as you well know."

"Oh, I know that one but no trick on my part," she protested. "I do have serious thoughts on the biblical names which I intend to share. Only if you are good, though."

"I'm all ears." He smiled broadly, glad to have eased past his confessional moment. "And I'm always good. I've got written reviews from all my girlfriends."

"You mean the girls from some escort service. I bet you do, and you do realize they are paid to write those." Rachel's eyes laughed at her small joke. "On the name thing, it was Mom. She had some deep spiritual instincts, mostly coming from her background, the family history at least. There are things that leaked out of her after you left. I became her sole confidante though it's not like we had mother-daughter chats all that often. Sometimes, I wondered if she rejected both of us for your sins. She couldn't talk to Dad, was too private to share much with friends, and was surprisingly lonely. She seemed so strong, so independent, but I guess we all have that needy side. In any case, she slowly started sharing just a bit with me. Thing is, there was much more to her than we ever saw. To us, she was the ice maiden—so self-contained. But she had all this history and a whole life about which we barely had a clue."

"What do you mean?"

"Like, she wasn't always Catholic. We knew so little about her early years, her family. She would say things, drop little clues. Her folks migrated around, mostly fleeing the civil strife and wars that racked the area. There were the Reds and the Whites, periodic skirmishes between Finland and Russia, all kinds of nationalistic, ideological, and ethnic strife. Pogroms were routine. Some estimate that ten million perished in the several years of civil wars following the Bolshevik revolution."

"Jesus, when did you learn any history?"

"Shush and listen, you really are such a cretin. I read some of the historical books you left around. I ate up anything that interested you. Don't forget, I was a kid and you looked God-like at times."

"I was God-like," he chuckled.

"Right." Her sarcasm was unmistakable. "In any case, her grandmother was Jewish, I figured out, and the whole family lived in Lithuania, a small village near Vilna, when she was a child. But that was not their original home. You know those times better than me. Life was hellish, a matter of survival. Their original homeland is lost, they moved a lot, driven by fear. A local pogrom pushed them from the Vilna area back into Russia. Then, not all that long after, the Russian civil war drove them into Finland. From the bits that she shared, her dad was killed in Russia or just died. That was not entirely clear, but I think he did fight. My guess is that he sided with the Reds but might have switched sides later which, now that I think on it, might just explain your twisted politics. Just surviving was a struggle."

"I bet." He exhaled.

"So, mom's mother had three kids that survived. That's what I put together from the scraps she shared, and no husband after a while. But she must at least have been a looker, mom got her looks from somewhere after all. Our grandmother nailed this guy in Finland, a fisherman I guess. Thus, the family name of Maki and the Lutheran religion. She might even have changed her first name to fit in. In any case, Ora and her mom were survivors. Guess you had to be in those days."

"Okay, so how did Ora meet Dad? He certainly never fished, and never mentioned Finland. Mom must have left for England at some point."

"Now that is an interesting question. It became clear to the world that both Hitler and Stalin had bad ideas about what to do with small countries like Finland. Mom was now grown and wanted out. She was tough and nothing was going to stop her. As a born survivor, she made it to England somehow. I've one thought on that. As I noted, we assumed our grandmother remarried in Finland and that is where the Maki name came from. But maybe mom married someone named Maki, someone who had a boat. Maybe mom brought the Maki name into the equation and her mother was never a Maki. We know nothing of the family from those days, whether they are alive or what they looked like. Nothing, just a black hole. My guess is that mom, as a teen, hooked up with some guy and used him to get out. There were some things she never talked about."

"Wait," Josh interjected. "That would make her a bigamist if she really married some mysterious benefactor and he didn't die."

"Yeah, I get that. Weird thought, huh. Somehow, she got there. Work was easy to find as war fever took over in the late thirties. She was young, strong, and smart. She might have had a smattering of English, but it would not have taken her long to pick it up. Think about her, she had such a quick mind. Our dad had all the charm, a typical Celtic storyteller and with wit to spare. But mom had the serious brains. There she was when dad made one of his Atlantic runs with the merchant marines. They must have met when he was in port and the rest, they say, is history. He must have been smitten, this gorgeous blonde who must have been like nothing he had ever met in South Boston. Though he had that charm and was handsome as hell, I suspect what she saw in him was a ticket to the promised land."

They arrived back at his place on Langara Street. He turned to his sister. "I just cannot believe I know so little about the family, about you. Really, what did I think about as a kid?"

"You were trying to get laid all the time, but I took care of that." She smiled impishly. "You forgot one of my favorite ways of torturing you. I would walk in on you and some bimbo. I would shout out to you about the girl that had called. *What girl?* You would ask, falling into my trap. I would go one about not knowing her name but she was frantically crying about being late and sounding terribly worried. And then I would act so innocent asking you what this girl could be late for that got her so worried. *Late for what?* You know, I'm not sure I knew the answer myself at the time, but I did love how angry you got."

"That only worked once." Josh tried.

"Hell no, you really were slow." Rachel laughed out loud for the first time that morning.

"God, you were a shit, I had forgotten about that one. Would it be okay if I hit you in the tummy?"

"Do it, and all you will retrieve is a bloody stump. Thanks for reminding me of those good moments. Teasing you was one of the few joys of my early years. I really was this nerdy kid who obeyed all the rules, the good child. But with you, with you…" She struggled where to go next. "Perhaps I was jealous. I desperately wanted your attention, to spend time with you. I would listen when you talked serious stuff with your friends, the political stuff. I just marvelled at your mind, you just seemed to grasp the big picture, you saw how things fit together. I tended to focus on arcane details, the specifics of things. You, however, seemed to get the meaning of things. I just wanted to suck everything out of your brain."

Josh sighed. "Funny, here I was, embracing all that nonsense of a brave new world, the revolution that was sure to come and that we would lead. And what did I miss, my own family, the things right in front of my damn nose. Seriously, it is like I never wanted to know anything about Mom and Dad. Maybe it was guilt, shame, fear, God knows what. Rach, I've spent over four decades running away from things." Then he stopped.

"Maybe, if you had got in touch, asked me to join you, it all would have been easier. I would have moved heaven and earth to get to you. You know that don't you." The way she looked at him permitted no dispute of how serious she was.

Josh shook his head. "No way I would have done that. I could not have stood the guilt if I ruined your life. That kind of selfishness would have pushed me over the edge. Think about it. I was hiding away in some student hovel in Toronto. I had nothing to offer you. Nothing!"

"We would have had each other," Rachel protested but weakly, as if she understood the weakness of her argument. "We would have made it, somehow."

"Nice try," Josh rebuked her as gently as he could, "the authorities would have tracked you down and dragged you back, after throwing my ass in jail. You were a minor, remember? In any case, we did make it, didn't we? And who knows, maybe I'm ready to stop … running away so hard. Thing is, I'm not sure I know how to stop. I really don't. Hell, I am damn old now, so it won't be easy. I have buried so much for so long I'm not sure I know what's real anymore. Lifetime habits are hard to kick."

"You're right there," Rachel mused.

"So, I'm kind of wondering if you can help me back. You know, for most of my life, I have felt so … exhausted, just exhausted."

"Dumb shit, running from everything and everyone can wear any man out, even an athlete like you were." she whispered.

"Were?"

Rachel wrapped her arms around him. "Yeah, past tense works. I can feel this spare tire developing. No matter, though. You are not running anymore. Do you hear me? I will follow you into the seventh level of hell to drag your sorry ass back."

"The seventh level you say. Well, you must know the way by now." He felt brave in the moment. He held her tightly so that she had no room to punch him. Still, it seemed prudent to advance an olive branch. "Guess I have no choice then. No more running."

"Is that a promise?" she asked hopefully.

"All I can promise is to try."

"Good enough," Rachel felt a frisson of warmth course through her.

Then Josh spoke as if to himself. "That last day and night, as I drove aimlessly around and sat in a diner trying to decide, I kept going over the same things in my head. I repeated scenarios of confronting you, dad, Mo and the others, my old friends from college and high school. I had these imaginary conversations where I explained everything. In my head, each of you understood. These were magical moments of the mind where everyone smiled at the end and forgave me. Then I would snap to. These conversations could never take place. None of us were that smart or forgiving."

"But you cannot possibly know that." Rachel protested.

"I suppose. In my head, though, there was no easy out. I was that lab rat with no escape, one of the ones doomed to become neurotic in the frantic search for an escape from an impossible situation."

"You were wrong about one thing, you know." Rachel murmured.

"How's that?" Josh took her bait.

"I was smart enough. I would have understood, forgiven you."

Josh was silent for many moments before responding. "You're right. Yes. But I wasn't smart enough to see that then."

Rachel wrapped him up even tighter. She never wanted to let go.

CHAPTER 3

Day 1- CONNIE

Josh showed Rachel around the campus during the morning hours, introducing her to several associates who happened to be present. It was end of semester. While a few colleagues had left the campus, most had not. Research universities did not shut down during the summer. The University of British Columbia was a top-tier school with a global reputation. In Canada, it ranked with McGill and the University of Toronto for prestige. Research was its major product and a full-time, full-year avocation for members of the academy located there. Few of the faculty paid all that much attention to the rhythms of semesters, teaching, or service to the public. Those who made it to the top of the academy knew what mattered. The cessation of classes simply offered more time for what each scholar had to value the most ... their research.

He was proud of her and was pleased there were enough colleagues around for him to show her off. She had accomplished so much and yet she remained the quintessential little sister in his mind. As kids, she would follow him around asking endless questions, the most common of which was *'what are you doing?'* That inevitably was followed by *'what do you want to do now?'* Early on, most specific queries were about the world around them, questions for which he really had no answers. *'Why is the sky blue? How do birds know which way to go when they head south?'* Such inquiries from her were endless. At the start, he simply would make up answers. Soon, though, he saw a quizzical, and then a doubtful, look in her eyes. He soon realized that she would not let him get by with transparent fabrications for much longer, no matter how creative. His run as the Wizard of Oz would soon be at an end.

In his mind's eye, he yet could see her running after him, her pigtail bobbing in the back of her head. In those early years, so long ago, she never seemed far behind despite his diligent, sometimes even desperate, efforts to lose her. Despite her seeming omnipresence, he rather liked the attention. It was the kind of adoration you rarely found in life, except from a dog if you're lucky enough to have one. Okay, it was true that some women could be obsessive, but he found that kind of cloying attention off-putting, and avoided them scrupulously. He prided himself at being able to spot the worst at fifty yards, those who would start planning the seating arrangements for the wedding reception right after the first kiss.

As a child, Rachel seemed to have this sixth sense about his intentions. Josh would wait until she was seemingly lost in one of her books and then creep out the door. He would get a half block away before hearing the door slam behind him. *Shit*, he would think, *how does she always know.* Over time, though, he realized just how attached he had become to her presence. He really liked this little pest, ever at his heels while looking up at him with wide, curious eyes. She was the sponge that hung on his every word, even when his words were crap. Seldom wishing to admit ignorance, Josh would simply make up plausible, or not so plausible, responses to her queries. '*I heard this phrase cut to the quick today,*' she asked one day. '*What is a quick?*' Not having a clue, Josh would say something like '*Oh, you have seen swords ... they have this piece at the end of the blade where the handle is. It is this round thing that protects your hand. That's what it is.*' Sounded good to Josh, and his little sister bought it. Three days later, she came running up. *A quick is not part of a sword.*' Uh-oh, Josh recalled thinking at that moment, my run as an omniscient God might well be at an end. She was beginning to do her own research.

He watched with some bemusement as she morphed from a total pest into something vaguely interesting. While it probably happened gradually, Josh was taken by the suddenness of the transformation. She discovered the public library with his help. In consequence, her literary world grew apace and an alternative to the faux facts he often fed her was now at her fingertips. It was another source of information to sate her unquenchable curiosity, one that mostly replaced his questionable reliability as an omniscient seer and source of all knowledge. In his Canadian exile, he realized that he missed her presence terribly, that bobbing pigtail and those wide, expressive eyes. But what really struck him in retrospect was the obvious maturation in her queries about the world around him. *'Do whales sleep?'* was replaced by more profound conundrums such as *'Can God create a rock so big that he cannot lift it?'* He had learned that his best response was *'What do you think?'*

Her eyes struck him as different from other kids her age he knew at the time, and even his own. Rather than looking out upon the world with studied cynicism as he too often did, she gazed upon the world about her with a studied curiosity. It was as if the palette of input about her was a smorgasbord of delights to be dissected and enjoyed. Even if it no longer overwhelmed her, the world of her youth became a laboratory for embracing new lessons and insights. She struck Josh as an absorbent sponge that could never be fully sated. He was so proud of her then. He was still proud now. He missed her wide-eyed innocence and never stopped loving her insatiable desire to understand the world.

As they ambled across the campus that bright and fresh morning, he pointed out various sites of interest until they encountered yet another of his colleagues. *'Oh, let me introduce my sister Rachel. She is the accomplished one in the family, a researcher, professor, and pediatric cancer physician at the University of Wisconsin's respected Children's Hospital.'* Josh's female colleagues would beam with delight at another example of their gender's obvious success while his male colleagues inevitably murmured something like *'Well, Josh, we would have expected your sibling to outperform you. After all, you did not set the success bar very high.'* Everyone would chuckle at the stale joke, and no one feared he would take any offense. Then they would go on to discuss her research in some perfunctory manner, which she realized covered up the fact that there was little else to connect them.

After some time, she rebelled by telling him in private not to parade her around like the prize hog at the county fair. "You have never been to a county fair," he argued.

"How do you know?" she retorted.

"Because then you would appreciate that they care for the hogs a lot better than I treat you."

As his official retirement celebration approached, he realized there would be many opportunities for her to meet the people in his life. There would be too many opportunities in his mind, a realization that wearied him suddenly. *That is odd*, he reflected. He was known as a witty, convivial sort, at least when forced to be among people. Though he preferred solitude, when in the public arena he was full of stories and vignettes that would keep people laughing and at ease. All the time, though, he was counting the minutes to when he could make his escape. Some get charged up in congress with others; he became psychologically depleted. It was as if all the energy drained from him in the effort. He found it remarkable that others never seemed to notice. They assumed that he loved being in the public eye, or at least around others. It all seemed to come so easy to him. Students loved him, he was a sought-after speaker, and invites to social gatherings were plentiful. Funny how the inside and outside can be so different, he mused. No one can really know what goes on inside another person.

At noon, Josh steered his sister to a small Italian place off campus. There, a striking Asian woman about fifty years of age was waiting. "This is Connie Chen," he said as they slipped into the booth opposite her. Rachel recognized the name from prior letters and e-mails. It struck her that this woman was a long-standing arrangement in her brother's life. She had to be significant to deserve any mention at all by her brother. Rachel looked over the person opposite her carefully. She saw a woman of delicate features, pure black hair, and bright, inquisitive eyes. Immediately, Rachel sensed someone who might go toe-to-toe with her brother. "Connie, like you, is plumbing the mysteries of the physical world. She is in the biochemistry department."

After the two women exchanged some details on their respective areas of study and teaching, Rachel smiled broadly. "Tell me, Connie, did you manage to pump some useful information into my brother's head? He fills it up with the most useless junk." Then Rachel wondered if she had been too forward. She assumed an intimacy between her brother and this woman, but why? They could have been just colleagues. But no, she knew she was right. The way this woman and her brother talked, looked at each other, almost finished each other's sentences, they were lovers, she was certain, or surely had been at some point. And she could see the attraction—the dark hair, olive-colored skin, and warm eyes resonated with what little she knew about her brother's taste in women. Best of all, this woman had a quick, easy wit. Rachel warmed to her immediately; her demeaner was fetching no matter the topic on the table and her humour bubbled easily to the surface in an unforced way. Yup, Rachel could easily see why her brother would be attracted to this woman.

"Oh, I would educate him if it were possible. But you know, he's just a social scientist and worse … a male. Most men are beyond help, just not trainable … like stubborn dogs. Now that I think on it, though, your brother is in a class by himself. Simply beyond reach I fear." Connie smiled broadly.

"I'm guessing you never gave up on his training regimen." Rachel persisted as Josh squirmed.

"Alas, no. It turns out that I'm taken with his focus on those larger political and philosophical questions. I mean, I do feel bad for him. It must be deflating to be in a discipline where nothing is ever resolved, where the core questions go on forever and never get answered, or so it seems. But it keeps those social scientists busy and out of the hair of us real scientists."

"Hey," Josh protested, "we have testable hypotheses."

"That's nice, dear," Rachel interjected patronizingly, "but let Connie talk. He is just so defensive, but what can you expect?" *No question*, Rachel thought, *this woman is a winner.* Her thoughts drifted to considering whether she might work on bringing Connie and her brother closer together. Perhaps they were an item, but she saw no evidence of any female presence at Josh's home. Then, she immediately recoiled at falling into a traditional female role of matchmaking.

"I think my interest in politics comes from my background." Connie turned serious. "My parents were professionals, scientists of sorts, in China. From what I gather, they faked being Nationalists and then Communists at one time or another to survive—not an easy task. But after the war, they knew they had to get out. Mao was certain to take control, and intellectuals like my folks would not fare very well. They got to Hong Kong but worried if that place would long survive Communist control, so eventually they made their way to Canada. I was a late addition to the family, right after they arrived here. Growing up, I would listen as they talked politics and the big questions that we all struggled with. You know, how do we create a just society yet permit freedom of action. After they passed, I latched on to Josh for my political fix. He even made sense but maybe that was because I thought he was good-looking at the time. Of course, that was before my cataract surgery and certainly before he got so old and crotchety."

Josh interjected, "Rachel, this poor woman was utterly besotted with me, thinking me so sexy. It was pathetic the way she followed me around, begging for any scrap of attention I might throw her way."

"Yes, dear," both women uttered simultaneously and then broke into laughter. Rachel was dying to ask more about this woman's relationship with her brother but kept her counsel. She saw her brother as a kind of Russian doll. There were many levels, and you treaded carefully as you entered the inner circles. He was clever by letting you in just a little before deflecting you with humour or indirection or one of his endless vignettes.

"Rachel, it is so good to have you here," Connie bubbled. "Now I can get the lowdown on what this guy is really like. He is one of those enticing layer cakes but where the outer layer is glued shut so you can't peek at the goodies inside."

Rachel looked at her brother. She was again reminded of how little she knew about him. Several decades of virtually no contact didn't help. But it was more than that. He was private but in a sophisticated manner … using many words to reveal little. He could be charming and voluble, but that was all artifice and designed to keep you at arm's length. What would she get from this woman if she pressed about her brother? Had Connie been successful at getting into the deeper layers of her mysterious sibling?

Then it hit her. Josh was his father—Big Jim. She yet could see her dad, tall and robust as he entertained customers in his neighbourhood watering hole. The Harp Bar, or the Haap Baah as the locals called it, was a popular hangout in the area for the Irish mafia and wannabe Irish revolutionaries. It was a haven for those reliving IRA battles from several thousand miles away. Rachel could yet hear the regular patrons waxing on about the Maze, the English prison for Catholic freedom fighters in Ulster, and the blanket boys who refused to wear prison garb as they went on hunger strikes. When the sons of the Emerald Isle touched on those martyrs to the cause, Big Jim would be driven to passionate eloquence of Celtic pride that, in turn, would result in a spontaneous eruption of patriotic songs—if they were not gulping down heaps of corned beef and cabbage with sides of potato that were a hit at Jim's place.

What could she tell Connie about this mysterious man to whom she was tied by blood? What did she want to reveal to a woman she instinctively liked, but hardly knew? Thus, she fell back on her favorite stories about messing with Josh's laboured efforts to woo women. Connie was laughing, but Rachel was beginning to pull back. Sure, these things happened, where she would break up a date with some outlandish fib, but that was rather rare in fact, at least in high school. Josh did not date all that much, not that she thought hard on the matter. He spent more time reading, playing classical pieces his mother taught him on the piano, and keeping his athletic skills sharp. Females seemed more interested in him than he in them.

"At other times, he wasn't so awfully bad," Rachel paused to find a positive memory as a way of seeking balance before continuing. "I recall this story about a girl in his high school class. She was apparently decent looking but shy and very studious and not that popular as a result. Academic achievement was not the way to social success. Then she was diagnosed with a virulent form of cancer. The chemo treatments of the times were harsh, and she lost all her hair. Of course, high school being what it was, she was the subject of further isolation and ridicule as only teens can inflict on one another. They can be so cruel."

"Tell me," Connie agreed, "I was one of the few Asians in my first western school. Now, Asians are everywhere in Vancouver."

"Then you know. Well, Josh's friend Jimmie told me that he and Josh saw this girl being teased by some girls one day in the cafeteria, the so-called cool girls. He went on to tell me that this brother of mine got up from his table, walked over and, in a loud voice, asked this girl to the prom. You must understand, he was the big man on campus, the big athlete. All the girls would have died to be asked to the prom by him. Some had even asked him already. I don't believe he intended to go, thinking those things silly. Yet he chose to ask this girl in such a public way, just to shut these creeps up. I yet remember him bringing her by the house on prom night. She was not a beauty, but I thought her lovely in a way … very delicate and sweet. So thin, though. You can tell that some have beauty that needs a deeper look. I cannot fathom the cruelty she faced." Rachel noticed the look on Connie's face and almost blushed at how serious everyone suddenly had become. "Well, I just wanted you to know that he sometimes rises to the occasion. Not often, I might add, but it has happened."

Connie obviously had been moved. "Can I ask what happened to this girl?"

"She passed a few months later," Josh said quietly. "But she had that night."

After lunch, Rachel returned to Josh's place to make some calls and work on the rewrite of a medical research paper for which the deadline for resubmission was approaching. There also were the calls to her clinical colleagues to check on patients. Any time away from her clinical duties involved the same struggle. Her staff would usher her toward the door with copious affirmations not to worry, that they would take care of her patients, and that all would be well. But she couldn't let go, not really. She knew they would roll her eyes at the sound of her voice on the phone but patiently address her anxieties. They were patronizing her, for sure, but she appreciated the pretense. Besides, there probably were some patients for whom her personal input might help. What bothered her colleagues is that she seldom took time off. Her professional life was pretty much her life. Taking a week off to visit her brother was greeted with awe and shock, and they all feared that she would return after two days, driven by some irrational belief that the medical world would collapse in her absence. So far so good though. Perhaps she might stay the course. It appeared the many bettors on an early return were about to lose their money in the office pool.

She had stumbled on to her interest in medicine early. When she reconstructed her professional journey, it inevitably involved an apocryphal memory, one so far back in time that she questioned its authenticity. She recalled coming across some budding psychopaths abusing a cat which sent her into a rage where she screamed and flailed at the miscreants with abandon. She had amazed herself but was relieved when she saw them scamper off. Then, she picked up the animal that whimpered in her hands. She felt so helpless. She desperately wanted to work some magic to restore health and vitality to this innocent creature. But she could not, and that reality tortured her. After one last gasp, it lay still. She stared for a while, trying to will movement into this creature that moments earlier had life. But she was impotent and hated the feeling. Now, decades later, she could not really recall if this was the moment her interest in medicine was born. Likely, there probably was no such moment, but this memory was vivid to her. What she did experience was this growing need to ease suffering, reduce pain, restore hope. At some point, preconscious understandings and emerging aspirations matured as fully formed ambitions. Once that took hold, nothing would hold her back.

Her mind returned to Madison, Wisconsin. She did cancer research at the Carbone Center and her clinical work at the impressive medical facility located at the far western end of the campus. When she had time, she would stroll from the hospital across the adjacent soccer fields to the path along Lake Mendota, one of five lakes that served as the physical template that defined the city. She loved walking out to Picnic Point, a peninsula that jutted out into the lake. At the tip, she could look across the water to the state capitol or toward the setting sun on the other side. The magic of the place never ceased to amaze her. She came across a piece in a national magazine once. It listed the twenty-five most romantic spots in the world, not just Wisconsin or the United States, but the world. Picnic Point was on the list. She laughed; there had been no romantic moments for her on this spot, just nature's glory.

Where did the years go? she ruminated. Her thoughts returned to an innocent time. She could recall sneaking into the back of her dad's bar. She would hide in a small stockroom to listen to the conversation drifting her way, desperately hoping Jim would not need a resupply of something or other. How would she explain to him her presence there? Already, her father thought her strange. Early on, she had been repelled by the smells of stale beer and the faint aroma from other sources she decided not to think about too closely. She remained, however. The world on the other side of the door fascinated her, spurred her imagination. The wistful talk of the Emerald Isle was particularly moving—a longing for a world the discussants neither knew personally nor likely wanted any longer if they were to be honest. Still, it was such a part of the myth that gave desperate lives just a little bit of meaning. She was drawn to what she heard and yet disappointed. They seldom looked forward in life. It was just talk, sentimentality, useless emotion. They obsessed about a world that no longer existed. It all involved looking back, as had all classical education up until the end of the 19th century. At some point, she realized there was nothing to learn here. Her world would lie elsewhere.

Her calls finished, she stared at her computer screen for a while, looking at data and numbers that she laboured to turn into a journal article. This one had *JAMA* potential or maybe the *New England Journal of Medicine*. But soon she slammed her computer shut. There was no way she could focus today or maybe this week. Seeing Josh again had unleashed all kinds of thoughts and emotions. She might as well let them run wild. And yet she felt a frisson of fear. Why? She had always been in command of her world. She really was like her mother—closed, self-contained, seldom showing emotion. It was her discipline and focus that had gotten her through college and medical school, mostly on scholarships and pure grit and drive. When others chose lucrative practices, she instinctively headed for research and the toughest medical questions to crack. Her divorce had been a professional blessing. She then moved to Madison where her medical research took off.

She smiled as she thought about the universal med school bromide about their being three tiers among would-be doctors. Those in the middle of the class, performance-wise, would make the best clinicians. Those toward the top would gravitate toward research and teaching. They wanted to make an enduring contribution. Those toward the bottom would make the most money, that's why they worked so hard for the credential. The worst students were in it for the dough. She had done fine money-wise. She had a nice home in Shorewood Hills, the small and rather exclusive enclave on the shores of Lake Mendota within walking distance to the hospital and university campus. Material things, though, meant little to her. That was one thing she clearly shared with Josh, a lack of concern about the usual trappings of success. It was the work that counted and her one daughter whom she did not see enough. Her ex-husband registered barely a ripple in her life. She should have conceived artificially. Much more sensible and convenient. Of one thing she was certain, if the triage based on medical school performance had any merit, she was top tier, the brightest of the bright that sought out new knowledge for mankind. Her laboratory work had always been special to her … a refuge from people. That feeling bothered her on occasion, though she didn't dwell on it much.

She shook her head and wandered into Josh's office. "Typical," she whispered to herself. Her eyes looked over a disaster area, piles of papers scattered without rhyme or reason. Yet she knew others like her brother. You asked for something, and somehow, they would dig deep into a seemingly random pile before pulling out the elusive object of desire. How did they do that? How did they live like that? She, on the other hand, was always organized. Everything was catalogued and cross-referenced. Such innate dispositions are the attributes that define each of us as individuals. She knew that he saw the world as an abstract painting. The colours and brushstrokes made little sense at first. She saw it a fully representative portrait, all clear with each aspect in its proper place.

Josh had always been able to see patterns in the chaos that looked simply like chaos to her. Where others saw random nonsense, he made connections. It was his gift, as if he were more of an artist than a scholar. She did not actually envy him; she was happy with what God had put into her, but she did admire him, even his miraculous ability to not drown in the chaos of his own world. He had always been a source of wonder to her, and great frustration. All her life, she had careened between admiration and anger. After casually thumbing through several folders and finding nothing of interest, she noticed a box on top of a cabinet. It had held pears in another life. Now, it held pictures which, like Josh's life, were simply thrown together without order or reason.

She hesitated, but only for a moment. She shouldn't invade his privacy, but here was little doubt that she could successfully practice restraint in the face of such temptation. After all these years, it was time to learn more about a brother who had remained such a cipher throughout her adult life. She poked through the box, carefully at first. Most of the pictures had that faded look suggesting age, if not neglect.

The first several were people she did not recognize, young and rather scruffy looking. *Probably from his early days in Canada,* she concluded. They were from a period where concern about clothing and one's grooming were easily conflated with some obsequious obedience to political, if not cultural, orthodoxy. In a couple, she found Josh, scruffy and almost unrecognizable. She looked three and four times to confirm it was really he. These were from that part of his life that had remained a mystery to her.

At one point, she came across a photo of Josh with his arm around a young woman. She was a natural beauty but had done nothing to accentuate her looks. Her hair hung straight down in disarray, no makeup, and adorned with a loose-fitting outfit that hid her body quite successfully. Rachel looked closely. She was certain there was chemistry between the two. This was something that even the highly rational physician could sense, part of what demarked the female from their less-developed male compatriots. She called it EQ, or an emotional quotient. Quickly, she put that one in her pocket, looking around for witnesses she knew were not there.

She continued deeper into the box. Almost immediately, she uncovered a layer that hit home. Here were pictures from her childhood—Mom and Dad, Josh's friends, and the little girl with the sandy blond hair and nerdy glasses. She bit her lip and immediately fought back tears. He had taken these with him, kept them all these years. That meant something.

CHAPTER 4

Day 1- LATE AFTERNOON

Time passed for her, she knew not how long, when she heard a sound at the front door. Quickly, she stuffed a photo into her pocket and put the box back onto its original perch. "Josh," she called out, "is that you?" Damn, she thought, her voice was forced, laden with guilt. And tears, how could she explain the moisture in her eyes.

"No," he replied, "it is the neighbourhood sex fiend. But don't worry, I only prey on broads still in their prime."

"Then I'm in danger." She tried sounding light as she emerged from his office. "I was just looking over your books, wanted to see what a fake scientist might have in his library." She was forcing it, wasn't she? She didn't want to start again with him not trusting her but then why did she pry? Damn it, this was more difficult than it should be.

"So, what is your judgment?"

"Just like I thought, a bunch of poppy cock." Why the hell did she say that? Were her eyes still moist?

But all he said was "Yeah, yeah, your envy of true genius betrays you. Get much done?" Then he laughed gently. "Poppycock? Where did you come up with that?"

"Enough," she looked for another topic. "Hey, tell me about Connie."

"Good friend," he said too quickly.

"That might work with your male friends, but any female would immediately see that there is a history there."

There was a silence. After apparently weighing several options, Josh went with honesty. He always thought that a questionable strategy since, in his experience, honesty was nothing but trouble. Still, in this instance, he might not have a choice. He had met his match. "This is going to be a tough week." He smiled.

"Bet your ass," she responded, "so buckle up, buttercup." Ah, she thought, she was back in control.

"Okay, Connie and I were an item for a while."

When he paused, she said, "More, much more."

Josh collapsed into an easy chair. "After Usha decided to be true to herself, I was adrift for a bit, more than a bit. I think it was the usual thing that happens in these closed worlds like academia. I was now unattached, and she had long returned to the single life. Someone schemed to bring us together, which I hate, but which is inevitable. We did not run in the same academic circles ..."

"Since she was a real scientist and you ... not so much," she interjected with a smile.

"Bite me." Josh quickly retorted but, to Rachel's relief, continued. "Someone decided they had to force the issue. Whatever subterfuge they used worked, and we started going out. At the beginning, it was just nice, concerts and museums and plays. These are things you don't want to do alone, well, most people don't. I was good with it, but she was different. She did not push, was funny and relaxed, and never seemed to have an agenda. You know how women are ..."

"Careful," Rachel warned.

"No, really, one kiss and most broads are picking out color patterns for the kid's room." Rachel smiled. He was right and she knew it. "She just seemed content with a friendship."

"Wait, not another asexual relationship?"

"No, no," Josh quickly responded. "We got to the sex stuff soon enough since, as is obvious, I am a stud."

"Barf bag please. Damn, where did I put the one that I took from the plane?"

"Funny gal. And despite the rumours, I'm not made of stone. It was nice. For a while we lived together."

"What?" She bolted upright. "I remember her name coming up, but I never heard about you living in sin."

"Living in sin? What's with that? Preparing for retirement in a nunnery?" Her reaction threw him off; lightness might not suffice here. "I didn't mention anything at the time, really?"

"No," Rachel asserted. "I would have remembered for sure."

"Hmm, my bad but that would have invited more questions. Besides, we both knew it would never get beyond a certain level. That's what made it great. The best thing was that pressure was off. You know, people put us together as a couple. We talked about that a lot. Everyone wants you married, or at least paired off. Oh, you look way too happy not having anyone to bite you in the ass every morning. We can't have that, so we got to make sure we line you up with a warden for life. When women asked me if I was content being alone, they would not believe it when I said yes. They could not accept that it was true. *'Look at my bright and ecstatic smile,'* I would say, *'do I look like I am suffering?'* But to no avail, they would insist on scheming me into a relationship. Now Connie and I could go about our lives in peace. We could focus on our work, have someone to chat with, or ignore if that is what was needed. It was an agreement of sorts. I'm not even sure we talked about it, we kind of slid right into it."

"Into what?" Rachel gasped. "I'm beginning to think you're a eunuch."

"Heavens no! Like I said, I'm not a stone. For a while, we had a damn good sex life, but we settled into a routine. No, that's not it. In fact, the sex was quite good. By good, I mean that I enjoyed it too much. It rather scared me. I focused on the company she provided and freedom that being coupled gave me. You know, I could ward off those women on the hunt ... I was in a relationship so not available as husband material. Worked like a charm." He smiled.

"You, sir, are a pig." Rachel thought of several questions, along with a few insults, but vocalized none of them.

"Well then, I might as well drive the final nail into that coffin." Josh had that lopsided smile again. "As time went on, Connie came to her senses and moved on. It was then that I found out that using professionals for sex was the best solution."

"Prostitutes." She laughed.

"No, professionals, women of quality who knew what they were doing. I mean, I didn't scour the streets for crackheads or anything like that. I did my research and found a reputable service that offered quality girls … err, women. I had a few regulars. I got to know several quite well."

"Interesting. I mean, even a schlepp like you could get laid on your own, without paying for it. I still remember the girls chasing you in high school and college. You had to beat them off with a stick, a fact which never ceased to amaze me."

"And that is the point, exactly. Life lesson number one, dear sister. You don't go to pros to get sex; you use their services so that you can walk away after the sex. Let's face it, with women kisses too easily become contracts, something men look upon with dread."

"Wow, and to think I looked forward to this visit." But she smiled. "Isn't that kind of sex demeaning, empty? Sorry, I just don't see the attraction."

"Just the opposite—it is great as far as the sex goes. You can focus on the sex rather than all the collateral crap. Of course, there are problems with the best of plans. Once, the girl that showed up was a former student. That was awkward. I remembered her all too well. She was studious, quiet, and dressed much more conservatively than virtually all the other coeds."

"Oh my God. How did you handle that?"

"After a moment of awkwardness, we talked. She explained that she had applied the analytical tools she learned in class to estimate various returns on investment for life choices after school. Hooking easily won and I could not argue with her logic. But she was aware of the short-term life expectancy at the top of her chosen profession. She now was in a graduate program and hooking made her much more money than being a teaching assistant. It also left her with more time for her studies. A very rational young lady."

"Did you …?"

"Oh no. We just talked on that occasion, but it would have been fine if we did and I still paid her for her time. Let's face it, all sex is an exchange. Women trade their goodies for affection, social status, protection, a good meal, or a date. If they get lucky, they negotiate their body for love. Men, on the other hand, use the appearance of love to leverage sex. Every young man knows that the key to the kingdom are the words *'I love you.'* Of course, back in the neighbourhood, nothing seemed to work with those Catholic girls. I think they all took a vow to St. Virginius of the body as a pure vessel of the Holy Spirit. They would have preferred diving into a vat of boiling oil than spreading their legs. You know the old Catholic version of birth control, an aspirin."

"An aspirin?" Rachel queried though knew what he would say. She wanted him to say it.

"Sure, just keep that pill pressed between the knees. If the aspirin didn't hit the floor, those legs were locked shut. No guy could possibly get to the promised land. I should know, I tried hard enough to get there with a few of them." Josh laughed at his little joke.

Rachel looked askance at him. "I refuse to believe you had that much trouble with the local girls back then. You were too much of a catch."

"I suppose I'm exaggerating just a bit for effect, but not much. Anyway, the way I look at it, sex for money is at least an open transaction. Each party knows the basis of the exchange, the price is set in advance, the parties know exactly what they are getting. There is no artifice, no disingenuous posturing. What could be better than that?"

"Love," she offered tentatively.

"Hah!" he snorted. "You remember Kit Olson, from my college days?"

"Of course, she was one of your groupies that followed you around like a sheepdog. I could never figure out her fascination—she was a real looker, cheerleader, nice body. She could have gotten a real man."

"Yeah, yeah, well, this story is not all that funny. She did always seem to be around. I just thought it was because I hung around with her best girlfriend's brother from my high school days, played ball with him. I also knew her brother, though much less well. He was older, and their family was from a different class of people. But even a putz like me could figure out she had the hots for me. But there was no way I would be interested."

"Why?"

"She was too obvious. I remember once, I weakened. I was horny of course, all of us guys were back then. Hmm, I suppose young guys still are. No matter, she was there one day, the big blue eyes looking up at me. I let my guard down and kissed her. I knew immediately it was a mistake. She fluttered her eyes."

"No, the nerve of her." Rachel could not help but chuckle.

"Not funny. Then she asked me what the kiss meant. What it meant! I wanted to tell her that it meant I was horny. I don't know what I said in the moment, but I stayed away from her after that as much as I could."

"Hmm, that was kind of you. I'm impressed." Rachel's expression mirrored her words.

"Don't be. Here is something you could not possibly know. She tracked me down after I left. I couldn't believe it. Here she showed up at my hovel of a flat in Toronto. I've no idea how she tracked me down. I did not exactly broadcast my location, but I guess she was persistent. It must have been that older brother of hers. He was working for the feds and chasing after draft-dodgers like me." He grimaced as if he remembered something very painful. "What could I do? She was adrift so I asked her to stay a few days and offered to show her around. I kept mentioning how busy I was with work and now school. But I knew the truth and dreaded it. She was hoping to build a nest at my place. I gave her my bed and slept on the couch. I thought that obvious but …"

"Oh, I have a bad feeling about this." Rachel looked away.

"You and me both. Anyway, I think it was the third day or something. I was sitting at my desk working on a paper and sensed she had come up behind me. God, I had been so lonely. I mean, the Canadians were great and all, they had a network for guys like me. Still, I was rather lost and felt so alone. And her smell, she always wore some scent filled with killer pheromones. I can recall it even now. But what killed me is that she brushed her breasts up against the back of my head. Wait, is that too graphic?"

Rachel found the direction of his story oddly embarrassing, but she was not about to admit that. "Keep going. No problem."

"It was just a suggestion of a touch. I even wondered for a moment whether it had happened or maybe it was just a mistake. It wasn't, of course, and I felt myself responding. I knew what she wanted. Really, I was not that dense. Don't say anything, Rach."

"Not a word." She held up her hands.

He leaned back in his chair, his eyes on some distant object. "I kept saying to myself … don't, don't, don't be an idiot. But that was my head, the one on top of my neck. The other one, the one between my legs that controlled my brain, was saying something else entirely. And that smell, it was overwhelming. I spun around and grabbed her, just lifted her up and almost threw her on my desk. The image of papers and books flying onto the floor is what I recall best of that moment. It really was a blur after that …"

Rachel saw his discomfort. "I can figure out the rest."

"I'm sure you can. Sex, for a man, is always a calculation between need and the price to be paid for satisfying that need. I knew this price here was large, incalculably large, and thus the terror. But all reason had fled."

"And next … not sure I want to ask." She looked away for a moment, then back at him.

"I'm not totally sure. I can't or won't remember details, just images of her clothes flying off and some sounds she made, or I made. Who knows now, they were more like grunts. That moment is with me.

Instantly, you want a do-over, but you know it is already too late to turn back. It is such an odd moment, to be in diametrically separate places physically and emotionally."

Rachel sat totally still, not quite comprehending the meaning of his last comment. Why was he telling her this now? He had revealed virtually nothing for decades and suddenly this painful moment from his past erupts to the surface. Was he confessing some deep guilt, sharing a cautionary tale, revealing some hidden dimension of his inner being? Confused, she did and said nothing. She decided to let him wander where he needed to go.

"Of course." She whispered simply to break the ensuing silence.

"It was over soon enough, a lot of pent-up need I suppose." He suddenly looked searchingly at her. "Wait, am I embarrassing you? You really don't need to hear this crap."

"No," she murmured. "I'm a physician for god's sake. There is nothing you can say that will embarrass me. Hell, I insisted that you open-up, and certainly didn't expect a Hallmark mini-series." She waited and hoped he would continue.

"Good, then you won't be shocked by the Stephen King script that is the rest of this debacle. There was nothing else but to take her to bed. I so wanted to scream that this had been a mistake. Can we just forget what happened? But I knew that was impossible when she wept into my chest. To my shame, we became lovers. That was so cruel of me, perhaps my weakest moment. I couldn't sleep that night. What was I going to tell her the next morning? How would I tell her to go away without breaking her? I doubt there is anything much worse than receiving unconditional love when you cannot return it. Then I wondered. Was she using birth control? Oh my god, I never asked, never used a condom. Most girls I knew were prepared, but Kit seemed so innocent. She probably thought it a sin to even consider using a contraceptive. Really, that would mean you were thinking about doing the deed."

Uh-oh, Rachel thought, *is that where he is leaving it?* "So, what happened?"

"Oh, she didn't get pregnant, at least not to my knowledge." He paused again, looking uncertain. "Tell me, did you ever love Evan?"

"Where the hell did that come from?" She was unsettled.

"Okay, here is why I ask. I never really knew him, but I never felt the two of you were close. In pictures, or when you mentioned him, I never felt warmth between the two of you. So—"

"Wait, where are you going with this?" But something about the look in his eyes told her that his story of Kit was finished for the moment. Funny, she thought. It had only been a day, and she was picking up his rhythms and signals. She was peering inside his head.

"Hey," Josh said, "I opened a bit, now your turn."

Let it go, she decided. He did have a point. If they were to establish a form of equity, she would have to reciprocate. "Love Evan?" She paused, realizing the question absent a response. "I suppose I thought I did, in the beginning. For a while I thought it was okay, until he started screwing around. Well, it was more complicated than just that, but at least I got Cate out of the deal. Thing is, I was clueless about what I was supposed to feel. I didn't know what married people were supposed to feel."

"Yeah." He smiled sardonically, looking at her with an intensity that unnerved her. "I think you know what I'm talking about."

"Of course," Rachel responded. Inside though, she was clueless.

Josh suddenly got up and strode into his office. She could hear him rumbling around the cabinet with the pictures. Rachel froze. "*Oh no,*" she said to herself, barely a whisper. *He is getting the pictures. He will know.* So? Why the guilt? She was just naturally curious, and after all, they were not hidden. Still her heart pounded. It seemed a violation of some sort to her. And she was the good girl, the one that obeyed all the rules. But he walked back carrying a single photo, a picture that had seen many decades pass since the moment it had been captured for posterity.

"I always loved this one," he said, sitting next to his sister. It was a picture of their parents, obviously looking at each other with affection. She looked hard at it, trying to gather intelligence from the scant clues available to her. The couple in the photo was young; children were a mere gleam in Big Jim's eyes at best. And they were not in the States. It was England, maybe Ireland, from the architecture of the buildings in the background. "It is hard to imagine they ever had such affection back when we knew them. But look, they were so attractive, so young, so vital. When we were kids, they were going through the motions. But here, look! Look at his face. He is besotted. No wonder he worked so hard to get her to the States. She was a beauty. Remember Ora giving those piano lessons, she even got me to play? Where did she learn to play so well? I was always stunned that there were so many scruffy Irish kids who wanted lessons. They came from all over."

"What she went through was incredible," Rachel whispered. "We will never know the truth, but I'm certain that she converted to Catholicism for Dad. She had that zeal of a newbie, but there were things she mentioned from time to time, little suggestions. I would ask her about the past, but it was clear she didn't want to go there. *It is past*, she would say, *no need to go there*. That would end any discussion. But once, she mentioned Dad and guns and the cause. The damn cause! Why would she give a damn about the cause? She doesn't have any Irish in her. Anyway, she was sick at the time, dying, and thinking a lot more about things past. She mentioned what she called the thrill of her life. I had to push and prod a bit, but she mentioned running guns into Ireland. She only said it once and then slammed shut on that topic. Can you imagine? But that's what she said."

"I'm confused," Josh said quizzically. "That would have been way after the Irish civil war and well before the Ulster troubles. I didn't realize this went on at that time. Then again, I never had Dad's passion for the history of the old country."

Rachel picked up her thoughts. "Remember that Europe was headed for war. Everyone knew it, except that dolt Chamberlain. I recall reading that the IRA thought this was their best chance to bring Ulster back into the motherland. They were getting ready. When England was distracted, they would strike. I think there is even evidence that the leadership was in contact with the Nazis who would have been more than ready to help stir up trouble on England's backside. Makes sense that the new Reich would spend a few deutsche marks to arm the rising, help the boys avenge the Easter debacle of 1916. If the Reich could get the Irish to rise-up and attack Northern Ireland during the planned cross-channel invasion, so much the better for the Nazis."

"Holy shit, Mom the rebel. Can't be, she was so, so domestic and almost meek when we knew her. That would explain so much though."

"Mom was never meek, just beaten down in the end. Our father had a lot to do with that, but you weren't around enough to see it all." Rachel added without hesitation.

"I don't want to know, even now." He said distractedly.

"By the way," Rachel decided to shift from a sensitive topic. "Do you think dad did his merchant marine thing just to help some crazy Irish uprising during the war?"

"No idea, but that makes sense at least." Josh shook his head. "It always confused me that he helped bring supplies to a people he hated so. You figure it out."

"Son of a ...," then she trailed off.

"In any case, the Germans footed the bill to run guns from Scandinavia to Ireland. Must have been dangerous, running past the British navy. Dad was working transport ships then and spent a lot of time in the UK. No way he would have ignored any romantic conspiracy that involved Irish freedom, either by intent or mere opportunity. Of course, that is how they met ... mom and dad. Can you imagine, the two of them on small boats, darkened faces, running in high seas at night with no radar or moon to guide them. The risks must have been horrific. Just think of a passionate man to be smitten by this ethereal and brave and mysterious angel from the roof of the world."

"Mom?" Rachel said with incredulity. "Our frail and quiet mother?"

"Don't think about her as we knew her." Josh enthused. "Just remember that everyone has a history, often one we will never know. When dad first met her, she is a young blond goddess who appears out of the North Sea mists like a dream. Someone like Dad would not have stood a chance against her romantic aura and mystery. And she? Well, he was a stud though I can never imagine that meant much to her. No, more likely she saw in him an opportunity. All the scraping by and near-death escapes of her past could have been behind her. With one stroke, she might get to America, the proverbial promised land. Must have been a powerful lure at the time. We always wondered why no pictures of a wedding. We joked that they were living in sin, which seemed so unlikely to us … good Catholics that they were."

"Hah, I can imagine what dad would have done to me if I had shacked up with some guy."

"I would have been placing flowers on your grave for sure. But hell, if they had gotten married, Dad would have thrown a blowout party at his wedding. He was a ham, there would have been tons of pictures with him in every one of them. I bet they got married over there. Now that I noodle this a bit, perhaps they dummied up fake marriage papers to get her into the States. Sure, that makes total sense. He had to marry her, or fake it, to get her over to the States. The IRA could have done that to reward them for services rendered. And if she were already married to some Scandinavian guy, then they might have thought a fake marriage the best alternative. Think about it, my logic is usually unassailable, that's why they pay me the big bucks."

"I am thinking about it, and my conclusion is that you are suffering from delayed acid flashbacks from the sixties. And yet, as much as it pains me to say this, you may be right. It fits."

"But here's the more important thing," Josh intoned. "We never saw any love, any affection. Did you ever see them kiss, embrace, hold hands?" When she shook her head, he continued. "No, neither did I. Hell, I used to joke that they had sex twice—me and you. They liked their first issue, me, but then seeing you, that was it."

"Ha-ha, your so-called wit still sucks." She was smiling, but it was forced. Her mind was elsewhere.

"But you agree, don't you, neither of us saw any affection between them. Neither of us had a role model for what a loving relationship might be."

"No argument from me." Rachel sighed deeply. "It was worse after you disappeared. They never talked. Dad seldom sang. Mom stopped playing the piano, mostly stopped at least. It was a perpetual wake. I tried but … you were the prince. No matter what I did, accomplished, the best I could get was the pat on the head. Top of medical school class at Johns Hopkins, and all I could get was a smile from Dad and a freaking handshake from Mom. What was with that? Dad would have thrown a goddamn ticker tape parade down Dorchester Street if you had gone to Notre Dame and scored one freaking touchdown. Mom used to brag about my grades when I was young, later she did not seem to care."

"I probably would have played strong safety, maybe line-backer."

"What?" She was annoyed he broke her train of thought.

"Those positions don't score touchdowns … at least not often."

"Not the point, nimrod." she shouted, but then her cell phone rang. It was her paper co-author who wanted to chat about a reinterpretation of the latest data runs. "This will take a while," she mouthed toward her brother.

"I'll do supper," he mouthed back. Rachel winced. Somehow, nothing in her past relationship with Josh suggested any confidence in his culinary skills was warranted. He soon would prove her snap assessment to be in error. Unlike her, he had gotten skilled in the kitchen.

"Josh," Rachel called out as he was about to leave the room and she covered the phone with her hand. "We will pick this up again another time."

"Oh, I know that." He smiled wanly. "I do know that."

She looked at him as he exited the room. After little more than a day, they already were in a different place. That pleased and unsettled her. She took a deep breath and then turned back to her call.

CHAPTER 5

Day 2 – GLIMPSES OF A LIFE

Rachel heard Josh puttering around the house the next morning. She thought about jumping up to join him but thought better of it. *"Come on, Mo,"* she heard faintly, then the door opened and closed.

A half hour later the door opened again. Josh paused at the smell of bacon sizzling in a pan. "My god, the domestic goddess strikes. Watch out, I can't vouch for how long that stuff has been around." Morris grunted, obviously displeased that his world had not returned to normal as he had hoped. The pug recovered quickly and waddled over to his bowl to find fresh food awaiting. He glanced back at Rachel with a fresh appreciation before his head dipped into the dish.

They sat down to the kind of breakfast he had not enjoyed in some time. "Good news to report."

"Oh," Rachel responded.

"Yeah, he had a first-class poop this morning. I think you threw him off yesterday. Mo is not a fan of change."

"Sure, great breakfast talk. Damn, I remember when I hung on your every word, you seemed to have the sagacity of a renaissance man of letters. Now you are reduced to the status of a world-class connoisseur of dog poop. I can see why you have trouble with the ladies."

Josh smiled. "I would like you to know there are still women who appreciate my beautiful mind."

"If they exist, my best guess is that their bra size exceeds their IQ."

"Sexist," he uttered.

"Pervert," she retorted.

They both laughed simultaneously. It was returning, their chemistry. That could never be turned off completely, no matter the litany of past sins. Josh could once again see her as the high schooler who no longer looked upon him with awe and wonder, absorbing all he said. Now that her razor-sharp wit was in full form, their exchanges would be quick and unforgiving. Outsiders probably would be taken aback, concluding that real animosity existed between them. The effect only served to motivate them further. For a time, they had kept score on who won each verbal parry but could never agree on the winner.

"Okay, point for you," he allowed. Josh looked at her closely as she smiled. She was twelve again, all ponytail and geeky glasses. He had slipped out of the house to head to a local playground where he would play some hoops. As he crossed the street, he heard the inevitable "wait for me." *Oh shit*, he had complained to himself, *why couldn't she be fascinated by boys, clothes, and gossip like the other girls her age?* He looked back as she darted between the parked cars. It was like a newsreel repeatedly playing before him, no matter how hard he pushed it all away. It all happened in seconds though it seemed an eternity in his mind. One moment, her face was wide with excitement, her legs churning to catch up with him. The next would be an excruciating horror played out in super-slow motion. He tried to scream, but nothing came out. His voice was frozen somewhere beyond his reach. Still, he heard everything else … the tires squealing, the thud, and her short scream.

His voice finally erupted. *"Fuck, fuck, fuck …"* came out somehow as he raced to her prone, bleeding body. He frantically tried to figure out what to do, but his brain was unresponsive. It was wrong, he knew, she might have fractures that any movement might aggravate. Still, he scooped her up and ran to the car he had recently managed to buy, his first one. With blind urgency, he sped through the streets like the madman he had suddenly become, pulling into the emergency room within two minutes. The inside of his new car was covered in her blood, but he could care less about that. His stomach surged up to his throat he could barely breathe. She could not leave him; he would not permit that!

He seldom left her side the next several days, often holding her hand and talking with her. At one point, when it looked uncertain, he kissed her forehead before whispering in her ear. *'Rach, don't you dare leave me. I swear, if you try, I will follow you wherever you go and drag your sorry ass back. Do you understand me, do you?'* He was certain he saw a smile briefly cross her face. She slowly started her comeback. His quick actions, he was told, might well have saved her life.

"Okay," Rachel interrupted his reverie, "I'm not coming with you today. I have got to get back to that overdue paper after last night's discussion."

"No problem, I've an end-of-semester committee meeting and a thesis defense. I would not be much fun in any case."

"Then it would be like any other day."

He smiled, appreciating anew just how good she was. "I really have to up my game again. Oh, and by the way, we're having dinner with a few of my friends tonight."

"Been to rent-a-friend again."

"Ha-ha …" He walked toward the door, then stopped and returned to his office. As he retraced his steps to the front door, he dropped the box of pictures in front of her on the kitchen table. "If you're going to snoop, you might as well do it in the open. One point for me."

"May your camels come down with a debilitating disease and your testicles wither to the size of dried dates," was all she could come up with while blushing profusely.

"Ow, I better stop at the burn ward on my way to school." She could hear his laugh as the door shut.

After he was gone, she stared at the box. Not yet, she thought. Her mind wandered back to Josh's much earlier question about her former husband. Had she loved him or any man? There was no easy response. She hardly ever thought of Evan; she never thought of him even while they were joined in matrimony. That level of indifference cannot be normal, she mused.

"This week is going to be tougher than I thought," she said out loud to Morris, "but at least we have each other." The dog merely eyed her with disinterest and curled up for a nap. "Typical male," she sniffed.

Alone with her thoughts, she wondered why she had married Evan. He was a bit like her, dedicated to his craft on the surface at least. He was more of a clinician than she but remained focused on being perceived as a successful physician, even if his clientele were drawn from the upper crust of society. As time went on, he spent more time seeking new medical devices in which to invest. That is where the money was, and his family had trained him well ... wealth is what defined a man and cemented relations within this family or, on occasion, drove them apart. Perhaps, she mused, it was too easy of a relationship for her and that's why it had lasted so long. She never had to explain why she needed to get back to the hospital, the lab, a medical conference. It was a shared understanding ... the work came first.

After several months of dating, he proposed. She saw it coming and yet was still surprised. Rachel fought hard to bring back the moment. What had she felt? It was not love, maybe a kind of comfortable understanding? Was there even affection? Not really. He was acceptable, an easy fit into her life. She was inexperienced sexually when they met. There had been nothing in high school. Ora had been firm with her to keep her knees locked together. Her message was clear. Under no circumstances do you give it away. You had something with which to barter. Negotiating a good deal was paramount. Perhaps her brother was right about women, not that she would give him the satisfaction of an easy victory. Sex is a negotiable commodity with a price. The dance between the genders was little more than an elaborate ritual for arriving at a suitable agreed upon arrangement. For the female, what can I get for my sexual goodies? For the male, what should I pay to get laid and, equally as important, what exchange currency should be used? Money and faux money were simple and direct but did not always work. Sometimes you had to go deeper where suggestion of an emotional attachment became the lure. That was hard to monetize in a conventional sense and for the male, Rachel presumed, this would prove way more expensive than a few costly dates.

When she got to college, she was beyond Ora's direct control. Something akin to a latent physical urgency interacted with basic curiosity. She started listening as a few of her female peers talked about their latest carnal experiences, late-night chats that she responded to with equal parts fascination and revulsion, though she admitted being drawn to the detailed discussions of techniques to achieve orgasm. On occasion, she felt as if she were listening to a clinical discussion of the best way to remove an appendix. Yet behind all the dialogue framed by the emerging feminist mantra of sexual equality, old emotional forms persisted. Even the more brazenly aggressive young women betrayed a yearning for intimacy. They might dissect various tactics for heightening their sexual response, but conversations typically returned to detailed examinations of various attributes of selected partners. So-and-so is funny but so self-centered. Or this one says he likes kids but doesn't seem ambitious enough. Sex may be the proximate topic, but the distal focus seemed never to stray from identifying a suitable mate for the long haul. With the nesting instinct firmly entrenched, the subtleties of better ways to secure the male commitment remained the favored topic du jour.

"What was his name?" Rachel wondered if she had said those words aloud, looking about her before realizing that the dog was her sole audience, and Mo did not care. For a moment, she blanked on the name of the boy to whom she lost her virginity. She had grown tired of fabricating the existence of a distant boyfriend who never appeared in her life. That tattered flag could no longer fly, and now she needed someone in the flesh so to speak to show her doubting sisters. Otherwise, the growing suspicion that she was a lesbian would become a full-fledged rumor or, worse, an assumed fact. She remembered the day a female classmate asked her for coffee. Rachel was prepared for a heart-to-heart about some intellectual topic or even of a personal issue.

But the words exchanged initially were innocuous and the girl, clearly nervous, suddenly reached out and took Rachel's hand. Stunned, she looked blankly at the face opposite her. Eventually, words like '*I find you attractive*' and '*I think we are so alike*' broke through the shield she had immediately erected. Without a word, she drew her hand back and fled the table.

Josh was sitting in his departmental committee meeting. They were dealing with end-of-semester administrative matters. Someday, he thought, he would have to calculate the number of such meetings he had endured. Surely, there were few activities conceived in the mind of man that were so tedious and utterly devoid of merit as a typical faculty meeting. Josh had never been shy about sharing his opinions. He often opined that it was a tragedy to bring very smart people together to consider rather trivial matters. Too much posturing, too many words to smother small issues, and surely too much preening among spoiled divas. Not only would everyone get their say, but they would also get to comment on what everyone else had to say. The most benign questions could be drawn out indefinitely. Too often, Josh would pass the time contemplating different ways to commit suicide. Hanging? Only if it broke his neck. A gun! Kind of messy, and he would probably only wound himself, never having fired one before. Poison? That had real possibility. He wondered if the Nazis had kept any of those capsules that Himmler and Goering had used at the end. Hmm, maybe Rachel could help him out there. At the termination of his ruminations, he would sigh. This was the price of faculty governance.

Today, his mind wandered in a different direction, back to the conversation of last night. He thought about Kit and the day he caved to her advances in a frenzy of loneliness and lust. The days and weeks after that had become unbearable for him. Kit was so vulnerable, innocent, needy. Couldn't she see that he was not hers? How could she love him so? He knew that there was nothing in his emotional tank at the time, at any time if he were honest. All worthy human sentiments had been depleted in the angst and drama that drove him north in the first place. Besides, who could possibly want such a wrecked version of a human being? He did not even like himself.

Still, she would look at him with such adoration. Each time he tried to draw back; she came on stronger. Each time he tried to find words to express what he felt, his courage failed him, the actual sounds trapped in the back of his larynx. He was, in the end, a prisoner of his own sensitivities, a people pleaser who could not hurt this innocent who would fall asleep in his arms each night of their brief encounter. Then, during the day, she would frantically try to please him with food or errands designed to ease his day. It had, of course, the opposite effect. She became even more of a continuing annoyance in what had been a lonely, but quite acceptable, existence prior to her unwanted intrusion.

Josh realized that few know the depths of Irish guilt. He often joked that his first words in the morning are *mea culpa* for transgressions that he surely was bound to commit and omissions that others could not possibly notice but he could not ignore. He had the full ethnic curse, that dark cloud hovering over every true Irishman. It would inform and color every dimension of his life. Two aspects of the Irish curse were particularly devastating. First, happiness had a temporal bound; any such feeling approximating this desired state would soon end. His God would not permit any joy to continue for long. Second, the magnitude of any ecstasy experienced must be paid in an equal amount of pain and sadness. These were part of a universal natural law like gravity, the speed of light, or Newton's laws of motion. Josh recalled how David Powers, President Kennedy's adviser, had reacted to his boss's assassination, not the precise words but the general sentiment. Powers said something to the effect that he knew that Camelot must end, but he thought that it would not end quite so soon. Every morning that Kit was with him, Josh woke up racked with guilt. What was he doing? He would push the guilt into his gut to survive another day. Aside from not getting close to anyone, his next abiding fear was hurting another person. Wasn't that precisely the reason he remained so detached.

Then one evening, Kit slid next to him on the couch as he poured through a reference book for a class. He gave her an annoyed look. "Not now, Kit, I have to look over this stuff."

She pouted for a few moments before melting into a softer pose. "You know, I can't really help myself." A deep sigh emanated from inside her, accompanied by an indecipherable sound. And then, "I love you … I am in love with you." He said nothing, staring intently into his book. "Josh, did you hear me? I said—"

The reference book he had been reviewing suddenly flew across the room, knocking over a lamp. "Stop, for god's sake, just stop."

"What …?" The shocked girl stammered.

"Damn it, Kit, I heard you. I'm not fucking deaf," he exploded. "And don't you think I know you love me? I would have to be a goddamn blind deaf-mute not to know. Hell, an idiot who could not predict the weather even if it was raining so hard his nuts were under water would know. For years, I've been looking into your moony expressions and ignoring your obvious ploys, or at least trying to. Its driven me crazy, just bat-shit crazy. You can bet your damn ass I know!" He wavered between wanting to take the words back and relief that they were out there.

Her face was melting into a frame of frozen horror edging on despair. "I…I…" but nothing more came from her.

He softened a bit. "Kit, sorry. I am so weak. I never should have made love to you. If I could take that moment back, I would … in a nanosecond."

"Why did you then?" Tears were forming at the corners of her eyes, but anger creeping into her expression.

Josh wavered for a moment but knew there now was no turning back. "Because men are pigs, Kit. Lesson number one that every young girl should learn before puberty. Really, before potty training to be frank, they should run all of you through a drill. Repeat one hundred times, all men are pigs. Sex doesn't mean anything to a guy. Someone should have taught you that. Damn, how did you grow up so naïve?"

"Well, excuse me for not being as depraved as you." She stood up.

"Listen, Kit, there is nothing I would like better than to have that night back. There is no horror worse than feeling someone's total love and having nothing inside to give back. I have felt like a total shit every second since. You cannot give to others what God never gave you in the first place. Don't you see? It's me, not you. I don't feel … complete. Not any longer. Forgive me."

"Nice try, asshole, you're always so goddamn glib." He had never heard her use strong language before. She was the last of the good Catholic girls. He slept in his office that night, though her weeping kept him awake for hours. She was gone the next morning. It was over, except for the guilt … that would never end.

———

Rachel eventually pulled the box of photos toward her. She would have time now, so she sat at the dining room table where there would be plenty of room to work. She pulled each picture out, looked at it, and intuitively put it into one or another pile. She was looking for patterns in the random chaos of her brother's life. There were many pictures of places and people she did not recognize. Occasionally, one would catch her up short. There was a picture of her and Evan, taken apparently in the one time she had brought her husband to Canada to finally meet her brother.

She was smiling, but there was something forced in her expression. What was she thinking at that moment? Frankly, her thoughts were not all that hard to infer. She was a prisoner in the proverbial gilded cage. Doctor Evan Ballentine III had been a catch—handsome, from a good family, and obviously headed for success in life. Everything had been meticulously planned for him: private grammar and prep schools, then the Ivy League, followed by the best professional medical training. He had toyed with business—that was where the real money was—but decided on medicine, his father and grandfather's line. Besides, a smart doctor would always find ways to capture some real coin. No need to waste his life toiling as an ordinary physician when his family contacts offered so much more. Still, a few years as a clinician to the wealthy and the connected could not hurt. That would confirm his *bona fides* before he segued toward his ultimate passion of accumulating more wealth.

She had first become aware of him in medical school at Johns Hopkins. He floated in like an Adonis anointed by the Gods. She had been a scholarship gal, graduating from the exclusive Smith College with honors despite working to make ends meet. The admissions people at Smith had been impressed with her academic potential along with her ethnic and working-class background. They had just started seeking non-traditional students, not just the issue from well-to-do and established families. They made her an offer she could not refuse. Still, she had little time for socializing or embracing the privileged airs sported by most of her peers at Smith and later at Johns Hopkins. She remained a hermit through college and paused long enough in medical school to notice that women behaved around Evan as most men behave around beautiful women—like total idiots. She would have none of it. She had ignored the pitches from conceited Amherst men earlier while at Smith and saw no reason to change now as she approached her professional goals. She did not care that he was handsome, or rich, or well connected. She had that working-class chip on her shoulder … you had to work harder and longer than those from the elite. Who cared about those entitled snobs, anyway? They were not worthy of her attentions.

Then one day she heard a smooth voice. "Excuse me, you are Rachel Connelly, are you not?" And there he was at her shoulder as she hovered over a lab specimen. When the shock subsided, she mumbled *'yes'* while thinking, *but you know that already, you dolt.* She instinctively had reservations about him with his assured notion of a superior place in the universe. Rachel was at a total loss to explain why he would stoop to acknowledge a plebeian like herself. Had he lost a bet?

Without a beat, he satisfied her curiosity. "This may seem presumptuous, perhaps even a bit impertinent, but I would like to invite you to a social event at my parent's place in Washington." Rachel blushed despite herself, a faint cloud of confusion spreading over her face. "Before you decline, this is not a date, I would never be so forward. I'm inviting several classmates. It merely is a way to get to know each other better. This process is such a grind we hardly ever socialize. I'm arranging everything. I'll have a limo pick everyone up on Friday."

"Why me?" she protested, bewildered. "We hardly know each other."

Evan flashed his broad smile, "Fair question. I know your lab partner in anatomy. She likes you a lot but describes you as a bit of a hermit. Let us say I am moved to do missionary work among the shy of the world. Just a chance to spread your wings, that's all."

Despite every instinct telling her to say no, she heard herself saying, "Okay." His thousand-watt smile flashed again.

For some reason beyond understanding, Evan Ballentine III had selected her to be his wife, and this was his first move, like advancing a pawn in a chess match where the outcome was predetermined. He spent that first occasion at his parent's soiree mostly talking with her, even as some other females tried out their best feminine wiles to lure him in their direction. In the background, she could see his parents eyeing her with great suspicion and what looked like disapproval. Before they even got back to Baltimore, he had asked her out on a real date. She did not need this complication. Her mouth opened to say *no*, but the word *yes* came out instead. She never did figure out why.

As Rachel stared at the picture at Josh's dining room table, she still struggled to interpret Evan's reasoning after all this time. She was attractive enough, but there were prettier girls. She was smart as a whip, but that seemed unlikely to be an attractive quality to someone like him. Worse, she was not only independent but bordered on the sassy, perhaps being described as obnoxious by some. How could she possibly fit into a wealthy and established family? As Evan's intentions became apparent, her insides told her to run away, escape, get back to her world and her tribe. But she didn't. Was she flattered? Did she just assume that he would come to his senses before anything final occurred?

Sometimes, Rachel mused, the big choices are the ones that we make with the least consideration. One day, Evan proposed at a fine restaurant, slipping a sparkling ring into her glass of expensive champagne. She almost laughed out loud but managed to stammer, "Are you kidding me?"

"I'm totally serious," he responded, somewhat nonplussed by her reticence.

"Evan, your mother thinks I am one rung above a street walker. I am Irish trash to her and a Vatican worshipper to boot."

He was, as the saying goes, a charmer and not one to be denied what he wanted. A month after graduation, they were married in a big DC ceremony. Several Washington power figures were in attendance. Jim cried and Ora beamed with pride. Rachel was achieving everything she never could. Later that evening, while changing out of her wedding dress, Rachel also shed a few tears for a reason she could not quite yet define.

———

Rachel snapped out of her reverie; there were things to do. There were calls from Madison and other colleagues in the academy, some work on her paper, walks in the neighborhood with Mo who was quickly coming around to accept her presence. She had discovered his weak spot—scratching his tummy. Between the distractions, there was time to develop a crude organizational scheme. There were pictures of the family. There were photos of Josh's early days in Canada and a few more recent pics. But what really captured her attention were the people who kept popping up in his life. From each pile, she selected a few and ordered them to create a collage of Josh's life.

There was Morris, not his dog, but the skinny and intense Jewish kid who became a presence in their home and Josh's closest associate in college. She banged her head. She should have guessed the origin of the dog's name right off. So freaking obvious. There was a picture of Kit Olson and a man she concluded was her older brother. They looked like they could be fraternal twins, but clearly, several years separated them in age. Both were exceedingly attractive with blond hair and bluish eyes.

There were more shots of Carla Shapiro, thin and dark haired. She always had an intense, focused expression. Rachel had met her during campus visits with her brother and wondered if she ever laughed or even enjoyed a light moment. Rachel had always felt invisible in Carla's presence and never once initiated a conversation with her. Rachel had been completely intimidated by her … to a degree few others had been able to do.

Next to Carla, Rachel positioned a couple of pictures of Sarah Kaplan. Rachel recalled sometimes confusing the two in her mind. They both were Jewish and had dark hair. Now, comparing the two, they were quite different physically. Carla was sinewy and thin while Sarah was bigger boned with a more sensuous body. While Carla had an incisive, if inflexible, intellect, Sarah had a more nuanced approach to issues and questions. Carla had answers while Sarah had questions. Rachel pondered the fact that Josh seemed to prefer the super bright gals. She knew why? He craved ideas more than sex. That did not prevent him from bedding a few gals merely for sexual gratification. All males did that. Those ventures typically were unsatisfying, if not disastrous. I mean, what would you talk about when the lust was sated? The one mystery was a third dark-haired beauty. She had never met her. Could she be his secret love? She would have to explore this mystery. Then there were Jimmie and Bob and a host of other young faces who looked so familiar but whose names escaped her at that moment. Some dated back to high school, others college. But they were the gang, the posse. They were the template that filled out Josh's simple childhood before things became totally complicated and irreversible.

Rachel jumped at a noise elsewhere in the house. It took a moment to figure out it was Josh returning. Wow, the day had passed quickly. Where had it gone? "Is it that late?" she shouted out.

"Not really but I am wondering if you're going to dinner in your sweats?" Josh smiled at her. "Now that I look more closely, this ensemble brings out your best side, kind of an early house frau."

"This comment on sartorial fashion comes from the man whose idea of style is to wear outfits colored with several shades of orange," she retorted. "You want me to clean up the mess on the table?"

He paused for several moments. Obviously, he was torn. "Noooo, I haven't looked over this stuff in ages. I guess retirement is a good occasion to dig up the past." After a short interval, Rachel emerged from her room wearing a stylish dress and a touch of makeup. "Damn," Josh exclaimed. "You do clean up well, and fast. Not bad for an old broad, not bad at all." He was being sincere. A touch north of sixty, and she remained slim and attractive without trying awfully hard. "And it only took you two minutes. At your advanced age, I'm stunned it did not take longer. With most broads in their dotage, it does." He did not quite make out the nature of the missile that barely grazed his head.

CHAPTER 6

Day 2 – THE DINNER

At the restaurant, there was some easy banter as they all sought out their seats. Rachel relaxed as she heard how familiar and jocular the interchanges were. This could be a fun evening. What did catch her up is that the cuisine was Indian, Josh's favorite. This was not Rachel's venue, and she looked around at the décor. There were paintings of various Hindu Gods like Krishna and Shiva, along with many depicting Indian matrons painted in vivid colors, each inevitably attempting to seduce some moonstruck male by employing seductive poses borrowed from the *Kama Sutra* she presumed. She leaned over to whisper to her brother, "You didn't mention Indian. You better help me order."

"Not a problem," he whispered back. "It will be good for you … clear out your intestinal tract." Josh hit his glass with a spoon. "Rach, let me quickly go around the table. Connie you know. Next to her, we have her significant other, Harold. He is a physicist so none of us can understand him. Then we have Ellison who is my department chair, a leader of men for sure. Next is Irv, an economist who studied at Michigan. Why I mention that befuddles me, other than it is next to Wisconsin. His spouse, Helen, is in the history department. Next, we have Timothy, Fine Arts department, and his partner Walter, who runs a gallery you must see." Josh continued, there was a sociologist, a political scientist, and a couple of non-academic significant others. Rachel decided that remembering names was not essential and merely nodded. At the end, she returned her gaze toward Connie and Harold. She was quite disappointed that they were a couple and tried to shake off her matchmaking instinct. Perhaps her brother was right, women hate to see a happy and unattached man while she, in turn, hated being a typical female.

Then Josh set about introducing his sibling. "Some of you have already met her earlier today, but this is my little sister who, by the way, hung on my every word when we were young. She owes all her considerable success as a world class medical researcher, clinician, and respected scholar to my mentorship. Let me note a couple of her achievements."

"Wait," interrupted Rachel, who was determined to stop her brother from embarrassing her with more praise. "There is another sister, one that actually listened to you, because I sure never did. Where do you keep her locked up?"

"Hah," Irv chortled. "None of us have listened to him either though getting him to shut up can be a challenge." Rachel relaxed, knowing now it would be a fun evening.

"Everyone is a comedian," Josh responded, "In any case, Rachel is now at the University of Wisconsin medical school, focusing mostly on pediatric cancer. And to think, she started out as an obnoxious brat who knew nothing, but modesty prevents me from taking too much credit for her success."

"True," Rachel interjected. "I did embrace every utterance from his lips as gospel … then I reached the age of reason."

Everyone chuckled. Connie Chen piped up. "We can see who got all the looks and wit in the family, and surely the smarts."

Josh decided he needed to change the conversation's direction. "Before we get further into this Rachel Connelly fan club adoration, did you hear the one about the two dutiful sons?"

"Oh no," came from around the table. "Stuff his mouth with naan."

"I'll take that as a no, that you haven't heard it and not that you don't want to hear it." Josh was in his element. "Two sons living in rural Kentucky were wondering what they could do for their dad's eightieth birthday. They concluded it had been a while since Dad had enjoyed any. So, they hired a fetching twenty-year-old vixen for the task. She arrived at the old man's cabin one evening, knocking on his door. *'What can I do your you, dearie?'* he asked. *'Hey, handsome, I am here to offer you some super sex.'* The elderly man looked puzzled. *'What's that, dearie, my hearing ain't so great anymore.'* The young beauty raised her voice and said in her best sexy purr, *'I am here to offer you some super sex.'* The old man now smiled. *'Oh good, I think I'll take the soup then.'"*

A loud groan went up. Looking around the table, Connie decided to stop the jokes before he went on. "I had the pleasure of getting to know Rachel earlier. It is clear she survived the trauma of growing up with a demented older brother quite well." Everyone chuckled louder except for Josh. For him, there was a bit of truth buried in that quip. "Tell us, Rachel" she continued, "what was he like as a young man?"

Rachel had them laughing with stories of Josh as a young lothario growing up in an Irish working-class neighborhood. Everyone was still laughing when the waitress appeared to take their orders. "My sister here will have the shrimp vindaloo," Josh said without hesitation.

Connie piped up, "Rachel, are you familiar with Indian food? If not, I would go with *tikka masala* or *tandoori*. Your dear brother is seeking revenge."

"Thank you, Connie, please order for me." Rachel liked Josh's former lover. She knew that they could be good friends if given the chance. Why didn't her brother marry someone like her? She obviously loved him, or at least liked him. The man next to her was monosyllabic and bordering on invisible. Connie could only settle with such a guy, Rachel thought. Immediately, she kicked herself for being so judgmental and so predictably female.

When everyone had ordered, Rachel picked up the conversation again. "Okay, really, Josh is such an easy target, maybe that's why I have always loved him so much." *God*, she thought, *why did I use that word, love, and right in front of him?* She paused, but then continued. "For much of my early life, he was sort of a demigod for me, though I'm aghast that I am saying that out loud." Her voice softened. "Even as a young kid when he did not know all that much, Josh clearly was just about the most sensitive, smart, and passionate guy I knew. By that I mean passionate about ideas. He might have been passionate about women, but that is a tragic drama we will save for another time. Sure, we were different. I never had his zeal for politics and issues of social justice, but he did teach me a few critical life lessons."

Josh was blushing when someone asked, "Like what?"

Rachel frowned slightly, wondering how the conversation suddenly had gotten to this place. "Well, he taught me about caring even when you don't always show it. Despite all my best efforts to ingratiate myself on him, I thought he detested me when I was a kid, totally. I'll admit, I was a pest. And then one day I was hit by a car. He … he raced me to the hospital and never even yelled at me for bleeding all over this piece of junk he had just bought and totally loved. Now that was a miracle. Still, his actions probably saved my life. My brain was swelling. If they hadn't intervened in time to reduce the pressure, irreversible brain damage was likely, possibly something much worse."

Wait," Josh interjected, wondering if his thinking about the same childhood event earlier had suggested it to her telepathically, "the jury is still out on that one."

"Bite me," she responded quickly, "my mom told me that this guy never left my side. I can still recall seeing him looking at me when I came to. What a let-down!"

"Let down … how so?" Ellison asked, missing the coming humor.

"Well," Rachel said, failing to suppress a smile, "if he was at my side, then surely I had not made it to heaven." People giggled a bit. "More importantly, he taught me bigger lessons, about how to be true to yourself and your principles. Without knowing it, he showed me what courage means and how to sort out what's really important."

The table was quiet. "Okay," Josh broke in, "too much wine, cut her off." Inside, though, he was continuing to marvel that she was reflecting on the same vignette that had crowded into his mind earlier.

Rachel continued. "I remember being at one of his football games in high school. He was quite an athlete back then, which is difficult to believe now that he is a frumpy old man. Our dad was already seeing him sporting the blue and gold of Notre Dame. I don't remember many of his games, but one moment stayed with me. The other team was about to score when I saw Josh hit this kid quite hard. This poor kid crumpled to the ground. I can still see this moment as if it just happened. The crowd was still cheering, and Josh was kneeling over the inert body of this player. The boy never fully recovered."

"Rachel, no ..."

She knew why, though, and continued. Though he had reminded her of this earlier, this was a moment from their childhood that had remained sealed within her heart. "Everyone told him it wasn't his fault, just the breaks of the game. It's a tough sport, bad things happen. But I could see a change in him, in his eyes. Not long after, he came into my room. You must understand, seeking me out was a major event. He spent most of his waking hours desperately avoiding me. I recall he just sat there for a long while, so long that I was confused. Finally, he asked what Dad would do if he stopped playing ball. I ... I literally did not know what to say. I'm not sure, but I guess he saw me as an adult in a girl's body. I remember waiting, hoping for the moment to pass. When it didn't, I told him the truth as I saw it. *'Dad will die if you stop.'* He told me he also believed that, but he did not think he could do anything else. That moment on the field just made him so aware of the violence in the game and in himself. That is not what he wanted to do in life, not who he wanted to be. And then he asked me if I would be ashamed if he quit. Instinctively, I knew what I said next was important. He never had asked my opinion before, not on something of consequence. *What was this all about?* All I knew was that the moment was momentous. I remember thinking hard and saying to him, *Josh, I'll never be prouder of you.*"

Josh reached over and took her hand. "Rachel, I remember that conversation. I remember warning you that I would no longer be the hero of the neighborhood, that your friends will give you a lot of grief because I was a quitter. There was nothing worse among the Irish than a quitter, except maybe a snitch or voting for a WASP. That's why I came to you that night. It wasn't just about me."

"Oh, I could feel that," she whispered as those farther away were leaning in to hear, "and that is when I started becoming me. Yeah, I was this little pest, following you around, sucking my worth from your life and reflected glory. Now, you were about to become your own person, whatever that was, not what our dad wanted you to be. You had to know Big Jim, what everyone called our dad, to understand the situation. It was his way or nothing. We would be in this together, until we weren't. I guess you wanted to know if I was okay with everything since we all would suffer."

"I'm not sure what I would have done had you not given me permission." Josh said abstractly, as if no one except his sister and he were in the room.

"That moment wasn't just about you, Josh. At some level, it struck me that I might need to be my own person in the future. That was scary for sure, but I realized that just might be what you were asking of me."

"I'm not sure I'm following." Connie asked.

"Sorry," Rachel looked at her brother. "I suspected at the time that I might lose him, that the family would fracture. I could not see how at that moment, but I could envision being on my own which … frightened me. He had always been there for me, my rock."

There was silence around the table, all had become aware that the conversation had become a confessional. Rachel was not talking to those gathered but to her brother, using the crowd as cover for a degree of honesty and openness that too often was hard to find.

"Wow," Connie exclaimed, "you two are really close."

"Naw," they both said at the same time. "We can't stand each other." Then they laughed at what must have seemed like a practiced routine to others. Rachel looked down at the table. "Well, sometimes yes, other times not so much." Only those near her heard the words.

At that moment, the food arrived, and they sat in silence for a while. Then Rachel spoke up. "This is not bad, tasty actually. Listen, everyone, so sorry to have gotten deep there. Sometimes I think it is easier to say things to someone in a crowd. Funny, isn't it."

"Spot on," Ellison, the department chair, piped in. He yet had a clipped British accent from his youth and training at the University of York. "Like everyone else, or everyone with any wit whatsoever, I give Josh a hard time. But that's because we all admire him so much. Sure, he is a competent scholar …"

Josh smiled. "Competent? Ellison, don't go overboard there."

"I want to say something I've never publicly admitted. Josh, you have one of the best minds around this place, any place. Most of us are like monks, working away in our little cells on our tiny questions. But you always saw the big picture, how things came together. Not everyone can do that, at least not without becoming superficial. To Josh." Ellison raised a glass and was joined by all. "But I am becoming aware of something here."

"Oh, oh," Josh expelled.

"We really don't know much about this man who has been among us all these years. Am I right? How many know that his real name is not Josh?" Most heads nodded, agreeing that they didn't. "No, his legal name is Jeremiah Joshua."

"Well, you try staying in one piece in an Irish ghetto as a kid with a name like Jeremiah. You might as well take up the cello as a musical instrument or join the chess club."

Connie picked up on the theme. "You're right, Ellison, I have been as close to this lug as anyone, and I know so little about his past. Hell, I think he knows when and how I lost my virginity and I know nothing of his past."

"That virginity thing only happened a couple of years ago and with Josh, right?" someone piped in. Rachel noticed that Connie's new partner, the quiet one, was not amused.

"As I was saying" the department chair paused as the laughter died down, "you really are a mystery to us."

"Hey, come on, folks, how interesting a life can any academic have? I ain't no Indiana Jones."

Classic of him, Rachel thought, he would use wit and distraction to keep from opening himself to others. Typical of most Irishmen, you never revealed yourself. You just left them laughing. Then Josh managed to get the conversation directed toward neutral academic topics.

As they all mingled getting ready to depart, Rachel found herself next to Connie. "Can I be very forward?" she paused, uncertain how to put her question. "You … you and Josh seem so good together. I … I can't help but wonder what happened."

"No great mystery," Connie responded in a low voice. "I couldn't reach him, and I decided I couldn't wait for perfection or Josh, whichever came first. Time to settle for something real."

"Settle?" Rachel wanted more.

"For a colorless but stable guy who at least gives me all that he has. Oh my, perhaps that came out a bit harsh. It's always that last glass of wine."

"No, Harold seems fine," Rachel lied.

"Don't humor me, Rachel. I know what I have and what I've given up. In the end, we make choices among the options presented."

"Ready, Connie?" the colorless man approached. As the couple walked out the door, Connie gave Rachel the universal hand signal for *'call me.'*

———

Back at the house, Rachel sat down at the dining room table and fingered the pictures she had arranged earlier that day. Soon, she heard a voice just outside the door. She smiled, recognizing Josh's voice chatting away with Morris as they returned from the evening walk. Rachel smiled as she thought, *what does a man need with a woman when he has a dog?* Moments later, his presence was at her shoulder.

"Are you mad at me?" she asked.

"For what?"

"For getting so personal, revealing a family secret. Wow! Talk about violating an Irish taboo. I don't know what the hell—"

"Forget it," he interjected. "No problem, though there will be a whipping tomorrow morning in the public square."

"I don't know." Rachel persisted. "I went into some very personal areas in front of others. That football game thing for one."

"Okay, that did surprise me."

"I suppose I wanted to thank you for coming to me after it happened, for asking my opinion. I never had a chance to thank you for that. It meant a lot, I guess more than even I knew at the time. So, I'm glad I got it out." After what seemed like too many moments of silence, Rachel went in a different direction. "Connie loves you. Really, what is she doing with that guy? She is so engaging and attractive. He, on the other hand, is a cipher. Did he say anything all night?"

"He is a physicist. Funny tribe, they have their own language, probably their own reality that mere mortals are not permitted to see. Don't the string theorists posit multiple universes. He might spend most of his time in one of the others."

Rachel would not let it go. "But the two of you ... maybe it would help if you would have someone to talk with besides Morris."

"Hey, don't let him hear that kind of talk, he is just warming up to you. He's very sensitive you know. Besides, that dog is more eloquent and sensible and ..."

"Mute! No, I'm serious, you moron. I don't feel it is healthy for a man to live all alone. You are a social being, look how you kept everyone entertained tonight."

"Know why I can do that, keep people laughing."

Rachel rolled her yes. "Your so-called Irish wit."

"While true, it is more than that." His face slid into that crooked grin she knew so well.

"It is because I am a content man. And do you know why I am a content man."

Rachel winced. "I'm going to kick myself for this. Why are you so content?"

"Because, my dear, I'm not hounded by a woman every day. I eat when I want, throw my clothes on the floor at night, clean the place once a month whether I need to or not, employ the smell test before deciding if a shirt can go another day, and walk around the house in my underwear. And if I want a bag of potato chips at night, there's no one to remind me of my cholesterol level. We call that male heaven."

"I call it the Robinson Crusoe complex. You have been without companionship for so long, you are losing touch with reality."

"The Robinson Crusoe complex … I like that." Josh chuckled. "Besides, isn't the pot calling the kettle black here? Personally, I never thought it natural for a woman to live alone. You can be social, like tonight. You had them laughing, weeping, everything."

"Easy audience," she offered.

"No, I'm serious. After Evan, have you even been with a man? Not sex, I mean a relationship. Look at you, you're well preserved for someone so long in the tooth." He looked at her closely. "Yup, no doubt about it. You are not bad for a gal on the cusp of her dotage. I noticed guys eyeing you tonight."

"Oh bull."

"No," he argued, "you must get hit on fairly often, if for no other reason than you have a hefty bank account."

Rachel thought for a moment. "I have Cate, my work …" And she came to a halt.

"Have you heard from Cate recently?" he asked softly.

"Given that she is living in Jordan, working at the embassy, I don't see her often anymore. Who knew I would have a daughter with a passion for languages and travel? I barely knew we still had a foreign service. But you're right …"

"I never claimed to be right."

She pushed on. "You don't need to be Sherlock Holmes to figure out that she was running away. From her teen years onward, she kept saying she wanted a job that would require a passport. She studied linguistics in school, taught English abroad, then did some work for international charities. From there she joined the State Department to work oversees. Now she is posted to places around the world. Where next, outer Mongolia? Sometimes I feel like such a total failure as a wife and mother."

"Don't beat yourself up, that is my job," he went to one of his standard one-liners. "If she's running away from anything, it is that loser of a father she has."

"Josh, we never learned how to love. Did you ever consider that? We're little more than emotional eunuchs," she wept softly. "Sorry about getting weepy, not like me. Perhaps the emotions of this trip are getting to me. I just need a good night's sleep."

He put his hands on her shoulders and kissed the top of her head. She recovered in a moment and picked up one of the pictures, one that had captured her interest. "I can remember a lot of the kids from the past, but this girl, she is so fetching." Her voice yet caught a bit.

Josh sighed deeply. "That is Eleni."

"Shit," she said softly. "I thought so, is this the girl you loved."

"That's her. Eleni Zahra. Okay, before you ask. Her dad was Egyptian, her mother Greek though a lifelong American. They met when he was studying engineering in the States. Eleni was their only child, and very protected."

"She looks, what, … exotic?" Rachel stared at this young woman with olive-toned skin and jet-black hair. "Her eyes are particularly striking, oval and dark. Even in the flat picture, they had special quality, that deer-in-the-headlights look."

"Nicely put. If you just looked at her, you would think she was worldly. But in truth, she was quite innocent, even naive. Yet she had a razor-sharp wit, almost as good as you in going head-to-head with me. I've gone around and around on this, what was the fatal attraction? I think it was this mix of innocence and insight. She knew so little about life yet so much about me." After a pause, Josh said almost mechanically, "I had one love, what about you?"

"But wait," Rachel countered, "if you loved her, why is she such a mystery to me?"

"We did not know each other long, never even had sex. Then I lost her … at the same time I lost … you."

Rachel thought about what he had said for a moment. She fought her next thought, but the words tumbled out in any case. "Did she come to despise you with the same white-hot hate that I did."

"Not now, Rach, it is late, but you might be on to something. I thought she did, for a long time, I feared as much. Another weight of guilt to pile on the scale. But what about my question? Have you loved anyone in your life?"

"You, dummy," she whispered, "until you threw me and the rest of the family under the bus."

CHAPTER 7

Day 3 - Morning

Josh was awake. It was dark, his face drenched in sweat. It took a moment to overcome the disorientation that comes with a sharp rupture of slumber. Was it time for Morris? He listened carefully and could hear the heavy breathing of Morris accompanied by low snoring punctuated by an occasional growl. Okay, too early for his walk. Mo was better than an alarm. At the appointed hour, he would awaken, shake his entire body, and then stare intently at Josh. If there was no response, *'he who must be obeyed'* would walk over Josh's body while issuing forth a low whine. If that failed, a frontal attack was in order including a full-throated bark. Josh would soon surrender, complaining that he would trade in the damn mutt for a hamster later that day, and the morning ritual would begin. On this morning, the dog was yet deep in slumber, yet dreaming at this early hour with his hind legs periodically thrashing about. Josh wondered what his dreams might involve—cute female dogs, winning a dogfight, finding a better home? The last one clearly was ridiculous. What home could be better than the one he now enjoyed?

He recalled the source of his present anxiety. He had experienced several of his nocturnal frights, those that had returned to him time and again. There was the one where he faced the end-of-semester final exam in a course for which he had missed every class and failed to buy the required texts. What was he to do? What would happen to him?

Fear and panic gripped him. Then, without warning, he transitioned into another classic. He had an appointment or a destination of some sort; The end was never important. What was critical is that he never made it. He would get so close, and then one diversion and obstacle after another would impede his progress. He could never make it to his goal no matter how hard he tried. These were classic academic nightmares, at least he believed that. He had never asked his colleagues whether they shared such nocturnal tortures. The academic world was based on anxiety, never doing enough, never achieving enough. No matter what you did and how hard you tried, only the ever-present possibility of failure and disappointment were your companions— the persistent anxiety that someone else was smarter or was working harder or, worst of all, was publishing more and thus advancing further along the academic treadmill.

He wondered if these frights were merely extensions of his youthful terrors, which usually involved being in some unfamiliar field or jungle lost, alone, and sensing horrific fates about to befall him. A few snakes would appear, then more, and more until they were all around him. The snakes might even morph into more sinister creatures if that were possible. He loathed snakes. As they crowded about him, he realized there was no escape. Concern melted into fear which turned to panic and then into outright terror. He felt a grimace take over his face. *The creatures would be at my feet, nibbling at my ankles. In moments, I knew I would be smothered and devoured. Then through sheer exercise of will, I would levitate, slowly. No matter how much I tried, there was no real escape. These monsters continued to snap at me as I hovered just out of their reach. Could I continue? Would I tire and fall to my doom? I was not sure. The effort took so much out of me. What was I to do if I were to relax my concentration or fall through exhaustion? Would I descend to earth and into the gaping, hideous jaws that awaited me? Just as this horrendous end was upon me, I usually awoke. The terror was yet present, but the fantastical nature of the fear was now apparent.*

He lay in bed thinking about that. These repeating nightmares must all stem from some primal or universal source, the newer versions having evolved from ancient themes now shaped by his adult vocational pursuits. No matter the context, they tapped a primordial terror shared by all. Perhaps they were a universal reminder that no one could fully escape failure, pain, and death.

Josh started to ruminate. He had never consciously pursued a career in the academy. After getting settled in Toronto, he migrated to the university as soon as possible to complete his undergraduate studies. His academic potential quickly was recognized, and he found himself enrolled in a postgraduate program, mostly because it was the path of least resistance. It was not a deliberate choice, more like a default position which offered him a paying research assistant placement. He never sat down and mapped out any kind of future. It was all casual, like waking one morning and deciding to go to the beach. He had to do something, and school was something both fun for him and socially approved by society. When he would be asked about his future, he would shrug his shoulders. Teach, he would say, but becoming a university professor struck him as overly ambitious for a nobody like himself. Without much thought, and no strategic plan, one thing led to another. Soon, he found himself finishing up his doctorate. It was all so … casual.

Now he was faced with an existential decision. He really should become an adult, get a job, embark on a career. He reflected on the students he mentored in recent years. How different they were from he and his peers when they were starting out in life. The kids today were more driven, vocationally directed, and concerned about debt and money. They would query him about the value of specific courses or various volunteer opportunities, not for the inherent value of such activities but for how they might look on a resume. Surely, the world had changed, had become more precarious and perhaps unforgiving. But had the students changed as well? Fewer seemed as concerned about the big issues that had consumed him back in the 1960s. Was that true or was he painting the past with a favorable palette of colors more to his liking. He could not decide even though he was familiar with those survey questions that documented sweeping changes in student attitudes and ambitions over the decades.

As he completed his studies in Toronto, he had been working for a community development agency. The pay was low, but he liked the people and it felt right to him. True, he distinctly felt that he was not optimizing his talents, but this was important work, he argued to himself. After all, he didn't need much money and this work felt useful. Still, he knew his peers in the academy did not approve of his vocational direction, or lack of direction. One day, his university mentor tracked him down to mention an academic opening in Vancouver. *You would like that place,* his advisor argued, *gorgeous area. Besides, if you don't make the jump now, you probably never will. It's damn hard returning to the academy once you stray.* At the time, he was not convinced of that but too unsure of himself to dismiss the warning.

These were halcyon days for newly minted members of the academy from a respected university, so there were choices, and others were mentioned to him. And perhaps his peers were right. He should give the academy a try at least. First, he had to battle this case of the imposter syndrome that he wasn't good enough. Moreover, he had never been to Vancouver. For that reason alone, it quickly rose to the top of the short list of employment possibilities. Besides, it was near water and the prospect of any position near the ocean was particularly seductive. That was what he missed in Toronto, no ocean. Sure, they had this big lake there but that was different. An ocean smelled different, felt different. The salt in the air added to the magic. After escaping from Boston there had been a void in his life. He was not near the sea. He missed it.

He recalled his first visit to British Columbia for his recruitment interviews. He drove around the city aimlessly until he came upon the Blue Horizon Hotel. On a whim, he stopped. The price was rather steep for his budget and he wavered. But the clerk, *sotto voce,* mentioned a lower price and suggested he might be upgraded. It was the off season, better to fill the vacant rooms at a discount. They put him in a suite at the top. The room had floor-to-ceiling windows with a magnificent view of the harbor to the west and the mountains to the north. Initially, he could not look out; his vertigo hit him with full force, and his legs became rubbery. Eventually, though, he peeked and then stared in wonder at the vista. That was the moment he decided. This would be his home. He would try like hell for this faculty position, a choice made even before he had stepped on the campus. Later, he wondered at how easily his commitment had been secured … a spectacular view. Was he that aimless?

It seemed ideal from the outside. Probably two classes most semesters, sometimes three, a beautiful campus, time to explore great questions, enjoying the admiration of young coeds. Best of all, the next generation would listen to him. They had to; He would have control over their grades and futures. Wow, instant respect! He had wondered what that might feel like after years as a supplicant student. Of course, the reality of life in the academy was different, less glamorous. Time evaporated under incessant deadlines. The pressure to publish was unrelenting, the competition in the academy at this level was harsh and his competitors extremely talented. Moreover, this teaching stuff was easier in his imagination, tougher in the doing. The damn students expected to be entertained as well as informed. And raising research money, what was with that? He would not be simply signing on to someone else's grants. Rather, he would be expected to generate his own resources. That, too, was easier said than done. It was during those days that the nightmares started. He would spring awake at four or four thirty each morning, filled with a diffuse anxiety that he was behind. The competition was probably up already, working to stay ahead of him. He would lose the race. Like all his peers, he was driven by the not knowing. One's imaginings can be the cruellest Hell of all.

His one disappointment came from what it meant to be a scholar though that was not apparent at first. Scholarship, defined as the quantity of publications in peer reviewed journals, evolved into a claustrophobic exercise. The issues being pursued in the academy seemed to be ever narrower and specialized, the techniques increasingly focused on a kind of technical facility associated with positivism. The social sciences were enamored with the hard sciences, which promised greater acceptance in the broader world and perhaps the adulation usually reserved for those making new technological discoveries that change the world. He played that game long enough to get by, until he was secure enough to go his own way. Still, he regretted not resisting the trends within the academy with more diligence than he had.

In the end, he did not lose the race. While the competition was fierce, most of his apocalyptic visions were overblown. He did well enough as a scholar, excellent as a teacher, and superb as a policy wonk, or what the University called public service. He embraced the teaching role after he realized that some students can never be reached. Then, the classroom became much easier. He found enough of them hanging on to his wisdom, and for the right reasons. He became a gifted and popular shaper of young minds. Most of his peers communicated information while he tended to focus on ideas, principles, ways of looking at the world. Perhaps what set him apart was his relaxed style, sonorous voice, and facility for integrating diverse materials into compelling narratives. Stories, he felt strongly, stay with students, while facts and data are ephemeral and were easily accessible in any case, even more so as the world-wide-web emerged. It did not hurt that he had an easy and slightly lopsided smile that seemed to make him accessible, particularly to those of the female persuasion.

His mind was such that he did not merely summarize the literature but distilled extant thought and theories through his own creative lens. What he shared had a value-added dimension to it. And best of all, he was funny. He would often start each semester by noting that it was fine to doze off in class; he was tempted to do the same thing himself. But he would ask them to stay upright in their seats since the sound of a body striking the floor tended to wake others who were napping in the vicinity. Some of them would be startled and have trouble getting back to sleep. Besides, there was always the risk of a cut head, excessive bleeding, and all the paperwork that would entail. He kept a sign on his office door with a chart depicting the effectiveness of various sleeping aids. Topping the list was *A Connelly class lecture.'*

At the same time, he was not an easy touch. He taught a variety of public policy, government, and program evaluation courses. He was passionate about the issues, both theoretical and substantive. Caring for the public good was something he brought with him from childhood. He was convinced that some attributes are at least partially hardwired. These were not specific beliefs and normative positions but basic dispositions ... like acceptance of change, the ability to engage in nuanced thinking and basic compassion. In the classroom, he was scrupulously fair and balanced. He presented all sides of an issue, often had the most liberal students argue conservative positions and vice versa. While he was approachable, he also was demanding. Sloppy thinking and unsupported positions were not to be tolerated. You could disagree with his views but must demonstrate your logic. Connect the dots with logic and evidence and you were fine in his book.

What he wanted more than anything else was to create independent and original thinkers. Of course, he knew that was not possible in every case, not even in most cases, but he recalled his own development. Early on, he was pretty much a typical jock with above-average, though not spectacular, grades. His early college years were an epiphany, a series of epiphanies. He would spend hours dialoguing with those peers he respected on the big issues of the day. It would prove to be a fortuitous and irreplaceable training ground for his whole career. He desperately hoped to replicate his experiences in the lives of these students before him. They should be pushed and transformed as he had been forced to question his prevailing world views. He would never tell them what to believe but rather how to think on their own. That is what education was all about. At some level, he knew that to be an impossible, or at least improbable, task but still. Yes, that was one blessing of this vocational path into which he had stumbled, he was able to reach across generations. And all this came about because he wanted a trip to Vancouver and then to be near an ocean again. Some way to embark on a new life trajectory.

If anything set him apart from his contemporaries, it was his attraction to the real world. The academy is a self-contained environment where members of the choir preach to other members of the choir. Ideas, theories, hypotheses, and analysis are exchanged through journals that are read only, or at least mostly, by other members of the academy interested in your narrow substantive or methodological area. That struck Josh as fine for many disciplines, but not his. He should be involved in the real world though not all his colleagues agreed. The culture of the academy was premised on the notion that anything that distracted one from pure scholarship was peripheral and to be avoided at all costs. The only audience worth considering were other scholars toiling in your disciplinary and theoretical areas. All outside the academic cocoon was irrelevant. The worst possible sin was expressing too much interest in the real world. It suggested you were not a serious scholar. Josh instinctively rebelled against such insular views.

Unlike many peers, Josh had taken a rather circuitous route through life. During his early days in Toronto, he needed a job. The network assisting American emigres at the time helped him find a low-level position in a human services agency. He did well, rising quickly even as he continued his studies. More to the point, he obtained a taste for policy and poverty issues. He got direct experience with families struggling to get by. Some were immigrants; others simply did not have the wherewithal to compete successfully. He thought he had seen desperation back in the Irish neighborhood of his youth, but he had seen nothing like this. It changed his life, gave him a kind of focus. Not since getting caught up in the civil rights and anti-war frenzy back in his college days had he felt so engaged. As he lay there wallowing in the blackness of night, he marvelled at the randomness of life, how small events can eddy into a river rushing to the future. Yes, he thought, that was his life, a river that carried him along, sometimes winding in unexpected directions, while never letting him see the destination.

Rachel sprung awake around the same time. Disoriented, it took her moments to get her bearings. Oh yes, she was at her brother's place

... this was his retirement week. Why was she so anxious? Then it came back. She also had been captured in one of her common dreams, one that had haunted her for years. They were paging her. *Code blue, code blue, will Doctor Connelly report to the operating room STAT, will Doctor Connelly please report to the operating room immediately?* The calls always became more urgent, insistent. She would move through very white corridors looking for the operating room. But each corridor looked the same, endless and indistinct. Surprisingly, they were empty of people. She would come to a corner and turn expectantly, only to find yet another endless corridor. And the calls continued, ever more strident. But it was no longer Doctor Connelly; the voice now was calling Rachel. It was a desperate utterance. *Rachel, please hurry, please. The patient is dying.*

She was running, but her legs felt as if they were mired in muck. She now could see people in the corridor, looking at her with disappointment, shaking their heads side to side. Still, she could not get anywhere despite her rising panic and desperate efforts to keep moving. Then it hit her; she would not know what to do once she got there. She could not recall going to medical school. She had been accepted, she intended to go, but had she? No matter how hard she tried, she could not remember being there, taking any courses or developing her surgical skills. Why would they ever let this working-class girl operate on people? Who in the world was that irresponsible?

She saw her goal, the operating room. Should she continue? Should she run away? Maybe she should roll into the fetal position on the floor. But her body would not obey her, and she continued to run faster as the voice from the ceiling screamed her name ever louder. The name Rachel rang through the halls. Just as she was about to explode, she burst through the operating room door. But she was outside, in the cold night, far from the demands of her chosen profession. The black she looked up into was the dark ceiling of her brother's guest room. She put one hand on her breast, which was heaving and wet with perspiration.

"Damn," she said to no one. It was always the same. *"Why is it that we focus on our weaknesses, our fears, and not what we can do?"* Fortunately, in the light of day, she would regain her confidence in what she could do. Besides, she was damn sure she had been to medical school.

She debated getting up to see if her brother had already risen. After a moment's reflection, she decided to lie there while grabbing on to the first thoughts that wandered through her mind, anything to escape her hopeless dash through endless hospital corridors. Ora came back to her, young and beautiful, her slim fingers flying over the ivory of the upright piano in their living room. When her mother was lost in music, her face lit up, her expression became effervescent. The eyes, Rachel recalled, the eyes would become even more translucent, and her aura emitted an ethereal glow. At those moments, Rachel knew that her mother had another life. It was not in that apartment, not in this country, not with her family. It was a life that had been snatched away by fate or decisions made a long time ago, necessary choices and yet so costly. Rachel sensed compromise and loss, and it left her sad.

Rachel would try to get her mother to open herself up. *What was dad like when you met? What did you do together when you first courted? Why did you fall in love with him? What was your wedding like?* But the responses inevitably were sparse and non-specific if she got anything at all. These big questions would remain a mystery. If she were lucky, Ora might share stories she had heard from her mother about a world somewhere across the globe and from an epoch that appeared to emerge from the dark ages, a world of pain and horrific brutality and senseless death. Rachel would grab on to these nuggets hungrily but was left unsatisfied. She wanted something personal, relational, but that was not to be. That would remain the essence of her relationship with her mother—an enigmatic mystery tightly protected against revelation and exposure. They each would live in their own worlds.

Rachel stared at the ceiling. Images danced in the darkness, but she settled on her childhood apartment above the bar her father owned. The furniture always struck her as from another era, perhaps borrowed from the set of a silent picture, an old Charlie Chaplin flic.

The living room was dominated by the piano and adorned by pictures of a religious bent, or painted scenes from the Emerald Isle. Several of the paintings seemed to capture the agony of the great famine of the mid-nineteenth century. In one that never left her, a desperate family begged for scraps on a country lane while a richly adorned carriage rushed by to a country manor that could be seen vaguely in the distance. The occupants of the carriage purposely ignored the outstretched hands of those who would soon perish. Rachel would stare at the picture and focus on the starving children, protected only by tattered rags, emaciated, and on the cusp of oblivion.

Rachel was always taken by the pain evidenced in the desperate family. Hurt and desperation motivated her. She wanted to reach out and bind up the physical wounds imposed by neglect and exposure to the elements. Clearly, they had been thrown out of their thatched cottage, ripped from their tiny plot of land. They soon would perish in the village lanes. There was no help for them. Not quite true, she corrected herself. Soup and bread might be had in some places, but only if the supplicant converted to Protestantism and the Church of Ireland. You could save your life but only be betraying your culture and forfeiting your soul. That price was too high for most.

Her brother, she was sure, focused on the carriage and the cruel indifference emanating from its occupants. More than once he told her how thousands of ships left Irish harbors to sell produce abroad as the native Irish starved or were forced to emigrate. Josh spent more time in their father's bar where old injustices were shared as if they happened yesterday. He had heard repeatedly how the British obsession with Adam Smith and laissez-faire economics had justified genocide on a brutal scale. It was simply God's will, the natural order of things. To interfere with free markets would thwart God's sense of order in the world. Besides, they were merely impoverished Papists, little more than barbarians, hardly worthy of a gentleman's notice and certainly not his charity. The lords of the land assumed the plight of the destitute was God's judgment.

What touched Rachel in the middle of the night was how her relationship with Evan touched upon Ora's sense of worth. Whenever her folks visited or met Evan's family, Ora would be renewed. This was the aristocratic world in which her mother thought she belonged, and which she had conspired to rejoin after the family had lost their elite position in society during the October Revolution. There were subtle suggestions of former glory and privilege, however vague and undeveloped. In her fantasies, Rachel could see Ora's family as descendants from Czarist lines, distant relatives of royalty who escaped the bloody revolution by fleeing and remaking themselves. Ora's heart never abandoned that desperate wish to make it back to her entitlement. Big Jim would never bring her to where she belonged, but perhaps her children might.

Josh held early promise but failed in a sudden and inexplicable fashion. He took up radical politics and then had fled. Now Rachel might succeed, not so much through her own success, but through marriage. Ora had a hard time appreciating that any female could achieve greatness on their own, even as she bragged about her daughter's successes. Being selected by this chosen family, however, was like being anointed by God. While Ora preened around the Ballentine family, Jim would smile through gritted teeth in the presence of his new in-laws, pleased that his daughter had landed such a 'catch.' He admired their success and, at the same time, bristled at their arrogance. Evan's family struck him as prime examples of the British autocracy that he so despised. Jim was gratified by his daughter's apparent good coupling. She was a girl after all and would need the protection of a strong man. He could not see how strong his daughter was, that truth was beyond him. Above all, he retained an ingrained reservation about all the rich. Jim would always be a salt-of-the-earth kind of guy, devoted to those who struggled through life. Those at the top of the heap would remain objects of internal scorn even as he smiled effusively during those moments spent with the Ballentine clan. He could never forgive the fact that they looked down on him, even as their judgment went unstated.

At first, Rachel was happy to bring some glimmer of light into her mother's life. The depression around Ora was seldom ever more than thinly veiled. But over time, Rachel realized that nothing she would do could salvage a life that had forfeited all hope and purpose in some distant, unknowable past. As Rachel sat listening to the silence in her brother's home in Vancouver, she visited a long-held lesson of life. You cannot make another person happy. She had tried with Ora. She was the daughter, the one that everyone else said was the look-alike of her mother. That was her mission in life, make her mother whole again. This became a peculiarly passionate mission after Josh disappeared, when the house seemed lonelier and more desperate. But it was a peculiarly hopeless mission, a reality resisted until it no longer could be denied. Rachel eventually realized that some would insist on their own misery, no matter what. You really cannot put in what God has left out. In the end, we are responsible for our own happiness or hell.

She had tried with Evan as well. At first, she balanced her own career to be available to his advancement. She prettied herself up for social events, smiled at people she thought dullards beyond all hope. She would make small talk with family members when she desperately wished to be back in her lab or on the ward. Not that her efforts at reaching to others in Evan's world did much good, Evan hardly noticed her efforts. He simply expected it from his wife, whom he never saw as anything other than an extension of his world. He not only possessed a trophy wife with looks, poise, and personality but also one that had achieved a position in life. That was a plus in his mind if it did not interfere with his agenda and, more importantly, his pleasures.

It did not take long for Rachel to figure out what was going on. She was an appendage and not an especially important one at that. But they were married long enough to have Cate, which, for a few months, seemed to make things better. Evan paid attention to the child and to Rachel. But that would not last; he soon became bored once more. He had made one mistake, which he eventually realized to his annoyance. Selecting a high achiever as a wife was a double-edged sword. What made her an especially good catch ... attractive and intelligent with professional credentials … also gave her a sense of independence. In the end, she did not need him. She had not even taken his name upon marriage, an outrageous act for the time and an unforgivable sin for the Ballentine clan. Still, it never occurred to Evan that he was the dispensable one. It was inconceivable to him that any woman could discard him like yesterday's newspaper.

Over time, their home became a quiet tomb. There were few fights. Evan stopped going through the motions of hiding his affairs. His flirting became obvious, and Rachel stopped attending those functions that were at all possible to avoid. That was one thing they did fight about since her absences increasingly were difficult to explain. One day, she came home early from a professional trip, deciding not to stay for the events of the final day of a singularly boring medical conference. She saw an unexpected, though familiar, vehicle in the driveway. It was a car she had been in several times, one owned by a colleague she considered a friend. Perhaps there was a professional reason for the visit. But then Rachel smiled to herself. Yeah right.

She remembered walking through the door and up the stairs, noticing two wineglasses on a living room table as she passed by. At one point, she stopped to listen, oddly smiling when the sounds confirmed her suspicions. Without stopping, she entered the bedroom. "Don't bother getting up, Jeanette. I don't want to stop your fun." As her colleague and friend died those thousand deaths associated with the embarrassment of discovery, Rachel continued in a matter-of-fact manner. "I assume Cate is at your mother's place. Of course, that would be a place to get rid of her while you fuck your whores. I am going to get her. Please finish up before I get back. See you at the staff meeting Monday, Jeanette. Oh, and enjoy this screwing. It won't be the only one you will get from him." Then she calmly turned and walked out the door. Rachel smiled at the memory of that moment all these years later.

She rather enjoyed the subsequent denouement. Evan made the expected overtures, the pro forma apologies and promises. She was flabbergasted. Did he believe her a total idiot? Even his mother was enlisted in the cause. She called on Rachel to seduce her back into the clan, using her syrupy sweet charm to best effect. She went on about how valued Rachel was to the family and how much she was cherished and respected. Rachel watched her with astonishment. In her heart, she knew she was tolerated at best, despised on most days. But since Evan had made this unforgivable mistake of marrying someone totally unsuitable, the damage had to be contained if possible. Public opinion and the aura of respectability must be assured. Rachel was tolerated only because to do otherwise invited ridicule and perhaps scandal. Social relations among the elite displayed all the savagery common among schoolyard children.

In a matter-of-fact manner, Rachel looked at the matriarch directly in the eyes and quietly stated that her son was a pig and she would never, under any circumstances, spend another day with him as his wife. *'No, make that as his slave,'* she added for clarity.

The mother's disingenuous charm instantly evaporated. Between clenched teeth, she spewed words out with a vicious relief, "I knew it from the moment I saw you. Trash wrapped in a nice package. You were never good enough for us, just the daughter of a drunken Irishman, as if there is any other kind."

"Dame Ballentine," Rachel said calmly, "please let yourself out. I believe you know the way but do be careful. Don't let the door hit your backside as you leave. You cannot afford any more brain damage."

Rachel could hear largely incoherent words as her mother-in-law exited, something about Irish trash like her would never get custody of Cate and that she would bury this ungrateful bitch of a daughter-in-law under lawyers and lawsuits. "You won't get a dime from this family," were words she distinctly heard. Rachel just smiled; she was ahead of the curve, having hired a private detective to dig up dirt on Evan's debauched personal lifestyle. She wanted Cate; She could give a rip about the family fortune.

Why had she married him in the first place? Was there ever any love? Did she know what love was? At first, there was comfort. They were both smart, ambitious, attractive, and directed. They fit well, had plenty to talk about. They could support each other professionally. Eventually, though, two professional couples face tough choices. Opportunities arise that would tear the existing situation apart, requiring one partner to sacrifice much for the other, especially in terms of where to live and whether to accept positions in other locations. Doing things to advance her husband's prospects was one thing. He fully expected her to advance his interests while he gave not a second thought to hers. Sacrificing what she had worked for was another. Rachel understood that Evan would never sacrifice anything for her.

Rachel kept debating whether she should get up since further sleep seemed hopeless now. But it was still exceedingly early, completely black outside. She could let her mind continue to wander. *Why not*, she concluded?

Perhaps she would have sacrificed more if there were any real affection. But it was never there. What always bothered her was whether it could ever be there. Had she loved any man? Then the cold fear hit her—she was becoming her mother. How many women had confided to her that the one thing they feared most was turning out to be their mothers? Men did not seem to share a similar phobia. They often aspired to be as good as their dad and worried more about not measuring up, or that is what she believed.

Women, she thought, often clash with their mothers. The process of separation struck her as far more difficult for females. Their relationships are more intense. Females generally require best friends, confidants. They needed relationships more desperately. She knew that her female acquaintances would process their relationships in excruciating detail for hours, pouring over each line and facial expression that constituted the interactional event they were dissecting. Men never seemed to do anything like that. She found that difference illuminating.

Moreover, social connections ran through females. Establishing oneself as an independent adult was not easily accomplished, the web of connections was set early for most women. Yet Rachel cannot recall any separation trauma with Ora. Her mother did not seem to care, particularly at the end. Sure, when Josh disappeared, she was paralyzed, first playing the piano for hours and not talking to anyone and then not playing at all. But Rachel could have run off to the circus, and not a drop of concern would have been displayed. Rachel mused that the Connelly females, both she and her mother, were bereft of commonplace human passions. It had all gone to the males. Did Josh really have a passionate side? She had never seen him in love or even pursue any female with a special interest. In any case, she was convincing herself that she could not feel basic human emotions like love or hate or even lust.

Enough of this, she thought. This was not like her to lie awake in the early morning wasting time in useless masturbatory self-reflection. Perhaps it was being around her brother. Yes, it was his fault. Always wise to blame her sibling. She slipped out of bed. If she could not sleep, she would wait for morning by doing some more snooping through Josh's stuff. She tried not to make a sound as she crept toward his study. She did not want to awaken him.

———

Her attempt at stealth was unnecessary. Josh had remained awake after his own night terrors. For him, this was not an unusual state. He often would lie in bed halfway between sleep and consciousness. He sometimes managed to find some comfort by using the time to imagine brilliant arguments on arcane topics. His insights during these nocturnal dialogues were deep and innovative, or so he thought. Often, he would debate whether to spring fully awake to write them down, not trusting his ability to recall these gems if he were to relapse into a deeper slumber. He seldom did, however, choosing the pursuit of rest rather than documenting what he knew to be another breath-taking insight.

On this occasion, he slid into more prosaic fantasies and images. He could not shake images of the saloon his father run. It looked like many other neighborhood joints, with a long bar and booths where couples could join up for furtive assignations or relive illusions of a united Ireland. Early on, he loved the old paintings of pugilists John L. Sullivan and Gentleman Jim Corbett and the tough depression-era Mick heavyweight champ Jimmie Braddock hanging above the bar. Josh smiled as he recalled that his dad once had violated ethnic rules by hanging a picture of the Italian heavyweight champ, Rocky Marciano, next to his Irish pugilistic heroes. Then again, Rocky had been born and raised in the Boston area, so this lapse of ethnic etiquette might be excused. He was at least a local hero. There were pastoral scenes of the Irish landscape along with paintings and faded pictures of those who made real and imagined sacrifices for Irish freedom. Josh could still recall a picture of Ian Paisley, the Ulster Protestant leader. It had been pasted over the tavern's dartboard and soon was shredded with righteous anger from the pub's patrons.

There was a room in the back where card games could be carried on with no possible detection. It also served as a convenient spot for revolutionary talk or other activities of questionable legality. During the day, the flow of customers was sparse, but regular. Some had their favorite spots and provided little evidence that they had any other dimension in their lives. In late afternoon, workingmen began filtering in to be joined by wives and girlfriends in the evening. At night, it was a lively place with laughter and singing and great camaraderie. Before he left, Josh played the piano on weekend nights. After, his mother was forced into the role, something she hated. This was not her crowd nor her culture.

Josh, on the other hand, had loved the place as a young man. He was fond of the characters that seemed to be part of the furniture perhaps, as he oft thought in those days, they were more a fixture in the establishment than the inanimate bar stools were. A few seemed plucked from central casting to play the wistful revolutionaries pining for the next Easter uprising when the bloody Brits would be conquered at last, and Ulster finally brought into the fold. Terrence Feeney was a fixture at the bar. He had that grizzled face, deep lines, and a stubble that always needed shaving. His greyish eyes were always watery, as if the tears for a bygone era could not be dismissed. And the brogue would always be there as if had had practiced the accent for a movie part.

"Josh, my lad, your dad is one of a kind, one of a kind I say. God never made better, you know. You should be proud, my lad."

"I am, Mr. Feeney," Josh would respond for the umpteenth time.

"You know, lad, he was a hero, a hero I say. He ran guns for the boys when Hitler was giving the goddamn Brits nightmares, not that they didn't deserve it. Yup, he and your mum, lovely woman that she is, ran the guns right past the noses of those Limey bastards. Irish in her soul, your mom, you bet she is. She helped him with the gunrunning, that's a fact. Never talks about it, but I know. Tis a fact, no doubt about it."

"What exactly did she do, Mr. Feeney?" Josh would ask.

"Oh, son, can't go into that. No, no, that would be dangerous. Can't be too careful, even now. Some crimes they never forget. Treason is forever. Never forget that. Yup, can't be too careful. Enemies are everywhere. Remember that, son. Some secrets you keep inside, forever. You think you're safe, but you ain't. No, you keep 'em deep. Take them to your grave, you do. In the end, you can only trust yourself, and sometimes even that doesn't work. Say, son, I have a powerful thirst here. Can you pour me another libation, I pray?"

"Coming up," as Josh poured him a free tap beer.

"And never forget, son, in the end you can only trust yourself."

During the quiet hours, when he wasn't in school or on the practice field, Josh ran the place. There was a buzzer to upstairs if Dad was needed and additional help would arrive by the middle afternoon. His favorite was Gert, a large woman who moved with amazing celerity when serving drinks to couples in the booths. She had taught him how to cook up corned beef and cabbage, with a side of spuds of course. She would give him a wink from time to time, *'you're a lucky lad, son. If I were ten years younger, I would give you a shot, I would.'* He would laugh at what he thought was her jest but always felt a bit of discomfort when alone with her in the back kitchen and storage area. He could never get around the image of having to explain to a couple of high school mates that he was doing their mom.

He felt rather proud that his dad trusted him with the place. He even ran a few numbers and took sports bets from the regulars. It was the Irish world; you trusted members of the tribe. No one would complain about a kid serving beer and booze or running numbers. It was good training, like an apprenticeship. Even local cops turned a blind eye. Besides, it was not long before Josh emerged as a local high school sports star. Now he was untouchable, a minor saint among the local deities. There were even rumors he might head to Notre Dame, the Catholic mecca of higher education. The worst he would do is Boston College ... a more local temple to young aspirants seeking social acceptability and perhaps membership among the Irish elite. More than one patron had tussled his hair while proclaiming *"you'll be mayor one day son. Mark my words, you'll be mayor one day."*

Some of his responsibilities were a little humorous. His dad usually was up late running the bar. Josh either studied or played sports. But there was an early morning flow of customers who wanted to be served before formal opening hours. Guys on their way to the day shifts, usually between six and seven in the morning. They needed a pick-me-up, or at least a balm for the previous night's hangover before heading off to the day's labor. They would knock on the back door, and Josh would be there to greet them. He would sell them shots and beers that would be downed quickly. Of course, it was illegal, but tribal customs are tribal customs. The law was something to obey at your convenience. Besides, Irish cops would never interfere with tribal customs. When done with this chore, he was off to school.

Josh realized what made him untouchable in the neighborhood. He was a fair reflection of his dad, not quite as stocky, but a bit taller with the same dark good looks and a V-shaped body with the muscular torso and reasonably slim waist of a trained athlete. His dark hair hung down just over his ears in that tousled way that suggested a casual sexuality. And the smile was a killer, the same smile that Big Jim sported most days. It was never forced, never fake. It came naturally to his lips in a way that invited people in, helped them relax. What differed Josh from his dad was his willingness to listen. Jim dominated most rooms, his strong voice and personality centering all attention on his presence. Josh was subtler, asking questions and drawing others out. Still, he had that innate aura of authority. People trusted him. Besides, he wanted to learn what others had to offer. Everyone had a contribution to make. You just needed to ask the right questions.

There was a difference between Josh and his dad. The son could see it plainly, he was never sure about his dad. It could be found on the inside where others might not be able to see. Jim was centered on himself, confident in who he was and his role in the world. He had been tested young and found himself adequate to all challenges. Josh was less certain about himself and the world about him. Things were a bit less black and white though only at the edges early on. If you were a son of the Emerald Isle, much was expected. In those days, that meant you loved the Catholic church, the Virgin Mary, the old country, unions, the Red Sox, and the Democratic Party. You hated the Brits, the Republican Party, the New York Yankees, and the WASPs who ran things. Italians were a bit suspect as well. Most days, traditional minorities never entered your mind.

The memory of iconic politicians such as James Michael Curley ran strong. As with many of his Irish peers and ancestors, Curley had fought for a place in this country. Members of the Celtic tribe had suffered the attacks and hate of the Know-Nothings and other nativist parties. Earlier immigrants had seen *No Irish Need Apply* signs everywhere. They competed with African Americans for the crumbs of society. Curley had risen from nothing to become mayor of Boston and Governor of the State. So what if he spent some time in jail, that was just a plot of those jealous WASPs to bring this sainted man down. Persecution, or the threat of it, made every tribe stronger. Jews were never more firmly bonded than when under attack. The same was true for the Irish.

At the same time, the sons and daughters of *Eire* slowly built up a strategy of self-promotion. They used the church as an institutional anchor upon which they constructed functional families and communities. They erected parallel education systems (parochial schools) and social service systems (usually administered through local political bosses). Best of all, they hit upon a wonderful strategy for community revival … politics. It worked for James Michael Curley, why not for many others. Their natural gregarious personalities and tribal allegiances made political advancement a natural tactic. Once they wrested control of local government from traditional WASP control, patronage was a boon for those seeking entry onto the first rung of respectability. And guess what? One of their tribe eventually had risen to the very top, the Presidency of the United States.

In many ways, the Harp Bar of the 1960s that Big Jim owned and operated played out the final chapters of this century-long struggle. The British spent several centuries trying to exterminate the Irish culture, particularly Popery, which they viewed as a wild and dangerous cult at best. Cromwell had savaged the land with the rallying cry of *'to Connaught and Hell.'* They would push the native population into the sea or, better still, into an eternity of brimstone. In the eyes of the Brits, worshipping God in the traditional Irish manner was an ultimate insult to the new overlords. They would spend several centuries doing everything to separate the native Irish from their own identity and culture. Of course, the exact opposite happened. The natives clung ever more fiercely to their church, which they would take with them into their diaspora of the mid-nineteenth century.

"My lad, have you ever been home?"

"Home, Mr. Feeney?"

"To the old country, my boy, to Ireland. Oh, you must visit. Every Irish lad must visit the homeland, son. It is *Eden* for sure. Walk through the meadows on a spring morn. Everything is so green you can just taste the very color of the place. And you can literally smell the dew-drenched grass as the sun peeks over the misty horizon in the morn. The rainbows, my boy, the rainbows. In the old country, they truly are God's special gifts. No wonder we all looked for that pot of gold at the end of such miracles, imaginary as it was."

"Sounds great, Mr. Feeney."

"Son, never forget where you came from, never. They can take everything else away from you, son, your money or your job or even your freedom, but they cannot strip you of your conscience or your culture. You don't face extinction and not come out hard, tough as nails. I was born the very week of the Easter uprising, that very week, in Dublin itself. I came into this world as those martyrs for the cause were leaving it."

"I understand, Mr. Feeney."

"Do you lad, do you?" Feeney's eyes were moist, a tear creeping jaggedly down his cheek.

"I do, indeed, sir." At that moment, Josh's black-and-white world was noticeably clear to him. There was nothing fuzzy in his early views. There was God and the one true and holy Catholic church. The Pope was infallible and sat in Rome. The Blessed Virgin was to be revered and served as a role model to most of the Irish lasses in the neighborhood, not an undiluted good in a young man's mind. The problem with that, Josh thought, was that it was harder to get laid, way too hard. As a young teen, the few peeks he got into the promised land was by checking out the reflection from their patent leather shoes at school dances. It was a good thing that there were some older women who took pity on him.

Out in the world, there was good and evil. We were the good guys, J. Edgar Hoover told us so, and he was the top G-man. Josh had read his book, *The Masters of Deceit*, more than once. Even as a young tot, he kept track on the back-and-forth battle front lines on the Korean Peninsula, or maybe he only imagined this. After all, he was so young at the time. No matter, he recalled how the Commie hordes almost pushed our guys into the sea, then the good guys pushed them back to the Yalu River. All seemed settled when the Chinese suddenly poured in, forcing God's defenders of truth and justice back once again. Korea was a metaphor for the universal battle of good and evil. The Commies were godless and bent on total evil. They all thought alike, plotting unspeakable things once they achieved world domination. Really, you had to know they were up to no good. How many times had he dived under his school desk to save his ass from the nukes the Reds were bound to drop on us any day now?

Josh recalled heading over to the Boston College campus one day to hear a talk by Tom Dooley, a graduate of Notre Dame and a missionary doctor who began practicing his trade in Southeast Asia during the chaotic decade of the 1950s. Colonialism was dying, but in a tortured way. The battle was on for the heart and soul of the people though few in the Western world, Josh would later conclude, gave a rat's ass for the people. It was all a matter of stopping the inexorable Red menace while, it might be added, ensuring continued access to the valuable commodities these countries possessed. Dooley brought the audience to their feet that night. He talked with compelling passion about how Catholics were being persecuted by Communist insurgents taking their orders from Moscow, or was it Peking? Young Catholic boys would be kidnapped and asked to renounce their faith and join the worker's cause. If they resisted, sticks were driven into their ears, breaking their eardrums. At least that is what Tom Dooley said. Josh would have joined the marines that very night had he been of age.

Josh's world at this time was hierarchical and very rigid. People and things had their ordered place. Truth was not negotiable and flowed downward, from the Papacy in Rome or the national government in DC, from the fathers as the head of the family to their wives and then to obedient offspring. These truths were not negotiable. The hierarchical order of things was not to be questioned. It was an inviolable attribute of the Irish approach to Catholicism, obedience to authority. The Pope in Rome, the President in Washington, the Patriarch in the home … the world was ordered according to God's wishes.

He had his first lessons out of the Baltimore catechism where a series of questions were followed by an answer, and not just any answer but THE answer. That was convenient, he thought at the time, an answer for every question. Of course, the natural and preordained order of things held for people and groups as well. Religions, colors, and ethnic groups all had their determined place. Even within the happy

Catholic family, there was a hierarchy of worthiness. The Irish were on top and on down the line to the Italians and Portuguese who hovered above the blacks and pagans but only barely. The first question upon meeting someone new was to ask *what are you?* Polish, they might respond. Okay, the Pollacks were not as good as the Irish, but better than the Wops. Most were higher than the Wops. Yes, he thought, his tribal caste system was more sophisticated than most. It was not just a bunch of racial divisions, but distinctions based on ethnicity, going back to when America was losing its exclusive Anglo-Saxon identity. That evolution had demanded a reordering of the hierarchy. Still, everyone had their place.

Yet, Josh recalled, even when he had embraced the truth of his world on a conscious level, he sensed doubt. The Irish Catholic church in the 1950s pounded into its flock this inflexible world view. Bishops and priests were seen, by the faithful at least, as demigods. Their word was law. It was often a harsh law, drawn more from the Old Testament than Christ's more loving message. The local pastoral authorities might well argue that non-Catholics were doomed to hell. If more lenient, they went to a place called Purgatory. Josh concluded this was yet a dismal final resting place where the temperature was at least a bit milder. A lucky few, those who had never heard of the one, true, and universal Church, were permitted into Limbo, wherever and whatever that was. All this struck Josh as unfair, even before he rebelled against his culture. It violated his emerging moral compass. The Protestant and Jewish kids he ran across were no different than he. They played the same games, had similar dreams, held to the same fantasies about the same girls as he, used the same profanities. Yet they were doomed when he was not. What kind of God could create such an inequitable system? As a young teen, he wondered about such things at night as he struggled to find sleep.

In his later teens, he was a voracious reader and found Pierre Teilhard de Chardin, the Jesuit scientist who spent decades in China exploring the origins of man and society. The restless and inquisitive mind that was developing in Josh was fascinated by the expansive vision espoused by Chardin. In this world, humans were evolving, undergoing transformation, perhaps becoming something altogether new. Maybe even our very concept of a deity was best located in the process of creation, in the miracle of evolution, a true understanding only to be realized in some distant future. Josh marvelled at the vision, so exciting next to the rigid and static world around him. But when he asked more well-read priests about his new favorite Jesuit author, he was told to be careful. Chardin had fallen out of grace with Rome despite doing his best to accommodate evolution with traditional Catholic teachings. The intellect, he was warned, could easily become the devil's workshop. This warning was shared with grave expressions on the messenger's face. *WHAT!* Josh recalled saying to himself. How can you be asked to think and study to be a success in life while fearing your intellect as the road to hell and damnation? It was all perplexing.

Josh now smiled as he drifted in and out of sleep. Yup, he recalled thinking early on that someday he would have to choose between the verities of his faith and the excitement spawned within his restless intellect. At some level, he recognized an irreconcilable chasm between faith and reason. Chardin and other intellectuals had bridged it, but he doubted he was that smart, nor did he possess their abiding faith. Someday, he would no longer be able to escape such Faustian choices, the decisions that would etch the final lines of his character and fate. He would ponder how he might deal with such fundamental choices that define a man before concluding that such things could be kicked down the road for a bit.

Suddenly, his reveries jumped a few years forward. Now he had a new faith, not Christ or the Virgin Mary, but a vision of revolutionary justice. He and his compatriots would nibble at a corrupt and selfish system to erect something new and fresh. For Josh, this was not a rejection of his childlike faith but a truer expression of it. What was Christ? He was a revolutionary, attacking the old regime and proposing a new order. No longer would truth be framed by a set of rigid laws carried out by religious fanatics. The old God of vengeance and retribution would be replaced by the beneficent vision of a deity who focused on love and compassion and justice.

How we treated others, and not just the others who looked and believed like us, would be the new morality. That message had always appealed to Josh. He never could quite envision a God of this vast universe counting heads on Sunday or calculating the evil associated with eating a hamburger on Friday. Nor could he embrace the Old Testament angry God who seemed little more than a militaristic avenger. No, he would sympathize with those priests and nuns who preached a form of liberation theology where a pure form of Christ's teachings would lead to a just and fair world. He adored the Berrigan brothers and Father Groppi of Milwaukee, priests who represented for Josh a pure and decent form of faith in which he could believe.

———

Josh was fully now awake. He looked over at the dog snoring at his side. Too early for the morning walk. He listened carefully. Yes, there were soft sounds coming from the kitchen, or was it his study. *Rachel is up, going through my stuff probably.* He did some quick calculating. Did the joy of getting to know his sister better after all this time offset any pain that she might experience by getting to know him better? No, he would lie here in bed a bit longer.

Josh winced at another ancient memory. He had tracked down Morris Greenstein just a few weeks after they had all taken a pledge to take things in their anti-war protests to the next level, whatever that meant. "Okay," he recalled saying. "You mentioned you needed money for the cause. Here, take this." He put a medium-size carry-on type bag onto the table in front of his friend who cautiously opened it up.

"What the…," Morris whispered. In the bag was an impressive pile of cash. His friend counted a bit and then gave up, mentioning in a low voice, "There must be thousands here."

"Over forty thou, maybe fifty grand, maybe more. I didn't have time to count it. I could've taken more, but I hoped they wouldn't miss this."

Morris looked at him with a *'are you completely whacked out'* look. "Where did you …"

"Don't ask," Josh interrupted. "I'd have to kill you if you knew. And if I didn't, there are others who would put a bullet in your head and bury you where no one would find you."

"Don't be so dramatic," Morris said but without conviction.

"This one time," Josh said without smiling. "This one time, I am deadly serious."

"Okay then, I'm deadly serious. This weekend we break into a selective service office and destroy records. Pour blood on the files."

Josh had looked at him long and hard at that moment. He recalled thinking back to the time they first met before responding. He was twelve or thirteen, playing a favorite stickball game in the local schoolyard. Here, you used a sawed-off broomstick as a bat and a tennis ball as a baseball. A rectangle was chalked into the school yard wall. If you did not swing at the pitch and it struck within the boundary of the rectangle, it was a strike. Arguments were fierce and commonplace. Hit it over the school yard fence, and it was a homer. There were other rules for singles and doubles.

Then Josh noticed a small group of kids picking on a slightly younger boy who was small in stature but brave in attitude. He was not backing down from their taunts and threats. *His freaking problem,* Josh thought. Then, inexplicitly, he stepped back out of the batter's box as the other players expressed their impatience. He could not look away. This was unfair, and he hated things that were not fair. He knew the potential assailants from school but not well. They were just a few of the local toughs. There were many of those, at least the ones trying to act tough. Bravado was the best way to survive in what was considered Southie, the Irish ghetto.

"Hey," he yelled over to the group, "leave him alone, you're bothering my concentration."

"Fuck you," came the response. "We're cleaning up the neighborhood of kikes."

Josh was never sure why he did what he did next. He disliked violence and had no views about Jews one way or the other. He really didn't know any, at least not up close and personal. But he slowly walked over and punched the spokesperson in the nose. That set off a melee where he and this unknown kid were outnumbered two to one. But his unknown companion was a whirling dervish, and Josh was already well built and athletic. The fierce battle was over quickly enough as the bullies limped or ran away, a couple leaving trails of blood in their wakes.

Josh didn't even ask the boy's name until they got to the Harp Bar where they would clean up. His dad laughed at the sight. "Let's get you straight boy and, for Christ's sake, don't let Ora see you. By the way, how did the other side do?"

"I broke at least one nose, for sure." Josh smiled broadly, which hurt his lip. "That kid must have been a Wop, his beak was substantial. I'm not sure I recognized him from the area. But what would a Wop be doing over here, it's not their turf. In any case, they didn't look particularly good at the end after my buddy here and I finished up."

"What's your name, son." Big Jim asked as Josh realized he had never inquired up to this point.

"Morris … Mo Greenstein. But tell me, why did you do that, come to help a Jew like me?" He directed his question to Josh.

"I don't know … they pissed me off. Besides, you fight great for a Jew," Josh said with a broad smile that hurt his split lip.

Mo smiled and winced, his left eye turning black. "Thanks," he said, sticking out his hand.

They had come a long way since that day.

Josh shook his head. Time to face the day, he said to himself. Then he turned to his dog, Morris. "Okay, you lazy mutt" he said to his Pug who immediately rolled over onto his back, four paws extended into the air. "You really are spoiled but I guess you have more sense than me. You get some more shut eye … I'm off to see what mischief my sister is into."

He spotted her intently reviewing a stack of pictures in front of her. He crept up behind her. "Boo!"

"Shit," she yelled, lifting off the chair. "Asshole!"

"My, my, you have developed a wicked tongue, and you were such a virtuous young girl."

"Oh, bite me." She smiled. "I should wear diapers around here; You scared the crap out of me." After she got her breath back, she started in on what she had been struggling with. "Tell me, what did you learn from Mom and Dad about love, about sex? I was thinking about things last night, my early years. Turns out, though, that even your pictures are better than those ruminations. How pathetic is that?"

"Well, based on what I saw, they had sex twice—you and I are the proof. But wait, there were those rumors, you know."

"What rumors?" She eyed her brother suspiciously. "Oh, why did I ask?"

"Rumors in the old neighborhood," Josh replied. "It is just that people thought you were too delicate to hear them. At the time I was born, there was a very handsome mailman working the block, a real Adonis that all the women loved. I am the living proof …"

"… That you're delusional, maybe."

He went on. "Now, when you were born, I can remember this ragman who worked the streets. He was ugly as sin—stooped, terrible personality. Ora apparently felt bad for him. And voila, we have you."

"Bite me again," Rachel sniffed. "To be serious for a change, there was never any love in the house, never. Did you ever see them hug each other, hug us even? Yeah, I know, it was not an Irish thing … any affection. I guess it wasn't part of Mom's inherited culture, whatever that was. I craved contact, touch. Remember Harlow's classic experiments?"

"Of course, I stayed awake in some of my classes."

"Maybe that is why love has come so hard to me." Rachel mused.

"To us," Josh corrected her.

Rachel looked at him with a soft expression. "I used to wish Ora would spend time with me, like a real mother. I hoped she would share herself, her feelings, teach me things that every other girl seemed to know. The only hugs I ever got were from you, now that I think about it, and I initiated most of them. Then … you abandoned me. Maybe I spent so much time in books because I was so ignorant about life, so convinced that what life had to offer was on a page, not in people. I mean, I couldn't ask other girls my age. They were so …"

"Silly?" Josh offered.

"Exactly!"

"Wait," he interjected, "you came out fine. As I used to tell my students all the time, don't be in such a hurry to get out into the real word, it's way overrated. And your opinion about people is spot on. The crap we found in books was way better, still is."

"Are you capable of love, Josh?" She wanted to stay on topic.

"Sure."

She looked unconvinced. "I'm serious."

His smile disappeared. "So am I. There was Leni."

"Leni, the mystery lass." Rachel whispered. "You must tell me more about her."

"But first, let me tell you how I lost my virginity."

"Was she expensive?" Rachel shot out as she realized that trying to get him back on point might be useless. Aside from humor, misdirection was his other go-to tactic when he tries avoiding an unpleasant topic. She would bide her time, not push it.

"Didn't cost a dime. Remember the music teacher at school?" Josh had a big smile.

"Oh yeah, she wore too much makeup and always fussed around the boys in class."

"Yes, and she wore loose clothing but all us guys knew she had a great body. It was a matter of great speculation among us as to how great. One day, she asked me to help with some band equipment after school. She got up on a stool and asked me to hold on to her waist while she reached up to a high shelf. Okay, that was fine until she mentioned how strong my hands were. I am thinking, what is going on here? As she stepped back, she grabbed my hands and pulled them around to her front, to her breasts. All my fantasies were real."

"You're kidding! Tell me you're making this up." Rachel eyed her brother suspiciously.

"No, I swear, and it gets better. She pulled me into a small room and locked the door. The next thing I knew, she was sitting on a table, skirt pulled up, panties off, legs apart. She whispered something about making a real man out of me. I almost crapped in my pants, but what the hell. I was getting nowhere with those freaking Irish Catholic lasses. She proved to be a dream come true, and I found I was damn good at it after a little tutoring though, my first trip to the promised land was too brief to recall. That was embarrassing but she must have forgiven me since we kept at it for a while. My god, I cannot believe it now. We took some big chances and I felt a lot of what … guilt or shame? I kept having nightmares about getting caught, and some big scandal. Then again, no one caught female teachers screwing male students in those days. I can't think of a single case. Why was that? I suppose no one could believe such a thing happened. Why would they since we all knew women didn't like sex."

"That's it, stop. Way too much information. Josh, you are a pig."

"What happened to *I'm a doctor and have heard everything*." At his retort, Josh laughed loudly, enjoying her mild discomfort.

They heard Mo jump off the bed, the noise disturbing his slumber.

"I'm not uncomfortable, just disgusted." Then Rachel paused, realizing she had fallen into his trap.

Josh tried to look contrite. "Okay, I'm being bad here. I am curious, though. When did you become a real woman? Surely not with Evan since he was hardly a real man."

She stood up and walked around the room, as if she were deciding something. The way to get inside of Josh was to open herself up, she finally decided. "Okay, okay, it was in high school. I was so naïve, no surprise there. I think this was my third real date and the first one I was excited about at all. He seemed like a nice kid. I would see him in church, and in the library. Perfect, I thought. Then when we were alone, he started in on me. I tried saying no, but he said something about it being time I got with the program. What program, I thought? Later, I found out that he had bet his friends he could deflower the ice maiden. I was a challenge to him."

"You were raped?"

"To make matters worse, I got pregnant. I did not know what to do."

"Damn, I wish I was there." Josh felt awful about making fun of his early experiences.

"But you weren't, were you?" There was a tinge of venom in her words. "Sorry. Can you believe it. First time and I get the brass ring."

"Did you tell Dad?"

"Are you kidding me? He would have killed the kid and then thrown me out of the house. He was still mad about you, kept bitching about having kids was his biggest mistake in life. I went to Mom. It killed me, but she did not blink an eye. It was as if she had expected something like this. In any case, she arranged an abortion somehow. It was just before Roe, so all this was illegal and in very Catholic Massachusetts. How she knew about such things is yet a mystery. I still have nightmares about this creepy guy and the pain and bleeding. I can remember sneaking down some alley and using a password at a nondescript door. Okay, maybe I'm imagining the password thing, but it all was clandestine. It was the worst moment of my life, well, maybe the second worst. But she covered everything up, and dad never knew. After, she hugged me. It wasn't warm, I don't think she knew how to be warm. But she tried and said something about knowing what women must endure. Some lesson I thought at the time, but her comment stuck for a long time. All my life really. That was my last date until college."

Just then, Morris waddled into the room, stretching, and looking a little confused. "Be with you in a minute, buddy."

"Poor thing," Rachel murmured, "we woke him up."

"He'll survive. Of the three of us, he'll survive." Josh then walked across the room and wrapped his arms around his sister. She breathed out deeply. "Listen, I have a plan."

"He has a plan." Rachel forced a light tone into her voice. "Now we are doomed."

"Just shush and listen. We have nothing planned for today, let's go over to Victoria, one of my favorite places in the world. We can take the ferry over, just the two of us."

"I'd like that," Rachel smiled. "I would … love that."

CHAPTER 8

Day 3 - VICTORIA

The sun slipped in and out of quickly moving clouds. A sharp wind, more bracing than expected, slapped them as they wandered up from where they had parked the car on the ferry. Josh and Rachel bundled up but decided to stay on the open part of the deck. Neither said much as they completed their water journey, Josh merely pointing out an occasional point of interest. Soon enough, they had reached the disembarkation point adjacent to the harbor, the center of Victoria and the seat of government for the Province of British Columbia.

"I've always loved this place the best of all. Well, it is among my favorites at least," Josh said. "It is so British. Oh shit, I hope Dad can't hear me, he would be appalled."

He gave her a quick car tour of the area, through Beacon Hill Park and then along the coast to Beach Drive and the Victoria Golf Club. He pointed out the men in their tweed coats and the posts warning that golfers might be crossing here, like the *Watch Out for Bears* signs one might see elsewhere. "Remember when we saw the Deer Crossing signs when in the car with dad on those rare drives into the New England countryside. He always used the same joke about how the deer could obey such signs. We would look at one another knowing what was coming. *How do they know to cross where the signs are? Do you think deer can read?* Then he would chuckle at his own little joke."

"Don't laugh, I took it seriously. I was a lot younger than you."

"And hopelessly naïve I see." He said while hoping that the fact that he was driving might save him from any further corporal punishment.

As they toured the area, Josh pointed out that dogs were everywhere along with men in their tweed coats. Many of the male walkers were sporting pipes, both lit and unlit. The only thing missing were English bobbies and those red public phone booths." He told Rachel about the Georgia Strait which separated the Island from the mainland. Warm waters coming up from the South Pacific provided the area with a temperate climate, even permitting a few palm trees to thrive.

After a tour of the University of Victoria, he swung north on highway 19 along the coast toward Qualicum Bay. He stopped. "I'd love to take you over to Ucluelet and Long Beach on the west coast. The drive is magnificent, just like the Scottish Highlands and the beaches over there are primitive and rough. I love it, but not enough time today. Rain check?"

Rachel looked at him as her heart clutched. He was no longer pushing her away. Rather, he was seeing a future for them. "Yes, rain check, for sure." She then wondered if she had responded with too much enthusiasm.

He turned and they headed back into the city center. It was a week or two before the primary tourist season would arrive. Finding a good place to park was not difficult. The crowds were light though a few street performers and vendors were setting up for afternoon performances on the steps leading down to the harbor. Numerous boats were found parked in their assigned spots. The wind was dying down, the water less choppy now. Perhaps they would enjoy some improvement later in the day, more summery weather. He pointed out the provincial government building, which seemed straight out of the British Raj, and the Empress Hotel, another reminder of the city's Victorian roots.

"Really," he enthused, "can you imagine any better example of the British Raj? I would not be surprised if we found some poor Irish lasses in service to the elite here. Hey, we can have afternoon tea at the

Empress later, but let's first walk along the edge of the harbor. I haven't done that in years. There is a walkway along the harbor."

"Tea at the Empress," Rachel smirked. "You are tempting fate. Our sainted father will strike you down with a lightning bolt. If not that, you will probably burst into flames as you munch on one of those tiny cucumber sandwiches."

"Cucumber sandwiches? You really don't get out much."

"No, I don't. I have been working my ass off for the last hundred years or so. Sad, really," she mused. "No regrets though, save one."

He guessed, this being the one aspect of her life she had shared in the past. Still, he asked to make sure. "Cate, I presume?"

"Hmm, you are not as dumb as you look." She did not look pleased with her retort. "I've been so focused on my career that I never gave Cate the attention she deserved. I missed too many of her school events, didn't spend time listening to her. Sometimes I feel like such a failure as a mother."

"More self-flagellation? Where is this coming from? Listen, Rachel, how many times have I told you not to be so hard on yourself? That's my job. I'm good at shitting on people. I've had plenty of practice. Ask generations of my suffering students."

"Okay, tough guy, you got the job of asshole in chief since I cannot quibble with your superior qualifications in that area." Then she smiled reluctantly. "I bet the students loved you, the female ones for sure."

"I suppose," he responded distractedly as they meandered along the water. "This is where I belong, near water. I looked at a position at the University of Victoria once, it was nearer a seat of government and near water. In the end, Vancouver had too much to offer, like a real airport. I love the doable size and the laid-back ambiance of this place but I'm glad I stayed put."

———

They walked mostly in silence for a while, slowing as Josh might point out a site of interest. Suddenly, he stopped and pointed to a bench. The abruptness of his actions surprised his sister, but she sat expectantly next to him. "Rach, I have a confession of sorts."

"Oh no, if you have violated and dismembered several of your female students, I really don't want to know. I would have to turn you in, or knock you off myself, whichever proves more convenient."

"This does involve a female. Hopefully, no violence is warranted unless you've decided to off me on general principles. God, you've threatened that enough. No, this is something I've been meaning to mention." He could see that she was eyeing him closely, trying to decide if this was another joke of his. "With all this talk about Cate … here's the thing. She's arriving tomorrow."

"What!" Rachel looked stunned. "My Cate?"

"Is there another?" Josh then spoke more quickly. "She left Amman a couple of days ago and is now on the east coast right now, seeing her dad. We have been e-mailing back and forth. She wanted to celebrate this, as she put it, milestone in the life of her favorite reprobate uncle."

Rachel stopped abruptly. "Why didn't …" Not knowing how to finish her thought, her right hand swung toward Josh's stomach, finding her target.

"Damn, I thought this good news." He managed to get out through a grimace.

"Yes, but you could have said something sooner." She knew her anger was rooted in the fact that her daughter had confided in her brother, not her. "Did she say anything about me?"

"Of course. She's all bubbly about seeing you … just wanted to surprise you, that's all. Perhaps I shouldn't have spilled the beans, but I didn't want you to go into cardiac arrest when she showed. She suggested I get you to the airport on some pretence and then she'd walk off the plane and yell *surprise*. I'm not great with surprises, rather hate them in fact. In any case, she has some news that she wants to share personally."

"What news," Rachel asked with a confused and excited expression on her face.

"I don't know, she has been totally secretive about that, I swear. Believe me, I asked, but she said I would have to wait as well. She's better at secrets than me. Maybe that's why the State Department likes her."

"I doubt she's better at keeping secrets than you. You could replace James Bond at MI-5."

"You might be right," Josh said. "No matter, she mostly wants to see you. My retirement is just an excuse. As you know, they want foreign service types stationed abroad, particularly in sensitive stations, to take leaves every so often. She was past due. Of course, it makes sense for her to come here since I am her favorite uncle. There's no doubt about that."

"You're her only uncle, you nimrod." Then after a slight pause, she said, "But still, I'm not all that happy that she seems closer to you than to me. I told you, I screwed motherhood up."

Josh grabbed her by the shoulders and spun her around. "Listen, you little shit, I can still put you over my knee. You have never been a whiner so don't start now. You did a great job with her. She is a wonderful girl, woman, person, whatever, and she loves you very, very much. She just found it a bit easier to talk with me, even if most of it was across continents. You know those mother-daughter things ... toxic. Not toxic, sorry, that was way too strong. Maybe complex is a better term. But whatever is on her mind, I am easier for her. Mr. Jokester, you know. And given what is hidden in my personal closet, whatever she comes up with could never compete with my sins."

"Good point. That makes sense," Rachel said softly. "Everyone knows you're a first-class reprobate and a big joke. So, do you keep those blow up dolls in your closet or up in the attic. I've always wondered where but forgot to look while you were at the university."

"Very funny."

Rachel felt a tinge of pride, she could recover through her wit as well as he. "Ha, so I bet that's where they are ... at your university office?"

The view was lovely, and the sun had made its way clear of all the intruding clouds. The air had warmed considerably. It was spring. Soon, Victoria would be swarming with tourists enjoying one of Canada's more delightful destinations. Today, though, they had some privacy.

Josh started up again. "My best guess is that she thought she failed you."

"That's silly."

"Not to her, now listen. You must understand. She never said this outright, but I can listen pretty well."

"Since when," Rachel injected and then immediately signalled her surrender. "Sorry, go on."

"The thing is, she looked up to you as a role model, thought that you wanted her to follow in your footsteps. But she wasn't into math and science, and the thought of playing around inside people's bodies made her slightly nauseous. I guess it was a little like the way I failed Dad. It doesn't have to make sense; it is just the way you feel. You know I have never ever forgiven myself for failing him."

Rachel looked deeply at him for a long time. "And me? Did you worry about failing me?" Then she added hastily, "Don't answer, that was rhetorical."

"No, I worried about that, failing you … every goddamn day of my life." Josh looked at the harbor, his face immobile. "I am so sorry I was not there when you were … raped."

Rachel turned her gaze toward the water. "Yeah, well, thank you. I'm not sure that even begins to cover it but still. Thank you. In truth, though, Cate never failed me, I wish I could get that through her thick head. I guess she's Irish too. You did fail dad, though. It was his fault, not yours, but the betrayal was real for him. It was like he died after you …"

"Quit football." He said curtly.

"That started it, then it got worse. Shit, it was like a continuous wake in the house after you disappeared." Her voice expressed sadness, not anger.

"You know, Rach, I thought about that for a long time. It wasn't just that kid I hurt so bad. That was bad, sure. I could've gotten past that. He was not the first kid crippled playing that silly game, particularly before the focus on player safety. Here's the thing. I might have been looking for some reason to escape the cage I was in … to change direction. Funny, looking back, it is so hard to recall what you were thinking, feeling. I see images, sense emotions, but they all seem like snippets on the cutting-room floor. What you don't get is the whole film, the complete narrative. You cannot separate the reality of then from what you now impose on it from where we are now. We're all great at revisionist history. It is one hell of a defense mechanism."

"Still, some things you can't forget," Rachel whispered. "I could never erase you and Dad screaming at each other. I cannot even recall what was said … just the emotion, the rage pouring through my door. I remember being in a ball under my covers, but I could not rub out the sounds. I would cry all night. Hell, I cried every night for a long time. It was like the household dissolved in slow motion. First, you quit sports. That was the first blow for Dad. Then you up and went to a school that was, at least according to him, a den of atheists and communists. That sunk him deeper into a pit of silence. It wasn't Notre Dame. It wasn't even Catholic. Even you probably could not see how much he lived through you. You were too close to it. But it was so obvious to me. Finally, you became a traitor in his eyes."

"Oh god, I kept beating him up, didn't I? I was so angry with him at the time. I'm not sure I noticed."

"Don't go there. There was no compromise. You would have had to sell your soul to reach him again, and that's way too high a price."

He looked upon her with immense admiration. "Yes, you're right."

"Remember how boisterous he was, how any room he entered expanded with his mere presence. He would fill it up and press the walls out. After you disappeared, fled, whatever, he shrank. They both did. The silence would often be deafening."

"Sorry," he tried weakly. "I …"

"Let me finish," she cut him off, "I need to say some things."

"I get that. Go ahead."

Rachel took a deep breath. "Those days were a bad dream. One day you didn't show when we were supposed to meet. I shrugged that off, but I soon realized I hadn't heard from you ... at all. You ignoring the folks was not universal, but you had not done that to me up to that point. Not a word from you, you were just gone. Panic until at least we knew you were alive. What, we got that postcard, a freaking postcard! Even dad freaked out at first, but soon it all turned to white-hot anger. Then the silence became something darker. It was not just dad. Ora slipped into the depths of her own personal darkness. Eventually, she stopped playing the piano. I wanted to scream some days, but who would listen. I could not stand the silence anymore. Christ, didn't they care about me at all ... was I merely chopped liver? Didn't I count? I was still there, but no one seemed to care anymore. And the worst thing was ... you never came back to explain things to me. I waited. For a long time, I waited. You had always been there to explain things ..."

"Rach, you remember the milk bottle thing we learned in Catechism class?"

"Sure. Venial sins put splotches in the white milk while a mortal sin turned the whole bottle black. So neat and simple."

"Right. My bottle was totally black. I felt so unworthy, of you ... of anyone."

She grabbed his hand. "Listen, I'm going to need more than a kid's metaphor for good and evil. I mean, I knew you were into the anti-war stuff, but then so were many of the kids back then. What the hell did you do that you had to run away and not come back ... other than the draft thing. It had to be worse than that. I do recall visits from Government men, maybe the FBI? They all looked the same in their suits. But I was always sent away, and never told what was discussed. You know, you have never said what really pushed you away, never. Over all these years, silence. Do you have any idea how deafening silence can be? It is the loudest sound imaginable." Her last words were barely above a whisper.

Josh lowered his head for several moments. Then he realized his sister would wait him out. He took a deep breath before starting in a low monotone. "I stole money. I destroyed government records. I started a fire and stole other dangerous stuff that ... that ..." And he stopped.

"What do you mean you stole money, like rob a bank?"

"No, for god sakes, though that was discussed. I stole from some Irish wise guys, you know, the Boston mob connected to the Winter Hill gang."

"Shit," she exhaled, her eyes wide. "Even I know that's worse than ripping off a bank. You could have gotten yourself killed."

"Tell me, I had diarrhea for weeks after."

"But how did you do it?" She stared at him intently. "Did you rob them with a gun? I can't possibly see you with a gun, ever."

"No guns, but it was easier than you might think. You must remember there were these wise guys always around the bar. They knew me, they trusted me. I even did them small errands and favors from time to time. I knew their schedules and routines, how they ran their games and scams. They would accumulate cash and, when they had enough, would launder it through legit operations or offshore. Often, it would go for a big drug purchase they could sell on the streets. Most locals never knew they sold drugs because they wouldn't do it within South Boston, mostly pushing them in Roxbury or among rich white kids. They protected their own, a matter of pride to them. From time to time, they had quite a bit of cash stored, and I mean a lot for back then. What was so freaking amazing is that security was so lax. It never occurred to them anyone would dare take them down. After all, to screw with Whitey's gang was a death sentence. How many people did he off, twenty at least?"

"At least, those are just the ones we know about." Rachel repeated, now staring at him.

"It was like this. I had a key to the place where they stashed their bankroll. Using banks would raise too many questions so they just hid it. I think they forgot I had this key from the time I did them small favors when I worked in dad's bar. I never told you, but I ran some small book out of the Harp Bar for dad. It helped with my expenses. A few of these wise guys were in dad's place a lot and I got to know them. I also did some gopher stuff, several of us Irish kids did. So, when we needed money for our so-called college revolution, I went back to see if there might be opportunities to secure a contribution for the cause. That's what I called it at least. I struck paydirt. This associate of Whitey's was drunk out of his mind one day and blabbed about all the money that had been accumulated. He complained that this was tough on him. You know, the temptation to grab some was too great."

"A crook with a conscience?" Rachel seemed dubious.

"Don't be silly. He was scared, that's all. What I remember was he mentioned that Whitey wanted to use it for *the cause*. And for Whitey, *the cause* was sacred. He might have been a cold stone killer, but he did believe in something."

"The cause?" Rachel asked.

"Yeah, to support the Catholic side during the troubles in Ulster, that's when the religious wars were starting up again. Bulger was a shit, but he had a soft spot for the old country. He also was taken with the dream of bringing Northern Ireland back into a unified country. Anyway, that gave me the idea of stealing some of this stash. In the moment, I thought this a win-win thing. I could finance our revolution and keep a few guns off the streets of Belfast. That was the last thing that poor city needed then, more ways of killing each other."

"You saw yourself as a good guy? Is that what you are saying."

Josh paused as if he were pondering her question. "I suppose. We're all capable of rationalizing what we choose to do. But I wasn't totally noble and knew it. I also wanted to strike back at dad. I'm sure he was never a real wise guy himself, but he surely would have helped Whitey in this Irish caper. That would be right up his alley. I suppose it didn't even matter if that was true, I thought it was and I wanted to get back at him for abandoning me, for not … understanding. In any case, I tried taking only enough so that they might not miss it. We were still talking about forty or fifty-grand. That was pocket change for them. Back in the sixties, that was a small fortune for us."

"That didn't work, did it?"

"No, not a chance and I shouldn't have been so stupid." he said. "Word immediately was on the street about the heist. It was awful. Let me tell you, I was sick to my stomach even during the heist itself. I recall sneaking up to the place, checking out each car on the street, each alleyway, every window. I have no idea what I was looking for, but I was sure my life was just about over. Even now, I can feel the tension in my whole body as I turned the key in the door. I was certain some alarm would blare, and I would walk into a front end of a .45 canon. But nothing, nobody. I had to jimmy another door. After that, my big concern was how much to take. Later I realized I was an idiot. Hell, the jimmied door was a dead giveaway that they had been taken down. I should have grabbed it all. But I thought at the time that if I only took some, they would only break all my arms and legs if they figured things out. I mean, they liked me."

"Not that much," Rachel whispered incredulously.

"Tell me. I sat on the crapper for a week straight. Later, a couple of minor Italian hoods disappeared. I remember thinking, maybe I got them killed, that they blamed the Wops. There was always this Mick-Wop thing going on in the streets. Whitey even used an old Southie buddy of his in the FBI to legally take down some of his competition from the North End by snitching. Of course, the Italians would be suspects number one for what I had done. I never knew for sure whether these two were whacked, never asked. If Whitey had thought about it, why would the Italians leave any dough behind?"

"And they never suspected you."

"I guess not. I was this harmless college kid and the sainted son of Big Jim. It probably never even occurred to them. Besides, most guys got caught because they could not keep their traps shut or started spending the money foolishly. Nothing advertised a big score like a two-bit hood suddenly driving around Southie in a big Caddy. Some of these clowns were not the brightest bulbs, getting liquored up and running their mouths."

"It has been a while, but I remember some of the young toughs. Future rocket scientists they were not." Rachel chuckled at her own joke.

"They reminded me of my high school buddies who scored with a gal, an achievement back then. Then these geniuses would proceed to trash her to everyone within hearing distance. I wanted to slap them upside the head. You idiots, you finally got some and now you want to cut off the supply by shaming the gal. Are you taking cretin pills? I was stupid, but not that stupid."

"Can we debate that?"

Josh rolled his eyes. "Damn, when did you get so quick. Now listen. I did worry, a lot. One day, a wise guy asked me if I still had a key to the place. When I lied, he insisted that he remembered giving me one and never getting it back. But I charmed him with a song and dance, the Celtic gift that Dad bequeathed me. That sent me back to the crapper in a hurry. I had visions of my body being dumped in the swamp with my hands missing and teeth removed. No one would know what happened to me."

"Did you ever find out if they ever suspected you for real?"

Josh shrugged. "I'm still alive so I guess not. In the end, I think it was beyond them that this kid had the balls to rob them. It had to be the Wops from the north end or some independent group trying to muscle in. I piled on to those hypotheses for sure. Still, I had nightmares for years, decades, about that damn swamp and me with a toothless skull and handless torso. No fingerprints or other ways of identifying me. DNA was science fiction back then. Wow, you would have been worrying about what ever happened to that worthless brother of yours for all eternity."

"Not really, I would have just presumed you had moved on to a real toasty destination, that place heated by brimstone." Rachel responded though her touch of humor seemed forced. "Tell me. Did you ever do anything irrevocable, something that could not be undone?"

"Like kill someone," Josh said, standing up. They started along a path. The sun was out now, and it had warmed considerably. "Well, there were the break-ins and Carla started a fire at more than one. Helen did at another when I was with her. But it was less what I did than what I knew I would do. We were escalating. Each action invited something more dramatic. No one seemed to be paying attention. I mean, we were getting media coverage, but the war went on and on. Our actions never seemed enough, or not enough in our naïve eyes. The insane killing in the war kept increasing so we felt compelled to up the ante. We talked about our responses as being proportional."

"Proportional?"

"You know how it goes. Oh, we destroyed those records, and they are still sending kids to die in Southeast Asia. Time for plan B or C or D. If the number dying went up by fifty percent, we should up what we did by the same. I yet think we had the situation analyzed correctly, but employed the strategic thinking appropriate to what we were … stupid kids. At that age, your passion runs away from your better judgment. It is just that the anger at the stupidity and passivity of those around you is overwhelming, so infuriating."

"If you're making the case that you were an immature moron, I will stipulate to that fact," Rachel threw out. Inside, she wondered what he was keeping back. She felt there was more. "Sounds to me as if you guys had a rather serious case of excess hubris. I worried about you back then but had no idea. I mean, you introduced me to most of them. I can recall the anger, the conviction. That was too obvious. Yet, I never guessed where it might lead. I could only see from the outside. That wasn't enough."

"Perhaps we had more conviction than brains, but I yet argue we were not morons. Christ, Morris was about the brightest guy I would ever meet. Carla was smart as a whip. The thing is that we cared, and we thought hard about stuff. We all did. Well, most of us did. One thing became clearer in those days. There is a huge penalty associated with caring about things, it is a curse. It is so damn easy to go through life absent passion for people or causes or even for life itself. I know. Look at me now. Life is now easy."

She stopped walking and turned to him. "Josh, I—"

"Rachel, you were not the only one to cry themselves to sleep back then. Not by a long shot. In the early days, after fleeing the States, I sat in a small room in Toronto, alone, scared, and without direction. You go from a life with all kind of supports around you to nothing. I was afraid to reach out to you, to anyone back home. I did not know whether the feds would show up at the door or the Irish mob, or maybe even the Mafia because I somehow got some of their guys whacked. You sit in a room and start seeing ghosts everywhere. Back then, the wise guys seemed omnipotent, now we know better."

"You have a point here," she agreed.

"Good thing there were others just like me, usually hanging around the university. They had an organization that helped us émigrés out with low-level jobs, housing, and counselling. The Canadians were against the war before us. These Canucks are as nice as people say. The government was quite inviting as well. They were becoming, even if unofficially, quite disgusted with our nation's militarism. For me, after I stopped hiding under the bed and wetting myself whenever someone knocked on the door, things slowly got better. I worked hard, earned some money, finally made it into the University. Then I just buried myself in work and study."

"And you forgot about me, us."

"Yeah, it must seem like that." He had a pained expression on his face. "You don't … it is hard … what I mean …"

She jumped in. "What you mean is that you don't have a fucking clue." He did not respond; they kept walking. She despised her brief bursts of anger and started again in a calm voice. "Josh, I hated you. I hated you with a white passion. I hated you beyond hate. Do you know why? Don't answer, that was rhetorical." She immediately answered her own query. "Because I loved you so much. Isn't that the way! We hate most those we love so desperately. You were my big brother, the hero that could do no wrong, the boy-man I admired without qualification. I was even jealous. Dad loved you. Mom adored her precious prince since the guy she married was no prize. Lots of families dote on the girls, but not ours. I was an afterthought but didn't care because I thought they were right to worship you. You were deserving of all that adoration and acclaim. And it was not just them, the whole neighborhood loved you. Hell, the whole damn Irish tribe had you on a pedestal. And then like sand in a sieve, it all slipped away and there was nothing…emptiness and an ignorance of what happened."

"Yeah," was all he managed.

She slowed her pace. Her temporary spasm of rage now had fully receded as she gazed out over the harbor. More small pleasure craft were now plying back and forth. Then she continued in a quieter voice. "I used to reflect in your glory, the little sister of the tribal hero. Yeah, I know, sounds silly now. But we lived in a small ethnic pond, and I was the younger sister of the best athlete and most popular guy on the block. Girls wanted to be around me because I was your sister. They would ask what you were like. I tried telling them you were a smelly, burping, farting messy thing, but they would have none of that, so I lied. Oh, he is just so cool, so sexy. It was nauseating. Some wanted to know what you looked like naked, naked for crying out loud, as if I spent my days trying to catch a peek when you were in the shower. I was appalled when a couple asked for pictures, you know the kind."

"Well, I could have posed for you—"

"You were a pig!" She half-shouted. "Excuse me, you are a pig. But what I didn't tell them was that you were good to me, always good to me, at least when you weren't trying to dodge me when you went out. I can still remember sitting on the couch watching television. I would stretch out with my head on your thigh. We would watch those silly sitcoms like *Gilligan's Island* and your favorite, *Rocky and Bullwinkle*. You would pat my head sometimes. I never felt safer, more secure, than during those moments. You were kind. I knew that. Whatever else you might be, you would be there for me. You really would be the knight in shining armor."

"And then I wasn't."

"And then you weren't. Maybe if I knew why at the time, I could've handled it. I don't know. I wasn't old enough to make sense of things or sort out feelings. I was a book-smart kid, but that does not give you a leg up on emotional maturity. I found myself wallowing in pity and trying to keep the family from falling apart. Try being a teenager and believing you had to be the adult. Damn, you grow up fast. Ora had been this pillar of quiet strength all our lives. Now she seemed a shell of disfigured desperation. She was hollow … unresponsive. I could not reach her, and that just killed me."

"My God," he managed to get out.

"Dad spent time in his bar, and I tried helping him out, but I never fit in. You were the natural. The guys would rub my head and say how cute I was. Sometimes, they would hit on me. They never talked with me as they did with you, though. They never confided, told stories of the old country, shared dreams of rebellion, or fantasies of female conquests that were sure to come their way that night, even when they hadn't all the prior nights in their pitiful lives. I kept trying, but you know your old saying about not putting in what God left out. It cannot be done. It just can't be done. I gave up one day."

"I never knew how bad …"

She went on as if he had not tried to speak. "I'm not exactly sure when, perhaps the day a couple of them hit on me in more than a kidding way, perhaps because I was developing. I left the bar and never went back. Dad yelled at me, but I told mom what was happening, how these guys were coming on to me. For once, she listened and put dad in his place. After that, I retreated further into my books if that were possible. The library was my second home. It was my escape and my salvation. But I never forgot you, nor forgave I suppose. I would always think back to those times I would be sitting at the table doing my studies and you would come rollicking in, full of life. You would have that easy, crooked smile on your face. I would bound up into your arms. After you went missing, I would stare at the door for a long time, a long time indeed. It never opened."

"Rach, would you like to twist the knife in a little deeper now?"

"Yes, I think I rather would. Does it hurt?"

"Of course, it hurts," Josh protested. "Contrary to the public consensus, I have feelings."

"Good! I mean good that it hurts, not that you think you have feelings. I need a hell of a lot more evidence on that score."

"I've no defense, but I still want to say something."

"Uh-oh," she said without mirth.

"Just shush for a moment." He paused, collecting his thoughts. A boat made one of those mournful warning sounds, and they both gazed off into the distance. "It is hard going back, even in my mind's eye. It has been over four decades, and a lot is lost or reshaped in one way or another. For me, two things remain, general feelings and sharp vignettes or these memories and conversations that seem as if they took place yesterday. I can feel the battle that raged within me after all these years. Nothing was simple. I wish to hell I could've been like most of the kids I grew up with, played ball with. Everything for them was simple, at least looked simple to me. You only worried about getting high without trouble with the law and getting laid without knocking a girl up. Everything looked so easy for these other kids, like what to believe and feel, whom to like and whom to hate. We had a pecking order. Irish on top above the other white Catholic ethnic groups with the Mediterranean types being down the list. If you ran into a white guy or gal, you asked what they were, Irish or Polish or Italian. Their response situated them within a defined world. You knew how to treat them, whether they could be trusted in a fight or date your sister or live next to you. It was a full-blown caste system, just like India."

"I remember," she interjected.

"Even outside the fixed rules of the Irish ghetto, you knew what to believe and why. America was number one without question. The Commies were total shit, and anyone who had not decided between good and evil, us and them, fell into the enemy camp by default. There was no quibbling, no gray areas. If you were needed to defend the eternal verities, the true church, our way of life, that's what you did, no questions asked. You defended your faith, country, and tribe. Not to do so brought your community and family into shame."

"Family and faith." Rachel whispered. "I remember dad telling us that. "Family and faith were everything, and faith meant country as well. There was no distinction in his mind. Ireland, America, and the Catholic church."

"Absolutely," Josh said with excitement, "and the church was at the center of everything, particularly the Irish version of the church. The native Irish hung on to Catholicism for centuries while the Brits killed their priests and stripped believers of all rights. You know the stories as well as I, Dad told them often enough. The soupers were shunned by their neighbors just because they renounced their faith for bread and sustenance to stay alive. The expected thing was to die a Catholic pauper rather than give up what was most dear. So of course, you hung on to that faith since it was the one anchor in a world so unjust that many a man went mad. There were approaching eight million native Irish before the potato blight, and maybe four-plus million after all the deaths and emigration. The Irish were little different from the Jews. Persecution brings you closer to core beliefs and your identity. You cling to some things with a desperation that others find naïve and childish. But it was not naïve and foolish to Dad, nor to me back then."

Rachel was looking at him intently. She feared saying anything as if it might shut him down. Eventually, she did fill in the silence with, "Why do I sense a *but* coming?"

"But I walked away. I broke the sacred code." His voice was flat.

"For a reason, something in which you believed." Rachel tried though without conviction.

"My beliefs? Who knows?" He forced a grim smile. "I do not say this lightly but God, in his wisdom, cursed me with a restless mind. Oh, I can't say it was a special mind. Hell, I knew kids who could whip through calculus and do all the Latin conjugations way better than I. They could even translate Virgil without cheating with a Trot. I, it turned out, was cursed with an inquisitive mind, the kind that always asks why, always need to seek a deeper answer. You must know that is a version of Hell. You are similarly cursed."

"What? I wasn't like you."

"Oh yes you were … probably are. All those questions you kept asking me. I knew you had the same affliction. And it is a sickness, make no mistake about that. I've watched the world very closely over the decades. How do most people survive? They simply live out programmed scripts. Essentially, they are unconscious, never questioning anything. Any little cognitive dissonance that might come their way gets buried out of sight. They push inconvenient or incompatible information far away or distort it to maintain the integrity of their existing world order. Change their worldview, forget about it. Think an original thought, not on your life. Conceptualize some new way of looking at things, you must be out of your mind. Remember talking with the locals in our neighborhood or in dad's bar. Every second sentence was punctuated with the phrase *am I right or wrong.'* You were always supposed to tell them they were right, the need for confirmation was universal and insistent. This is what I grew up in, what I lived and believed in for a long time."

"Me too, and then …" She waited for her brother to complete her thought.

"For me, small shit happened, especially after I met Morris and Carla and Peter Favulli and some others. We would talk about the larger world. None of my friends did that when I was a teen. Foreign policy would have been what was happening on the other side of Route 128. Mo Greenstein, though, knew about what was going on across the globe. He got me reading stuff, things that our world had never seen. I was shocked to learn that we overthrew other government leaders like Arbenz in Guatemala, to help United Fruit, I guess. Then we engineered a coup to overthrow the elected prime minister in Iran, to help British Petroleum. So much for democracy and fair play. We failed to allow elections in Vietnam in the mid-1950s because we could not guarantee the outcome and feared the Commies would win in a fair contest. Democratic processes and national sovereignty were only permitted on our terms and only if the results we wanted could be guaranteed. That was crushing stuff for a naïve young kid raised to believe we always wore the white hats. But I didn't waver right away in my childhood beliefs, that took a long time. I would argue with Mo, and so did Peter. The more I sensed my world view crumbling, the harder I argued. But all in vain. I was doomed."

"I think that's always the case." Rachel said in encouragement.

"We had some great fights—verbal ones. Mo made me think. To this day, I don't know if I loved him or hated him for that. No, I loved him, but it was painful. I can still recall some of the conversations. Why were we supporting colonial powers trying to hang on to their oppressive overseas regimes? Why would we support the French in Indochina, the French goddamn it? They were not exactly benevolent overlords. Was it all just our anti-communist obsession, or did we implicitly back the exploitation of commodities from countries that could not fight back? Why weren't we fighting for democracy and self-government, for the right of people to find their own way? Were we not the ultimate hypocrites?"

When Josh paused, Rachel jumped in. "I really don't know. I was busy with high school biology, chemistry, and calculus at the time. Then, as an adult, you weren't around to keep me informed about a world beyond the human body. I think I became a technician. What have you called me, a plumber of the human body? How sad."

"I was asking a rhetorical question, kiddo, and you are way more than a freaking technician." He stared at the harbor again. "You know, we should have been holding up the North Vietnamese as heroes, not villains. They were the ones trying to create a strong independent nation free from foreign control. I remember seeing cartoonish depictions of Ho Chi Min in the Boston papers as if he were some ghoulish monster with fangs and long fingernails. Hell, the guy was educated in France, was lied to, and screwed by the Western powers repeatedly. But he never gave up. He fought the Japanese, the French, and the Americans for decades. George Washington fought the Brits and the Hessians for seven years and had the French army and navy on his side at the end. Hell, France went bankrupt, and Louis eventually lost his head after he bankrupted his treasury mostly to give us freedom while embarrassing the Brits. Sure, Ho had supplies from China and the Soviets but no real fighting assets. It was really an amazing story of David versus Goliath. But what did our geniuses do? We came up with the domino theory. Yes, if Nam fell, could Australia be far behind, then New Zealand and Hawaii? In a month, Californians would be speaking Vietnamese. Okay, I exaggerate a bit, but it was all so insane. Still, people lapped-up this crap."

Rachel looked at him intently. He was not present to her at that moment. He was focused on something unseen over the harbor somewhere in Victoria. He was back in his youth reliving old struggles. She said nothing. Perhaps she was understanding him just a little bit better. *Shit*, she thought. She was beginning to feel sorry for him, how did that happen? "Damn, you piss me off."

"What?" Josh said, confused.

Rachel sighed. "You are way too charming and glib. I just hate that."

"Also a curse, dear sister. In any case, the more I read and talked, the angrier I would get. At times, I would become enraged at the stupidity and simplistic patriotism around me. Didn't anyone have the balls to question what we were doing? Didn't people question anything we did as a country? My god, how could we possibly hold any high moral ground when we held people of color in economic and legal bondage? How could anyone watch the fire hosing of blacks who just wanted to sit at a goddamn lunch counter and not go ballistic? How could people stand watching black churches burn or young girls get blown up in a church basement just for asking to vote and not be enraged. I went ballistic inside myself when I saw those images. This was America, goddamn it. In whose universe could we claim any moral authority? Later, I was to become even more familiar with the courage of those who protested and the evil of those who oppressed them. Remember the Freedom Riders, mostly kids who braved death by riding interstate busses into the heart of Dixie to use segregated facilities?"

"Yes. Vaguely."

"Did you know they made out final wills before getting on the buses. What courage! And the establishment at the time, surely in the South, embraced violence and fear and red baiting as they prayed to their God on Sundays … the pathetic hypocrites! What did they not get about Christ's message? What was going on in their heads with all their talk about freedom and opportunity and democratic principles and faith?"

"I have no answer." She stammered, recognizing that he was venting long repressed emotions. She sensed he was no longer talking to her, but to himself.

He paused then looked at her as if recalling she was there. "Of course, I'm making this sound a lot more linear and inexorable than it was. Inside, I was engaged in a constant internal battle. I would conclude something and then immediately doubt myself. Maybe I was just being a kid. I mean, really, the adults must know more than I. Perhaps they had information on what the Communists were doing that was classified. Really, it seemed impossible to me that they were as narrow and brain-dead as they appeared. My reservations ran deeper than that. You don't just shed the scripts of your youth overnight. It is not like someone hits a switch and you go from good Catholic altar boy to long-haired revolutionary over the course of one afternoon."

"Josh, you never shared what you were going through with me. I never saw your anguish, never knew. You kept that part of your life secret, probably to spare me. Shit, I should have seen."

"Rach, you were barely a teen at the time." He looked at her as if surprised that she had grown so old. "There was an article I read once, a long time ago. But it always stayed with me. It was by a New York State Supreme Court justice. He'd come of age in the 1930s in the Big Apple. Like many of his peers, he was taken with the suffering and despair around him. Like so many of his friends, he searched for solutions. They argued for hours about what must be done and, in due course, stumbled on socialism, even communism, as possible solutions. Oh, he matured out of these early infatuations and went on to an exemplary judicial career. But he wrote that he was forever grateful for growing up in such a difficult decade. He had to think hard about things. He could not just take what his parents told him as the truth. No, he had to work out his own view of things, his own philosophy of life. All those late-night discussions, the intellectual sparring, it is not a waste of time. It was not for this future Justice. It is how you learn how to think. Think about it, most of school is absorbing facts. That is not what real education is all about, not simply memorizing crap. It is developing analytical skills, being able to ask tough questions, think more deeply about stuff, and pursue issues with creativity. In retrospect, he was convinced that he would never have become the deep thinker that he became had he merely survived a conventional and traditional childhood. But he hadn't, he was one of the lucky ones. He had grown up in a crucible of turmoil and challenge. Well, the sixties were the same, a decade of turmoil and challenge. Despite all, maybe I also was one of the lucky ones."

Rachel's phone rang. She glanced at the number and said, "Sorry, I must answer this one." After a discussion on medical matters about a patient back in Madison, she hung up and looked directly at him, "I used to welcome these calls, they told me I was important. Suddenly, they are a nuisance. Please, go on."

"I'm sure Dad thought I lost my mind or had become a druggie. Of course, he could not see what was going on inside. He blamed Morris, hippies, Commies, whatever. It had nothing to do with that stuff, not much at least. I never fully appreciated why others didn't see the world as I did. I think I somehow thought dad and you might magically understand. But how could you?"

"He couldn't. That was hopeless." Then she surprised him my smiling. "However, if we had had this talk back then, I would have straightened your ass out in no time."

"You are a smart ass," he laughed, breaking the tension. "But you have a point. You and I could have understood one another. Even as a bratty kid, you were beyond your years. I see that now. We possess an ability to dissect the usual scripts, see beyond them. I used to think about Galileo challenging the church in Rome."

"I was just thinking the same thing."

He looked quickly to see that she was teasing. "Yeah, yeah, you are hilarious. Anyway, he probably said something like this to the Cardinals that were persecuting him. *'Okay, you have centuries of consensus and the authority of God, but I have my reason and curiosity. You see, things as you were told must be where I see things differently, as my reason and observation tell me they are.'* I can see Galileo telling them that he sees things as God really wanted us to see them."

"Foolish man, indeed." Rachel tried a smile. Inside, she was thrilled that he was sharing so much.

Josh sighed. "Can you imagine the courage that took? It's hard arguing with people who think they know God. Dad would rail against me. He could not understand my disloyalty, to him and the church and the country. What he never understood is that I was like him, too much like him. I had inherited his integrity and his passion for stuff. Hell, he broke the law to fight for what he thought was right. He plotted revolution and ran guns for a cause, for a cause that he believed in. Why could he not see that in me? He and I, we were the same in some fundamental way, the same. We may have had different gods, but we were the same inside."

"He realized that," she whispered though not believing her own words.

"No way, he didn't. I tried reaching out, even after I left. I sent letters, even called. I kept hoping you would answer but mom usually did. She always told me you were out, and that dad was busy. Once, he answered the phone. I said, 'Dad, this is Josh, your son, can we talk?' Do you know what he said?"

"I think I'm afraid to know."

"I can still hear his voice. *'Sorry, you must have the wrong number, I have no son.'*"

Rachel thought there was moisture clouding his eyes. "Josh, why didn't you try harder to reach out to me?"

"I did, sort of" he said weakly. "I sent notes to you, quite a few, but got nothing back. I thought you'd written me off as well."

"I never saw any of them. Shit, shit, shit! They kept them from me. Jim or Ora got the mail every day. I guess you were persona-non-grata for sure. I think Dad controlled Mom on this. She was strong in her own way, but not when he had dug in. I think she lost some of her independence as she aged, lost her … beauty. And he could be stubborn. You know, the typical Irishman."

He laughed bitterly, wanting to correct her on what their mother really thought about her son back then. Instead he said, "Ya think, I suppose I could be just a bit stubborn myself. Like I said, we were the same."

"I suppose." She conceded his point.

"But sometimes it took me a long time to get where I was going," he paused to decide where to go next. "There is one life lesson that took me a long time to embrace. For a while, when I was young, I thought my intellect was the magic key to things. I was the smartest guy in the room, except for Morris."

"And me, except I guess I'm not a guy," she added with a grim smile.

"Right, that was the only reason, now shush. I was convinced that I could bring everyone else to my way of thinking through evidence and reason. Hell, all the arguing we did to sharpen our critical thinking skills had to be good for something. I proved a natural at policy analysis, embracing the challenges of sorting through complex trade-offs, detecting externalities, and figuring out the nuances of the *cui bono* question. Others saw the surface of things while I could get to the heart of any issue. I could distinguish correlation from causation, think through the direction of causal paths, mine data for hidden meanings. All that came second nature to me."

"I see that." Rachel nodded. "I was impressed with your mind when we were kids. Not so much now though."

"God spare me." He tapped her lightly on the arm. "The thing is, and being full of myself, I thought that was all I needed, all that counted.

But the bitter truth is that it is not. Smarts and formal training can take you only so far. In the end, values matter. Imagination matters. So much is post rationalization. We decide, or merely accept, and then construct complex rational edifices to support what we want to believe. And where do those core values come from? Where should we look for vision and truth beyond calculated reason." Then he paused.

"I await the answer with bated-breath."

"By the way, I intend to ignore all sarcasm from a mere plumber of the human body. Seriously, I am convinced that some of what we believe is hardwired, at least in how we process input and information. Our brains are configured differently. Some of us see threat everywhere where others of us like new things and diverse stimuli. Why did the hard-right see Communists everywhere in the 1950s? Shit, the Birchers thought Eisenhower was pink for Christ sakes and that fluoride in our water was a goddamn Commie plot. You cannot dispel such beliefs with reasoned argument. Why did I go and save Morris from getting the shit beat out of him by some Irish thugs? I bristled at the thought he was being treated unfairly. Unfairly? No one else in my neighborhood would have done that, would have given a shit. He was a Jew in the wrong place. Period. But I could not look away. That should have been clue number one. The head is important, but the heart, you know, is everything."

"Dear Josh, you're not quite as dense as you look." She kissed him on the cheek. "I really despise the fact that you make it so hard to hate you."

"Why, thank you, Rach, that's a big concession on your part. And by the way, the good guys will win in the end."

She looked at him with slightly narrow eyes. "I know I'll kick myself for asking, but who are the good guys again and win what?"

"Glad you asked, sis. The good guys are those that think like me. And we'll win because we are on the right side of history and, more importantly, of evolution. Darwin never said that the strongest would survive. No, those who were more adaptable, those capable of responding to new things, would do the best. That's us, or people like us."

"Hmm, this helps." she murmured, not sure she agreed but deciding to let his hypothesis pass. "I still can't figure out why you stayed away after the pain subsided and you established yourself as an academic. For many years, you were a virtual stranger … a ghost to all of us in the States. You never returned to the States for a long, long time, not to ply your craft or even for a social visit. What was with that?"

"Part of it was that I was scared, at least at first. Yes, scared. It wasn't the selective service problems or at least not the only issue. Okay, I fled the draft. That would have been problem number one. Then there were the break-ins and other stuff."

"Was a warrant ever issued?" she asked. "Were you a real fugitive."

"Frankly, I never knew for sure. I knew I was a person of interest for many things. I did wonder if they had just forgotten about me. If I did try to enter the country, I worried it might trigger something buried in a file somewhere. That was one worry I had. It turns out Kit's older brother was with the Justice Department at the time. I got word that he was keeping an eye on me. I suppose that's how Kit found me when she did. I feared that if I ever returned, I would be brought in for questioning at the least. The Canadians would protect me from most of that, or so I thought, especially after I had become a citizen. They would at least drag their feet on stuff."

"But not everything?"

"There was other stuff." Then he went silent, and Rachel sensed he wasn't ready to go there. But I think I know the real reason I stayed away. Guilt! Good old fashion Irish guilt. It overwhelmed me and I… just could not face it, not really." His lip quivered.

It was Rachel's turn to back away. "Maybe we should head back to the hotel for the funny sandwiches and tea."

———

When they made it back to the steps to the harbor, the scene was in full bloom. There was a group playing haunting sounds from South America, street artists of amazing technical skill, imaginative body art, and jugglers and others vying for the crowd's attention. Rachel observed aimlessly that it was amazing how much talent there was and how many of these people survived on near-starvation wages. They said little as they made their way out of the immediate harbor area, crossing the street to where the iconic Empress Hotel stood guard over the boats bobbing in the gentle and protected waters. Here, Rachel thought, the elite of the Empire might stay if they had made their way to this very British outpost on the western edge of Canada. Rachel's gaze was drawn to the right and the Provincial Capitol building, obviously erected in an era when projecting power was important. She had always admired the state capitol building in Madison, where she had practiced her trade for so many years. That public building had a central dome second only to the one found in Washington D.C. But this symbol of power put that to shame as an iconic representation of authority. The Victorian architecture gave this place a unique ambiance that made it the most British of all cities in North America. Finally, she took in the flowers. There were effusions of flowers everywhere. What was with these people, Rachel thought, they seem obsessed with flowers. Then again, after a gray and overcast winter, this had to be an expression of liberation associated with spring. She liked it, all of it. And once inside, she was taken with a sudden rush that she had been transported in time. Yes, this was the late 1800s … the waning days of the Victorian period.

"Listen," she suddenly said with too much assertiveness.

"Uh-oh," Josh responded before she could continue. "Suddenly I sense doom."

"No, no, at least I don't think so. You mentioned Kit's brother being with Justice. Wasn't Peter Favulli with the FBI at this time?"

"Yeah, after law school, he went right in."

Rachel grunted. "I knew he was with the agency. He had something to do with your situation, right?"

"You know that." As they reached the hotel, Josh looked at her with increased suspicion. "So, why do you ask?"

"Let's get seated. Yeah, better you be seated." When the logistics were completed, she resumed. "Earlier, you mentioned not liking surprises. Guess what? You had a secret with Cate. I also have a secret, so we're even."

"Oh shit, if you have something that makes us even with Cate's secret visit, I'm screwed. What?"

Rachel sighed. "Peter is coming."

"Coming where?" Josh sounded confused.

"Coming here, you idiot. I take back that thing about you not looking stupid. He wants to see you again."

"But what … how? What the hell is going on? Why didn't he call me?"

"And why didn't Cate call me?" Rachel blushed. Why had she waited so long to tell her brother? Then she knew; she wanted to get a handle on where her brother was before springing any surprises. She felt rather embarrassed that his old friend had been in touch with her for some time. She should have mentioned his intended visit earlier than this. Unlike Cate, Peter had not told her this was a secret of any kind. "Peter and I have kept in touch over the years. He first reached out to me after it was apparent you were gone for the duration. I can't recall when this was, but for several years he worried you might go underground. He cared about you and thought I could be a conduit to you if you disappeared. We've been communicating to trade notes on our favorite revolutionary."

"Or he wanted to use you to nail my ass when and if they had enough evidence to come after me," he said the words in a matter-of-fact way.

Rachel pushed back at a bit of anger that tried to surface. "Never considered that, good thing I never went into the spy game. Anyway, Peter and I have stayed in touch and we would share what I knew about you with each other. I don't think he ever stopped caring about you. I'm positive of that."

"Hmmm," Josh growled. "After he joined the bureau, he did stay in periodic touch. Whatever his motives, the bottom line is that he was involved in my situation, officially. I could never be sure, but he might have been protecting me, at least until something awful surfaced about my so-called revolutionary activities. I was never sure what was going on."

"No matter," Rachel tried to assume control. "I called him and told him you were dying to have him at your retirement."

"But I didn't want anyone—" Josh tried to protest.

"I wanted him here, so shush."

"Yes, ma'am." He knew not to argue.

"By the way, he's bringing someone."

"Who?" Josh asked. "His wife?"

"I don't know, but someone he thought you would like to see."

"Hmm, so not his spouse. I never met her. Maybe Sarah," Josh speculated.

"Who?" Rachel queried, then it registered. "Sarah from college."

"Right, my other college flame, before Eleni. I liked her, and Peter knew her from those days. She also knows I'm retiring. She tracked me down through Facebook a while back."

"Well, stop the presses, you liked a girl! Will wonders never cease."

"Hold on, you liked her as well. I introduced you to her and you said you liked her."

"Of course," Rachel's eyes brightened. "I remember. Sarah was attractive and smart, not only real bright but focused. I never could quite understand what she saw in you."

"You are hilarious, my dear. Still, you're right. I couldn't figure that out either. I mean, she actually studied while I got by on my charm and wit."

Rachel guffawed. "And you graduated, really?"

He ignored her. "Best of all, she was engaged to someone else at another school three states away. So, I was a perfect proxy. Can't be near the one you love, love the one you're near, and all that. We studied together, had some good …. times. We drifted apart just a bit when I got deeper into the political stuff. Not so much drift apart as I had less time. And then Eleni came along, and I know Peter is not bringing her. I can't think of who else it could be."

"I don't know who it is. He was coy about that. Apparently, he didn't want to say anything more because it was not yet a done deal."

"Well, as long as we are filling in the dance list, Usha is coming as well and without her partner."

"That's nice," Rachel responded. "You sound surprised. She was, after all, a big part of your life."

"I am, a little." he said with a slightly raised brow.

"Maybe she finally realizes the gem she had in you," Rachel said, laughing as if that prospect was absurd on the face of it.

"Everyone is a comedian. Still, this whole thing is getting out of hand. I expected a typical retirement event. You know, a couple of dinners and a boring final party with the usual speeches about what an amazing human being I am and some adulation about my contributions to posterity. Now it is turning into Jeremiah Joshua Connelly, this is your life. Remember that show?"

Rachel smiled; she could barely recall a TV show by that name. "Hmmm, let's consider your contributions to posterity … that would take at least thirty seconds" Her joke was cut short by another phone call from Madison. No matter how much she tried, her professional responsibilities always caught up to her. She might complain outwardly but, until now, she was thrilled by them. They had signified her importance to the world, justified her efforts to get where she was. At some level, she realized her colleagues could handle most of these matters, but she had trouble giving up control. They often called in anticipation of her approbation if they did not. When she finished, she looked up at him to say. "Maybe it's Eleni. Maybe Peter is bringing Eleni. That would be something. I'd love to meet her."

"Yeah, it would more than a surprise."

"What," she asked, seeing something in his expression.

"Nothing, but Peter did not know her, she was my secret." The food and drinks arrived. "After a few moments of silence, Josh started up again. "I can't believe this … freaking amazing."

"What? Personally, I think the fare here is overrated, but the ambiance is nice. Thank you."

"No, no," he said. "I really don't share much. I'm a private person, really I am."

"I'm not arguing, I've learned more about you in two days than I did in four decades."

He looked perplexed. "What's going on … between us. It feels like someone turned on a spigot, all this stuff coming out of my mouth. Could it be that I like sharing stuff with you? No, that can't be it. More likely you've been spiking my food with some secret drugs you docs know about, just to get me to talk."

"Or just maybe I'm the only person you can be open with." She reached out and put a hand on his. "Listen, when I came here a few days early, I didn't know what to expect. I had hopes but … hell, maybe you would give me a local tourist guide and tell me to enjoy myself. But this … this has been, I don't know."

"A surprise." He smiled.

"More than that," Rachel insisted, "a revelation. I thought I had lost you, forever. A few times since I've been here, I have had this feeling … God, you will hate this … that we are being reintroduced. I … want that."

"You know the best moment so far?"

"Tell me," Rachel pushed.

"That first morning when you ran after me when I was taking Morris for his walk. It was such a déjà vu moment."

"Really?" She seemed surprised.

"Absolutely." He smiled. "Once again, you were this obnoxious ten-year-old pest always running after me. Really, you always caught up to me no matter how quietly I snuck out of the house when I was a teen. Did you have some advanced GPS tracking back then? I just could never shake you. What a freaking pain you were." He now laughed out loud.

She picked up a piece of bread roll and launched it at his head. The missile bounced off his forehead and onto the floor. Several nearby patrons looked quizzically but realized that the two apparent combatants were smiling. No real drama here.

Later, they were back on the ferry, standing at the rail. Rachel entwined her arm in his.

"Careful," Josh warned. "People will think we get along."

"Not to worry," she responded. "All will be clear to them when I push you overboard."

Josh started in a low monotone. "I remember the first time I saw Leni. Well, not the situation or location exactly, but my response. She walked into a room, maybe it was a classroom or a social event, not sure, really. But I looked at her slim body, her longish black hair, deer-in-the-headlights eyes, soft lips, and inviting smile, and it was over. I knew immediately that this was the one. I knew it with a certainty that would never be challenged."

"Oh my god, you're sounding like a Hallmark card again. You could not possibly have known that soon." Her countenance suggested incredulity.

"Says Ms. Romance herself."

"Fair enough, but all you experienced was a rush of dopamine, which is what makes one dopey. And believe me," she smiled, "you need no help whatsoever to be dopey."

"I know, I know, this defies everything I am—Mr. Cool and the rational ultra-detached guy. But it happened. I swear. As I got to know her a bit, the attraction became even more intense if that were possible. It was this incredible balance of things. She was very bright but humble, innocent but with a sharp wit, attractive but absent any vanity. She could go one-on-one with me, make me think, keep me on my toes. When she looked at me with those big eyes, I collapsed inside. It was devastating. I loved her deeply. And you know what, I never slept with her—well, once but no actual sex. She was the innocent, and I didn't have to go there to figure out the depth of my feelings, there was no need."

Several humorous responses had occurred to Rachel, but she realized this was not the time. "Why did you leave her behind? How could you leave someone like that behind? Somehow, I know I'm not getting the whole story, am I?"

He just looked toward the Vancouver ferry port as it approached. "I left her behind because I did not want to drag her into my exile. That did not seem fair."

"Any regrets?"

"I've regretted that choice every day of my life."

Rachel finally responded. "I understand, I think. You know, you're still on probation with me. I still might whack you upside the head."

He smiled but kept his focus on the distant port. Rachel joined his distant gaze. She sensed that this was all she would get right now. But she was struck with how much alike they were. Neither had found love, or at least could not keep hold of it once in hand. It was as if both were adrift. But she was with him, at least in the moment. She held on to her big brother even tighter.

He did not pull away.

CHAPTER 9

Day 3 - Evening

After dinner, Josh retreated to his office and Rachel to her room. She was restless and it was not long before she made her way to the doorway of his man cave. "Mind if I join you?"

Josh had a smile on his face. "Please do. I've just been thinking about those good old college days since we got back from Victoria. What's happening to me? I'm getting mushy."

Rachel smiled back at him. It had gone well, this first full day that they had spent alone, just the two of them. Thinking back, she could not recall any day quite like this since Josh fled north. "My professional diagnosis is that you finally are exhibiting signs that you are becoming a human being. Should I nip this affliction in the bud? Otherwise, it might take over all of you. Perhaps it is time for me to perform a humanectomy and return you to your preferred robotic state."

"Hmm, I bet you have emasculated many a poor lad in your time."

"Only the deserving ones which, it turns out, were most of them." Rachel swept into Josh's office and sat on an old couch opposite his desk. She was wearing a tattered robe that had seen better times.

"Where did you find that relic?" Josh asked with a half-smile.

"In the closet in your guest room. Left by one of your exotic working girls I assume?"

"No, they dressed very well, and I prefer to think of them as professional services providers."

"Blah, blah, blah, mind if I join you?"

"No problem, I'm about finished with these papers … final semester grades and I'm running out of time to get them in."

"Forever?"

"Hell no," he asserted. "They will drag me back to teach some courses for sure. Most scholars don't want to teach anymore. They don't have the time."

"Nor the inclination." Rachel added. "I know."

"On the other hand, I rather enjoyed it. In the classroom, someone listened to me, if only for a grade. No question, the powers that be will be begging me to teach."

"Wow, reeking of desperation, are they? By the way, I listened to you. I was always looking for a good laugh." She wore her broadest smile.

"Hmm, I think I preferred you before you found this wicked wit."

"Really?" Rachel momentarily thought he might be serious.

"Hell no, you got it from me after all," Josh laughed. Before she could respond he got up and left to make them drinks, wine for Rachel and something stronger for himself. She looked around the room. It really was an academic man cave, books, and papers everywhere with no semblance of order. You could barely see the floor. Only his swivel chair and the couch offered places of sanctuary from the clutter. He sometimes would sleep on that couch after working late into the night. His bed often seemed too far away.

"You need an organizational scheme," Rachel observed upon his return.

"I need a match," he responded. "Still, I can usually find what I want. I'm like an archeologist. I have a general idea what lies at each layer of detritus."

"Yeah, sure. Now tell me more about those happy school days of yours?" She asked her question without conviction. Too pushy, she wondered. "The ones you mentioned thinking about, I mean."

"Ah, Poirot on the case."

"Who?" Rachel missed his allusion.

"No matter," he responded. "Agatha Christie character. You really should get out more." He took a long sip of his drink and breathed out heavily.

"If Poirot didn't publish in the AMA, he would remain a mystery to me." She frowned. "Now, back to your musings."

"Retirement, and you being here. It is hard not to reminisce. My college days, back in the States, were a relatively brief escape from reality and yet so transformational as they say. You know why they call universities repositories of knowledge."

"I fear you're about to tell me," she added.

"Someone has to, you didn't learn much of use in medical school. It turns out that all these kids enter as freshmen thinking they know it all, and they leave school four years later realizing that they know nothing at all. The smarts gotta go somewhere."

"I desperately hope you have another bottle of wine." She smiled with a look of forced desperation.

He doubted she would get to a second glass, knowing her, and never a third. "But it is true. I walked in a fresh-faced naïve Irish Catholic kid and fled a couple of years or so later as a bewildered proto-revolutionary. You can't find that kind of change at the bottom of a box of cereal. By the way, which cereal had the surprise at the bottom. I would eat a whole damn box to get to it."

"Got me, I ate healthy."

"Suck up. You always obeyed the rules … made me look bad."

"My dear, you did that all on your own."

"Hah, you should've enjoyed the sugary poison, like me. After all, you can't live forever." He paused that half second that usually signalled a shift. "First thing I recall from school, from college, was the diversity—Jews, Protestants, some minorities. In some ways, I was the minority at this well-known den of atheists and communists. That's why I went, of course, to cheese off dad and the fact that Mo was going there. I was shocked to see Pete Favulli my first week there, thought he would go Catholic. I'll have to ask him how he got there when I see him. Perhaps he told me, but I no longer recall."

"I did," Rachel offered and then regretted her honesty, perhaps suggesting that she had replaced her brother in Peter's life. "He was upset that no major Catholic school offered him a football scholarship."

He got up to top off his drink. "He really was slow for a running back, but strong. He should have gone on the defensive side of the game, but let us not digress. All these new ways of looking at things confused me at first. Mo had already nibbled at the edges of my cultural edifice but now I was surrounded by learning opportunities. Wow, I was going to have to figure things out all by myself."

"Have you started yet?"

Josh gave his siter the finger as he continued. "I so remember Mort Silverman, one of the first profs to get to me … in a good way. He ambled around campus with a cigarette hanging out of his mouth and looking as if he had just slept three days straight in his clothes. He had that avuncular and yet dishevelled air, like the dissolute uncle that the family griped about when he showed up for Thanksgiving and whose cigarette ashes wound up everywhere including in the cranberry sauce. But he was brilliant."

"Josh, you thought Rocky the squirrel was brilliant."

"He was, and *Peabody's Improbably History*, great stuff. Anyway, Mort had this way of getting us to think. The first day of his class, he threw the main text across the floor. Shit, we all jumped a foot. He said something about all of us being smart and we could read it on our own. Then he just started talking about the game of pool, asking us if we could infer causality from a billiard ball moving every time it was struck by another. We all looked at him stupidly. Well, I did at least. That somehow led to a deeper conversation of causality and theory building and other epistemological insights and mysteries."

"Okay, I'm hooked." Rachel admitted.

"Sometimes, he would amble into the student lounge and sit with us. Wow, a professor who knew we were alive. I recall one day eavesdropping on a conversation between he and a colleague. The colleague was an empiricist and was using rats, white mice, in a psych lab experiment. I was just a gopher in the lab. He called in Mort since, though more a theorist, he had a reputation for thinking outside the box. The experimental subjects, our rodent friends, were being trained to run through a maze in a certain way while being exposed to differential reward regimes. Hmmm, I wonder if they still do those silly experiments."

"No idea," Rachel smiled. "Are you forgetting that I am a real scientist?"

Josh extended his middle finger skyward and continued. "Anyway, the empiricist asked Mort and me to think about the ways in which our search for truth might be corrupted, thus having their internal validity threatened. Maybe the independent variable of interest, intermittent reward schedules, were not the only possible explanation for any observed results. What other confounding influences could we imagine. I stumbled for a while but eventually got into it. Hey, maybe smell had to be eliminated, we should cleanse the maze after each trial. Maybe we needed a top to the maze since they could not get cues from the ceiling. Or time of day and who the handler was or something so obtuse that it might otherwise escape even a diligent researcher's attention. I recall piping up, by suggesting noise factors which seemed to make sense. Do we need deaf mice?"

"Does this have a point?" Rachel yawned for added effect.

"Listen and learn, you Philistine. I walked away from this session, and others like it, a wiser young man. Such informal sessions helped us think about things more deeply. How do we really know what we think we know? What is truth? The epistemological mysteries were laid before us. Maybe there are other explanations for what we accept as fact. Never stop questioning. And never assume that you have the final answer. Science is not believing you know the truth. It is the attitude that you must keep searching for the truth. That was a first baby step toward critical thinking. Keep digging. Never stop at the first answer."

"Damn," Rachel said. "If you only had taken that second step. You might have had a chance at being a real scientist."

Josh threw a paper clip at her, grunting as it veered off course. "Damn, next time a paperweight."

"You could, but never forget this. I know thirty-seven ways to do you in that are untraceable." She cocked her head with a knowing look.

"That many, really? Remind me to be nice to you."

"I'll send you a memo." She deadpanned.

"Back to my point ... sometimes Silverman would throw out the simplest correlations. Okay, poverty is related to poor physical health. We would nod. But what is the causal direction? Does poverty cause health problems? Or do health problems cause poverty? Is the relationship more complex? Maybe the causal path goes both ways or differs by subgroup. *'Think hard, gentlemen,'* he would suggest, *'what's your underlying explanatory theory? Can you really know anything absent a plausible theory?'* He then would tease us with an enigmatic smile." Josh himself was wearing a semi smile.

"What's so amusing?" Rachel asked.

"Just reflecting. These lessons stuck. I would examine something that seemed obvious for example. You might consider the correlation between smoking and health care costs. The relationship is obvious, no? Smoking causes health problems, which increases costs. Who could argue with that?"

"Seems right to me," Rachel agreed knowing that the obvious answer likely was wrong.

"But think about it for a moment. Maybe smokers die sooner, which they do of course. And we know that the preponderance of health costs goes to offset end-of-life care where we spend fortunes extending one's pain for a few weeks or days or even hours. This is where you guys pull in the big bucks."

"Hey," she protested.

"Just yanking your chain. Think harder though. Maybe smokers cost us less since they do us a favor by dying off sooner. Hell, they do themselves a favor by avoiding years of languishing in expensive nursing homes. I don't know for sure, but that is a possibility. I learned that nothing has a simple answer and that, my dear, is a huge life lesson. Think deep and hard about everything."

"Great idea, when do you intend to start?" She was enjoying herself tonight. They were talking, even sharing. It was like the old days.

"To add to your levity and confirm your low opinion of me, I'll admit to not being the most conscientious of students. I approached college with the same casual attitude I did toward life in general. I would work hard on subjects I liked and then skate on the ones in which you needed to know something. Statistics courses were the pits, and the sciences were not much better. How did you not want to off yourself in those boring courses?"

"I loved them," she protested.

"Shit, I always knew you were demented. Know what I took to meet my science requirement, botany or some such thing? Even there I could never figure out how to use that damn microscope. I was always using the kid's scope next to me. He was this little nerd from New York who seemed on top of things. It must have cheesed him off no end when, as I vaguely recall, I did better than he in the course. Still, I really was clueless. The lab instructor was a tiny Asian gal with a heavy accent. I could never understand her. Just shoot me, how in hell did I get through college?"

"Beats the hell out of me." Rachel could not resist the opening.

Josh gave her the finger once again before continuing. "On the other hand, I loved sociology, political science, psychology, history, English lit, everything that was not defined by numbers and equations, courses where charm and bullshit could take you a long way. You probably actually worked in college."

"At Smith, in premed? Yeah, you could say I worked hard. I can say one thing, there were never any all-night bull sessions. We just had cram sessions for exams, at least among my crowd."

"The nerds I suspect. Too bad, the continuous bull sessions for me were like an ongoing tutorial in current events and a proxy-type preparation for becoming a policy wonk. I even learned a few things in my courses. Some of them kept setting off small epiphanies in my head. It was never like we were consciously exposed to propaganda of any kind. Still, you kept hearing facts and interpretations that challenged your priors about life. It was as simple as learning what we did around the world that was less than kosher. No one had to come out and say that *'we are assholes like everyone else, maybe bigger ones than the other guys.'* You could connect the dots if you wanted though not everyone wanted to."

"Sure you're not remembering things through rose colored glasses?"

"Yeah, I've worried about that. Anyway, I recall one professor asking from time to time what causes some effect. When we paused, as was often the case as we frantically tried not to look stupid, he would throw out *'did God cause it?'* It was the casual way he did this that was effective. It was offered as a clearly absurd response, but no one ever challenged his cynicism about religious matters. For a young man in his last days as a Catholic devotee, nothing could be more effective. I walked around with my brain exploding as if it was beset by some mental storm. At night, I sometimes just let my thoughts wander in internal dialogues as I sorted things out. I often thought these personal discussions brilliant and would tell myself to write everything down upon arising the next morning. When that failed, I brought a tape recorder to bed and tried whispering thoughts, but it all sounded like gibberish the next day."

"So, no different than your so-called academic papers." She was enjoying herself. This visit suddenly struck her as being so familiar. *Don't become overly optimistic,* a small voice in her head cautioned. Still, she had not felt this level of connection in such a long time.

"I am ignoring your pathetic attempts at wit, in case you have not noticed. Remember, I'm the master of the deft, yet devastating, insult. You, grasshopper, are the mere student. So, to continue as if you had not been so rude, things eventually became more defined. My little group formed. It started with Mo, Jimmie, and Peter from the old world. Then additional students gravitated toward us like Carla and Helen and Bob, and Kit for a bit. There were others of course. The war was escalating as was the desperation of the male students on the left who faced a year or two fighting in the jungle. We thought we could change the world. We really believed that we were a vanguard to the future. We were the smart ones, the enlightened ones. When we matured into adulthood and took power, we would run things differently. It was only a matter of time. In retrospect, that particular prediction theory was big time bull hockey."

Rachel now chuckled aloud. "I am sorry. You remember, I did visit you on quite a few weekends. Was I even in high school yet? I know I wanted to feel what college was like, and I missed you. I really was young and impressionable, wasn't I? I was impressed by your group by the way. Wow, I must have been young. I even was impressed by you. My judgment clearly was suspect."

"I can't argue with that one," he murmured.

"Still, I recall you guys talking among yourself, touching on ideas and issues beyond my world. Sure, I was younger but advanced for my age, way beyond my peers for sure. Yet, I felt intimidated, like an idiot among savants. I knew that your group was special, particularly Morris, Carla, Bob, Peter, and you. The conversation and ideas would just sparkle, you often finished each other's sentences. Later, at Smith, I met smart kids. Not just smart but whip-smart kids. They struck me as shallow though. It was as if someone had given them a script and they were merely spouting the lines. They were … cynical and book smart, not inquisitive. The few years that separated you and I made a huge difference."

"Yes," Josh almost shouted. "I noticed that too. The first wave of dissenters had to create their own world view, develop their own moral center. Then, almost overnight, followers came along. I sensed most of them never got it, not really."

"Yeah, your crowd was clever in a different way, always seeking those deeper meanings. You did see connections among things, you're right about that. I found my tiny glimpses into your world quite special before it slammed shut. When I was in college, I noticed that the Smith girls were ambitious, driven, most hardworking, but they had a lot of answers and fewer questions. And they cared for little beyond their own worlds, very self-centered. Of course, most were from privileged backgrounds, so what would you expect. Perhaps I'm being unfair and, of course, I hung with the science nerds. Maybe if I had walked over and talked to the kids who dressed like hippies, who knows." The words were strong, but her expression was soft.

Josh mused on her words. "You know, in retrospect, I could see there was a downside to my world back then. It was a continuous high for sure. But it all took place in a bubble. Something you said reminded me of what I missed at the time. We could finish each other's sentences. After a while, we did not spend enough time with people outside our circle, too easy to slip into groupthink when you isolate yourself. You need to keep reaching out to contrary opinion, that is vital. But I wasn't wise enough to see that then. I obsessed on what fit into my new world view. We call it confirmation bias. We have a term for everything, don't we? In any case, perhaps the brave new world we were creating in our heads wasn't strong enough to face much contrary evidence. We might not have been strong enough to deal with much cognitive dissonance."

Rachel looked at him without a smile. "We were kids. Well, you were a kid. I think I went from twelve years of age to thirty-two, missing my teens and wild youth. I spent all my time, after you left at least, parenting our parents."

"*Mea culpa.*" Josh whispered.

"No more of that apologizing stuff," Rachel waived a dismissive hand. "Karma will punish you enough."

"Like how?" he asked

Rachel cocked her head. "Hmm, probably by reincarnating you as a Republican."

"Oh, god forbid. I'll take the brimstone please," he responded with mock terror.

Rachel grew serious. "I tried too hard to impress our parents so they might get over the perpetual mourning that was going on in our house. God, it was a nightmare ... a wake that never stopped." Josh started to say something, but she raised her hand. "When I was at my seven-sister's school, I would think about what I saw of your college experience and wonder if I was missing out. I looked at the kids sitting out on the campus lawn discussing whatever and thought I should join them."

"But you didn't."

"No, I didn't. I was a kid from a working-class family surrounded by the elite. I assumed I was always behind and had to work my ass off to just stay even. It just seemed a continuous grind of class, lab, library, study groups, and class again. I should have realized I belonged at Smith when I saw my class ranking, but it's hard to shake that imposter syndrome."

"Tru dat," he affirmed.

"In the end, I realized one thing. You and I were not the same intellectually. We were attracted to different things, neither approach was necessarily better."

"And we both made contributions to the world. You did for sure."

"A concession on your part, thank you," she smiled. "You for sure made a contribution, if your colleagues are to be believed."

"I paid them off before you arrived." Josh then looked at her seriously. "I have to ask … no guys, no fun?"

She paused. "I need another drink."

"Okay," he said, getting up, "but I am not holding your head over the toilet bowl again."

"That happened only once, when I was just a kid."

"Yeah, but it was disgusting, and I had to change your clothes." He grimaced.

"Which caused me no end of shame."

"Shame?"

She grimaced. "Yeah, you saw me naked."

"You were a scrawny young teen at the time. And remember, I had seen real women, the music teacher and our neighbor and—"

"Again," she inserted with feigned disgust, "way too much information. Wait, which neighbor? Never mind! Hah, do you have any idea how bad they were?"

"Who?" Josh asked, surprised at the sharp transition. "Are you talking about the extra-friendly neighbor ladies?"

Rachel went on. "No, silly, the gals in my dorm. They badgered me to date some guys they knew, or to go to some horrible frat party at a nearby boys' college. They told me to relax, that guys would just love me. Anyway, I tried, a little at least. Mostly, it was awful. There was the guy who started reaching for my crotch the moment we were alone. I punched him in the nose. And there was the guy who could not stop talking about himself. When I tried to insert something about myself into his monologue, he looked at me like I was irritating him. I got up and walked out of the restaurant. There was the sports freak who kept watching the game while I tried to engage him in conversation, and the one who flirted outrageously with other girls at the party he took me to. I could go on, but you get the picture."

"Hey, these guys sound like winners to me. You just described all my favorite moves."

"Well, now I see why you need to pay for professional '*service providers,*' or whatever you call them." She said the next four words slowly. "I … just … gave … up. Maybe I didn't really try. I went through the motions because I thought it was the thing to do … if you were an attractive gal in college. Then at some point, I said, what is the point of all this crap?"

"Searching for love is crap? I am shocked." Josh added with an exaggerated smile.

"Sarcasm I presume. You should not even try faking at being a romantic," she said with a generous amount of false incredulity. "The man who never has had a conventional relationship with a woman is lecturing me on love. Really!"

"Point taken, But I'm not made of total stone. I did have my moments." Josh paused as if he were deciding something. "Let me tell you about Sarah. It was not love, but it came close, at least for me. We met my first year there, I think it was early in the second semester. I studied quite hard at first, wanted to make sure I would keep my scholarship. Back then, probably like you, I had my share of insecurity.

When you come from an Irish ghetto, you wonder if you can compete in the real world with kids who had all the advantages. Then, of course, I looked at my first-semester grades and they were good, great even. Bad lesson for someone like me. I immediately relaxed, fell into my old habits."

"I seriously doubt that." Rachel observed. "After all, they did not throw your ass out of school."

"Hah, hah! Anyway, one day I'm sitting in class and this attractive gal was seated next to me. I had noticed her around but, you know, it was clear she was highly intelligent, way too smart to put up with a putz like me. It did not help that she was not flirtatious in any way, extremely focused on the class. She was friendly enough but did not invite any familiarity as some women did. Don't laugh but I really was shy and, by now, no longer the school jock. It never occurred to me to speak to her. Frankly, I could never figure out why women might be interested in me."

"Neither could anyone else," Rachel slipped in.

"Anyway, asshole, one day I raised my hand and made a comment on some class topic now long forgotten. She turned to me with a shocked look and whispered that what I said was brilliant. Then she added that she thought I had been sleeping through the class. It was a common mistake that a lot of people made, including my professors."

Rachel chuckled. "I am shocked, just shocked."

"For me, the ice was broken. She had acknowledged my existence. So, we started talking after class, which turned into coffee in the student union, which in turn became a long walk and that was that. She was open with me about being in a committed relationship with her high school boyfriend who was going to the University of Pennsylvania as I recall. That was a plus with me, I thought at the time."

"Of course," Rachel managed.

"But what fascinated me was her background and her smarts. Her parents had been caught up in the Nazi holocaust. They had escaped to Vichy France that kept them safe for a while. But the killing of Jews started. Though the French, to their credit, mostly dragged their feet on cooperating in the slaughter, things still looked bad. Her dad managed to bribe officials to get her mom and older sister out, Sarah was in her mom's womb at the time. Unfortunately, her father did not make it. He had stayed back to get some other family members out. It was one good act too many. That story got to me. Maybe it struck me as familiar to our folks, danger and intrigue and trying to keep their heads above water. The causes and circumstances were different, but I could feel some similarities. I always thought there was this connection between Irish Catholics and Jews."

"Yeah," Rachel nodded. "I can understand that."

"She also seemed to respond to my story, especially by mom's mysterious past, the possible gunrunning, the glamorous way I described mom and dad's early relationship. Perhaps I made things just a little more exciting than they were, or at least by adding more than we actually knew about things."

"What you're saying is that you lied to impress a woman. Again, I am shocked."

"No, you shit, I embellished stuff. You know, I am Irish, a natural storyteller. I could've convinced her that dad was Whitey Bulger's right-hand man if I wanted. What would she know about the underbelly of Boston? But the other thing was that she was so smart. I could tell that from our first conversation. She was a lot like you, not physically of course, but personality wise."

"No wonder you liked her."

"And she believed my BS, like you." Instinctively, Josh covered his stomach.

"You better cover up."

"On the other hand, unlike you, she was really nice…not some obnoxious little shit who needs a spanking." Josh wagged a finger at his sibling.

Rachel raised a fist in mock anger. "You try that, spanking me, and you will need that toe tag sooner than you ever imagined."

Josh raised his hands in mock surrender. "Got it. Thing is, she listened to me and pretended to care. She probably did care since she had her man nailed and wasn't on the hunt."

Josh was smiling. It suddenly struck him. He was enjoying this. It reminded him of long-ago times he thought lost forever.

"Oh," Rachel uttered to intrude on his private epiphany, "I'm quite sure she pretended a lot of things."

"There was that, for sure. I wasn't naïve. Yes, I was fortunate to have these wonderful older women, but girls my age were uptight. Some put out, but often it seemed a bit forced in my mind. Could never shake this impression that they felt compelled to do it, not something they always enjoyed. Well, you know as well as I that we all develop these scripts based on early experiences. These become so ingrained they are hard to erase after a while. My impression was that girls my age let you get to the various bases, because it was expected or necessary to bargain for what they really wanted. I sometimes wondered why they put up with us at all. Whenever I was about to make a move, I would become paralyzed. I kept thinking the girl was thinking *'oh no, this letch is going to make a move'* and hoping desperately that I would not. Sometimes I would and sometimes I would not, never quite sure how I decided which way to go. But the whole thing always made me guilty. I did not want to be just another horny guy. I did not want to be someone they had to deal with, handle. I wanted to be different."

"It never occurred to you that the girl might also have needs."

"Nope, that seemed beyond the pale," he said without hesitation.

"Wow," Rachel expressed incredulity. "You really were damaged goods. But from what I saw, you came across as confident."

"Just a good actor." He laughed. "But this is where Sarah seemed so different. When I first kissed her, she responded. It was not the going-through-the-motions response either. It struck me as real and spontaneous. She enjoyed physical intimacy. I was shocked. I never felt guilty with her. She always seemed genuine during sex, I never wondered whether she was faking it. I suppose, though, she might have been. The sad thing for a guy is that you never know."

"I think I know this girl, not her personally but her type. She wouldn't fake anything, too much integrity." Rachel observed.

"Hmm, perhaps you're right. In any case, she would continue to tremor for a time after we finished. It was like aftershocks. What a release, for both of us. I will forever be grateful." Josh looked over at her to see if he had wandered into a taboo area. All seemed well. "We did so much together, beyond sex and studies I mean. We would go to Tanglewood for the concerts, museums, lectures, and talk about ideas for hours on end. But it was not just the political stuff, I had others for that. Sarah participated in the anti-war rallies. She never lost her hold on reality, never became obsessed like I did. Still, she became a close companion. I don't know what she told her boyfriend or how she explained me to her girlfriends. Now that I think on it, we were rather circumspect, but people knew. I stayed out of the way when he visited, and everything would return to normal after he left. It was perfect."

"A relationship without commitment, it does sound sublime. I am shocked they didn't make a Hallmark special about it."

Josh wagged a finger at her. "Now, don't knock emotionless relationships, they are the best kind. Now we call it friends with benefits. Strikes me that you never inspired the writers of those insipid Hallmark romance movies. Did you ever have any feelings for a boy during those years, ever?"

"Well," she paused for a long time. "There was a guy. We met in my junior year of college; he went to a nearby school. He was smart, and nice, and seemed sensitive. But the poor schmuck was so shy. It was clear he was interested in me, or I thought he was. Still, it took him several weeks to make his move. He kept showing up but doing nothing."

"Only several weeks? Wow, he moved fast."

"Whatever. When he asked me to a lecture, my immediate reaction was to say no. But he looked so uncertain and nervous I couldn't turn him away. He would have been crushed."

"Wait," Josh asked, "exactly what kind of expression did he have? I've always wanted to perfect the pity sex look."

"As I was saying," she said loudly to communicate her annoyance, "I reluctantly agreed to a date. Then, to my surprise, I had a good time. He was a bit like you ... funny and smart."

"And sexy."

"Yeah, I'll get to that. So, we continued to see each other, nothing heavy but nice. I even met his family, which bothered me a bit though they seemed thrilled to meet me. I did think it odd when I took the initiative regarding sex. After a while, I thought he would never get to it, that he was too shy. To make a long story short, we were alone one night in his room. I just started taking my clothes off. For a moment, I thought he might faint. Was he a virgin? Were there any of those left?"

When she paused, Josh blurted out impatiently, "And? Surely you're not stopping there."

"Of course not, and please don't call me Shirley." She chuckled at her own joke. "Okay, that last part I added on just now."

"Yup, too much wine." Josh reached to take her glass, but she kept it from him.

"Well, let me just say that the earth didn't move during sex. In fact, I did all the work. The whole thing seemed rather strange to me, but he seemed happy. And like you, it was all convenient. It took all the pressure off about not dating and reduced the possibility of lesbian flirtations."

"Why do I sense that the denouement is upon us?"

"Ah yes," she said, throwing her head back. "One day I stopped by his place unexpectedly and found him in bed with ... ta da!"

"Another boy." Josh threw out.

"You guessed it. He looked much happier than he ever looked with me."

"I can see that ... makes total sense to me." Josh said, trying to stifle a giggle. "But really, talk about awkward. Were you hurt, disappointed? What did you do?"

"Well, I didn't propose marriage. I walked out. It was no big thing. At least I knew what was going on. He tried his best to explain, but what was there to explain? He was gay, and this was at a time when being such was not all that cool. Same as Usha though I can see it in her case. Traditional Indian families are tough. And that was it for the boyfriend experience." Rachel had not finished her second glass of wine but did get up to top off her glass. "We are two sick puppies. Why am I thinking of the song about *looking for love in all the wrong places*?"

"Well, there might be a second career for both of us as country songwriters. But don't forget, Sarah and I were getting along fine."

"Yeah, but only because she was not a threat to you. If she pushed for any kind of commitment, you would still be running. Hell, the Great Wall itself would not have kept you from finding refuge in some monastery in the backwaters of Mongolia."

"Wait, wait, not so fast there. I grew to like Sarah, a lot. She was an anchor for a while. You've got to understand that my world was spinning under my feet. It is a dizzying experience to find your childhood givens crumbling under you. When I first drifted leftward, it all was exciting and fun. We did stuff like teach-ins, wrote articles for the school newspaper, held informational sessions, staged rallies, and stuff like that. We had Abbie Hoffman in. Remember him, he later launched the Yippie movement with Jerry Rubin. This was early and Abbie wore a suit and tie and gave a detailed talk on how we were destroying the very country we purported to be saving. We had Senator Wayne Morse from Oregon in to talk about how Johnson engineered our way into escalating the conflict through outright lies. Imagine, our government was lying to us. Back then, we were shocked. We held a protest rally when Vice President Humphrey came to campus to speak at a graduation ceremony."

"And the *but?*" she prompted.

"The *but* was that frustration soon set in. You know, we were young. We expected the world to fall over and get in line. How could they not be bowled over by our insightful analysis and overwhelming passion? The State Department sent a representative to one of the early teach-ins we sponsored, they went to a lot of colleges to quell the discontent. We buried the poor bastard with our facts and analysis. Worse, their arguments came out of this narrow, tunnel vision of things. But, you know, we were ignored, totally. Our so-called leaders went about their work of killing and maiming while ignoring us completely. How could they possibly do that? Didn't they care? What was wrong with them? I could not believe it. A rage developed inside, slow at first but flashing up with this bright intensity over time. I found out that I really cared. What kept them from seeing things as we did? We were killing people by the tens of thousands, mostly because they wanted foreigners out of their country. Was that such a sin? Of course, not many felt things with such intensity. Sure, we had a lot of fellow students who were in part way, the ones who worried about the draft and getting their asses shot off. They seemed committed if it didn't screw up their weekend social plans. The number of true believers was small and became my alter ego."

"And Sarah?" Rachel felt he was drifting off point.

"Sarah gave me a connection to reality. She was against the war for sure but realized that life was more than that. She kept pulling me back to reality, served as a kind of anchor, for a while at least."

"I have to ask," Rachel threw out. "Did you love her?"

Josh looked at her. "Me, love? Did you forget who you were talking with?"

"Don't make me come over there. I'm small of stature but I pack a wallop. And just in case you've forgotten already, I still have those ways of doing you in that no one would detect. It totally will look as if you expired from your dissolute lifestyle." She was laughing now. "So many choices. Which one will I choose?"

"Don't be so cocky, I watch those crime shows. They uncover everything."

"Not the way I'll do it." She was smug.

Damn, he thought, he really missed not having her in his life. "I … I thought I was getting there, with Sarah that is. We became close enough to scare me. She wanted me to meet her folks and all. I even envisioned us together from time to time. I could see it happening. That really scared the shit out of me."

"Hmm, she sounds way too good for you. How did you screw it up?"

"Eleni."

"Oh." Rachel kicked herself for not guessing.

"I'm going to let you in on a secret. Everyone thinks that men cannot commit, *constant to one thing, never*' as Shakespeare once said. But that's not true. Really. Men can look at a woman and just know. I don't think the reverse is quite true. Women vet a potential mate more completely, audit his stock portfolio at least. You're sceptical, I know. But here is the thing. I think we poor males have an archetype ingrained in us, imprinted if you will. When we see a woman that fits that fixed image, we respond. It's irrational, primal. And it's not just lust. Hell, I would fall in lust a dozen times a day. I had a friend back then who was working his way through school as a part-time assistant manager at a McDonalds. He mentioned that when bored, he would count the number of times he fell into lust during the lunch hour. Oh, I forget his winning number, but it was into three figures. It was a busy place."

"But what if this dream girl turned out to be a psycho which, if she liked you, was a high probability?"

Josh gave his sister the finger with gusto. "Good question, asshole. I have thought about that one. It seems improbable, but part of that initial reaction involves intuiting what they are like from the start. I looked at her eyes. They were soft and warm and vulnerable and inquisitive all at the same time. You just know." He was digging in.

"Let me get this straight. The fact that the woman of your dreams might be carrying a bloody axe under her jacket would not bother you," Rachel queried. "Once bitten, it was forever no matter what."

"Only if she intended to use the axe on me. But I'm convinced there is something to initial responses, very scientific. Never forget … the eyes are portals to the soul, as they say. From her eyes, I could see immediately that Eleni had a deeply sensitive side. We would be soul mates."

"Only if opposites attract," Rachel countered. "Your eyes are bloodshot and vacant, not sensitive portals to some deep soul."

"I'm sure that's the wine talking. Just give me fair warning so I can get you to the toilet bowl in time because you, my dear, are cleaning up your own mess this time. And you'll sleep in your own mess because I'm not changing you."

"Good!" Rachel rolled her eyes.

"In any case, I knew I was besotted from the first moment. But the problem was that I froze, even more than I usually did. This was not like hitting on some broad with big boobs, this was a shot at happiness. I must have circled around her for weeks thinking of smooth lines but realized I didn't have any. My only progress was getting myself introduced to her so that she would not call campus security if I talked to her one day. Then we ran into each other when no one else was around. We stumbled around an awkward conversation. My god, normally I was smooth, but I felt like a sweaty teen. I could feel myself flush. Just to end my agony, I blurted out some event I was attending and asked if she would be interested in going. She looked embarrassed and I knew. I wished the ground might swallow me up."

"I can't believe this; I'm feeling sorry for you."

"Of course, she murmured something sweet about that sounding nice but couldn't on that day ... some conflict. It never occurred to me that she really might have a conflict. I just assumed she was thinking that this putz had made his move and it was time to put him in his place."

"Josh, you know I never say anything nice about you, but even I knew you were one of the better-looking guys on campus, and you still had all your hair back then."

"I know that now, but it was different then. I thought I was unlovable, that no goddess like that could ever be attracted to a mope like me. It never crossed my mind that she felt the same. Much later she confessed to always feeling she herself was ugly and unlovable. I never put it together that I never saw her date or be with guys. It turns out she was very shy and was shocked that I would be interested in her. I did what came natural to me. I licked my wounds and sulked for weeks. Normally, I would never take a second run at a gal. Why endure the pain? But I could not get her out of my mind, so I did the unimaginable. I tried again. My ploy was that I needed subjects for a class experiment. We often volunteered for each other's class experiments. This was not like asking her to come to my room to look at my etchings. When she agreed, my heart started racing. I was sure she could see it beating a mile a minute through my shirt."

Rachel leaned back, enjoying the moment. "This is delicious."

Josh relished that Rachel was enjoying his confessional moment. That was okay in the moment. He also found the experience liberating. He had never told this to anyone before. No one. "As my ruse unfolded successfully—well, not exactly a ruse since I did not make up the psych exercise—I panicked again. It took everything in me to ask if I could say thanks with a cup of coffee at the student union. I thought my heart would burst when she said yes. I have no recollection about what we talked about, but I did not let go of her after that."

Rachel wrinkled her nose. "And what about Sarah?"

"She understood, totally. We stayed good friends and did things together, but the sex petered out, no pun intended."

"Wait!" Rachel's nose remained wrinkled with suspicion. "You gave up sex for romance. Oh, be still my beating heart."

Josh smiled as he wagged his index finger in her direction. "Keep it up, cupcake, and your heart will be completely still."

Rachel laughed aloud. She had not been this relaxed with her brother since they were young. It felt so warm and right. She noticed that Morris had curled up next to her. She started to pet him, and he turned over on his back while she rubbed his tummy. "Oh, sweetie, you're so cute." Morris grunted with undiluted pleasure.

"Morris," Josh exclaimed. "You little traitor you, she won't be around forever. Bread and water for you when she leaves."

"Hmm, maybe I'll stay. I like this area, as good as Madison, and Morris needs to be rescued. Look at his pathetic expression."

"That expression never changes. It is his go-to look." Josh reached to his dog who moved slightly away.

Rachel laughed aloud. "Good dog. Listen, dear brother, I am still struggling with this no-sex thing."

He smiled and immediately she knew she had lobbed him a soft one. "No problem, sis, I know some guys who would be happy to service you."

"Hysterical, your no sex thing." She gave him the finger again. "I mean as a young man. You sounded almost celibate."

"Well, in addition to Sarah there were a few one-nighters, and Carla."

"Ah-ha," Rachel issued in a triumphant voice.

"I mean, it was the most casual sex imaginable. Carla was part of our rebel alliance as you know. She also had dark hair and was bright as hell. But she was so intense, no humor. She would look at me sometimes and I would know. If I ignored the look, she would just come up to me and say outright that she was horny. As I look back, she just assumed I was available, not an outrageous hypothesis since all males are horny morons. Please excuse my graphic language.

"No problem," Rachel said, "I'm not your little sister any longer."

"No, I suppose you're not, that's hard to get used to," he responded pensively. "In any case, she would start taking off her clothes and pull me down on top of her. If she were in the mood, she would turn me over on my back and ride me like the last of the Valkyries."

"Valkyries?" she asked.

"You know, the beautiful maidens that brought slain warriors to the Scandinavian God Odin. And believe me, if you had been there, you would know how close to death I came on occasion. Wow."

Rachel made a fake gagging sound. "Maybe I am still the little sister. Moving on, though, I think my mind's eye has gone blind at that last image. Really, how could I have forgotten about Odin. I was just discussing him the other day with my surgical nurse. Tell me, how do you know some of this trivia?"

"I'm a prime source for all useless information, trust me. In any case, I really got to know how women must feel given the way men treat them, like pieces of meat."

"And Eleni was okay with this … arrangement."

"Oh, she did not know. I think that would have ended it. After meeting her, I ended it with everyone else. To be accurate, I tried to end it with Carla but she never took no as an answer. Man, she was a tough broad!"

"You couldn't fight off a woman probably half your size. Really?"

"Yeah, well, you should meet her someday."

"I did meet her bozo. And I'll give you that one. She intimidated the hell out of me as well."

"I'm sure," Josh then tried to get back on track. "Eleni was, how can I say it, a marvelous mix of attributes … feisty and innocent. She admitted that what she knew about life could be fit into a small ring box. And yet she was so quick and witty. Perhaps better than any other woman I have known, outside of you my dear. She could go one-on-one with me and take no prisoners. Moreover, she was very smart but humble, almost reluctant to show her intellect to the outside world. Most of us made a sport of demonstrating our intelligence, not her. And she had this sensitivity about her. I remember one time we were driving somewhere and came across a family stranded by their stalled car. I stopped and helped them out. After, she looked at me with such love. It was the first time she had looked at me like that. I have never ever forgotten that look. It melted my soul. Those eyes, wide and deep, I can never forget them and what they reflected."

"Can I ask? What am I saying, of course I can ask! Did you ever try for intimacy with her?"

Josh laughed. "I suppose, but in a half-hearted way. One time, I argued that it would be better for her not to wait too long to lose her virginity, intercourse would be overly painful if she did."

Rachel guffawed. "Smooth, most guys would try flowers or liquor. Really, how could she resist that pile of shit?"

"I know, really. And I didn't even smile or giggle as I tried that one. Now. I grimace at the memory. But she ignored me as did most women. I can't believe that women did not fall for my crap, I really was smooth."

"For sure, a real mystery there," Rachel added, shaking her head.

"In the end, I was not unhappy. I just wanted to be with her. I didn't want to push her in any direction that made her uncomfortable. She made me happy. No one else did, at least not like her. Maybe Sarah to some extent. And I liked Eleni's family as well. Maybe I mentioned this, but her dad, an engineer, was from Egypt who came to the US to study. When the war broke out, the Nazi war, his technical skills were valuable to the government. He did well as an engineer, but I think he really wanted to be a poet. At least he had a poet's soul, in my mind at least. He was thin and good-looking quiet and very widely read. I liked him; we could talk about things for hours. He had been raised as a Coptic Christian, which was not an easy path as Egypt was buffered by various sectarian winds. Coming to the States probably was as much an escape as it was an opportunity. There was less risk of being on the wrong side of things as the winds of change altered direction. At some point in college, he met this Greek woman. She was everything he was not ... exuberant, outgoing, and passionate about life. Of course, she was Greek Orthodox and took it very seriously. Her upbringing was overshadowed by religious ritual and belief. But that did not keep her from seeking out some adventure, and somehow, she ran across this quiet Egyptian. Maybe opposites do attract because she fell in love with him."

"And he with her?" For Rachel, this was a question.

"Good catch," he responded. "I was never totally sure. There is a chance that he saw her as an opportunity to stay in the States after the war ended. For him, it could have been a marriage of expedience. He never said anything like that, but he never struck me as someone who would fall easily in love. I suspect, though, he came around over time, and he seemed devoted. For her, it was clearly a love match. It had to be. She went against all her traditions and expectations. Eleni was born not all that long after the marriage so there must have been talk. Despite all the chatter and speculation, by the time I met them, they had a genuinely nice relationship. They certainly adored Eleni. She was the only child, and they poured everything into her."

"I presume she must have been spoiled like you were as the Irish prince."

"You know, I'm convinced I am an only child. You're such a shit that you must have been adopted."

"Absolutely," Rachel deadpanned. "Mom and Dad saw what they sired and decided to try something different the next time around." Morris was now on her lap and clearly in dog heaven.

Josh thought about retrieving Morris, but inside, he concluded that the dog was an excellent judge of character. He gazed at his drink for a few moments. "Visiting Eleni's home was so different. At our place, dad was seldom there, and mom was remote. I recall the first time I went home with her, to her place. Her mother was genuinely nice, could not shove enough food into me. I was treated like a visiting prince. The next visit was amazing. I walked in the door, and she rushed up to throw her arms around me. I almost backed up through the wall. We never hugged in our home. Do you remember any hugging?"

"Ah," Rachel thought, "not really. Ora would have thought someone was assaulting her and dad was Irish after all. I've never known either one of them to hug anyone, certainly not one another."

"Nor us. With Eleni's family, her mother and aunts, it was this Greek thing. Life was a celebration. But there was another part to it. They loved me. I am not totally sure why. I was not Greek, and that should have been important to them. But later I learned that they, particularly her mother, were convinced that I would be good to Eleni. That was everything to her, to them. I thought about that a lot. In the end, I concluded that they could see that I loved her, loved her with a depth that mattered. Then again, I always did good with mothers, the daughters were a problem. I think I struck the mothers as a clueless schlepp who could never harm their daughter. Good thing they could not see inside my lecherous head."

"No question about that," Rachel offered.

"There was one more thing. Eleni had hardly dated at all. Amazing, really, she was a lovely girl."

"Not that strange, I was reasonably attractive and didn't date, not much anyway."

"Yeah," Josh said immediately, "but you had a rotten personality while she was nice."

Josh got up and sat next to his sister where he started to pet his dog. "I don't like the looks of this at all. I think Morris is abandoning me for you."

"Oh, he has a such an instinctive appreciation for good people. It is amazing he never ran away earlier." Then she assumed that mischievous smile. "He asked me to take him away that first day, poor thing."

"Shit, he will love anyone that scratches his belly and fills his bowl with chow. Listen, I'm heading in. I still have a couple of papers to do. I'll get up early to do them in the morning before running over to the university. We pick up Cate early afternoon."

Rachel had a quizzical look; She was still confused why Josh knew more than she. "Did she visit Evan on the East Coast?"

"I suspect so but I'm not certain. I really don't have much info, just the basics." He fibbed here, wanting to minimize his connection to his sister's daughter.

At the same time, Rachel pondered whether if he had said that to spare her feelings. "Josh, I'm actually nervous. She is acting weird. I hope everything is all right."

"Well, we both will find out tomorrow. It will be okay, trust me." He knew that sounded rather stupid so he kept talking before she could ask how he could be so certain. "One more thing before I go. This is something that bothers me, I think. Well, it must since I need to mention it." But then he said nothing, just stared at her.

"So," Rachel prompted.

"Yeah, okay. Damn, I am not sure why this is so difficult." Josh teetered on the cusp of going where his suspicions lie. There, his convictions stalled. Rather, he went to a safer place. "The thing is that I could have easily married Sarah until Leni came on the scene. It would have been an easy relationship to envision. Two academic types, shared interests, plenty to talk about, compatible personalities."

"Wait, you didn't love her."

"Oh, don't be such a romantic. I liked her a lot. And I respected her. She was honest. That is what counted. But I could never tell her how I felt. I suspected even at the time she was waiting for me to open, say how I felt. She was waiting for an opportunity to respond. I suspect she might have dumped this other guy. But I never told her how I felt, didn't want to go there. I hid behind her so-called engagement. Maybe I knew then that commitment for me would be a big problem."

"No shit, Sherlock."

"I do state the freaking obvious, don't I?" He continued quickly as she opened her mouth to respond. "The biggest wound I endured, my open sore if you will, was not in telling Eleni about possibly leaving, not giving her a choice to join me. I did love her, the whole nine yards. There were times the words were right there, on my lips. But I could never do it. In the end, I could never say those words. In fact, I cannot recall ever using the word love with any woman, perhaps not even mom. I did not use the magic words even to get laid. Talk about stupid morals."

"Magic words?" Rachel knew but wanted to make sure.

"The words that were the keys to a woman's magic kingdom ... *I love you.* All guys knew this secret. But me! I would rather pay money than lie to get what I wanted. Still, not to say it when it was true, that was something I regret. But maybe it was for the best. What good would it have done to say, 'Eleni, I love you, and by the way, I'm running away from everything tomorrow.'"

"Josh, you could have given her that choice as you say. Everyone deserves that."

"No, that would have been too cruel." Before she had a chance to respond, he leaned over and kissed her on the forehead. "Thanks for listening." Then he stood up and started toward his room. "Morris," he yelled back, "come on."

Morris looked at Josh but didn't move, his legs straight up in the air, his belly open for more scratching.

As Josh disappeared down the hall, he yelled back, "Dog, you better learn how to use the damn toilet on your own. I ain't getting up to take you out."

CHAPTER 10

Day 4 – MORNING MUSINGS

Josh sprang out of bed the next morning. It was light. Why hadn't Morris harassed him at the usual time? That's right, his traitorous pup had abandoned him for his sister the night before. He must consider some suitable revenge, like bringing a kitten into the house. He smiled at this wicked thought as he quickly got ready. Then he ran out to look for his pup, hoping not to find a pile of poop on the living room rug. But there was Rachel sitting at the breakfast table, Morris at her feet looking quite satisfied with himself.

"Would you like some breakfast?" she asked. "Most important meal of the day."

He grimaced. "Food in the morning, how gross."

"Ah," she responded, "I see that you're one of those who works hard at shortening his life expectancy."

"Been trying but failed at that too. Is Morris set?"

"Yup, we went for his walk, he ate, and we had a long talk."

"This is definitely treason." Josh pointed at his content pet. "Listen, you canine Benedict Arnold! Give her only your name, breed, and dog license number." Josh scowled to no effect. The dog cuddled next to Rachel's foot simply sighed and rolled over on to his back.

"Good boy. I'll protect you from the mean man." Rachel scratched his tummy.

"I'm off." Josh intoned in an admission of defeat. "End of semester stuff as I mentioned. However, the beatings will commence upon my return?"

"Fine," Rachel smiled. "Morris and I will be over the border by then."

"Very funny." Then, as he opened the door, "that was a joke, right?"

Josh walked toward campus while the late Spring morning air was still brisk. The sun bounced off the campus buildings as he approached. But his mind was not on the pleasant weather, but on thoughts of Sarah and Eleni. He mused on an ancient issue involving them, are one's early relationships the most profound? He wondered if that was true of everyone. It surely was true for him; everything felt common after college. Perhaps it was simply because the feelings and emotions were fresh and new during those early years. Had he met these women later in life, they might not have stood out in such a compelling manner. But this was a counterfactual beyond testing. An opaque sense of raw emotion remained along with specific vignettes of them that were oddly vivid, if not indelible.

He stopped before reaching his campus building, enjoying the rising sun. With the spring semester over and summer school and related activities yet to begin, things were quiet. It was an annual, if brief, hiatus that the permanent residents of the insular city of any academic campus might enjoy. The morning rays bathed his face as he relaxed on a bench normally occupied by lingering students. It was empty this morning.

He recalled looking up at the same sun many, many years ago. Sarah and he were arriving at the scene of the planned anti-war march. He had been glad that it was in Worcester, not Boston … less chance of being seen by friends or family. These events would become routine in future years as the war became more unpopular, but this was early on. Any sign of protest was viewed with suspicion at the least, outright hate in these days. He remembered thinking how foolish it was to worry about pissing off his dad. They already were at war. How much worse could it get. Yet, he did worry about such things.

Sarah and he were joined by a group of co-conspirators including Morris Greenstein, Carla Shapiro, Jim Dailey, Peter Favulli, and Bob Wilson. There were others in those days, drawn from the liberal element on campus and the community. Many were still conflicted and frankly confused. Then, it proved quite difficult to admit that their country was wrong. They had grown up in the aftermath of World War II when we wore white hats and the Soviets defined evil now that the Nazis had been vanquished. Josh had been a relatively recent convert to a firm anti-war position. For months, imaginary conversations had raged within his head punctuated by real conversations with his peers. The group would dissect every argument from several perspectives and, in the end, came away convinced that their country was engaged in an evil and indefensible conflict. It was not a matter of the United States being evil but engaging in evil. This was a critical difference in Josh's mind. The country was confused, not ethically bankrupt. The bankruptcy conclusion was something he would arrive at much later in life, after his hope for a better America had evaporated. Back on that long-ago day, the moral high ground could still be envisioned as achievable.

As Josh looked around that morning of his first major college protest, he grew concerned. While he saw many familiar faces, he also saw many more faces that were unknown and, quite frankly, hostile. Many a good citizen had turned out to defend America from what they saw as a bunch of Communist sympathizers who had no right to tarnish the American flag. Josh saw a lot of working-class types, many of whom might well have fought in WWII or Korea or, worse, had sons in the military right now. He saw business types who worried that this new generation was out to undermine the greatest economic engine the world had ever seen. And worst of all, he saw a few too many delinquent types wearing biker jackets. To Josh, these seemed intent on finding fresh meat to pummel and torture. Oh well, he thought, time to put his principles on the line.

As they started to walk in a big circle, Josh pulled Sarah close to him. He whispered to her that things might get ugly and not to get separated if possible. She was incredulous; This was America after all. They were just exercising their rights as citizens to express their opinion. And that opinion, on that day, would be expressed in the politest terms. There were no chants of "Hey, hey, LBJ, how many kids did you kill today." That would come much later. No, today there were calls for "giving peace a chance" and calls for more understanding and less violence. The appeal that day was to the *better nature of our angels.*

Josh, however, had grown up in the kind of working-class neighborhood that spawned uncritical devotion to flag and country. He knew that many of the folks surrounding them would not engage in nuanced thinking, would not look at both sides of any issue. Their world was given, black and white, right and wrong. You were not permitted to become mired in complex analysis. Beliefs were not debated but continuously reinforced. Groupthink was the norm. Josh had drifted far away from that world, but he remembered it well. It was a world toward which fond, if increasingly fragile, sentiments remained in his own heart. The tribe in which he had been nurtured increasingly struck him as primitive, unknowable, perhaps barbarian. That was an insight, if correct, that struck him to his core.

The protestors moved well at first. There were a few calls of *"go back to Moscow" and "love your country or leave it,"* Soon, references to *Commie fags* were heard. It was not long before things became ugly in a more noticeable way. First, Josh saw something flying in his direction. He ducked instinctively, but the egg struck a gal just beyond him. Then another and another. Several marchers were struck with eggs that burst upon contact. Okay, a wash job. It could be worse.

Then he saw something different, a beer can. It must be empty, but he heard a sharp cry go up when it struck someone ahead of him. *Oh shit*, he thought, *this is going to get ugly.* Now things went into slow motion. His mind raced, what to do. Out of the confusion, he could hear a voice: "Get the tall one in the glasses." Josh didn't have any doubts. He was the tall one, and he wore glasses, which he quickly took off. He started looking around for an exit if what he thought might transpire next happened. There was no escape; they were surrounded.

His thought process was interrupted by a mostly empty beer can hitting him in the shoulder, the remaining liquid spraying up on his face. A moment later, an unopened can smashed into his forehead just above his eye. The world spun as Sarah grabbed for him, blood oozing into his eyes. He felt a punch to the back of his head … peaceful protest, the expression of civil dissent, had evaporated into unreasoned hate. A blind rage against those on the other side had erupted among many of those who saw themselves as defending country and flag.

"Sarah, down," he uttered in a weak voice. He grabbed her and managed to place his body over hers as kicks found their way to his sides and head. In that moment, he thought he might die. What surprised him was his acceptance of this presumed fate. He would be free, at peace. That would not be bad at all. Just as consciousness was floating away, he felt arms pulling him to his feet. His rescuers were wearing blue. He tried to thank them but was pulled to a nearby squad car and spread-eagled to its side as handcuffs were snapped on his wrists that had roughly been pulled around to his back.

"What the fuck, they were the ones trying to kill me. Arrest them!" He could hardly see through the blood seeping into his eyes. "What are you doing?"

A hostile voice came back at him. "Should have thought of that before you attacked this country, buddy. We can't protect you from red-blooded patriots."

Josh could not believe it; Rage replaced fear as his head cleared slightly. "You morons, I was exercising my first amendment rights. Do you bastards have the first clue what this country stands for?" Then it hit him. That was an argument that would carry exactly zero weight in this situation.

They shoved him into a squad car with a warning. "Better not bleed on the goddamn seat, asshole."

He felt someone slide in beside him. "I'm going with him." It was Sarah's voice.

"Girlie, out!"

"Your call, buddy, but my dad is a federal appeals court judge with close ties to the Justice Department. I will be on the phone to him one way or another, and he will be on the phone to the top Justice people in Washington. Soon, someone's ass will be in a sling, and you look like a perfect candidate." She looked directly at his badge which the officer then fumbled to take off. "Too late, I have all the information I need, officer Sheehan. This boy needs medical help and you, my friend, have been abusing your authority. Think carefully about what you do next. Think very, very carefully. I just hope you have career plan B lined up." Sarah cradled his head and began mopping up the blood from his face.

Vaguely, Josh could hear a heated discussion among the officers punctuated by profanity-laced exclamations about hippies and Commies. Then a decision was reached; they would take the SOB to a hospital. They pushed Sarah and Josh out of the cruiser in front of an emergency room while warning them to get back to their studies. As Sarah helped him in, Josh asked, "I didn't know your dad was a judge."

"You really are out of it. You know he's in finance and a staunch Republican. If I called him, he would probably tell the cops to put me in the slammer with you and throw away the key."

"Good plan then," he moaned, "but at least we would be together."

"Nice thought but not the kind of romantic get-away I had in mind," she said sarcastically. "And don't forget why your ass is not in jail. You owe me."

It took over two dozen stitches to sew him up. While the medical staff suggested staying the night to see if there were any internal injuries, Josh insisted on going home. Later, Sarah fed him some soup and put him to bed at her place. She sat next to him.

"Sorry, honey, I have a headache tonight." He tried smiling at her.

Sarah smiled back. "You really are an Irishman, still making jokes after your head was split open and your body used as a punching bag."

"I'll be okay as long as I don't laugh at my own jokes."

"Do you mind if I lie next to you? I can sleep on the couch if that would be better."

"No, I would like you next to me."

She slid onto the bed next to him and rolled her body up against his. "Ouch," he winced visibly. "My body really was a punching bag."

"I'll be able to give you more pain pills in an hour."

"Hey, Florence Nightingale, I'm hurting now."

"Half hour maybe, if you're nice."

"I'm always nice … all the girls say that. I've got reference letters and everything."

She instinctively elbowed him, and he let out a howl. "Oh, sorry, but you deserved it." They lay in silence for a while. "Thank you," she finally said.

"For what? I talked you into getting involved in something that put your life in danger. I think you could do much better in the boyfriend department."

"Hey, you talked me into nothing. Got that! You're not that charming. I wanted to be there and, as you know, I already have a much better boyfriend."

"That's nonsense. How could anyone be better than me?" He winced with the pain, anticipating another blow from her elbow that never came.

"My thank you was for trying to shield me, protect me. Okay, you did a rather shitty job of it, but you did try. So, thank you." Josh did not reply; he just closed his eyes. Sarah looked at him tenderly before continuing. "Josh, this is like a moment that takes you out of yourself. I don't know. There are times when I could see myself with you. And yes, I'm being unfair. You hate serious conversations, and I do have you trapped here. Anyway, fantasies of us as a couple have crossed my mind which I know will never happen." Sarah saw Josh press his eyes shut, but she decided to continue. "You're a hard man to reach, and I've concluded that I am not the woman to do it. I know that. I'm not sad, not angry, not even disappointed. I'll take what's offered and be grateful. Besides, I've a man who loves me in the more conventional way, at least as long as I can keep you a secret."

"Can I ask," Josh finally spoke. "Do you love him?"

There was a long pause. "I like him enough. Can any of us ask for more? The thing I realized early on is that you're missing something. You have so much to offer … charm and intelligence and wit and passion. But …"

"But?"

"You're … incomplete." Sarah carefully snuggled against him; her head curled onto that part of his chest not bruised. "Something has been taken out of you."

"Or never put in," he replied in a whisper.

———

Josh looked up into the morning sun. Oh yeah, he was in Vancouver, the smell and touch of Sarah was only in his mind. Maybe he should get going. But no, the pull of the past still held him. He wondered about Sarah's long-ago words, about him being an incomplete man. They never picked up that conversation again. Maybe he should have gone to a shrink back then. Members of his tribe would never do that … it would be an admission of weakness. Besides, what would a trained professional have said? Hell, what does it even mean to be incomplete? Just because he didn't want a traditional relationship didn't make him damaged. He simply knew what he wanted. He recalled two girls talking one day on this very campus. He loved catching isolated snatches of conversations. One told the other that her boyfriend had a commitment problem. Josh had laughed to himself. The young man did not have a commitment problem. He knew exactly what he wanted … sex without any complications. The young gal had the problem; she was not able to rope him in. It was the age-old struggle between the genders.

Then Josh laughed to himself. Had Sarah been right? Had he lost part of his humanity? Was he incomplete as she said? Sarah was not a silly coed who would bitch about a boyfriend who kept wiggling off the hook. She had been one of the sharpest pencils in the drawer, straight As, the top of the class. He could have gone to Carla for advice. She would be direct and honest. He could still envision her looking at him, wondering why he was stupid enough to ask her if he was incomplete. *"Absolutely, you're a goddamn man, aren't you? All male assholes come up short. So just screw that self-pity crap, cupcake, and just strap on a pair."* That would be the end of her analysis into his deeper psyche.

Josh was again back with Sarah in her bedroom. He managed to doze for a bit until the pain woke him again. This time he was successful in coaxing some pain pills out of Sarah.

"Florence Nightingale, I need your help. I have to pee."

"Hey, you're a big boy so I've always assumed you were potty trained."

"No, help me up. I am hurting. By the way, I should call Morris, find out if the others are okay. He must be frantic."

"It's okay, I called him earlier when you were being treated. Everyone escaped in better shape than you. You must look like a real Commie. I talked them out of coming by, you need the rest."

Amid many groans, the task was accomplished. He took off his T-shirt and looked at his body in a mirror before getting back in bed. "Yikes," he managed.

"You're a mess, maybe you should have stayed in the hospital overnight." She sounded concerned now.

"No, I'm a tough guy. Hell, when I played football, I looked like this after every game." He smiled through gritted teeth.

"Josh! I didn't just fall off a turnip trick."

He quickly added, "Okay, not this bad, but I would have bruises sometimes."

"These are more than a few bruises. You look like shit."

"Well, thank you, Sarah, I thought you would never notice." He started to chuckle but groaned at the accompanying pain. "The price of being on the right side of history, I guess."

There was a long silence and then Sarah added quietly. "Are we?"

More silence, then he responded. "I struggle with that question every day, every single day."

"Maybe that's why I … like you so much. More than anyone I know, you care."

Josh smiled bitterly. "Caring is not a blessing, let me tell you. It's a freaking curse. I saw first-hand where caring about things can lead. My dad. He was a passionate man, about Ireland and his tribe but also about life. His opinions were held fast."

"I've never met him, have I? Doesn't he visit?"

"No, and you won't meet him. He never forgave me for giving up football and not going to Notre Dame. Now he thinks I'm the antichrist. We only interact to scream in each other's faces. Not a pretty sight. I feel bad for mom. She is tough, well, came from a tough background, but this gets to her. I feel the worst of all for my sister. She doesn't deserve this."

"I knew things were not good but never imagined them this bad," Sarah whispered. "I should have guessed … you seldom talk about family except for Rachel. So sorry."

"Oh, everyone has a story. I'm lucky in some ways. I think my folks gave me some special gifts. Really! My dad was a classic Irishman, great storyteller, a romantic, holding fast to his principles. And I look like him. But I also got things from my mom. She was deeper, more thoughtful, someone who saw beyond the surface of things. I think she did, at least. Truth is, she never said much, played the piano a lot. Maybe I just assumed the depth from her musical talent, and her silence. She could even do Chopin, some at least."

"That can happen," Sarah said.

"What?"

"I mean you can interpret silence for wisdom. You were quiet when I first noticed you in class, but assumed you were simply dumb."

"Thanks a lot." Now he managed a small laugh. "Oh, that still hurts. Here is my dilemma. I'm passionate and analytical at the same time. I want to commit, but then see all the nuances and shades of grey in everything. It drives me crazy. This war thing. There are moments when the stupidity and injustice of it all overwhelms me. And then and then …"

"And then?" She prompted.

"Then I begin to question everything. You know, McNamara, Bundy, and Rusk are smart guys. Bundy was a prodigy at the best schools, and McNamara is known as the whiz kid both in the corporate and government worlds. They are no one's fools. And they have access to information that I don't. Maybe I'm just a foolish kid, still immature and too easily fooled. I fear getting up one morning and finding out that I'd been a total idiot."

"Josh, let me tell you right now. You are a total idiot. Got that, so stop worrying about it."

"Don't do that anymore, it hurts to laugh." He paused to let the pain in his chest subside. "The thing is that I feel torn between my head and my heart. There are people who strongly believe we should legalize abortion and others who think it is murder. I want abortion legalized, we should get rid of the coat hangers for sure, but I can see how those who oppose abortion could be outraged if it were, in truth, murder in their eyes. If you thought it was murder, what would you do to stop it? If you thought that thousands of lives were being snuffed out, hundreds of thousands in fact, could you stand by and do nothing?"

"I hadn't thought about that."

"I look at the damage we're doing over there in Nam and ask, what should I do to stop the slaughter? What should I do? Is any act forbidden or immoral if I believed in my heart that we were committing systemic murder, abetting the destruction of an entire country? What would I tell my grandchildren? Oh yes, my country was guilty of international war crimes, but I could not be bothered. I looked the other way, just like the good Germans who looked away as the SS stuffed Jews, Gypsies, and the disabled into ovens."

"But—"

"No, let me continue. This struggle is not a matter of calculation. There's no equation, no sums of pros and cons that will give you an answer. Reason convinces me that we are engaged in an immoral and surely counterproductive war. We're killing people by the tens of thousands for the flimsiest of reasons. Really, do you believe that the Commies will be in San Diego if Saigon falls? And the Vietnamese, except for the elite who are getting wealthy off the killing, are sick and tired of being told what to do by foreigners. Come on! It is as if a whole generation is taken with some viral infection that saps our ability to reason. There's the rub. What if we continue? What if the war continues to escalate? What if the damn war spills over into a broader conflict? Right now, I try to reach out and educate and convince others. But you saw what we experienced out there. They hated us. They spit and threw crap and really tried to kill me. How can I reason with such hate?"

"It takes time, Josh."

"I'm afraid…terrified that we're living among idiots. They will never see reason. They are incapable of connecting the most obvious dots. Sometimes, I think they are driven by fear, an irrational fear. They see a bogeyman everywhere. And they lash out at someone who comes along and says, *'Hey, you moron, you're afraid of things that are not real—illusions.'* It's as if they need their fears to be substantial and real. Fear and hate are what gets them up each morning. And fifty years from now, nothing will be different, not a goddamn thing."

"You're too young to be so cynical."

"Perhaps. But let me make one prognosis here and now. One day, we will lose this war. Will we be beaten on the battlefield? Probably not! More likely, our patience simply will run out. The fiscal cost will be too much to bear, and too many of our kids will have come home in a box. Then, we will just leave, just like the British abandoned the colonies in 1783 and India in 1947, or the French departed Nam in 1954 after Dien Bien Phu. Decades later, I bet Americans will be visiting Nam and even retiring there. The people are so nice, the weather warm, the beaches unspoiled, and the cost of living so reasonable. But, in the meantime, our unreasonable fears and self-destructive impulses are driving us to madness and mass murder."

"But you're afraid of something, aren't you?"

He paused. "Yes."

"What?" She asked when he paused.

"I desperately fear that my resistance to societal madness will become rage. My frustrations will mutate into fanaticism. I'm afraid of what I might become, what I might end up doing. It's like football all over again."

Sarah decided to ignore his football comment which escaped her immediate understanding. Rather, she spoke in a firm voice. "Listen, I've come to the same conclusion about the war. But there is a difference, I think. I don't expect perfection in our policies and our politicians …"

"But …" he stammered.

"Shush, my turn." She slid her hand down his stomach slowly until she reached her destination. He looked at her with a hint of surprise but said nothing. "Listen, you're in no shape to make love in any conventional way, but this is not so unconventional." She started stroking him before continuing. "I see our political world as messy and not very rational. You throw in your best shots and cannot expect to win them all. But of one thing I'm certain. You had better be damn sure about the things for which you might be willing to sacrifice everything. That is precisely what might be on the line … everything."

He sighed. "There it is. How can anyone be sure of things that matter so much?"

Sarah paused a long time. "I wish I knew. What I do know is that you are a passionate man. That's what makes you so attractive to me, among other things" She chuckled a bit at her private thought, then turned serious again. "At the same time, I know that passion could destroy you. So do you. I'm not sure I've said this before, but I am in awe of you. I know I'm at the top of the class in terms of grades but, in many ways, you have the better intellect. I just work harder at it. You're quite brilliant, you know. Why do you think I take all these chances to be with you … the sex?"

"Of course that's it."

Sarah laughed aloud. "Don't flatter yourself, stud. I take these chances because you make me think. You touch my mind." Her voice caught. "For my sake, don't screw everything up. Don't sacrifice

everything for lost causes. The price is too high. I'm scared for you."
Josh barely heard her final words; her ministrations were beginning to
have their intended effect.

"I bet your prince charming doesn't have family jewels like mine,"
Josh murmured before realizing how vulnerable he was. He was glad
she ignored him, continuing her ministrations as he sank further into
a sense of well-being.

Wow, Josh thought, so much was lost to him from those years. Some
things simply are gone, others repressed, many recalled through opaque
filters. Yet, some images remained vivid, alive. Many involved Sarah,
others involved Eleni, which surprised him not in the least. Incoherent
scenes with her flowed through his head without pattern at first but
soon slowed and assumed some coherence.

Sitting on that campus bench, he struggled to recall the first kiss
with Leni. That was odd, he remembered first kisses with women
whose names were now long gone. While the kiss was gone, he
could summon up his early feelings for her. There was a deep pit
in his stomach where reason and detachment had disappeared. Mr.
Cool had lost that which marked him as unique and lost it in a big
way. He could not determine whether this was the first real date, or
it happened later, but he saw her sitting next to him in his car. As
they chatted, he pushed Leni's longish dark hair back, revealing a long
neck. She stopped talking in anticipation. It mattered not; he had not
heard anything she had said for some time. Then he leaned over and
kissed her below her ear, very gently. It was no more than a touch. He
detected a slight shiver through her body. More kisses followed until
he touched her lips. He expected her to run away, maybe even smack
him upside the head. But she lay her head on his shoulder. He was
relieved she had not decided to cuddle against his chest. If she had,
there would be no missing his wildly beating heart. He felt like the
most innocent teenager imaginable.

In some ways, looking back, that whole relationship was surreal. He would never be sexually intimate with the one woman he completely loved. How could that be? Was that accident, chance, or was there some causality working here? Was this a cynical joke by a malevolent God? After all, his most persistent image of God was comedian Don Rickles, whose humor took no prisoners. Just as youthful relationships seem more real, perhaps unconsummated romances are the most intense. Familiarity just might tarnish the emotional luster a fraction, take away the sharp edges of anticipation. He could never hope to sort that conundrum out. His sample size was way too small and hardly representative. He only had this one subject. And yet the intensity of those kisses, of her finally indicating an interest in him, yet overwhelmed him after all these decades. That same hollow feeling settled where his heart was just a few minutes ago. Need did hurt, desire struck one down with unimaginable intensity. The poets wrote magnificent odes to love. In truth, it was a feeling that sucked the big one. Her haunting deer-in-the-headlight eyes were still available to his mind's eyes.

She had been the only girl whose family he had gotten to know. He had steered away from such familiarity wherever he could ... too intimate for him. When Sarah suggested he meet her folks, they mutually concluded that was not a good idea. But he had embraced Leni's. What did that say about her, about them as a couple? Her dad's family had connections in Britain, and several in his extended family made their way there from Egypt as war broke out. Her father then made the even more improbable jump to America where he volunteered his engineering skills to the military and continued his education. He was living a lonely, monkish existence in a time when men were scarce. One day, an exuberant and lively Greek lass came across him and decided he would be the one. It was speculated later that she would have clung on to any man in those lean times for young women. Still, most thought she really loved him. In any case, this pairing of opposites worked.

What Josh found remarkable was the general ambiance of the household. There was hugging and noise and general mayhem. Eleni was an only child, but there were aunts and uncles and cousins and neighbors in the house all the time. Every one of Josh's visits was an excuse for a party. He was embraced and fussed over as soon as walked in the door. Some of the female cousins he thought hugged him with a special exuberance. He usually tried to seek out her father who seemed an island of sanity in a sea of craziness. This refuge never lasted long; he would be dragged back into a vortex of familial activity. What was a private Irishman who froze at casual expressions of affection to do?

Josh came to from his reverie. He sensed he was smiling as he sat on this university campus bench and quickly looked around to see if anyone had noticed his odd behavior. No one seemed to be paying him the slightest attention. He chuckled to himself. Odd behavior on any university campus was not likely to stand out. That is why he loved this place, the unconventional was to be expected. With his anxiety that he stood out as strange being assuaged, and satisfied that all was fine, he returned to his reverie.

The chaos in Leni's home was so different from his own habitat. His family life seemed an ongoing wake. He loved Rachel, but she often retreated to the sanctuary of her books. His mother was the usually quiet, ethereal presence who floated through life trying not to attract attention to herself. Josh presumed that she had depth and untapped mysteries to be explored. Unfortunately, he never found the key to unlock those secrets. His dad was gregarious and a great storyteller, but he was never around even when Josh were a part of the family. Big Jim was usually entertaining people in the bar or with his fellow Irishmen yet plotting revolutionary acts that became less likely by the year, or with female acquaintances who would remain shadows to the rest of the family. Day to day, it was an icy and silent world.

There also was this superb cuisine to be found in Leni's world. His own mother could play the piano. She could even be coaxed to play in the bar on weekend nights though she hated this demanded servitude. She also kept the house orderly and very neat. But one domestic skill that had eluded her was cooking. She had neither flare nor imagination in the culinary arts. His dad didn't seem to mind. He was one of those classic Irishmen who favored boring foods—a piece of meat, a vegetable, and a potato. The three food groups were not to touch, and no seasoning was permitted. The meat was often fried, the vegetable out of a can, and the spuds mashed to death. Dinner was consumed quickly and often in silence. He had learned to eat to live and not live to eat.

Now he was exposed to a cornucopia of wondrous foods—spiced lamb, Greek potatoes that he loved and which surprised him to no end, moussaka, souvlaki, cheese and spinach pies, soups, assortments of goodies on long spits, and amazing desserts. And the conversation was sparkling and enthusiastic. They were always interested in what he was doing, what he was thinking about, what he was planning to do. After he quit football, his dad seemed singularly uncaring. He thought Ora might care, but she never bothered to reach out by breaching this wall of silence and isolation into which she retreated. Well, there was the one time that she looked at him and said, *"Son, I will be proud of you whatever you do."* When he tried to pick up that conversation, she walked away. Had she really meant it. Had she even said the words or were they in his imaginings. *Mom*, he had screamed inside, *talk to me*.

He wondered why he found Eleni and her world so enticing. It was alien to him, perhaps the newness was the attraction. No, then it hit him. It was the oldest reason in the world. He had found love, and not just with Eleni. The family loved him, were treating him as a son. Like the proverbial moth to a flame, he was drawn in. One day, he found himself with Eleni's favorite cousin, whom she treated as the sister she never had.

"Tell me," Josh asked her. "Why does everyone treat me so nice? Did the family treat all of Eleni's boyfriends this well?"

"Hah," she had burst out, throwing her head back. "This is Eleni you are talking about. You're the first guy that mattered to her. Frankly, I think everyone is shocked she is not a lesbian though it would never be discussed, at least not among the parents. They would love any guy who paid attention to her and, most importantly, that she liked back."

"And all this time I thought I was special," Josh said.

The cousin paused a moment. "Okay, you should know that you're not really the first. There was a Greek boy who has pursued her since she was in high school. But he was older, and no one liked him very much."

"Why?"

"Hmmm, he was a bit into himself, obnoxious. I think the bigger thing is that Eleni didn't seem to like him that much. He was aggressive, pushy, wouldn't leave her alone. And she was being Eleni. She didn't want to disappoint him. She would not push him away because that would not be nice."

"Ah," he had responded, "that explains everything. She is dating me out of pity."

Then the cousin leaned in quite close, making Josh a bit uncomfortable. "Listen to me. Leni loves you. We all know that. She would never say those words, but I can see it in her eyes, the way she looks at you when you're not paying attention, the way her voice changes ever so slightly when she talks about you. And if she loves you, then we all love you. In truth, if she wasn't head over heels in love with you, I would give you a shot myself." She gave him a mischievous grin.

Josh recalled the wave of panic that swelled over him. Eleni never said that to him, never hinted it. She was nice, responsive in her asexual way, but she never revealed her feelings. Maybe that is what had drawn him in. She did not push, she never pursued him. He had come to her in his own stumbling manner. He had always hated girls who flirted or dressed provocatively. He despised the ones that bared almost everything and then shamed the boys who made passes. How obviously disingenuous could you get? But then he was hit with another feeling, a strange one. Was it true that she really loved him? Normally, that should send him running. But it didn't. He rather welcomed this possibility. How could that be? Why didn't she tell him? Could she not get the words out? Did she know he was a flight risk?

Was she unaware of her own feelings? Did she feel the same as he did, that love was a toxic illusion? He did not quite know what to make of all this. But one thing was sure. He had no intention of running away from this woman. Whatever was going to happen, he wanted to see what would come next. This woman had vexed him in frightening and seductive ways. This family had shown him what a family could be. He was entranced.

"One more thing," the cousin said, "if you hurt her, I personally will break your kneecaps. She is the nicest, and most vulnerable, girl I know. I love her to bits. We all do."

Before Josh could stop himself, the words escaped, "So do I."

Many specific memories were lost from that time but not the internal struggle. On one hand, he saw at last what love and affection were all about. He was drawn to the laughter, the acceptance, being part of a larger family. He loved simply spending time with her. She dragged him to see a movie one night called *A Man and a Woman*. It was subtitled if he recalled correctly, but the plot seemed achingly familiar. Man meets woman, they dance around each other through several near disasters. The man is a race car driver. He has had many women and tries to run away from a commitment with this one but is having a difficult time. He is confused and torn, and not entirely sure why. Then one day, after winning a long and gruelling race, he accepts in his heart how deeply he feels about her. Immediately after accepting his trophy, he drives through the night from wherever the race took place to Paris where he runs into her arms at daybreak. True love is found, and the world is again at peace.

When they left the theater, she asked him how he liked it. He should have noticed the moisture in her eyes. Of course, being a typical clueless male, he didn't and dismissed it as a silly chick flick, though the term may not have existed at the time. She stomped up the street as he ran after her, trying to make amends. When he caught up to her, she waved a fist at him, saying, *"Connelly,"* her term of affection when she was scolding him. But that was the thing. She never got mad. She was always kind and funny and loving in her innocent way. She always seemed to treat him as a gift that had fallen accidentally into her life. But she never did it in the fawning way that turned him off. The banter was always there, and it never failed to make him happy. And then it hit him. While he was kidding her about the movie just to get a reaction, the story line hit home. OMG, he really had been the protagonist in that flic, trying to run away but getting nowhere. That's why he had found the story so unsettling.

———

"Professor," someone said to him, breaking into his private space, "big day today."

"Can't wait for it to be over," he responded truthfully. He never did recognize who had disturbed him.

Josh pushed his mind back to Eleni. She would step into his troubled political world on occasion and only tentatively. She might come to some of the protest events but only for his sake. She was never part of that world, and he knew it. She was a science major, after all, and they were too busy to get involved in political nonsense. One day, as the early fall season was upon them, he convinced her to come away with him to Cape Cod. She could miss some time in the lab for a day or two. She hemmed and hawed for several reasons but eventually relented. Inside, she was excited by the prospect and nervous as well. She hated deceiving her family, but the thought of being with Josh excited her. She really was innocent about so many things.

"Where are we headed?" she asked.

"Provincetown."

"Never been there, can you imagine?"

"Well, that's my job, to make you a complete woman," he said with a smile.

"When are you going to start?" They both chuckled but she had a wary look on her face.

He noticed her wariness. "Don't worry, I'm only working on getting you out being a total nerd, we can wait until next week to turn you into a wanton vixen."

"Did you bring a book on how to do that?" She smiled back. "Or maybe take a fantasy class."

"Woman, in a couple of days, you will be—"

"Begging you to take me back to campus." Now she laughed aloud, and he did too. He glanced at her. His heart fluttered.

Provincetown was a favorite place of his. He had come here alone more than once, just to get away and be with his thoughts. He loved the remoteness and isolation of the place after the summer crowds had exited. Ted Kennedy had secured protection for large areas of the nearby dunes and beaches; these unmatched sites henceforth would be protected from predatory entrepreneurs, their beauty preserved from ugly developments motivated by greed. It was a special place.

He knew of some cottages outside of the town itself and amid the dunes. There was no natural protection, only scrub grasses, so the winds blew with few impediments to slow their journey. The air was brisk and fall-like, crisp and dry. The sky was an azure blue. The setting sun would sparkle off the choppy water as would the almost full moon that night. The town was situated at the end of a long hook of land so that you could look westward over the water back toward Boston.

He had picked a good time to bring her here. That late afternoon, they first walked through the town. A few of the boutique shops were in their last days before boarding up for the off season. They found a restaurant in which to enjoy some fresh cod. Later, he thought that maybe he should have sprung for the lobster, but he knew that Eleni did not care about such things. She did not have a materialistic instinct in her makeup. As the sun sank lower, they walked away from the town and along the beach. It was sweatshirt weather now, and she pulled the one that had been draped on her shoulders over her head. They walked for some time holding hands, talking about things big and small, laughing at their constant banter and mirthful insults. Her hair would whip about her face in the gusts, sometimes covering her face.

"I should cut this stuff," she complained. "It can be such a bother."

"No," he raised his voice. "Anything but the hair."

"Why should you care?" she asked.

"Well, I like it long. It makes you, what, sensual."

She laughed. "Sensual? Me? No way, that is the last thing I am. In any case, Betty Friedan would not be happy with you. You're treating me as a sex object."

"Which no one ever did to her. Maybe that's why she is so angry."

"Shush, you're terrible."

"Okay, as a favor to me, keep the hair long. I … I like it that way."

She stopped and he did as well. "Okay, I will, just for you." Then she inched up and kissed him before leaning into him.

Later that night, she undressed but left her panties on. She snuggled up to him in bed, and he felt a profound peace settle over his body. He sensed something wrong, small tremors from her and wetness where her head lay against his chest. He wondered if he should ask but kept silent.

"I must be such a disappointment to you," she whispered.

He was relieved that she said something. He would not have to guess at her mood or the source of her despair. Figuring out women was something men simply could not do well. In truth, they are simply hopeless. Now, however, she had opened the door. "What? Why do you say that?"

"You should be here with someone who can give you what you need. I want to, but you know, the way I was raised. There is all this pressure about the wedding night, the jokes and the songs and the expectations. Yes, it's silly, but I am who I am." Then she sobbed aloud, just once, and jumped out of bed.

"Wait," he managed as he followed her. He gathered her in his arms at the window. For a few moments, they just looked out the window. The moon was nearly full, its reflection shivered off the bay waters and bathed Eleni's face in a pale light. He could see a tear making a path down her cheek. Her eyes were moist and deeply sad. Her hair fell in disarray around her face. She brushed it back.

"Sorry, I'm acting like a child." She looked him directly in the eyes. "Josh, you must know that I feel deeply for you. Sometimes I'm scared about what I feel. It is just this world of mine, my culture. I …"

"Not another word. Eleni, I don't care about the sex. All I know is that my heart beats insanely when I'm with you. It feels light and free, as if all is new and fresh in the world. Can you imagine how much that means to me? The rest of my life feels so heavy, so serious. You're my refuge." He stroked her hair. "Eleni, I-I … care for you deeply." Inside, he cursed his cowardice. If he said the word, there was no way back. He could walk up to the word, look directly at it, and then would back down. He pushed his heart forward, against the usual resistance. "Leni, I …"

She cut him off. "I know you care. I wouldn't be here if you didn't. I'm better now." Had she anticipated his next words?

They returned to bed as he cursed his cowardice once again. Almost as a consolation for the unstated words, he tenderly kissed her entire body, occasionally nibbling her ears to make her squirm and giggle. He spent forever exploring her body with his hands and mouth. It was all in slow motion, done with infinite tenderness. Why not, there was no urgent sexual destination to reach, just the journey to appreciate and savor. The wonder of the moment left him in awe. It was not lust; it was something way beyond that, something that frightened him to the core. Perhaps this is what the poets talked about all the time. He had never appreciated all the fuss before. He thought that romantic feelings were an affliction suffered by the weak of will and the slow of mind. He was beyond all that nonsense. He was better than that. He was a superior form of *homo sapien* because he was in control of his feelings. That, he thought, was not a shortcoming, not an incompleteness, but a strength.

Eventually, she sighed and nuzzled into his body. The next morning, Josh woke to find her still intertwined with him. He had never felt so alive. For a while, he watched the shallow morning light bring the room to life. The curtains billowed out in the morning breeze. He loved the crisp morning air. He loved Eleni. Why could he not say the words?

He knew that this moment would stay with him forever. What he could not predict is that it would be the last such moment.

CHAPTER 11

Day 4 – THE FAMILY GATHERS

A familiar voice pierced Josh's reverie into long ago days.

"Professor Connelly, still slacking off, I see."

Startled, he looked up to see Usha standing before him.

"Ah, the plot thickens, now enters the former spouse" he said. "All the ghosts from my past are returning for the wake."

"Retiring is not the same as passing on, my dear friend. Besides, we all know what academic retirement is for research types … the same amount of work absent the dreadful faculty meetings." Then she grimaced a bit. "I e-mailed you that I was coming. Don't you want me here?"

Josh jumped up and hugged her. She clung to him for a rather long time, giving him a chance to recall the appeal of her body. "No, no, I'm thrilled you're here. I've missed you, really missed you. Just a little nervous, I suppose?"

"Nervous? About what? I don't bite."

"True, you were never into kinky sex."

Usha groaned. "I see you still think you're witty. I was hoping that Connie might have beaten that out of you."

"First," Josh countered, "there is absolutely no doubt about my wit. More importantly, my dear, I'm facing a personal horror show."

"How so?" She asked with a big smile, knowing that Josh would entertain her with some fabricated crisis.

"Don't laugh. This is bad. I have spent my adult life running away from social gatherings, and now a whole bunch of them are showing up to haunt me at this event."

"Oh, the horror." Usha mocked.

"I see no sympathy here. This might as well be my wake except for the inconvenient fact that I'm still alive. This really does not bode well, though I'll get no sympathy from you. It strikes me like a slasher movie where I'm offed right after I volunteer to go outside and see what happened to Suzy."

"What? That makes no sense."

"Sure it does, Ush. Everyone in the audience knows I'm doomed except me. In those horror pics, we all know Suzie's fate except her, and that the poor schlepp sent to find her. He also will succumb to a similar, dastardly fate. All these people are coming to watch my demise, make sure I go away."

"Is Suzy another gal you disappointed? Never mind, there are too many of those to count. Listen, it is so good to see you again, Josh, even if I am cast as a villain in a horror movie. And besides, retirement is not death. Marriage, though, is another matter."

"Okay, bad metaphor. It is great to see you as well. Hey, you look damn good for an old broad."

She smiled. "It hasn't been that long. Did you think I would decay in a few years? But I see a few more grey hairs up top on you and some lines on the face. The problem is that it just makes you a little craggier, even more handsome. I hate that about men, getting sexier as they age. And I can see you still working so hard to be charming. Alas, still not happening."

"Yeah, my lack of friends is easily explained, isn't it? But if I were nice to people, everyone would be confused. I believe in meeting expectations, no matter how low the bar is set."

"Dear Josh," she said in a serious voice, "it really is good to see you and I'll not ever admit this in public, but I do miss that Irish wit."

"And good to see you, my dear. One question, why didn't you bring, ah ... what's-her-name."

"Very good. The woman I left you for and you cannot remember her name. It's Rose."

"Right, I knew it was some flower, or vegetable, or fruit. But I should've gotten her name down. I wanted to send her a thank-you note, for stealing you away. But wait, you're avoiding an answer, why didn't she come with you? I could have thanked her in person."

Usha forced a smile. "What's-her-name and I are no longer together."

"Oh … sorry," he said with meaning.

"These things happen," she offered.

"Still, it hurts I bet. What happened? Or should I not ask?"

"The oldest cliché … a younger woman," she said with a small, bitter laugh. "And here I thought only men, vile pigs that they are, did that." Instinctively, Josh pulled her into his arms. He feared she might pull away, but she melted more deeply into his embrace. Then she continued, "I suppose I was not very available, busy with work, preoccupied. I never noticed the signs. Too busy even for that."

Several clever responses flowed through Josh's mind, but he decided not to be cute at this moment. He just held her and once again was surprised how good her body still felt to him. *Too bad she is on the other team*, he said to himself.

"Well," he said, "no argument from me on the 'men being pigs' hypothesis. The evidence is overwhelming. But I'm super glad you're here. We'll have a good time at my retirement wake. Rachel is here. This will be the longest we have been together since we were kids. She really is quite a woman."

Usha looked at him quizzically. "You seem surprised at that."

"Hmm," Josh appeared surprised at what he had just said. "I guess … I suppose I am getting to know her again." He paused. "Wait, more like I'm getting to know her for the first time, as an adult."

Usha leaned over to kiss him on the cheek. "My dear, you always were a bit slow. Think about it. Someone had to get all the talent in your family. I suspect she is well worth knowing."

Josh smiled at her observation. "And we will be picking her daughter up at the airport this afternoon. A freaking family reunion. How did that happen?"

Usha pulled away and looked up at him. "I remember meeting your sister, but we never talked that much. She was quite lovely as I recall though noticeably quiet. I never got to know her then. This will be nice, an opportunity to meet the talent of the Connelly clan."

Josh laughed. "Don't let her quiet ways fool you. She is a pistol when you get to know her."

"Then I am really looking forward to it." Usha smiled.

"Come with me. I've a few odds and ends to do here and then we'll head back to my place."

———

That afternoon, Josh, Rachel, and Usha waited in the international terminal. Rachel was nervous, but she and Usha kept whispering to each other and laughing. This was not good, Josh thought. His sister and ex-spouse had immediately bonded and undoubtedly were amusing themselves at his expense. Then he caught himself. *Now that is paranoid*, he concluded. *Not everything is about me even though it should be*, he mused. He noticed both glancing in his direction and giggling like schoolgirls. It really was about him. Still, he was happy they had connected so easily.

Then a familiar voice reached him. "We made it." Cate ran up and hugged her mother. "Oh, Mom, so good to see you but I fear this is not a surprise for you. You don't look appropriately shocked."

"Sorry, my dear, your uncle folded like a cheap suit."

"And speaking of my favorite uncle," Cate pivoted toward Josh. "I forgive you for not keeping our secret."

"Sorry I blew that; I never could withstand torture. Good thing no one entrusted me with any state secrets. And to be accurate, I'm your only uncle."

"Details, details, but I suppose you're lucky not to have any competition." Cate laughed excitedly. "Still, I brag all the time about my brilliant, funny, handsome uncle who is a great intellectual."

"Cate," said Rachel with a serious expression, "how many times did I warn you against taking those hallucinatory drugs."

Cate threw her head back and laughed again. "Not to worry, Mom, the foreign service makes me pee in a cup from time to time." Then she noticed the third member of the group.

"Oh, do you remember Usha?" Josh added.

"Of course, how nice you could make this. I am so thrilled to see you again." Cate walked up and surprised Usha by embracing her. Then Cate turned to a young, attractive woman standing uneasily about ten feet behind her.

Cate walked back and took the uncertain woman by the arm, urging her forward. They all focused on a striking woman in her mid-twenties. Josh took a deep breath. If he looked quickly enough, he could see Eleni standing there as she was some four decades ago. He tried to shake the image out of his head, but it stayed there, discomforting him. "This is Meena Muhaisin, my … good friend." While Cate's hair was light brown and shortish, Meena had long black hair, dark eyes, and caramel-colored skin. Her facial structure was well articulated, fit for a Vogue pictorial.

Meena flashed a tentative smile. "I am glad to meet you all." She had a recognizable clipped British accent. "Cate has told me so much about you." She nodded toward Rachel and Josh.

"Well, in my defense, there is another side to that story," Josh added.

"No, no, it could hardly be more flattering than what Cate has already told me," she said, emitting a nervous chuckle. Her eyes were guarded in that moment, betraying some uncertainty, if not fear. She turned to Usha. "I am sorry …"

Usha picked up on her confusion. "Let me introduce myself. I was married to Josh for several years. We had been colleagues and have remained friends." Meena's confusion continued as Usha spoke up. "Long story, we can get into that later."

"Okay then, now that we're here, let the party begin," Cate announced. As they walked out, Josh glanced quickly toward Cate and Meena. His niece grabbed Meena's hand for a moment and mouthed the words *"It will be fine, don't worry"* to her. The light went on in Josh's head. *Oh, so that is how it is. That explains a lot.*

Then Cate broke an awkward silence. "It's so wonderful to be here. With Meena being Mid-eastern, Jordanian and all, I feared the paranoia going around would cause us problems, particularly in the US. The Canadians generally are more civilized. But it helps that I'm with the service, that seems to work. And speaking of the service, I've been angling for my home leave for a while. In the Mideast, getting leave can be a touch-and-go proposition, there is always some situation or another and we always seem to be on call. I know I should have given you more warning, Mom, but I wanted it to be a surprise. Hope you're not mad. I wasn't totally sure I could make it until recently." It was obvious to Josh and Rachel that Cate was talking fast. It was as if she feared that someone else might take control.

Rachel jumped in at her question. "No, sweetie, I'm not mad. Maybe a bit surprised, but that was the point, I guess."

Meena looked as if she might say something but could not. Josh picked up the slack. "You were on the East Coast? Did you see your dad?"

"Yes." Then silence. "We can chat about that later. Meena has never been to Vancouver. Let's point out some of the sights on the way."

That they did until, in a lull, Josh asked out of genuine curiosity now. "Meena, tell us a little about yourself."

She took a breath, as if recalling a prepared script. "Yes. Well, I grew up in Jordan, in Amman. My father was in business and government, quite successful. I was shipped off to school in England as a teen. They thought I was clever enough to warrant an investment, so I spent time in a rather exclusive public school. It was difficult at first, but I adjusted. After some time, I thought it all rather brilliant once I got to gather some friends about me." Yes, Josh thought, more British than Jordanian. "Then I matriculated at Oxford where I read Political Science and Economics. By the way, I loved England though the winters always were a bit depressing. I never could quite get used to the endless winter dark, such short days. After finishing my studies, I was ready to return to my home, my family, and the real world."

"What keeps you busy?" Josh inquired.

Meena seemed to be relaxing with each word. "My father wanted me to join him in business, but I sought a position in government. Simply making money has never held much attraction for me. I did some tourism stuff at first and then development projects, particularly with refugees. That's where my heart is, and it involves a great deal of work with foreign governments. I love it. That is how I met Catherine" Josh did a double take. He had never heard anyone call Cate by her full name in a long time.

"Yes," Cate chimed in. "We hit it off right away. Meena has made my stationing in Amman a joy. She won't say anything, but she is related to the royal family."

"Oh shush, it is a distant connection."

Cate picked up the thread again. "Close enough to get me invited to the palace on some social occasions. Have you ever seen the queen? She has been interviewed on US television. She has to be the most beautiful woman in the world, and so articulate."

———

Later that afternoon, they were getting ready for a celebratory dinner at Josh's home. Josh was surprised when Connie showed up. When Rachel learned that Cate would be visiting, she had called Connie with whom she had chatted a couple of times since they first met. In the back of her mind, Rachel could not quite push aside a deep feminine impulse that Josh was lonely, and Connie just might fill that need. She would then kick herself for being a homewrecker. Still, it was apparent to Rachel that Connie and Josh made a better pair than Connie and the cold, remote physicist whose name already escaped her. When Rachel asked Connie for help in getting the dinner planned, she went further to suggest that her new boyfriend probably would be bored and was relieved when Connie readily agreed.

Even at this moment, Rachel could not fully acknowledge her nefarious plans even to herself. She had a nagging sense that she was behaving like a manipulative female but pushed such thoughts aside. Nothing untoward would happen and she liked Connie. They were sister scientists. Everyone crowded the kitchen for a while as a general and superficial conversation continued. Then Josh asked Cate and Meena to accompany him to his office using the excuse of showing them some family pictures. Cate recognized many but was thrilled at the prospect of sharing with Meena old pictures of Rachel and Josh and herself when they all were young, as well as scenes that brought back fond memories. It was one of those sentimental tours that the audience must pretend to enjoy no matter what. Meena displayed the expected enthusiasm, oohing as expected and asking many questions. Josh wondered if she were trying a bit too hard.

After some time, Josh suddenly put the pictures down and quietly asked, "Okay, young lady, when are you going to tell your mom?"

"What?" Cate stammered, stalling for time.

"That you two are a couple."

Cate and Meena looked at each other. Meena then glanced at the floor with an expression that screamed she wanted to be somewhere else, anywhere else. "What gave us away?" Cate asked.

Josh smiled. "First, I'm not as dumb as I look. You have been visiting me periodically since you were a teen. I know you way better than I do your mom, my own sister. You never talked about boys, not once. Okay, that might be just a healthy sense of independence or just maybe you're smart enough to realize that we're all worthless. I thought about that on occasion but decided not to jump to conclusions. Then I get these texts and e-mails, all mysterious-like, about this visit. Bringing a friend on your leave, someone that had never been mentioned before? What nailed it for me was a gesture I caught as we left the airport. A brief look, the joining of hands, words mouthed silently, expressions of anxiety. The real giveaway, Cate babbling when she got off the plane."

"But I always babble … Okay, Sherlock …" Cate looked for words. "I, we …"

Josh pulled Cate to him in a big hug. "I so hope that you did not doubt for one moment that I would love you a scintilla less. You're the closest thing I will ever have to a daughter. I'm just ecstatic that you have found someone. But why in hell are you worried about your mother? You must know she will feel the same."

"Well," Cate said slowly, "it did not go well with Evan and his family."

"That prick," Josh uttered spontaneously and then regretted it. "Sorry, no need for that."

A tear formed in Cate's right eye. "No need to apologize. I agree. He is a shit, and his mother is a stone-cold succubus. He has this new family, and I am sure he saw me and Meena as an irritation. But that wicked witch of the west wanted us out of the house. She treated Meena like crap, I was freaking furious. And Evan, my own dad, did nothing to support me. He just stared as if I was not even his child, as if I were some irritating neighbor's kid who had defiled his damn flower garden. I could barely convince Meena to come with me here, she feared it would be the same."

Josh kissed Cate on the top of her head and turned to Meena. He took her hands. "Meena, welcome to our family. If Cate loves you, then I love you."

Meena lowered her head. Josh could see her shoulders heave a bit before she looked up with a tear winding down her cheek. She surprised him with an impulsive hug. "Oh my, that was bold of me."

Josh thought back to the time when Eleni's mother hugged him, his surprise at the gesture. But now he welcomed this universal sign of affection. He wrapped his arms around the young woman and wondered at the ease with which he used the word *love*, a word that had never ever come easy to him. That was irrelevant, though. It hit him that this young girl had been deathly afraid of this moment, and that her relief was genuine. So was her affectionate hug. It was a good thing.

"What the ..." They all looked around to see Rachel at the door to his office. "I mean, my brother can make anyone cry, but this is impressive even for him."

Meena let Josh go. "Rachel," he said calmly, "I think these two have something to tell you."

Cate took a deep breath and wiped the tears from her eyes. "Mom, there is something I've been wanting to tell you for a long time, one of the reasons for this trip, other than to celebrate with uncle here. Damn, I just hate myself for being such a coward ... so freaking fearful. Damn!"

"Cate, just say the words," Josh whispered. "Just ... say ... the ... words."

Cate took a deep breath. "I ... love Meena. We want ... to be together, adopt children, have a life together." Now the words cascaded out. "I have known for so long a time that I'm attracted to women. As a kid, I was confused, sure. I went through the obligatory boyfriends and relationships. But inside, you know, I had that emptiness, that feeling of something being wrong. But I can't do that anymore. It is not fair to you, to me ..."

Rachel did not blanche in the slightest. She held up a hand. "Whoa! I understand, Cate, I really understand. Believe me. You think I did not suspect? Why didn't you come to me earlier? Did you think I would be mad, turn you away? I don't understand. Why keep this inside, my dear?"

Cate stood there, immobile for a few moments. "It seems silly now, but I was ... afraid. Well, not afraid that you would reject me so much as you would be ... disappointed."

"But why ... I don't understand." Rachels voice was plaintiff, perhaps pleading.

"I just never felt I measured up, that you hoped I would be ... more. You had been such an achiever, the gal that worked her way out of the Irish ghetto to become the top doc. I barely made it through high school chemistry. And now I was going to fail you in the biggest thing of all, being a real woman. No husband, no traditional marriage, no children. Sometimes I would imagine just faking a marriage to be the nice child. At least I could measure up in that way."

"My god," Rachel blurted, "was I such a monster?"

"No, no, it was me."

"Listen, Cate, you have no idea the hell I've endured thinking I had failed you. I could not stick it out with Evan, then I was so busy being that hotshot doctor you so admired that I was not always there for you. How many school performances did I miss? I can't help but wonder how many conversations we did not have but should have. I just wasn't there. We never had mother-daughter talks, not really."

"Mom," Cate pleaded, "please …"

"No, it's true. I was too much like my own mother, every girl's nightmare. I see that now. Oh god! And how many times did you ask me to join you when you came to visit Josh? How many? I always found some work reason to put you off. In the end, my brother got closer to you than I ever did. You know Josh better than I. Now that is a dagger to the heart."

Josh broke in, sensing the conversation would spiral down into a sob fest. "Well, to be fair, I'm not such a joy to know."

After a tiny pause, the small group broke into a laugh, more from relief than in response to any humor. All were relieved when the call came from the other room that dinner was ready.

Rachel walked to Meena and hugged her. "Let's eat. I will have a long time to get to know you. Believe me, I'll take the time to get to know you." She glanced at her brother. "I suspect we are all sorting stuff out this week."

He nodded in her direction. "I can vouch for that."

They all settled down to eat, which started out with too much silence for this crowd.

"Good food," someone said.

"Sure is," came a response.

Usha and Connie looked at each other with a *what the hell is going on* look.

Rachel broke the silence. "I'm not sure, why but I can't get an old patient out of my head. In truth, I am not sure she is my patient or whether I just consulted, but no matter. This was a long time ago. She was a young lady with one child, but wanted many more, like eight or so. But she was having a great deal of trouble with her second pregnancy. Yes, now I recall, I didn't become involved until later but heard the whole story." Everyone watched her now, curious, as they continued eating. "She kept consulting her attending physician to save the pregnancy. Eventually, her doctor told her that an abortion was probably called for to preclude further complications for her. But she couldn't face it. That was not her, given her background. Her doctor became more insistent, she now was risking her own health. It was very possible she might not survive. Still, she couldn't do it. She was so devout. Aborting something that was so important to her was anathema. If she died, she died. Then someone pointed out that her personal decision was not for her alone. If the worst happened, her two-year-old child would grow up without a mother, and her fetus likely would not survive. Could she live with that? This young woman finally decided to go ahead and abort. She could not let selfish principle interfere with what was so important. As the day of the procedure arrived, it turned out that the anti-abortion fanatics were in full throat. They were harassing the women and the staff, physically trying to keep the patients away. To counter the pressure, they had the women arrive quite early and had supplied passwords to each so that protesters would not gain entry pretending to be patients. It was all very clandestine and tense."

"Did she go through with it?" someone asked. They were all now listening intently.

"Oh yes, she did. In fact, she would become a proabortion advocate. But I get ahead of myself. What happened is that she got pissed that others presumed to assault her for a choice she arrived at after so much agony, indecision, and pain. During the procedure, they found that the fetus had already stopped developing and saw other worrisome signs. So, they did other tests and found that she had uterine cancer. That's where I came in. Among other things, she had a hysterectomy as part of the treatment. She would live to raise her only child but could not have any more. But what she realized was that her decision to go ahead with the abortion saved her life. Had she waited, we might not have been able to save her."

She paused, realizing that people around the table were both intrigued and perplexed. Josh got up and began refilling wineglasses. "I think we need more cheer."

Usha asked, "What happened to her?"

"She made a full recovery. She raised her biological child. And she even got to have all those children she wanted. She became a foster parent to special needs children. Her life became an inspiration, and in some way, her life trajectory could be traced to an act of courage that violated her basic principles and outraged many around her." Rachel looked around. She could tell that those assembled were struggling to figure out if the vignette had any relevance to them or, more importantly, to Rachel, who just smiled. "A lesson for all of us, one should never free-associate when wine is being served."

"Ah, this is what happens when an abstainer has that second glass of wine," Josh offered but wondered if the story was about him. He was not sure. Maybe it was for Cate, that made more sense. In any case, humor was needed. He sensed that the group did not know where to go next. "Perhaps I should tell the story about holding your head over the toilet when you got smashed as a kid."

"Only if you're on a suicide mission. By the way, that story is not a total *non-sequitor*. Sometimes things happen that result in huge life changes. You never know, you never know. I almost did not come to this event. To tell the truth, I've mostly ignored my brother over the past decades though I suspect we both were complicit in this mutual avoidance dance. Cate pointed out an inconvenient fact to me ... I often found excuses to stay away. The truth is that I was mad at him.

Even when I decided to come, I was not sure if it was to celebrate or to give him hell."

"I vote for giving him hell," Connie asserted without hesitation.

"I'm definitely opening another bottle," Josh offered.

"Careful Josh. Don't leave any empty bottles around," Usha offered. "Rachel might whop you over the head while the rest of us cheer her on. Hell, I might take the first blow. Yes indeed, you are so vulnerable here surrounded by all your so-called loved ones."

Connie joined in with a smile. "I suppose, though, we should keep him alive until after his retirement party. Perhaps a vote on that?"

Rachel also was smiling. "You know what the problem is. This useless sibling of mine is way too charming. Look at that crooked smile and those dimples. Who can stay mad at him? Besides, I sense he and I may be approaching a rapprochement."

"You mean you're not going to bludgeon him with an empty wine bottle?" Usha looked disappointed. "Damn! Why do you think I came all the way from Toronto?"

"To be honest, my urges to assault him with the nearest bric-a-brac are receding, but not gone." Then Rachel's voice lowered bit. "Maybe it's happening?"

"What?" Cate asked when her mother ended there.

"I'm thinking ... maybe we ARE becoming a family again." The table fell silent as if pondering Rachel's sentiment. She spoke again. "And speaking about family beginnings, do you want to share anything, Cate? I'm thinking it's time."

Cate blushed. "Is it okay?"

"It is more than okay. It's wonderful news to be shared."

"Okay, then." Cate cleared her throat and took a deep breath as if searching for the right words. "Here's the thing. Meena is more than a traveling partner. We're more than just friends. We are ... you know ... a couple, partners, lovers. We hope to marry."

"Fantastic." Connie enthused.

"Perhaps we should have said something right away, but ..." She wasn't certain how to end her thought. "That was part of the reason for the trip, to tell my dad and mom and that favorite uncle of mine, maybe even get married, though everything is so complicated."

"A toast to the couple," Usha interrupted. Glasses clinked to great cheers. Morris, snoozing in a corner, raised his head to the sharp sounds of glass on glass before dropping back to sleep. "May you find love with each other and happiness in life."

Connie looked at Josh. "You never mentioned that your niece had found a partner. This guy is hopeless. He talks a lot and still says nothing of interest. When we were together, I would ask him how his day went. All I would ever get was 'fine,' whether he nearly died that morning or won the Nobel Prize that afternoon. Men are so frustrating. You are making a wise choice, Cate."

"Though I agree that Josh is hopeless, I'm guessing that he didn't know until today, that no one did. That's what I am thinking. Am I right?" Usha said in her still slightly lilting Indian accent. "You just found out, right? Perhaps no one knew."

Cate looked at Meena, who nodded imperceptibly. "I want to be fair to uncle and my mom. They did not know a thing. They had never heard of Meena until I dragged her off the plane today. And let me tell you, prying her out of her seat on the plane was not easy. I needed the help of two flight attendants."

"Cate, please." Meena lowered her head.

"Okay, only one. In any case, this is my coming-out, at least with people who might care. In fact, this is our coming-out of the closet moment, technically the second I suppose, though we're not sure who on Meena's side has figured things out yet." She took another gulp of wine.

"So, how did you meet?" Connie enthused.

Cate now brightened. "By chance, though we think it was meant to be."

"Not another Hallmark story." Josh smiled before ducking to avoid a half-eaten bread roll thrown in his direction by Connie.

"I fear our story is not exciting enough to warrant a movie. We did some work together. We hit it off and soon did things socially. As an

American in the Middle East, particularly a female alone, you can be isolated … lonely. Most of the other staff were married or paired off. Well, some guys would hit on me, but that was not my thing, as you can imagine. Besides, it usually was the married ones that showed the most interest. There was another female on the staff that I wondered about, but the risk seemed too high and I was never sure. The Service can be tricky in these matters. I guess I had a date or two for show, but they ended awkwardly, if not badly."

Usha made a sound, then added *"nothing"* when people looked in her direction.

"I suppose Meena sensed I was lonely. One day she asked if she could show me around, things that were off the beaten path. One thing led to another. We have been close friends for eight months, quietly, and then we decided on this trip as a motivation to announce ourselves to the world. That was the reason for the last-minute thing, working up our courage and all. Up until we got on the plane, it was a touch-and-go thing."

Now the conversation flowed. It was as if a dam had burst. There were more questions and answers on how they met and what it might take to find someone to marry them. For a while, the discussion revolved around knowing who the *'right one'* is, a discussion that had Josh rolling his eyes to Rachel's delight. Then it segued into more practical issues. Would their marriage be recognized in every state and in which other countries? People talked about citizenship issues for Meena and a host of other issues.

What struck Rachel was that no one questioned the relationship in the least. She thought back to her own home, to Jim and Ora and the Irish neighborhood in which they lived. Her family would have preferred death and a wake to a family member coming out of the closet. The penalties for straying from a rigid orthodoxy were clear and certain. The old Catholic world bridged no form of sin, and anything that brought one pleasure surely was a sin. Scandal was to be avoided at all costs. They existed in every family but fanatically hidden from public view. She could recall her dad making references to some bar patron being a fag for sure or some female who rebuffed his charms just had to be a goddamn dyke. As a female, she shrunk at such labels but would look upon the targets of his ire with suspicion and wonderment. What was their world really like? How did they feel about life and others? On rare occasions, she might ponder how her internal world differed from theirs, or if it really did. That illicit gay life remained a delicious mystery to her.

Rachel noticed that Meena was sitting immobile with her head bowed slightly. Rachel got up and walked to her side. "Is something wrong, dear?" Up close, she could see that a tear had run down her cheek. Meena, realizing that everyone was looking at her, abruptly rose and walked into the living room. Rachel and Cate followed. The others cleaned away the plates, and Josh, when finished, peeked inside.

"Josh, tell everyone they don't have to hide. They can join us," Rachel said.

When all had gathered, Meena gave a big sigh. "Sorry about that. I am not upset. Just the contrary, I'm quite good." She had that delightful crisp accent of someone who had spent much time at university in Britain. "Well, this is hard. You see, all my life I've been silent about who I am. It is so difficult being from my family, a public family in a Muslim country. We cannot hide, not really, since we are close enough to King Abdullah that what we do reflects on him and the government. You can see, I am sure, how sensitive our politics are. Jordan is mostly Sunni though we're not Wahhabi or one of the extreme sects. Still, people are conservative, and the monarchy is always being watched. The King has been safe recently, but his father and grandfather were the targets of assassination on several occasions. Even when things look calm, you know that rumblings are just under the surface. Can you possibly understand?"

Josh broke a momentary silence. "Rachel and I sure can. Sounds a lot like an Irish Catholic clan."

"No, sounds more like your typical Indian family," Usha offered.

Cate took up the narrative. "Funny, we live in this sophisticated age. We have gay pride everywhere, gay marriage is on the verge of acceptance, gay couples are popping up on TV commercials, and gay partnerships are announced in the *New York Times*. But believe me, all this is not universal. My uncle is right, I have been weighed down by my culture almost as much as Meena. My granddad, Big Jim as everyone called him, seemed larger than life to me as a child. He spoke of gays as if they were diseased. This was someone huge in my young life, his words weighed on me like an anchor. I wasn't sure, but I knew something was different inside me. You push feelings aside, go through the motions with guys who do nothing for you, steer conversations away from those uncomfortable topics like *'when are you going to find Mr. Right'* and *'isn't it about time to settle down.'* I always had that *'but I need to see the world first'* gambit, or maybe the *'I need to focus on my career'* thing. But I am approaching thirty and that would soon fail to do the trick." She considered something for a moment. "Mom, I'm so sorry I never opened up. You raised a coward."

Josh could see the moisture in Rachel's eyes and a slight tremor on her lips. He was about to add something, but Meena took over. "At University, I came across female students that I suspected might be responsive. I could tell that some were feeling me out. We make guessing gay or straight way too hard, especially among certain groups. Anyway, there were occasions when I wanted some human contact so badly, our lips would be just inches apart and our eyes locked. It would have been so easy to kiss, so seemingly easy, but I could not. My head would not allow me to go where my heart wanted to be. I would think to myself, what is the real danger here. If I am discrete, who back home would find out?"

"But you could not do it, right?" Usha added.

"Not even close. I was in a self-imposed prison, that's how it felt at least. Then I returned to Amman after my studies, I thought that would be it. My family would insist that I marry, and I would have no choice. The night before I was to fly home from England, I cried bitterly. For the first time, I considered ending it all. I was not serious in that. At least I don't think I was … just miserable beyond words."

"So sad." Connie said in a whisper.

"I found myself avoiding friends and family, withdrawing into myself, knowing they were talking about me, plotting the future of my life, a life I could not accept. Once again, those thoughts of ending everything returned. But then …"

"Then what?" Connie pushed, caught up in the narrative.

"Then Cate and I met. My world turned upside down. Well, not right away. Fortunately for Professor Connelly, this is not a Hallmark movie. No rushing into each other's arms from across the room."

"Professor who?" Rachel laughed. "You mean Josh? You can call me Professor Connelly, but not him … just kidding about that, Meena. Calling me professor that is."

"Guess I'm not used to the informality, but I'll get it." Meena took a deep breath. "When we did meet, it was like sensing daylight for the first time." Cate was smiling at her and reached out to take her hand.

"Tell us about the first meeting." Usha asked.

"I liked my new work in Amman and all. But I could sense disaster lurking. My parents had picked out what they considered a suitable mate. The suicide fantasies were nibbling around the edges of my mind again. And then, and then …"

"Magic struck across a crowded room." Josh added with a bit of a smirk. "I just knew it … Hallmark it is."

Connie's next missile, a piece of hard candy, hit him in the middle of the forehead. "Bullseye!" She announced with satisfaction.

"Professor, I mean Josh, is correct. I was in a meeting when I looked up and saw Cate. Her smile was so warm, and she seemed so bright and personable. I thought, she might not be gay, but I wanted to spend time with her no matter what. Since she was new to Amman, I offered to show her around, as we mentioned earlier. We did things for a while, just the social and cultural things that friends do. She was so open and had this laugh that was … genuine. It was the first time in a long time that I felt alive, that I felt strong enough to resist my family."

"Okay, I'll admit to this. I like this Hallmark story, but all the others suck." Josh offered. "And get the freaking candy away from Connie. She'll put out my eye."

"Shush, and let her talk, you chauvinistic nimrod." Connie picked up another piece of candy but refrained from hurling it.

Rachel nodded toward Connie. "Thanks. I'm tired of trying to civilize him by myself."

Meena smiled, now relaxed fully. "One day, we were walking early in the morning. We were alone. We were sitting on a bench, talking about who knows what. Then we stopped with the nonsensical chatter. It was like all those times in college when I came so close. Our heads seemed to inch closer. That's where I would stop in the past. I had never allowed myself to cross that line."

"And then," Cate added, knowing Meena would soon be embarrassed to go further in their story, "we knew. I remember as if it happened five minutes ago. Our lips approached and we kissed. We did not let fear take over us, did not pull apart. I'm not sure we talked about it that day, the kiss and what it meant." It was as if Cate and Meena were suddenly talking to one another, as if the rest of the room had disappeared.

Meena then added. "Still, we knew a line had been crossed. The next time we were alone, it was easier. We found places to be alone. But the fear was there, ever present. We never moved on past those innocent kisses. Jordan is relatively free, but there are spies everywhere. Each morning, I was afraid I would be asked in for an interrogation about this foreign she-devil."

"How delicious and exciting." Usha gushed.

Cate gave a short laugh. "More than exciting. Hell, I feared that I would be kicked out of the foreign service, or at least shipped home. They tend to take a dim view of personal behaviors that cause embarrassment to country and particularly the service. Yeah, they are surprisingly picky about such things. Go figure."

Meena took another glass of wine. "Don't let me have a third one of these. I am not good with the devil's brew like you are."

"We must make you an honorary Irishwoman," Josh offered. "And that infectious laugh that Cate has, she gets that from me."

"No uncle, I think I got a slight case of narcissism from you." Cate laughed aloud before continuing, "Meena and I soon found ourselves on this wild emotional ride. We went from professional acquaintances to sometime friends to close buddies to an exciting romantic dance and finally to lovers. It seemed all in slow motion and yet so quick. Once there, we were ecstatic and distraught at the same time."

"Distraught?" Rachel asked.

"Face it, every day we feared discovery. Males get away with far more in that culture, but not women. When you hide from society, your family, your own self, it all gets out of proportion. You don't know what is real anymore. Everything said in your presence takes on a double meaning. Every glance or gesture can be twisted into some nefarious plot. What did that last comment from a colleague mean or that last glance from a friend? It is hell."

"Oh, I so understand." Usha injected.

"But we continued. Once we found each other, there was no going back. You cannot, it's impossible. It's like being released from your personal Hell. No fucking way are you going back into that private prison again." Then Cate realized she had let out a profanity in public. "Oh sorry, Mom."

"No problem." Rachel's voice was heavy with emotion. "Just good to see you happy at least. But we will talk later … about your potty mouth."

"For sure we'll have to wash out your mouth with soap," Josh added to lighten the mood a bit. "No swearing in my home, except for me. *Mea cathedra, meae regulae.*"

"What?" Connie inquired and immediately kicked herself for doing so.

"Essentially, Latin for a house rule." Josh responded as he carefully eyed to see if any missile was headed his way.

Cate continued as everyone ignored Josh's attempt at wit. "When I had this opportunity for leave, I took it and insisted that Meena come with me. We needed to be where we could breathe and be ourselves, figure out what we wanted to do. Good thing I'm in the service, I could expedite Meena's visas and stuff. There will be no hiding things when we return, though. We simply will face what must be faced. But we are good, we know what is important for us."

Rachel leaned forward. "And what's that?"

"Well, aside from getting married, we want to adopt a couple of children. One is a Syrian orphan girl, and the other is a Palestinian girl." She searched through her wallet and picked out two small pictures. As they circulated, there were a few exclamations as to how cute they were. "We can't save them all, but we can start with two. We came across them while working the refugee camps. I wondered for a moment if Mom's story earlier was about this, but that would have been impossible. She didn't know. In any case, I suspect all this may result in the end of my tenure in the service, but ..."

"There will be other things for you," Rachel added softly.

"So, Mom, you don't mind if I throw away my career?"

"What? Me care? Are you kidding? I sacrificed so much in the pursuit of fame and fortune as a physician and academic. I was not there for you so many times when you were a young woman. I can see everything now. You would want to talk; I could feel it. And I would think, okay, let's do that this weekend after I get this journal article off, or when I get back from this conference where I am giving a paper, or when the grades are in, or whatever seemed so important at the time was past. And you know what, none of that stuff was all that important, not at all. I'm so ashamed." She wiped a tear from her face.

Cate jumped up and ran to her side. "Please, Mom, I love you."

"Why?"

"Well," she said, "relatively speaking, you're a saint."

"What?" Rachel asked.

"I said this was our first coming out in a technical sense. Let me tell you what happened when we met with Dad and his mother, the grand dame? Without most of the detail, I explained about Meena and I being a couple and touched on the adoption plan. When I finished, dad said nothing, sat there looking at me. Brunhilda got up and left the room."

"Is that her real name?" Connie asked.

"No," Josh whispered back to her. "That's what we call her. A real bitch."

"Then … then," Cate stuttered, having trouble getting the words out, "my own father asked me how long I planned to stay. What he was asking is how quickly could he get rid of me. Meena was sitting right there, right there. Why not just shoot me, really? That would be kinder. He was shutting me out in that overly smug and superior way of his."

Josh looked over at the couch. Cate was now sitting between her mother and her lover. Her ever-present smile was no longer evident, her effervescent personality gone for the moment. And yet, there was a serenity to her look, as if something heavy had been lifted from her. Meena offered consolation. "Please, Cate, do not be hard on yourself. You told me what it would be like, or what it might be like."

"It was worse than even I imagined. I thought I had prepared Meena for a worst-case scenario, but I was not bleak enough. My own father turned his back on me. I knew that succubus might, but I never imagined dad … And don't tell me that it didn't get to you, Meena. I had to drag you out here kicking and screaming." Suddenly, Cate looked around the room. "Oh, this is terrible. We have ruined my uncle's night. I didn't … we didn't …"

"Are you kidding?" Connie smiled. "Do you have any idea what you saved us from … an evening of your uncle's tedious stories. Number one, we've heard them all before and, number two, we know he just makes them up in the first place. And then there are the jokes. You know, when we were together, I kept something on my person at all time for protection."

"What?" Rachel asked. "Mace, pepper spray?"

"No, silly. Earplugs."

"Still," Cate insisted, "you all have been so kind. I'm sure it is hard for you to understand what we have been going through and how wonderful you've been."

"I understand." It was Usha. "I understand totally."

"Sorry," Cate countered, a bit confused at her tone.

"I understand totally. I'm a lesbian as well."

Cate stammered, "I'm confused, you were married to uncle … I thought you just drifted apart."

"No. I never stopped loving your uncle. We just had an arrangement until I found the courage to be with someone I was meant to be with or, more accurately, thought I was supposed to be with. Bottom line, you cannot deny the biology you are given. Josh knew all along it might happen, but like you, it took me a long time to take the plunge. And like Meena, my reticence to come out was rooted in my family situation. Conservative Muslim or conservative Hindu makes little difference. The shackles are the same."

"So, the marriage was a sham?" Cate asked.

"I … would not say that. Day to day we were like most couples. Hell, we probably had sex more often than some heterosexual couples we know. Yes, I would take pity on him in that arena on occasion."

Josh let out a chortle. "Pity? We can discuss that later, my dear."

Connie let out a harrumph. "I've always wanted to trade notes with you on what he is like in the sack."

"Okay," Josh said lightly, "I'm nipping this in the bud. I can end all debate about my prowess. I have the body of a Chippendale dancer, the technique of a top-flight gigolo, and an above-average wand."

"Wand?" Meena asked, confused but enjoying the banter now, glad that the conversation had lightened.

"He is talking about his penis size," Cate added.

"Oh," Meena exclaimed, clamping a hand over her mouth.

Josh raised a hand to make a point. "But remember this, gals, it is never the size of the wand that counts but how the magician summons its powers."

"Okay, I'm a good Indian gal, enough talk of wands," said Usha with a smile. "Seriously, I did want to tell Meena that she is not alone. I think that is the biggest curse we face. We too often endure our feelings and fears in isolation. We simply cannot believe that what we confront has been faced by so many others for so long."

"So very true." Meena murmured.

"And then," Usha exclaimed with emphasis, "we withdraw into our own personal agonies. Such loneliness, self-loathing, confusion. The memory of those days is horrific. I remember crying myself to sleep at night trying to figure out how not to disappoint my family. They were putting increasing pressure on me to either marry or come home. Good Indian girls could not be on their own. While I read at Oxford, I could put them off, and even through law school. Then the pressure ratcheted up, but I got a faculty position, and that saved me for a while. After tenure for sure, I argued to put them off a bit longer. But it was becoming unbearable, and I was running out of excuses."

"And then came along Mr. Right and his magic wand," Josh threw out.

"Forget the stupid wand, too small to notice in any case," Connie added.

"Let me finish this," Josh said. "I forget where we met, but …"

"A university-wide committee, we served together. I remember."

"A mere detail. Thing is, I was always attracted to beautiful dark-haired women, but Usha inexplicitly resisted my charms. I'm sure we can all agree that was inexplicable."

"Anyone here agree with that?" Rachel proffered as all except Meena nodded their heads side to side.

"I really am stuck among Philistines. Shush. Then one day, I breezed into her office and found her crying. Now getting the story out of her really took all my charms. Fortunately, I am a miracle worker."

"Oh god, shoot me," Rachel moaned.

"Anyway, after she poured out the whole story, I thought for a while and popped the question."

"What question? Meena asked meekly, not sure she was following.

"Asked her to marry me, of course. She had reservations, of course. She even asked if we shouldn't love each other. Love? That's not important. I did have one condition, though, a deal breaker for me. I posed the biggest question of all." He then paused for effect.

"Which was?" Connie pressed, though she hated playing into his game.

"Would she cook me Indian meals? It was a done deal after that. And we were happy until some younger woman lured her away from our happy nest."

"Don't joke about that," Usha reproved him gently.

"Sorry." He said contritely, recognizing he had stumbled across some line.

Cate still looked confused. "But did both of you get what you wanted. I can't see …"

"Yes," they both answered at once.

"But we're drifting off topic again," Usha said with conviction. "The point is that I understand. Better than that, I'm a lawyer and know way too many other lawyers. If I get the drift here, you'll need a lot of legal help. There will be marriage issues, international adoption issues, citizenship concerns. Given what you want to do all at once, you have tough choices to make, like which country will make all this easier."

"Oh my god, Usha, that would be so great," Meena said. "We have been rather confused about what to do next."

"You, young lady, just focus on your family and how to open up with them. What I found in the end is that my fears were overblown, but alas, you cannot know that for sure until after the fact. Your experience with Evan and his mother remains the bad outlier I hope."

"More wine?" Josh asked. No one responded. "What about you Morris?" The dog perked up at the sound of his name, but his head did not stay vertical long. With all the excitement, he had not gotten his daily quota of beauty sleep. He was exhausted and most upset that his routine seemed upended these days. He had led such a quiet, sheltered existence.

"I feel like Morris," Connie murmured and added that she had better get back home. Usha took that as her cue to leave as well. There were hugs all around, and Usha loudly stated that she would be back in the morning to work with Cate and Meena. Rachel grabbed Usha's arm as she started out the door. "Thank you so much," she whispered. Then the two embraced deeply.

Cate collapsed on a couch. "I'm bushed, too much today. And we have to get a hotel."

"No way," said Josh. "Downstairs, I can pull out a sleeper bed. That way you can clean up the kitchen in the morning. Women's work!"

"Cate, throw something at him." Rachel suggested.

"He's going to luck out, too pooped. But one question. How come your former partners get along so well? That looks a little unnatural to me." Cate was looking at Josh.

"I am the Teflon lover; women cannot resist my boyish charms."

"And I remain the nauseated sister," said Rachel, "is there a vomit bag available?"

Cate and Meena laughed aloud. It was a laugh that signalled the earlier tension had been fully dispatched. Then they all went downstairs to get things ready for a night's slumber.

Later, Josh sat on the couch in his office with a last glass of wine. He had a folder that he was glancing through without really looking at the contents. Rachel came in and sat next to him.

"Good wine," she offered. "Maybe one last glass."

"Don't make me have to get that barf bag," he admonished.

She tucked her legs under her and leaned her head against his shoulder. "I promise. From this moment on, I'm going to be a better mother. Hell, I've done all the professional stuff, achieved all that I ever wanted. Okay, I might need to work a bit longer since it probably will cost me a pretty penny for a hit man to take out Evan and Brunhilda, but that's it."

"Is it Brunhilda or Brumhilda?" Josh pondered without caring.

"Whichever version I used is right."

"Of course, what was I thinking. Listen Rach, you keep forgetting one thing. Don't beat yourself up. That's my job and I do enjoy it so much. It is one of the few joys remaining to me. Besides, you're a great mom, not such a good sister, but a great mom. So, you can stop fishing for compliments. And Cate, she is a total gem, for which I take credit."

"Yeah, I love her so and Meena seems very nice."

Josh smiled. "I'm a little surprised about no sounds of noisy sex coming from downstairs."

"Hadn't thought of that," Rachel grimaced.

"Face it, they are young enough to get excited about that stuff, unlike us withered old prunes." He scrunched up his face.

"New topic."

"You know, Rachel" Josh noted, "I could barely look at Meena. She so reminded me of Eleni. The same black hair, olive-colored skin, dark oval-shaped eyes, and full lips. Every time I looked in that direction, my heart would stop for a moment. Some things never end."

Rachel raised up and kissed her brother on the cheek. Then she stretched out with her head on his thigh. She would do that when she was a kid and they were watching television. She had always felt safe in those moments. Rachel was turning something over in her head. "If you are looking for redemption, you won't get it from me. You were a class A jerk with that woman. You ran out on her and the best things in your life. It doesn't mean I don't love you, but you were a total jerk."

"I paid the price," he whispered.

Rachel had a small desire to dig her knife in a bit deeper but hesitated. "I suppose."

They sat in silence for some time. Josh stroked her hair as he had done decades ago. She almost sank into sleep. "Rach, am I incomplete?"

"What? I'm not sure I understand."

"That's what Usha and Connie and Sarah, among others, have told me over the years, that I am incomplete or something that amounts to the same thing. Apparently, I'm missing something, but I am not sure what?"

Long silence. "Josh, this is not freaking rocket science. You've never had a single real relationship with a woman. You ran away from mom and dad and me as a young man, and none of us really knew why. You and I hadn't had a real conversation in decades, at least until this week. You pretty much cut yourself off from old friends, and from what I can see, you have a bunch of colleagues in your life that like you or appreciate your contributions, but with whom you are not close. You married a woman with whom you could not have a complete relationship. And the one woman who seems perfect for you, and with whom you lived, you let slip away or perhaps pushed her away. The jury on which is still out."

"And your point is?"

"Just think about it. You're a smart guy, or smarter than you look. Even your dog, not the smartest canine on the planet, could connect those dots."

He gently pushed her head aside and got up, walking into his office. She heard drawers open and files being moved. Out he came with an old manila folder bound shut with twine. Without a word, he placed the file on the table in front of her.

"Listen," he said, yawning. "Big day tomorrow, they are throwing the big going-off extravaganza so that I don't change my mind."

"Not to worry, Connie told me that your colleagues already changed the locks on your office door, and by the way, your parking space is history. Oh, I should mention that I got another text from Peter. He said they might be a bit late, but that they would be here for your final party. Apparently, they are driving up."

"They, who are they? How mysterious." He kissed her on the forehead and handed her the file he had been fingering without comment. "All this cloak-and-dagger stuff is driving me a little crazy."

She thought about asking what he had given her but decided against it. As he headed off to bed, she decided, rather, on one last insult. "Not to worry, you're already there and beyond on that bat-shit crazy thing."

CHAPTER 12

Day 4 - Evening

Rachel sat on the couch after Josh went to bed. Her mind, racing in response to the day's events, resisted any inducement to sleep. On one hand, she was elated. She felt more connected to her daughter than she had in some years. Cate had always been a warm child but often held back in an indefinable way. It bothered Rachel at times.

As a younger woman who enjoyed her witty and charming uncle, Cate would ask her mother to accompany her to Vancouver. Rachel almost never went, and seldom stayed long when she did. Why? The reasons were never candidly admitted, nor privately explained in any coherent way. Rachel had never forgiven her sibling for abandoning her when she was a young student entering high school. She had been vulnerable when it happened, and she felt betrayed. That was difficult for her to admit, however. In her mind, it betrayed some form of weakness.

She had always known the obvious reasons for his actions, the war, and his opposition to the draft. But there was no evidence they were after him, and certainly not for the duration of his exile. He just disappeared. There seemed no acceptable reason, and then he stayed away without explanation long after others who fled had returned to the States. Okay, she knew more about why now but remained unconvinced. He was holding something back, she was certain. His wounds were there, unhealed, buried under his disarming wit and charm. What did he lack? Where was this incompleteness he talked about? These things frustrated her and yet she still loved him dearly at some level. He made her laugh, got her angry, and prompted her to think hard about things. For better or worse, he got under her skin.

Worse, she knew why Cate liked his company. He was so damn intriguing. Josh was like his dad in that way, the good storyteller and affable wit. While she also could be witty, it was somehow different. Her humor surfaced occasionally, usually around and in response to him, as she was now realizing. It was as if he could draw out a part of her that had long been buried under the need to achieve and excel and be professional. It was clear now; she liked herself more completely when around him. In her heart, she had come to see him for a reason … to find out why he had abandoned her and surely to let him know what that had done to her. She had harbored a bitterness she seldom admitted for over four decades. It was repressed most of the time, hidden under a frantic professional career, but it was there. On the plane to Vancouver, she had a series of imagined moments when she put him in his place by fully venting the strangled frustrations she had buried for decades. And yet, they had gone unused, at least the better ones she had rehearsed in her head. He was charming her to death. Damn him!

Rachel knew in her heart that Cate saw only the funny, bright, insightful Josh. She could envision Cate's visits to him in Canada during her college years when she studied linguistics at the University of Minnesota. He would show her the sights, take her to exotic restaurants, introduce her to his fascinating and literate acquaintances, let her watch him regale impressionable students, and awe her with insightful stories and lessons for life. He was the dad that Evan never was. Every once in a while, Rachel considered the possibility that she was jealous of her daughter's affection for her brother. She would reject such thoughts as ridiculous, and yet they continued to linger.

Her ex-husband was another matter entirely. Evan pursued Cate's loyalty at first as Rachel removed herself from the marriage. He subtly and gradually turned on his daughter when he failed to turn her into his ally against Rachel. Cate would have none of that. She initially was confused and then saw his actions as part of his petulant response to not getting his way. Rachel was supposed to be a trophy wife, a pretty appendage. Cate was there to complete a picture of this perfect family. He had fallen into a classic mistake for a narcissist. He initially saw his spouse's professional aspirations and success as a bonus part of the package in securing her as a wife. What he missed was that she saw these attributes as essential to her own life, not his. When that became apparent, he quickly understood that he hated this arrangement. She was supposed to be pretty, compliant, attentive to his needs and yet successful enough to be another bragging point for him. Of course, she was supposed to do all that without trying, as if success as a doctor and a mother and a wife might be achieved with the effortlessness of Gods. Nothing was to intrude on the satisfaction of his needs.

Brunhilda, what Rachel had always called Evan's mother, ruled over the extended family like a potentate, symbolically castrating all males within her purview. She wanted everyone to play their assigned role. For Rachel, that role was to be the supportive handmaiden to her favored offspring ... the crown prince of the family. For Cate, it was to play the role of the adoring and grateful child. Perhaps that is exactly where Evan disappointed Rachel the most. He came across like a confident, successful, ambitious man who was in control of his life and destiny. But around his mother, he dissolved into a sniveling child. If she told him to quack like a duck while waddling down the middle of the street, he would wet himself as he scrambled to the center of the road. At least her brother Josh stood up for the things in which he believed. He had not caved to either of his parents, at great cost to them all.

Funny, she thought, how the scripts embedded in us early in life can be so crippling. As Brunhilda concluded that Evan had erred in taking Rachel as his wife, the matriarch began treating her with increasing disdain and obvious disrespect. Rachel could just imagine what she told her intimates at the country club. She undoubtedly painted Rachel as a self-centered bitch who caused her precious son no end of grief. Rachel could see the change in how Evan's siblings and the extended family interacted with her. At social events, it was obvious that the wider family, including social acquaintances, had distanced themselves from her. She could see them looking past her during conversations as if seeking an escape route. Sometimes she wanted to scream at them that she did not have leprosy, that she was a good person, that she was worth knowing beyond being the trophy wife to the scion of family royalty.

At some point, she concluded she was being gaslighted. She'd begun to doubt her own worth. Perhaps she didn't have much to offer on her own. Could she cut it on her own? Were her accomplishments insufficient to warrant attention and respect outside the protection of the Ballentine clan? How pathetic we are to seek affirmation from even these shallow people. She was disturbed at how easily we respond to the negativity of others. Ultimately, there was only one way to address these doubts, cut the cord. She could only save herself, and her daughter, by removing herself from the toxicity of her family drama.

What disturbed Rachel the most was that her apparent sins might be visited on her daughter. Evan, after the divorce, waited a suitable period before remarrying. He chose one of the many women he had bedded during their marriage. His choice was everything that Rachel was not, the compliant trophy wife whose hair was always perfect, her adoring gaze always directed at her husband, and her day filled with charity events and social interactions. *That woman was a brainless twit with big boobs*, Rachel mused. Yet, Brunhilda loved her willingness to conform to family expectations. Evan was also content, able now to pursue his extra-marital flings while tethered to a woman who would look the other way. It was then that Rachel most feared he would come after Cate. He now had a wife to look after his first issue. That would make it convenient. At this point, Rachel had geared up for a custody fight that, though threatened, never materialized.

That worry dissipated further after wife number two sired two children, a girl and then a boy. Rachel and Cate now were little more than a youthful error to be ignored as superfluous baggage. Evan did find time in his schedule to see Cate periodically. As his new offspring matured, Evan seemed to lose all remaining interest, going through the motions with his first daughter as if she were an unavoidable and irritating obligation to satisfy. Even that level of interest diminished. Rachel could see the disappointment in Cate's eyes. He did not even show up at her college graduation … too busy. But he did send a nice gift. Cate bravely maintained a smile while Rachel's disdain for her ex-husband turned to a bright hard hate. Cate was tainted stock by virtue of her association with the despised first wife. She might prove to be excess baggage in such a prominent family. Besides, she would always serve as a reminder of an unconscionable lapse of judgment on Evan's part.

These memories were beginning to sour her good mood from the day. In response, she turned to the folder Josh had left behind. Apparently, she never would have found this on her own. It was well hidden, she concluded. That is why he had retrieved it; He wants her to look inside. This was his way of revealing himself. *Typical Irishman*, she said to herself once again, *easier for them to communicate through the written word*. He had handed them over and then ran like hell, such a coward. Still, she was intrigued, very much so. There must be something here, something that might unlock more keys to her brother.

Why now? Had he decided to open up fully, reveal those things she suspected he had kept inside? The evidence suggested as much, but she remained guarded. He really was a private person despite an easy public presence. His easy joking manner was the perfect cover for a world zealously protected. No one would be permitted in without a struggle. Attempts to bridge the impenetrable wall were rebuffed by a joke or a story or a roguish smile. And it worked or likely had worked for most of his life she thought. She doubted if Connie or Usha had penetrated his defenses effectively. Suddenly, her wandering train of thought settled on Usha. She wondered what her relationship with Josh had been like. It seemed rather clear to her why Josh would enjoy sharing his life with her, to the extent he could. She was smart and kind and interesting. Rachel could never understand how couples thought they could make it on physical attraction alone. You can only screw so much. The other 99.9 percent of life needed a deeper connection. If Usha had not found someone to love, they still would be happily coupled, she was certain of that. Her brother would have thrived in a relationship that demanded little of him.

As she thought about Usha, Rachel knew why Josh would find her appealing. She had that dark beauty that he found seductive, black hair and copper-toned skin with high cheekbones and perfectly proportioned facial features. Yes, Josh must have been physically attracted to her. She wondered how he dealt with a sensual relationship that essentially was one-sided. But maybe that was not such a mystery. A lot of relationships were like that in her experience. Besides, he had this steel core about him. She recalled his high school days when girls threw themselves at him. He generally rebuffed them, gently of course. Any girl that tried to be coquettish was toast. Those that flaunted their bodies never got near first base. He wanted something more and found cloying or obvious seduction moves off-putting. Of course, he would grouse endlessly about these girls teasing boys while secretly paying homage to St. Virginius of the of Holy Incorruptible Body, a secret cabal of Catholic girls who would prefer martyrdom over actual sex. While she eventually determined that he had overstated the issue, his attitude was not without merit. He had joked about it so often when she was young that it had taken her a long time to discover that no such saint, nor society of young girls, ever existed. He seemed so firm in his opinion that it was all real even as Rachel saw little evidence to contradict his beliefs early on.

Rachel could not quite shake the image of Usha out of her mind. She liked her soft voice, mild demeanor, and still-present British-Indian accent. Close to Rachel in age, a bit younger, Usha looked even younger than her years with few age lines marking the passage of time. Then a vague sensation hit her with disturbing force: was she feeling a physical attraction to this woman? That is stupid, impossible, out of the question. She had shut down her body years ago. Okay, she pleasured herself to be sure, but that was just a rare necessity, more a pointless diversion than anything else. Since Evan, she had been pursued by several men, dallying with a couple when their pursuit did not cease upon her early avoidance and outright rebuffs. But they had left her unmoved, detached. Odd, she now considered that these suitors were perfectly nice; most women would be delighted by their attentions. It was as if she were incapable of any conventional response. Now, this feeling in her body would not go away. It was a kind of yearning. This was not good, she thought.

Rachel awoke with a start, realizing she had drifted off to sleep. She turned to the material Josh had given her. Like his life and his office, the folder was haphazard and disorganized. Still, Josh wanted her to plumb whatever mysteries were to be found. Herein lies some key into his inner life, she was sure of this. She selected some items from the mess. There were letters and newspaper clippings and computer printouts. She decided to spread out some of the contents in front of her and grabbed a letter that happened to be at the top of the pile. It was lengthy, but one paragraph caught her attention.

January 7…
Dear Leni,

One aspect of my new life here is time, time to think, time to reflect on what I have already done and what I intend to do. There is time for long walks through the streets of Toronto. My life at present is relatively unfettered by the proliferation of distractions considered essential in American life for someone seeking conventional success. As a result, it is rather impossible to prevent oneself from becoming more reflective and perhaps a bit more aware.

If you dwell upon your own behavior and that of others and further the relationship between the two long enough, then it becomes increasingly more difficult to maintain the superficial differences by which we shore up the soft inner self. Of course, the inner self can be described, itself, as little more than a plethora of patterned roles arranged to respond to specific cues. But I yet tend to believe that beyond the potentially numerous responses which one organism is capable of and ordinarily does emit, there is a consistency or uniformity which usually appears when the individual faces stress.

The upshot of all this is that I've faced another little bit of truth about myself with what I hope is a degree of honesty … when I reflect upon some of the letters I have sent, many of them seem designed only to evoke pity or sympathy or admiration through the emphasis on the loneliness, deprivation, or accomplishments in my young life. It has all been a rather semi romantic escapade through some of my philosophical stream of conscious meanderings.

Wait! Rachel said to herself. Was this the real Josh or someone pretending to be him? She glanced at the other letters. They were all to Eleni, the mysterious gal that neither Rachel, nor any of her acquaintances, had never met. They were written over a series of months during his early stay in Toronto after he had fled the States. This was the period he had never talked about to any extent until this trip. She had asked, more than once, during the few times she had seen him in the intervening years. But he never had opened up to her. Any exchanges about what she considered his *'missing years'* were all rather strained. She remained dissatisfied with his silence but struggled to maintain a semblance of sibling civility by not pushing the issue. For years, they had gone through the motions of a cordial relationship, being polite but distant, leaving so much unexpressed and unstated.

Rachel sat back for a moment. They really had been children to each other, simply acting out youthful roles. Both were dressed in the garb of adulthood and professional authority, yet inside, they had remained little more than pouting kids. She knew her problem. She never saw him as an equal. He was the older brother whom she idolized. And he betrayed her. It would have been different had she been abandoned after reaching adulthood. Damn him, he had done his worst before she was fully armed with the weapons of maturity. She didn't have the tools to respond at the time. It was different now. Okay, he didn't plan it that way, she had to grant him that. And yet, her pain had never expired. She could suppress it, but not eradicate it. The hurt lay deep inside as did most of her human feelings.

Then, she had her epiphany. This was his way of *'talking'* about those years.

January 17, …

Dear Leni,

I know a fellow émigré named Michael. His girl in the States has not written in about two weeks now. Her husband has probably returned from Vietnam, and the situation is tense all the way around. It is another case of the shifting sands of human emotions, the liquidity and vacuity of which never cease to amaze me. The course of human involvement typically seems to run from the improbable to the absurd. The grasping, hoping, seeking become inevitable frustrations and unfulfilled aspirations. Today's bliss and ecstasy are tomorrow's despair and emptiness. To maintain your purpose and direction, you must love and believe in that love. And out of the deepest despair of its reality evolves the highest respect for its necessity and appreciation of its existence.

Partially, one may say that love is an illusion or some form of selective reality, and further, that distance perpetuates these illusions. But the emotional character of love is only the superficial surface. Its real nature lies in the contract made between two people. It is the arrangement between separate individuals to share common excitement and joys and accept each other's burdens and fears. It is the merger of their identities as well as their bodies, an investment of themselves and their trust in the other. It is perhaps the most incredibly difficult goal to accomplish and yet the easiest thing to convince yourself that you are doing it. It is something that cannot be manufactured but rather must simply exist. Yet it cannot be taken for granted but rather nurtured and cultivated with all the strength that can be mustered.

As you know, this kind of investment has been particularly difficult for me. The exposure to and investment of self in other human beings is a noble aspiration, perhaps ultimately unrealizable yet seemingly the only reality worth pursuing.

In rereading this letter, I've realized that it is extremely ambiguous and unintelligible. It is just so incredibly difficult to verbalize emotions in general, never mind probing one's own thoughts and feelings. Beyond that, such thoughts are alien to my analytical, pessimistic nature. Perhaps there is a kind of metamorphosis, a maturing which is taking place, and I am neither able to analyze it nor describe its direction.

There is something I want to say now, that I must say or forever hesitate. I do want to marry you. This is an incredible confession for me, and I know it will freak you out. Before you retreat into your shell, let me assure you that I don't believe it will ever happen. Circumstances, time, distance, and certain common weaknesses will, in all probability, prevent it. But let me also assure you that I mean it and that if you ever, at any time, feel strong enough to make that arrangement, that contract of identities, real, then let me know.

Rachel sprang up on the couch. He proposed! He proposed! My god, he proposed! This wasn't some fake proposal or arrangement, but the real thing that normal people do. Who is this woman? Where is she? Why isn't she here? Why hadn't he talked about her over the years? Here was the evidence that she existed. This was the woman he loved. Of course, she had one answer to all her questions. They hadn't shared much since he left. While there were times when she was struggling with Evan that she wanted to reach out to her brother, she was never sure she wanted his advice on anything. No, maybe not his advice but his comfort. What she needed during those difficult times was to lie on a couch with her head on his thigh, his hand gently stroking her hair. That had always calmed her. The world had never been scary when he was there, stroking her hair. But he wasn't there, damn him!

She shook her head. *Does Connie and Usha know about this Eleni? And what about Cate who knows Josh so much better than she does? She had talked with him over the years.* Perhaps they had talked about this mysterious woman who touched her brother as no other. Rachel desperately wanted to meet this woman. Obviously, she had once reached her brother in some deep and special way. How did she do it? Why did he let her get away? But of course, this was so long ago. Perhaps it was merely a youthful flame that time and maturity would extinguish. That was improbable, however, and she knew it. He would not have shared this stuff with her. She picked up yet another note from the pile, her eyes fixed on the following passage.

January 25 …

Dear Leni,

Both the genius and stupidity of man are beyond comprehension, both his humanness and depravity inexplicable. In the past, the relative powerlessness and isolation of man guaranteed that a delicate balance could be maintained between the extremes and that somehow the human species could perpetuate itself. But now we seem to have reached a point of incipient desperation, of incredible gaps between the species' technological prowess and its limited wisdom. Between its science and its conscience, we have allowed ourselves to become enmeshed in a morass of fear and frustration, increasingly thrashing about with incomprehensible violence, struggling over inappropriate decayed symbols.

In Vietnam, we sap our strength, prostitute our sensibilities, and potentially precipitate a holocaust. It seems to me that the sensible thing to do would be to establish our commitments along a pragmatically defensible perimeter, e.g., Australia, India, Taiwan, the Philippines, and Japan. This would not only rationalize our military posture but liberate the dynamic energies of both the Western and Eastern worlds to confront some of the critical questions of our generation: food production, population control, socioeconomic inequality, and the quality of the human condition.

It will do absolutely no good if we destroy every single communist in Asia while the rest of the world is devoured by famine, disease, and pollution; while society disintegrates under the tensions of social inequality; and while civilization is crushed under the mass of its own weight. At home, our response to the Black revolution is to modernize our riot responses with the latest, most sophisticated equipment and techniques. Mace, automatic weapons, armored vehicles, and improved gas attacks do not appear to be an appropriate reaction. But then again, there is no reason to break with tradition and adopt a thoughtful humanitarian approach.

Rachel could feel her eyes moisten. For her, Josh was this rock. She had never seen him sad or weak or confused. Yes, she had seen him angry, but only with his dad and she could understand that volatility. They both were stubborn Irishmen. That was a toxic mix. It had been okay when Josh followed his ordained path, but all amity dissolved when he struck out on his own. No football, no Notre Dame, no church. That was the height of insanity and insufferable insolence in Jim's eyes. The screaming had driven Rachel into her room, where she buried herself under the pillows. But she could still hear. A couple of times she heard items crash and feared that the inevitable violence finally had broken out. Other times she heard Ora's pleading voice beseeching for calm. Usually, the row went on until the door slammed shut. She knew in that moment that Josh once again had fled. And then she would cry herself to sleep.

In these notes, she now saw a bit of what drove her brother during those days. She could see his passion and commitment. These were not his reflections on what he thought four decades ago, dredged up from faulty memories and filtered through an adult mind. No, these were his feelings committed to paper in real time and thus had a special authenticity. This was a raw and real version of her brother.

January 28 …
Dear Leni,

I heard the music from Zorba the Greek the other day. As usual, it sparked a flood of memories. I am reminded of Zorba's recommendation that we all must possess a little bit of madness. Madness that has brought me to this situation, madness that may never permit us to see each other again, but most importantly, the madness by which we dare to hope. But the ultimate madness of them all is the one by which we desperately learn to survive and, in the face of all this increasing insanity, seek the kind of futile happiness that our elusive dreams pretend.

Yet maybe, just maybe, we can make it.

I want to say something now, not out of fear or lack of trust in you, but simply to clear up any ambiguity. While I love you, and do hope the relationship will endure my absence, the reality of the situation is that we are in separate countries. For how long is indeterminate. I also realize that my irascible moodiness, chronic immaturity, and impractical leftist politics, hardly make me an ideal catch. If you have any doubt about how you feel about me, or change your mind, please feel completely free to communicate this to me. Perhaps, given my Irish pessimism, I anticipate it anyway. And of course, if you are insane enough to like me, you are also allowed to tell me that as well.

Rachel had never considered that her brother would pour his heart out to anyone. Of all his considerable gifts, they did not include any evidence of sentimentality or romanticism. He had been the ultimate self-contained man. If he had experienced doubt or pain as a young man, she had never seen it. Rachel thought he had things figured out and had pursued his dream with confidence and passion. So, who was this man in the letters? This was someone who felt deeply and passionately, a man searching and feeling his way through life. It was a person she had not been permitted to witness nor know.

March 14 …

Dear Leni,

Your "Dear Josh" letter must have been an unpleasant experience, one which finally having been done would be difficult to repeat. Writing again was a brave thing for you to do. I'm not sure it was a wise thing, but it did please me, immeasurably. Thank you.

You mentioned that sometimes you break into tears without reason. I must admit there are times I become misty-eyed. It is not so much for what might have been but rather for what was. My times at college and with you were extremely pleasant. The time we spent together were the most pleasant of all. There was a warmth and comfortableness there, and a sharing and excitement which now strike me as unique and which never again can be duplicated. In truth, they were unsurpassed in meaning and passion.

The days we shared are past now and will never return. But we are in no way to blame for it had to be that way. The times and the people who fill in those times do change, inexorably, and without apparent direction and there is little, so damn pitifully little, that we can do about it. We, as a couple, would have evolved irrespective of my leaving. I suspect that what we were to each other or what we might have been to each other is a simple function of time and place that cannot be duplicated.

In my Irish pessimism, there is no room for happiness or hope.

Perhaps I shouldn't start this tonight. For one thing, I have been drinking. Right now, I feel pretty washed out. I kind of feel like a hunk of fruit that has been squeezed dry. The juice is gone. All that's left is the bitter emotional rind that is stale and repugnant. Nothing much is left of the idealism, the kinds of commitment that occasionally made me a bearable (or maybe the opposite) person.

At times, I can still sense the processes that seem to make the whole thing go, but like many others, I reject the acceptable labels (probably political) and systems that define our little world. Unfortunately, my rejection is complete to the extent that the possibility of replacing the rotting thing with new generative institutions or of achieving any kind of adequate escape from the impact of reality is amusingly absurd.

You and I and every single other person, we are all alone and, by the curse of God, we must face the total intensity of existence in that state. Not even the booze I pour into my body can dull it into anything approaching acceptability. There is a kind of ultimate frustration that hovers about me, that makes me reject so much yet does not provide me with the illusion of escape or the delusion of utopian possibility. There is just this incessant and inescapable Pascalian sadness, redolent of vast empty spaces in the universe, which reflects on the immensity of the world and in the infinity of our absurd realities.

It would be nice to capture and describe this insanity that has captured this futility and make it understandable to others. Sometimes I am motivated by a kind of revenge, as a way of exposing the preposterous joke that has been played upon us. Yet in a kind of ultimate irony, I am not foolish enough to take even my own confrontation (more likely my interpretation of the existential) with the world around me seriously. It is a product of my inherited pessimism (the Irish curse) and cynicism (my pseudo-intellectual pretensions). But if out of this maelstrom of contradictions an understanding might emerge which could touch others with an emotional impact, an interpretation of existence which makes no pretense of coincidence with the actual world but could possibly make a few people stop and think, then maybe I might be satisfied. That is the classic pipe dream, no? I am dominated by that kind of gnawing hunger, that loneliness, which leaves you directionless. All I have is a very intense suspicion that futility is programmed into our experience of what is little more than a cosmic tragedy we call life. In the end, no one, no one at all, ever gets to the pot of gold.

She put the letter down. It was clear, Eleni was not joining him. Had he asked her, by phone at least? Was this there only communication? Had she said no? If so, it must have felt like a total rejection to him. For a moment, she considered a mean thought: *Well, a just karma for him. He had abandoned her after all, which must have seemed like a rejection to her. Rachel knew well such rejection.* She pushed that thought aside as mean-spirited. His agony touched her. He sounded so desperate, so lost. He did have feelings, real feelings, like a human being would have. Now, she had a response to his earlier query, he was capable of being a complete man, at least he was back when these words were put to paper. She felt a shiver of pity course through her. Wow, he had proposed, and she had turned him down or not responded at all. Of course, that's why he had given her these letters. These were the parts of him he could not talk about openly. This was the only permissible avenue toward revelation.

A sad thought struck her. Had she rejected him? Perhaps that had broken him. Had this rejection forced him deeper into some shell where others could never reach him. She was not old enough to know him well before he disappeared from her existence. She had been too young to see him through adult eyes. Perhaps he was never as together as he had appeared, and this lost love had crushed him. It would be tragic if he had been a whole person and this lost love had amputated part of his soul. How might she figure out what had happened and come to know him again?

But where were her letters to him? Why had he saved these and not hers to him? How did he even get these since they looked like the originals, not copies? She examined them carefully, they had to be the originals. She shuffled through the contents of the folder. All she could find were letters to her. They looked original, old and worn. They obviously had been read and reread many times. Why would he have these and not whatever she had sent him? They obviously existed, the Dear Josh letter and one where she had written to him after that. She was sure there were more. One does not pour their heart out into a vacuum, or does one?

April 11, …
Dear Leni,

Aspirations such as graduate school, careers, things like that don't seem very important. My cynicism, my amorality, my lack of practical ambition have left me with a huge void that only suggests more drift. Find something else to take up next year and something else the year after that. And after you've successfully completed the prerequisite number of solar revolutions, you are permitted to withdraw in some complete sense. There doesn't seem to be any real place to go, and on top of that, it probably isn't worth getting there.

The overwhelming irrelevance of it all forces upon me an inescapable sense of ennui. Things seemed just a bit easier back in the days when the big sweat was a paper for class or some other some nonsense. Perhaps if it were not so conventional these days, I would retreat to some religious ashram in the Himalayas where I couldn't possibly be bothered by revolutions, war, sick societies, traffic jams, starvation, middle-class neuroticism, or four years back to Republican normalcy. Then again, I probably wouldn't like that very much either. The future is a void. Here, futility prevails, overwhelms me. The loneliness has taken something out of me.

I am tired, very tired.

She shifted through a few more letters that reflected similar themes and sentiments. Rachel could not quite envision the writer of these words. Her brother had always been light-hearted and upbeat, a crooked smile across his face. He was the handsome athlete that the neighborhood girls fantasized about and whom the guys wanted to emulate. He was the guy who made others laugh, brought cheer to any room he entered. In those years where she knew him best, it appeared he saw life as an adventure to be seized, opportunities laid out before him for the taking. But that was on the outside which, she ruefully admitted, could be mere illusion.

Rachel had always seen him during those years as a rock on which she would always be able to count. She remembered one time when she was in middle school and he in high school. Rachel realized she was developing physically, which would please most young girls but basically annoyed the hell out of her. Rather than wearing clothes designed to attract the opposite sex, she preferred loose-fitting ensembles dedicated to hiding her physical charms. It was to no avail; it was already apparent that she would be a beauty. Her soft yellow hair fell to her shoulders. She wanted to cut it short, but mother would not permit that. Her eyes were that inviting pale blue that tended to melt the insides of male onlookers and generate jealousy in her peers of the female persuasion. Her features were delicate and almost perfect in symmetry and proportion. When she looked in the mirror, she saw her mother. She was Ora in form, though remained unsure about substance. Her mother was careful never to reveal her substance nor her body. Ora was steel, a self-contained enigma. No one was permitted inside her mother's reality. No one could ever get close.

Who was she, Rachel pondered about her own identity? To her mind, Josh seemed the classic Irishman, genial and witty and a good storyteller. She, however, did not feel Irish, but what? She was reserved and private but could summon a biting wit when necessary. That skill was Irish for sure. Perhaps all that ancestral nonsense was silly, simply designed to foster intimacy among members of a clan where none existed. Yet, she could see attributes from each of their parents sprinkled in different proportions within each of them.

Wait, she thought excitedly. Maybe that was the key here. Could it be that Josh had taken some attributes from their mother? He looked, and talked, and conducted himself much like his dad, but maybe there were things he had taken from his mom. Perhaps there was a need inside him to keep others out, to bury a truer identity deep within and use the old misdirection ploy of humor and charm to deflect the curiosity of others. Perhaps, she thought to herself, no one would be permitted to see his true self, surely not his little sister. But what was worth hiding so fanatically? Perhaps there was no sin inside, no flaw that could not be revealed. Perhaps what he was hiding was vulnerability, an intense fear of being hurt once again, as this mysterious woman had done so many years ago. Perhaps this brash Irishman she had seen back then was illusion, the strong athlete a mirage. She suddenly saw him as a little boy, insecure and uncertain.

Her mind had wandered again. She returned to that awful period where her developing beauty drew the attention of young boys like bothersome pests. Perhaps the other girls found these attentions desirable, but she was unmoved. In fact, she was annoyed no end. They started following her home from school, trying to provoke a response with those nuisance tactics that insecure males fall back on when unsuccessful in the pursuit of the opposite sex. The more she ignored them, the more they escalated their annoying tactics. Eventually, they slid into their final assault, forms of verbal aggression designed to trigger a reaction when milder teasing failed. '*Rachel is a prick tease,*' they yelled, or '*a cock sucker.*' They would yell such insults aloud as if they were common knowledge shared by all. Everyone knew that she was '*doing it*' with an ever-changing array of lucky guys, names picked at random in truth.

Josh had found her crying in her room one day. It took him many strokes of her hair and a soothing voice to get her to tell him what was bothering her. Her story came out through deep sobs she could no longer contain. "I see," he had said several times. Inside, he had raged. Nothing touched him like seeing his sister in pain.

"There is nothing you can do," she wailed.

"We'll see, kiddo."

The next day, as she made her way home from school along familiar streets, the boys appeared as she feared. The routine started once again. Rachel had had enough. Rather than run away, she took one of her books and hurled it at a tormentor, who merely laughed. Immediately, she knew that was exactly what they wanted, her attention that could be secured in no other way. In her act of defiance, she admitted their existence … a huge error on her part. However, she had passed over some social threshold. She could no longer back away, perhaps there was a bit of Irish fury within her.

"Come closer. Yes, you with the tiny prick and I'll take that smile off your face." Her face was crimson, but she could not hold back the tears of rage that flowed down her face. Suddenly, they stopped laughing. Had she gotten to them? Wow, that was easy. Too easy. Then she realized that a larger presence had come up from behind her. The boys backed up, their faces frozen with concern and then fear. As they turned to flee, Josh ran past her and grabbed the biggest boy by the back of his jacket. There was no way that any of them could outrun the school's best athlete.

Josh's prey squirmed and pleaded to be let go. Fat chance of that happening. He dragged his victim to a nearby building and, picking him off his feet, slammed him against a brick wall. Rachel stood frozen with shock. For a moment, she panicked that her brother was going to kill this kid. His face was immobile in that visage she had seen only on game day.

"Listen, you little pussy," Josh said. "You get the word out to all your buddies. If anyone bothers my sister again, I will track them down. When I find them, and I will find them, I'll separate their shriveled balls and tiny pricks from their bodies and shove them up a place where it will take a team of surgeons a week to retrieve them. Do you understand?"

"Yeah," came back a quiet whine.

"I want to hear a *'yes, sir.'* I want to hear that loud and clear."

"Yes, sir." The whine was a bit louder.

"Not good enough, my patience is running out."

Now came a full-throated "yes sir, understood." That was loud enough to be heard by the boys who lingered well down the street waiting to see what might happen to their buddy.

"And you tell them that all I need to hear is that any one of you little shits came within a block of her and I'll get all of you, one after another. And I will enjoy every moment of it. Make no mistake about that. I will enjoy every fucking second of that." He stared at the boy for at least thirty seconds before dropping the young man to the sidewalk. He noticed a urine stain on the boy's crotch. As his victim scrambled to get away, he turned and took Rachel by the hand and walked her to his car.

Inside his car. He turned to her. "Remember this. You can always count on me. If you have any trouble with anyone, Come to me. Got that?"

He had been her rock then. What had Josh asked that first morning, something about a tendril? *Oh,* she murmured to herself, *a tendril is something that anchors a fragile flower to something solid. Of course.*

Somewhere and somehow, though, their tendril had snapped.

CHAPTER 13

Day 5 - Morning

Josh awoke to discover Morris missing once again. It was time for his morning walk, past time in fact. His faithful companion had always been there, a creature of habit. In a small panic, he swung out of bed and threw on some clothes. The mystery was solved as he walked into the living room. His not-so-faithful companion was curled up with Rachel on the couch. While papers from his private files were scattered about suggesting activity during the night, the two were fast asleep.

"Hey, Benedict Arnold," Josh whispered, "up and at 'em. I just want you to know, dog, that you can be replaced by a hamster at any time."

Morris lifted his head sleepily but still managed a wag of the tail. He rose, shook his body, and lazily jumped down to waddle over to his master. There he sat waiting for his leash and the initiation of the morning ritual. The commotion woke Rachel, who looked around with momentary confusion.

"What time is it?" she managed.

"It is noon, you overslept."

"What?" She bolted up. "Why didn't you wake me? Where's Cate?"

"Oh, she and Meena left hours ago. They said something about letting the old broad get her beauty sleep, that you really needed it."

Suspicion replaced confusion on Rachel's face. "Okay, what time is it really?"

"Early," he finished, putting the leash on his pug. "The sun is coming up though, and I assume the girls did not escape during the night. On the other hand, you know the younger set. They might well have snuck out for a Stones concert if Mick and the others are still alive. Are they?"

"How would I know." Rachel was yet sleepy enough to be irritated by her sibling's jocularity.

"Of course, they could be sleeping in until the drugs wear off. Kids today … sex, drugs, and rock and roll. No work ethic like we had."

"Like I had," she corrected him. He threw that crooked smile at her, and she instinctively smiled back. *Damn it*, she said only to herself. *He is so freaking charming*. In a loud voice, she stopped him as he reached the door. "One question. I fell asleep before getting through this stuff…" She swung her arms out to indicate the papers about her. "I only found letters from you to Eleni. She wrote back, she must have. Where are they?"

"Long gone."

"Gone? Where?"

Josh paused for several moments. "I threw them out a long time ago."

"But you have all the one's you sent her?" It was more of a question than a statement.

"She kept everything. I guess women are like that. Anyway, she sent me everything she had before …" He did not finish, turning and heading out the door with Morris.

Rachel momentarily considered running after him but caught herself. No need to look desperate by running half naked into the street. She did not want to be mistaken by his neighbors for one of his 'professional service workers,' as if any reputable agency would send someone of her age. Rather, she turned to the papers in front of her. She rustled through them some more. There were notes as far back as college, short messages of no significance. She had kept everything to do with him, but he had thrown away all her communications. What was with that? Is the difference due to gender, to different levels of affection, to something else? All men are jerks, that had always been a satisfying explanation for virtually every stupid thing they did and said, at least among her female peers. Well, those conjectures would have to wait. Then a note caught her eye. It struck her as different, less a letter than a short story. Curious, she picked it from the pile.

Dear Leni,

My mind's eye turns to you all the time. This sunset this evening moved me. There is something special about those quiet moments when the brilliant orb shades to orange and red before touching the horizon. At such times, I'm drawn to what might have been, toward moments beyond reach but still within our apprehension. Of course, that is the same as saying that I'm drawn to the possibility of us.

I think of the Cape often. I cannot push away that first morning together, just about our only morning together, when the breeze pushed the curtains and the sun fought its way into our room. I can yet feel the texture of your body against mine. There was something special about realizing that the closeness was a new experience for you, that you were saying by your actions that you found me special. You never said the words, but I knew at those moments you loved me. And for the first time in my life, that realization did not scare me to death. I welcomed it. I will forever hate myself for not saying the words that were in my heart that morning.

Now, we can only capture those moments in our imaginations. I have a friend from India. He told me about a special place on the West Coast and had lots of pictures. It was a place he loved in his younger days when he dabbled in a free, hippie lifestyle for a bit. It was a place called Goa, the old Portuguese colony until the Indian government kicked them out not that long ago. The culture is more Western than the rest of the subcontinent, and when he was there, the beaches were undeveloped. It was paradise. The sand was pure, the palm trees curved in response to the gentle breezes, the waters were azure blue reflecting the cloudless skies. Usually, only the local fishermen worked the beach. He said the evenings were magic, the sun would dip its magic into the Indian Ocean with splendor and majesty. In one picture was a small chapel, built into the sand not far from the water but nestled in a few palms.

I've never forgotten his words about the place. You could get lobster dinners for next to nothing and eat dinner at a small restaurant located a few feet from the surf. So many times, I have envisioned us being there, together. We would watch the sun expire in all that boisterous color before dining under the stars as the surf roared nearby. Then we would walk along the shore, hand in hand, talking about a future together or just the nonsense of the day. I never tired of exchanging nothings with you. Your long black hair would twirl around your face in the warm, wet sea breezes. On occasion, you would look up at me with those doe-like eyes, and my heart would melt just a bit more if that were humanly possible.

Eventually, we would find a quiet place near the beach where the world was all ours. The only witnesses would be the canopy of stars above us. We would disrobe and lie next to each other, your body seeking mine as it did that night on the Cape. I would feel small tremors of anticipation as you surrendered any remaining resistance. As I rose over your prone figure, I realized the depth of my own needs, my brain struck dumb with desire and my flesh fired with compelling passion. With effort, I would suppress those most essential impulses, seeking a gentle path to where we both wanted to be.

Rachel put the letter down. Should she be reading this? It seemed too personal to her, as if she were a voyeur into a private tryst. Part of her scolded her conscience to put it back. But he had given her the file. He must have known the contents. But maybe not; he struck her as so disorganized that she wondered how he had managed to survive adulthood, get tenure, and achieve some professional notoriety. But that was too harsh, she eventually concluded. Einstein was disorganized, or so she imagined. No, he wanted her to read about his inner life. This was his way of reaching out. She could read or not as she wished. He would not force himself on her. If she did continue, she would choose to embrace his world. If not, they would continue as if nothing had changed. After a pause, she picked up the note once again.

You looked deeply into my eyes as I leaned over you. I thought I sensed your lips trembling but that must have been my imagination. I would start by kissing your forehead and then your nose and cheeks and then your soft, accepting lips. Each touch would be gentle, exploring, as if I were mapping your body to store in my head for a long absence, perhaps anticipating that I might never see you again. Eventually I would move on to your ears, which always would generate a giggle and a squirm from you before moving down your long neck. Here, my tongue would reach out to sense the surface or your skin and taste the tangy sheen of salt from the sea air.

Your shoulders and chest inexorably led to your breasts where my mouth and tongue elicited a spontaneous gasp from you. I cupped them in my hands as I played with your nipples, my tongue flicking across them lightly, then running small circles in ways that fired your senses. Involuntary gasps continued as you grabbed my head and hair. I sensed you guiding me down your body and obeyed. My mouth slowly found my way along the length of your stomach and hips until they located your inner thighs. Now the gasps were frequent and more pronounced. I was close, so close to where you wanted me, but I tarried longer until I thought I heard one tiny word, "please."

I navigated my mouth to that place between your legs where nerves fire with uncontrolled savagery. Now I felt increasing urgency as my mouth frantically sought out your clitoris and the surrounding tissue and flesh. Your whole body was now squirming and tremoring, the gasps becoming audible groans. I wanted to stay there forever, pleasuring you, but I could hear above the roar of my own brain the word "now, now please." And so, I raised up and thrust myself slowly into you. Your whole pelvis arched in acceptance and need. It is always difficult to recall the acts of completion. The rhythm of our bodies being one moved from slow appreciation to frantic need and back again, several times. Eventually, we found a rhythm that matched the pounding surf nearby.

Later, we cuddled as we often did, with bodies spent by the ultimate expression of intimacy. Your body would be intertwined with mine so that I could imagine our separate identities merging. It would not be you and I but us. We could look up through the swaying palms to the moon and stars above, wondering what the sky would look like if we were back near Provincetown among the dunes. Would we notice any differences? But what would it matter, we would be together?

With all my love,

Josh

She stared at the letter for some time. *This could not possibly be her brother.* How many times had she uttered this phrase silently over the past 24 hours? She had never seen him express much passion in his life, at least not for the opposite sex. Oh, she was certain he would make efforts to satisfy his momentary lust, as do all men, but little beyond that. That's how it seemed to her.

Why did she think that? He had had plenty of women; they had always flocked to him. And, if he was to be believed, he had purchased the services of many others, even though she remained unconvinced of that. Perhaps he had been pulling her leg about using escort services. He had never lacked the opportunity for physical release. But that was not the same as emotional intimacy. Every woman knew that though she was not sure what men understood. Men struck Rachel as being woefully dense and irretrievably shallow. Why did women bother with them? A mystery for sure. Then it struck her. He had been honest with her. His professionals were a way of obtaining what was necessary without any emotional baggage. He was just a typical male … a conclusion that saddened her.

A disturbing thought struck her. Nowhere else had he ever intimated love in his life. Perhaps this was it—he had confessed as much at least obliquely. But if the only intimate congress between he and Eleni was in these written testimonies, that would be sad indeed. He had left Eleni when he had abandoned the family and his life in the States. He had abandoned everyone, even this woman he obviously loved. That reassured her in some odd way. Knowing how much he had loved this woman, there must have been compelling reasons for his actions. Maybe it was not a whim, merely avoiding the inconvenience of the military draft, the search for new adventures, escaping his family battles, or becoming bored with an ordinary life. She had imagined all kinds of reasons for his behavior back when he had broken her heart. Maybe, just maybe, there was something deeper that could justify his callousness. She now knew that he had sacrificed … everything.

She selected some letters from adjacent areas in the pile. She glanced at a few before selecting one that talked about him and Eleni spending time in various parts of Europe. There was Prague, and Barcelona, Salzburg, and Dubrovnik. For each such destination, he would describe what they would do in each place, depicting streets of charm and history as well as locations that should never be missed. He talked about each in an intimate way as if he were using the written word to share what was most special to him. She read the Dubrovnik description with care. In luxurious language, he described looking down at this Yugoslavian gem, the red roof tiles of the ancient walled community set against the pale blue Adriatic Sea. His writing captured the charm from before the Balkan Civil War when most of this priceless site had been senselessly shelled. Rachel could almost feel what he was describing. He was even more enthusiastic about a small seaside village, which he called Primostin in the letter. This ancient walled town, little more than a village, was situated on a hill that rose out of the water, connected to the land by a narrow bridge of sand and rock. From the shore, the outline of the village was pasted against the sunset's amber hues. It sounded magical.

In another, there were long drives through Ireland, Scotland, Wales, and along the Adriatic Sea. These were destinations of beauty, charm, and historical significance. Again, he wove personal narratives that were his best attempts to share a virtual reality with this person he had loved so passionately. He had been to Europe many times, often in lieu of trips to the States, which he had avoided out of caution, justified or not. *That must have hampered his career*, she mused. But why was he writing to this woman he loved about such adventures rather than sharing them with her first-hand? These letters were written long after the notes exploring his angst and despair, and after he had been to all these places. There was no way he could have spoken about them with such undeniable authenticity had they not been rooted in personal experience. Rachel concluded that he must have been in contact with her over a long period of time, even to recent times. The questions mounted within her.

She thought she heard sounds from downstairs. The thought crossed Rachel's mind that Cate and Meena were having noisy sex as her brother had joked about. She wondered if Josh had earplugs, which she would borrow. Listening to her daughter would be like listening to her parents, which fortunately did not happen often, a fact that made her thankful. But the noises were probably just the sounds of them getting ready for the day. She jumped up, wanting to be ready when they emerged from downstairs. At the same time, she wanted to spend more time with Josh's letters and notes. She scooped up all the material and deposited them in her bedroom. Then she slipped on some clothes and moved to the kitchen to make coffee.

Cate and Meena soon emerged from the lower level. They looked refreshed and more relaxed than the day before.

"Morning, Mom." Cate kissed Rachel on the cheek.

Rachel looked over at Meena, who seemed uncertain about what she should do. Rachel walked to her and kissed her on the cheek. "Good morning, Meena, hope you slept well."

"Just great," she replied with a broad, infectious smile. "A lot better than the night before."

Josh came through the door with Morris, who stopped as if he were surprised once again by the presence of others in his domain. But the dog recovered quickly and waddled over to his food bowl, which he found full, thanks to Rachel. Josh, on the other hand, wandered over to Cate and Meena to kiss them on their cheeks and wish them a fine day.

Cate laughed. "What is going on, affection among the Connelly clan? Someone call 911, at least the EMTs. I think this is late breaking news with film at 11."

"Sarcasm, my dear," Josh said with a smile, "will not get you a free breakfast."

"Thank God! I do remember my uncle's morning culinary offerings. We are spared, Meena." Before Josh could respond, Cate turned serious. "By the way, everyone, I am legally changing my name."

"To what?" Josh asked and then realized the likely answer.

"To Connelly, of course. I want nothing more to do with the Ballentine clan, nothing. This is my family, right here, the two of you, and Meena of course."

Rachel and Josh looked at each other. "Okay," Josh replied, "but remember that there are many horse thieves and miscreants among the branches on our family tree, such as it is."

Cate laughed and looked directly at Josh. "Oh, I think that the biggest family miscreant is in this room, the lug standing by the stove, which I doubt he knows how to use." Then Cate noticed a slight change in Josh's face and went silent.

"Okay," he said, "I have to hide in my office now to work on some brilliant comments for this afternoon. You will all be there, right, when they say all those lies about me and give me a gold watch or whatever. My gift watch will probably have a cute image of Mickey Mouse on it."

"And that would still be more than you deserve." Cate beamed. "I would not miss this for the world. Why did you think I came all this way?"

Rachel followed Josh into his office. She wanted to catch him outside of Cate and Meena's presence. "Listen, you can enlighten me on one thing."

"Rachel, you underestimate me. I'm sure I can enlighten you on so much. You're merely a technician of the body while I am an observer of God's wonders."

"Yes, yes, we all know you're a genius." She was not to be put off by his transparent deflection. "These notes and letters you gave me. I can't quite figure out what's going on."

"Really, my tortured soul eludes you?"

For a moment, she considered slapping the crooked smile off his face. "A lot of these were from your first year or so in Canada. But some of these messages look as if they covered a long-time period, after you had an opportunity to travel the world. A number strike me as quite recent given some events covered. I'm confused about the timeline of everything."

He leaned back in his chair, looking at her. She had her game face on, he could see that. She would not be dissuaded by a cute quip. "The first reality is that she would not join me in my exile in Canada. I'm not sure I even asked her outright."

Rachel protested. "But you asked her to marry you."

"True," he uttered the word slowly, "but it was a rather pathetic proposal. You read it. I wanted her, true enough. At the same time, I was desperately afraid she might want me back. Does that make sense?"

"Yes … maybe … hell, no!"

"I wrote these letters, but I never went back and looked in her eyes. I never asked her up in a way that she might come and join me, or even visit me. I always had excuses in the moment. At the time, maybe I wanted her to turn me down. But that was hard since everything inside me wanted her. But if she had joined me, that would have been worse."

"You were a mess, weren't you?"

"You think? Let's face it, forgetting me was the best thing she could do. That was my gift to her, making sure she said no even though I communicated my love. Then she married someone else. I died inside but I was relieved. I thought it was over. Best of all, it seemed to be her decision. In a fit of relief, or maybe it was grief, I destroyed all her letters to me. Then, for the next three decades, I thought of no one except her, despite all else. I have kicked myself for my cowardice every day."

"But the descriptions of Goa, and Dubrovnik, and Scotland, and all those other places."

"Oh yeah, easy enough to explain. Several years ago, after a decades-long gap, I found her on Facebook. Wonderful tool it is, except for the fact that they occasionally throw me in their jail. Their so-called community standards program is the epitome of incompetence."

"To the point, dear brother."

"Of course, I remember agonizing over sending a message to her after all that time. It was like asking her out on our first date. But I did, a kind of *do you remember me and how is life treating you* message. I wasn't sure she would respond. She did, immediately, and we were bonded as we had been back in the 60s. It was as if nothing had happened in between, as if our last interaction occurred the day before."

"Let me cut to the chase here," Rachel inserted.

"You always were a no-nonsense gal."

"Why isn't she here? Why aren't the two of you together? Damn it, I've never seen you want a woman ever, not like this. The stuff you've shared, and how you've shared it, seems more designed to drive me nuts than help me understand. I just don't understand. I want to, but … I wonder if you're playing games, teasing me."

Josh winced a bit. "I really should work on my communication skills."

Rachel scowled. "You know what? Stop being childish here. Just tell me."

Josh's eyes widened a bit. "Wow, you have become the big sister here, a parent. You make a good one by the way … a good parent."

"Flattery will get you nowhere, buster." She was not smiling.

"Listen, I wasn't sure you would be interested in all this. We've been apart for so long. I suppose I started giving you these things as if they were breadcrumbs. If you followed them, I would give you more. It would mean you cared."

"I care, nimrod, get it. I have always cared. I cared when you were part of my life, I cared when you disappeared. Okay, then I was pissed, but I cared. I cared all those years when we passed each other as if we were no more than casual friends. I always cared. Every day of my goddamn life I cared. I may not always have shown it, but I cared with every fiber of my being. Just how many brothers do you think I have?

Besides Cate, you're it for the people I care about." She caught herself, fearing her rising voice would carry.

He looked in her eyes before turning once again to the deep archeological site composed of detritus that captured important moments of his life. After some brief digging, he pulled out another file. "Look at some of these. Then we will talk. But not now, okay? Later … please."

Rachel took the folder and, without another word, exited his office. *In his own good time*, she murmured to herself. An hour later, Josh made his goodbyes and left the house. As he backed out of the driveway, another car pulled up in front in front of his place. It was Usha, arriving to help Cate and Meena as promised. He jumped out to greet her.

"You have arrived to save the day, I suspect," he said as he gave her a big hug. It once again surprised him that his body responded to her touch. He made a mental note to call one of his professional women after all this was over. It had been a while, too long in fact. Still, he had to admit that her body had always been attractive. She had always been slim and shapely, which sometimes posed a problem when they were nominally married. They slept in separate rooms, but there were times when his needs and the sight of her alluring body presented him with a temptation that he worked damn hard not to act upon. On occasion, though, she must have guessed his desires and would take him by the hand to her bedroom. *'You don't have to do this,'* he would protest. *'I know,'* she would respond, *'but some of this is quite nice, actually.'* He was never totally sure which part she was talking about or whether she really was thanking him for providing cover to her lifestyle. No matter, he was grateful. Often enough, one or the other wanted human contact during the night. They would share a bed for the sake of intimacy, simple human touch, as opposed to sex.

"Saving the day is what I do best," she responded when the hug was over. "However, I'm glad I ran into you."

"Funny, that's what all the girls say." She gave the briefest smile to his witticism. If she had any shortcoming, she was not totally comfortable with the easy exchange of insults. Her proper Indian upbringing gave her a somewhat more formal approach to things. He looked her over. "You are striking today, even wearing some casual though very chic Indian attire. Anything special planned?"

She was wearing a colorful form-fitting outfit with white leggings that were far more comfortable than a sari, the more traditional formal attire she had long retired from her wardrobe. "One of my favorite people is retiring today." She smiled.

"Do I know him?" Josh deadpanned.

Usha ignored him. "Seriously, I have a question, so shush." But then she paused, looking uncertain.

"And that is?"

"Oh, this is difficult." She paused once more.

"Ah, we have seen each other naked. What can't we talk about?"

"For me," she said, "that makes it more difficult."

"Usha, it is just me. You can be open. You know how much I care for you."

"Here goes," she said with more conviction. "I want to ask you about Rachel. What is her ... sexual preference?" She started talking faster. "I mean, from what I know, she hasn't had any male attachments since her marriage. So, I was just wondering. She seems so nice, like you. Oh God, what did I just say? She's much nicer than you."

"You are rattled. And there is absolutely no doubt about her being better than me. But let me get this right, you want to hit on my sister." Josh had a devilish smile on his face, but inside, his mind was racing. "Is that where you are going with this?"

"Oh please, don't make this more difficult than it is."

"I'm sorry, Ush, really. That damn wit, you can't take out what God has put in, as the saying goes. But the reality is, I don't know. I really don't and I'm ashamed about that. Rach and I were so close as kids. Siblings usually fight and we did tease each other, but we were darn close. And now, I'm finally getting to know her as an adult. Scary, but nice I think. However, there's so much I don't know about her."

"Perhaps I should not even consider ..."

"No, don't go there, that's the easy out." He paused to consider his next words. "Listen, I had my suspicions about Cate for a long time. About my own sister … nothing. Yet, that possibility now hits me as distinctly possible. Go for it."

"Oh … I don't know."

Josh's mind was slowing to a conclusion. "Ush, you're lonely, I can tell. You need to be with another person."

"Everyone does, except you apparently."

Josh considered this and could not disagree. "You want my advice. Well, it does not matter since I'm giving it no matter what. Go for it! All she can say is that she is not interested. But if she is, you just may be the answer to a question she probably has not permitted herself to ask."

"Are you sure?" She remained uncertain.

"No, I'm not. But I am very, very certain that she needs someone in life. No man has ever made the cut. I was supposed to be that someone, at least a long time ago. Talk about counting on the wrong horse." Josh then turned serious.

"I'm not talking about a good friend or close family member. I'm talking about … you know?"

"Yes, Ush, I know. What I can share is this. She's not like me. She is tough and independent, but I sense she wants someone in her life. She hasn't said so as such, but I get the feeling that she has done everything professionally that she wanted to do. My best guess, and it is just a guess, is that she's looking ahead and sees a lonely future, especially now that Cate has found someone. She had no love in her marriage. This time around, she wants to connect with someone who will love her. Will you love her?"

"It is a thought …" And with that, Usha continued into the house.

———

An hour later, Josh was hiding in his university office when he heard an insistent knock on the door.

"I'm not here," he tried.

"Josh, it is Ellison."

Josh grimaced. "Do you know the password?"

The door opened, and in walked a tall man with a distinctly avuncular air and a slightly British accent. Josh wondered why everyone around here seemed to have that accent. His father would have been outraged at that fact.

"Oh, I will miss your humor, Professor Connelly."

"And I'll miss one of my favorite targets, Dr. Howard."

"But I hope not totally, which brings me to my request," the tall man added, then cleared his throat. "I am hoping we can keep you a part of our happy family on a part-time basis, just a little teaching and stuff."

"And stuff?"

At that moment, the door opened again and in walked Connie Chen. "Oh sorry, I was hoping to catch Josh, but I can come back."

"No," Josh almost yelled with a hint of desperation. "Stay, this won't be long."

Ellison Howard continued, now with a slightly annoyed look. "Yes. We might need someone to teach both the policy and the evaluation courses next fall."

"I'll do one—the policy course."

"Can I—"

"No, Ellison, you cannot. The policy course is fun, usually interesting students or perhaps it is more accurate to say students in which I am interested. That, my dear friend, is the only reason I will do it. And what's with the younger faculty, don't any of them want to teach anymore?"

The tall man cleared his throat. "Let me suggest one other contribution you might make, and don't turn me down until you hear me out. I want to start a thorough review of the department, a kind of strategic-planning exercise. We are juggling several degree programs, a community outreach effort, and a full research agenda. And we're doing this with increasingly limited resources. I need someone to guide us through an exercise that will engender enormous uncertainty and, how shall I put it ..."

"Turf protection and interminable whining. I know the drill, you can change anything you want except what I do, which is anointed by God and cannot be touched."

"See," Ellison said with a broad smile. "You understand the character of the challenge right off. As an emeritus, you will be viewed as neutral. You won't be perceived as having a personal oar in the water as they say. Besides, everyone likes you. You have a way with people, even those you insult all the time."

"That's only because I'm an equal-opportunity insulter."

"Nevertheless," Ellison tried to retake command, "I need you; We need you. We should have done this years ago. Can I impose upon you to take up this challenge?"

"I will think on it, Ellison."

"Josh, what can I do to—"

"I'll think on it, Ellison," Josh raised his voice slightly for emphasis. "Now I would like to spend a few minutes with this young and lovely colleague, well, maybe not so young anymore but still not bad looking."

"Yes, of course." The distinguished man arose. "I will be in touch."

After he left, Josh started to say, "I bet you will." He never finished as he was distracted by a pen whistling past his head. "Hey, what was that for?"

"Not so young anymore, not looking bad. As if you would still have a shot."

Josh looked over at her. She was also dressed up for his event, wearing a real skirt that revealed a pair of very good-looking legs. Josh again made a mental note to look up the number of the escort service. It really had been too long. "Cut me some slack, okay. I did admit that you were not bad for a broad so long in the tooth, or is it teeth? Where does that come from, by the way? It is how they check the age of horses, no?" Another missile passed over his head.

"I really have to practice my aim." She smiled. "I am curious. Are you going to help poor Ellison out with his strategic-planning thing? They are pure misery."

"Oh, of course I will. I just want to make him squirm a bit. I still have some concern for the flock. I cannot imagine leaving them to his inept ministrations. World War III would erupt. Anyway, what brings you to my lair? Most women only enter my cave with an escort or a can of mace. Should I check your body for cans of pepper spray, or maybe a hidden camera to catch a chauvinist pig in the act? Perhaps a strip search is in order."

"That is so bogus, everyone knows you're totally harmless, though a pig to be sure. But I have wanted to catch up since the party the other night. And, in the interests of full disclosure, I did phone Rachel to get the lowdown on you."

"Hmmm, this does not sound good. Have you forgotten the old rule, never ask the aggrieved sibling? Besides, she doesn't know that much."

Connie shifted in her seat. "She knows enough and cares a lot more. She loves you, Josh."

"I-I ..."

Connie bailed him out. "But you know that. Not even you can miss something that obvious. She wants to be your sister again. Do you understand that? She is trying."

"I'm getting there, quickly in fact." He decided to avoid humor which he knew would elicit a missile aimed at his head. "It takes me a while."

"Well, don't take forever, none of us is a spring chicken any longer. In fact, biologically, you could be my father if you had reached puberty exceedingly early."

"You mean as a toddler." He interjected.

"Hah," Connie exclaimed triumphantly. "I'm just pointing out that if you leave things unsaid now, they may never get said. That would be a tragedy." Connie paused to decide on her next words. "I ... I like you a lot, but I also know you better than most. Beneath the jokes and light banter, in that quick and agile mind lies a very lonely and searching heart."

"Come on, Connie, my shrink, my butcher, and my favorite bartender have seen far worse. I'm not a tortured soul, just a pathetic putz."

"Don't, asshole," she barked. "You cannot charm me, well, not often at least. While I might concede that you're not exactly tortured, and only mildly pathetic, you are infuriating beyond measure. There is no question on that score. I can see it all now. You will be that destitute guy shuffling aimlessly around campus with his fly open with people wondering about that derelict who looks vaguely familiar. Wasn't he someone important at the university once upon a time?"

He paused and looked at her without mirth or artifice. "You have always been my closest friend. I … I … I've wanted to thank you."

"And don't go maudlin on me." She said this with a softer voice.

"Wow, kiddo, you're not leaving me much wiggle room. Going straight for the jugular. Besides, I wasn't going maudlin. I was about to ask a favor … whether or not you would zip up my fly."

"What?"

"You know," he smiled, "when I'm wandering around the campus with the front door open, so to speak."

Now she smiled. "Wooo, I came this close to losing it moments ago, but you have this thing you do."

"It's called charm."

"No, it's called bullshit," then she laughed aloud. "Josh, I have no idea why I like you so much. You do bring out my Chinese temper, and the Chinese don't even have one. I must have learned about this temper thing from the Irish master though in all honesty, I can't say I saw it much. Just the opposite. You were … passive. I remember trying to rile you up on occasion. All I got was that crooked smile … exasperating."

"Well, I'm half Russian or Lithuanian or Finnish or something we are not sure about, maybe that dilutes my Irish blood. I just look like a roguish, romantic lad of the Emerald Isle." Then he cut off the witticism that was sure to come from her. "Hey, by the way, when are you getting married to that physics guy, what's-his-name again. Hope I am invited, I always cry at weddings … such sad events."

Connie leaned forward. "Still can't remember his name?"

"I always wanted to call him Mr. Pencil Neck. It is just that he always walked around with a slide rule inserted up his …"

"Stop it … you are so mean. Harold is a nice man. He treated me very well."

"Oh Connie, his personality could stop a watch."

"Be nice," she shook a fist at him, "he was just a bit conventional."

"And the wedding?" Josh ignored the opportunity for another witticism. "Wait, are you using the past tense?"

"Yeah, good catch."

"Which means?" he asked even though he guessed the answer.

"No wedding, it is over." And during the pause where Josh absorbed her news, she added, "Slide rule? Just how ancient are you?"

"No wedding," he echoed with a serious expression reaching out to take her hand. "I'm really not sure how to respond. What happened?"

Connie shrugged. "After the dinner the other night, and a chat with your sister, I accepted something that has been there all along."

"Oh god, you talked with my sister. Bad move."

"Just listen, damnit! I think I just wanted someone to be with. Harold seemed okay. But in truth, he isn't. It was time to accept that. I also need laughter and stimulation, and not just sex you pervert. I hate to admit this, but women love men with senses of humor. It is sexy. And don't say anything stupid like that makes you a stud. There is a huge difference between being funny and being the joke itself."

"I said nothing, nothing."

"But you do understand, don't you?" Connie's lip trembled a bit. "No need to settle. I need more than a body on the other side of the bed."

"Connie, I understand more than you realize."

"I know, Josh. I was not whistling Dixie when I said you might be about the loneliest guy I know. You're surrounded by admirers, colleagues, students, female adorers, and I bet you do not have a single friend. Not one. I'm talking about a good close friend, someone to share stuff with and confide in, other than that ugly mutt of yours. Maybe you even want someone on the other side of that bed and the paid service workers don't count."

"Well, they should, given what they cost."

"You don't have a single one, do you?" Connie remained resolute. "Am I wrong? Am I?"

Josh sighed. "Yes, you're wrong."

"Okay then, I want names, names." She tried to sound light but clearly was not.

"You nailed it … Morris?"

"How about one that can respond with more than a growl." Now, irritation surfaced.

"Okay then…you. You are my friend." Josh didn't smile, then adding more as she remained silent. "I hope you know that."

Connie sat there, immobile. Josh still held her hand and slowly got to his feet. She followed tentatively. With measured motion, he inclined his lips toward hers until they touched. She murmured what sounded like a faint protest but yielded immediately. There was a noise at the door as they jumped back and laughed.

"Just like kids kissing in the school corridor," he whispered to her.

She continued to laugh. It felt good to her. She wanted more laughter and more touching.

"Where is the man of the hour," came from the other side of the door. "Your adoring fans are getting quite restless."

"The man of the hour has gone over the border with a sexy bio-chemist."

"Shut your mouth." Connie whispered. "Are you trying to ruin my reputation."

"Oh my dear, that will only enhance your reputation."

"In your delusional dreams," she shot back as she threw the door open to several people gathered outside while exclaiming in a loud voice. "For what it is worth, I give you the man of the hour."

Several colleagues gathered outside his door broke into a hearty cheer. Josh groaned inside. He faced social events and public responsibilities with a bit of dread even as he knew he was good at these things. He could schmooze with the best of them, run meetings well by involving everyone, and by using humor at the right moments. His ability to deliver an entertaining and provocative talk was well-known. On social occasions, he seemed to pitch his interactions at the right level, relaxing others and even mesmerizing them with his vignettes and dry wit. Yet he inevitably approached these expectations with some dread, having to pump himself up for the effort. From discussions with others, he had concluded that there were two kinds of people. The first were like him. They would have to psych themselves up and then expend energy during their public exposure. The trick was to have enough stored up in advance. The second type tended to accumulate additional energy during social and public events. They embraced what was being given off by others in their orbit. Somehow, Josh had managed to be a very public person with a very private core. He would have to think on how he pulled that off one of these days.

Okay, Josh said to himself, *it is showtime.*

CHAPTER 14

Day 5 – RETIREMENT SURPRISE

A large gathering had convened in the social sciences conference room. It was a perfect venue for special events, and Josh could not think of any event more special than his retirement. The room was expansive and adorned by pictures of selected academic luminaries from the past. Perhaps he will hang there one day, though he doubted that. If he were to be so honored, he could be ignored by visitors more attracted to the scene of the water and mountains visible outside the large windows rather than portraits of stodgy scholars few now recalled.

He slowly worked the room, shaking hands and exchanging *bon mots* with peers, acquaintances, students, and assorted others whom he suspected had wandered in mostly for the free food. The biggest challenge involved thinking up clever responses to the inevitable question about what was next in his life. He could not believe how many accepted his line that he was about to embark on a climb of Mount McKinley, or Denali if you prefer, as a start to conquering the highest point on each continent. Most nodded admiringly at his alleged plans unless they knew him well enough to detect the absurdity of this claim. Did they not know that he could not get across the suspension bridge north of the city? His vertigo was too bad even for that modest challenge. But most would respond with wide-eyed admiration while sharing words of encouragement.

Eventually, he made his way to a platform that elevated the university dignitaries and others chosen to say a few words. Someone tapped the microphone and called the room to attention. A roomful of eyes looked expectantly toward the dais.

"Let's get started here. The sooner we start, the sooner we can finish and reassign Professor Connelly's parking space." It was an old joke but never failed to elicit a laugh. The standard line about university faculty is that they are a bunch of independent academic entrepreneurs held together by disputes over office location and parking spaces. In Josh's view, this ancient aphorism was all too true. In the academic world, at this level, you pretty much had freedom to do what you wanted, at least if you could raise the money to finance it. It was not paradise, though. One downside was that very smart people too easily became entrapped in trivial departmental disputes about comparatively small matters. Should the next recruit be another positivist, or should they look outside the box and seek an ethnographer for methodological balance? Should they approach the administration for another faculty position or more research money? How should pitiful amounts of flexible resources be allocated among departmental priorities? The debates on such issues could rage for weeks or months or even years. When considering additions to their individual departments, perhaps they should follow the strategy of many sports teams. Just select the best talent available whatever their methodological preferences. But that would deprive the combatants of hours of faculty meeting conflict and hallway intrigue. Josh was popular because he typically rose above such petty arguments. He put them in perspective and could sort out and differentiate the important from the tangential. It helped that he was in the academy but not of the academy.

The master of ceremonies spoke into a microphone. "This is an auspicious occasion, the retirement of one of our most beloved colleagues. Before we begin, I want to announce that he has graciously relinquished his prized parking spot, a perk of having emeritus status that he is giving up since he lives within walking distance. The winner of the lottery for this spot will be announced at the end of the festivities. And yes, you must be present to claim the prize." Chuckles and a groan went up from those assembled. "However, without further ado, I want to introduce our distinguished Provost who will make a few introductory remarks."

It was starting, where were Rachel and the others, he wondered. Josh looked out over the crowd and sighed with relief when he spotted the group together toward the back of the crowd … Rachel, Cate, Meena, Usha, and Connie. Oh, there was Peter Favulli. He had made it. He was looking even more successful than he recalled from their last interaction. Peter was occupied in a side conversation with a couple he did not recognize … a mostly bald man, slightly stooped, wearing rimless glasses, and looking very much like a retired accountant stood next to a woman with short, curly gray hair and wearing a stylish pantsuit. It was obvious that they all were together, but who the hell were these two unknowns? He pressed his memory to no avail even as a sense of recognition lurked just beyond his immediate grasp.

He pushed his confusion aside when a short, somewhat portly, Asian man stepped to the microphone. "For me, this is a sad occasion. We're losing a valued member of our university family, Professor Jeremiah Joshua Connelly." Josh could see looks of surprise on the faces out in the audience. Few knew his real name; he was Josh to everyone. "When I first came to this wonderful institution from Hong Kong a dozen years ago, I soon heard one name over and over, Joshua Connelly. His reputation as a scholar was secure. His skills at negotiating academic politics were legendary, however, along with his public service work in various wider political arenas. I personally asked him several times to move up the administrative ladder to no avail. He was too committed to his students, his research, and his consulting work."

Josh faded out. It was agony for him to listen to people comment on his so-called gifts and contributions. His view of himself bore little relationship to the glowing terms in which he would be described that day. Who was this guy they were talking about? Inside, he always felt like the impostor. When he was presenting an academic paper before his peers or consulting with top government officials in Ottawa, he always kept looking around for the adults to enter the room. They were sure to be lurking about, waiting to pounce and eject him from the proceedings. *'Son, you will have to leave. We only allow adults here. Playtime is over.'* But that never happened. They never burst in to rectify this colossal error. After all this time, he could not believe that they still listened to him as if he really knew something. Even after years of apparent success, he would pause amidst a public talk, a serious discussion with government officials, or even a typical lecture as he was overcome with doubt. *Was he really making sense*, he would ask himself? *Isn't this total drivel*, his internal muse would say. Apparently, if history was to be believed, it never was.

The Provost was still talking. "On those occasions when I required incisive input regarding delicate matters, whether retention packages or the inter-disciplinary collaborative initiative, or recruitment efforts, Joshua was always willing to help out. He was a critical go-to guy. Therefore, let me extend the best wishes of the administration and personally wish you well in your future endeavors which, as I just heard, will involve mountain climbing." A trickle of giggles rippled through the audience as Josh suppressed a smile. Undeterred, the provost proceeded to end with a rhetorical flourish.

Next came a junior faculty member who had recently been voted tenure. She praised Josh as a wise mentor who guided her through the tenure perils with patience and kindness. How nice of her to lie about him like this, Josh thought. She had needed no mentoring. She would have achieved tenure on her own without any assistance from him. Her empirical skills were stronger than his for one thing. He did consider the possibility that his success in the academic world probably was a great comfort to her. *If this klutz could make it*, then she had to believe that she would experience little difficulty. That insight could only boost her confidence, Josh concluded. Yes, that was his contribution to her; he calmed her down when she became overanxious about her prospects.

Then a student was called on to make a few comments. Josh listened at this point. He was a minority student who had done his undergraduate work here and now was in the graduate program. He had taken several courses from him, and Josh had overseen his senior thesis. Josh recalled how that he had divided the disorganized rabble of so-called students into three groups for the service classes at least, those involving larger numbers of students. There were those who sat in the back of the classroom reading the student newspaper, texting, or dozing in their seats. He always warned the dozers that a snooze was okay but to do it with discretion. He encouraged them to sleep with their eyes open, as if listening, and to try their damnedest not to fall to the floor. The second group sat in the middle, managed to stay awake, and would take some notes, but little more. The final group sat toward the front, took frantic and copious notes, and asked many questions. They seemed to care. How quaint! This student was a member of that group.

Josh suddenly realized the student was looking at him while praising the impact he had on his life. His words were heartfelt and touching, sending a flush of embarrassment suffusing through his neck and face. When the young man finished, he walked toward Josh and hugged him. He expressed his thanks, but his voice caught, much to his embarrassment. This was something Josh could never fully appreciate. Many of these kids really listened and cared about what you had to say. You might be trying to get through another fifty-minute lecture, but they were being thrilled and motivated by what you considered throwaway comments. You just never knew. He had a vague sense that many transformed lives were out there, but the actual numbers would remain unknown.

Ellison, the department chair, next took the microphone. He focused more on Josh's academic successes. "Our Professor Connelly contributed so much to the better understanding of social issues in Canada and across the Commonwealth. He was heavily involved in the basic income guarantee experiments in cooperation with the prestigious Manpower Development Research Corporation out of

New York. He did extensive evaluations of various work programs for assistance populations at the national and provincial levels. He engaged ground-breaking work on the theory and practice on integrating human service systems. He helped us develop new ways of understanding how complex human service and rehabilitative systems might be organized ..."

As Ellison droned on, Josh tuned out, as was his want during such laudatory exercises from his peers. Josh was glad when the Divisional Dean took over to segue into alleged university wide contributions that he had made. Josh brightened since this might well signal an end to this embarrassing exercise. Drifting through this list of accomplishments were words of praise for the help he had given to various interdepartmental budget struggles. Those were the worst, Josh thought, the downside of academic life. He snapped to full attention as the Dean arrived at a conclusion and shifted to the gift giving. There were a series of serious gifts along with the gag gifts to elicit the expected laughs. He noted a photo album of his career and colleagues over the decades. He would treasure that. "And now some words from the man of the hour."

The room burst into prolonged applause as Josh took the mike. He sought out Rachel and the others. They were clapping vigorously. His eyes wandered again to the couple with Peter Favulli. He knew them. They were so familiar. But he could not quite make a connection just yet. It gnawed at him.

"Okay, okay, calm down now. I know that you believe the louder you applaud the less likely I'll change my mind. And for those of you eyeing my parking space, a plain envelope filled with cash, small and unmarked bills please, is the best way to advance your prospects. That lottery promise is a sham, just another fund-raising scheme by the cash strapped college." More laughter. He was Josh being Josh. He had a habit of picking up on previous comments, and this would be no exception. "First, I want to sincerely thank the previous speakers. I thought they did a superlative job of delivering the comments I wrote out for them. It was hard holding back on the words of praise I supplied them, but my innate modesty prevailed." More laughter and he saw Rachel roll her eyes with a *same old Josh* look. Who were those two next to her? Now, it was really getting to him.

"As I look back over such an illustrious career, who could forget those budget battles. These are the things academics live for. I do remember one conversation I had with an economist I know and love. He was lecturing me on why my department's resource request was overly ambitious. I was a bit taken aback since the economic department's request was multiple of ours. I argued that if they were granted everything they were asking for, there would be virtually nothing left for any other discipline, including our modest request. He looked totally perplexed and asked what my point was. He was serious. To his mind, only the economics department counted. The rest of us were no better than chopped liver. You have to love that sense of unbridled entitlement." The non-economists in the room exploded with laughter. "But really, I do love practitioners of the dismal science. After all, someone has to."

Connie was laughing. Rachel looked on with admiration. He was the Teflon academic. He could insult anyone yet leave the room loved.

A half-dozen other stories and vignettes flowed through his mind. "Whoa, I better put a break on this. If I start with the jokes, we may be here for a while." A couple of people yelled encouragement, but he held up one hand. "I will admit to having the Celtic gift of bull … err, storytelling. It was something my father bequeathed me." He sought out Rachel's face again. "He and I did not see eye-to eye on many things, but he did bestow a few treasures upon me. Not money, to my regret, but things of far better value … a quick mind, a sense of honor, and the gift of the blarney. That last bequest of his helped tremendously with my government work, with academic politics, and even with the writing of academic papers. My story-telling gift may well be useful in retirement. If I don't scale the great mountain peaks in the world," he smiled broadly at this point, "I will surely try my hand at fiction. When I mentioned this dream to my closer colleagues, several noted that they thought I had been writing academic fiction all along." That drew howls of appreciative laughter.

"No doubt," came a voice from the audience. "I ran across your works in the science fiction section of the local bookstore." More appreciative laughter.

"Get that person's name." Josh laughed deeply. "another one off my Christmas list. More seriously, Allen was so kind in his remarks of me as a teacher." He turned in his direction and smiled. "If people only knew how unprepared I was for so many lectures and seminars. The students probably would have asked for their money back. There never was time to do it all or do it all well. Oddly enough, my best talks often were the ones for which I was least prepared, like this one." More laughter. "I would draw on this vast repertoire of anecdotes and vignettes to make my points in the most vivid terms by drawing on my experiences in the real world. Early on, I learned a valuable lesson. All knowledge is not to be found in the literature. Much of it resides in the real world and among real people. You just have to know where and how to look for it. That insight must have served me well. After all, the University never fired me, and I kept getting invited to give talks. Of course, it helped that no one wants to teach anymore. In fact, I believe the non-English speaking janitors are being pressed into teaching service these days. Hard to get fired in that environment."

"It also helped that they couldn't find anyone else to teach as cheaply as you." He saw that the quip came from Connie while those around her guffawed. He smiled at her until his gaze caught that couple next to Rachel and Peter. God, they looked so familiar. Damn it, he knew them—a sense of unease quickly overtook him.

"Ah yes, everyone is a comedian. My dear colleague is right though. With the pittance they paid me, they were sure to get their money's worth. It was hard not to." He had shifted back to Connie and smiled at her. "But I am reminded that I have been surrounded by so many inspirational colleagues throughout my career. I would introduce those I admire the most, those that have meant so much to me as a professional and as a person." A pause for effect. "Unfortunately, none of them could make it here this afternoon. Guess I'm stuck with this crowd." Groans and more laughter. "And now you know why I don't have many friends."

"That was no secret to the rest of us." Connie was on fire. Many in the large assembly knew of their past relationship and laughed appreciatively.

"Could we have security escort that young woman from the room? I thought only real scientists were permitted in here." Josh said with a hearty laugh. "Okay, let me be serious for a moment before I lose total control. I've been very fortunate. I am not sure how many know of my background. I grew up in a working-class ethnic neighborhood where my father ran a bar and did other things better not revealed in public. But he was a charming, witty man who passed on many of his special gifts to—"

"His daughter." This was Peter getting into the swing of things.

"And speaking of his daughter, that woman next to the rude man who just spoke up is my sister Rachel, or should I say Doctor Rachel Elizabeth Connelly, a member of the medical faculty at the University of Wisconsin and distinguished pediatric researcher and clinician." This was accompanied by a robust round of applause. "As you can probably tell, Rachel did get both the looks and the brains in the family, and I do love her dearly." The final words just slipped out. Rachel stood there, suddenly embarrassed, with her mouth open. Usha reached out for her hand. For most in the room, this was an expected sentiment. But for a few, the significance was clear ... the remote and unreachable Jeremiah Joshua Connelly had used the word *love*, and in public no less. "Next to her is her daughter Cate, my niece, who is visiting from Amman, Jordan, where she is posted by the US State Department. And no, she is not a spy, at least that's what she told me to say ... or else. Next to Cate is her...partner, and who will become the newest member of the family. We are so thrilled to welcome her though I remain perplexed as to why she would consider joining this nefarious clan."

He quickly moved on as Cate suddenly wiped a tear from her eye, smiling broadly. "While touching upon reprobates from my youth, I also want to point out a good friend from those early days—well, a friend at least. The now pudgy gentleman standing next to my niece is a connection from my youth. We first met on the high school athletic fields in the Boston area. Hard to believe now, but he was a running back then. I'm sorry, he tried to be a running back. I still remember racing him down from twenty yards behind—"

"Ten yards," came the reply from Peter.

"From fifteen yards behind where I tackled him on the five-yard line. He was so surprised he fumbled the ball and we won the game. I give you Peter Favulli who spent his career with the Federal Bureau of Investigation." Josh's gaze turned once again to the couple standing next to Peter. The man was looking at him with a familiar smile on his face. He knew that smile. He knew it. Yes, it had been a big part of his youth, of what he had become. His body then felt as if it had slammed into a brick wall.

"Oh shit …" The words just escaped him. Some laughed thinking it must be part of another joke. But the laughter petered out as the crowd saw the intense look on his face. He remained silent for what seemed like an eternity as people began to fidget.

"Sorry," he murmured as he pulled the standing microphone out of its holder and sat on the edge of a table that was positioned to serve no obvious function.

People looked confused, uncertain. Josh looked directly at Rachel, who mouthed the words "It is okay." She had a big smile on her face.

"Listen," he started again, "forgive me for not thanking everyone for making my tenure here so memorable. Consider yourself thanked." He paused again, obviously looking for a place to start again. For a man who was renowned for thinking quickly on his feet, this surprised most of the audience. He started off again slowly, as if searching for new words and thoughts. "You know, some people look at the world and see unicorns and wondrous possibilities. I am Irish, in part at least. In case you have not noticed, there is a dark cloud over those of my tribe. I look around and see failure and challenge. I still do that today, at least in some larger arenas. I spent my professional life working on policy challenges in Canada, the UK and EU, Australia, New Zealand, and even India. And you ever wonder why I avoided the States, my home turf? On the surface, that didn't make sense. Our social problems pale by comparison to theirs, at least by all the metrics we ordinarily employ to assess national social health. Think about what is happening south of the border. Just think about it." He paused, apparently trying to decide what to do next.

"Go on." The encouragement came from the man standing next to Peter who now struck Josh as an aging accountant.

"Okay, here it is. One of the richest countries in the world permits 50 million to exist in poverty with one in five children included in those ranks. That is a rate that would spark outrage in virtually all our peer countries, but not there. They have income and wealth inequality not seen since just before the Great Depression with the share of all income enjoyed by the top 1 percent back up to 24 percent in 2007, or right before the most recent economic collapse. It had been less than 10 percent prior to the Reagan revolution. While inequality in most advanced countries is up, the United States still ranks fourth worst out of thirty-three countries in terms of the concentration of income at the top. Not surprisingly, social mobility rates in the United States have declined to the point where we have fallen behind their so-called 'socialistic' peers in that regard. By some measures of social mobility, the probability of moving up the income distribution, the U.S. ranks dead last compared to their European peers. The States have health care outcomes that are middling at best while sporting the forty-seventh-highest infant mortality rate in the world. Outrageous! Kids in the US are falling further behind their primary economic competitors, particularly in math and science. Moreover, they have the highest teen pregnancy rate in the world. No wonder America is well down the list when they do hedonic surveys, assessments of aggregate national happiness."The data rolled off his tongue easily and effortlessly, statistics that were second nature to him.

"Why didn't you help them out more … the country of your birth." The question came from a colleague who knew his work well.

"There were … complications." Josh responded uncertainly.

"Perhaps they wouldn't let you in since you were a known Canadian radical." It was the woman who looked like a granny now, also standing next to Peter Favulli. She was smiling warmly.

"Could be. Could be." Josh seemed to regain his footing. "Think about this. What if you looked to the south from the perspective of a real Canadian? What is the big deal for us up here if America screws up things? That's their problem. Who cares if they choose to be selfish and indulgent and engage in short-term, destructive behaviors? Why should we care?"

"I take it you have an answer." Rachel asked with a warm smile, as if encouraging him.

"You know I do … that very tempting perspective would be short sighted indeed. To use a popular cliché, we are all be in this together. We are a global village. You know what we always say, the US sneezes and we get the flu. What I find particularly troubling is that our easy strategies for dealing with declining economic opportunities, by that I mean stagnating incomes for most families along with growing inequality, appear exhausted. We have already delayed marriage, had fewer children, thrown our spouses and partners into the labor market, saved less, and borrowed more while using housing equity as personal ATMs, and added more advanced educational credentials after our names. In addition, our children often delay establishing their own households, good luck in kicking them out of the nest. And still, economic outcomes grow more unequal. Yet so little outrage! When new policies are posed, not enough ask about the impact on the more vulnerable. Think of the trends over the past several decades that would be expected to exacerbate poverty and increase the economic struggles for so many. We have seen demographic changes and a sharp rise in single-parent households raising children. We are witnessing rapid globalization where firms seek to lower labor costs by outsourcing higher-paying jobs overseas. We're battered by technology-driven changes, automation, and computerization in which tasks formerly done by humans are now done by digital technology and robotics. Can self-driving trucks be far off? And look at immigration where the US saw the proportion of the population being foreign born jump from 5 percent to 13 percent, many of whom are low-skilled individuals. How has Canada changed, how might it change, in a world under constant stress and migration flows? Unionization has almost collapsed south of the border since Reagan killed the air traffic control strike almost three decades ago. The percent of unionized workers in the private sector fell from about one-third of the workforce in the 1950s to about 7 percent in recent years. We're seeing distinct signs of a fractal economy where, even within specific sectors of the economy, compensation has grown wildly unequal even in the face of modest differences in talent and contribution. A typical CEO's remuneration went from twenty-seven times the average worker's pay in 1973 to over two hundred and sixty times the average in 2008. Can we in Canada continue to provide a sense of community and compassion when the colossus to the South becomes a Dickensian horror show? When you consider the adverse trends around us, and others that might be cited, maybe we did better than many of us had thought in at least moderating the adverse effects of an increasingly hostile world for the less well-off, especially given the piss-poor performance of our American neighbors. How long can we get by if things fall apart next door. How long can we ignore climate change if the world's biggest users of fossil fuels continue as if nothing is amiss? What has happened to a society that has more guns than people, that has about a quarter of all incarcerated prisoners with only four percent of the world's population. As my friends who practice the dismal science always remind me, there is such a thing as externalities. We have long border with that dysfunctional country, and probably cannot build a wall to keep out the Americans when their society implodes."

"All the more reason for you to have come south and try to help us out." The question came from Cate.

"Yes, so right … you are so right." Josh looked to the ceiling as if looking for his next thought, as he reflected on how much about him Cate did not know. "I remember asking a visiting colleague from the US many years ago why he thought America had such an impoverished safety net for the disadvantaged. He gave a one-word answer … *heterogeneity*. I initially thought that a simplistic response. Over the years, I came to appreciate his wisdom. We Americans were too tribal and had no common identity, nor a unifying culture. It is too easy to say, and to believe, that the less successful are *'them'* and not *'us.'* They did it to themselves. For too many Americans, their tribe is all, whether defined by race or ethnicity or class. We are not all in this together. Society is degenerating into a horrific contest for survival and dominance."

"You'll find that up here as well." The comment came from Connie.

"Oh yes, I see discrimination toward indigenous peoples and jealousy toward affluent Asians." He glanced at Connie. "Believe me, not to the same degree though. It is instructive to note that Americans are much more likely, by some thirty percentage points, than our European counterparts to respond positively to questions that assign success to personal efforts as opposed to luck or social environments or family fortunes. In the end, these are not just U.S. challenges, they are North American challenges, global challenges, our challenges. To address them, we will have to get beyond business as usual." Josh stopped, wondering how he had fallen into such a polemic. He had not meant this to happen. He had meant to keep his final remarks light and hopefully short. However, his Irish anger had risen for reasons he could guess. He was angry at himself. In this moment, he was forced to confront his own cowardice. Perhaps he should have stayed home four decades ago to keep up the fight.

"Yes," a colleague from his department asked during the pause. "I've always wondered why you spent virtually no time in the States. It would seem a natural environment for you. You're correct in saying that their failures and problems are likely to be our future challenges. They challenge us now in fact."

Josh did not respond to the questioner. "I want to introduce two people standing next to my old college friend, Peter. They are Morris Greenstein and Carla Shapiro. I knew them from another life a long time ago … and I had long since given up hope that I would ever see them again." His voice caught. "Wow, this is a surprise…a shock. Permit me ramble a bit for a moment or two. I know some will say that is all I ever do." He looked at Connie. No smile broke over her lips at his quip. She was looking back at him with wide and open eyes.

It was Rachel who spoke soft words. "It's okay."

"Most of you know nothing about my past … how I got here, to Canada. I think I told people I liked freezing my fanny off and that seemed plausible enough." A small titter made its way through the crowd. "But the truth is more personal, and perhaps a touch tragic. We, Morris and Carla and I and Peter for a bit, were among a small band of passionate students opposed to the Vietnam War and other policies in the US back in the crazy decade of the 1960s. We were young, full of ideals, and driven by a strong sense of purpose. We let ourselves be sucked into the extremes imposed by the times. I've thought back to the things that we did, and did not do, many times. I've tried to sort out whether what we did was moral or not and whether what I did were acts of rationality, idiocy, cowardice, or outright felonies. Believe me, the smart money is on the idiot wager."

Josh suddenly feared that he was talking nonsense. He looked out over the crowd. He could see that many in the audience now were confused, uncertain. Still, no one moved. All remained focused on him.

"Okay, most of you have not a clue what I'm talking about. In our pursuit of peace and justice, I did things best not remembered with any clarity, and probably not revealed with any honesty. If they had been known when I applied for a position here, I doubt I would have been hired. More likely I would have been turned over to the RCMP. Hell, I should have spent time in jail and for sins way more important than lousy lectures and poorly written journal articles." A smattering of laughter. "In short, I rationalized both violations of the law and common sense for a higher purpose. Is such behavior justified? Is it ever justified?"

"Yes," came from the man Josh had introduced as Morris. "If done for the right purposes, yes."

Everyone looked on in rapt attention, most putting together what he was trying to say. "I hope you are right, Mo. I could not answer that question then and, for over forty years, I continued to struggle with the choices I made ... that we made. Some questions simply are beyond rational calculation. Our empirical methods and sophisticated equations cannot answer problems of the heart nor matters of moral culpability. This is where our science is useless. We have to find answers within ourselves if we can." He looked directly toward Morris and Carla. "All those years ago, I made a choice. I fled my country, my friends, and my family. I could not bear the thought of sliding further into the violence toward which we inexorably were being drawn. And yet ... I could not look my best friends in the eyes and tell them I would not be with them any longer. In the end, I fled. I ran north, to your wonderful country, and I do mean wonderful country. I remain so thankful for your willingness to take in such damaged goods."

"It was to our advantage, something we have never regretted." The words came from Ellison which shocked Josh. He would have to tell his old adversary that he would help him out.

"I came here mostly out of cowardice though, being a clever sot, managed to dress my reasons up in more saleable rationales. In escaping America, however, I left my closest companions, my sister, my parents, the woman ... I loved, the life and culture I had known forever. It was all like ripping part of me out. Why didn't I go back, someone asked earlier? Probably the pain ... the pain. Surely the guilt."

"Josh, don't go there, don't beat yourself ... We were all at fault." It was the woman he had called Carla. The words had just slipped out of her.

"Too late, Carla, too late. That ship has long set sail. I have been beating myself up for four decades."

CHAPTER 15

Day 5 – REFLECTIONS

"I could tell you didn't recognize me, at least at first." Morris smiled at Josh in the post event chaos.

Josh was still taken aback by the surprise. "Well, it has been … forever"

"Longer than forever, a different lifetime. I was rather afraid how you would react when you finally realized who we were. But know this, my friend, for the longest time, I blamed only myself for everything."

Josh looked confused. "I don't understand. I sent letters when I got to Canada. I tried to explain my feelings. I blamed you for nothing, I was the one wallowing in guilt."

"Well," Morris sighed. "I never read them. Sorry. They would arrive but I destroyed them. Truth is that there was a lot of bitterness at first and just not wanting to deal with stuff. I mean, I knew you had doubts, concerns about where we were headed. We all could see that. But then you just disappeared. I felt abandoned, I guess, we felt abandoned. No warning, no explanation." Morris glanced at Carla, who nodded. "The way it happened just didn't seem like you."

"I felt guilty. I wasn't man enough to face you, any of you." Josh looked stricken, fighting off the moisture forming in his eyes.

"We all were struggling … I suppose." Morris looked abashed.

After a moment of silence, Carla spoke up. "And I know you had no idea who I was."

"No kidding," exclaimed Josh. "You went from this fierce revolutionary to … to …"

"A gray-haired old granny, you can say it, Josh."

"Well, yeah, but still an attractive old granny."

"Sure, nice try. And you even got the name wrong."

"Wait, let me guess," Josh jumped in. "That name I used to call you …"

"The raven-haired Valkyrie?" Carla threw out.

"Yeah, that's it."

"No longer," Carla corrected him. "My name is now Carla Greenstein."

That stopped Josh. He looked at the couple. "Wow! Go figure."

"What, are you that shocked that I married Mo."

"Hell no, more that you took this loser's name." Josh was quickly relaxing.

"Awfully conventional, isn't it? And guess what, I am a grandmother, for real. Can you believe that? I'm a granny and loving it."

Josh looked skyward. "Right now, I'm checking out whether flying pigs are about to attack us."

Peter had been looking on with a broad smile. "Josh, you have no idea how close this came to not happening. Until I got them in the car, Mo was backing out. He really thought you would not want to see him again, that you despised him. Carla was much more optimistic. But what finally worked was that Rachel mentioned you named your dog after him. There is no higher honor, none that I can think of at least. Still, Favulli would have worked much better."

"Oh god, no freaking way. Favulli? True, the dog is ugly as sin, but not ugly enough to curse him with an Italian moniker. Listen, we have a lot to talk about, but not here." Josh turned to Connie nearby. "Can you lead them out to the common area? There will be few students around now, and we can find a comfortable place. I still have some people to see here, I can see them hovering, trying to decide if they can interrupt this love fest. I'll be out as soon as I can."

"Sounds good." Connie said. "Follow me."

"Wait Connie. Better still, take them home … to my place. This may take a while. Oh, and use my car as well if you need more room. I want to walk back in any case." He handed Connie all his keys.

"As always, my master," she said with a broad smile, "your wish is my command."

Josh went through the motions of shaking hands and exchanging small talk with those that had remained after the ceremony. He paid more attention to the students that stopped by. He had always cared about them, even those he had not seen for years. As was his wont, he remained interested in what they had accomplished. Several mentioned how he had changed their lives. He wondered how that might be possible, but not for long; the blanks often were completed as they rushed to fill him in on their successes. *You shared principles for life that I have never forgotten*" or "*You excited me about public policy*" or "*You helped me see things in an entirely new light*" and "*you gave me a sense of direction in life.*" Then they would add what they were doing now. In some cases, he was surprised. The long-haired hippie student now looked like a banker and served as the CEO of a major nonprofit organization. The quiet, prim gal who wore long dresses now looked chic and sexy, obviously using her seductive assets in her work as a political lobbyist, or so he surmised. Another former student who had struck Josh as a seductress in terms of dress and demeaner now headed a series of safe houses for battered and abused women. *You never know at the beginning of the race,* Josh mused.

He recalled how he had looked upon a few professors so long ago in college. They seemed so prescient and all-knowing. But when he was behind the lectern himself, he realized that those iconic sources of wisdom had been real-life people just like he was now. They had problems and uncertainties and dimensions of their lives that were beyond their full command. Yet he would look out over the faces in his classrooms and just knew that some, not all, but some were hanging on his words. Why didn't they realize he had feet of clay? He had thought that his struggles and vulnerabilities were like scars all over his face. It seemed so obvious to him. Why didn't they ever see them. Talk about being an impostor. But they did not know that. They saw intuitively what he could not. He was a thoughtful and insightful man. He did have things to share with those coming behind him. They had been correct in their decision to pay attention to him.

"You were an inspiration, even if you choose not to believe that. So many have shared how you influenced them." It was a middle-aged woman whose name he retrieved from a brief glance at her name tag. Then he recalled she now was a student counsellor at the university.

"Thank you, Joan, you're too kind." He felt himself flushing with embarrassment and quickly moved on, only to hear similar sentiments. It really did make everything worthwhile. Each seemed so sincere and, given the number, impossible to discount. Still, he found any praise hard to accept. His every instinct was to deflect praise with his sharp wit but that would be unnecessarily cruel. Most wanted to thank him. The least he could do was accept the good words.

Finally, after he had exceeded what he calculated was his embarrassment quota, he felt free to head home. He took a somewhat longer path along the shore; he needed the extra time to decompress. The sun was lowering in the western sky, reflecting off the mountains to the north and the city skyline ahead. He loved the way the bay waters sparkled as the sun's diffusion shimmered off distant windows in downtown Vancouver. He needed these moments to clear his head. There had been so much this week. He was fine with crowded schedules; he had always been known as someone who could juggle different tasks simultaneously. But those were professional challenges, all this was personal and emotional. He had kept smiling and joking, but if he were honest, it was taxing him.

In his mind's eye, he suddenly was back home as a young man. Was it his last visit before he fled? He was not sure, but it was close. Why had his mind drifted to this dark place? Perhaps the good vibes of this day had to be seen from where he started. This could well be his benchmark for how far he had come. He thought back to a moment when not everyone was impressed with him or his virtues or his accomplishments. His father's face was creased in anger, his voice choked with bile.

"You're goddamn useless," his dad raged. "Fucking useless. What are you doing with those criminals?"

"Criminals? Are you kidding me, Dad? Criminals? You are accusing me of hanging around with criminals. You have been breaking the law all your life. If I went downstairs to the bar right now, all I would find are a bunch of Mick hoods and probably a few old IRA assassins."

Jim's face, flushed with alcohol, burned bright with anger. "Don't you dare, don't you dare, you ungrateful son of a bitch. Sure, I broke the law, but for something worthwhile, for Irish freedom. The rest is a harmless diversion, no one gets hurt. People want to gamble, goddamn it."

"Oh my god, you do everything for noble principles and what I do is not. Is that what you're saying? I'm not getting rich fighting against a war that I feel is stupid and whose human and fiscal costs are incalculable. This goddamn war is tearing the country apart. Is that what you want?"

"No, you piece of shit," his father spit out the words. "You are tearing it apart."

"Dad, can't you see that we are the same, fighting for what we believe is right?" Josh's voice had lowered to a plea. "Don't you see it? We are the same."

"The same," Big Jim raged. "The same? I don't think so. You are no more than a worthless pile of piss. I raised a coward, a sniveling coward who fled from the football field, from his church, and now from his obligations. At the first sign of trouble, you shit in your pants and run away from anything tough. You're weak, and I hate weakness."

"Well, Dad, thanks for being so understanding. I appreciate the support."

Drunk as he was, Big Jim could still identify sarcasm. His right arm shot out. For some reason, it caught Josh by surprise, the moment for evasion was past. A broad fist landed on his left cheek and nose. "Shit," he exhaled as he spun back to the wall. He shook his head clear and thought about retaliating. He could take his intoxicated father, that was certain. But he leaned against the wall mute, blood leaking from his left nostril.

"Come on, you little shit," Big Jim spit. "You turned out to be such a coward." With that, his dad moved forward and grabbed Josh by the throat, pushing his head hard against the apartment wall. He cocked his right arm back while Josh passively waited for the blow.

Ora screamed, "Jim, stop, for god's sake, stop! Do you want to kill the boy?"

Rachel had burst from her room at the sound of violence. Her voice, thin with terror, joined her mother's. "No, Dad, please!" She rushed to him and tried to pull the big man from her brother.

Big Jim lowered his arm and roughly pushed his daughter away. He stared at his son, clearly teetering on the edge of another attack. Then imperceptibly, he relaxed. "Get the fuck out of my sight." He turned and went down to his bar.

Ora quietly got up and began dabbing away the blood with a damp towel. "Son, tell me one thing. Why are you doing this?"

"What do you think I'm doing, ma?"

"You have joined up with some damn Communists." She said the words with great sadness.

"Communists! No, Ma. Why do you say that?"

"Don't tell me that." There was a distinct tone of anger he had not heard before. "I know Communists. They did unspeakable things to my family, things not in your imagination, things I can still see each night, things from when I was a young girl."

"Ma, I'm fighting for what's good in this country."

"Bullshit!" she screamed. Josh recoiled; he had never heard her swear before, ever. "Don't say such things to me. You are being duped. That's how they work. They fill your head with silly words and dreams. Then … then twist and turn things around until you're no longer the same person."

"Ma, will you just listen?"

"No! You're no longer my son."

"Ma, please."

"The Communists, those animals, I cannot believe what has happened to you. Just go away."

"Ma."

"Get out!"

Josh recalled being totally exhausted at that moment. He went over, hugged his sister who continued to sob, and walked out. Was that the last time he saw them? He could not recall a later image. How could he not remember exactly when this happened? Too much pain, he concluded.

———

He looked up to the sky. Dark clouds were blowing in toward Vancouver from the west. Maybe a storm tonight. He tried reflecting on the good moments from earlier in the day, but the face of a young Morris Greenstein intruded. He could not shake moments from those decades ago when all seemed vivid and emotionally iridescent.

"Josh, you're the glue that keeps this together."

Josh remembered protesting, "That is silly, Mo, it is you that inspires everyone. You are the group's Trotsky, Che, Malcolm X, Saul Alinsky, and maybe even Eugene Debs all rolled into one. Hah, I'm probably Kerensky, or a Sydney and Beatrice Webb, a hopeless and confused Socialist at best."

"Listen to me." Morris did not smile at Josh's attempt to lighten the moment. "I can move people intellectually, in their head. But you can move them in their heart. They like you. They may respect me, but they respond to you. And that is what we need now, someone who can tell a convincing story, reach people's hearts."

"Mo, this sounds like a pep talk. What's wrong?"

"I worry, Josh, I worry about you. There is a lot of pressure on you with your family and that girl you never bring around, I forget her name."

"Eleni," Josh whispered.

Mo looked at him intently. "Remember when the two of us first met, you saved my ass. I never forgot. You were this tough Irish kid who whaled away at guys from his own people to save this skinny Jew. I knew at that moment you were a special kind of guy, that you would always have my back. That meant a lot to me. Do you hear me? That still means the world to me."

"What could I do, you were so scrawny. Those thugs would have killed you."

"No way," Morris shot back. "They were Irish pussies. I can take six of them at a time."

"Sure, tough guy." Josh smiled. "Truth is, they would still be scraping pieces of you off that sidewalk."

Morris smiled warmly. "You're my best friend. I feel closer to you than my brother. But what we are doing is above all that. Remember this, each generation selects just a few to hold to the highest values. For this generation, it is people like you and me. We can be a vanguard."

"Like the vanguard of the proletariat?"

"Don't mock me. Never do that." Josh recoiled at the anger in his friend's demeaner.

"What we do now is small and symbolic, but it is a start. It is only meant to catch their attention. No one is paying attention. Everything is business as usual. We need to inflict just enough pain to get them to listen. Do you understand? I can't help but believe that things will change if we just can get people to listen. They can't be as stupid as they appear."

"And if they never listen or, worse, listen but never change." Josh stared at his friend.

"Then, we have no choice. We must move on to the bigger things."

Josh recoiled slightly. "That's what worries me, that there will be no choice."

"There always is a choice," Mo asserted confidently. "The thing is that choice is theirs, not ours. We must respond if they continue. In the end, though, they will see we are right. You watch. The people will prevail. After all, we are on the side of the angels, on the side of history."

Josh recalled looking directly into Mo's eyes, nodding imperceptibly. Mo acknowledged the nod but was uncertain as to its meaning. Was it a sign of agreement or a recognition that things were reaching some point of no return? In truth, Mo did not feel the confidence he displayed in the moment, not in the least. Neither did Josh.

That image of Mo Greenstein segued into a memory of his days as a student in Toronto. He was sitting on a campus bench on a spring day when a warm sun competed with cooler breezes off Lake Erie for dominance. He sat trying to focus on a reading assignment when he noticed a figure walking across the green quadrangle. What caught his attention was that the figure, ambling slowly with a distinct limp, seemed to be heading directly toward him. He didn't recognize this man but there was no mistaken that he had Josh in his sights.

As this man drew near, Josh rose. Uncertainty fused into something closer to shock. "Holy shit. Terry Mahoney. You are a ghost from the past."

"How's my favorite Commie doing," the limping man said as he stopped, hesitated, and then threw his arms around his former friend.

"Still vertical and taking nourishment. But you, your so much thinner, and the limp. I almost didn't recognize you. You must have stories."

"Well, it hasn't been that long but lots of water under the bridge, lots of water my friend. Obviously, our life choices made a difference. I suppose they do for each of us. I'm not sure we are that special."

"Yes, they do. We choose, and never know the consequences. Frightening!" Josh hesitated, wondering where to go next, what their connection might still be after their youthful friendship had dissolved in recrimination and anger. Neither could understand each other's choices when they were in college. "I'm sorry, Terry, for what I said at the end when we were in school, before … Anyway, how did you find me?"

"Long story but I'm living in Ottawa now, working with kids who, like you, fled to escape the insanity…" He hesitated.

"But you were so gung-ho, that's what we were always fighting about, that's what broke our friendship. You wanted to go and fight the Commies."

Terry looked across the campus as if a thousand miles away. "Yeah, I was that guy, all rah, rah and flag waving bullshit. It took me six months as a second louie in charge of a squad to change all that. Josh, it wasn't the heat or the fear or the intense boredom followed by sheer terror. All that was bad but seeing what it was doing to the kids looking to me for leadership. That overwhelmed me. You cannot imagine."

"No Terry, I cannot."

"For Christ's sake, Josh, we were turning good kids into monsters and there was nothing I could do to stop it. We were in the fucking twilight zone, nothing made sense. There was no front line, no victories, no sense to it all. There was just this body count. Can you imagine? We used to joke about getting to count a gook cut in half as two on the paperwork. I mean, you could not separate the good guys from the bad guys, not really. A body was a body. Sometimes they were so disfigured you could not tell age or sex. Still, they counted on the daily body count sheet. That's all that mattered."

"I'm sorry." Josh was at a loss.

"Your sense of humanity evaporates under the pressure to produce. Just kill more and don't ask any questions. What really did it was slowly becoming aware of what was happening inside me … inside each one of us? If you were in leadership, even at my low level, the burden was greater. You knew inside what you were doing to our kids over there. You were turning them into monsters. That is what Hell does to a person. I still feel the guilt."

"That bad."

"Worse than that. Nothing made sense in the end." Terry's eyes moistened. "You see villagers beheaded for being friendly to us. A day or two later, you are torching some farmers hovel because of a rumor that he had helped the VC. But you didn't know shit. You just went and did it to please the fucker up the line of command. Next you are wading chest deep in water with snakes slithering by and every twitch in a nearby tree stopping your heart. These eighteen-year olds get so hyped that they are ready to explode. Half were stoned most of the time. We were all so unprepared. That Viet kid who just smiled at them might have planted an explosive device on the trail we will use that day. How could you tell? Ever seen someone with a blown off leg, begging for his buddy to shoot him. I did that, Josh. I did that I swear. I killed my friend because I could not stand seeing him in such pain. I mean, I told myself there was no hope for him. I didn't know, not really. I wasn't a freaking medic. Thing is, I could not stand his screaming."

"Terry ... don't."

"I have to. Maybe I need your absolution. You saw it back then and I didn't."

"It wasn't that clean. We both made mistakes."

Terry became reflective. "I should have read more in college, like you. But I was more the jock I guess. After, though, I caught up a bit. I read about the German SS troops sent into Poland, the Ukraine, Russia, and the Baltic countries to follow up the Wehrmacht troops heading east in June of 1941. They did the same thing we were doing in Nam. They were killing people, Jews and local partisans, and filling out forms. Promotions followed bigger body counts. You got a prize if your area became *Juden frei* ... free of Jews. We got medals if we could claim we had made a village VC free. It hit me. I had become just another fascist killer."

"Except you were killing Communists, the enemy."

Terry sneered. "Really, you think that makes any difference."

"No, not a bit." Josh put an arm on his old friend's shoulder. "You have to step back from that. You must."

Terry seemed not to hear him. "Ever see a boy, and most were boys, go from a clean-cut high schooler who had attended mass with his family to a butcher who bayonetted a young woman because he thought she looked at him cross-eyed. I saw that, and worse. You cannot imagine."

"I'm sorry." Josh was at a loss.

"No, don't feel sorry for me. I should have listened to you, Josh. But I made my own choices. That's the thing about choices. You must live with the freaking consequences. But, in the end, I was lucky, or so everyone said. We were on patrol. I took the lead because that was my job. I only wanted to avoid the enemy, period. Body count, my ass. But there was no way to avoid some things. I thought I was getting good at this stuff, but it was a crap shoot in the end. One day, I heard something. By this point, I could separate the normal jungle sounds from what you had to hear. But there was no time. That's often the case. Before I could react, I was on the ground screaming for a medic. Like I said, it's all a crap shoot. I survived, crippled but alive."

"How did you get here, to me."

"After I rehabbed, I knew I had to leave the states. It was falling apart, and I could not stand the bullshit anymore. I came north to help others escape the insanity. I had some work here in town and learned you were here. The ex-pat community is a rather small world if you are looking for someone."

Josh winced at the perceived slight. He was into his own world these days. He hadn't searched for his old friends, the opposite really. "I really am glad to see you and ..."

"At least I've finally seen the light. It took me a while, too long." Terry issued a forced laugh. "Yeah, you were the smart one. I got through college because I was good on the football field. And Josh ..."

"Yeah?"

"You made the right choice. You were fucking right all along. I was wrong. At the time, though, I was so ..." Terry trailed off.

Josh lowered his head. "Not that easy, my friend, not that easy. I came within a whisker of ending my life in the early days here. The guilt can be overwhelming. That's the agony of it all. There was guilt no matter which choice you made back then. If you cared about anything, there was no exit."

Terry looked taken aback but recovered. "Want to know why I came up here to do this work. I saw others returning while in the states. I would try to help but the pain was often too much. Some are bringing demons back with them that they will never exorcise. One day, I couldn't reach a kid I was counselling. Such a good kid, nice, you know. I finally went to his place to see what was up. Found him slumped on the floor with a hole in the side of his head. Some of the lucky ones died where and when they were hit on the battlefield. I'm not kidding about they being the lucky ones. Others died a slow painful death long after they were patched up and sent home. And there are the wounded without blood. They are stricken with the invisible wounds, perhaps the unluckiest of them all. They relive the horror inside their heads forever, and that's a long, long time man. But no one sees their wounds … no one understands."

"Terry, I'm …"

"No need to say anything. I just wanted to find you to say you were right damn it. You made the right choice."

They sat for a long time, Josh recalled.

He jerked that image out of his head and wiped the tears from his eyes. The wind picked up, stinging the salt that the tears brought with them. He wiped his face with his hands. He was getting close to home, but his mind wandered off again. This time it was Sarah Kaplan who entered his mind's eye. He recalled banging on her apartment door late, hoping she was still up. One of her roommates answered, looking decidedly unhappy.

"Josh, what the hell are you doing here? It is the middle of the damn night. Oh, never mind, come in and I'll get her."

When Sarah emerged from her room, he sounded contrite, which was exactly what he felt. "I have to talk, so sorry. I know it is late. I'm a shit, but-but …"

She grabbed his hand and pulled him into her room. "This is for privacy, not sex."

Josh had not thought of sex until that moment. They both sat on her bed, and her robe fell open a bit, revealing one of her breasts. Now the thought of sex rushed throughout his body. He waited for the hormonal wave to pass before starting.

"Sarah, I'm so sorry. Things are piling up, overwhelming me. Sometimes I feel I will explode. What's happening to me? Remember when everything seemed so clear? We joined that first anti-war protest. Sure, we almost got killed, but it was more of an adventure. We felt proud, superior to those so-called patriotic clowns throwing things at us. We saw the world in ways they could not, or so we thought. We were more insightful and certainly had better principles … and superior IQs. At least we were not moral reprobates who got their rocks off killing people whose biggest sin was looking different from us. Now … now it has all become so serious. Life is spinning out of control. I just know I am going to disappoint everyone … everyone I care about. It used to be that people loved me. Okay, they liked me. Now I fear becoming a pariah, up for the most despised man on the planet."

Sarah leaned forward to smell his breath. "Nope, no booze. I guess this is real hurt."

He sighed. "I've tried booze and pot, the usual anaesthetics. No luck, nothing is working."

She tried a weak smile. "About being the most despised man on the planet … what the hell is with that? Wake up, you idiot." She whacked him on the arm. "You're not that important. I think Ho Chi Minh still got you beat but keep it up, buttercup. You just might have a shot at the title. I will say one thing. Showing up at two in the morning is not helping your cause. You can cross Carol off your list of possible future sexual conquests. She looked pretty pissed when she came in to get me."

"Thanks, that's what I needed to hear, and just when she was reaching the top of my co-ed conquest to be list." He offered weakly, trying to counter his heaviness. "Do apologize for me when you see her."

"Do your own dirty work."

Josh realized Sarah was unusually angry with him. "I will. Now that I think on it, I'm shocked she did not slam the door in my face."

She reached out to take his hands in hers. "So am I. Then again, she thinks you're cute. Apparently, there is an epidemic of poor taste going around. But since you are here, and I'm now awake, tell me what's going on inside that confused, complex head of yours."

Josh acknowledged neither the compliment nor the insult. "I feel I am in this impossible place."

"Oh God," she moaned. "This ought to be good."

"Earlier, I was thinking about that psychology experiment we worked on? We set up the maze wrong and the rats were shocked no matter which way they ran. The poor bastards ran this way and that. It took us a while to figure out what went wrong, the current we used to shock them likely was too high. They could not learn because the pressure was overwhelming. I can still see the poor frantic things rushing about but there was no escape."

"I get it," she said softly. "Now you're a pariah and a rat."

"Yes! I know your mocking me but that's how I feel. I'm the rat with no way out." He let out a deep breath, fighting a feeling that he was suffocating.

"Can I ask you something? Why are you telling me? Why aren't you sharing all this with Eleni? Why come to me?"

He shrugged. "I don't know what to tell her. I suppose I could run the following by her. *By the way, Leni, I am fucking up my life totally, but I love you so why don't you throw everything away and join this train wreck in motion?* Wow, what woman would pass up an offer like that?"

"No, I suppose that's not the suburban house or the white picket fence. But, and this is a big but, females are known to evidence atrocious judgment when it comes to selecting male partners. It is the only weakness in my gender of which I'm aware. If she loves you, she might accept anything."

He looked at her blankly, "No way she likes me that much. Think about it. I'm not that much of a prize."

Sarah was irritated. "Damn, I can't believe you're making me say this. Just in case you dropped off the turnip truck last night, let me make one thing clear. She loves you. Got that, you moron, she loves you. Even an idiot like you must see that. I believe there was a piece on that very topic in the college newspaper."

"She's never used that word. I don't know if she does or not," he said weakly. "Sometimes I'm not sure she even likes me all that much."

"Well, have you?" Sarah asked as she rolled her eyes.

"Have I what?"

"Damn it, don't be so dense. Have you ever told her that you love her?" Now she was very exasperated. "Women don't like to go first."

Josh paused. "Yes … I think. Perhaps not exactly."

"You, sir, are a dumb shit. I am speechless. No, not just a dumb shit but a colossally dumb shit. I have been with the two of you many times. It is obvious to me you love each other. You know, sometimes you are brilliant. Other times, it is like talking to a freaking turnip. Oh, never mind."

After some silence, Josh asked in a low voice, "Did you love me?"

"What?"

"Did you ever feel that way about me?"

"Why would you even ask that?"

"I need more guilt. I don't quite have enough yet." Josh tried a smile.

"I should tell you that I burn incense to a shrine dedicated to you every night. But I won't." She paused to consider her next thought. "Josh, you were never disingenuous. You never promised me love or devotion or commitment. You gave what you did promise, companionship and intellectual stimulation and the sex was okay as well."

"Sensational."

"Sorry?" She was not sure what adjective he had inserted.

"The sex, it was sensational."

"Ah yes, what was I thinking? But my point is that you were always honest. That is rare for a guy. I shouldn't say this, but I could have fallen in love with you. No way would I let myself go there, no way. I held back. I had to. Who wants to be rejected, disappointed? I did not get to the top of our class by being stupid. Want my advice? Go to Leni, open yourself up. Ask her to be your life partner. If you don't, you will be the sorriest-ass guy on the North American continent."

"Can I lay next to you for the night? I need a … human touch?"

After an exceptionally long pause, she lay down and pulled him closer to her. They snuggled, wrapping one another in their arms.

"Thanks," he said. "I needed this."

"Yeah, dammit." She was irritated with herself. "This is rather nice."

Soon, Sarah could hear a change in his breathing. He was asleep, she was sure of that. Then she permitted herself to say what was on her mind. "Yes, I love you," she murmured softly. "Dear god, you really are such a moron."

CHAPTER 16

Day 5 – CONNECTING

Josh snapped out of his reverie as he neared his destination. He realized he now was just a few feet away from his home. He was not conscious of making this trip, it was second nature by now. Perhaps that is why he liked walking this route, he could accomplish the task while musing about larger issues. He slowed his pace to avoid what would come next. He always was more comfortable with ideas and issues. It was people that tended to bother him. They were messy, inconvenient, and inexplicable. Still, he guessed they were essential in life. He would give that conclusion more thought on his next walk. He took a deep breath and walked through the door.

There was, however, no greeting of the day's hero as he anticipated. Rather, most were looking at Cate, who was engaged in an animated conversation on the phone. She was walking about in the center of the living room, her face set in that look of determination. It was the same look that Rachel often had as a young girl when displeased. Suddenly, he was struck with a connection. She was her mother's daughter.

"Yes, yes, you have made your position clear … No, there is no room for negotiation, it is not like we're closing on a house here … Ah-ha … I am sure I know exactly how your mother feels." Cate turned and gave the finger to the world in general, making it clear how she felt at that moment. Rachel closed her eyes tight while Meena put her head in her hands. "Listen to me … No, no, just listen, goddamn it. I am marrying

Meena. We are adopting the orphans I told you about, assuming we can pull it off. Forget that conditional shit, we will adopt them no matter what, even if we must help them escape from that damn camp. You remember Usha? Yes, Rachel's brother's ex-wife. Good for you, I'm surprised you remember anyone outside the Ballentine circle … Okay, unfair. Anyway, she is a law professor and is helping us with everything. It is happening … Fine, do what you must … No, you can just stop now. There is nothing more to say. Goodbye, Father." With that, she terminated the call and took a big sigh.

Josh broke the ensuing silence as the others searched for an appropriate comment. "So, I take it that was not a telemarketer selling time-shares."

Cate laughed aloud despite herself and walked over to hug her uncle. "Glad you've escaped to join us. Welcome officially to the ranks of useless retirees, which I hope to join someday. Sorry for the dramatics, I thought about taking the call privately but having all you about me gave me strength. So, again, thank you." Her gaze swept the expectant faces of the group gathered about.

Rachel sighed. "I can guess his side of the conversation but want to share the bottom line?"

"Of course," Cate's anger was yet evident. "I am pleased to announce that I have been officially cast out of the Ballentine clan and cut out of the family fortune."

Rachel joined her and kissed her on the cheek. "What should I say, sorry? Want me to talk with him?"

"Of course not. We both know who he is. I do wonder what you saw in him, though."

"He was cute, and all the other girls wanted him." Rachel said absent conviction.

"Hey, I'm cute and all the girls wanted me" Josh tried.

"What girls?" Connie asked. "Usha, can you think of any?"

Rachel smiled appreciatively as Usha nodded a negative response. "To be totally honest, I have no freaking idea what I saw in Evan. I was young and foolish and more than a little insecure. He really was a callous prick from day one. I used to think he had charm, but it was nothing more than … oily disingenuous manipulation."

Josh raised a hand. "Hmm, Rachel, you always said I was charming."

"I never said that, more like you are clueless which sometimes is confused with charm."

Cate joined in. "Uncle, I for one think you are charming."

Rachel put her hands to her face in mock shock. "Cate, please." Inside, she was proud of how her daughter was handling all this.

"But men in general," Cate suddenly groaned aloud, "surely we can live without them." Cate then gave a forced smile. "Still, I wish I had a better relationship with dad, but that ship sailed a long time ago. His choice, damn it! However, mom, I do have bad news."

"What?"

Cate broke into a smile that reminded Rachel of her brother. "You will have to labor in the operating room until you're ninety to make up for my lost Ballentine fortune. I assume you know that I expect to continue in the life of leisure to which I've become accustomed."

Rachel smiled. "Don't count on it, kiddo."

Cate noticed the stricken look on Meena's face and took her into a corner to chat privately. Rachel joined them.

Connie broke the ensuing silence. "Josh, you're now retired and officially useless. I mean, you were always useless, but now it is official. In any case, we have been catching up with your friends. Morris runs a bookstore in Seattle while Carla is a nurse or was a nurse."

"Now part time." Carla snuck in. "Working with dementia patients. Really hard but most fulfilling."

"And Peter is retired from the FBI, no longer protecting us from the bad guys."

"That I knew," said Josh, finding a seat, "but the rest is news. A bookstore? Somehow, if anyone had said you had finally stopped trying to save mankind, I would have guessed you became a clock fixer."

"What?" Morris thought that amusing.

"Sure, I could see you having a little shop filled with half-repaired time-pieces. You would be sitting behind your counter wearing those granny glasses and working on a cuckoo clock. I would bring my broken timepiece in around May, and you would promise to have it fixed by October. Then, before I left, we would talk politics for three or four hours. Of course, I would come back in October and you would be behind the counter working on that same cuckoo clock you were tinkering with six months earlier. You would tell me to come back next May for my clock and again we would talk politics for three or four hours. No one would bring a clock to you to have it fixed, just to sop up your wisdom."

"Funny man, you have not lost that wit, thank god." Morris chuckled.

"Bookstore … how, why?" Josh wanted to know more.

Morris sighed. "For someone with my … colorful background, options were limited. Fortunately, Carla had a sister who married very well. She and her spouse were in the computer field and rode the digital age to considerable wealth, had some innovation they sold to Bill Gates. I finally realized that capitalism is okay when you are related to it. Anyway, they asked us out to the West Coast and set us up, helped pay for Carla's schooling. They never judged. Nice people, very liberal. I discovered that not all rich folk are assholes."

"Yeah, wisdom comes to those who wait." Josh observed. "Tell me, how and when did you two finally connect?"

Carla picked up the narrative. "You mean after you escaped my evil designs." She chuckled at her comment. "I got out first. I started visiting Mo. He had the longer stretch, being our leader and all, not that he could ever control some of us."

"I would have had better luck with a herd of feral cats." Mo said with an impish smile that surprised Josh.

Carla continued. "I visited him as often as I could and we finally talked seriously about all kinds of things … about you, and life and what we had become. By the time he was released, we were in love. I was ready for that by then, something permanent. And he … loved you again, finally." She looked at Josh.

An awkward silence was broken by Usha. "Got out? Is it okay if I ask … out of what? I am lost?"

Morris and Carla looked uncertainly to Josh, who returned their gaze.

"Go ahead." Carla disrupted the uncertainty between the three of them.

"Time to fill in a few blanks." Josh said. "As college students, we were committed to stopping what we considered an immoral war, as you now know. I mentioned that part earlier during my impromptu retirement remarks. We forget now, but the Vietnam conflict tore the country apart a half century or so ago. Many students protested, either because of the draft or because they really hated what was going on there. But a few went beyond protest. A few did things that were against the law, that edged over into violence. Some," he looked at Peter, "were wise enough to run off before things became … extreme. Others stayed with their convictions to the end. You can guess who the coward was, Morris and Carla went to prison for their beliefs while I ran away."

"That seems unfair," Usha inserted, looking at Mo and Carla. "Being imprisoned for one's beliefs. America is known for free speech."

Josh held up a hand. "Let me finish. There is something I need to say." He poured himself a drink. "Back in college, there were a couple dozen of us or so who were more committed than others protesting things. Even within our group, there was a core…Morris, Carla, Helen Mueller, Jimmie Daily, Bob Wilson, and me. Peter also was with us in the beginning but had the sense to bail early. We grew frustrated with teach-ins, marches, petitions, and the usual student BS. That was the free-speech part. We were generally treated as spoiled brats and just maybe that is what we were." He looked quickly over to his friends, but they seemed not to object. "We got inside our own little bubble. For hours, we would discuss politics and causes and why past revolutions for social justice failed. We went through the Wobblies and Fabian Socialists and the Bolsheviks and Mensheviks, the old Reds and the new Reds, Gus Hall, Caesar Chavez, Malcom X, Che, and for sure Tom Hayden and the SDS, which I joined for a while … before they descended into nihilistic self-destruction. The search for ideological purity was an obsession back then. In truth, it has always been like that. The Stalin purges were a case in point though the goal of ideological purity was little more than a transparent rationale to consolidate power."

Connie smiled. "I must have led a sheltered life. I escaped most of that except for Mao of course. He was too close to home."

"For us back in the 60s, it seemed so real and urgent. So many were being killed for no reason at all. I remember thinking a bit later when the abortion debate exploded that those opposing abortion and those opposing the war were alike in one respect. While they differed on almost every political question, they felt a special calling to oppose murder as they defined it." He paused to take a sip of his drink. "I never bought their view of things but I saw the conundrum they poised."

"Conundrum?" Cate asked.

"Yes, what do you do to stop unwarranted killing? What if you believe that thousands or hundreds of thousands are being murdered for no justifiable reason whatsoever? This is the rage we felt back then, many of us at least. Now, of course, Vietnam is a footnote in history books. Ask a college kid on this campus about the meaning of Vietnam and they give you a blank look. How many students today could tell you what the Tet offensive was? That is the irony of reality, isn't it? The most important moments of your life are soon lost to our collective memories, little more than a hard question in a game of trivia-pursuit."

"I'll drink to that." Peter Favulli said, raising his glass.

"Hear, hear!" The others chimed in.

Josh smiled but continued. "Still, you can't deny it. That war was the defining moment for our generation. It is what many of us cut our teeth on when we were shaping our worldviews and erecting our moral cores. I recall a few old regulars in my father's bar talking in low voices about the brave and illegal actions my father took to liberate Northern Ireland and forge one Irish nation. In that divinely blessed cause, nothing was illegal. I think, at some moments, I also felt that nothing was illegal for my youthful cause."

"How true, Rachel offered as she joined this discussion. "I can still remember the old guys in dad's bar going on about the 1916 Easter uprising. They were kids, no more than tots at the time, but it seared them for life."

Josh was nodding toward his sister. "Maybe more than events is the power of culture. I was raised Catholic. You can stop believing in the peripheral stuff, like the saints and the holy days, but what sticks with you is the moral obligation to do what's right. You cannot escape your core responsibilities, or your innate guilt. When we Catholics talked about original sin, we meant guilt. It overwhelmed us; we could never escape. And my own version was to rectify this blight of an unjust war that corroded our collective souls. Sure, there were all the other battles for black rights, women rights, Native American rights, and so forth. They were also important, but somehow could be sloughed off to others, like blacks or feminists or the tribes. Vietnam was my cause, our cause. And we knew, just knew, that our generation would change the world for the better. We simply had to speak truth to power. I recall so vividly our discussions back then. It was just a matter of time. As we evolved into adulthood, we would take over the positions of power."

"I think you missed on that one." Usha shook her head.

"You think? I guess our powers of prognostication were a bit lacking. When Goldwater was buried in the election of 1964, we felt that the forces of decay and evil were finished. Progressive ideas were on the rise around the world. What was to stop the preordained and inevitable rise of social justice and peace and good will. It was merely a matter of staying the course. Hadn't the President just declared a national war on poverty. That would replace the war on yellow people halfway around the world, wouldn't it?"

"Can't predict them all. If we could, I'd be making book in Vegas." Peter smiled.

"Okay, wise guy" Josh waived a finger at Peter, "we were off, just a bit, on that one. Now we can look back and see things more clearly."

"And you see … what?" Connie asked Josh.

"The hard right began a systemic push to take control of things. It started after World War two but got serious in the 1970s. With Reagan, their takeover became a reality. They were backed by limitless money and laser-sharp focus. Some trace the initial push of the right, at least in a strategic way, to a memo written in the early 1970s by Lewis Powell. This future Supreme Court justice laid out a multipronged strategy for taking control of both the institutions of power and, more importantly, the central tenets of the political debate. Others go back to the creation of the Virginia School of Political Economy by James Buchanan after the public schools were desegregated in 1954. Still others go further back to when Friedrich Hayek gathered three dozen free market extremists to a confab near Mont Pelerin in Switzerland where they initiated a conservative intellectual revolution that is with us today. Wherever you start, the message was clear. Government was not the solution to problems; it was the problem. Get it out of the way so those born to lead might rule absent accountability. Free markets would protect us. And maybe, in our own misguided way, we contributed to that shift."

"How so?" Carla asked. "I'm not sure I follow."

"By feeding the fears of the common man since we leftists gave the right a perfect straw man. We were the cause of all the problems faced by joe six-pack, to be feared and marginalized and even hunted down. Meanwhile, the right went about their campaign to reorder politics in America. Systematically, and over several decades, they erected the Federalist Society, the Leadership Group, the Club for Growth, ALEC, a host of right-wing think tanks like Cato and Heritage and the Hoover Institute and so many others. They created Fox News, Newsmax, One America News, and a media empire that has spawned a host of ever more radical outlets. They worked tirelessly at the local level to alter how people looked at government. And they went about attacking anything that smacked of the public good. America pioneered free public education. In a few years, that great public good will largely be swept away by privatization. Everything will be about making a buck, prisons and health and schools and probably what we call national defense. What did we do, what did we do?" He stopped realizing that he was rambling a bit. He looked around, but people seemed mesmerized.

"Wow," Cate murmured.

"So, a bookstore?" Josh said to Morris when there was no further response. It was as if his rant had not taken place. "By the way, what happened to Bob and Helen? I have always wondered."

After an awkward silence as people tried to shift to a more mundane issue, Carla spoke up. "Funny story about both. When they caught up to Helen her family rallied to her defense with their wealth and the best legal defense. She did spend time in jail but not much. She is now a pillar of her community back in Philadelphia. She is a staunch Republican, advocates for conservative causes."

Josh laughed, a bit too loudly to his mind. "Well, not surprising. Her leftish passions always struck me as disingenuous. I recall a colleague of mine always saying that the political spectrum is not a straight line but a horseshoe or even a circle. The ends curve back to each other. If you're at either extreme, you're more likely to slip to the other side rather than back to the middle."

"Bob," Carla picked up, "is an interesting story. As some of us know, he had been in a Catholic seminary before college, the Maryknoll Catholic Foreign Mission Society. He was serious about his spiritual life and a devoted adherent to what we called liberation theology back then. Apparently, some of the Maryknollers embraced socialist principles in their work with poor indigenous populations in Central and South America. Some of them gave their lives in that cause, not being liked very much by the right-wing juntas in charge of things. Anyway, when Bob got out of prison, he tried several things before finding his place."

"Which is?" Josh asked.

"He is in a monastery, in Iowa. Mo and I visited him. He is very content."

Josh took in her words. They had visited Bob? Then why had they never sought him out until now? Had he been the unforgivable traitor in their eyes? Did they really hate him but were too polite to say so? He almost asked when Connie raised her voice. "Listen, everyone, it is getting late. Some of us snacked at the big event, but Usha and I want to run out and pick up something substantial to eat. I can guess there is nothing in his refrigerator. So, we are off on this errand of mercy but shall return and … that's it." Cate, and Meena had re-joined the main group by this time. Meena decided to join the search party seeking the evening's sustenance.

Cate looked around the group waiting for someone to say something. Finally, she spoke up. "Okay, I am sorry but, arriving to this discussion late, I'm not following all of this. Prison, why prison? Lots of students protested the war. Some got arrested, maybe spent a few days in jail at most."

"Josh apparently never told you," Morris intoned, slightly surprised.

Josh jumped in. "This clown named Josh is a first-class idiot in case no one has noticed. I've shared some of this with Rach over the past few days, but maybe I need to finish a bit of family history for Cate."

"Uncle, really, it is not—"

"It is, dear, you might as well know about the horse thieves in the family tree, especially now that you have severed ties with the Ballentine clan. I walked up to the truth back at the ceremony but still could not quite do it. I keep asking myself why. Is it fear? Peter, can you still arrest me?"

"That moment, I hope, has passed." The FBI man responded. "Depends on how big a schmuck you were."

Looking in the direction of his sister and niece, Josh went on. "Here is the thing. Morris, Carla, and the rest of our merry band went right past protesting and, after collecting our two hundred dollars, did all kinds of things that landed us, all but one, in the pokey. We broke into government facilities, destroyed records, committed arson.

I've mentioned some of this to Rachel the other day. There's a more, though."

"I knew it." Rachel said. "Then, embarrassed that the words were not silent, she quickly added. "Go ahead, sorry."

He took a deep breath. "We had gotten to the point where we started making bombs. Yeah, we got that nuts."

"Not my finest hour." Mo murmured.

"Well, our intentions were noble." Carla suggested softly. We weren't bad people."

"No, we weren't, not by a long shot." Josh added in a less than convincing tone. "Still, we started making bad choices, and they have consequences."

Another awkward pause, broken this time by Rachel. "Consequences?"

"One of us, poor Jimmie, killed himself building one of those damn things. A woman in an adjacent flat was gravely injured, and her fetus died when the shock of the blast caused a miscarriage. It became quite a legal tangle at the time with the abortion debate beginning to percolate. Losing Jimmie ripped my heart out. He was one of my first friends in the neighborhood. He followed me everywhere, to college and even into the revolution. I killed him just as much as if I put a bullet into his head."

"Oh," escaped from Cate. Rachel now looked on, mute.

Josh could see that Mo and Carla were going to take issue with his implied responsibility for Jimmie's fate, so he hurried on. "And we broke into government offices to disrupt the selective service operation which we saw as fuelling the war machine."

"Anything I don't know?" Peter now asked.

"Nothing big. I stole some money to finance our little revolution. Told you Cate, you just might want to look for a new family on Craig's list."

At that, Peter perked up. "What, you stole money? How? Was it an armored car heist, the one where the guard got shot. We thought some terrorist group did that one. Maybe I don't want to know."

"That's okay. We're past the point of caution here." Josh seemed resigned.

Peter was not smiling. "No, you would never shoot anyone. It was a bank, right. Which one?"

"Not a bank."

"Shit, I really am not sure I want to know, but I guess the Statute of Limitations has expired." Then Peter blanched. "I'll ask again. You didn't shoot a guard, did you? Please tell me you didn't."

"Nothing that prosaic, my friend. I just stole some dough from the Irish wise guys."

"What! Are you fucking crazy?" Peter Favulli realized his language and started to apologize but realized no one cared. "What I mean is … you stole from the freaking mob? Was it the Winter Hill gang?"

"Yeah." Josh admitted sheepishly.

"Why aren't you dead? That is a death sentence, no question! How much?"

"I think thirty or forty Gs."

"Josh, it was well over fifty thou," Morris corrected.

"Shit," Peter groaned, "that was a fortune back then. You're lucky you are not part of a Boston highway somewhere. If they knew, they would have killed you dead, real dead, no matter who your father was."

"When I was in Toronto, I died every damn time there was a knock on the door. I would walk down the street looking over my shoulder, wondering if that tough-looking guy behind me had a contract on me. I became totally paranoid. When someone did knock, I prayed it was Chuck Olson with a warrant for my arrest."

Peter issued a gurgle that tried to be a cynical laugh. "No, Chuck wouldn't bother. I would have been sent and I'd only shoot you in a kneecap for being such a dumb schmuck."

"Maybe, but after I despoiled Chuck's sister, all bets were off."

"Kit?" Peter asked.

"Yeah, she tracked me down. She also had hung around our group for a while but mostly to be near me, I guess. She never did anything illegal, as I recall. I lost touch. What happened to her?"

There was a silence. Then Peter spoke. "Well, I might as well be honest here. Old habit, keeping things close to the vest. I did know about Kit and Toronto." Josh looked surprised so Peter continued. "We tracked you during the early years, don't ask how. Sad about Kit, so sad indeed. She was a very lovely girl but spiralled down into drugs. No one could turn her around. She was a walking shell toward the end before she died."

"Chuck surely would have shot me if he had the chance. He must have blamed me for that."

"I don't think you had a worry on that score. Let me put it this way, he had no reason to at the end. Kit was hot on you no doubt, but she went after lots of guys as she spun out. She even hit on me and I was happily married with three young kids. By then, she was strung out which might explain her interest in a schlepp like me. Still, Chuck Olson really did hate your guts so he might have fantasized about rubbing you out, an arrest gone wrong. That was harder to pull off in another country."

"Yes, no doubt about it. It was personal," Josh mused as he considered whether Kit's brother would have set him up for a hit by government men. "And those other guys, that's hard to imagine. She had been so pure. She came on strong to me and I cast her aside. I suppose ... that started it."

"Hmmm, maybe I should arrest your sorry ass for being a heartless schmuck," Peter shot back.

"What did happen to her in the end?" Josh was curious.

Peter opined, "My guess is that she was always searching for things that were not there, and thus remained very unhappy. She was the well-scrubbed sorority sister who never found her way into a sorority, could never figure out if she wanted in. Then, as you know Josh, she fell in with this exciting but twisted group who were hell-bent on saving Western civilization. It lured her in and chewed her up. She said all the right words, dressed in the correct uniforms, but did not belong. In the end, you cannot fake conviction. It takes too much out of you. Each of us fought to find out who we were. For some, it took a long time. Too bad you don't get an instruction book at the start. That is where God screwed up. He didn't give us an instruction book, not that I ever could understand those damn things. Ever read those come-ons for do-it-yourself crap, *even a child can put this together*. Well, maybe a child but no one over twelve. But I digress. Anyway, I looked her up toward the end. Her brother asked me to do it. Now he really was a useless piece of shit, the older brother, I don't care how high in the DOJ he rose. I think he was afraid to see her in case it ruined his damn career. She was in terrible shape, thin as a rail, nervous, distracted, all the signs of a junkie playing out the end game. I could not get her into treatment and had no leverage, not being family."

"Her own brother didn't try?" Rachel was astonished.

"Nope. You might well ask why Chuck ignored her in her darkest hour. My guess is that she probably embarrassed him."

"Wow," Rachel exclaimed. "This guy Chuck reminds me of Evan, self-absorbed."

"I had the same thought." Cate enthused. "Funny, some of the people who go through life with these impeccable reputations and all kinds of public respect turn out to be the biggest assholes."

"Cate," Josh said lightly. "I'm really afraid I'll have to wash your mouth out with soap in the morning, another violation of my no obscenity house rule."

"Well, unc, you can try. But the service taught me some great self-defense tricks."

"Hmm, hadn't thought of that. Okay, I'll put your mother in charge of your punishment. But you do have a point my dear. We always seem impressed with arrogance and entitlement while ignoring those with pure hearts and noble purposes. Look, Chuck rose to the top while Peter, despite having a solid career, was overlooked in my opinion."

"Hey, I wasn't totally invisible." Peter said awkwardly. "Besides, I never minded."

"Really? I'm pissed that life gets things so backward. Peter, you are good people," Josh said.

"You don't know the half of it," Morris intoned.

CHAPTER 17

Day 5 – SHADOWS OF A REVOLUTION

Later, several continued to chat while nibbling on snacks after sending out a scouting party to secure the evening's repast. Those remaining behind were digesting the events of the day while waiting for more food. Mostly, they were from Josh's college past. The discussion, not surprisingly, drifted in that direction.

"Do you ever think back to the old days?" Peter looked at Morris.

"More often than I should. Sometimes, when no one is in the bookstore, which is far too often, I tend to reminisce. I see us back when we all were young, full of vision and so righteous in our purpose. It is almost as if all that were someone else's life, as if it did not happen to us. Who were those idiots who thought they could change the course of history? I mean, it needed changing but why did we think we could do it."

"Hubris on steroids." Josh mused mostly to himself.

"I know what you mean," Carla said. "Remember our first so-called action? What were we thinking? Who would have thought we were among the brightest in that school, except for that Jewish girl you dated, Josh, the one who was at the top of the class."

"Sarah. But she doesn't count."

"Why's that?" Morris asked.

"She studied. The rest of us were too busy storming the ramparts of futility. I'm surprised she took time out for me."

"We all are," Carla continued.

"Ah," Josh laughed, "you were just jealous of her."

"Not Sarah, it was the other one … the one you kept secret."

Josh was about to respond when suddenly the door opened and Connie, Usha, and Meena stormed back in laden with quantities of aromatic foods.

"Hope everyone likes spicy food. We got Josh's favorite, delicacies from the sub-continent. That's only because this day is his. He had better not get used to this."

Peter wrinkled his nose. "Not that Indian crap. He's always getting that stuff."

Josh issued a belly laugh. "Come on, you ignorant Wop, time to try new things, not everything can be smothered in marinara sauce."

"Don't listen to him Peter," Connie added, "we also got some pizza for normal folk." Everyone found their way to the food and loaded up. People ate and exchanged pleasantries about the day and how Josh obviously had his colleagues fooled. Josh was aware that Cate and Rachel kept glancing in his direction.

"What were you guys talking about?" Connie asked as the dinner wound down.

"Oddly enough, we were still thinking back to our youthful adventures." Josh explained.

"Ooh," Usha exclaimed, "I'd love to hear more about those. Josh never shared any of his youthful misadventures with me. I concluded he was hatched fully formed as an adult."

"Don't feel bad. He never shared with anyone," Rachel added.

Carla spoke up. "Remember this, guys?"

"Boring!" Josh tried.

Carla glared at Josh to silence him. "We were just starting on our first so-called action. We picked out a selective service office and decided to break in to destroy records. The three of us, Mo and Josh and I, were dressed in dark clothes. I'm surprised we did not put boot black on our faces like all those covert guys. We were no longer settling for doing something symbolic, this was to be the first strike of an uprising that would take down the war machine. God, we took ourselves seriously. I think we parked some four blocks away and crept along in the dead of night?"

"What I remember is that Mo stumbled on a curb and I almost crapped in my pants," Josh said.

"Was that the time a cruiser pulled around the corner and we jumped behind some bushes?" Carla asked.

"No, that was later at the facility in Ware." Josh added. "That's a small city in central Massachusetts, for the uninformed."

Mo picked up the story line. "I remember as if it were last night. This was the first when we were even more jumpy. So, we finally get to the door and what do we do … start to argue. What if an alarm goes off when we pry it open? Carla here still wanted to do something to indicate we had struck while Josh wanted us to get the hell out of there. Finally, after much discussion, we got to work to prying the door open. Since we were the gang that could not shoot straight, I tried first. As you can see, I have the arm strength of a wet noodle. After struggling, Josh just grabs the crowbar and gives the damn thing a good yank. When it broke, we were sure the resulting crack could be heard in downtown Boston. We wait, no alarm sound. Next, we start our assault on the war machine and my good wife asks if anyone considered the possibility of a silent alarm. We all froze to think that one through but decided we were screwed so we might as well keep going. Once in, we started debating what to focus on. I remember us checking out various file draws, this was long before computerization. Amazing now that we had no plan going in. We did come across something that looked like pending draft decisions where the status was under dispute. Those we piled out onto the floor and poured red paint all over them. Then we ripped up stuff and did other mischief before getting skittish and deciding to get out."

Carla laughed in a way that pleased Josh for some reason. "Oh yes, and we got about a block away and our discipline broke down. We started running like mad. Talk about looking guilty. International jewel thieves we were not."

Rachel looked on with a bemused expression she could not suppress. "Why didn't you stop? Clearly, you were out of your league."

"We were on a mission and we did get better with practice," Carla noted. "Not perfect, though. Later, we were doing an office in Lawrence. It was sandwiched in between several businesses. Obviously, now being pros at this, we were not going to break in the front door facing the street. With great stealth and consummate cunning, we snuck down the back alley. But we counted the doors wrong. So then, when we broke in, it was the wrong place It was not a government office at all."

"What was it?" Cate asked.

"A lingerie store!"

Silence, then everyone laughed as Cate said, "So you knocked off Victoria's Secret?"

"Well, I did grab a couple of lacy bras before we left." Carla's lips were curled in a thin smile. "Funny now, not so funny then."

Josh chortled. "Ha-ha, you didn't even wear bras back then, I suppose I could've used the sexy nighties, though, when seducing the ladies. Hey girlie, what can I get for some sexy lingerie? Let's face it, my charms alone were not going to get these gals into my bed." His earlier reluctance had completely evaporated.

"They still aren't." Connie offered while chewing on a slice of a pepperoni pizza.

"Don't eat and talk at the same time." Josh reprimanded her. "It's not becoming of a lady."

"What lady would that be." Connie stuck her tongue out at him.

Josh already had shifted and missed her attempt at a humorous insult. "Things soon got serious, or more serious at least. Jimmie and Bob had big plans. They came and asked me if I could get them dynamite and stuff like that. This was nuts, but I didn't even ask why. I was the go-to guy. I had the connections, through my dad's bar, so I showed them where they could get the stuff, a small construction company owned by a guy who frequented my dad's place. I had done some odd work for him and knew the layout and a bit about explosives by this time. God, I wish I had that moment back. Stupid, stupid, stupid!" He got up and poured himself another drink. "And then there was the time that Helen came up to me and said I should help her on an action … we called them actions back then. She told me Mo wanted it done."

Mo shrugged. "I doubt that. I never would have gone on an action only with her. She always was a wild card. I doubt all her marbles were in place."

"I took her at her word and drove her to a place in Worcester. Don't ask me what I was thinking. This was too close to home, our college home at least. She had a big bag with cans inside. I thought it was paint. I was getting nervous now. We had been lucky, moving around and hoping to remain lost amid so much growing anti-war stuff. But patterns would not be overlooked forever. I had a terrible feeling in my stomach from the start." He took another sip. "We get inside, and all seemed okay. We open some files, and she gives me a can. I pour the paint, and she takes another can. As she pours the liquid out, I stop in my tracks. That is not just paint, even I knew it was laced with an accelerant of some kind. The smell is unmistakable. Before I can say anything, she strikes a match and the place goes whoosh. I thought my freaking eyelids were gone. That moment got me thinking about backing off."

"In what way?" Cate asked.

"I could see that the logical imperative was to become more extreme. You felt you had to ratchet up when there was no response. And even a numbnut like me could see that no one would suddenly end the war, nor would there be any general uprising. We would be alone, and we would eventually get caught. But for what? Up to that moment, no one had been injured. Fortunately, the fire was put out before anyone was hurt, there were apartments next door. It could have been a disaster."

"On the next action, with the usual team, an alarm did go off. We barely got our asses out in time. They were beefing up security, that would not be their only response. We now forget how much low-level terrorism went on during that period. Catching domestic terrorists, even amateur revolutionaries like us, was becoming a big push. That insight, that our time was running out, was catching up with me. My damn conscience also was causing me no end of grief."

"Hmmm," Carla murmured. "you did an action with Helen. I forgot."

"Was that important?" Josh asked.

"Not sure, maybe." Then she shrugged.

Josh smiled as he looked at Carla and Mo. "Funny how our youth morphs with time. What we loved or hated or feared is reborn in our imagination. But I wonder, I have always wondered about whether we really were so wrong? Were we? Damn it, we were among the brightest of our generation. I'm convinced of that. Yet we became outcasts in our own land except for Peter."

Peter put his plate down. "You, Josh, were not an outcast, but an exile. Not sure which is worse. Hey, remember that night when Mo asked us to make a kind of bond with one another? Sure you do. We all do. I left, the only one to do so. Funny, even though that decision probably saved me untold grief and gave me a shot at a good career and nice family and all the trappings of middle-class success, I still don't know if I did the right thing. I wanted to be with you guys. I thought you were right. For me, the choice was one of excess common sense, which just might be another word for cowardice."

"Don't beat yourself up," Morris quickly added.

"No, damn it, I didn't have the guts to do what I thought was right. When pushed, I chose the easier path. It wasn't even like I gave it great thought. At the time, I had no idea how consequential that choice was. Later, though, I thought about it a lot. It was my whole life. But who knew in the moment?"

Josh leaned back. "You were not alone in your doubts that night. I came within a whisker of joining you. These things, these life choices, were just made with little or no thought. Funny, you spend all kinds of time trying to decide what movie you want to see on a weekend and almost no time on the course of your life. I bought this house after walking through it once. Okay, it had a roof and I could walk to the university. Good enough. Of course, it was affordable back then, but that's the thing. Have you ever observed real decision makers? They will spend time on small matters like whether to hire an extra secretary for the office and then pass a huge entitlement budget without much debate. They can get their head around the small issue, but the big stuff is too big. Events carry you along. You flow along day by day and suddenly, you find yourself facing something big, perhaps irreversible. But you never know at the time."

"Yes," Cate said distractedly, "some choices we make. Others, it seems, are made for us. All the same in the end, I suppose."

Josh smiled at his niece. She could make him regret not having children of his own, but only briefly. His kid would probably rebel and become a Republican. "I suppose there are major roads taken and not taken where we never appreciate the consequences. Other times, we think of something as being small, yet which turns out to have enormous import. How does one ever know? But that night, when Morris asked for our pledge, it seemed a major fork in the road. And I just decided, perhaps with trepidation but not great consideration. None of us said, *give me a week to think it over* or even *let me sleep on it overnight*. That would have made sense but not one of us did that. How odd."

Morris sighed. "Perhaps you have a point. I was carried along by everything in my life. My heritage was all about fighting oppression, seeking justice for working people. Hell, I was weaned on the holocaust, and heard stories from my grandad about the brave new world the Bolsheviks envisioned at the beginning of their uprising against the Czar. Righteousness is what I was fed as a child. Other kids ate oatmeal, I was spoon-fed revolution. By the time I was eight years old, my fate was determined. There was no other choice, so I never thought hard about things. Not quite true, I thought hard about how to justify my core choices after the fact."

Carla then chimed in. "I grew up in a religious family, my dad was a rabbi, and I took it seriously. I absorbed the guilt at least, that I needed to do the right thing and fight evil."

"I always knew you wanted to be a Catholic, Carla." Josh chuckled.

"What?"

"Come on, think about it. Most of the left-wingers in our generation were either Jews or adherents to the one, true, holy and universal faith."

"The one true what?" Carla seemed dubious.

"That is what we called Catholicism when I was young." Josh got up. "Like all of us, I have gone over those times repeatedly in my head. Rachel wonders why I hid up here for so many years, even after I could have come home. It was fear in part. I always worried that a warrant would be issued for my arrest and that coming back to the States would end with my ass in the pokey. Since I never changed my name and the RCMPs never came to arrest me, I suspected that was just paranoia after a while."

"I don't know." Peter chuckled. "I had a lot of fantasies about throwing your ass in jail."

"Funny man. Seriously, most of my paralysis was simple guilt. In my head, I had committed to my friends and then I ran away. I would read about Jimmie's death, arrests, trials, prison sentences, and think only that I was the coward that ran away. What did Shakespeare say, the coward dies a thousand deaths, but the hero dies but once? That is so freaking true. I just could not face anything for a long time. By the time I relaxed, I had a new life but still could not shake my fear that there would be a knock on the door. I guess I was beyond paranoia, I had wandered well into the land of the delusional."

Peter rose to put his plate away. "Listen to me. While I do subscribe to the belief that you are a little bat-shit crazy, you were not as paranoid as you think. Chuck Olson was, in truth, after your ass. Oddly enough, we were both assigned to a joint task force on domestic terrorism. You were in our sights, and Chuck seemed to have it in for you. If you had asked me in the 1970s, I would have advised you to stay up north. It was personal with him. And he was in a position to at least try to nail your ass."

"His sister, I'm so sure he blamed me."

"Yeah, you did have a way with the ladies, and I can't discount that. Not that I'm looking for praise, but I kept trying to deflect him."

"You did?" Josh seemed surprised. "Why?"

"Damned if I know." Peter waived a dismissive hand, then grew serious. "Maybe loyalty, I guess. The friendship … the bond we had. Besides, I knew you were harmless, or thought so. In my mind, you would never be a terrorist even though you were on one of our watch lists which, in those days, was easy to get on. Of course, I didn't know about all your misdeeds, that you were stupid enough to steal from the mob nor the arson thing. And getting explosives, that blows my mind. Frankly, I'm glad I did not know about all of it, I would have been conflicted. That would have been a tough call at the time. Good thing you escaped early. When you did, I only had you pegged as a stupid Mick, as most of your tribe were. Nothing more."

Josh thought for a moment. "We all had our moments of struggle, of decision. Hmm, I wonder if we thought ourselves invulnerable. Is that why we just made these … choices. Did we see ourselves as anointed in some way? It seemed like we would sit around chatting up things like…oh well, I guess I'll try to bring down the state next week. Unless it is nice out, then we'll go to the shore for some sun? Were we naïve or stupid?" He paused as if seeking to answer his own query. "No, in the end, we were neither. Damn it, we were right in our analysis but wrong on tactics. That is clear now though it was not then. We were right on the war, but more violence in response to violence was plain stupid."

"Amen." Connie added.

"But it goes deeper even than that." Josh continued his inner dialogue.

"What do you mean?" Morris asked. "I'm losing you."

"We were raised in interesting times, as the old Chinese curse says. We did not know it, but we came of age when the American dream was real. From the war—the Second World War—through the early 1970s, America enjoyed almost unprecedented growth. But what marked the period as unusual was that the growth was shared equally by all. Not only did real incomes double but those at the bottom also shared in the good fortune as much as everyone else. In fact, they did better than the wealthy by historical standards, so inequality fell. What did that mean, you ask? Well, kids like us could go to college. We did not worry about getting jobs. We assumed jobs would be there. So rather than focus on survival, we obsessed about the higher-order issues like justice and equality and the good society. When I was in school, stateside college I mean, I never worried about what courses to take. I selected the ones I thought I might enjoy. Same when I came up here. Now, I look over the anxious faces of kids who are worried sick about their futures and what it holds. It's worse for the college kids in the States. Those poor SOBs are up to their asses in debt. If they don't get a good job straight out of school, they will be off their parent's health insurance and screwed if they have an accident or get sick. It is a different world. We were a fortunate generation and a cursed generation."

"Fortunate." Carla simply said the word, neither a question nor a confrontation.

"Yeah," Josh responded. "We had this deep belief that all would turn out right, if only we stood up to insanity. We had a Teflon future before us. Nothing bad would stick. Truth and justice would prevail. Too many B movies and superheroes."

"Some of us were not blessed with rose-tinted glasses. Some of us were even more cursed with an excess of conviction than others." Morris grimaced.

"Yeah, for sure," Josh agreed. "we couldn't ignore our sense of commitment. Yet, we still sinned."

"Meaning?" Rachel asked.

"I think our biggest sin was to focus on the wrong thing. Now, give me a minute to see if I can get this right. We vented our spleens on the war. That was easy. Kids, the males at least, had some real skin in that game. But the real issues were bigger I suspect. Remember that the

Port Huron statement, the signal call of our generation, was framed before Vietnam was on anyone's agenda. It basically decried a lost generation dulled by success and lacking consciousness and direction. We lost that issue in our fury about the war and, in truth, lost our way. Vietnam was easy. It was so wrong, so stupendously stupid, that it became the low-hanging fruit … the easy target. It was the Iraq war of our generation except the cost was greater both there and at home. There was even our WMD moment, the Gulf of Tonkin fabrication. We had been attacked, or so the myth went. It was easier and easier to rally some support against the war as it dragged on and on with mounting casualties and increasing numbers being placed in harm's way. We were on our own slippery slope, though. There would be no easy exit once we started. After all, we could not end the insanity. That was way beyond our meager abilities, and yet the psychological assault on our reason and sanity continued unabated. We were trapped by our own sense of right."

"Having principles is such a curse, who knew?" Carla growled softly.

"It is. Especially when you pound on the wrong nail." Josh stopped. "Where the hell did I come up with that metaphor? I don't even have a tool kit. Anyway, those who never forgave Roosevelt and the Great Depression for evening out the odds of success in society were just waiting for their revenge. The elite wanted a return to their full privilege and entitlement. They loved an unequal society with few real winners. Remember, as late as the 1950s, the top tax rate hovered around 90 percent, education at public universities was a deal, unions were protected. The working guy had a chance, and his kids, like us, had every opportunity. We assumed that we would sweep away the remaining detritus of injustice, like de jure segregation, and that all the economic gains that had been made would remain intact. Little did we know."

"Yeah, I guess our crystal balls were a little cloudy," Morris said.

"While we frittered our energies away on something that would end in any case. Face it, America would eventually lose in Vietnam. That was a certainty, and for the same reason the Brits lost the Colonies. It was too expensive to fight against a determined foe thousands of miles away. We fought a symptom while the core of the elite began to focus on the war that counted. They systemically went about reframing the political debate and electoral protocols to dominate US policies."

Rachel tilted her head. "I'll need more. Remember, I'm just a plumber for the human body as you keep saying."

"I only said that once, and you are a very talented plumber." Josh chuckled. "Still, think about it. How does a major political party that essentially serves the interests of the top sliver of the economic pyramid retain such a hold on power? It makes no sense. Huge numbers must vote against their own interests. There is one county in Kentucky that is virtually all-white and dirt-poor. Something like 90 percent are on food stamps, and their kids are on free or subsidized lunches. Yet they vote overwhelmingly Republican, the party that would eviscerate those benefits they desperately need to survive. Why would they do that? I guess because they still believe that the GOP will make it hard on those they despise ... minorities and immigrants. The strategies of the right are not all that brilliant. They use the oldest misdirection plays in the book ... we will give you permission to hate the guy that looks a little different than you while we steal you blind."

"Just racism, then," Rachel said thoughtfully.

"A bit more complicated. It is more like a full-blown caste system that's being protected ... a deep, cultural divide composed of many layers." Josh intoned. "This goes back to John C. Calhoun and the early 1800s. The South had more millionaires than the North, and great income inequality. The elite even then knew they had to control what was called democracy to maintain power, in effect prevent democracy from maturing. With poll taxes and literacy tests, they could ensure that only propertied whites would have power up through the 1960s. Harry Bird, and his class-based dynasty, ran Virginia just before World War II with less than 20 percent voting in elections. Rule by oligarchy. In the 1960s, that was under attack, with the voting rights act and all. But we focused on the war while they continued to focus on keeping democracy from becoming a reality. They had to keep the masses impotent and they knew how to do it."

"Sure, easy to see now," Mo said. "We focused on the elephant in the room while the real issue went unaddressed."

"Not so fast." Cate looked sceptical. "After all, we did get the voting rights act. There was broader progress at the very time you guys were doing your so-called actions. There were lots of protests going on."

Mo spoke with a deliberation Josh did not recall from the old days. "True enough, Cate. Our problem was that we dissipated our energy and focus too easily or were foolish enough to get thrown in jail. The right systemically went about reframing the underlying political dialogue in this country and restating the default political narrative for most Americans. Markets are good, government is bad, the cause of all your problems is the black or brown guy and all those foreigners. They gave people fear and simple answers, a convenient narrative to distract them while the elite picked them clean."

"Like I said at the ceremony," Josh was warming to the topic, "the top 1 percent of the pie has seen their share go from less than 10 percent to almost one-quarter in recent decades. That constitutes a tectonic change of historic proportions. The shift started when Reagan took power, but the groundwork was being laid after the big war, in the late 1940s. The right-wing elite saw collectivism everywhere, from the new Deal in America to the energized Labor Party in England, to the rampaging Russian Bear across eastern Europe. The met in Switzerland to alter the trajectory of history, to start a transformational process to ensure that free markets operated absent any government oversight. Common people were the enemy. F.A. Hayek, Ludwig Von Mises of the Austrian School, and Frank Knight of the University of Chicago were elected as the titular heads of an invitation-only group that had a vision. They would stamp out and eradicate anything that smelled of the public good in the name of individual freedom and the protection of private property and wealth. Knight subsequently mentored James Buchanan whom I mentioned earlier, then an economics student at Chicago. He founded the Virginia School of Political Economy, largely in response to so-called federal overreach in desegregating public schools. Back then, it was the William Volker fund, headed by Harold Luhnow, that supplied the money. Now it is the Koch brothers and the Mercers and the Adelsons and the Uihleins and so many more. They have stayed the course decade after decade to cut away at democratic processes and convince folk that an economic elite will govern in their best interests. How sad is that?"

"And we, who only wanted to make things a little better, ended up in jail," Carla said bitterly.

"Sucks, doesn't it. Today, we have those cute facts like the richest 100 families have as much wealth as the bottom half of the world's population or that .00025 percent of Americans have as much as the 150 million poorest in their land. And yet, it still is not enough. The Koch brothers continue to spend enormous amounts of their treasury to further tilt the rules in their favor. When is enough, enough? Is there no limit to greed, to outright avarice? They won. We lost. How about a truce? But no! You would think that such smart guys would figure out that there is a limit to the share of resources that they can command. What will happen when the overwhelming masses cannot buy the crap they produce, when their desperation becomes overwhelming? When that happens, the system will collapse in an apocalypse. Either that, or climate change will turn the earth into a crispy wasteland. If we were smart enough, that is what we should have seen coming. That is what we should have dealt with. But that would have been way too difficult for us to take on, way too difficult. The war was simple, insane, and right in front of us."

Josh looked around the room. He saw Morris and Carla sitting together, Cate and Meena. Then he noticed Rachel and Usha together. It suddenly struck him that this was not the first time he had seen them paired off. Was that just in his imagination? He thought not, recalling Usha's question. Connie was next to him. She was looking at him intently. Only Peter sat off by himself. But that was okay. He had always been the sensible one, with the loving wife, three kids, and seven grandchildren. Josh realized he had fallen into a monologue. "I probably should apologize for the lecture."

Several protested that there was no need for that.

"Okay then, at least this material will not be on the final." He smiled.

"Good," said Peter with a chuckle. "I wasn't listening."

Josh went on. "Right or wrong, for good or bad, there's something about those days that are unforgettable. Every insight seemed fresh and unassailable. Every emotion was heightened by a sharp intensity. All things and events since those days seem pale by comparison. It was our war, our crucible in which we were tested. I guess I needed to say that. Otherwise, what I want to say next won't make sense." He paused before looking at Peter, Morris, and Carla in turn. "I love you, guys. You know, we picked the wrong target, used the wrong tactics, and screwed up our lives. Still, in the end, I would never give up those memories. We had something precious."

"What, for god's sake?" Mo looked puzzled.

"We cared for Christ sake. We gave a damn. I should have stayed, maybe tried to talk us on to a different path. I should have had the balls to stick with it." He paused to realize he did not quite know what to say next.

Those watching Josh could see the tear find its way down his cheek. He did not bother to brush it away.

Carla got up and walked over to embrace him. Morris was right behind her. Now, there was more than one person brushing away a tear. "Oh," Josh added, "you aren't bad either, Peter, for the slowest running back in eastern Massachusetts."

Peter joined them. "I really should have let Olson throw your sorry ass in the pokey. What was I thinking?"

"Listen, everyone. Tomorrow, road trip to Whistler. It is a must-see for the out-of-towners. Time for some laughs." A cheer went up.

— —

Later, Josh drove Peter, Morris, and Carla back to their hotel where he spent some time catching up with what was going on in their lives. When he returned to his place, it was mostly dark though he could tell that a light was still on in Rachel's room. Probably catching up on e-mails, he thought. As he pulled into his driveway, he noticed Connie's car at the curb. She emerged as he exited his vehicle.

"Can't find your way home?" he queried her lightly.

"Not sure I could fall asleep. Then I remembered, Connelly always puts me in a coma. I'll listen to him some more."

"And so, you thought you would harass me a bit." He tried keeping it light.

"My favorite pastime if you remember. Besides, it just struck me that you might need some, what shall we say, comfort tonight and it might be a little late to get one of your professionals. Besides, my prices are better."

"Oh no." He laughed. "You may not demand cash, but there is always a price. That's the one lesson about women emblazoned firmly in my soul."

"True enough," she responded. "the question is, are you willing to pay my price?"

He paused, as if thinking deeply. "I might. Need to see what you've got to offer first."

"You've seen it buster. Best offer an aging lothario like yourself will get these days."

Later, they slipped into his bed. He merely held her, her head nestled onto his chest and their legs intertwined. Neither moved in a way that would signal that sex was imminent. It was more a moment of intimacy, not passion.

"I miss this," he said.

"Me too. Then again, I don't go around seeking the services of male professionals. I'm sure gigolo services are of higher quality, but you will do in a pinch."

"Why did you dump me, by the way?" he asked. "And it was you that dumped me."

"Yeah, I suppose," she breathed deeply. "Thing is, you were too detached. Perhaps I let my female protective instincts overcome my earlier lapse of judgment. A temporary yielding to lustful fantasies unfortunately can short-circuit the brains of the best women."

"Ow, then you didn't stand a chance in the face of my Adonis-like body."

"Shows what you know," Connie whispered. "You want the real story?"

He paused before saying, "Yes, I do."

"The truth is that I read some of your e-mails to this girl Eleni one day. I should not have, I am sorry, awfully bad of me. Can't remember what I was looking for, but I ran across them just sitting on your computer. Wow! I realized how much you loved her. That was okay, but I also realized something else … how little you would ever love me."

He considered several responses before settling on a question. "Why tonight, then?" He realized that was not what he wanted to say.

She snuggled even closer to him, kissing his neck and face. "With all my education and experience, I remain a dumb shit. Ultimately, there is no accounting for taste. My question is *why did you let me get in your bed?*"

"As you say, there is no accounting for taste." He smiled.

She stroked his face. "I watched you over the past few days. I guess I remember why I … was drawn to you. But today, you looked different. How long have we known each other? No, don't answer, it reminds me that I'm on the verge of becoming a fossil, just like you. But in all that time, I never saw the intensity that was there today."

"Like what? Frankly, I thought I revealed little."

"But inside?" she pursued. "You couldn't hide what was there. It struck me … you can feel things."

"Inside, I died several times. Even I found it hard to come up with an occasional quip. With time, pain and guilt subside but those things never go away entirely. Perhaps the sharpness mutes into a dull throb until you cannot run away anymore. I could hardly look at Morris and Carla without falling on my knees … begging for forgiveness."

"But they ..." Connie started to protest.

"I know, I know, that made it worse. They didn't betray a trace of disappointment, never mind disapproval. I could not believe it. How could they be so good? How could they so easily forgive?"

"Josh, listen to me." She raised herself up on her elbow to look at him. "I am a scientist, not an expert in the human mind. But I have learned one thing that I sense you know all too well. Do not judge others by what is in your heart and head. Do not kick your psyche senseless because you believe they must secretly despise you. I looked at them hard all day. The only thing that I saw was anxiety."

"Anxiety?"

"Yes, that you would reject them. My guess is that they saw themselves at fault. My guess is that they felt they somehow dragged you into something you did not really want to do. And my best instinct tells me that you didn't want to do some of those things. Oh yes, your Irish blood was up, I've no doubt about that, but I don't think you would have gone there just with your anger. In the end, they believed they screwed with your life. They felt they led you astray, or so they believed."

"What do you think?"

"About?" She was not quite sure where he was going.

"What do you think about what I did?" Josh needed to know.

She leaned back into his chest and arms, tightened her legs around him. "It makes me like you even more. You're even more of a bad boy in my head."

"Hah." Josh chuckled. "I never understood that bad boy thing. I'm so lucky it comes easily to me."

"So, Mr. Bad Boy, are you going to make love to me? I am practically jumping your bones here, and I should be way too dignified to do that."

Josh stroked her hair with affection. "Not tonight, I feel spent. Too much today. But I'm so glad you're here. And there's this other problem."

"What problem?" Connie asked with genuine confusion.

"You're a groaner."

"A what?" She propped up on her arm to see him better.

"You shout out when you orgasm, you might upset the houseguests."

She took her free arm and punched him in the stomach. "Groaner, my ass. Have you ever listened to yourself?"

Between deep breathes, Josh managed a few words. "Damn, you have been talking to Rachel. That's her favorite trick."

"Rain check, then?" she asked, now smiling.

"Rain check for sure," Josh promised. "I think the discussion earlier has put me in a mood."

"A mood? And all this time I thought you only had one mood … horny."

"No, my dear, you are thinking of all those other guys you have known."

"Careful. You must now realize I'm within striking distance of what you refer to as the family jewels."

"Josh chuckled. Good point. No, I couldn't help ponder what I might have done differently, if I could go back as I am today."

Now Connie chuckled. "You're not claiming you are older and wiser now. Well, you are older for sure but that's it I'm afraid."

"Another good point. You are on fire. I think some of us are born with wiring in our brains that is way too complicated."

Connie leaned up to kiss his cheek. "And with hearts that are way too caring. A toxic mix for sure."

"Who knows?" Josh sounded far away. "All my life I kept struggling with one conundrum. If I had had children, and they asked me what I did when we were faced with some political or moral crisis, what would I say. *'Oh, my child, I went to war and killed a bunch of people fighting for their futures.'* Or would it be *'I followed my conscience and fought against what I thought was evil, even if the effort was the height of stupidity and which, by the way, rather destroyed my family.'"*

Connie lie next to him for some time, simply listening to his heartbeat as her head rested against his chest. This is what she had missed since their breakup. He frustrated and infuriated her but, in the end, she felt alive when with him. He made her think and feel. "You do realize, don't you, that this is a hypothetical that probably defies a rational answer?"

"Spoken like a true scientist." Josh moved so he could kiss her on the top of her head. "And yet, for me ... I'm not sure I could live without such questions. Does that make sense, or have I gone around the bend?"

"Oh, my sweet Joshua, you went around that bend a long time ago. But that's why I ..." she paused, not daring to complete her thought.

"Why what?"

"Why I've returned to take another shot at the most dysfunctional relationship of my life." Inside, she kicked herself for not saying what she wanted to reveal. "I guess women really do make bad decisions."

"I know one woman who does." Josh sensed all kinds of long suppressed feelings rising within him, only to be ignored one more time. "Just hold me tonight if that is enough. Thing is, my head, the one on top of my neck is too full of stuff, preventing my other head, located between my knees to function as it should."

"I get it, you men are just so emotionally complicated." she murmured with a small laugh as they sank into sleep while making love only within their separate imaginations.

CHAPTER 18

Day 6 – EARLY MORNING

Rachel could not sleep. At one point, she heard voices. One sounded like Connie, but that was probably her imagination. It must have been the TV in Josh's room or maybe Cate and Meena finally were enjoying some noisy sex. She squirmed at that thought, a response she dismissed as silly. After all, intimacy was natural for those in love. Then again, how would she know? She had never been to that place called love, did not even know if it really existed. Perhaps she was missing that part of the brain where such feelings originated or had been short-changed on the necessary hormones. Oh well, no real loss. That love business seems way overrated in any case. More trouble than it is worth.

That tangent dismissed; her thoughts returned to her brother. All afternoon and evening, she had examined his face looking for clues to his deeper emotional condition. She realized at some point that their separation had weakened her confidence in her ability to read his moods. At this point in his life, she was not sure about the idiosyncratic tells that might reveal his inner thoughts and feelings. It always is possible to detect these tells but you need exposure to the target. That had been missing for so long. On the surface, he revealed little aside from his occasional soliloquies which reflected his political views and not his emotional character. She wanted more than public words that might, after all, be staged to obscure deeper feelings. That, however, would have to wait until they were alone.

She turned over, trying to get her mind to settle down. She sometimes could work on her breathing, slowing the pace and trying to sense various parts of her body relaxing. She did this on nights before heavy surgery schedules, those moments when REM sleep was particularly desired. For a bit, her tactic seemed to be working. Then suddenly, the image of Usha flashed through her mind. What is this all about, she wondered. She liked Usha from their first introduction when she played the role of Josh's spouse. But now they were talking more, particularly around the situation of her daughter and Meena. She was so grateful that Usha was willing to bring her considerable legal knowledge. Though she knew Canadian law best, Rachel assumed that Usha could navigate computerized law files for the UK and the US. Besides, she had many contacts across the legal and government worlds who could fill in the blanks.

But gratitude for her help is not what was keeping her awake now. It was Usha's smell, the periodic touch of her fingers on Rachel's arm, the look that lingered longer than it should. Once, when they were attending to a computer screen together, Usha brushed up against her, her breast resting against her back. Rachel squirmed ever so slightly, expecting the woman to pull away. Usha had not, however. Rachel was glad; a warm sensation suffused through her body.

She jumped out of bed, confused. What was she thinking, feeling? She had assumed control over her body years ago. She had been irritated when she sensed males circling about her, seeing an attractive single professional woman who was affluent and unattached. She was a catch or, at the least, a wonderful target for a dalliance. But she would summarily shut them down; her shields were unmistakable. Rachel thought her capacity to want another person was gone. She had convinced herself that she was self-contained, that her independence was to be valued and protected. Perhaps she was more like Josh than she realized. Nevertheless, she remained convinced that she was now the stronger of the two. She did not need others, he did.

In her confusion, she required a distraction. She looked around the room for the place where she had stashed Josh's file earlier in the morning. Every time she considered peering into his private life, she felt more than a twinge of reluctance despite having his permission. Then she would remember, he had kept her out of his life for four decades. To hell with her reservations. After all, he had given her the file in the first place. Her reluctance lay elsewhere. What further secrets lie inside the magic kingdom of her brother's life? Some of what she had learned has been less than pretty. With a sigh, she forged ahead once more into her brother's past.

She picked up the latest material, the breadcrumbs as he put it, that he had scattered in front of her. She went to a different stack of paper. She immediately noticed a difference. This material was not from the distant past, but rather recent. Moreover, these were printed copies of e-mails which, while all with Eleni, went in both directions. She would now be privy to a dialogue between them, not just his side of things. She would get to see inside Eleni's head, and perhaps heart. How exciting. At the same time, she felt nervous.

This was an almost mythical relationship in Rachel's mind. In fact, there had been moments when she had wondered if this Eleni existed. Perhaps Josh had made her up out of whole cloth, a fictional creation to replace the hole he had created in his own life by running away from all who had loved him. At first, she dismissed this as ridiculous, but the possibility never entirely disappeared. He had never mentioned Eleni, not in the distant past nor in her recent memory, not once. No one else in his orbit seemed to know about her. She was certain that Cate knew nothing of her and could not recall his college friends mentioning her. Now, there were emails to him from this Eleni. They must be from the period after they had reconnected, somehow, through cyberspace as he had claimed. She paused, caught between excitement and caution. What other secrets lie in his life, in this portion of his world hidden by design or innocent omission? What was going on in her brother's twisted head? Perhaps a clue or two to such mysteries was in these exchanges somewhere, but only if she dared look.

Carefully, she picked up some of the pages as if they might burn one at the mere touch. She rifled through them, looking mostly at the dates. No order, she cursed her brother's lack of discipline. Typical male, one reason she preferred to work with female colleagues, especially in her research and writing. Males wanted to use her as a gifted administrative assistant mostly because they were easily distracted and lacked all discipline. Yet, they tended to ignore female colleagues in ways that mattered. Their hubris prevented them from acknowledging any intellectual contributions from female associates. How sad of them. Could they not see that medicine was the next profession to be dominated by women? If you looked at medical school rosters, it already was. Hah, she mused to herself. The male gender quickly was becoming irrelevant. She wondered if that side of the species might soon become obsolete, with a few being preserved as a source of sperm until procreation can be turned over to machines when the singularity was realized. Then she shook her head clear. *Focus*, she told herself and grabbed a couple of letters with earlier dates and started reading.

To Leni:

I thought I might respond to your comment about being perplexed by our time together, how the "we" of our past was such a mystery. Perhaps we are both looking for clarity. I have thought on these questions from time to time over the years. I doubt I have any insights, but I thought I would start an answer. Bear with me, this may be a bit "stream of consciousness" style.

After forty-plus years, I can still feel the moment I first saw you. It was some event toward the end of semester or during the summer break. I could not understand my reaction, very intense and frightening. Let us say I did not like emotions of any stripe at the time. I knew they were strong because I waited until that fall, screwed up my courage (after weeks of procrastinating), and then asked you out. Of course, you said no and had some kind excuse. Normally, that would have been it, but I tried again (after weeks of angst). That was a big clue that my sanity was gone; I never tried a second time.

The relationship was intense and baffling to me. Dating Sarah was cool and easy, kind of detached and cerebral. I liked that. With you, it was intense, volatile, and uncertain. I know I tried pushing you away emotionally to maintain my sense of order and control and that I felt you doing the same to me. You know, I cannot recall ever saying that I loved you and I cannot recall you ever saying that to me. Maybe we did, but I cannot recall, not a single time. I'm not sure I would have heard the words back then.

I think you don't know if you love someone until much time has passed. For the next four decades, there always remained a sense of loss, a dull ache, a bit of sadness and regret. Occasionally, I would fantasize that we would somehow reunite. Then I snap to and think, hell, she is probably a fat shrew by now, with seven kids, and bad body odor. You can't go home and all that. I rationalized that those feelings were most likely a product of time and place and lack of maturity—a childish puppy love.

I'm not one to live in regret, to whine about what might have been. We make choices and we live with them. From where I am now would I have done things differently? Yes, I think I would. I would have at least given you a shot. Would it have worked? I don't know, maybe passion and intensity are the worst foundations for a lasting relationship. Maybe we could not have found a core on which to build a life. But it would have been fun to try. I recall spending one night with you on the Cape. I have an indelible image of you waking up in the morning with a breeze blowing into the window and you at my side. I've never recaptured that moment. So yeah, something rather irreplaceable slipped beyond my (our) grasp.

Josh

To Josh:

Sure. Go ahead. Enjoy yourself while I sit here stewing, agonizing, ruminating, and rationalizing. Don't worry about me—I'll be fine :-)

Thank you for sharing your thoughts and memories so freely—I'm incredibly grateful. You're a brave man. I'm totally useless after reading your emails, but I needed to prepare for a meeting after the last one and didn't want to give you a hurried response. As if a hurried response were even possible.

That was yesterday. Today, after much thought (okay, obsessing), I still don't have a clue where to start. The most natural place for me, always, is to beg forgiveness. I think I've always understood your ambivalence, but I wasn't as aware of my own. I know I have a selective memory, but I don't remember any of the bad stuff—the volatility, the pain, the pulling away. I'm so sorry about that!

One of my favorite memories (apparently indelible, thank goodness) was that morning on the Cape that you also remember. It was beautiful and magical and fleeting. As I was thinking about all this over the past day, I think I finally understood something that had escaped me before— "we" just didn't have enough time to develop. Duh! We were together so infrequently and briefly that we didn't have time to get beyond the exhilaration that any new relationship creates or to figure out that maybe it wasn't so perfect after all.

In my convenient selective memory, things seemed to be on track until you left. I just felt I never had a chance to say goodbye. That wasn't a great start to any long-distance relationship. I cherished your letters (still have some of them) but talk about mixed messages! I've always wanted you to know that the night before my wedding, my mother came into the room and closed the door behind her. I was afraid she was going to launch into a dreaded "wifely duty" kind of talk, but she didn't. As we attempted an intimate chat, she finally came out with it. "Eleni, whatever happened to Josh? He was such a nice guy." The night before my wedding! Score one for the away team!

Leni

A sense of shock shot through Rachel's mind. Whatever they had was far deeper than anyone knew, than she ever experienced herself. Rachel scoured her memory of any mentions of this woman, or of anyone in their mutual circle mentioning her. But nothing. The first time she even heard the name was earlier this week, and in a throwaway sentence, until she dragged more out of him. This was different. These messages had an immediacy that was not lost in the retelling. This was like getting an unexpurgated view into her brother's core. She grabbed some more.

To Leni

Something hit me this morning during our brief telephone chat. When you said, "I love you," I thought to myself, she really means it, I can hear it in her voice. She is not just being nice! This is a breakthrough for me. Before I lost my virginity (and after), I could not imagine any woman "wanting sex" (or any physical contact) with me at least. It was unimaginable. If they did, I wondered what they really wanted? If a woman seemed to like me. I was perplexed and confused. When they said that they loved me, which happened often enough, I was suspicious, no, incredulous. At some level, I thought I was doing gals a favor by not having sex. Okay, in your case, I was right. Point is, it has always been hard for me to accept affection and love as genuine. But I feel it from you now. Feeling that love sent a shiver through me this morning.

I love you … xoxoxoxo.

She hungrily grabbed a handful of pages and began to devour them. It was as if she needed to absorb all that might be contained here in one sitting, before she might be interrupted. Some messages caught her attention for one reason or another.

To Josh

I need so much forgiveness from you it is scary. You mentioned that you thought I had a type A personality. I may have a type A schedule, or wish list, or to-do list, but if any part of me is type A, it is trapped in a type B body and brain. I'm totally overwhelmed. You are an island of comfort. So, forgive me again? It is the story of my life … attending to what is right in front of me and easy rather than what I know I should attend to. Thank you for being so patient.

I am so hooked on you. I know I didn't explain enough for you to understand, but I still love your easy forgiveness. You are so good.

Much love & xoxoxo

Rachel sat back. She brought the pile she had collected over to the bed. There she got under the covers and thought about what she was looking at. He did love this woman. And she loved him. At first, her mind drifted to the usual defenses they used with one another, a witticism she might employ to discount this transparent affection being directed at her brother. Perhaps this female was developmentally disabled. That was absurd. Eleni obviously was a woman of quality and her expressions of love were genuine. To Rachel's mind, she had to admit that Josh was deserving of such affection. Eleni had reached him, drawn out things she had wondered even existed. She desperately wanted to go find a picture of her but decided that would be unwise. They were in that box, back in his office. She hesitated. She did not want to disturb anyone, and the quest might well prove futile in any case. She pushed on with the email printouts.

To Josh

Just a couple of thoughts before becoming a focused, brilliant strategist. Right, that's not bloody likely to happen but I got a difficult meeting in the morning. I hope your day went well. During my breaks, I'll be thinking about who should get to play the role of Connelly ... stud ... womanizer or, should I say, Connelly the gallant Romeo. That should be fun.

But what I really wanted to say is thank you for granting me a pass for my role in our doomed relationship. I hope you know that I feel the same way about you. What I can't stand, though, is that you won't give yourself a pass! Even I have given myself a pass! We were all we could be, to ourselves and each other. That is my story and I'm sticking to it. I'm going to be so mad if you don't agree soon. You should be very afraid.

Love, hugs, and a g'nite ... Xoxoxo

To Leni,

Morris, my pup, is a treasure. I really love that dog. I keep thinking of the line from the Wizard of Oz where the Tin Man says he knows he has a heart because it is breaking. I know I only have a few years left with him ...

I am chagrined just a bit about my long rant this morning, my only rationale is that I feel better and that is what counts. One addendum, though (there always is one). Beyond the fear of being shot down, the universal male concern, I struggled with the possibility I might feel something. Love for me was weakness. With all other women, it was not an issue. Take Sarah, she was perfect in that I merely enjoyed being with her and she was already committed to someone else. There was never any pressure. But you were real trouble, did I want to ask for more? I know I did …

Sweet dreams … xoxoxo

To Leni:

Dear whack job #1 (you have beaten me out for the top spot), when I asked whether you thought you would be alone after your divorce (no man would want you or something like that), I knew what the answer would be and I also said a monosyllabic response would not do. I wanted to scream … how could you not know that men would throw themselves at you IF THEY THOUGHT THEY HAD A SHOT. You were, and are, so attractive it is probably illegal in forty-four states. And I don't mean just on the outside. What you have inside counts for so much more. Let me say this (well, I guess you really have no choice), while I've been shot down by many women (as all men have), I have also been blessed with attracting some very beautiful and successful persons of the female persuasion (there is no accounting for taste). You are the only one I have loved. That must mean something. If you were not immediately hustled by guys when you became available, it is only because you walked around with the "do not touch" sign on your forehead. I've known many women with that sign. It is highly effective though I doubt you were conscious of what you were doing at the time.

My god, we were both pathetic. It would have been merciful, back in college, if we were taken out back and put out of our misery. I will probably beat you up more later, but I do have exciting news to share. I found my favorite recipe loved by women everywhere. Oh wait, that's my secret sexual technique. It is called Josh's surprise!!! Had to end this on a light note.

Much love and many hugs.

Rachel smiled. They obviously had a warm relationship. They joked with each other, called each other endearing names even if they might sound odd to outsiders. Rachel knew that her brother reserved his biggest insults for the people he liked the most. Rachel sensed that Josh was upset with someone when he became nice to them. It was an odd male quirk particular to those of the Irish tribe.

To Josh:

I won't be sending this until the end of the day (so you can get some work done), but I need to get it off my chest so I can get some work done. God knows there's enough weight on my chest. It is inconceivable to me that you don't know this, but given our other misunderstandings, I guess anything's possible. You do know that I never have ever, for one minute in my life, not just back in college, considered myself attractive. You had to know that, right? Surely this won't be the kind of information that will bring EMTs to your house, will it? I don't want to dwell on it, I just wanted to make sure you knew. Surely you did!

Xoxoxo

To Leni:

One other thing now. I'm sure some other people connect after four decades and experience something like we have, but I guess it is quite rare. I now would like to be in touch with Sarah, but it would be more out of curiosity, how they are doing and what they accomplished in life. This is qualitatively different. There is no emotional overlay with the others. For us, it is like making up for all the stupid things we did that somehow prevented us from getting to know one another. And the thing is, I want to get to know you as deeply as I can. There is no one else about which I have that kind of feeling. It is simple, there is no one else I have loved.

I'm staggered by how broad the misunderstandings were between us. Oddly enough, I give myself credit for being able to get people to open up. I never had any ambitions to be a counselor or therapist (listening to people whine for a living would have driven me over the edge), but I always thought I was good at getting others to talk, to reveal themselves. Maybe it is my deep voice or honest face ... really! And yet we spent hours together, I pawed your body endlessly, I fell deeply in love with you, and yet I still failed to get to know you at all. How pathetic is that? Aaargh!!!! To use the old male metaphor, I came closer to hitting a home run sexually than I did getting inside your head, and I barely got to second base in the sexual game.

You have stayed with me even as I have revealed my political escapades and some of my all-too-casual way with women (in the past). You are a nice person, not a "bad girl" at all.

Much love ... Josh

To Josh:

Greetings guy. Your emails remind me of the Connelly I knew in college. I remember how intimidated I was by your intellect in college. You often seemed immersed in thoughts that I couldn't quite get my mind around. In the beginning, I just accepted the obvious inferiority of my own intellect but think that as I matured (?), I could rationalize that the differences in our knowledge base and thought processes were due to our ... ready for this ... different majors. I told you! I can rationalize anything. I told myself that maybe if I weren't taking organic chemistry and comparative anatomy with all their labs, I too would be able to worry about and converse about the John Birch Society or oppressive regimes in Africa and Asia. Even with my superior rationalization skills, though, it was humiliating to be so ignorant.

I've told you this for a reason (I know ... that's different). As I started to think about it, I realized that my feelings about being so outclassed most of the time likely affected our relationship. Maybe I was so certain that discovery and rejection was inevitable, that I reflexively held back. Of course, that would only be a piece of the story, but it makes sense that such feelings played a role. I thought you were too good for me. I love telling you that! Is it new information to you?

L&H ... xoxoxo

Rachel could understand how this girl, any woman, would fall in love with her brother. He was a charmer and handsome with his dark hair and rugged good Irish looks. His blue eyes, what were called bedroom eyes, worked with many of the gals. It struck Rachel that Eleni was not overly impressed with his looks or his sexuality. The connection was deeper than that, on both sides. She loved him, she loved him for him, not his athletic prowess or his casual good looks or the fact that other females were after him. She loved him for him. Eleni loves him for the same reason that she does … the quality of his soul. How special is that?

The way they talked to each other struck Rachel as extraordinarily intimate and meaningful, the way people who loved deeply would communicate. It was natural, unforced, and spontaneous. Rachel thought about several of the romantic movies she had seen. The dialogue between the so-called lovers went beyond insipid. She kept thinking as their drivel continued … *what would these people have to talk about after the lust wore off?* That thought was replaced by images of her marriage to Evan, the long silences in the tomb that had become their so-called home. At that moment, she was desperately jealous of her brother. He had enjoyed real intimacy, even if only at a distance.

To Josh:

So, help me out, Big Guy. I'm looking for a word that expresses the concept of slower with more meaning than glacially slow. That epiphany was yesterday's? Really? It's hard for me to get my mind around how you felt (feel?) about yourself. But then, you quickly pull me off my high horse by reminding me that I have similar, okay, identical … um, to be kind, can we call them "blind spots"? I'm so happy to be part of your epiphany. And I thank you for being part of mine! I guess you're never too old for epiphanies! Oh, please keep talking to yourself (and me!). I finally decided to hunt down and start answering those questions you asked some time back. BTW, do you have any idea how much and how often we write? Good thing we don't have real lives.

You asked how I met Nick. Easy … a friend introduced us. What attracted me to him at least relative to Dennis? Not so easy. Dennis was an important stepping-stone in my rejoining the world after my divorce. He was the head of a department (mental health) in my building and was a friend of one of my friends. We bumped into each other occasionally on campus, but he didn't know anything about my personal life until he saw me off campus one day where we had privacy and talked. He was bold and funny and enjoyed life. We started dating, and I could finally imagine that there might be life after divorce. That was extremely valuable to me, but I knew we were incompatible on many levels. I had decided that the positives greatly outweighed the negatives and that my relationship with him was a positive influence on my evolution into a post-divorce adult. Our major incompatibility is a long story, but he was evolving into an Orthodox Jew. I am flexible, but he was getting increasingly committed to rituals that were difficult for me to embrace. He even went as far as to introduce me to his rabbi, perhaps for his blessing? As he evolved beyond Orthodoxy, because of his hopes for his spiritual afterlife (I think), he learned that according to scriptures, he was compelled to marry a Jewish woman who had never been married (widowed was okay). We continued to date as he pondered all this. I knew "we" didn't have a future (for many good reasons), but my feeling was that dating him was doing no harm to either of us.

When I met Nick, I was upfront with him and with Dennis, but dating nights became more difficult to share and I "chose" Nick. Obviously, it was time to be pushed out of Dennis's nest. Nick was different from anyone I knew or had known, I guess. Hard to believe, but for all my years of adulthood, I had only known and socialized with people from academia. I saw Nick as possessing great intelligence, integrity, and humor. I respected the way he ran his business, the way he dealt with his two teenagers as a single parent, his closeness to his Arizona family. Most amazingly, my PhD did not intimidate him. I think one of the reasons I made the cut is that he saw the bad girl in me. That is not so easy to find in the south. I also think he assumed that because I was a "scientist," I could always satisfy his need for logical straight-line thinking. We were compatible on an emotional level. We both had learned a lot from our histories and knew that wasn't a given. Eventually, I passed all the tests. He tended to interview me. He kept looking for inconsistencies. He is a very careful man.

How did I reel him in? I don't think I did. I should mention that I learned early in life that "indifference" was a safe place to land. I am pretty sure I had that "dubious talent when we were dating." Nick, on the other hand, recalls the night of the "reeling in" and refers to it as the night I made "The Speech." My view is that we were talking about our lives in general, what seemed natural to us, etc., and I casually said that I saw myself as comfortable as a partner. Not necessarily married but committed to and with someone in life. I guess I think there are people who can't imagine that and see themselves with lots of people or other people who prefer to be alone. It was not "The Speech." My closing argument to him was that if I had planned to make a speech, I wouldn't have chosen a restaurant as my venue. I guess he proposed shortly after that (I do not remember).

I love knowing you are there.
BH! xoxoxoxo

To Leni:

Yeah, we finally agree on something. You ARE dumb, inexperienced, fearful, and repressed. Oh wait, that was back in college. Now, of course, you are worldly, sophisticated, and sexually savvy. I'm sure you could teach me a trick or two, heh, heh! Anyway, as I waxed eloquently yesterday, I wondered about the contradiction of fearing that women would fall in love with me at the same time as feeling that I was unlovable. The answer to that conundrum was easy, though. I concluded that women were infatuated with the notion of love; it was not that they really liked these poor schmucks with whom they were stuck.

But that was not yesterday's real epiphany. That came in my text about how you would have fallen madly in love with me had you known me longer and presumably better. I texted it with a distinct "tongue in cheek" attitude. But then, I thought, she probably would have. Sure, there are reasons why we might not have worked, but a bunch of reasons why we might have worked beyond imagination. And it hit me, a lot of quality gals who are smart, successful, and attractive have liked me, some an awful lot. I must have something to offer. More than that, I really feel a lot of affection coming from you now. I believe it is sincere and real, something I could not have considered back then.

And so, my epiphany was just how far I've come from this totally insecure and self-hating schmuck I was all those years ago. And it struck me that you made the same kind of journey. In your heart, you know that people admire your competence and smarts (even if you backslide momentarily on occasion). You know that you are likeable and attractive to others. You can now accept the fact that you are loved. So, if we now could go back in time, I'm sure you would have fallen madly in love with me. More than that, I would have been able to admit my love for you, without fear or reservation. All these epiphanies are liberating. Thanks. You really are better than the gals they send over from Rent-A-Friend.

Big hug … xoxoxoxo

My god, Rachel thought, they sounded exactly like soul mates or what she thought soul mates might be like, at least in her mind. Then again, how would she know? She certainly had never had one, not even a best female friend. But to Rachel, the banter reminded her of the way Connie and Josh related. It was easy and natural, what two very quick people who trust and respect each other would do. This must be how people in love relate to each other. It is not found in grand passion, but in the small intimate communications. It is the laughs, the mutual discoveries, the ongoing connecting. It is less the mighty and flashy oaks and more the tendrils that loop around and bind one object to another. They appear fragile but cling with a remarkable tenacity. Suddenly, Rachel felt an ache in her own heart. It hit her. She was missing out on a big part of life. Talk about being incomplete. Perhaps she was the one that suffered this affliction. Suddenly, she felt a pain deep inside.

To Josh:

My dear Josh, I know that you asked me to just humor you about wondering what would have happened if I professed my love to you. I understand the value of your dialogue with the blessedly silent me, but your thoughts prompted me to wonder if I could ever have said I love you back then. I've said this all before, I am sure, but just in case one of us learns something, maybe it's worth repeating. I had never said "I love you" to anyone. I understand the superficial reasons (I was taught to never be the aggressor, that love meant sex, sex meant marriage, that love was a commitment), but since you've been pondering this, I've been forced to wonder whether I truly understand love, especially back then. I don't think I had a clue. And it's not "understanding" love that I really mean. I guess I wonder if I really felt it … ever. It seems to me these days that if you feel it, you say it, one way or another. Although I understand why I never told you I loved you, it saddens me greatly to think that you did not sense my affection for you. I do know that I'm all about affection.

I am convinced that you and I were just much too immature to commit to each other … or, sadly, to even help the other. The question about love? It is still a question for me, but, with your permission, I am going to put off getting any deeper into those murky, scary waters.

Much love to you, You are a gift … xoxoxo

To Josh:

Hey, you are still there! You're such a good guy … and such an easy sell. I like that in a person. Regarding the 17 years of my first marriage, perseverance has always been one of my stronger traits. But whenever I see that trait as only positive, I remind myself of someone's definition of insanity … doing the same thing over and over and expecting a different result.

Thank you for your thoughtful (and very kind) insights on my abbreviated saga. Two comments struck a chord with me. One led to a strong confirmation, the other to a question. I fully agree that expectations are the root of most disappointments, and I must take responsibility for much of that. As the kids of this generation would say … "my bad." I never discussed or questioned much before getting married. I just assumed. I never asked Jack for his thoughts about children, monogamy, housing, retirement, or … ? Let me count the questions I never asked. I just assumed that our compatibility was sufficient to get us through future questions. I have no idea where that idea came from, but there it is. As I think about it now, part of my naïve thinking may have come from never hearing a rational two-sided debate in my family. I thought there must be a better way to decide things. Some things would just happen naturally; everything else could be decided by a rational discussion. That plus the fact that as we have already determined, I was as dumb as a rock.

The second comment was about males and redemption. That reminded me that one of the final very strong protests about the divorce was that there would be "no chance for redemption." That was and remains a total puzzlement to me. At the time, I thought that maybe it was the attempt of an avid Wagner fan to live out a "Flying Dutchman" fantasy. I did not get it at all. After 17 years of trying???

MLMH … xoxoxoxo

To Josh:
Good morning and good grief, Connelly! It will be impossible to answer your questions and still sound sane. I know … so what's new and I should trust you, you are a doctor of sorts. I can't wait until it is my turn to ask questions. Soon, right?
Question 1: "Did you really love him when you got married?" I thought I did, but right away, your second question becomes important. I don't think I knew what love was then. I knew I was happy and very comfortable with him. Seemed like love, but how does one ever know? I also knew that our relationship seemed infinitely better than my parents. We had fun together, similar tastes in people, books, movies, lifestyles, no skirmishes. Not a bad start.
Question 2: "After you became suspicious (or at least received allegations that he had been unfaithful), was the trust bond irrevocably broken?" No, it

took me almost 20 years to get to the irrevocable part (duh!). I was infinitely forgiving and unrealistically hopeful that our professionals were going to solve our problems. They often commented on our obvious affection for one another. Somehow in their comments I saw approval to keep trying. No one ever talked about us calling it quits, as I recall.

Question 3: "Were you always suspicious after that, checking, and was that the source of your distress over time?" The checking didn't start right away. I started doing that when something didn't feel right and when I finally understood that direct questions were useless. Checking is a god-awful humiliating process!

Question 4: "When did you know it was over?" The first round of therapy ended with triumphant success and the unmistakable symbolism of buying our first home. I mean, what's more romantic than a 30-year mortgage. Can't remember what precipitated our return to the psychiatrist as I was about to walk out the door. Psychiatrist # 1 sent us to shrink # 2. We bought ourselves a lot of time (and probably a couple of boats and cars for these guys) with that round. More tears, denial, and lots of delay of the inevitable with this round of therapy. The breaking point was when I found undeniable evidence. I had really, really given the marriage my all. After all those years of counseling, forgiving, being duped, not understanding, not believing, I finally understood! It was over! The therapy had been totally useless. Jack was never straight with the therapists either. Aaargh! I took some comfort in the fact that both had been duped too. After all, they were pros.

Well, that was fun. Jack was totally distraught by the divorce, suicidal. You'd think that he would feel liberated. All that is still impossible for me to understand. My new life is such a blessing. I sooo appreciate Nick's directness.

All my love … xoxoxo

Rachel put the papers down. For a moment, she felt as if she were prying into someone else's life, their deepest secrets, on some unethical level. *This is wrong,* she thought. Would Eleni want anyone other than Josh to see this? Rachel sensed she would not want anyone seeing her private longings or anguish if she were the author. But Josh knew what was in these, and still gave her permission to look. This was his way of revealing himself, letting her peek inside his soul. He could not do it while looking directly into her eyes. Should she chide him for being a coward. *No*, she told herself. She would walk with him at his pace.

But what if she meets this woman someday? Can she be friendly with her without revealing the level of intimacy to which she was exposed? That could be very awkward. No, once again she fell back on the fact that Josh had given his permission. There was no doubt about that. Of course, she might be giving this dolt, who was a clueless male after all, way too much credit. He had probably forgotten just how revealing this material was. In any case, she was hooked. Besides, despite what she called him from time to time, her brother was no dolt.

To Leni:

I still think of what would happen if we had a do over (with the advantage of knowing a little bit about what we would be as adults). I'll have more to say on this (don't I always) but I have no doubt I would have given you my best shot. As I said before, I had no idea that I would never again feel that depth of feeling for anyone. There were, for sure, the moments of strong attraction, much lust, and even affection but nothing that was so complete and enduring. Having said that, there would still be the same impediments and insecurities, my "marriage is death" phobia, and the pull of protest. Still, if I had even an inkling of what I would uncover about myself over time, I would have tried my best to spend more than one lousy night with you. The night wasn't lousy, only the fact that there was only one.

Love … xoxoxo

To Leni:

What! No self-flagellation permitted, but I do it so well. Yeah, this rush of rather raw emotion took me by surprise. My friends and colleagues here would find it amazing, hilarious. Surely, everyone sees me as totally laid-back and unemotional. Hell, I've been erroneously declared clinically deceased on at least six occasions.

But this has been good for me, really. For you, not so sure. I clearly had stuff inside that has been floating around on some level all my life. I am grateful to finally have had the opportunity to get it all out, if rather clumsily. Otherwise, I would someday be sitting around the nursing home saying damn, never had the opportunity to tell Leni how I felt about her. Now I can sit around the nursing home and focus on the important things, like chasing the pretty nurses up and down the aisles. But alas, they will surely outrun me.

Reconnecting has been just a little like ripping open old wounds. A little pain, sure, but then some real healing. Hell, I bet most people go through life never having suffered a grand passion. The poor bastards are doomed to go through life happy …

Love … xoxoxo

To Leni:

When did I get in touch? When I looked over the emails since then, I was taken with how far we came in a short time. It is almost as if we recovered the best of what we had 45+years ago and then immediately started moving beyond that point. Remarkable! When I decided to send that first message (and I did hesitate), I wondered if you would even recall me. I envisioned you sitting there going … Josh Connelly? I should know that name from somewhere … was he from Harvard?

But you did remember and, amazingly, you apparently retained strong memories of certain traits I had back then. It strikes me that is why this dialogue may be important to us. It seems precious and rare to find someone with whom you want to share core feelings and thoughts. It is like finding a special place (and person) where you can go and feel again; here you can dig inside and better understand yourself. You can't manufacture that connectedness. Perhaps our struggles with one another over so many years gave us a way to get to that special place. I do hope this makes some sense.

All of this is one of those indefinable things. I see the words you send to me and I can see you, the way you smile and joke and care and look sometimes vulnerable and sometimes emotional and sometimes unreachable. That is a unique package. We may look older and we may be beyond our innocent days. But at some level, I think we both retain qualities that were special then and remain attractive now. I think the important things have not changed.

Love ... .xoxoxo

Rachel paused again. He was a good writer, a great writer. It was something she remembered from their childhood. She would ask him what he wanted to be when he grew up. She thought he would say an athlete, the dream of many kids in their neighborhood. He never did. He would talk about becoming a writer, of painting with words. Then he would warn her not to laugh at him, that this was their secret. No one else would understand. Later, she took some pains to locate his academic publications. What set him apart was the quality of his writing. He found a way to keep his early dream partially alive.

Fatigue struggled with curiosity. She recalled reading about this phenomenon where lovers from their teens reconnect a lifetime later and find they are as emotionally attached as they had been as teens. It is if they last chatted six hours ago, not six decades. The connection she now was exploring seemed different somehow, and she struggled to figure out why. It all seemed so unlikely. Josh and Eleni had a very brief, incomplete relationship back as college students. Her brother never seemed incapable of deep attachments despite many opportunities. She knew little about Eleni other than she resisted both physical intimacy and remained aloof from her brother's political obsessions at the time. They did not even study in the same disciplinary areas. *Where in God's name is the connection here? How did it happen?*

It all seemed so unpromising. If anything was unique, it is that it happened early in their lives. Was this its unique feature? Perhaps if everyone could find their early love, they would experience the same intensity. Of course, she had no such love. No one had touched her so. She could not possibly know but found it all fascinating. Perhaps, just perhaps, if she had not pushed away those girls at Smith who fluttered around the periphery of her emotional barriers. If she had only let one or two inside? That would have been impossible at the time. She had no choice in that matter even if she had taken the time, or had the courage, to sort out her feelings.

Unlike her brother, she never felt brave enough to take an unconventional path. But was that true? After all, she had taken all kinds of risks, leaving her working class culture to compete with elite girls from privileged backgrounds at a seven-sister's school, taking on her professional training at the premier medical school in the country, and then specializing in pediatric surgery, a specialty only for the most gifted and self-confident. Yet, all those felt like easy choices to her. Then she smiled. She would not confide this internal dialogue with her brother. She knew he would yell at her for not appreciating her own strengths. That's the thing, though, isn't it? *Most of us never do see ourselves objectively. We can't.*

To Josh:

You've given me such a great gift in reconnecting and sharing your memories and feelings so openly. I'm incredibly grateful. I had never really understood how you felt. The mystery of "us" has been clarified greatly. There may be strong twinges, but for me, our connection has replaced the question marks with treasured, positive feelings.

How do I really remember you from college? You were kind, sensitive, super smart, passionate about causes, and the best kisser ever. Frankly, I was awed by you.

I am sure that my own insecurity and naiveté fueled your ambivalence. We were both just beginning to evolve. I was afraid to say the words "I love you" because back then, back then I had this dumb idea that saying it was a total commitment. Total, as in body and soul. I was scared.

I must admit. You write beautifully. I was blown away by what I read—from the beginning to the end. I had such a swirl of thoughts and emotions. As I read it, I'm not sure I'll ever get my thoughts together well enough to respond. When I found it almost too painful to continue reading, I reminded myself that pain was my guarantee that I was still alive, that I still cared a lot. That's a good thing, right? Sometimes you remind me of the old lyrics ... the honesty is too much; I have to close my eyes and hide. You do take my breath away.

The emotional dust hasn't settled yet, and the worst thing is that I don't have enough time to do your writing justice. I want to read it again, and probably again. Please forgive me for going first to a negative. I do know I'm overly protective and private, but I really would like to understand how you think about your "pieces." All the "what-ifs" are choking me. What if, years from now, or tomorrow (!), you were incapacitated and some helpful family member, friend, or colleague found pieces of your work that related to them. Am I wrong to imagine that some of your details would be very hurtful? I'm sure I'm missing something. Maybe I'm missing the freedom of a totally honest life.

One other great fear is that I will disappoint you. Just know ahead of time that I really, really didn't want to. I hope to be able to read your piece again, this time with less emotional white noise. You knock my socks off. Thank you for taking the plunge and hanging in.

So much love to you ... xoxoxo

Rachel stopped. For a moment, she wondered which writings Eleni was praising? But the lack of organization prevented any linear understanding about what was going on. Still, there was so much here that her head was spinning. She was stunned by the intimacy, what it revealed about a brother she had not known since she was a young teen, and thus had not known at all. She was also afraid about what this journey into his heart revealed about her. *'Enough for tonight,'* she whispered to herself as she lay down on her bed.

———

Morris walked over her, suggesting that it was time for his morning constitutional. The pup had bonded with her; She was not sure why. The morning air gave her a chance to think about her brother. He was capable of love, it appeared. Caring for another human being was possible for him. Who knew? It was such a shock. She had thought that perhaps there was a genetic anomaly in the family genes, that neither she nor Josh could fully commit to another person. Yet, when she asked, Josh had casually mentioned loving this mystery woman from college. That had seemed improbable ... the connection too ephemeral, too casual. *Be serious*, she thought. What kind of lifelong obsession could possibly arise out of a short unconsummated relationship in which there had been no physical contact since the 1960s? It struck her as ridiculous, a soap opera drama. But here it was ... laid out in black and white.

She shook her head. Focus on the comfort and serenity of the morning, she insisted to herself. Josh had been right; this was a special time and place. She now appreciated why her brother took the dog on a daily walk at such an hour. The remaining city lights yet gave shape to the outline of Vancouver's skyline. They would soon be extinguished as the sun rose to fulfill its daily obligation. At the same time, the emerging sunlight promised an interesting day. The group would journey north, through the city, and up into the mountains that framed the northern edge of the metropolis. They would spend the day at a favored tourist spot, particularly for the winter sports enthusiasts. She would prefer to journey to Tofino and the adjacent beach area, a location that Josh had described on occasion. It was an isolated, wild shore on the western edge of Vancouver Island, remote and subject to incessant assaults from a demanding surf. It sounded divine. Perhaps she could get Josh to take her someday. She might have to extend her stay a day or two, but she had never anticipated how well this visit would turn out. Before arriving, she had wondered if the two of them could get along for a few hours, never mind days. She was getting her answer.

After Morris did his business, they headed back. "You're such a cutie," she said to the dog that waddled along next to her feet. He looked tough with his pugnacious face and strut, but he really was the sweetest thing. "I am taking you with me, is that all right with you?" *Okay*, she thought to herself, *this confirms that I have gone around the bend to join my idiot sibling.* The chief of pediatric surgery is talking to a dog. *I knew this would happen if I took a few days off.*

The breeze blew off the waters. She found it refreshing; it tingled her skin. That previous evening, as she drifted off to sleep, her mind had wandered in a different direction. She could not get Usha out of her head. Just as the breeze now caressed her, the feel of Usha's hands touching her skin flooded incessantly across her head. She tried driving it away, but the image would not disappear. How childish, she scolded herself. She was not a schoolgirl. She had complete control over her emotions, needs. What's this she is now feeling? For years, now decades, she had exercised command over her inner self. Why now when she had decided all that nonsense had been finally buried?

Perhaps what she was feeling was some empathic association with her daughter. Don't some husbands experience pregnancy symptoms? Maybe this was a similar condition. She so wanted to connect with her daughter, she was associating with her offspring's life choice. *How silly was that,* she concluded? Then another thought crowded in. She had been taken with her brother's experience with love. He knew what it was, he had experienced it first-hand. She had assumed he never had this experience, even if incomplete and unconsummated. That she was wrong about this shocked her. Worse, she was jealous. Yes, that was it, she was jealous. She wanted to know what it was like to be in love.

Back at Josh's house, Rachel fed Morris, who alternately devoured his food and looked up at her with growing appreciation. The dog liked her, that was something. Perhaps some members of the male tribe were worth the effort. The secret to finding them was to avoid humans and stick with canines. As she contemplated her latest insight, Josh emerged from his room.

"Ah, I see my traitor of a formerly devoted pet has been satisfied. Morning, Benedict Arnold," he said in the direction of the dog happily licking an empty bowl.

"Sit," Rachel insisted.

"The dog or me? You know, I'm thinking that maybe you should take the dog since I could never train him to do anything."

"Same as with the women in your sorry life?" Then Rachel caught herself and returned to the task at hand. "You, Josh, sit!"

"What's up, you have your game face on this morning."

Rachel looked at him for a moment while she gathered her thoughts. "I couldn't sleep. I looked over some of the e-mails, the ones with Eleni."

"I suppose that's why I gave them to you," he responded without expression.

"Why did you do that? You did not have to, I didn't ask. Hell, I don't believe you ever mentioned her until now…Leni that is. If you had, I probably would not have recalled her name if asked. You never indicated that she was as special as … she is."

Josh reached down and picked up Morris. He scratched the pet's ears. "I don't know how to talk about certain things. Hell, there are things I can barely even think about without my head hurting. Leni has been inside my head for most of my life. No one has known about her, other than perhaps her name."

Rachel looked confused. "Tell me one thing, why isn't she here? Is it because she's married? I do not understand, she loves you and you love her. It pours out of those e-mails. How can you stay apart? You never struck me as that principled. No, scratch that. You are selectively principled. You would never let a little thing like a marriage contract stand in the way."

"Selectively principled? What? You do not know me, do you? I have many faults, but I always thought my biggest problem was being too principled. A conscience is a terrible thing. In my addled head, it was a quantum leap from my high school music teacher to this." He tried a smile but could not quite get there.

"Be serious or I swear I'll greatly diminish the quality of your life by taking your dog away with me. Then, you will be totally alone, more alone that you are now."

Josh sighed. "Okay! Obviously, you didn't get through all of them. Not surprising, they were probably all mixed up. I found her on Facebook, by accident as it turned out. It was quite a shock. Several decades had passed with no contact. I stopped writing letters to her about a year after she married someone else, husband number one."

"That one ended unhappily?"

"Yeah, but after about two decades of her trying to keep it together, commitments being sacred to her, she gave it up."

"Seventeen years," She stated. "It was in one of her messages."

"Right." Josh looked impressed. "She did have better luck the second time around. In any case, when I found her again, it was like asking for that first date. It took a while to work up the courage to send that first message, but she seemed thrilled to hear from me. Literally, within days, we were far more intimate with each other than we had been back then. The chemistry was amazing."

"I could feel that. It exuded out of these exchanges," Rachel interjected.

"But from the beginning, we developed a DNH rule or Do No Harm. She was married, and I was living with Connie at the start of this reconnection. This all emerged after Usha had found true love, or thought she had. No matter what we shared, we vowed not to harm existing relationships. In truth, I probably used Connie as an excuse to make it seem as if we were on equal footing. It seemed safer."

Rachel shook her head. "I don't see how that's possible, married couples don't have connections of this depth." Her voice was laced with incredulity.

"And this from the original ice maiden."

"You are a shit!" she shot back. "But okay, I'll stipulate to that."

"Okay, that shot was a bit sophomoric … sorry. In the end, though, it didn't matter."

"How could it not matter? You loved this woman, she loved you. How in God's name can you be so cavalier about all this?" Rachel sensed her Irish temper rising. "Are you totally made of stone? Don't you have a single thread of humanness in you? It had to matter."

Suddenly, a voice came from another direction. "I want to hear the answer to that one." Connie stood in the door of Josh's room.

"Oh," Rachel exclaimed. "I didn't know …"

"No matter, Rachel, we were chaste despite my best efforts." Connie gave Josh a disapproving glance. "Yes, I want to hear this. Turns out that I saw a couple of his exchanges with this Eleni, some time ago, when we were still a couple. They were on his screen one day. Though I felt awful about peeking, it was also a relief. It explained why he never seemed fully there to me. I think it does a least. You know the old female fear, was there someone else? In the end, I never figured out whether someone else was better or worse than not being good enough."

"Don't apologize, Connie, a reasonable fear among all women." Rachel said, welcoming an ally.

Connie came into the room and took a seat. "To be honest, I suppose that is why I started withdrawing from you, Josh. I assumed you would get together with this woman, that I was in the way. I was surprised when nothing happened after I exited. The one thing I knew, or thought I knew, is that you didn't love me as you did her."

Josh put Morris down and got up. He looked directly at Connie but had trouble sensing her mood. To Josh, she looked somewhere between wary and enigmatic. Damn inscrutable Asians, he thought. "What started as e-mails morphed into texts and phone calls. I should have told you, Connie. But I didn't know what to say. I'm a coward."

"Hold the presses on that one." Rachel said with a dollop of sarcasm.

"Okay, I avoid conflict if I can. This was confusing to me. It was intense, all-consuming, but in a limited way. We would never meet, touch, experience the things lovers do. Above all, we were committed not to disrupt each other's lives. That was our prime commitment. I had blown my chances with Leni the night I chose to head north, damn coin flip. There really is no going home again."

Connie remained enigmatic. "Make me understand. Would it have been impossible to ask her here, for this milestone? You have so much of your life here, and she is such a part of your heart. I'm losing you here. You're a clever guy, you could have figured out something. Hell, people manage affairs all the time."

Josh permitted a look of anguish to cross his face before pushing it away. "Well, the 'Do No Harm' rule failed. Her husband discovered the e-mails, and she promised to stop. But neither of us could. That would have been like cutting out our hearts. We talked about elastic hearts a lot, being able to expand to let in more love. Then he found out a second time. That was it, it had to end."

"Then, for sure you should have gone after her. Even I would have understood. After all, we just had … an arrangement."

"And you could walk away?" Rachel asked. "I would have thought that would be difficult beyond measure. More than most, you know what losing loved ones means."

Josh winced at her observation. "What was hard was not being there for her, not being able to make her laugh … at the end." Then he just stopped as if hung in mid thought. "In my whole life, I only experienced such pain one other time."

"When?" Rachel asked.

"For God's sake, sis, you know very well when."

"What end? What pain?" Connie asked in frustration. "What the hell are you talking about?"

"The end, the ultimate end! Leni was dying from cancer at the time. She passed about a year ago. Her last words to me in her final e-mail were *I do love you.*'"

CHAPTER 19

Day 6 – THE ROAD TO WHISTLER

As planned the evening before, the group assembled at a reasonably early hour. They were excited, perhaps less by the trip itself than by the prospect of spending time together doing something entertaining. Josh assumed command and, to his sister's surprise, managed to organize the day's adventure with minimal confusion. It takes a bit of time to get from Vancouver to Whistler, primarily a winter resort nestled high in the mountains north of the city. The place looks and feels much like an Alpine ski destination, an ambiance Josh always loved even if he was not into the sport himself. The journey itself is a big part of the attraction to him, a winding road up through rugged peaks. That was part of the charm of the area. Crowded together was a cosmopolitan city, a diverse population, the ocean, and rugged mountain peaks. *God had His A game the day he created Vancouver and its environs*, Josh often exclaimed. He missed Boston, particularly the accent and edgy people, but loved his adopted home perhaps even more.

Two cars set out: In Josh's SUV were Rachel, Usha, Meena, and Cate while Connie volunteered to drive Peter, Morris, and Carla in her vehicle. The small caravan drove through the center of Vancouver to pick up Highway 99. Turning west, they wove through Stanley Park, across the bridge, and up into the craggy peaks that guard the city's northern border. It is a magnificent drive, replete with inspiring vistas. He had taken Cate at least a couple of times during previous visits, but

Rachel never stayed long enough to venture up this way. Either her brief visits did not permit much sightseeing, or the prospect of spending so much time together had not proved much of an inducement. It was different now. He was wondering if he could convince his sibling that her future was in the great northwest. It was a thought that surprised him.

Rachel sat next her brother and remained silent as Josh talked about what they would be seeing and possibly doing during their journey. When she put her head back, he wondered if she had spent too much time the night before exploring the written documentation of his relationship with Eleni. Was she fighting off a need for sleep?

Suddenly, she turned to him and broke into his travelogue. "It must have been difficult at the end." She uttered the words *sotto voce* so those in the back seat might not notice. The passengers were busy commenting on the majestic scenery.

"What end?"

"What do you mean what end? The end with Leni, when she was sick, and you could not stay in contact."

"Yes," he murmured, irritated that she expected him to follow her internal dialogue. It was something he recalled from their childhood, one of her few annoying traits. *No*, he then thought, *all women really were like this.*

After a pause, Rachel added in a more insistent tone. "Listen! I will only say this once. If you think you will get by with monosyllabic responses, there will be one less occupant in the car on the return trip. You do realize that it looks very much as if there are remote places ahead of us where they will never find your body. Just promise to reveal more when we can find a better place to talk. Deal?"

Josh sighed. "Sorry, you deserve more. I gave you pretty much everything that's in writing. Funny, I am not even sure why I gave you that stuff. I've never shared that with anyone."

"Not such a mystery. I'm guessing you didn't want to carry the hurt alone anymore." Inside, Rachel was thrilled to hear this. Perhaps she was special to him.

"Yes, Doctor Phil." He flashed her his disarming smile.

"Just talk about it when you … we can." Rachel wanted to slap him for being flip while she was finally feeling warm toward him … needed even. On further reflection she decided that attacking the driver might prove unwise. There were places where the drop off at the side of the road was dramatic and deadly.

As his smile faded, his next words came out slow, measured. "I'll say this right now. It was agony. Throughout our reconnection, she had worried that someone would get hurt, one of our significant others would stumble on to our relationship and misunderstand, or worse, understand."

"Does he mean me?" Usha asked from the backseat. Those in the back seat suddenly started paying attention to the conversation up front.

"Shit." Josh said softly as he realized his words were public.

Rachel also regretted pushing her brother where others might witness his pain but had assumed the backseat occupants were occupied with their own interests. She now realized they must be clueless about where she had taken the conversation. "Sorry back there, selfish of me," Rachel tried to apologize. "I was obsessing about something."

"This must have something to do with your idiot brother, he is a lightning rod for drama." Usha added.

Josh decided to resolve Usha's confusion while ignoring another witty shot at his expense. "No, Usha, you had already dumped me and were in Toronto when I ran across a woman with whom I had a relationship in college. I never mentioned her to you when we were a thing since I thought it long over by then. I was with Connie when I stumbled across this college flame in cyberspace. It was one of those Facebook surprises that opened old feelings and wounds. Eleni, that was her name, but I called her Leni. I knew within days of reconnecting that the old feelings had never disappeared, so we imposed a Do No Harm rule regarding the people in our lives. I didn't want to hurt Connie, and Leni was happily married."

"Did the rule work?" Cate asked.

"No, do they ever? Her husband found out about our renewed connection … not once but twice, as did Connie."

"You screwed up, I suppose," Usha offered.

"No, oddly enough, she did on her end, that's how her husband found out. But I was careless as well I suppose since I found out that Connie also stumbled across some emails."

"Wow, how soap-opera like." Cate offered.

"Deception never works forever." Usha added.

"I suppose. Toward the end, we were communicating daily … e-mails, texts, and discreet phone calls. She must have gotten careless as she weakened. When he found out a second time, we had to stop. For me, the agony was not being able to give her any comfort as her condition worsened, even from afar."

"Condition? We're clueless back here." Cate asked, trying hard to catch up.

"Sorry, she was dying … cancer," Josh interjected, "I keep forgetting that you are not on board with this."

Rachel emerged from her private thoughts. "We are talking about my brother's one love in life."

"Besides you and Cate and Usha and …" Josh corrected her, ecstatic that Connie was in the other car.

Rachel cut him off. "His one romantic and passionate love in his life. But no one is far behind in this loop. I've just found out about it myself."

"To be honest, all I wanted to do when we reconnected was to ease her end days … maybe figure out went wrong when we were kids."

"Oh my god, this is a Hallmark movie." Cate said and then kicked herself for being so flip.

"If I am not intruding," Meena added timidly, "I would like to hear more."

Josh then spoke as if he were addressing mostly himself "I could always make her smile, laugh. It wasn't always easy as the disease progressed, of course, but still I could do it. She was so courageous, so brave. A couple of times, when we were still connected, she had bad episodes where she almost died, but her bright outlook never wavered. When she was terribly sick, she had a saying that she was *down a quart of oil.*' Brave gal, she always worried about inconveniencing others. I would have been whining uncontrollably. But she never lost her optimism, her brightness." His voice quavered, and he tried to hide it with a cough.

"She does sound special" Meena said.

"She was, believe me. Her husband once sent me an e-mail after Leni and I ended our cyber-relationship for the second time. He warned me against contacting her again. Of course, I had no such intention. It would bring way too much anxiety to her at a time that she did not need it. But I knew there was no chance of seeing her before she passed. It could not happen. I told him that the most important thing, the most important thing by far, was for her to be comfortable in her last days. I just hope she was. Damn, it killed me I couldn't do anything."

Cate spoke up. "I'm still lost here."

"I'll fill you in later, dear." Rachel turned to her.

Josh continued. "She had one of those sites, I forget the name now, where people can keep track of what is happening and send best wishes. Maybe it was Caringbridge, that sounds right. God, I cannot even recall now how many people sent her notes and thoughts and prayers. There were thousands. If I were in her situation, I would not reach double figures unless I went back to Rent-A-Friend."

"Those escort service girls might remember you or your money at least," Cate offered to lighten the mood. Rachel was glad for her daughter's biting wit, and surprised that Cate knew about this part of her uncle's life.

Josh chuckled. "They better given their prices."

"What about Sarah?" Rachel suddenly became afraid that talking about Leni would get too deep for a public discussion, though her interest remained compelling. "That was his other college girlfriend," she added for keep the others in the loop.

"What about her?"

"Did you invite her to all this?"

"In fact, I did. We talked. She is still some kind of Dean at Rutgers but beginning to think about hanging it all up. Maybe a couple of years, she told me. She thought it would be a blast to come out to this, but it conflicted with her own graduation responsibilities, heading the School of Education and all. Everything I would have predicted for her came true—good career, strong marriage, successful kids, and now grandkids. She married a different guy from the one she was with when I knew her. That didn't surprise me. Perhaps that made it possible to connect with me back in school. It turns out she didn't love that first guy all that much. Either that or she wanted to move up in class though, after me, all guys would pale in comparison."

Rachel guffawed. "Right! Here's a breaking news flash, dear brother. Compared to you, any man with a pulse would be a step up."

"Mom, you are being cruel." Cate tried without giggling. "I've met several guys worse than uncle."

At that, Meena came to his defense. "Personally, I think your uncle is wonderful, and so handsome for an older man."

"Older?" Usha guffawed. "Don't you mean ancient?"

"Hah, hah, good thing Connie is in the other car, I would be dog meat by now." Josh laughed.

"Still lost back here. I'm going to need a scorecard if we're heading down memory lane about Uncle's female conquests. I know, let's talk about his use of prostitutes. Really, what was with that? Frankly, I was rather shocked when I first learned about that," Cate chuckled lightly but with a bit of truth attached. "I don't know why but I was, probably had you on a pedestal."

Rachel turned to Cate. "Dear daughter, you will be sorry you went there. Now, he will go into his speech about male-female relationships. Pure BS. That pedestal will crumble to dust as he drones on."

"Not prostitutes! And not BS! I only pontificate on sound insights that clearly emanate from a brilliant, intellectual mind, supported by empirical evidence. These women were professional service workers, exceedingly high class, and who told by the way?"

Cate laughed. "Hell, it is all over the internet. Okay, I cannot tell a lie, Connie did. She is a pistol. She couldn't stop laughing as she told me … funny as hell and incredibly open. She told me so much about you. The ammunition I have now. Oh, and by the way, from which brilliant academic mind do you steal all your ideas. Surely, you don't think them up on your own?"

"You couldn't wait to get that one in" Josh offered though glad the conversation had lightened up.

"You should be nicer to your uncle." Meena tried.

"Hah, no harm Meena. My uncle has always been fair game." Cate laughed again.

"Why me, oh Lord? Please spare me. Why am I surrounded by a family of malevolent female jokesters? I feel like Job."

"You're just lucky I guess." Cate continued. "Tell, me, what line of crap did you give my mom about this prostitute thing making sense."

"Oh shit, I should've trained you when you were young and malleable. Now you are getting more like your mother every day." Josh sighed. "Listen carefully, I'm only going through this once. Ready?"

"Ready," Cate replied. "Shoot."

"Take notes now, this material will be on the exam."

"Got that." Cate stifled a laugh.

"Okay, payment for sexual services rendered is the bedrock of our way of life and our economic system. It is capitalism on steroids." He tried not to smile. "These professional women perform an essential social service in a way that corrects the supply-demand imbalance respecting sexual gratification. Moreover, it makes sense in terms of economic principles and interpersonal relations. The exchange is transparent, the price known, and the interaction ceases upon service delivery, or orgasm, whichever comes first. Then, and this is most important, both parties walk away without complications."

Meena let out a small noise; she seemed embarrassed. After Cate whispered to her, she smiled. Meena then added, "So you reduce love to an economic exchange, do I understand you correctly? Sounds sensible."

"Absolutely," Josh affirmed with excitement. "See, Meena gets it. What's wrong with the rest of you?"

Cate shook her head. "She's just being nice. She really thinks you are an idiot."

"No, I don't." Meena tried to no avail.

"Nevertheless, almost all human interactions have an exchange calculus as their foundation where some sense of equity is realized. Here we are talking about sex, not love. Vastly different. Viewed objectively, both sex and love are transactional activities, an exchange."

"You mean men see sex and love as unrelated, things that are bartered?" Rachel proffered. "Makes sense, I suppose. We all know that men, when all is said and done, are chauvinistic pigs."

"Hmmm, as I think on this, I'm really outnumbered in this car. Only Connie is missing from the usual gang of my female torturers." Josh concluded that a strategic retreat might be prudent. "You know, the men-are-pigs comment does remind me of a great joke."

Versions of '*oh no*' came from all the women except Meena who simply looked on uncertainly but mostly bemused. Then she added her '*no.*' She had come a long way in one day.

"Is there an eject button somewhere in this vehicle?" Usha asked.

"I will take your response as encouragement." Josh went into his joke mode; he had a slightly different lilt to his voice when he did so. "So, a man is driving down a country lane where there is such little traffic that he picks up his speed. A car approaches from the other direction. As it passes him, a woman leans out her window and yells out in a loud voice, '*Pig!*' The guy immediately shouts back, '*Bitch!*' He was still wondering how she knew he was such a male pig as he negotiated the curve just ahead. There, he found a huge pig standing right in the middle of the road which he desperately tried to avoid but, unfortunately, failed to do so. His funeral later that week was attended by many of his girlfriends, each of whom spit in his coffin."

The ensuing groans contained some grudging chuckles. "Be honest, uncle," Cate persisted, "do you really think of intimacy in bartering terms?"

He responded without missing a beat, "Not so far-fetched. There is an established equity theory of relationship that was developed in the 1970s at Wisconsin by someone in the sociology department ... Walster, I believe. Later, a Chicago Nobel Prize winner in economics named Becker developed an elaborate economics approach to most human behavior including what we call love. But let me educate you on the basic points here."

"Oh goody, I can't wait." Cate managed as she gazed in increasing admiration at the surrounding scenery.

Think about this. Aside from setting the terms up front, as I pointed out to my sister when she attacked me on this very point, the act itself is more honest. The female service provider still fakes interest, and even orgasm, but you know it is a paid for response and she knows that you don't believe her. Now, everyone knows the game, no pretense. Moreover, it is easier on the guy, one of the several benefits of paying in money up front. You don't have to work so hard to please your partner, she's all set with the payment going in. Therefore, you can focus on your own pleasure, which should be paramount in the first instance."

Usha interrupted. "Isn't that what all males focus on, their own pleasure?"

"Oh, look at the pretty mountains," Rachel next tried.

Next Cate laughed. "Meena's desperately looking for a way out of the car. I thought she was about to jump for it a moment ago."

"Not finished yet." Josh struggled to regain control. "Here's the best thing ... you can walk away after the act is complete. And with no complications. There are no false promises about calling tomorrow even as you know that pigs will have mastered flight before you ever call this woman again. There's no disingenuous BS about what the moment meant. You don't even have to endure the mandatory post-coital cuddling. Done and done, what can be better than that?"

"Methinks the pedestal that my daughter had you on has now crumbling away rather completely. Want to dig yourself in any deeper?" Rachel added.

"Just one last point. Sometimes you don't want sex. Lots of times you don't. You just want companionship, someone to talk with who, and this is critical, won't argue back. A professional is great here as well. It is your dime, so you get to call the shots. You can wax eloquent and she will agree that you are brilliant. This is even better than having control over students with grades since teacher evals are anonymous. You know, I've always thought they should make those end of semester evaluations public and signed, make those pissants tell you that you suck to your face."

Usha laughed. "Now your being absurd. I know you got great evals. They loved your BS and were too young to know better."

"No changing the subject. And here is another thing. With pros, I mean service workers, there are no excruciating discussions about sofa-covering swatches. Those discussions are how women get revenge on us for having to endure sex."

"Endure sex?" Cate puzzled. "Sofa-coverings? Has uncle lost it?"

"Oh Cate, that ship has long sailed." Rachel added quickly.

"If I may proceed absent interruption, the sofa-covering choices are emblematic of the pure torture we males suffer."

"Oh brother." Usha moaned.

"It goes like this. Your significant other shows you two pieces of fabric. *Which one do you like, dear, this one or the other one?'* Of course, you don't give a damn but are required to pick one, hoping it is the right choice. Alas, it never is and now you must explain your ridiculous selection for the next hour. Talk about agony! I mean, you're not allowed to say, *"I meant the other one."* No do overs permitted. There are other points I might make, but I would start fearing that my future tenure among the living would be brief indeed."

"Anyone got some chloroform?" Cate asked, smiling.

"Or maybe a bat?" Usha threw out.

"Too bad it's so hard to get a gun up here." Rachel ended that theme. "Easier in the States. We should lure him back there."

The conversation wandered for a while as the group paid more attention to the scenery. They were winding up farther and farther into the craggy sentinels surrounding them. Snow yet capped the highest points. The air was fresh and brisk while the sky enveloped them with brilliant clarity. *This is God's country*, Josh thought as he pointed out selected mountain peaks and gave some local color.

"So," he said at last, "what do you think, Rach? It is as advertised, is it not?"

"Sorry, yes, as advertised." Rachel noted abstractedly. "I had some stuff on my mind. Just being a little selfish here. But tell me, Cate and Meena, tell me more about how you came to know about yourself, about discovering who you were. If I'm being too personal, just tell me to mind my own business. I can be rather direct and even intrusive. I'm sure Josh will confirm that about me."

"No, mom, not at all," Cate hastened to say, "though I should not speak for Meena."

"Oh no," Meena added quickly. "I don't mind chatting about this at all, especially among the group in this car. It rather helps me … us. In Amman, we felt as if trapped in a prison where we could not be open."

"Good then," Rachel was relieved. "Go for it."

Meena started, which surprised the others. "Sometimes we feel that the past few months have been a dream, that everything has happened to someone else. And it all has been going so fast, I wake some mornings and wonder what has been real and what is not. Cate and I chatted about this last night. Sharing with others makes it real for us. I certainly cannot talk to my family. Not yet at least."

"That's the other thing," Usha added. "We'll have to work out a strategy for bringing your family on board. Sometimes it is not as bad as you anticipate, but you never know. It took me forever to confront my family. As you know, I hid behind a fake marriage with Josh for a while. But you can't hide forever, not without great damage to all involved."

"Damage?" Josh evidenced surprise. "I thought it was a pretty successful marriage. We never fought, not that I recall. We were good companions, did stuff together. You would cook me great Indian meals on occasion. The more I think on it, it was better than most hetero partnerships."

Usha did not disagree. "It was great for what it was. Yet there was one thing missing, and it is a big hole. We had respect, could communicate, had common interests, but there was no spark, no real intimacy of the kind you dream about. Our hearts did not race when we were together. I am right, am I not?"

"True enough, I suppose. Okay, to be honest, mine raced on occasion, but that was mostly the lust." Josh chuckled, hoping that Usha would not smack him from the back seat. "On the other hand, I doubt that happens for many couples over the long haul, that spark thing."

No one responded to Josh's observation. Rather, Usha continued. "In the end, our marriage probably could not last. But when I did fall in love, or thought I had, I knew I could not put off the inevitable any longer. I went back to India and fessed up. I will always be appreciative to Josh, for his kindness and courage. He came with me for support. I might have lost courage once again were he not there at my side, encouraging me on."

"When you did tell your family, what happened?" Meena asked.

"Well, there was shock at first and all kinds of emotions. They had been so proud of me. To them, I was a successful academic in a successful marriage. The one blot was the lack of children, but that was still possible in their minds though time was running short. In any case, the news was a shock. I think it was a shock, you never really know. They surely had their suspicions early on but the so-called marriage to Josh had them fooled. Thing is, they really liked him."

"His one talent … fooling people." Rachel whispered mostly to herself.

Josh spoke more clearly. "Of course they liked me. You were getting long in the tooth, so they would have loved any guy you managed to reel in."

"No, they really did like you. They saw your kindness behind those awful jokes, not all of which they even got by the way." Usha paused for a moment, then continued. "It would have been more honest to come out earlier when I first came to realize who I was. But I did not have the courage. In the end, I just explained the best I could what I had gone through. Like all parents, there was concern about what everyone would say. Their peers, those from the older generation, could be savage, at least some of them. Then Josh took over; He was great with them. He spoke about me in such admiring terms, and he told them about how much I loved them and how deeply I suffered at the very thought of hurting them. Mostly, he focused on what their love and acceptance meant to me. It was his finest hour."

"Wow," Cate murmured. "Uncle is making a comeback in my mind. I just knew he had to be more than your typical, debauched pervert."

"Funny," Usha was finding her voice, "it turned out to be my grandmother who broke the ice. She pointed out other gay couples in their acquaintance and said that she would love me no matter what. I so admired that shrivelled-up old woman. It took a lot of talking and tears, but only a few in the extended family did not come on board. For me, it was like experiencing freedom for the first time. Even though I picked a partner poorly, she did provide the incentive to publicly admit who I was."

"Were there any negative consequences to coming out?" Meena inquired with genuine interest.

"Not for me, or not for long at least, and things have gotten even better. Being an academic makes it easier. You're in a liberal community to begin with. Still, general attitudes are changing rapidly though a lot yet depends on your situation. Living in a major cosmopolitan area like Toronto or Vancouver makes personal choices less of an issue. People just do not care. But I would not want to live in rural Alberta. That would be quite different. You, Meena, must be acutely aware of your culture, as we began to discuss yesterday. On reflection, not even the Islamic world is monolithic on this matter anymore."

Meena sighed. "I know, I know. It is not as simple as many might think. It remains subtle in my world. As Usha said, if I were from the Jordanian equivalent of Alberta, loving another woman would be impossible. In some places, the family might sacrifice me as part of an honor killing. But we're of the so-called sophisticated elite. Many of my extended family were educated abroad, and some have settled in the West. But there still is a code. You can do what you want when there is little chance of it getting back home. I probably could be an exotic dancer in London, so long as no Jordanian nationals frequented the establishment. At home, however, we must be careful indeed. You can stray from the cultural rules a bit in private. Still, that's always risky, for women especially so. You find yourself looking over your shoulder all the time. I think my family had suspicions."

"Usha was curious. "How did you deal with that?"

"With my sister and female cousins, I tried to fake an interest in boys, but I always felt I was trying too hard. People must know when you are faking it, at least that's what I thought. After a while, I'm sure they knew but never said anything. My good parents were always trying. While at Oxford, they could tell the relatives that I would marry after my education was complete. For a while, I think they simply told folks that I had high standards. My poor mother was always suggesting so-and-so or some guy from an acceptable family. That was so important to them ... the respectability of the family Of course, they were always such nice boys, or so she would insist. For show, I went out with a few, and believe me, they were not so nice. The good ones were married off early. Those left were no bargains, pretty much party boys or damaged in some way. Among male elites, even in Jordon, there are few boundaries."

Rachel had been staring at the mountains, an enigmatic expression on her face. "I still find it amazing that you two connected. I mean, that you made it through all the ... barriers."

To this, Cate responded, "It amazes me as well though, barriers remain until we are officially joined together. Then I'll relax. For now, I simply cannot fathom why I hid from myself for so long. People were open all around me. What was I so afraid of? I blamed dad, my career, even you, mom."

"Me?" Rachel was surprised, more that Cate would say that aloud.

Cate sounded a bit defensive. "Stupid, I know. You never suggested you would have a problem with such a thing. It was more that I didn't want to disappoint you, of all people." She sensed that Rachel was going to say something. "Let me finish. You know I always felt like a disappointment to you. I mean, you were always nice about my choices, even my not so good ones. To be totally honest, I hid my worst choices well."

"Thank god." Rachel smiled. "That must have been easy for you. I was too busy to notice."

"Not true, you kept an eye on me, or so I thought. But I was too clever by half. I really didn't want to disappoint you any more than I had."

"Wait," Rachel sputtered, "what does that mean? You never disappointed me."

"Oh mother, please. You were top doc and a world class researcher. I did linguistics at Madison and some grad courses in international affairs. Not bad, of course, but hardly on your level. You were perfection in my eyes. I hated what you might be thinking of me. It was worse that you never said anything. I could well imagine what you were thinking. Hell, I could not even get my sex life right."

Rachel twisted around to face her daughter. "Stop. Just stop. Cate, you're the best thing that ever happened to me. I've loved you from the moment you came into this world. And you know what? My love for you has grown with every passing day. You have always been sweet, and caring, and funny, and committed to doing the right thing. And you did all that without much help from me and absolutely nothing from your father. And never forget this, you are not too old to put over my knee."

The car was silent for a moment. Josh ended the disquieting silence. "Cate, I can tell you from bitter experience that you don't want to piss off your mother. I may have to have surgery to put all my organs back in their proper places after she leaves."

Rachel reached back and took Cate's hand. "Love you, kiddo."

"Love you, Mom," Cate murmured.

Josh turned to Rachel with his smile. "Rach, do you love me?"

"Of course not," but she broke into a broad smile, "you're a total ass."

Cate sighed loudly. "Funny, but when the time is right, when the person is right, all the fears and concerns melt away. They don't disappear, but they aren't as overwhelming anymore." Cate retrieved her hand and took Meena's. "There were so many times in the past when I would develop a friendship with a woman. The feelings were there, sexual and romantic, whatever. They were feelings I never had with a man, but I always found a way to minimize or dismiss them. Life went on, and I was busy seeing and saving the world. No room for human intimacy."

"I know the feeling," Josh said the words so quietly that they were overlooked.

'I can vouch for that.' Rachel immediately wondered if these words were only in her mind or whether she had said them aloud.

"I still remember the first time I saw Meena. She was wearing an all-white outfit that set off her dark hair and complexion. It was a professional meeting at the Embassy, but I mentioned that before. I was supposed to be in my official role. At first sight, I melted inside. A current of something went through me. What was that sensation? Then I realized I could hardly breathe. I thought for sure that everyone in the room could see, but no one seemed to notice nor, thank god, said anything."

"I remember that you looked professional, very attractive but professional," Meena added. "You showed nothing but I, on the other hand, could hardly take my eyes off you."

Cate laughed. "We hid it well I suppose. I got through the meeting, but all I could think of was how to find some excuse to be with this vision before me. Meena, I was lost as you talked about the issues that day with that clipped British accent. You clearly were competent and quick, and I could even sense a little wit. You were damn lucky I didn't dive across the table to attack you."

"Oh, my," Meena chuckled, "that would have been awkward in the extreme given the people in the room."

"What devious plan did I concoct?" Cate knew but wanted her partner to share the moment.

"I remember. We needed sign-off from your embassy for what we were proposing, I forget why. It was all routine, I thought, but there was some small resource issue you raised. I recall being disappointed since it seemed unnecessary. Then, however, you said that you would need more input before you could approve our project. You suggested some site visits. For a moment, I thought you were being an obstructionist."

"You're kidding, no way."

"Absolutely, this was rather a small initiative that sold itself. I believe we were only requesting in-kind resources, not real money. I was rather disappointed in you at that moment." Meena laughed. "I thought perhaps you were just an officious bureaucrat throwing her weight around."

"Hey, I was desperate. If you walked out the door, maybe I would not see you again. When did you figure things out, that I was trying to get to know you better?"

Meena thought for a moment. "Oh, pretty quickly. How many site visits did this stupid project demand after all? Then you were suggesting other possibilities … as soon as you could no longer drag out the first one. Something was up, but neither of us made a real move. In retrospect, we were circling one another."

"Hallmark mini-series for sure," Josh interjected, "but one I'd watch."

"Duct tape his mouth, will you Rachel."

"No problem, I expect no less from Mr. Romantic." Rachel hit her brother lightly on his shoulder.

Cate chuckled lightly at her memories. "My first big step for me was asking you to do something social, nonwork related. It should not have been that difficult. I recall asking you to help me out with the local culture. That should have been so easy. I had done so in other postings. But it wasn't since I knew what was inside my heart. Funny, when you know what's in your heart, even the most innocent acts become something totally different. I felt like a high school girl with a terrible crush. I went through the exercise of asking you in my head a hundred times. When I asked for real, I know I blushed."

"Yes, you did." Meena laughed once more. "I recall thinking you might be ill with a fever."

Josh added. "I agree. It really is hilarious how something innocent can turn sinister given a slight change in intention. I've been there for sure. You meet a colleague for lunch, and it is a so-what event. Meet the same person in the same restaurant as a prelude to a sexual tryst, and you're looking around as if you are in a spy novel. I mean, I've frisked many a waiter to see if they were wearing a wire."

"Says the depraved pervert who should know," Rachel observed.

"Ah, depravity is in the eyes of the beholder," he countered.

"Anyway," Cate assumed control again, "I finally mumbled something along the lines that it would be nice if someone could guide me through the Jordanian museum so they could give me an interpretive tour, not the stock stuff, but an insider's view. After I got the words out, I think my mind went blank."

"Hmmm," Meena considered. "I thought I jumped at the chance to say yes. Maybe I hesitated for a moment, just so my eagerness did not look so obvious. Your uncle is right about how even simple things are interpreted. People looking on would see nothing more than a simple request for help, very innocent. But we knew. We knew even when we could not say the words. I sensed it was more than a casual request for information. Did I want to go there, to that place I had contemplated only inside my head, and heart?"

"Was it hard to decide? I thought you hesitated forever." Cate asked her partner.

"Not then. I was ready. At last, I was ready to try."

Cate looked directly at Meena. "After the museum, we walked over to Nakheel Square and just talked for a long time, remember that. We shared our histories, even started talking about our hopes. Not a word about our longings though. My god, I thought my body would explode that day. My heart was beating so hard."

Meena spoke but seemed far away. "Then I asked you if you wanted to walk around the square, which, by the way, is a big circle. That always confused me as a child. No matter, that gave me an excuse to take your hand."

Cate quickly added for the larger group, "Women holding hands in public, even men holding hands is not a problem, quite common. But again, I knew by this time it meant more than friendship, at least that was what I was hoping."

Cate and Meena were talking to each other now. "You were hoping right," Meena said softly. "I don't recall when I figured out what was happening. But I could see something in your eyes that spoke to me. Your gaze was too long, too deep, too meaningful. Finally, toward dusk, we knew we had to part. We were yet walking, our hands clasped, and our bodies occasionally nudged one another."

Cate was still far away, back in Amman's Nakheel Square. "Each time we touched, I felt that same current surge through me. I was not letting you walk away, but our time together that day was slipping away. I stopped thinking and walking. When you turned to me, everything in me wanted to kiss you, wrap you up in my arms. But we were still in a public place. Instead, I invited you to dinner at my place for the following night."

Meena picked up the story, as if forgetting they were among others. "By this time, my heart was lost. I had not let myself really believe that this beautiful American would be interested in me as a woman. Now I was certain. I said yes. And to make sure no misunderstanding remained, I leaned over and kissed you on the cheek before whispering that I could not wait."

"I so remember that kiss; I almost lost it." added Cate. "Did I say anything at that moment? I cannot recall now."

"Neither can I except I knew those would be a very long twenty-four hours," contributed Meena as she giggled a bit. "I had some wonderful imaginings that night."

Usha laughed. "Hell, I am having some wonderful fantasies right now. Oops, that was brave."

Josh briefly glanced toward his sister. Her eyes were shut; her lips seemed to tremor ever so slightly. What was she thinking? Josh wondered. This was supposed to be a dull week, a ritual milestone to be endured as one transitioned toward the so-called golden years. But it now was spinning away from anything he could control with his wit. Those around him seemed to be changing as he watched. How did he feel about that? He was not sure. He liked his life for the most part, it had become known and predictable. He could sleepwalk through the days, reflecting an oft-stated insight of his ... life was mostly a set of prescribed scripts that demanded little thought and less effort.

"I think I now have a vision of what Hell will be like." Josh managed during a pause in the conversation.

"Good to get a head start, uncle," Cate inserted. "But what vision?"

He glanced in Rachel's direction again. He could see she was engaged in some internal struggle. He knew what it was; he just could not guess at the resolution. She was no longer the bouncing kid following behind him, lapping up both his wisdom and his BS. Now she was a mature, successful woman perhaps on the cusp of discovering something essential about herself. Somehow, up until now, she had followed him on an ill-considered path. She had cut herself off from life, from others, much as he had. She had become too self-contained. Did he see a tear in her eye? Maybe neither of them could hide from life anymore.

"What vision." Usha asked when he did not respond to Cate.

"In Hell, I will be tortured by being forced to watch Hallmark chic flics for all eternity."

With that, Josh pulled into a Whistler parking lot. When the car came to a full stop, Usha immediately wacked him on the side of the head.

CHAPTER 20

Day 6 – WHISTLER

The tourist destination of Whistler was in that awkward period after the ski season had wound down yet just before the summer tourist mobs showed up in force. The crowds were light.

"This looks lovely," Rachel observed as they walked into the main village square. She had pushed aside her private struggle with the last conversation and worked to engage with the group. Of the group, she was certain that Josh alone had noticed her discomfort. Their old childhood bonds were returning.

Whistler was a needed distraction. It had the boutique shops and upscale restaurants enjoyed by the well-heeled. Nestled on a niche at the top of the world, they would be surrounded by craggy peaks with air that was unadulterated by the usual urban effluent. You could not but feel alive. Privately, Josh thought it had grown way too big, with much of the charm he recalled from his initial visits sacrificed to developer's greed. Now, big chain retail outlets were forcing out the smaller shops. The local establishments were still there, but you needed to know where to look.

"Usha, do you remember where David's Tea House is?" When she nodded, Josh went on. "Why don't you bring the group over there. There are plenty of shops in that area. I'll head back to the parking area to wait for Connie. Then we'll join you."

About twenty minutes later, Josh noticed her pale green Prius pull into the main parking area where they had agreed to meet.

"What took you so long? I thought you had gotten lost."

"No, they wanted to stop and enjoy the scenery, take some pictures."

Josh smiled. His old revolutionary comrades had evolved into your average tourists. As they headed off to join the others, Connie maneuvered her way next to Josh and whispered, "We had a fascinating discussion on the way up. They talked a lot about the investigation."

"What investigation?"

"Of you, silly. Fascinating details about pressures they were under to give you up, and things along those lines. You know, sometimes paranoia is justified because people really are after you. Get them to talk about this." Then they re-joined the larger group.

As with all groups with varied interests, they decided to disperse and meet again later at a given time and place. Josh asked Peter, Carla, and Morris to join him for lunch. At the last minute, Connie asked if she could join them, which Josh thought a bit odd. Then he kicked himself inside for presuming that women would prefer shopping. *Could he really be a chauvinist?* Perhaps she had bonded with them on the drive north. He took the group to an Indian restaurant that he knew would not be crowded and where they could spend time talking. It occurred to Josh that all he was eating this week was Indian fare. He would have to diet next week or, worse, exercise more.

"You know," Carla said at one point, "there is a real cute blouse I saw on the way over. After we finish, I want to look at it again."

There was a pause before the men broke into laughter. "From Valkyrie warrior to purveyor of designer clothes." Peter joked.

"Oh shush, assholes," she retorted. "You guys don't look as if you're going to mount any barricades soon."

"I don't know." Josh chuckled. "I was thinking about starting the revolution after tea this afternoon. "You fellows with me?" Peter and Morris indicated they were game.

"Oh, bite me," Carla responded.

"Now that's the Carla I remember," Peter chuckled.

Connie piped up. "It was a cute blouse. I'm with Carla."

"Before the women go off on a shopping spree, I've got a question." Josh collected his thoughts and spoke. "Please don't blame her but Connie mentioned that you guys were talking about the old days in the car. Okay, let me ask straight out then. There are things about what happened when the arrests and trials took place that remained a mystery. The thing is, why didn't I go to prison? I waited and waited. Nothing happened."

There was a long silence. He needed to know this. It was a question he had obsessed about for years. How did he, of them all, escape?

Peter finally spoke up. "Well, to tell the truth, it was a close-run thing. Chuck Olson was never a fan of yours. He was one of those rigid super-patriots who saw Reds behind every tree. But the more I think on it, you might be right about Kit being on his case after you dumped her."

"It wasn't like that." Josh protested.

"No matter," Peter pushed on, "you pissed her off … the woman scorned and all. His venom toward you increased over time as our attention to small-time revolutionaries like you went in the other direction."

"Small time?" Josh looked hurt. "That hurts."

"Lucky we didn't know all the shit you did. You still had a problem for another reason … beyond Kit's wrath. Chuck was always an ambitious prick. Damn, I think I've called him a prick so many times I sometimes think that's his real name," Favulli smiled at some private bit of humor. "You may recall that he and I eventually were on a joint terrorist task force shortly after joining the bureau upon completing law school. By then, the war had wound down, as were any fears of a serious domestic uprising. All the Vietnam stuff was circling the drain as an issue. People wanted to forget about it, so they put me as the new guy on this mostly moribund task force. But Mr. Prick was still after you, he kept your name on this list of active persons-of-interest. He wanted to squeeze one more headline victory out of this dead horse."

'I knew it,' Josh muttered under his breath.

"Hell, when I read the files about your group, I understood what character and personal integrity were about."

"Sorry?" Josh was afraid he might stop.

"Character, Josh!" Peter hesitated as he realized that Josh was clueless. "Shit, I guess no one ever told you."

"Told me what?"

"Well, after all this time, you should know something that apparently we all kept a secret." Peter took a deep breath.

"Shit, this is embarrassing." Mo murmured. "Do we need to go into this?"

"Yes," Peter asserted. "Time Josh knows the whole story."

"What story?" Josh wondered if he was ready for whatever might be coming.

Peter started. "Olson, my favorite prick, was after you like a pit bull. But the evidence against you was circumstantial. Most of the hard evidence had been gathered after you headed north. In consequence, most of what we had was circumstantial shit that you had hung around with unsavory characters, nothing direct."

"Unsavory?" I resemble that remark. Mo tried to look aggrieved.

"Still, Olson thought he was so close. He just needed one person to flip on you to get a warrant and start extradition procedures. Get a couple of your associates to flip, and a conviction was a snap. He went through them all. Helen was a good bet, but she was so lawyered up with high-price talent that with her family's connections, she was in for a sweetheart deal without flipping. Besides, he would still need a second and she didn't have much direct knowledge of your, shall we say, crimes against humanity."

"What about that arson caper?" Morris asked.

"Oh yeah, that would have done it. But no one knew about that one at the time. Somehow, it fell through the cracks or was blamed on someone else. You guys weren't the only wannabe revolutionaries running around so it was sometimes hard to pin the blame on specific individuals. In any case, our vendetta guy, Chuck, moved on to the rest of the gang that couldn't shoot straight."

"Hey," Morris complained, "I resent that remark even if it is true."

"Sorry, Comrade," Peter smiled and went on. "The bottom line, Josh, is that Carla, Mo, and Bob didn't sell you out. My guess now is that he felt Helen might be persuaded but needed that second corroboration before trying to get through all her lawyers. He went back to the others several times. He promised lighter sentences during their trials. Even when they were in prison, he would offer promises of early release. All they had to do was give you up. No one did. Not Mo or Carla or Bob … none of them. Olson was befuddled. He never understood."

"Narcissists can never understand integrity." The comment came from Connie who looked on with amazement.

Josh was dumbstruck. He looked at Carla and Mo, neither of whom would look at him directly. "Why, in heaven's name … why? Think about it! I ran out on you. When crunch time came, I fled. You know I thought you hated me. You know I did. That is precisely why I almost crapped in my pants when I saw you in the audience yesterday."

"It's complicated," Morris said quietly. "As I mentioned, I was conflicted at first. I hated what you did, but I never stopped loving you."

"I still can't …" Josh could not finish the sentence. He could not get over how much Morris had changed. His intensity and fervor were gone, or at least diminished. He was quiet, reflective, soft-spoken. He had not decided which Morris he preferred, but he was leaning toward the current version. Mellowness is a good thing later in life. Obsession and passion are vices best enjoyed by the young.

"Josh, you simply saw reality earlier than the rest of us did." Morris took off his rimless glasses. "By reality, I mean you understood that you don't fight violence and hate with violence and hate. We were spiralling downhill, losing all perspective. You're leaving, if nothing else, slowed us up. If you had been around and encouraged our, what shall I say, adventures …."

"I for one quickly would have been out of control," Carla added, "more than I was already."

"We would have been the ones blowing up a campus building and killing someone, not Karl Armstrong and his buddies. One of us was going to get there, it could easily have been us." Morris reached out to take his wife's hand. "You said something once back in the old days that I didn't fully understand until much later."

"What?" Josh managed.

"A man that raises his fist in anger is the man who has run out of ideas."

Carla smiled. "We were young. We were into group think. All we needed was support from one another to justify ... who knows what. You remember how things were. We would feed off one another. Had we continued as we were going, we probably would have killed people for sure. You saved us."

"How the fuck did I save you?" Josh struggled to understand.

"Can't you figure that out? You're the professor." Morris shook his head. "I had more passion back then, but you were always the analytical one. Your level head held you back, and that was a blessing. In many ways, you calmed us down. I mean, you had that silly smile. It kept us from getting too serious. And when you left. Well, that got us thinking, a lot. Perhaps you had made the right choice. Just perhaps." Morris gazed at the distant mountains as if they were another reality before returning his gaze to Josh. "Besides, I owed you. You saved my ass from those Irish toughs, remember?"

Carla again spoke up. "I think, Josh, you touched us in different ways. All jokes about Irish toughs aside, I was a wild woman back then. I talked like a trucker and, frankly, could be rather a freak in bed. But that wasn't me. Not really. I acted as I thought a revolutionary should. Oh, my passions against the war and injustice were real enough. They are still there, just more proportional to the way the world works. I'm less impetuous, we all are. We discovered, in the end, that you simply cannot will utopia into existence."

"So true," Connie contributed. "If wishes could be made reality, all of my experiments would work."

Carla nodded toward Connie. "Truth from a real scientist, Josh. If you were smart, you'd keep her." Josh opened his mouth, but Carla cut him off. "The thing was, deep down, I liked you. I admired you. I never said it back then—it would have been way too sentimental. But you saw the world for what it was, not as we wished it to be. There was no way I would give you up after you left … as a friend that is. You were in another country, but I knew that we were still in your heart. That was my story at the time. Sometimes, in my cell, I wondered if I was nuts. Sure, I had my doubts. I wavered more than once … the joint sucks. In the end, though, I kept true."

Morris picked up on his spouse's theme. "Oh, I wavered at times. My weak point was when Olson threatened to have me sent to the worst of the worst prisons where terrible things happened to guys like me. I was panicking inside but just kept smiling at him."

"Did he do that?" Connie piped up, her expression revealing how taken she was with the discussion.

"Send me to a hell hole, no," Morris said. "Waiting for that shoe to drop, though, was hell enough."

"Now I'm sure we all did the right thing," Carla added. "Face it, you were worth protecting. Some people are. Besides, Olson was a slimy prick. I wouldn't have flipped on Jeffrey Dahmer to help-out that monstrous creep. In case your confused, the creep is Olson, not the cannibal guy. Never could decide which one of those two was worse."

"From time to time," Morris added, "Peter would get in touch and fill us in on your life. It was a comfort to know you were doing well, that you were shaping minds and doing your bit to improve society. The one thing we all agreed after is that we never gave our favorite prick the time of day."

"Hah," Peter laughed aloud. "I have my favorite Mr. Prick story."

"Do tell," Carla encouraged.

"He asked me to stay after a meeting one day. By now, things were winding down and he still had not flipped anyone and he was getting desperate. Besides, people were forgetting the old battles, more willing to forgive things. But not Mr. Righteous. He started in on me. *Favulli, you are holding out on me. You know what that bastard Connelly was up to back then. Hell, I always thought you might be guilty yourself. I think you are protecting him. I know you two go way back, all of you guys from that Mick neighborhood had one another's back.'* It didn't help when I pointed out that Josh and I were from different tribes, that the Micks and the Wops hated one another. He thought all ethnic working-class types looked and thought the same, and he definitely did not like being told he was wrong."

"No doubt," Josh inserted. "He would have been with the Know-Nothings back in the 1850s, attacking destitute Irish immigrants escaping the potato famine."

Peter continued. "He was in a lather. He accused me of hiding or destroying evidence, of not helping to flip you guys, and of abetting a traitorous miscreant to escape to Canada. I recall his face turning bright red as he built to a crescendo while screaming that he would bury me, ruin my career, and have me chucked in the pokey. I think that poor guy had anger management issues."

"No shit," Morris said. "How did you respond?"

"He wanted a confrontation, which is what I would not give him. I yawned in his face and told him that I was a busy man. As I walked out the door, I yelled back that he should get in touch when he had actual evidence of my wrongdoing. Until then, he could stay out of my fucking face. Good thing, Josh, that I did not know about all your misdeeds back then. I might have been conflicted or at least worried. But now our old friend is enjoying the fruits of a long career pursuing phantom threats to our country. He was a paranoid fuck. I believe he has a retirement home in Naples where he can consort with all the other right-wing crazies and greedy geezers."

"I … I …," Josh didn't know where to go next.

"Forget it, okay" Morris insisted. "We're only glad that we all did not have suffer for our youthful, what to call it, exuberance. And by the way, your life trajectory has motivated the rest of us."

"Really?" Josh stammered. "How?"

"Obvious, isn't it? If a pitiful screwup like you could make it, there was hope for all." Everyone chuckled and the tension evaporated.

"So true, my friend." Josh mused. "We probably are the lucky ones. Guys I played ball with, hung around with, went over to that Hell in Nam. Some never came back. Other's came back with terrible wounds, not all physical. There was one guy, Terry Mahoney. Good football player on my high school team. Got a scholarship to B.C. Funny as hell, and always in trouble … a typical Mick. Joined ROTC in college and went off to Nam as a second lieutenant. It only took him a few months to see the futility and waste, but he had no escape by then. He came back with physical wounds, but they were nothing compared to the damage to his soul. What was in his head was much worse."

"Oh, oh, I don't like where this is going." Connie sighed.

"Yeah, sad but common. Terry did try to atone for his sins. He emigrated up here to work with guys like me who had made a different choice than he had, one he regretted not making. He never could escape the pain and the nightmares. I think, in the end, guilt got to him. He was ashamed of what he had done over there, what he had become. I tried to stay in touch, but he was in Ottawa. The contacts became fewer and then stopped."

"Suicide?" Peter asked.

"Yeah, jumped off a building. That wall in Washington with all the names of the fallen. It is not nearly long enough. So many, many names should be on it," Josh's voice trailed off, "and never will."

Peter groaned. "I saw some of the others, several that joined the agency. They came back from over there all fired up, angry that they were held back. It struck me as something like an overwrought conviction in the righteousness of the cause. I could never understand those guys."

"Perhaps those guys were reacting to their internal doubts in the only way they could, by embracing the war with even greater fervor," Connie suggested.

Carla looked at Connie with growing admiration. "Hmm, I see why you and Josh click. You're more than just a scientist."

Mo seemed contemplative. "You know, we all made big choices back then without really thinking about the consequences. They were so casual, really. Some didn't think about it. Others never stopped thinking. It was remarkable when you consider it."

"I think," Josh said slowly as if just formulating his words, "that most of us decided and then spent all this time justifying what we did or didn't do. Some of us came up with convincing explanations, at least to our own minds. Others never could … and paid a huge price."

"I think you are right," Mo said just as slowly, "but not the decision about whether to flip on you. Those consequences were pushed right into our faces. Yeah, we knew the costs and it was worth it. That was a choice none of us regretted."

"You were one lucky bastard, Josh," Peter said quietly. "Is that what people meant by the luck of the Irish?"

"No Peter, none of us were lucky. Some of us were survivors though."

Peter sighed. "I suppose you are right. Could have been worse for you though. I think Olson finally was convincing his colleagues that it was worth nailing your ass and go for extradition. They wanted to get him off their backs, he was such a pain. But Carter set a different tone in his presidency. He was a real Christian … into forgiveness. Besides, people were looking for reconciliation, didn't want to think about the war anymore. It had become a painful memory. Hell, we got our asses handed to us by a freaking third-world country. Think about that! And priorities had changed, we started going after real problems, like the Mafia. And no WOP jokes, understand? I still know made guys who owe me favors." Peter broke into a big smile.

Josh rubbed his face with his hands. "I wonder what we have learned from all this, other than the *luck of the Irish* thing has a bit of truth to it. I mean, while our actions may have been ill advised tactically, were we wrong? What if we faced something similar today, if some maniac got the White House and went off the deep end? Would we act any differently? Would we make different choices?"

They all sat in silent meditation. Josh wondered if no one thought his query worth a response.

Morris was the first to respond. "Now, there is one counterfactual I hope to avoid. I'm too old and tired to confront evil again. But I will say one thing. Like you, Josh, I see that struggle between the analytical side and our emotional side. Our analytical gifts enabled us to identify flaws in the rationale for an essentially insupportable foreign policy."

"And on the domestic side." Carla added.

"Exactly," Morris enthused. "We could connect the dots with lightning speed, or at least quickly, and could spot where their causal explanations fell apart. It was infuriating to be told that you were too immature or lacked the capacity to understand complex matters. That pushed me over the edge—my personal vice of youth was excess hubris."

Josh stood. "Except, goddamn it, we were smarter than those around us. We were! Hell, I suffer from the impostor syndrome as much as the next man. And sometimes I did wonder if the other side was right, that we were the ones foolishly pursuing false illusions … like being the Don Quixote of our generation. Perhaps we were tilting at windmills."

"Have an answer to that one yet?" Connie asked.

"Yes, I think I might. Eventually, I became one of those adults, the person inside rooms making public policy. I came to two conclusions then. Yes, the world is more complex on the inside than from the outside. That is true, undeniable. But second, we were right back then! Nam was a colossal mistake. Apartheid was an unacceptable evil. A society where women are prohibited from enjoying equal opportunity and rights is a weaker society. And the list goes on. Our fault was not being ambitious enough. The war was a horrific side show, but we let it consume us."

"What strikes me," Carla added, "is that we are missing one critical dimension. Analytics and simple caring are important, but so is one's moral compass. You need all three, sort of like a trinity of inputs into our calculations."

"See," Josh beamed, "Carla is a secret Catholic. She is on to the Holy Trinity."

"Bite me." Carla said with a smile, extending her middle finger skyward in Josh's direction.

"Actually, more like the ego, id, and superego," Peter added thoughtfully.

"Yes, good analogy. For a G-man, your kinda smart," enthused Carla with a smile. "Ego can be analytics, id is emotion, and superego is the moral compass. It strikes me that individuals have different combinations of these factors. Evangelicals probably have high, but rigid, moral compasses. However, they are low on analytics. Tea party types are like evangelicals but have some super-high emotional juice. So, they would be high on a rigid but highly skewed moral system combined with a pathetic ability to connect the dots and easily swayed by emotional arguments. We would have to play with this, but it might work."

"I miss these discussions, how I miss them," Peter complained. "At the bureau, we talked about sports and sex until they got too many damn female agents. Then all us guys would take long potty breaks instead."

"Face it, G-man," Morris said. "You would never have survived with us."

"What the hell are you talking about?"

Now Morris smiled. "Think about it. You would have lost too much time recovering from all the beatings Carla gave you for being such a sexist pig."

"That would have been such fun." Carla smiled.

Josh returned the group to a serious point. "One more thing disappointed me from those days ... how brief the moment was. The kids who became involved right behind us mouthed the words and sentiments, but they did not understand. It was like someone handed them a script ... off the pigs and power to the people."

"Power to the people … sure. I remember seeing kids shouting that. The first thing the people would have done is to throw their sorry asses in jail," Carla added.

Morris agreed. "No shit. The point is that these kids did not go through the hard process of figuring things on their own. Each generation must figure things out for themselves. No shortcuts. You cannot get by just borrowing slogans from those who have gone before you."

Everyone assented.

Josh then spoke up. "One thing is clear to me. What has been going on in the US disgusts me. You heard my spiel of growing inequality and declining opportunity. You would think that people would be outraged. Some are, of course, but they are the educated elite who are doing rather well. Those suffering the most are more likely to remain angry but misdirected. Poor whites vote against their self-interests all the time. You cannot reach them with evidence. Reason is the part of the human experience to which Obama appeals. He is high on analytics, which is death to most national politicians. He's different. People also like him on an intuitive, emotional level. In short, he has some cross-over appeal."

Josh paused to consider his next point. "True, Obama has a personal appeal. However, perhaps not the kind of broader, ideological message that will fire up progressives. He suggests it, touches real progressive ideals on the edges, but his instincts are centrist. On that broader level, most liberals respond to reason and rationality. They like science and numbers. They believe that evidence-based policy making can make the world just a little better. But conservatives go directly to the gut level. They tell people what they should fear and whom to blame. They focus on primal emotions, the id if you will, and never get beyond palatable nostrums that any thinking person should reject out of hand."

"Like what?" Connie pushed him.

"Okay, take health care financing for example. We have by far the most expensive system in the world, yet our health outcomes are average at best when compared to our peer countries. And how does the American electorate deal with this outrage? They punish the very people who try to help them. Look at what happened to the Dems in Congress in 1994 and what they face this fall. They are going to lose Congress again, mark my words. Obamacare will torpedo the Dems in 2010. Then watch Obama struggle. Unbelievable."

Morris spoke up. "But this goes exactly to our point. Conservatives have thrived on non- thinking slogans. Government is bad, the private sector is good. There is an ism always on the shelf to scare the crap out of people—Communism, Secularism, Socialism, Humanism, or Islamic terrorism. And there is a solution, safety in more killing, particularly if the people we kill look or believe differently. And of course, lower taxes will solve everything. Cure cancer, lower taxes. Don't like the weather, how about another tax break? Didn't get a raise, cut taxes for your bosses. Of course, the bulk of the rewards go to those at the very top. Your average working stiff gets a twenty-dollar tax break while Warren Buffet, as he has pointed out many times, pays proportionately less in income taxes than the secretary who keeps his damn scheduling calendar."

Josh picked up the narrative again. "The elite have seen their share of income and wealth soar past levels not seen since the 1929 crash when government had far fewer tools to manage the economy. Other countries, many of them, do much better. They provide security and opportunity and have happier citizens. Think we ever will look to these places for inspiration. Hell, no! Americans never look outside their own bubble. If it works in Canada or Europe, it must be tainted, everyone knows those Euros are damn Socialists."

"I don't see Canadians pouring over the border for the American dream." Connie joined in.

"Hah," Josh laughed, "I have never come across any of my fellow Canadians wanting to move South for the American health care system. Who the hell wants to pay five times as much for the exact same drug?"

"I can never figure out why some of us up here admire Americans at all," Connie added.

"I never forgot the vignette about Eisenhower when he was pushing the interstate highway act in the 1950s. When he saw the initial plans, he dismissed them out of hand. They were designed as three-lane roads with alternating passing areas. He sent the planners packing with one piece of advice. *'Give me the German autobahn.'* Think about it, the president wanted to copy the nation that he defeated in total war just a few years earlier. And then to get the Republicans in his own party on board, he had to justify the system as necessary for national defense."

"Really?" This seemed like news to Peter. "What was that all about?"

"Ridiculous, but true. Here was an infrastructure investment that was essential to the future development and prosperity of the country, and he could only sell it to the conservatives as a plan to get our tanks quickly across the country in case Canada decided to invade. As if my fellow Canucks would want to be stuck with such a sorry lot of assholes. What in God's name is wrong with right-wingers? Why do they so hate anything and everything that is for the public good?"

"I could see moving up here." Carla mused.

Josh continued. "What really worries me is what happens after Obama. On the one hand, some challenges are approaching the apocalypse stage. Global warming is an example. Conservatives will deny science on the matter since to address it will demand public action on a scale not seen since the last total war. They will only sanction such a concerted effort if it involves killing on a monstrous scale. They love death and destruction among those who do not look like them. But soon we will be past the point of no return. What scares the right the most is that demographics are going against them. Given current trends, we're not that far away from the day when white America will be the minority. Their fundamental nightmare, and what drives their hysterical fear, is that these *others* will take over."

Mo shook his head. "The right will bring the country down, or try damn hard, to prevent that from happening. My guess? They know in their hearts the sins they have committed over the decades, the centuries. They fear justice or, worse, retribution."

Josh nodded in agreement. "Your average working-class slug sees his economic world collapsing as globalization saps a way of life. Attacking free trade will just replace new problems for the old. A guy looks at his son, who may just be able to graduate from an underfunded high school that provides a second-class education compared to schools in Asia or Scandinavia. His primal fear is that his progeny will be the member of the new minority racial group, whites, and permanently underemployed. Can you imagine his panic?"

"Oh yeah," Morris echoed. "No political power. No presumed superiority. No gratuitous racial entitlement. No matter how crappy their lives were, they could always feel above another racial or ethnic groups deemed inferior. Talk about anxiety. Hear this! Someone soon will come along with a message of perverse populism that will sweep up the hopes of white working-class America. This demigod will tell them that they have every right to be afraid and that they have permission to hate again without any guilt. It will be 1930s Germany all over again except it will be *'make America great again,'* not Germany."

"Hey guys," groaned Carla, "will you listen to yourselves? *Will you just freaking listen to yourselves?* Another half hour of this crap and we will be back to plotting the revolution. After all these years, not a damn thing has changed."

"And this time, I will arrest your asses *before* you can do something stupid." Peter laughed. "Okay, this crowd is guaranteed to do something stupid, and I mean *really* stupid."

Josh laughed out loud. "Not to worry, one lesson I've learned is that I'm not going to change the world. Few in history have. Sure, some make temporary ripples, severe ripples in some of the usual suspects … Lenin, Hitler, Mao. Their impacts are severe to be sure. but temporary. They seldom last. Shit, Genghis Kahn created the biggest empire in the word, from China to modern day eastern Europe, and it was mostly gone just a couple of generations after he bought the farm."

Peter asked, "Okay, does anyone make your list of significant contributors to change?"

"Well," Josh considered for a moment "Hugh Hefner, of course. Oh, and Charles 'the Hammer' Martel."

"Who?" Peter asked.

"The problem with Italians is that the only historical figure they know is Columbus, who proved to be an arrogant genocidal monster." Josh ignored Peter's obscene gesture. "Charles stopped the armies of Islam at Tours in the ninth century. We might all be worshipping Allah if he hadn't. But I will give you one Italian, Peter. Constantine. He made Christianity work as a political institution. That had lasting consequences."

"That's the only Italian you can come up with." Peter feigned outrage.

"Yeah, and I'm not totally sure he came from Italy. He might have come from the periphery of the Roman empire by that time. Oh wait! Da Vinci was a cool dude. But that's it. Oh, and there is that Russian sub commander during the Cuban missile crisis though there was no evidence he had ever been to Italy, and certainly was not a WOP."

"Who?" This time it was Connie.

"I forget his name but check this out. They were off Cuba during the height of the standoff, in an old diesel sub armed with nuclear warheads. Worse, they were at ground zero where no Soviet ships were permitted to pass. The US navy was depth charging this sub to get them to surface or leave. The Soviet commanders had no contact with anyone on their side. For all they knew, World War III had already started. They had to decide, should they launch their nuclear weapons? Three people on the sub had to agree—the boat captain, the ranking political officer, and the group-commander who happened to be on that vessel. Two of them agreed to launch. One held out. Again, it was like 120 degrees down there. They were under attack and they had no idea what was going on. But this one guy said no, he was not going to destroy the world. If he hadn't sucked it up, exercised some courage and reason, we might all be walking around sporting an attractive orange glow."

"Is this the crap you taught in college. I would have asked for my money back." Peter wisecracked.

"Shit, you wouldn't have been admitted into my classes in the first place." Josh responded.

"Okay," Carla intoned. "That's it. I'm going shopping. And the first guy with a wisecrack will become the next candidate for the Vienna Boys' Choir. Connie, come with me."

"Now, that is the Carla I remember," Josh said affectionately.

It was Connie, however, who gave Josh the finger as the two women departed.

———

Not far away, Rachel had spirited her daughter away from the rest of the group. They sat outside a Starbucks drinking those expensive, fancy drinks. The sun was warm and comforting now. They had peeled off their sweaters and enjoyed the warmth.

"Cate," Rachel started hesitantly, "a question."

"Sure, Mom. The answers are that I don't do drugs and always use protection, though the latter is rather a moot concern."

Rachel laughed. "Oh my god, I did always ask you about those things. But hey, it was Madison after all, Mad-Town as they say. Many a young girl went the way of all flesh. Guess I didn't have to worry about the sex thing, did I?"

"Not entirely, there was pressure to look normal and a lot of boys willing to whip out their weapon at the slightest invite."

"Weapon?" Rachel tried not to react. "I suppose you have a point; Guys do come up with some suggestively aggressive names for their genitals."

"Yes, they do, but to your question. The others will realize we are missing soon."

"Yeah … wow, this is difficult, it was easier in my mind." Cate waited for her mother to continue. "You ended your story about Meena and you with asking her to your place. So … what happened there?"

"Ah, we had wild sex after a bit of fumbling around and never got to the food I had prepared. You never taught me how to cook so the sex seemed a better option." She thought of extending her remark into a risqué area but backed off.

"I knew I let you hang around with your uncle too much—his so-called wit spilled over on to you, and I tried so hard to raise you right. Okay, let me start again. What I'm getting at is how exactly did you get through that fumbling thing? I mean …" Rachel stopped, uncertain.

"Hey, Mom, I know what you're asking. I'll try but think I lost some of the details even though it was not that long ago. I was such a wreck that day. Several times I almost backed out. I kept thinking of reasons why I should cancel. I was so nervous I even had a couple of dry heaves waiting for her. Seems funny to me now. But at the end of the day, I understood one thing. I had to go through with this."

"How … why?" Rachel was not sure what question to ask.

"My body was telling me what I needed to understand in my heart, why I reacted as I did when she was near? It was a sense I had felt dozens or hundreds of times before but never in such a compelling way. I could no longer push it away. What's the old saying, *'know thyself?'* Wise counsel indeed. Just before she arrived, I looked in the mirror and told myself that if you don't do this now, find out for sure, you will regret it for the rest of your life. You're a doctor, you must know that one cannot repress their chemistry without some serious emotional blowback."

"And then?" Rachel then stalled.

Cate smiled. "I did it. I made the move. Exactly how is hazy in my head … too much emotion going on. But mom, I felt what eroticism means. I could sense what a complete love means. Every day, I pinch myself. Sometimes I recognize that little bit of Irish coursing through me, the Irish curse that uncle always talks about. You worry when you are happy because you know it probably will be taken away, somehow you don't deserve it. But I do deserve it, goddamn it, and so do you."

Rachel embraced her daughter. "Honey, I love you so much."

"Mom," Cate whispered as they embraced. "I love you as well, more than you know. But listen to me. Time for me to be the parent in this relationship. I need to practice for the day when I'll be changing your diapers. Go after it. Do not cheat yourself … do you hear me? You've raised me, and well. You've done all the good doctoring stuff. Now it is time for you to find someone to love and have a freaking life."

"What are you talking about, dear? I've had love and have a great life." Rachel, however, knew exactly what her daughter was talking about. Her protest sounded stupid as the words escaped her mouth.

"Mother, I have a brain. Don't try to be cute here. You have had a successful professional life. But ask yourself. Is that all?"

"I think I have."

"I doubt that very much. There is more than that and you know it. I doubt you have ever experienced any real love of another, and I don't count and neither does uncle. That would be filial love. I'm talking about full-out romantic, erotic love, the kind that causes your blood to rise and every sensory connection in your body to explode. Be honest—you never loved Dad. Shit, I knew that as a kid. The two of you went through the motions like some terrible country song. And face it, you are no spring chicken anymore. If not now, then when?"

"It's just so … hard."

Cate paused to take a deep breath. "Look, I've watched you and Usha, the way you look at each other, the way you respond to each other's words, presence. I know what all that means because I have been there."

"Oh, Cate, … I don't know."

"Hah!" Cate exclaimed.

"What dear."

"Funny, now that we are talking about this, *the* moment with Meena is coming back. I thought I had lost it. Yes, we had eaten some of my terrible meal, and I decided we needed more wine. I got up and went to pour two glasses. Then I sensed her behind me. I could smell her, feel her breath on my neck. I struggled not to faint. Then she said something like *'Catherine'*—she still called me by my full name then— *'please, oh please forgive me if you are offended.'* I was about to ask what she meant when she lightly kissed my neck, her lips just brushing my skin. I remember whirling around so quickly that she jumped back, thinking I was angry. Before she could say anything, I walked to her, took her face in my hands, and kissed her. It was an uncertain, tentative effort, but the flood was about to be unleashed. Softness became sensual became need, all in a matter of moments."

"Wow, you are suddenly a poet."

"Poetry comes easily to those who can feel life." A small tear formed at the corner of her eye.

"And then?" Rachel pushed.

"I'm not sure you want to know or that I want to talk about it with my mother." Cate laughed lightly. "Let me just say that we did not even reach the bed for quite a while and that miserable meal went uneaten. That was one blessing. The other blessing was the sex. I thought my body was on fire and that my head might explode. But maybe that's too much information."

"Yes, you are a wise daughter, that would be way too much information." Rachel laughed at this point but was thinking hard on her daughter's words. "Let's go back and find the others."

"One last thing, Mom. You cannot run away from what is in your own heart."

"But my dear, that's what we Connelly's are best at."

"Not any longer. Deny your own feelings and I'll put you over my knee. Face up to it, dear Mother, you are approaching your dotage and I'm sure I can take you on now if you continue to act like a child."

"You probably could." Rachel smiled. "But remember this. I can always change my will."

Cate let out a belly-laugh.

———

Later in the afternoon, the various smaller groups found one another after Carla and Connie stopped at a few shops and made several purchases.

"Where were you guys?" Connie asked.

Josh responded, "We would have found you sooner, but didn't want to detract Carla from boosting the Canadian economy all by herself."

"Careful," Carla growled at him.

"And we Canadians are most grateful." Josh smiled. "But I will desist from any further comment since I'm most interested in keeping my testicles attached to my body."

"What?" Connie asked.

"Private joke, Connie. Ever since I've known Carla, she has threatened to separate me from the family jewels, too many times to count." Then, before Carla could respond. "Are we ready to head back?"

"We could, but Rachel and Usha have disappeared." It was Cate.

Josh looked at his niece closely. He saw an enigmatic look on her face as if she were privy to a private confidence that would not be shared.

Josh grabbed his phone to call his sister to let her and Usha know they were thinking of heading back. Cate saw him. "Are you calling Mom?" She already knew the answer and shook her head back and forth while giving him the look.

He caught himself immediately. *Think, you idiot*, he said to himself. Cate does know something, so just give his sister a little more time. Putting his cell phone away, he looked around at the group as they shared small talk about the day. It was an eclectic composition of past and present. Yet they were melding together.

"Everyone have a good time?" Josh shouted.

"Yes," came from several directions, as they returned to private conversations.

Josh reflected on the earlier conversation with Peter, Morris, and Carla. It suddenly struck him how little things had changed. They were the same as they had been forty-plus years earlier. They had slipped seamlessly into a discussion of deep issues that meant so much to them. The back-and-forth, the mutual respect, the intellectual spark, and the tired old insults all were the same. If anything were different, they were more comfortable with one another perhaps because they were more comfortable in their own skins. Yes, the early connections and discoveries are the most compelling. He could engage in conversation with contemporary colleagues, but it was not the same. There was a qualitative difference, the level of intimacy and sharing could never be duplicated. He knew these people would not leave his life again.

Then an inescapable analogy struck him. How obvious! It was Eleni all over again. He had fantasized about reconnecting with her for years after the letters stopped and he lost track. But he had always been reluctant. His reservations were several. She would resent him. Or she would barely recall who he was. And most of all, she would not be the same. He would be disappointed in what he found. He always joked internally about finding that fat toothless harpy with a half-dozen kids, most of whom belong in some public institution of one kind or another. Worse, he would find her outwardly unchanged but totally uninteresting. He would now find a woman who was pedestrian and ordinary and wonder what in god's name had attracted him in the first instance. But no, the magic had never left, the passion was undiminished almost from the first words. He did not have to be with her, touch her. It was Leni, the same woman who once captured him totally and did so again. Some connections are eternal.

It had been similar with Morris and Carla. From Peter, he knew when they were released from prison and could have followed up with Peter on their doings and their whereabouts. Contact had always been possible. But he never did. He was afraid and for similar reasons. They would hate him, or he would find them insipid and disappointing, or they would reject him. But none of that was true. He was changing his mind about Virginia Woolf. Perhaps she was wrong, and you can go home again.

Not far away, in a reclusive area where privacy might be preserved, the two missing members of the group sat on a bench. From their vantage point, they could view some of the peaks about them. It was calming, relaxing. Proximity to such majesty somehow put life into perspective, permitting each to see their lives with more honesty. They were comparatively small, insignificant, considering the vast world about them.

After many minutes, Rachel breathed deeply. "Usha, I want to share something. My daughter told me more about her first moments with Meena, how scared she was, how uncertain. It really is rather amusing when the daughter suddenly becomes the parent. You look upon her as a child long after she is grown. Then one day, you see the adult person you created. Amazing."

"That's not what you wanted to tell me, is it? We all know that Cate is wonderful. That's … that's so obvious to all of us."

"No," Rachel admitted. "It isn't. Of course, it isn't." Usha waited patiently. "She shared with me what it felt like the first time Meena touched her, kissed her. It revealed a new world to her, physically and emotionally. My god, she is so like me in some ways. We are way too Irish. We stuff feelings in and then hide from ourselves. I retreated into medicine. Damn, I might be worse than my brother. Is that even possible? Cate, on the other hand, ran around the world, never slowing enough to give human contact a chance to take root. She knew who she was for a long time but kept pushing it away. I guessed and should have asked. Damn it, I failed her once again. I should have paid more attention, been a goddamn mother for a change."

"Rachel, stop it." Usha took her hand. "You are sounding like a broken record now."

"You're right. I've got to work on that."

"You do," Usha said warmly, "I fear it is a family trait."

"I suppose, in the end, it does not matter how you get where you need to be nor how long it takes. The only thing that matters is finishing the journey."

Rachel took another deep breath. She felt her heartbeat, a tingling over her skin. Then, slowly, she leaned over and kissed Usha on the lips. It was soft at first before subtle movements explored different possibilities and settled upon an emotional connection that spoke of meaning and possibility. Eventually, Rachel drew back as a tear coursed down her cheek. She sighed deeply. "Something is happening between us?"

"Of course, it has been happening almost from the moment we met the other day."

Rachel's voice caught "What?"

"We are rediscovering love."

"No, that's not right." Rachel said quietly.

Usha pulled back, flummoxed. "Sorry."

Rachel lowered her head. "I am discovering love for the first time. You are rediscovering it … was your first time with my brother?"

"Heavens no." Usha expelled a brief laugh. "I love that man but, as they say, not in that way."

"With Rose?" Rachel tried.

"I thought Rose might be it. After all, I left him for her. But I now know that there was nothing there. That proved to be mostly lust, an experiment that went south. Getting to know you has taught me how shallow that connection really was. It lacked …"

"Completeness."

"Yes," Usha looked at her with wide eyes. "How did you get that?"

"Oh … that's something I've been discussing with my brother, the original incomplete man."

Usha touched Rachel's cheek. "Bottom line, this thing that has possessed me over the last couple of days is something beyond my understanding. I am very articulate, the best legal education in Britain. And yet, I am mute at this moment. There is no sense to it. We are entering that part of the human experience where cognition is quite useless."

"Yes, I know what you're saying. I'm a doctor. I know the chemistry of emotions, how estrogen and dopamine works, how the nervous system works. But I'm a total idiot about what's inside me now. On one level, I realize this is fundamentally chemistry and can be rationally explained. On another level, this is all a complete mystery. I am falling in this thing called love at this very moment."

"Just like kids though we missed out then." Usha whispered the words as she leaned in for another kiss. "Maybe I know what's happening. You're so much like Josh, don't argue, and I did love that guy in that incomplete way. With him, it was just … nice. But with you, it can be … awesome. I feel like a kid again."

The ring of Rachel's phone shocked them apart. She noticed the number, grimaced, and answered it. They both could hear Josh's voice. "Sorry to bother you, but it is getting late. People want to get going so we're headed to the parking lot. So, finish up … whatever you are doing. Okay."

"Yeah, okay … see you there in just a few minutes."

"Rach, … everything okay?" Josh's voice came through the phone.

"Yes, everything is okay, better than okay," Rachel responded while smiling at the woman opposite her.

CHAPTER 21

Day 7 – BEFORE DAWN

Josh awoke to a low growl. He looked at his watch. Midnight. His faithless watchdog, Morris, was back with him and staring at the bedroom door.

"Hah, you traitor, couldn't get a better offer tonight." The door opened, and he could see Connie's familiar shape. "Damn, I was hoping you were the gal from the agency."

"Laugh now," Connie responded, "but wait until you get my invoice."

"I see I should have changed the locks. You apparently kept a key."

She stripped off her clothes and slid into bed next to him. "Maybe I should have asked first. You aren't going to kick me out of your bed, are you?"

"Hey, how dumb do I look?" he quipped.

"And I repeat my question …"

"Funny girl." He pulled her to him before continuing. "It is good to have you here, really. And I'm thinking that you just might get lucky tonight."

"Oh, that's what all the guys say. Then I realize they are only talking about sex."

Josh chuckled. Connie was as good at trading insults as Leni had been but, then again, how are comparisons of quality on such matters made? "Let me ask you something that has been on my mind."

"The answer is no; I ordinarily don't do this on a first date."

"Where is the freaking off switch," Josh said with a twinge of exasperation. "Seriously, has it been uncomfortable to be around Usha at all this week?"

"You mean because we both saw you naked? Not to worry, it is not that big a thrill, fella, your body that is. Now, if you were George Clooney…"

Josh began to think his question stupid and wanted to take it back. But it was out there. "Well, even before this week. Did the two of you ever, like, talk about me?"

"Why Josh, all of us girls talk about you boys." She tried to look coquettish.

"Why do I feel like a teenager?" He blushed. "However, I have noticed you are evading my question."

Connie regretted being so flip. "Okay, I'll be serious. Yes, Usha and I did discuss who would get which Connelly. I drew the short straw and got you. Usha got the brass ring … so she gets your sister. Lucky duck."

"Does everyone know about Usha and Rachel?" Josh asked.

"Oh, there are a few lost souls in the Northern Territories who won't know until tomorrow. It has been rather obvious given how they have been looking at each other. Really, did you see them when they finally re-joined us? They're acting like a couple of schoolgirls experiencing their first crush."

"Perhaps they are." Josh mused distractedly.

"By the way, when I passed the guest room, the door was open, and your sister was not there. The bed was still made."

"Really?" Josh was a bit surprised. "When I packed it in, she and Usha were chatting in the kitchen."

"Not to shock you, my dear, but my best guess is that they wandered off to Usha's hotel room for some privacy. I can easily understand that she would not want her brother and daughter to hear her having wild sex."

"Why am I having trouble with that image?"

"Your sister having wild sex?" Connie asked the obvious.

"I know, stupid. But she is still 14 years old in my head. That's … when we were so close or, more to the point, when she liked me."

"Not to worry, big guy. She likes you way more than you deserve." Connie purred. "I can't believe how easily you fool women."

Josh massaged the side of Connie's head as it lay on his chest. He looked at the ceiling, hoping desperately that his sister was finding some measure of happiness, even if he rebelled at imagining how. "I so hope she finds what she is looking for. She has been so lonely for so long."

"I have great confidence in Rachel. The greater concern is her hapless brother?" Connie countered. "You talk and act as if you have got your shit together but let me set you straight on something, kiddo. Do you know why I drifted away from you? No, don't answer. You will just make me mad." Josh thought she sounded rather angry already. "I listened carefully this afternoon. Do you know what I heard?"

"Ah, some political B.S.?"

"No, I heard a man who had a sense of conviction, someone who had principles and passion. I saw a man who cared deeply. That man excited me."

"I don't understand. You had that man and walked away from him. I never asked you to leave, remember?" Josh realized his error the moment the words were gone.

"You are joking. Tell me you are joking. I never had that man. I had some guy named Josh who, at his best, was funny but so remote. Face it, you were like half a man. Listen, I'm not a kid anymore. I have few romantic illusions. But you were not even meeting my low standards. At least Harold tried."

"Who is Harold?" And Josh immediately realized his error.

"The man I was supposed to marry, the physicist. You're just being obnoxious here. Stop it!"

"Come on, Connie, cut me some slack. That guy was invisible. No one could be expected to remember his name. Hell, even at half speed,

I am more of a man than that guy." His words came out overly harsh and he was not sure why.

She jumped out of bed. "You goddamn Irish prick!" Josh was stunned. He had never seen her angry, not this angry. "You can be such an arrogant asshole. Just because you're glib and charming does not make you a man. Sure, Harold is rather plodding …"

"That doesn't cover the half of it." Josh had no idea how those words came out. What was he doing?

"That man did his best to be there for me. He tried. Do you hear me, at least he tried!"

"Connie, listen …" Josh got up, reached out to her. She backed away.

"No, you listen to me. Did you ever tell me that you loved me? The answer is no by the way. Not once." Connie's words carried with them a tide of rising frustration.

"I didn't think that meant all that much to you." But his words came out weakly. He suddenly felt very alone.

Connie's anger remained crimson and right in front of him. "Really, did you ever ask? Did you ever say, *'Connie, what would you like from this relationship?'* Did you ever ask me if I wanted more than a companion for the symphony and an occasional fuck? Again, the answer is no, you never did. Not once! Don't even try to charm your way out of this one, asshole."

"But—"

"But nothing. My god, couldn't you even figure out that I had fallen in love with you?"

"I had no idea," he protested without conviction.

"No idea! No idea! Of course not, you probably think I select the men I want to screw from off the rack at Target. God, you're such an incomprehensible ass." She started picking up her clothes. "I'm sleeping in Rachel's room. I doubt she will be back tonight. She, at least, is with someone who cares about her. Damn, I wonder what that would be like." Then she disappeared out the door.

Josh sat back on the bed, putting his head in his hands. "You are a total fucking idiot, Connelly," he said aloud to himself.

"You won't get any argument from me."

Josh jumped back up. Connie had reappeared in the door. "Just so you understand. I am not some weepy girl, nor am I one of your escorts. I am a scientist trained to think analytically and with great rigor. I make decisions based on evidence … most of the time at least. But no matter how well trained you are, no matter the methodologies used, even the best of us make mistakes. I thought we had gotten along so well that love would happen. A lot of couples start off slow but grow into each other. We laughed, we shared, the sex was good. I even thought you were bright, for a social scientist I mean."

"Thanks," he whispered. He wanted to say the sex was great, not just good. He struggled to keep this wittier quip buried. What was wrong with him, he wondered?

"Not one more goddamn word from you, time for you to just listen! I knew you were damaged goods. I could sense something was missing. Apparently, everyone who gets close to you figures that out. Usha cautioned me that you were perfect for her because you would be imperfect for any straight woman who was moronic enough to prefer men. But like too many women, I had convinced myself that you were salvageable. What an idiot I was. I foolishly thought that anyone who was so kind to others must have a spark of decency and humanity somewhere inside him, perhaps a bit buried, but it had to be there. I mean, those working on robotics have made great strides recently, but could they really have produced a Josh Connelly? I kept betting that you were, in fact, human and not concocted in some lab despite all the overwhelming evidence that you were nothing but wires and a mother board. How stupid could I be? I thought you were real. But no, turns out someone can simulate a human being, just not perfectly. Turns out they can make someone who looks, walks, and talks like a real person and yet still not have a damn clue about what it takes to be human, and certainly not a real man. You are nothing but a goddamn machine.

If I ripped open your chest, I bet all I would find are computer chips and wires."

"Connie, I—"

"I told you … not a damn word. Do you know why I came back this week? Your sister called me after that first night at the restaurant. I liked her. She apparently has all the decency in the family. She called to tell me what a great couple we made. That, I thought I knew but then she said something else. She said you needed me. She asked me to give you another chance. She felt bad about Harold, and yes, she remembered his name. Still, she wanted to press the case for an us, you and me. I told her that Harold would hardly realize I was missing which was a lie. I broke his heart, and for what?"

"Connie…listen."

"No goddamn it, you listen. Rachel was convincing, I must give her that. *'You guys are a real couple, you guys are like peas in a pod,'* she said. Then she closed the deal by saying how damaged you were, how much hurt you were feeling, how lonely you are. Still, she argued, there was something good inside you … something worth saving. It just needed a little help from someone to get it out in the open. And I believed her. I freaking believed her. I mean, she is your sister, after all. Who better to know? What an idiot I was? I just had no idea how little she knew about you. I get it now, though. You had shut her out as well. Your own sister, and you shut her out for decades. How cold is that?"

"Rachel is pretty damaged herself," he said quickly when she paused a second.

"Oh my god, don't even go there. Don't you dare go there." Connie's anger was peaking. "Maybe she is, but that woman is trying. She is trying this very night. Think about that! She is giving life a damn try."

"I … I have no excuse." He managed to get out, his face displaying obvious pain.

Connie's anger dissipated a bit. "Listen, I know Cate and your other friends are leaving tomorrow. If you don't mind, I want to be around to say goodbye. I like all of them."

When she paused, Josh thought for a moment she might join him in bed again. "You … you can still sleep here, with me."

"You must be joking. I will stick with Rachel's unused bed. Even with no one else there, I will find more human comfort than here … way more. Okay, I'll leave you alone now so you can power down and reboot in the morning." And she was gone.

Then Josh noticed Morris, his pug, stir and jump down from the bed. Out the door he pattered, apparently following Connie. *Et tu, Brutus*, he thought. He tried sleeping but could do so only fitfully. She was right on so many levels. They did get along better than any other married couple he knew. They complemented each other perfectly. There were times when positive feelings bubbled up, catching him unawares. Feelings always surprised him. He recalled her snuggling in bed one night. They had returned from a concert and had capped off the evening with some great sex. He could sense her heart beating against his body, still elevated from the orgasm she had just experienced. The moment felt perfect, too perfect. He gazed on her as his feelings took over. It took everything in him to push the feelings back down, but he was good at it by then.

Josh got up and quietly made it to his office where he recalled that the file of cyber communications between him and Eleni had last been deposited. When Rachel had finished with them, she had left them in plain sight. Josh recoiled at the possibility that others might have stumbled over them. He was getting careless. Then he made his way to the guest bedroom.

Connie was on top of the bed lying on her stomach. She sensed his presence and looked toward the door. "Go away," she barked.

"Just one moment, please." He sat on the edge of the bed. "Connie, I have printed versions of hundreds of e-mails between Leni and me. You saw a couple on my computer one day. We never talked that out, but you started drifting away after that. The end was a drip, drip, drip where the connection simply disappeared. I never saw the anger, the disappointment, the residual feelings. What did you walk away with … mostly disappointment and hate? Until now, I've never seen such things in you. Believe me when I say that you are a kind, smart, and gentle woman. I, I, …well. Anyway, I shared this stuff with Rachel. Now I want you to look if you wish. Perhaps, just perhaps, this is the clearest path to my insides. I'm hoping it suggests that I am capable of … caring, maybe even more." He walked to the door. "I would like you to tell me, I really would."

"Tell you what?" She managed to get out through her emotions.

"That I'm more than a machine."

She said nothing. He could see her body tremor in silent sobs. His heart broke a bit at that moment. He was such a shit. Back in his room, he looked in the mirror, thinking perhaps he would see the Tin Man from Oz in the glass. But it was just him, looking immensely sad. Was he so irrevocably damaged?

Perhaps, like Connie, he should look at the evidence. He never went to his father's funeral. What was with that? Sure, he feared being detained for questioning if he went back to the States. But he had checked with Peter, who assured him he was on a list, but Peter would be the one notified and he would do nothing with that information. Peter advised him to do it. Still he did not go. Perhaps if Big Jim had died slowly, perhaps then he could push himself to go to his side, apologize. Maybe there could be a deathbed reconciliation, the mea culpas exchanged, the tears flowing in copious exculpation. But that was not to be.

His dad was in his bar one day, joking and arguing with the same guys from his tribe he had known forever. He told a joke that had several laughing as he went to pour someone a beer from the tap. Then he disappeared. It took a few moments for anyone to sense that something was amiss. When a customer checked behind the bar, he was on the floor, still holding the beer glass. Big Jim was already gone. He had been struck down by a massive heart attack. At first, Josh was furious with him. Why had he been so stubborn and unforgiving? They could never reconcile now. Their last days as a father and son would remain little more than stormy rages at each other from positions forged in brittle righteousness. A few weeks after his dad's passing,

Josh suddenly cried uncontrollably. What might have been would never be. There would never be redemption, forgiveness, closure.

Ora survived Big Jim for a few years. She grew thinner and even more ethereal if that were possible. She kept the bar, bringing in Big Jim's much younger brother to run the place. It survived but never was quite the same. One day, Rachel called to say that the end was near. He could come or not, as was his want. She would take care of everything. His paranoia had lessened but not disappeared. Still, he got on a plane and flew to Boston. As he walked through immigration control, he fully expected to be detained or arrested. The official looked at his passport and checked his computer screen for what seemed an eternity. He was certain the next words would be for him to stand aside and be escorted to a private room. But nothing happened; the official wished him a good visit. No one cared about him any longer. Perhaps no one ever had, he thought at the time.

As he sat next to his mother, she would look uncomprehendingly at him. Occasionally, she would grimace. Was that pain or recognition? He recalled Rachel telling him that their mother had never forgiven him for becoming one of them. She could not forgive those Communists who had ravaged her family as a child. It was a primal hate. She had never explained to others what had happened back then, in the birth of Bolshevism. It was all locked in a mystical past where fact and fantasy merge. It must have been horrendous, unforgettable. It is the emotional residue of early events that count, time cannot possibly heal all wounds. He patted her hand as she labored to breathe. He said *sorry* several times as Rachel sat on the other side of the bed. Suddenly, his mother looked at him, as her eyes widened as she then pulled her hand away. Then, after one final breath, she died. He cried one more time.

After they buried Ora, Rachel drove him to the airport. Rachel kissed him perfunctorily on the cheek, and he left. That had been their relationship over the decades. They would exchange information and on rare occasions physically see each other for some bigger event like Cate's college graduation. It struck Josh at that moment, as he lay in bed reviewing the debris of a life half lived, that he really had worked hard to keep Rachel away. They were cordial, never argued or had disputes, but shared little. His age-old question returned ... *why was that?* He could tell that she wanted more. Many of the women in his life wanted more. So many times, he saw her looking at him, considering some action that was never taken. It was as if they hated their assigned scripts but had no other choices. Well, he felt he had no choice; he was never certain about her.

He knew the problem; he had always known. He was racked with guilt, a deep and overwhelming guilt, the same dark pool that overwhelmed him whenever he thought of his old life. It had sat on him, suffocating him, for decades. It was the kind of existential despair that brings most Catholics to the highest ecstasy of religious meaning and, at the same time, to the depths of personal self-loathing. Ecstasy and agony, two sides of the same coin. He had been a coward. He had abandoned her, all of them, and he never said he was sorry, never tried to explain why. He had thought about a sharp knife on several occasions, but who was he kidding? He knew from experience that he would not go there. At other times, he formulated a long and articulate contrition in which he would pour out his heart and beg forgiveness. That had even less a chance of happening. For all those decades, he had been embarrassed beyond words just to be in her presence. Distance and silence were his solutions.

It was the same with the old gang, particularly Morris, Carla, and Bob. Jimmie was the worst. He had known Jimmie the longest, a boy from his tribe and neighborhood. The two had played ball on the streets, flirted with the Catholic girls with whom they had no real shot at scoring with, and studied together. They ate at each other's houses, and shared secrets and dreams. As Josh became the local sports hero, he eclipsed Jimmie in attention and popularity. He never abandoned his early friend, though, keeping him close. Jimmie, in turn, would have followed him to Hell. And, in the end, he did. Jimmie was just your average Irish kid, but he loved Josh, the iconic image of Josh, and followed him into the labyrinth of the leftist world of the 1960s. Even then, Josh knew it was less about conviction and more about hero worship, wanting to impress his personal icon. For Jimmie, this was about doing more than the others. Perhaps then, Josh might be impressed.

It was Bob who had come to him about getting blasting materials. Bob Wilson, the slightly older member of the group who had spent two years studying for the priesthood and a year doing volunteer work in Central America before arriving on campus. His revolutionary spirit came from a deep moral compass. Christ, for him, would have been a Socialist. And so, he set Bob up with an Irish friend from the old neighborhood who could help for a price, with money he had stolen from an Irish gang. Josh now twisted in physical agony on his bed. He should have known what they were doing. He should have known what might happen. How could he not? It was where they were headed. It had to be.

He could see an inevitable disaster in front of him. It was a classic Greek tragedy. The players carried out their roles, spoke their lines, as everyone knew the inexorable denouement, what had to be. Perhaps this was the line in the sand, the proverbial final straw. Then, one day not long after his escape, what he feared happened. Jimmie blew himself into small pieces. Bob, after his stint in prison, went back to God. He entered a monastery where he prayed to expiate Josh's sins, and his own. Josh never had a chance to tell either of them just how sorry he was.

He could have contacted Morris and Carla during the years of his exile. Peter had asked him to do this on several occasions. But he put him off; there was always an excuse. Was he merely afraid? They would spit at him, deride him, remind him that he had run. He abandoned them; He left them to their own fate. He could not stand the possibility that they might look upon him with disgust, throwing his weakness back in his face. That is what his own father had done, called him weak and useless. That was a pain that could not be ignored. That shame would overwhelm him, only because it was true. He had dissolved from a strong, confident young man to a pathetic coward.

In the end, when he finally saw them again, they did none of that. No anger was directed toward him, no rejection, just acceptance and sharing. His fears were smoke, insubstantial, a mirage. They yet loved him. How could that be the case? How could they be so forgiving? Even that added to his anguish at this moment; why didn't they punish him so that he might experience the despair and personal revulsion he deserved? Isn't that the lot of all transgressors of human decency and personal loyalty? You must be punished, ostracized, cast out. Where was his hair shirt, or the monks to flail at his flesh as they whipped Henry II after he had his best friend, Archbishop Thomas Beckett, murdered on his alter at Canterbury. Hell, Morris and Carla weren't even Christian, but they practiced Christ's message more deeply and fully than those disgusting evangelicals who run around praising God's son all day.

Of course, he had been punished. He had beaten himself up daily for over forty years. He functioned well in the world, achieved considerable success and public recognition, accumulated a decent amount of wealth, had many acquaintances who laughed at his endless wit and self-deprecation, and enjoyed waves of adoration from colleagues and the many students who credited him for changing their lives. How can one appear so normal and content on the outside and yet wallow in such self-loathing on the inside? Yes, that was it—he was punishing himself. He pushed away the people who had the power to complete the man. He used distance and cunning to isolate himself and avoid the need for real human contact. He buried himself in work, traveled around the world to consult, and either faked or purchased relationships just so he could avoid facing himself and others who knew what a sniveling coward he was. Yes, he had wandered in the desert for forty years just like Moses but alone, without any pathetic band of followers.

So many from his old and new lives could have been his connections to the world, attaching him to others with love and connectedness. They could have helped him embrace others as whole people do. He had refused to let any intimate embrace happen. He was frightened they would let him go, tease him with hope and then abandon him as had his father and mother and sister and Leni. Caring was inevitably associated with panic, a primal connection forged before reason could be applied as an antidote. When he was spurned, as he knew he would be for not living up to the standard of a deity, he would surely fall to earth and perish from abuse and neglect. What an idiot! He had succumbed to irrational fear. He anticipated rejection, so he never got close to anyone. The dangers were palpably real to him but, in the end, false.

What was he, an amoeba perhaps, just responding to whatever was in his environment? Had he ever thought about any of the big choices he had made … to give up football, to reject his culture, to run away to Canada, to pursue an education or become an academic, to marry Usha and to not marry Connie, to push away the people from his early life. He thought about all these milestones. Hard as he tried, he could not recall thinking hard on any of them at the time. A choice was before him and he responded, just like some single-cell organism. It was only in the aftermath, when doubt or pain or regret or loss caught up to him that he realized the enormity of the moment that was long gone. *What an odd way to conduct one's life,* he suddenly thought.

Josh looked at the ceiling. He had been drifting in and out of sleep and had lost track of time. People would arrive early this morning. Peter, Carla, Morris, Cate, and Meena would be leaving. There was much to do, words to exchange, promises to make, goodbyes to say. He sensed that the others would want to savor the last hours together. They would seek each other's company. Josh just stared at the ceiling as the morning light pushed out the gloom of night. He should get up, but his body would not move. He simply permitted the salty tears to flow over his face onto the pillow.

He knew, when the time came, he would grimly push himself out of bed and face the day. It was what he had done every day since that cold and snowy November morning when he had fled north.

CHAPTER 22

Day 7 – DAYBREAK

Connie was immobile the next morning as she lay on the bed Rachel had been using during her stay. As with Josh, she had not slept much during the night and now had trouble getting herself to move. She felt lethargic, depressed, and emotionally drained. Why had she let him get to her? Perhaps she should have left last night. It would be difficult looking that bastard in the eye during the light of day. Still, escaping the night before somehow seemed like a defeat in her mind, giving that man a victory of sorts. She wanted him to deal with her presence this morning; She would not make it easy for him. Besides, she meant it when she said she wanted to be there for the others to see them off. She loved Rachel and Cate and had warmed to Meena almost immediately. She also found Josh's old friends fascinating and would love to spend hours probing their views on the world. Their stories of their revolutionary college days enthralled her.

Connie pondered her own world. It revolved around high-level science and scientists. Her colleagues were all brittle bright but could be provincial about the broader world. They seldom had time for things beyond the next published issue of *Analytical Chemistry*. Josh could provide her with access to this broader universe. While she ridiculed him incessantly as just a social scientist, she loved when he discussed politics and international affairs. At some level, she appreciated that his world was more complex than hers. While her research was technical and beyond the reach of most, he functioned in an arena that ultimately defied measurement and thus could not be totally quantified. The human element made it both challenging and, in the end, frustrating. She had always admired his fortitude and patience as he labored over intractable social problems.

And then, it was true that Josh was physically attractive. She could not deny that. This is what drew her to him when they first ran across each other on some university-level committee. On one level, she understood that looks were a shallow basis for assessing a man, or any other person. Still, she was not made of stone and could not totally discount her physical reactions to him. What had sealed the deal for her was that he struck her as a mini renaissance man. He knew so much about so many things. His mind seemed to flow over topics and ideas, making easy and yet beguiling connections. And it didn't hurt that he made her laugh and that she loved going one-on-one with his wit. She shook her head in disgust. Why couldn't she evict this worthless piece of trash from her thoughts. Damn, he was stuck in her head.

No, enough of that. She lay there resolving herself to what needed to be done. He could be George Clooney himself, and that would not change things. She would not accept half a man. She did not need to compromise. She knew that men would always be attracted to her, she would have options. But even that was not important. She did not need any man. She had known that for years, ever since the divorce from her first husband. That experience taught her that choosing a life partner was not as easy as it looked and probably not worth the effort. The odds of identifying a soul mate were astronomical.

She and her first spouse seemed compatible even if he were Western and she Asian. They were both educated and cosmopolitan. Their friction, however, emerged from a source she had not expected. He was not in the academy, but a successful businessman. At first, that did not seem to matter, but it did over the long haul. The intellectual and practical worlds were distinct cultures. Members of each group had their own language, motivations, rewards, and visions for the good life. They drifted apart until the separation seemed inevitable. It was amicable, and each were grateful for the product of their union, their daughter Erika who now labored as an economics professor at Cal-Berkeley.

No, she reaffirmed in her head. She would be rid of Josh. She had no reason to settle, and she had concluded during the night that he would never change. You are what you are. She had seen so many women, very smart and accomplished females, waste time and emotional chips on the futile quest of turning a croaking toad into Prince Charming. Why did women willingly embrace this impossible challenge? Men were unteachable. That was apparent, undeniable, beyond dispute. Most of her female colleagues agreed. You could put a tuxedo on a frog, but it was still a frog. She would not be one of those fools to pursue the impossible, not Corinthia Alicia Chen, the Edna McMurtrey professor of biochemistry.

Suddenly, she was stirred from her wandering internal discourse by pressure moving across her body. Oh right, the dog had joined her last night. He must need to go out. She stroked him until he flipped over on his back, displaying his manhood for all to see. *Finally, a man worth having around*, she thought. Minutes later, she was out the door and a bit surprised that the sun was up. *Sorry pup, my fault that we are late this morning.*

As she followed the route in which the dog led her, it was immediately clear that she needed to make no independent decisions. Morris waddled ahead of her along the path to which he was long accustomed. Soon, they were across Marine Drive walking along the beach. When Morris did his primary morning business, Connie realized that she had not brought along a poop bag. *"Sorry, guy, let's move on before the doggie poop police descend upon us."* Just then, a car pulled to a stop. Connie blushed; for half a second, she thought maybe she was about to be scolded for despoiling the community.

Rachel jumped out and turned to the driver. "Here is a key if no one is up yet. I want to talk with Connie a bit. See you soon." Then there were words shared in a lower voice.

As Rachel leaned down to scratch the dog's ears, she said, "Hi there, did I catch you attempting to purloin this fine animal? You look awfully guilty to me."

"The guilt, I fear, is real. The cause is lies elsewhere, though. I forgot a poop bag and left his morning contributions behind."

"Punishable by death in many neighborhoods," Rachel replied, "but your capital offense is safe with me."

"Well, you're a good friend." Connie looked at her as she said the words. "At least I hope so."

"You know, it is my hope that we become more than that, maybe even family." Rachel blushed a bit at her bold impertinence.

Connie did not reply to that, knowing full well Rachel's insinuation. Rather, she shifted in another direction. "Tell me, how did it go last night? All the other girls will be asking me at lunch break." She tried to sound light, but it felt a bit forced.

Rachel paused, not sure that she wanted to change subjects from the topic of Connie and Josh. "Gee, I'm not one to kiss and tell … But then again, I'll probably have an aneurism if I keep this in." Another pause. "Okay, I'm thinking of you as a sister. I know that Cate will ask, but I would have trouble with that. Besides, I am torn up inside."

"Why? That makes no sense."

Rachel disagreed. "She will always be my daughter."

"That's true. I feel the same about Erika. Here she is, tenured at Berkeley. Yet, I still see her in pig tails. That never changes until they become the adult and we the child. But I don't think you feel conflicted only about opening to your daughter."

"Damn, I had not considered our girls taking care of us, not until you mentioned it. Dastardly thought! We are only about six months from senility." Rachel looked at Connie as the two effortlessly changed direction and started to walk slowly along the beach toward the university.

"Back to the question at hand. Why are you torn?" Connie pushed.

"Here's the thing. When we got to her hotel room, I surely felt like the child. Here I am, on the north side of sixty and I was trembling like a schoolgirl. But Usha was so kind, tender. When we started, I recall looking beyond her, wondering if I was still in my own body. There was a surreal sense about me and the situation. Funny, I could sense a dimension of life I had avoided for so long emerging. It surprised me that such things existed. Talk about becoming weak-kneed, my legs were rather wobbly. I'm being a teenager again. I mean, I'm reduced to babbling like a teenager. Am I embarrassing you?"

"Hell no, don't stop now, though this is too G rated. I probably need a little porn this morning."

Rachel paused to consider her remark, which struck her as a non sequitur. "Well, we stumbled toward the bed at this point. Connie, you and I both know the chemistry of sexual arousal. But when you experience it, really for the first time, forget the biology. What happens is so primal that it is beyond analytics. In any case, Usha brought me back, slowed me down. She knew this would be a moment to remember for both of us and should not be rushed. My response was …well, let's say it was my first orgasm in … far too long."

"Like ever?" Connie looked at her with incredulity.

"Oh no … the first in response to another. I can't say that is quite true but true enough. Of course, I could be kind to myself. This, however, was like being reborn. As a woman of science and accomplishment, I thought myself beyond pleasures of the flesh. As a female with real feelings, I am a child yet exploring the world. At that moment, I knew how much growing I had to do."

Connie then asked, "That's it, I'm changing sides, enough of men. But what's next? The two of you cannot just go back to your ordinary lives. I mean, you are no spring chicken."

Rachel intertwined Connie's arm with hers, and they continued walking. "People keep pointing out this spring chicken thing, I've checked several times recently and have yet to see vultures circling over me. Still, I don't know what is next. Therein is the conflict!"

"What conflict? I don't see it."

Rachel breathed deeply. "The truth is that I'm afraid. I am scared. My fear has nothing to do with what people will think or say. We know that no one in our circles cares."

"Then I'm not sure I understand."

"It is something in me, very hard to talk about." Rachel stopped and leaned down to pet the dog. It was a way to escape for a second. Connie went after her, pulling her up. Rachel sensed there was no easy escape and relieved that was the case. "It is me, Connie. I am desperately frightened of being abandoned. If I give myself over to someone, they will reject me. Or I'll be disappointed somehow."

There was silence which Connie chose to end. "Is this about Evan, your husband."

"Heavens no. Evan left no scars. No, it goes back deeper, back in time as well."

"To when Josh left for Canada, right?"

Rachel nodded, "and being rejected by my parents?"

"So much now makes sense." Connie looked pensive.

Rachel nodded. "I was never sure whether mom and dad's anger toward Josh spilled over to me or whether I earned their enmity and avoidance all on my own. Perhaps that is irrelevant. As an adult, you can put things in perspective. But I was a teen when all that happened, Josh fled. Things had fallen apart at home, raging arguments between Josh and my dad, between my mom and dad. I had always looked upon my brother as my anchor, my lifeboat as one storm after another threatened to drown me. Then he was gone."

"I get it." Connie said while wondering if anyone understands another's pain.

"Not a word from him for a long time. He was gone. It was weeks before I even knew he was still alive. His disappearance scarred me deeply, as it did my dad. I only found out this week that he sent letters to me that my mom and dad kept secret from me. But I don't really know if that would have made much of a difference. Then, after he was gone, my folks checked out. They never had much time for me before but after there was none. I tried so hard but there was nothing. Ever experience total loneliness, ultimate rejection?"

Connie embraced her. "I want to say silly things like that was a long time ago and that your brother is a well-known shit but that would be just stating the obvious."

"No Connie, Josh is not so bad. I'm the one lacking … something."

"Bullshit!" Connie yelled, causing Rachel to jump back. "Trust me, he is *that bad*. In any case, this is my message. Do not throw this away. You hear me? Do not throw away your chance for a relationship. You will regret it forever, and more importantly, I will be so pissed."

Rachel pulled further away. "Maybe I have already blown it. This morning, when we awoke, I was distant to her. To be honest, she awoke as I had been going over things in my head most of the night. That's always a bad idea. For some reason, I just wanted to run away. Usha had to notice. I felt myself curling up in some dark place…" Rachel stared off toward the mountains. "I didn't have any words for her, nothing rational at least."

"Don't be silly. Just be honest with her. Usha is worth it. Just talk to her, work it out."

Suddenly, Rachel's expression changed. "Wait, wait just a minute. What about you and Josh? What do you mean that Josh is … *that bad?*"

Connie looked away. "Maybe we should head back."

Now Rachel knew for sure that something was wrong. "Something is wrong. What about you and Josh? He needs help; You know that."

"Rachel, here is the thing. I appreciate your concern for your brother but I'm not ready to be a babysitter."

"I have no idea what that means."

Connie rolled her eyes. "Oh, I bet you do."

Rachel's eyes narrowed. "Maybe! Tell me anyway."

"Okay, we had a fight last night." Connie's chest heaved. "Now I can't quite recall what started it, something about Harold. That doesn't matter. It brought to the surface so many feelings and fears I had tucked away, more like buried. He is so exasperating!"

Rachel nodded. "That he is."

"By the way, I slept in your room, I left it a mess. Sorry! Damn it, I'm just way too old to start a reclamation process. You think he would have become an adult before he retired."

"Oh, I love him but he's such an asshole," Rachel looked anguished. "I should break his kneecaps."

"No need, I think he's suffering enough."

"I hope so. Let me ask one thing. Did my brother argue back? Never mind, I know the answer. He was mute, maybe a few random words spoken with a stutter."

"Yes, how did you know?" Connie was impressed.

"That's what happens when he's forced to face his emotions. Either he's incoherent or evasive or he tries to joke his way out of things. One question for you. Do you love my brother?"

"No," Connie answered quickly.

"Really? Look at me and say that."

"No…" the word came with less authority.

"Don't bullshit me," Rachel stared intently at her. "And remember, I've had male doctors try to bullshit me my entire career."

"Okay," Connie exhaled. "I give. It is much worse than that … I am in love with him. I was back when we were together. How bad is that? Damn him, I hate myself for that … makes me feel weak, dependent." They walked in silence for a while, letting the breeze move over them as each remained deep in thought.

"Love sucks." Rachel said to no one.

Connie let out a cynical chuckle. "I'm not sure about that but I will say one thing with confidence … we both know the common denominator for our misery."

"Yeah, my idiot brother," Rachel responded immediately. Both women laughed.

"He came into my room, well, your room, and gave me those e-mails to Eleni which he had given to you earlier. He encouraged me to look them over."

"Really?" Rachel was curious about this.

"Yes, and I did for a bit. Frankly, I had trouble reading them … My tears kept getting in the way." Rachel put an arm around her as Connie continued. "But I got through enough. I was stunned that he could feel anything so deeply. I did not think him capable of that. Where is that man?"

"Surprised the shit out of me as well." Rachel agreed.

"I want that man. At some point, I jumped to the end, but it was hard … too sad. She was ill and then it seemed over."

"I know," Rachel murmured. "But here is what I take away from all this. He wanted you and I to look at those messages for a reason. Like any man, he does a lot of stuff without thinking, but this was not one of those things. You could say that he was motivated by the most callous of reasons. You could conclude that he was laughing at us. Here, read these and see that I can feel things but not for either of you."

"You don't believe that, do you?" Connie had a doubtful look. "We agree he is an idiot, but the jury is still out on whether he is a total asshole."

"No, I don't believe he has a malicious bone in his body." Rachel stopped walking, and the two women faced each other. "I believe he is telling us something quite different, that he can feel but is afraid."

"Of what. For Christ's sake."

"Of letting go, trusting. Connie, this is his way of asking for help. He's reaching out in a way that makes sense to him. He can't ask like an ordinary person. I believe that. I suppose I must believe that. And Connie, you are the key. He needs you."

Connie looked directly back at her. "Well, you can take one thing to the bank. I'm not going to let you throw away your chance at happiness."

"Right back at you sister."

Morris started pulling on his chain. He had done his business a long time ago, at least in his mind. Now these women were wandering around without purpose as far as he could see. It was time for his food, and he was running out of patience.

Several of the group were milling around the kitchen making coffee and looking for what food might be available as Rachel and Connie came through the door.

"Mom," Cate yelled with a slightly exaggerated voice. "Usha has just been giving me a blow-by-blow description of last night's, what shall we say, booty call."

"What?" Rachel feigned ignorance, looking at Usha.

"She guessed and is pumping me for details. Oh, you are such a bad girl." Usha was shaking her head from side to side with exaggeration. "Your poor mother's hair will soon be grey."

Cate groused with a chuckle. "No problem, I'll get the whole story somehow … I am a patient woman. Of course, it will be back into therapy for me."

"Hah." Meena laughed, whose tone was light and upbeat. "You should be nicer to your mother."

Cate went on. "I'm always nice. But mark my words, I will get all the gory, disgusting details one way or another."

"Instead of torturing your good mother, I think you should read silly romance novels like all the other girls," Meena went on, enjoying the moment.

Cate focused on a different target now, looking at her uncle who stood oddly quiet against a wall. "Uncle, you're such a typical bachelor, don't you have any edible food in this place?"

"Well, I think I can scrounge up some stale donuts, maybe some week-old pizza." His voice was flat, lacking his Irish-born humorous lilt.

Cate noticed but went on. "You, sir, need a woman. I'm totally amazed you survived to your advanced age." But Josh did not respond. He was looking at Connie with a sad expression. Cate was confused and slightly flummoxed. "Okay, I'll find some edible loot. Help me, Meena."

Connie walked up to Josh and pulled him by the arm into the guest room where she had spent the night. "Jeremiah Joshua Connelly, … listen to me, people are leaving today. The last thing they want is to see you standing around making fisheyes at me."

"But—"

"Shush. We will fight after they leave, when I'll have a clear shot at tearing you a new one. Understand?" Connie looked at him without expression.

"Gee, that's something to look forward to."

"Until then, you be yourself. People will know something is wrong if you're not insulting them." She started toward the door. "One last thing. You better thank your sister that you are not seeing my backside walking out the door, at least not yet."

Connie and Josh walked back into the kitchen. Cate straightened up from her food search. "Hey, where'd you two go? Getting in a morning quickie?"

"Hah," Josh responded with something closer to his usual demeaner; he was trying hard. "If that were it, I would not finish up until you were halfway to wherever you're going today."

"Oh, he got you there." It was Meena, laughing again.

Josh looked at the dark-haired beauty. How much she had changed from the moment she shyly followed Cate off the plane. It had taken her a bit to understand the dynamics of her new situation … at first being a bit taken aback by the casual banter and the good-natured insults. She had been raised in a family where everyone was more formal and polite, at least in public. Now she saw people who played with one another through soft insults delivered with undeniable affection. Josh realized at that moment just how good Meena would be for Cate whom he looked upon as the child he would never have.

"Thank you," he said, looking at Meena.

"For what?" Meena responded, a smile remaining in place but muted a bit by a quizzical look.

"For being here, for being who you are, for becoming part of our family." Josh walked over and kissed Meena on the cheek. Then he reached out and pulled his niece closer. "You two are meant to be together. You love each other. I can see that; feel that. Never lose that love. It is the most important thing in life."

"We won't," Meena whispered back to him.

"Thank you, Uncle." Cate looked deeply into him with her pale blue eyes, mystified by the unsolicited sentiments but grateful nonetheless. She mouthed the words "I love you" before speaking up to change the mood. "Okay, we have our plans finalized. We're flying to San Francisco this afternoon, one of my favs. A couple of days there, and then I'm taking Meena to Vegas. She wants to see Sin City for some reason. If we have any money left, it will be on to Chicago and then up to Madison, Wisconsin's Sin City, to join Mom who should be back home by then. Usha has agreed to come down from Toronto to spend some time and work on getting our adoptees to the States. I'm going to pull every chit I have in the service, and Usha will help on the legal side. Meena can pull some strings in the refugee camp through her family connections. We'll get this done. Of course, somewhere along the line, I'll need to decide what to do about my career but one step at a time." She turned toward Meena. "Hey, gal, we better not lose all our money in Vegas. Getting the kids here will not be cheap as Usha has stressed, including the baksheesh that will be needed."

"How much?" Josh asked.

"What?" Cate asked.

He persisted. "How much might you need? Moneywise."

"Not sure, it could be quite a bit." It was Meena. "I know how things work in that part of the world. All is possible if you can help things along."

"You got it, whatever you need." Josh stated.

Cate jumped on him. "Uncle, don't be foolish. We could be talking many thousands."

"You have it. End of discussion."

"Josh, I can ..." Rachel started.

"End of discussion I said." He was resolute.

This time, Meena leaned up to kiss him on the cheek. "Can I call you Uncle?" Josh nodded. "Cate so often talked about you. She loves you so much. Now I can see why. Not your generosity, that doesn't matter. I can see your love. There is so much love here. That's what counts."

Connie brushed something away from her cheek. She was about to say something when the door opened. In poured Peter, Morris, and Carla bearing bagels and other goodies. "The cavalry is here with provisions," Peter proclaimed with gusto. "We knew the owner of this modest establishment is way too disorganized to be prepared for hungry travelers about to set on their journeys."

"Food," Usha yelled, "call off the search for the donuts and stale pizza. Even if located, they would be as hard as a rock though good enough for this guy I am sure." She nodded toward her ex-husband. "When we were married, I could not believe what he would eat. He would pull something out of the refrigerator that looked green and could walk on its own. After a quick smell, he would pass judgment, *'probably won't kill me,'* and in it would go. I kept waiting for him to keel over, but on he went."

"That's because he only looks human." Connie added, forcing a smile.

Josh managed a laugh for the first time this morning. If anyone had looked closely, they would know it was false. "By now, you should all know that the really evil never die young."

"True-dat," Cate offered.

———

Later, Josh gathered in the living room with Peter, Morris, and Carla. They would soon be off on the road back to Seattle.

Peter asked at one point, "Okay, are we better off now or back in the 1960s? I have my thoughts, but I want to hear what you Commies think."

Morris took the first stab at it. "The great thing about owning a bookstore in a time where fewer people read real books is that one can think about such useless questions. No offense, Peter."

Peter smiled. "Considering the source, none taken."

Morris leaned back. "Most people looked fondly on the good old days. That's because their memories suck. A half century ago, when we were in high school, a lot of things were in the crapper. We talk about cyberbullying today, but I had to physically fight my way through gangs of Irish toughs just to survive. That's how I met Prince Charming over there, he saved my ass from some Irish thugs."

"Now there's a moment I'd like back." Josh smiled.

"Very funny. But think about this. The air was polluted. You couldn't hardly see L.A. Lake Erie was so junked up it could be set in fire. When water burns, you just know you have a problem. We had apartheid in much of the country as bad as South Africa at the time. Half of all kids dropped out of high school, older people died because they had no money to pay for health care and no insurance to cover the cost. Workingmen perished from accidents that could have been prevented. Babies ate paint off peeling porches laced with lead. Coal miners died early from black-lung disease unless their lives were mercifully cut short by a cave-in. Women had few professional options and were routinely harassed without recourse. The jobs open to them paid poorly and, by definition, had less status. Our cars were death traps because everything went into stylish frivolities like tail fins and nothing into safety. You never heard of child abuse or women being beaten daily, not because it did not happen, but because men essentially were free to prey on those who were deemed to be private property. I could go on, but you get the picture."

"As bad as that was, never forget that a century earlier we were killing each other by the tens of thousands just to end the barbaric practice of slavery," Peter added. "If you were wounded in a limb, a former butcher posing as a doctor likely hacked it off for want of basic antibiotics and with no pain killers."

"And yet," Josh jumped in, "we came of age in an economic renaissance of sorts. The middle class had grown rapidly in the forties and fifties and sixties. Factory workers could own a car, buy a small house in the suburbs, think about their kids going to college. Poverty was falling though we did not see it at the time. We expected the rich to pay their fair share, and they did, for the most part. And we were about to see a decade of progressive policy making that would expand the federal government's role in education, health, the environment, racial justice, expanded social opportunities, the economy, workplace safety, and just about every other aspect of public life. If we had taken the time to look back then, we might have despaired less about our failings and worked harder to preserve our successes."

Josh realized that everyone else had joined this group and was listening now. Somehow, all were drawn to this conversation. He did not know how Usha, Connie, Cate, Meena, and even Rachel initially had looked upon these people from his past. They were all friendly, but it was a respectful cordiality at first. Now they were listening with rapt attention. "As I think we touched on up in Whistler, we have a conundrum before us."

"Which is? You do realize that we were not all together while up in Whistler," Rachel noted. "I've noticed my brother needs to be prompted to share his wisdom. When we were kids, he talked all the time. I couldn't shut him up."

"And I've noticed that my sister is still an annoying little shit even after all these years." Josh responded with a big smile. "And here's my wisdom. Take notes Rach. Things were bad then, but we had such hope. Now, many things have improved but so many of us despair. Did we win many battles but lose the war? What is the real bottom line? Is there some disconnect between reality and perception?"

"Uncle, you're losing me." It was Cate. "Barack Obama was elected president not that long ago. Surely, that says something about continuing progress, in fact and in terms of our view of things."

"Perhaps the last gasp of a liberal impulse," Josh countered, "though I desperately hope I'm wrong on that."

Carla shook her head. "Don't forget. A sinister form of Republicanism controls much of the country, not the GOP of our youth but something totally scary. They would not hesitate to turn back the clock to 1930's Germany and are not that far from doing just that."

"I hate to say this but Carla's right," Peter chimed in at this point. "I still keep tabs with old buddies in the bureau who get together on social occasions. You would be frightened to death if you knew of the rise in hate groups since 08. There are almost a thousand such groups out there now and ten times that number of hate crimes annually. In truth, we don't know the half of it. The nut groups are deadly serious about the end days being upon us, that a massive showdown must take place to determine who will own America. The white nationalists are consumed with a fear of being replaced by minorities. Worse, they are arming themselves to the teeth. Freaking scary times."

Morris smiled. "Peter, you forget that we were a nut group back in the day."

"You guys," Peter was deadly serious, "were misguided but driven by the best of intentions. These whack jobs are straight out of a moral and ethical swamp. Worse, a lot of so-called average Americans tacitly, or overtly, support them. They no longer are the fringe. They are mainstream now. Just think about that."

Josh agreed. "I'm not sure I want to know what you know, Peter. The hate has always been there. Our turf wars back in our day between the tribes—Irish, Italian, Jewish, minorities—were all part of a melting pot where little melted together. It is part of our fabric ... the Know-Nothings and the Klan. Hitler's Nazis gave it a push with Fritz Kuhn and the German American Bund along with William Pelley and his Silver Shirts. By the fifties and sixties, we had the Birchers and Norman Lincoln Rockwell with the American Nazi Party. Those were the visible symptoms of a deeper rot. The disease was below the surface, except in the South. What we missed at the time were the big money interests who would be most willing to use the fears of average men and women to stir up hate and distrust for government and liberals. The push for a kinder America was exactly what they needed for their counter revolution. The 60s, with all the progress made then, ignited a fire on the right that burned slowly and steadily until it burst into the open with Reagan."

"A fire that's on the verge of consuming us all." Carla sighed.

Morris picked up the thread. "If Josh is right about the demographic trends, and if white working-class Americans feel as threatened as we think they feel, things could get awfully bad, awfully bad indeed. I can see a right-wing populist soon riding to power. Already, the Republicans are consolidating power at the state and local levels. They are one vote away on the Supreme Court, on the verge of a congressional sweep given the negative animus generated by Obamacare, and who knows what will happen in future presidential elections? They have been working steadfastly for this since the aftermath of Goldwater and now they can feel it. And if they succeed, then what? They could dismantle all we just talked about just as the world teeters on the verge of a real crisis ... apocalyptic climate change just as one example. Josh was right earlier when he said, in his own way, that we went after the shiny bauble as the whole tree was about to fall over. That, however, is the next generation's windmill to attack with righteous indignation. We gave it our shot in our time and what did they do?"

"I threw you in jail." Peter lowered his head in contrition. "Well, not me personally but my people did, to my everlasting shame."

"And think about this ..." Carla tried.

"Nope!" Peter said. "That's it! We are off to Seattle. Another half hour of this bullshit and the bunch of you will be off on one of your crazy apocalyptic adventures."

"This time," Morris looked at him, "maybe we could get you to join us, Peter?"

"This time, you just might," the retired G-man chuckled.

"Welcome to the revolution, old friend." Carla walked over and kissed him on the cheek.

As they all filed out to the waiting car, Peter said loudly. "One last thing I never understood."

"Only one?" Josh faked a look of shock.

"Just remember, I did take notes on all your crimes."

"Ooops," Josh chuckled.

"I can remember when the GOP started drifting further right. With each election, the more right-wing element of the party would argue that the candidates were not conservative enough. They had to take even a harder extremist stands, nominate even more radical nut jobs and whackos. I thought that argument insane. But son of a bitch, it worked. Oh, the wise men kept saying that the Republican Party was shooting itself in the foot. They were becoming a regional party, appealing only to those backward provincials in the Deep South. Remember those guys who never, and I mean never, get anything right and yet they get paid to spout off crap that even dumb kids would be embarrassed to utter in public?"

"Don't be so harsh, dear," Carla admonished her husband. "We wouldn't seem like sages if we had to fill up all the hours on those talk shows."

"Okay, I suppose they are not that stupid, they just keep saying stupid stuff. What they did not consider was the deep wellspring of anger and hate out there among the unwashed masses. It is there, bubbling and gurgling in places the wise men never bother to visit. They stay in their bubble, far away from reality and those places where the real folk survive."

"You know why we will see a revolution from the right?" Carla suddenly asked.

"I didn't know one was in the offing," Peter responded as he opened the door to his car.

"Oh yeah, I can guess why." Josh said with a hint of resignation. "Demographers predict Caucasians will be a minority by the 2040s. As whites see their position of entitlement slipping away, they will rise up to preserve the traditional caste system, even if it means destroying American democracy. Do you know that white Americans have not given a Democratic candidate the plurality in any election since 1965 when the voting rights bill was passed? They won't share this country with anyone else. My old country will become the new South Africa before apartheid ended. Poor whites gladly would blow the whole thing up rather than risk their perceived entitled position in society."

"Rather harsh, no?" Peter tried.

Josh did not smile this time. "No, not nearly harsh enough. It cost me a lot but oh God, I am so freaking glad now I left when I did."

"Aprez-moi, le deluge," Morris offered.

"Aprez-Barack, le deluge." Josh countered.

There were hugs all around amid general confusion. "Listen," Josh spoke above the final chatter, "I want to come down and see you guys. Better still, let's take a road trip to see Bob. He can have visitors, right? It is not like solitary confinement. I really want to see him again. I just want to see if he is happy. I hope he is happy."

"We would love that," said Carla. "We really would. And by the way, I think he is."

"Happy?" Josh wanted confirmation.

"Yes, I really believe he is happier than he has ever been," Morris added.

Josh's expression changed. "I still cannot believe you guys didn't spit in my face."

"Wait till next time." Carla laughed as she got into the car with the others after giving Josh one final hug and kiss.

As Peter Favulli circled around to the driver's side, Josh called out to him. "Hey, how the hell did anyone as slow as you make the varsity football team?"

"You always were a classless Mick, Connelly. Should have thrown your ass in the slammer. What was I thinking?"

"Wait," Josh yelled as Peter was about to duck into the car. "A serious question, one I wanted to ask decades ago. Why didn't you go to a Catholic college? I was shocked you went to the same den of Commies and Pagans I did. What was with that? Someone said it was because you never got a football scholarship."

"Not true! Holy Cross did offer me a football scholarship. I'm not sure why I turned it down since it pissed off my family royally. Got up one day and said to myself that I had had enough of this religious crap.

Time for something different or maybe it was my youthful rebellion … just to piss off my dad. If you think an Irish dad can get pissed, try an Italian one. Now that you mention it, I never really gave it all that much thought. Funny choice, no?"

"Like flipping a coin." Josh said and saw Peter react with confusion. "Forget that comment. Listen, I'll for sure come and visit. We'll sort out all our crazy choices then, especially the one where I befriended this lame-ass Wop."

Peter flashed his warmest smile and slipped into his vehicle. Josh still stood watching after the car was long out of sight. The others had gone inside to give him time alone. They suspected he would want time for the tears in his eyes to dry.

————

"Who do we get rid of next?" Josh asked with excessive bonhomie as he burst through the door. "Oh yes, my pesky niece. However, her new friend is welcome to stay if she wants."

"No luck, Uncle. She is my fiancée and she has you pegged as a debauched pervert already."

"Oh, no I don't," Meena protested.

"Meena," Cate chastised her with exasperation, "We talked about this earlier. Never say anything nice about this man. He has this oversized ego that needs to be whittled down to size."

In an exaggerated whisper, Meena said, "I think you are great. I am definitely calling you *uncle* from now on."

"You better!" He smiled broadly. "That would be several steps up from what the rest of the family calls me. I'm beginning to think my first name is cretin or is it idiot."

"Both work." Rachel quickly noted. "However, I personally prefer nimrod."

Josh chuckled at the cut. "Of course, I usually prefer monetary expressions of adoration, but terms of affection will do. Some days, I'll even settle for not being whacked in the stomach."

"Speaking of your tummy, dear uncle, stay away from a steady diet of spicy foods and week-old pizza. We want you around for a long time." Cate patted his stomach. "Connie, I'm putting you in charge of him, okay?"

Josh shot a glance at Connie. She smiled at Cate's request but did not respond. Had her expression softened? He was doubtful, but he had hope.

Usha and Connie had said their fair wells to Cate and Meena at Josh's home. Josh, Rachel, Cate, and Meena arrived at the international terminal in plenty of time. Cate's foreign service credentials usually expedited things at immigration, but you did not take chances these days. They could only accompany the travellers so far, but they savored each moment.

"One thing, we're going to be a family now," Cate enthused. "I don't know exactly how things will work out with the service, but I am determined to be closer to you two."

Rachel thought about that for a moment: *you two*. Cate was joining her and her brother together as one. That struck her as qualitatively different from the past. Then, her daughter seemed to be a peacemaker, trying to keep two individuals joined by blood from spinning off into their own orbits, usually absent great success. Had something happened that even she had not fully apprehended? Was there now an observable filial relationship that had been absent to this point? Of course, they were good at public display. This was Josh's business in part, to reach students and political actors. Similarly, her public role as the face of medicine in professional communities had sharpened her people skills, at least to a point. Perhaps they had hidden their inner tensions well enough to avoid detection even by those closest to them. On the other hand, perhaps the tensions were no longer there. Such questions kept circling through Rachel's head.

While Josh took Meena to a nearby shop to buy her a souvenir of Vancouver, Rachel jumped at the chance to be intimate with her daughter one last time. "I want to thank you once more for opening me up, you know, about relationships."

"Mom, I don't know what to say. I want to joke about all the other lessons I have planned for you in the future, but I suspect that a spanking would soon follow."

"Wait, did I ever spank you?"

"No, mom, but you should have. I was a bit of a handful, more than a bit."

Rachel cupped her daughter's face in her hands. "You were a treasure, always."

"Well, thank you. Listen, you've already given me one gift by, how to put it, repairing things with your brother. You cannot imagine the joy that brings me. But if you really want to please me even more, don't screw up your chance for happiness. Understand me? If you let Usha slip away, I will track you down and make your life a living hell, even more of a hell than in the past."

"Why is everyone threatening me with doom?" Rachel asked, even as she knew.

Josh and Meena heard the last comment as he and Meena rejoined them. "Because the Connelly clan are known screw-ups. I've seldom seen people so devoted to snatching defeat from the jaws of victory."

"I have something to remember Vancouver by." Meena grinned, showing off a touristy trinket.

"You won't need it since you will be back," Josh asserted. "We'll all be back. I'll make damn sure of that."

"Gotta go, I'll start crying if I don't. So, a big hug." With that, Cate threw her arms around her uncle. "Same message for you, don't screw things up."

"What?" he started to ask, but the two women were walking into the area off limits to the public hand in hand. "Want any money for Vegas?" Josh called after them.

"No, save your money for our future children," Cate shouted over her shoulder. Then she stopped and turned. "Besides, I already got the biggest gift of all."

"What's that dear?" Rachel yelled.

"Isn't it obvious? You've given me a real family again." She flashed her big smile, took Meena's hand, and continued down the runway.

Josh put his arm around his sister as they watched the two retreating figures disappear. "You raised a treasure there."

"As did you," replied Rachel.

"Me? What did I do?"

Rachel gave him a mock blow to the stomach. "You really are as dumb as you look. Why do you think she visited you every chance she got in recent years?"

"Well, I am charming. All the girls say so."

"Yeah, right!" Rachel retorted. "You replaced her worthless dad, her biological dad. As he had less time for her, you became the male role model parent in her life, the one she looked toward for guidance. Oh my, God help us all now that I think on that. But she loves you. I suppose that's what counts."

"And I love her," he said, still looking after her.

"It's a mystery."

"What is?" he asked absentmindedly.

"She is so smart and yet, she never saw through you. I tried to warn her but…"

Josh laughed and kissed the top of his sister's head. "I'll tell you one thing, I'm not so smart."

"You just figuring that out now." Rachel said as she squeezed his hand.

"Afraid so! I spent a lifetime avoiding so many people out of shame, thinking they would reject me. And then, in the end, they didn't, not at all. It was all in my head. Remember all the stuff said at my retirement thing about me being so smart. Well, that was total crap."

"No," Rachel said softly. "It's just that each of us is smart, and dumb, in different ways. I suppose each of us is scared in our own way as well. We all have our blind spot."

They turned and walked away as Josh mused about how often he was using that word: *love*.

"One more thing, dear brother, we have an issue to discuss."

Josh winced. He knew he was about to receive another scolding. This one undoubtedly was quite serious. After all, she had not whacked him in the stomach. So, this issue must really be serious.

"Hey," he tried in a tone dripping with desperation. "I think there's a Midwest flight directly to Milwaukee leaving in an hour. Sure you don't want to be on it?"

"No way, bozo. I've got unfinished business right here."

"Oh shit." He replied but with a smile.

CHAPTER 23

Day 7 - DENOUEMENT

"Connie! Usha!" No response. The house was empty when Josh and Rachel returned from the airport to see the couple off. Not even his Pug was in his customary spot.

"Where are they?" Josh asked. "Do you think they ran off with my dog?"

"Truth is," Rachel replied, "your dog is desperately looking for someone to steal him. But my guess is that the two are running away from us. We've both been less than our best. Your ugly mutt is just an added benefit."

"Ungrateful cur, after giving him the best years of my life."

Rachel tried a strangled laugh. "You trying to blame your mutt? He's the only sane Connelly among us. Love comes easily to him."

"Yeah, he'll love anyone who'll rub his belly." Josh said with mock bitterness.

"I suppose," Rachel mused. "I will say one thing for him. He's happier than the two of us. He doesn't fight it."

"Fight what, Rach?"

"Happiness, of course. Whenever given the choice, he goes with happiness or maybe pleasure. No indecision and agonizing for him." Rachel paused as she noticed a note addressed to Josh and Rachel in large block letters. "According to this, they took your unfaithful canine for a walk along the shore. Apparently, he literally begged them to take him away from all this."

"Begged to be taken away from this heaven on earth. No freaking way."

Rachel looked up smiling. "Come on, Josh, let's go find them before they get away. We have a lot of grovelling to do."

"I'm not sure I ..."

"Listen up! We both have a lot of grovelling to do. Understand!" Rachel's tone brooked no counter argument. "Time to suck it up."

"I hear what you're saying." Josh replied ambiguously.

Rachel wanted to ask her brother if he also agreed, not just understood what she had discussed with him on the trip back from the airport. She remained silent, deciding that, in the end, he must determine his own future. She was not her brother's keeper, though that job attracted her. "Good, let's go find them."

A few minutes later, Rachel and Josh saw their prey walking along the beach. Josh yet marvelled how well his two former lovers got along. Apparently, he was not worth fighting over. They had not gotten far along the beach. Walking was not their purpose after all. When they realized that the Connelly siblings were trying to catch up, they stopped and moved toward them.

"The kids off okay?" Usha asked, leaving Connie's side to approach Rachel.

"Yes, they are great. I've never seen my daughter so happy." There was more than a hint of tension in Rachel's voice.

"That's nice," Usha said in a wistful tone. "Everyone deserves ..."

Rachel interrupted. "Usha ..."

"Rachel, let me finish before I lose my nerve." Usha moved toward Rachel. "When you left my room, I sensed the tension in you. Hard to miss. You obviously wanted to be somewhere else, as if you wanted to escape. Perhaps we should have talked more rather than ... . In any case, I want to talk more now, about how I feel about things. This has all been so fast and so unexpected. Hell, I just came to make sure this lug would, in fact, retire. His colleagues got in touch and begged me to help push him out the door."

"I'm sure they did …" Rachel reached for a light tone that she did not feel.

"No, of course they didn't. People that don't really know him, like you and I, love him."

"I can see that," Connie said just above a whisper looking away from Josh at her side. "That's what makes it hard."

Usha took Rachel's hands in hers. "You, Rachel, were his barely remembered sister. I'm not totally sure, but the last time I saw you in person was when I got married to Josh and you were still with Evan. I had only the faintest recollection of this attractive and bright woman who seemed so distant and untouchable I suppose. I can tell you now, but I was uncomfortable around you then. You were…"

Rachel let out a small cry. "The ice maiden! Even Josh called me that. I am, or was, and who knows what I was called behind my back. I was going through the motions of being a dutiful sister at the time, as if it were an obligation. I had shut down … for a long time. It was my way of hiding."

"Yes, that's obvious now." Usha reached out and took Rachel's hands. "I could feel the chill at the time, hard to miss. Let me say this, though. When we met the other day, I saw something vastly different. Suddenly I met this warm and funny woman. It wasn't your physical beauty that captured me, at least it wasn't the first thing. Rather, I saw someone who was caring and loving while being so accomplished. You captivated me. Yet, I was wary."

"Wary?" Rachel asked.

"Well, I thought I had fallen in love before. That is why I left Josh and took up with Rose. But it proved a stab at what I thought was intimacy, and not a good one in the end. Still, it was necessary. It proved to be the biggest step of my life other than the moment I finally stood up for what I was as a woman. But I think that was the thing. I was more enamored with taking this stand than I was with the person

I was standing with. I had convinced myself that I loved her. In the end, she was more honest, more honest than I was at least."

"Can I …" Rachel tried.

"Just a bit more, please. Rose eventually found someone where the spark was real for her … where feelings were not consumed like yesterday's leftovers. You know, like one of Josh's week-old pizzas." Usha tried to smile. "I suppose we'll see but I think she has now found the real thing. I was hurt, a lot. Rejection is always hard, but I knew it was for the best. And once again, I was lonely."

"So sorry," Rachel whispered softly.

"Want to hear something hilarious? In the back of my mind, I wondered if Josh might take me back. How is that for desperate thinking? Why not put an ad in the paper or on one of those silly dating sites? *'Desperate and aging broad who cannot get things right looking for a woman who will help in getting her life straightened out, desperate enough to take some poor male schlepp who will fake at being a lover and husband, if willing.' All considered, even total whackos.'* Pathetic, no?"

"Please …" Rachel reached out and took Usha's hands in hers.

"Then you were suddenly there. You look a little like Josh, maybe just the eyes. And the smile, definitely the smile. But here's what hit me. The two of you are alike in so many ways, in ways that counted, inside. I don't know if you noticed this that first night, but I could not take my eyes off you. I cannot recall being attracted to another person so immediately and so fully. I kept thinking later about my response, what was happening. Then it struck me. I already knew you, even if we had only exchanged a few words. This was the person with whom I had shared my life for a few years, that I loved in an incomplete way. This is the one other person I might love completely, if only she would accept me. At this advanced age, I would finally have that complete relationship. Wow, what are the odds? All I knew is that you had been married and had this adult daughter and were a top-level physician. I stuffed that brief hope inside."

"What happened?" Rachel whispered.

"We talked. I … got to know you, saw how you looked at me. I sensed a reaction in you when we brushed against each other, first by accident and then … who knows after that. The heart senses these things. Listen, Rachel, I know you have doubts. I know you are scared. This morning, you wanted to get away from me. That broke my heart. I didn't know what I had done wrong but … but …"

Usha never finished the sentence. She was not certain there was a finish. Rachel moved forward and kissed her deeply. The embrace remained after the kiss dissolved. Josh reached for Connie's hand, but she did not respond so he let it go.

Still holding Usha, Rachel continued in a voice breaking with emotion. "Last night, you can imagine. I did not know how much of this cursed Irish blood was within me. I suddenly felt that I could not possibly deserve such happiness. I was not worthy. No, it would be yanked away from me again. Some wicked deity lets you peek at happiness before snatching it away. We Irish believe that. I do at least. I don't know. Maybe that cloud comes from the way I saw my brother and our sorry relationship. If I got too close, he would abandon me again. It is so hard to escape irrational fears, the ones that get deep inside. Odd, our ability to reason is such a tenuous faculty. We can be so fragile inside no matter how tough and accomplished we look like on the outside. Today, a terrible reality hit me."

"What's that?" Usha asked.

"That I was reacting just like my idiot brother would, by running away from any chance at happiness. I had borrowed that Irish black cloud that hangs over his head that whispers *don't love, don't love, don't love! It's too dangerous. It will hurt you.* That's what he did for four decades. Perhaps, and this is hard for me to say, I was not so different."

Usha stroked Rachel's face. "Rachel, I am not walking away. Neither of us are kids anymore. To walk away now would be the worst mistakes of our lives." She forced a thin smile. "Well, that's my story and I'm sticking with it."

Rachel tried one last weak protest. "There's so much to think about and deal with, of course. Lots of choices to make."

"Oh shush," she chided her. "Look at what your daughter is doing. She might abandon her career, commit to another human being from the other side of the world, and adopt two foreign children. You cannot let her show you up. We can work everything out. We can for sure."

They were holding each other again.

⸻

Connie grabbed Josh's arm and pulled him along the beach. The sun was beginning to settle onto the western horizon. It was a light and breezy day; puffy clouds hung in the sky, and a spring cool breeze pushed against them. Josh loved this time of year. The winter might bring unending cloudiness and wet drizzle. Summer could have a bit of heat, at least for him. But he loved the transitional periods when the extremes could be avoided, and when seasonal climactic patterns were in flux. In Vancouver, you might have four seasons in one day.

"They should have some privacy, though I seriously doubt they realized we were there." Connie said before lapsing into silence. They walked a considerable distance without saying a word. Finally, Connie broke the silence. "I promised Rachel I would be here today. I am here. I promised to listen. I am listening."

More walking and silence. Josh stopped and looked back toward the city. Usha and Rachel, with Morris in tow, were walking back to Josh's place. They were hand in hand. Josh watched with mixed feelings. They were a couple. He knew it now. At last Rachel was accepting a complete life. How special was that, how thrilling. His heart burst for her.

Where was he though? Connie might well be beyond his reach now. Perhaps she was lost to him. He was accomplished at running away from things. He ran from the law, from his country, from his family, from relationships, from human feelings, and from himself. This was his personal strength, running from things. The walls of his personal cocoon were well constructed, impenetrable. What could he possibly do at this late stage in life? It was too late. He was a lost cause, one of the walking dead who would play out his days looking and talking like a functioning person but hollowed out inside. In his mind's eye, that was what he saw. He had seen this most of his life. He looked like a human, walked like a human, talked like a human but, in the end, he was not a human. He was that freaking robot that Connie saw.

Until this moment, that reality, when he allowed himself to admit to it, never bothered him all that much. It was simply how he survived. But Rachel, his beloved sister … she had done it, hadn't she? She had crossed over to the land of the living. Yes, she had. Perhaps… perhaps it was possible.

It started somewhere in the pit of his stomach, an emptiness that was undeniable. Slowly the unease moved up through his body. His chest began to heave, and then his throat became restricted. Was he going to choke? Was this a heart attack? Perhaps it was a stroke. He had to get it out, this overwhelming tension, this oppressive and crushing burden. Is this what the end felt like? Perhaps, after the intense pain, he would find oblivion, peace.

"Josh, are you okay?" It was Connie's voice, as if from a thousand miles distance.

In his head, he felt a harsh choice pushing itself upon him, screaming for some form of resolution. He could yield to the pain and oblivion on the other side, or fight toward that human voice in the far distance. Indecision seemed about to drown him when he threw his head back. Out it roared, no longer capable of being contained.

"Gaaawd Daaaaamn Iiiiit!" His primal scream hung in the air. Connie stepped away, looking down the shoreline. Usha and Rachel had turned to look in the direction of the sound but were too far away and could no longer make any sense of what they thought they heard. With a shrug, they continued their journey back to Josh's place.

Connie looked at Josh, her face ashen. "Are you all right?"

"Wow," he said with a wry smile. "That felt good."

"Damn, you scared the crap out of me. I thought an aneurysm had burst or something," Connie said as she stepped toward him and looked closer to see if he was okay. She put a hand on his face.

Josh spoke through deep breaths. "Well, this hurts like an aneurysm, not that I know what those things feel like. Wow, I now see how psychological wounds hurt the most."

"Good to know you're not too old to learn something new." She was not smiling.

"I know. I mean … you crush the things inside of yourself, things you feel. You grind them all down and push the detritus in between your bodily organs. But they continue to build up and up until they squeeze the life out of you. Then, everything seems … dead."

"Yeah, maybe I understand," Connie said cautiously. "It's the things we try the hardest to deny that do the most damage."

"No shit. In the end, you manage to grind all living matter into dust. What you have left is a hollow excuse for a guy just going through the motions. Anyway, if you again see me bellow again, you know … like a pregnant cow giving birth … don't be alarmed. I'm simply getting the rest out."

"What are you babbling about?" Connie now wavered between annoyance and concern. "Damn, you're making even less sense that usual."

Instead of answering, Josh grabbed her hand and led her across Marine Drive. "Come with me."

"Where are we going?" She asked with a hint of irritation.

"Across campus …."

"Where across campus?" Now her irritation was back.

"…to Wreck Beach. Hah, that sounds appropriate," he smiled tentatively. "Did you know it is named that after all the shipwrecks in olden days."

"What?" Connie tried to pull her hand away, but Josh held tight.

After they walked in silence for a time, Josh spoke first. "Connie, I should've been open from the beginning, I mean about my past and all the crap that I kept bottled up. I guess I hadn't grown up yet, the *boy in a man's body*' thing. Hell, I came to a place where I wanted to drive you away. I didn't realize it then but I'm sure of that now."

"But why for God's sake?"

"Isn't it obvious? If you had remained part of my life, I would have to face up to my feelings for you. If I faced up to how I felt about you, there would be Rachel, and my college friends, and even my dead parents. Running away from my friends and family, I never forgave myself for that. I did what we Irish do. I put it aside and kept busy with life. Most of all, I told a lot of jokes. But I never had the guts to confront things. Facing all that would have been, how shall I put it, inconvenient."

Connie tried to speak. "I would have called it …"

"Shush, my turn."

"Fair enough," she said, her words still clipped.

"Rachel and I grew up in a very normal working-class household, at least from the outside. You never met my dad, but you know he owned a bar. He was boisterous, a natural leader, a man of great conviction who would spare no words letting you know where he stood. We were not poor, but money was tight. The bar did a great business, but I think Dad was not a businessman. He gave away drinks and money to those hard up and the remainder to his causes, all about Irish freedom. He was a believer. Our mother, Ora, was so different. If he was fire, she was ice. Rachel looks so much like her, with the light hair, the delicate features, the pale blue eyes. Men would pant after my sister, but she kept to herself, mysterious and disciplined and focused on greater, or at least different, things. I cannot even think about the successes Ora might have achieved had she not been born when and where she was. Rachel and I could see that our mother was very bright but, at the same time, hard inside. She had needed that hardness to survive growing up amid untold dangers as her family wandered about in Russia, Lithuania, Finland or wherever just to stay alive. That part of the world was tearing itself asunder in those days."

Seeing a colleague, he pulled her in a different direction to avoid any disruption. "Wait, where are you dragging me now?"

"Shush, listen. There you have Rachel and me. We were the bookends. She reflected Ora, our mother, and I, on the surface at least, was Jim, my dad. And early on, we seemed like two quite different siblings … physically for sure. I was dark and athletic, she was blond, aesthetic, and analytical. Strangers could hardly believe we were from the same family. And yet …" Josh paused as if he just thought of something for the first time in his life, "we were so much alike."

"Hah! She's nice and you, not so much."

"Oh, all kinds of small things. I never dated much in high school, didn't have a single real girlfriend as such. Girls were around and, as an athlete, I was the catch."

"Really?" Connie could not resist the dig. "Standards must have been lower then."

"That's what I was told, anyway. Neither did Rachel, date that is. She had a reason, turns out she was gay."

"And you?" Connie asked with growing interest.

"I was just damaged, even then. It was as if I needed to protect myself all the time. I could never get by the notion that they wanted something other than me. It could have been security, or social status, or a free meal or movie, or this elusive thing called a relationship, but none of those things meant they wanted me. I represented stuff to them, but they did not want me as flesh and blood. I kept wanting to tell them that here is twenty bucks, go and have a great date with yourself and then you won't have to put out to pay me back at the end of the evening. I am sure you think me twisted. Well, you are probably right. Damaged from the get-go."

"I don't see the connection with Rachel," Connie slipped in.

Josh pushed on. "Connie, let me just babble. A lot of me, and Rachel, came from what we saw at home. We would joke that our folks had sex twice—we were the proof. But then I would argue that one of us came from another union. I used to piss her off by saying that I looked like Dad and came from what must have been the one occasion where their union was consummated. I would tease her about which neighborhood miscreant was likely her real father. She would get so mad at me. But that story had a kind of logic. After all, there was no evidence of any love between my folks. They wandered about in the same house but in separate worlds, hardly communicating. Dad used whatever family love he possessed on me … likely because I was an extension of him, or so he thought."

"Okay," Connie's voice had softened. "Expectations are tough … they certainly are in Asian families.

"I bet. You would think my dad might dote on his daughter. But no! I wondered if maybe Rachel looked too much like Ora. In any case, he hardly paid attention to Rach. Hell, she was just a girl, she couldn't score touchdowns. You might think that Ora would take up the slack, focus on the one who reflected her beauty and intelligence. But she didn't. I could never figure that out, not really. Eventually, I decided that she could not love anyone—the hardness that permitted her to survive her harsh youth would not let her love any longer. Her isolation was a life sentence, something to suffer for the remainder of her existence. For her, Big Jim was a convenient ticket to that better life, not much more, except perhaps at the very beginning. She did not love him and hardly noticed us. Her life was an interior journey, only her piano served as a life raft."

Despite her effort to remain angry with him, Connie was responding to Josh's words. "That is so … unspeakably tragic."

"To be fair, there was one moment she showed feeling, at least to me. When she became aware of my anti-war stuff in college. That set her off. Her once heartfelt feeling toward me was … disgust. I figured out that her early life had imprinted in her a fierce hatred of Communism. She carried images and emotions from her childhood forward, from family stories. I have no doubt that those around her as a child suffered greatly. Many did in those terrible times. I recall her yelling at me toward the end of my time at home that Stalin had killed 4 million Ukrainians. *'That animal starved them to death,'* she repeated several times. I've no idea why she fixed on that, though Rachel and I speculated that her family might originally have been from there. People moved all the time to escape death."

Connie reached out to him, touched his arm. "Josh, it's okay."

He continued as if she had not spoken. "I thought she was making it up, just to give me a hard time. I looked it up. Turns out she was wrong. Stalin starved 5 million to death. She was right about what she experienced as a child, the horrors her family endured. She was simply wrong about me. She somehow thought I had become a Communist, because of my protests. I was her son, damn it, not the enemy."

"I am sorry."

"I couldn't reach her. Neither could Rach. I've thought long and hard about those days, especially this week. What Rachel and I experienced was gentle compared to what so many other kids endured. We knew of kids who were abused, physically and sexually, neglected by parents who battled addiction or worse. We knew kids who largely raised themselves or were trained in the family business of breaking the law. I saw guys who drifted into one of the gangs because they saw no other options. The gang was their family. Am I making sense?"

"Absolutely." In truth, Connie had no idea what gang life was like but forced herself to be quiet as Josh continued his monologue.

"Okay, Big Jim decked me a few times, but I always knew why. Usually there was no lasting damage, other than a broken nose and a few stitches. Sometimes I even agreed that I deserved the whack. But other kids were randomly beaten for no reason. It was routine stuff in working-class Irish households back then. Getting beaten toughened you for life as it was. That was the prevailing theory then. Now, it would be a major story deserving a Presidential Commission and a miniseries. In my day, it was business as usual. Yet, most of these kids grew up to be normal, well, relatively speaking. They got married, had kids, got jobs, paid taxes, and thought little about the meaning of their existence. They just did the stuff of living. So why did Rachel and I make it so difficult? Why have we struggled so? I don't have much of an answer, just a guess."

"Which is?" She asked gently now, softening to this new person in front of her.

Another pause. "Maybe it's more like a theory."

"Josh, I'm just not sure this is an intellectual exercise."

"Let me try. It just might be that Rachel and I are burdened with these enlarged moral compasses, like enlarged hearts if you will. We've been over this several times this past week. *We care too much.* I think it is called a conscience, a soul. Do you have any idea how easy it is to go through life without being burdened with one of those damn things? You just happily live out your years. Thing is, if you care that much, it is way too easy to feel pain, real pain."

Connie looked at him softly. "I think I see … finally."

"You can't live with that pain all the time, with so much failure. You push it away, people away, thinking that might help. You fill in the time between birth and death with stuff … work and eating and crapping and enduring endless trivial events and then fucking when you get a chance. And work, that really fills up the hours. Rachel became the dedicated doc, I the popular teacher and gadabout policy wonk solving everyone's social problems. Those are good things but what is the meaning of all that? Who cares? Why care if you don't include others on your journey? Without others you become one link in an endless series of relatively meaningless lives. You do little more than follow the script someone hands you, find your mark on the stage, and read all your lines. That's it. End of story."

"My dear, that sounds way too cynical coming from you. You touched a lot of people, more than you will ever realize."

He took one more deep breath. "I suppose. For sure, Rachel and I tried to do good. I think she was much better at redirecting her inquisitiveness into science and her caring into a healing profession. I got stuck in the labyrinth of the primeval, metaphysical forest and policy and political theory. We both tried to make sense of stuff, impose some moral certitude on a senseless world. Neither of us could just accept things. I know I always had to think about stuff, figure everything out for myself."

"Oh my," Connie said, with a smile that reached through to Josh, "that sounds exactly how I would see you as a kid." He now recognized that she was touching him, that her eyes again were softer, more inviting.

He smiled back at her. "I always was a softie, from as early as I could recall. I remember walking down the tough streets of my childhood Irish ghetto thinking that we had so much in this country. Why weren't we giving our excess food stuff away to places that needed it, those godforsaken countries where children were starving to death every day? Why were we not turning over heaven and earth to help? I kept thinking that we should be working toward one government for the entire planet. All these separate nations were silly. Anything that kept people apart was ridiculous and counterproductive."

"Big thoughts for such a small boy."

"No shit! This was when I was like ten or twelve years old and living among an Irish tribe that thought the entire civilized world was contained within the borders of South Boston. Even then, I was appalled by the way we treated blacks … another cause not particularly favored among my Irish tribe. Wow, I can still remember arguing that the Supreme Court had a right to end school segregation. Not long after, South Boston blew up when they tried to bus kids for the sake of school integration. Even Whitey Bulger got involved in that to save his Irish tribe, in his mind at least. Do you know how many other kids in the hood thought such things? None, zero, nada, zip. Those kinds of feelings are a curse, a terrible disease that needs to be cut out like a fetid tumor. Perhaps if I had, I could have been … normal."

"Josh, listen to me. That is just stupid. Can't you see? That enlarged moral compass you keep talking about is why I love you." She stopped. It had just come out, just as it had the previous night when she was so angry. Now she had done it again, used the word never spoken between them. She had not meant to confess it again so easily. But it was out there, and she wasn't even angry anymore.

"You do?" Josh stammered.

"Damn it to hell! I do. Do you really think I would have exploded last night if I didn't love you so? I would have just kicked your ass to the curb. Guess I'm not as smart as people say. Damn it, Jeremiah, Joshua Connelly, you have gotten into my head. Now that's a horrific curse if you want to talk about such things."

In silence, they started walking again through a wooded section near the west end of the campus. Connie put her arm through his without ceremony. He did not react outwardly but felt a warmth throughout his body as she moved against him, her breast pushing against his side. He was surprised by his reaction, a kind of peace that seldom accompanied any sign of affection from a woman. In the past, it would have elicited anxiety, suspicion.

Josh went to his sure thing, his wit. "Sure wish I had a buck for each girl that had thrown themselves at me because of my compassionate soul."

"And what would you have now? A buck?"

Josh laughed. "Little you know. I have done research on this topic. After years of intensive field work, I've found that deeply felt ideals and a five-million-dollar bank account will draw women like flies."

"I want to warn you, old man, that your sister has given me detailed instruction on where to best whack you in the stomach." Then Connie stopped walking. "Wait, you have five-million bucks?"

"That's for me to know and you to find out." Josh cracked a huge smile. "You know, when we were young, when I wasn't playing ball or the piano or hanging around my dad's bar listening to stories of *'the troubles,'* in Ulster, I would watch television with Rach. She would lie next to me with her head on my thigh. I would stroke her hair. We watched *Gunsmoke* and the *Cisco Kid* and the *Lone Ranger*, all those westerns. My favorite show was *Rocky and Bullwinkle,* a cartoon collage of characters but with sophisticated humor. Her favorite show was *You Are There*, where Walter Cronkite would narrate some great moment in history. We would discuss the historical moment we had just watched. I could tell that she was precocious, that she was going to be a star. I felt such affection for her. I can stand a lot of pain but running out on Rachel was the hardest thing I ever did in life, even harder than losing Eleni. It was so hard. I remember sitting in a small room in Toronto, drinking cheap wine and crying into the night. I cried for a lot of reasons but for none more than my sister. She meant so much to me, she means so much."

"And she knows this how?"

"I think. Doesn't she?" Suddenly, Josh was concerned. He was sure he had expressed his feelings to her, but the more he searched his memory, the less certain that he was. Why did he assume that people knew what was inside him? How would they know? There was no running story line across his forehead. It was just that expressing himself was not the easiest of tasks. "I do hide, don't I, behind that damned wit? You know, the wit is real. It just comes out naturally, unconsciously."

"I was afraid of that." Connie leaned in closer as they walked. "I mean, I looked all over for the off switch. Could never find the damn thing."

"Yes, it is a blessing and a curse," Josh noted, "but what it enabled me to do is avoid saying what I feel. I guess I did keep people at arm's length, make them feel that I was happy and content even when I was dying inside. Those ancient Greek and Roman actors would run around the stage wearing masks which revealed the emotional content of their character. I ran around life's stage wearing a comedy mask. Perhaps that's the special burden of funny people, to turn sadness and worry and pain into humor. Laughter hides a lot. Still, I must say it is a special gift from the Gods that I would never give up. I could always leave them laughing."

"Yes, that you did," Connie agreed, "and there surely are worse things in life."

They reached the far western end of the campus, where Marine Drive separates the university from the bordering trees and beaches. After they crossed, they stopped on the compact sand of Wreck Beach. The sun was now in the final stage of that day's existence. The rays found a way through puffy clouds in the west before reaching darker ones on the distant eastern horizon. They stood silently for a few moments watching the display as if they had never seen it before.

"You're full of shit, you know," Connie finally broke the silence.

"A well-established fact, I concur. But you bring it up now because …"

Connie now spoke with warmth. "Because I watched you and your friends closely and I talked with them on my own. Have you figured out why your friends were able to put things behind them? Of course not. Well, you must remember Jacob Marley, from Dicken's Christmas Story? Jacob was destined to carry this ponderous chain around for eternity for the sins he committed during life. To me, and the others, you are Jacob. You are dragging all this guilt and failure with you. Think about your college friends for a moment. They are not carrying all this crap around with them. In fact, they seem pretty damn happy."

"They are not Irish," Josh tried weakly.

"They are Jewish, for crying out loud, just as bad in that guilt thing. Okay, Peter isn't, and I confess not to know what neuroses are found among Italians. In any case, kiddo, it is finally time to put that Irish crap behind you. Hear me! You don't hear me blaming stuff on my Chinese heritage."

"Hmmm, I thought that Chinese stuff was what made you so inscrutable." Josh kissed her on the forehead. He was relieved when she did not pound him somewhere in the stomach area. Feeling spared, he went on. "In truth, I'm not sorry about the guilt I felt. Had I not felt such things, it would have been a clear sign that I was a sociopath. Everything comes back to the golden rule, the Aristotelian sense of proportion and moderation. Some guilt demonstrates that you are a real human, but too much paralyzes you. The trick here, as in everything, is finding the right balance. I can get there now. I'm sure of that. I will thank Peter for the rest of my life. He probably kept me out of jail and brought my college friends back to me. It is funny, thinking back doesn't hurt anymore, not much at least. I still remember being in so many sessions where we were trying to figure out what we would do about the war we all hated. Our emotions followed along the escalation of the war. Everything back then took on an apocalyptic aura. That age-old question … what would we tell our grandchildren about what we did to stop the insanity?"

Connie erupted in a short, cynical chuckle. "Turns out that the current generation cannot even remember that war. It is little more than a paragraph in their high school history book."

"If that much." Of course, I avoided any possible prospect of explaining myself to my own children by getting a vasectomy soon after getting to Toronto. No offspring for me. If I could not prevent the insanity, at least I could avoid exposing more victims to it in the future."

"Oh my," Connie murmured, "you were hurting big time. You would have been a great dad."

He looked dubiously at her. "I recall this night when Morris asked us all to make a commitment, the choice of a lifetime. Now, I can see that it meant little. We were just kids. We were making no legal commitment. But we felt as if it were a moral statement we were making. It seemed so real to us. As I have reflected many times, those days were so compelling. Every moment seemed fresh and unique. Every idea was new and exciting. Every relationship was monumental. You can never relive those early experiences, they are unique. Little did we know that all else in our futures would be pale reflections of those moments that had come before."

"I had to make a choice once, as a child ... between science and music. I couldn't do both ... not as well as I needed to."

"Really? Tell me more."

"Not now, though." Connie was sorry she mentioned it. "I will tell you all about it, some other time. I will say one thing, it is still with me today, after all these years. You know, did I choose the right path? But for now, tell me about yours. I now know we will have time for me to bore you with my tale of woe."

Josh thought about what she said, they would have time. He smiled and continued. "When I had to make my choice to follow Mo that night, I knew I should not do it. That was not me. I abhorred violence and saw us headed there. I saw Peter get up and leave. He was always the sensible one. I stayed, but not out of total conviction. I did it from a sense of loyalty to those I loved so dearly. I did not know myself well enough. Hell, maybe I thought I was being my dad in that moment, fighting the just cause. In truth, I was not authentic to myself. You must believe in what you are doing, not just who you are doing it with."

Connie poked him gently on the arm. "For Christ's sake, you were what ... 20? Brains are not fully developed yet. How would you know your authentic self? Do you know what that tells me? You consider things beyond yourself. There can be no doubt of that, none whatsoever. And that, my dear, is a good thing."

"I suppose," he agreed distractedly.

"But Eleni, what about her? She has always been the big question in my head. She still is. Let me be clear about this if I can," Connie spoke in a low, yet careful voice. "From what I can figure it out, she was the one for you. Like you said, most of us have some early crush that we never forget. But this is different. You appeared to have something missing inside yourself after you lost her. It really was like someone excised that part of your brain that controlled feelings." She paused. "This is important, Josh. It surely is important for you and, I suppose, for me. Can you restart that part of you?"

"Is that your real question?" He asked.

"Shit, you are clever. I suppose not. I'm wondering," Connie paused to consider her next words, "if you can love me like you loved her. Is your quota of love spent, gone?"

"I understand." But then Josh said nothing. He looked out over the water. He loved this place, the serenity that water always afforded. It brought him peace and, when needed, focus. "Connie, I won't lie. Losing Eleni is something I'll always regret, never get over entirely. This sounds like nonsense coming from a guy who could never commit. I had thought for a long time that maybe we all have just one great love in our lives. I know, most guys go from pillow to post so that sounds ridiculous. But I only know what I felt. It was as if this were that one connection that could never be replaced. Why did I prefer my professional escorts, why did I jump into the fake marriage with Usha? Why did I never suggest a real marriage to you? I thought I could never fill in that hole where my heart had been. I patched all the wounds over with the anaesthetic of humor, the narcotic of work, and a few diversions."

She stepped back a half step. "Josh, I—"

"Connie, let me finish, please. Your question after all." He looked at her with an intensity she had not seen before. "Remember when we first got together. It was so casual and relaxed. We almost fell into living together. It was like, gee, this is a nice segue from Usha. Please forgive me for this, but one attraction you had for me was that you were not a threat. I didn't think you cared for me all that much. You hid yourself from me, that inscrutable Asian thing. Yes, I know now that was not true. Then, I saw myself as a convenient person to share some things with, what the kids would call a friend with benefits. How great for a guy like me, the man who is deathly afraid of a real relationship, the guy who had never seen a mutually beneficial loving relationship in his own world, a man whose one loving connection was the source of unending pain."

"But those e-mails, so much love. A man incapable of love could never have written those words."

"And an equal amount of pain. I was never sure I wanted to feel anything again. You know, a child that burns his hand on a hot stove doesn't touch the stove again, unless that child is an idiot like I was. Thing is, I never wanted to feel that kind of pain again. But then, I found that my simple and convenient arrangement with you was not working out."

"Not working? I remember walking away from you."

"Not working because you were too attractive to me. We laughed too much, could talk about so many things. You weren't like those narrow, hard scientists I would meet in university committee meetings. One night, I remember waking up feeling uncomfortable. I got up and started pacing. Then I watched you for a long time. It was coming back, that caring. You were becoming Leni for me. I wasn't sure I could handle that."

"Josh, did you leave those emails on your screen for me to find."

He sighed. "I'm not positive but I think so. In the back of my mind, it hit me that you might walk away if you saw them. I would not have to push you away: You would do the walking. Then I could wallow in another rejection."

"Your plan worked."

"Yeah, some plan. Thing is, I didn't know you had just come across Leni's e-mails. You never said anything. I had no idea you were pulling away from me until the fat lady had already sung. When I finally noticed, I wasn't sure how I felt. As you began to disengage from me, Leni revealed she had cancer. Her decline started and then she died. For a while, I thought that it was all for the best. You rejected me by walking away and she by dying. Isn't being alone what I wanted?"

"Was it," she asked quietly?

"Of course it wasn't. You have no idea how lonely I was after all that. It was like my early days in Toronto all over again. My jokes kept coming though. They never stopped."

"Why didn't you come to me, tell me all this, you dolt?"

"I couldn't, no way." Josh protested. "If I had, I would have had to admit the truth."

"Truth?" she asked. "What truth?"

"That I had fallen in love with you." There was no smile on his face.

"Oh," is all she managed.

"Now, it strikes me that Leni came back into my life for a reason, to remind me how to love. She would leave the stage all too soon, but I would be left with an understanding about myself. I would be reminded of what I was looking for in another human being. It is you ... the smarts and sensitivity and wit and caring. I had found it all again. Simple in the end once you get it. When you walked away, I knew I was in love with you. My sin was not chaining you to the house."

She put her head on his chest. "Josh, you have to understand. I also need to trust. You know I don't need a man in any traditional sense. But yes, the thought of having someone in my life, an anchor, a center if you will, a ... what is the word I am looking for?"

"The word doesn't matter. We know what it is." Josh whispered. "That's what I will always be grateful to Leni for. She showed me I was capable of love, but I was not man enough to grab on to it with her. She came back into my life, just before passing, to whack me upside the head. *Don't miss it this time around, you nimrod.*"

"You almost did, you know?" She kissed him on the cheek. "You came within a whisker of fucking it up a second time."

"Connie, you know the old saying about 'we get old too fast and wise too slow' or something like that? Well, that's me. This week woke me up. I can see what a moron I've been."

"No, Josh, you're being way too kind to yourself. Besides, it is my job to make you feel like a shit, you hopeless idiot." She had taken one of his favorite lines and turned it on him. "I'm really looking forward to that."

Josh laughed out loud. "There it is. That is exactly why I love you. You know me as few others do."

"And yet," she responded, "I'm not running like hell in the opposite direction. Go figure!"

Everything stopped for a moment as each looked at the other. Josh repeated his words slowly: "That's why I love you, Connie." He took a deep breath. "Wow, I can say the word without breaking out in hives."

Connie stood still for what seemed an eternity. Finally, she moved against him and pulled him close. She had missed him, his body. She realized she was rubbing up against him ever so slightly. "You are on probation, you know."

"Okay, is it like a civil service thing, six months and then I am off for life?"

"No, the probationary period is indefinite. But I'm sure you will screw things up in six days or less. In the family betting pool, Rachel has six hours before you screw up. And about Eleni. I had to ask. I understand … not totally, but well enough. I'm glad you had her in your life. Without her, I would not believe you would be capable of love. You would not have even made it to probationary status."

They took one last look at the western sky. The horizon was shading toward pink. Then they turned for home. "You do realize that you still will be subject to the withering Connelly wit?"

"I do," Connie said solemnly. "We Chinese have suffered much. I can take it."

"Good, because you cannot take out what God has put in." Then Josh assumed a serious tone. "Thanks for giving me another chance."

Connie put her head on his shoulder. "I know. I could feel your appreciation rubbing up against me. It was hard to miss, pun intended. And while I admit that the very thought of you inside me makes me, how shall I put it, moist with anticipation, we were never going to do it on the beach."

"Damn," Josh murmured. "That is a kinky thought, two old farts going at it on Wreck Beach as the sun sets."

"No way, Romeo. First, it would have been one old fart and one totally foolish but younger and still ravishing woman. Second, all I would need is for a colleague to drive by and see me screwing my brains out on a public beach. Think that would look good for the next chair of my department?"

"Really, the next department chair? What sins did you commit to warrant that sentence to hell?"

"Falling in love with a putz," Connie responded.

The big Irish smile was back on Josh's face. "Do I know this loser?"

They continued walking hand in hand as they traded insults. Any random person passing would assume this was a long-married couple enjoying a lovely evening.

———

They found Rachel and Usha nibbling on some food when they got back.

"Good to see you back. We were just about to give Morris your scent and use him to track you down," Usha said.

"My bet," declared Rachel, "was that Connie was burying your body somewhere along the shoreline."

"And you wanted to rush out and save me?" Josh asked, knowing the answer.

"Hell no, I wanted to help her," his sister laughed.

Rachel then took Connie's hand. "Come and help me in the kitchen. We're putting something together."

Off the two went. Josh was certain that Rachel would be grilling her on what had happened. Wow, he thought. She does care about him. No matter how badly he behaves, people care. Then Usha walked over to Josh and kissed him on the cheek. "I take it all is okay with Connie."

"Yes, but I'm on probation. I guess there really is no accounting for taste."

Usha smiled; she was exceptionally fetching when she smiled. "I'm so happy, and Rachel will be thrilled."

"I have often thought about this."

"About what?" Usha asked.

"Why do women want to punish men by getting them into relationships?"

Usha started to chide him and saw his crooked Irish smile. She had never fully embraced his humor, mostly deadpanned and dry. Connie was perfect for him, she got him. Usha then went to the issue foremost on her mind. "You are okay with Rachel and me ... with us as a couple. We haven't talked, and I don't want anything under the surface."

"Well, there is one thing that bothers me." Josh looked profoundly serious.

"What?" Usha was concerned.

Josh looked at her with a pained expression. "You have heard about all the prior women with whom she has had relationships." Josh was delighted when Usha looked confused. "I mean, you won't have to worry about running into them since they are all deceased. Oh, and I'm sure those rumors about her being a black widow serial killer are exaggerated. I am certain of that. After all, nothing has been proved in a court of law, and you are innocent until adjudicated guilty. Right?"

Suddenly, Josh cried out as Usha's wacked him on the head. "You are a shit, … Jeremiah Joshua Connelly. After all this time, I still fall for your crap."

"Rachel," he called out while holding his head, "your girlfriend is hitting me."

"Good," came back from the kitchen. It sounded like two voices.

"Leave these two alone for a few minutes and see what happens. They start fighting." Rachel and Connie came into the room with more food.

"Rachel, are you giving lessons to all women how to assault me for maximum pain? Wow, that still hurts."

"Obviously, my lesson plan needs upgrading. You're still vertical and taking nourishment."

"The jury is still out on the second part of that." Josh tried to chuckle. "Morris, get over here and try this food they are giving me. I want to see if you flop in five minutes."

"Don't worry Morris. The poison only works on human males," Rachel jested.

They sat down around the dining room table. Normally, it would have been piled with unread mail, paper, reports, and other reading material on Josh's must-read list. Now it was being used for its intended purpose. *Yes,* Josh thought, *this is the price one pays for having women in his life.* Now, he will probably have to throw dirty clothes in a hamper and not on the floor. And damn, he would have to forego his sniff test to see if an article of clothing were still wearable. But he was smiling as he had such thoughts.

Rachel mused with a thoughtful demeaner. "Amazing. Several days ago, I landed late at night and was met by the brother I had not really known for decades … a funny but remote and distant guy. I spent the first couple of days here communicating with Madison and wondering how they were going to get along without me. And what happens? First, my useless brother turns out to be someone whom I find tolerable, the very same guy I remembered when I was a kid."

"I didn't know you had another brother. When are you going to introduce me to this nice sibling?" Josh inserted.

"More to the point," Rachel wrestled control of the conversation back, "and much to my chagrin and shock, I discovered that the medical world could survive without me. Patients survived, there was no outbreak of bubonic plague. All these years, I was afraid to take real vacations, except for professional responsibilities. My big excursions were long weekends in Chicago or New York. I'm beginning to think my colleagues are happy I'm gone for a while. I'm not pestering them like a mother hen. Really, how inconsiderate of the world not to appreciate a control freak like me."

"Welcome to the world of the irrelevant." Josh raised a wineglass.

"To the irrelevant," they all toasted, laughing amid the clinking glasses.

"The real point is this, Rach. Are you happy?" Josh asked. She looked down at the food for a long time, saying nothing. "Rach, are you okay?" he asked.

When she looked up, her eyes were moist. "I've not been this content since those days watching that Walter Cronkite show asking you to explain the background of whatever historical event we were watching. Lying next to you, hearing your commanding voice, the world made sense. You and Walter seemed like the voices of authority. Of course, back then I didn't know you were making it all up." She chuckled but her voice remained thick with emotion. "That first morning, when I caught you sneaking out to walk Morris, I feared this would be like all the other visits. We would go through the motions and that would be it. I would get on the plane again and fly back to Madison. We would not have talked, not really. Everything would be the same, this polite but distant relationship. Now, our worlds are turned around. What happened? It was all so fast."

Josh looked pensive. No quip was coming. "I've been thinking about something. It is little more than a metaphor for a critical aspect of life. Okay, I slept through botany in college, but I can remember pictures of tendrils. It seems that they were the thin filaments that flowed out from vines as they struggled to find a direction or even survive. If the vine didn't have these things, these tendrils, or there was nothing for these lifelines to grasp, I presume the vine would fall then wither and die. The tendril was as critical as the vine itself. It gave direction, even hope, to life."

"I remember you asking me about that the first morning … I thought maybe you were finally losing it," Rachel said.

"It probably seemed so. But no! I was thinking of you at the time, even before you ran to catch me. I was remembering my days in Toronto when I first came up here, escaping from all that angst and conflict that had overwhelmed me in those initial months on the run. In addition to the guilt, there was loneliness. I was so lost, no direction, no future I thought. Oh, there were helpful folk for American émigré kids escaping the war, but they could not substitute for family and friends. One day, it was cold and rainy. I was just about broke by now, and just drifting. I had no plan about how to move forward even if I knew where I was headed. In short, I had hit bottom. I got in this bathtub with a knife. I remember thinking that it would be simple. You slice the wrists and let the blood flow out. It wasn't supposed to hurt that much, at least that is what I had read. And surely that pain would not match what I faced every day."

"I never knew" Rachel managed.

"But obviously you didn't do it," the comment came from Connie.

"No, I didn't. I had made a mistake that day. Peter had sent me some letters. You were desperate, Rach, and had given him a letter for me. I got it, but I couldn't open it at first; I had been too afraid of what it would say. I was certain your words finally would nail me to my cross. I had the water ready, the knife in hand. Then I thought, it will all be over very soon so I can take whatever is in the note.

"You read my note?"

Josh let out a soft sob as he nodded yes. "In that moment I knew I could not do it. Your words wrapped themselves around my heart.

I just sat in the water crying. Rach, you were my tendril. You never knew, but you stopped my downward spiral. When I could not sink any lower, I clung to your memory. That proved to be enough."

"Oh my god," that was all Rachel could get out.

"You saved my life that day. I wanted to tell you that first morning. That was why I brought up the tendril thing. Then I couldn't. I suppose I wasn't quite ready to talk about things. I was not sure I would ever be ready. Rach, I owe you everything. Today, for the first time in almost a half a century, I have a family. I have woman I adore, a sister I love dearly, a niece who is like a daughter, and even a daughter in law. I can call Meena that, can't I."

"Sure," Rachel raised her glass and the others followed, "to family."

"Funny," Josh mused, "you think back over your life, any life, and see all these points where choices might have gone one way or another. What if I hadn't put myself back in that football game where I hurt that kid, it was such a spur of the moment choice. When I agonized about coming north, I flipped a coin. Think about that, a life-changing decision based on a coin flip. Even coming to Vancouver, I liked the view from the hotel I picked at random and from an upscale room they gave me because it was the offseason. Hell, I married Usha because she promised me Indian curries."

"That was all, just the curries." she laughed.

"Pretty much," he responded. "So many choices made so…casually."

"Perhaps," Rachel said quietly, "but I think, my dear brother, you would have become the same person you were meant to be, no matter which roads in life were taken. In the end, it may not be the choices that count, but what each of us brings on the journey, what one makes of the path they have stumbled upon. A wise man once told me that you cannot take out what God has put in you."

"Hey, I know that wise man." Josh chuckled.

"Yeah, you do." Rachel reached out to take her brother's hand. "And finding love with him again has just been so … brilliant."

They pondered Rachel's thought, continuing to sip wine while they talked and shared long into the night.

EPILOGUE

It was a late August day at the University of Wisconsin in Madison. Early morning joggers could start at Memorial Union where generations of students had consumed beer, flirted, saved the world from itself, and even worried about their courses, though probably not too often on that final item. The terrace on the Union, arrayed with distinctive brightly colored chairs, looked out over Lake Mendota, the largest of the five lakes that made Madison special. These joggers could then amble along the lake path past the limnology lab, the social science building up on the hill, Elizabeth Waters Hall, and various other campus buildings with the lake hugging them on their right. Most mornings, even before dawn, the University crew would be out practicing, the coaches barking instructions as the long, sleek sculls slithered through the water with the morning sun peering over the eastern shore.

Eventually, our joggers would reach the entrance to Picnic Point, that fabled peninsula that one national magazine had identified as one of the top 25 romantic spots in the world, though its inclusion on such a prestigious list remains a bit of a mystery. The journey from the entrance to the end of the point was approaching a mile. The view to the right could be captivating, particularly at night when the capital city's isthmus was twinkling with lights dominated by a Capitol dome bathed in an aura of white marble. To the left across the waters were the gentle rolling hills and farmlands to the north of the city, the beauty of which resulted from the glacial movements of many thousands of years ago. Mountains of ice and snow pushed debris aside as it expanded south during a recent ice-age and left deep lakes and hillocks in its later retreat once again to the north. More recently, in the 1830s, Illinois militia chased Chief Blackhawk and his beleaguered band of fighters along these very shores west to the Mississippi River where they would meet a violent end despite several attempts at surrender. Effigy mounds in the shape of birds and bears yet dot the area as silent reminders of a lost past.

Rachel had convinced them that this would be an excellent place to have their ceremony. Events had gotten away from them after they all departed from Vancouver. It all started about two weeks after his retirement when Josh interrupted Connie as she intently focused on her computer screen. Many of her belongings were still sequestered in boxes waiting to be unpacked as she relocated to his place once again.

"We have to talk," Josh said.

"Uh-oh." Connie looked up. "Kicking me out already. Well, at least most of my stuff is ready to go."

"Don't you wish. Nope, I want off probation."

"You really think you have earned it?" She looked cross.

"Hey, I've been good for two weeks now, virtually an eternity for me."

"Well …," she demurred, "the jury is still out on that one."

"Marry me," he suddenly said.

"Stop kidding around, I have work to do." She looked back to her screen.

Josh dropped to his knee. "Corinthia Chen, will you marry me?"

"Where is the ring?" she asked suspiciously.

"Okay, I didn't think of everything, but I am serious."

"Really?" Her tone was changing. This was not his usual banter.

"Connie, I have never been more serious about anything in my life."

"Oh, I suppose I could do worse," she replied, "though that's really hard to imagine." A week later, they were married in a small civil ceremony.

———

Cate and Meena spent the weeks following their Vancouver visit furiously trying to get their two war orphans out of harm's way. Cate had taken a leave from her work. Fortunately, they had the kinds of contacts that could cut through the endless bureaucracy. Cate used the State Department and Meena the Jordanian royal family. At some point, they legalized their relationship, believing that might speed things along though they were not sure how. They were married in a civil ceremony in Toronto, where they had been working with Usha on the international adoption issues. Josh flew in for the ceremony, which pleased Cate no end, and Rachel came in from Madison. As they all celebrated later that day, Josh casually asked his sister why she and Usha were still waiting. Rachel looked at him for a long time before saying anything. "You know, some things take time."

"No they don't, Rach. Even an idiot like me can tell when two people are in love."

"Usha," she called out. "My idiot brother has this idea that you and I should get married."

"Sounds good to me," came the response from the next room. "Your sibling is not nearly as dumb as he looks."

Josh laughed, thinking he was the object of their humor. But Usha joined Rachel, and they began making plans. "Holy shit," he murmured, "now that was casual."

"Don't let this go to your head." Rachel smiled. "We've already been talking about this."

"Wait, I have an idea," Rachel exclaimed enthusiastically. "Let's all get together," she proposed, "everyone who had been in Vancouver. Usha and I can tie the knot, and the others can redo their vows. We should have this very public commitment. That way, everyone can participate." With that, a plan was set in motion. Peter, Morris, Carla, Josh, and Connie all flew into Madison. The day before the ceremony, Peter, Morris, Carla, and Josh took a rental car to Dubuque, Iowa, where they visited a nearby monastery. It was about a two-hour journey through bucolic countryside where the famous Wisconsin cheeses were made.

At the monastery, they met with Bob, who now was known by a religious name that meant nothing to his visitors. He was still Bob. Josh hardly recognized him at first. His head was shaved, and he had the aesthetic look of someone who daily focused on transcendental matters. He seemed to float over the ground rather than walk on it, perhaps a skill they perfect as they move about the abbey without making a sound. As soon as Bob began to talk, however, Josh recognized his old friend with whom he had shared so much of his childhood tribe and faith. His calm words were soothing yet insightful. There were no unthinking platitudes. This was a man Josh could respect, that he did respect.

After a group discussion, Josh steered Bob off while the others looked over wine and cheese locally made available for sale in the visitor's room. They walked to a quiet grove of trees where Josh could envision the monks communicating with their God in peace. Earlier, they had been permitted to listen as the monks sang Gregorian chant as part of their daily ritual. The beauty of the sound reflected by perfect acoustics was soothing, tranquil. Josh understood what had drawn his old friend to this place and life.

"Bob, tell me. What was Jimmie like at the end? You were closest to him."

"If I had been that close at the end, I would not be here today." Bob looked at him kindly. "It sounds to me as if you're looking for a bit more guilt, the Catholic stock in trade I fear."

"Only if you're Irish," Josh responded.

"The truth? He was hurt by your leaving, no question. But he still felt very connected to the group. Of all of us, he needed that connection, that sense of belonging. Alienation and loneliness are powerful motivators. Please don't blame yourself for what happened. He never stopped loving you. And if anyone is to blame for his death, it is me. I was supposed to be with him that day. He should not have been handling the explosives alone."

"I cannot help but think I would have been able to talk him out of this craziness that killed him."

"No, you probably would have joined him in eternity. Our moral vision was correct, it was our actions that were impetuous." Bob grabbed Josh by the shoulders. "You all think I am here out of guilt, that I'm running away from the past. That's not true, at least not true any longer. Back then I was searching for a larger cause. We all were. It is what I've found here, in my own way. Between you and me, I don't buy all the personal God stuff. But the search for enlightenment, nirvana, truth, meaning remain vital to me. At night, I look at the vast sky and think about quasars and pulsars and the possibility of infinite universes. Who cannot be moved and humbled by such mystery? Pascal was. By the way, Pierre Teilhard de Chardin remains my favorite thinker. Remember how we used to discuss his works?"

"I have never forgotten. You really can find meaning here?" Josh asked.

"My boy," Bob said with a smile, "you can find it anywhere. Remember, we used to make fun of kids who said they needed time off from school to find themselves. Hey, for ten bucks, we would joke, we could tell them exactly where they were. But we were too flip, I fear. I am convinced each of us has a place, a center, where they need to be. You must be quiet and listen, you will know when you feel it. And when you do discover it, you will have that peace you seek."

As they drove from Dubuque to Madison, the four spent much time discussing how delighted they were in the visit and in their reconnection. Suddenly, Peter exclaimed, "Oh, I almost forgot. I tried Helen again and did get a response. She gives everyone her love and e-mailed a pic. It is her with three grandchildren. I believe it was taken at one of the Disney parks. Very matronly, I just know she is the president of the local Republican club."

Josh admonished him. "Peter, don't be cruel."

"I'm not kidding. In 2008, she sent me campaign stuff for McCain and that Republican candidate for governor in Pennsylvania, Tom Corbett."

As he handed his phone around, Morris exclaimed, "Oooh, she looks a bit chunky these days."

"I think the word you're looking for is fat," Carla responded.

Everyone laughed. They settled into a banter about how they remembered one another. It might have been a discussion of their senior proms. Of course, they soon were debating vigorously a comment that Josh made about knowing that the concept of global Communism would never trump provincial nationalism in the hearts of men and women. That debate was soon replaced by whether they had predicted the collapse of the Soviet Union as a first-rate power. Josh insisted that they saw how the internal contradictions of the Soviet-planned economic system would never satisfy internal consumer demands as long as they tried to maintain a superpower presence in the world. The core of this debate was whether they were really that prescient or were merely rewriting history to accentuate their perspicacity. After considerable back-and-forth, they decided that they were, in fact, very smart and more insightful than the people in charge of the world back in their day, and perhaps even today. It was a point on which they could all agree.

Eventually, silence embraced the car as they gazed at the countryside. Each reflected on those golden moments. Those were days and memories that were priceless to each of them. They all agreed on one fact. The early bonds are the best, the most permanent. As the lush farms and picturesque barns flowed past their car, cows munching leisurely on a grassy lunch, Josh reflected with deep thanks on how fortunate he had been to discover his complete life again. And yes, he thought, they were as smart as he recalled.

By noon the next day, everyone had gathered at the end of Picnic Point. The ceremony would be officiated by the minister from the local Unitarian Universalist congregation. Their place of worship was adjacent to the west end of the campus and had been designed by

Frank Lloyd Wright himself. The U.U.s were noncreedal and thus could draw upon the Christian, Islamic, Humanist, and Buddhist traditions, the last preferred by Usha even though she had been raised as a Hindu. A cool, refreshing breeze blew off the lake. Meena chose some appropriate Islamic words of wisdom. Often, August could be sultry. But this day suggested the fresher days of autumn that lay ahead. Rachel had been right; this was the place. They could always have used the impressive U.U. church if they were rained out.

Josh was incredibly pleased that Sarah made it to the ceremony. She had a son on the faculty of the University of Minnesota and used a visit to him as an excuse to stop by for this occasion. She had aged, they all had, but again Josh was taken by how familiar she seemed to him. He immediately could see why he had gotten so close to her in college. Had choices back then been slightly different, he reflected, they might have married and spent their lives together. It would have been a good partnership but likely not a special one. Which is better, he wondered, an ordinary and predictable life, or one that demands engagement and struggle? He knew the easy response but had no final answer.

Others collected to watch this special ceremony, students and university staff and nearby residents from Shorewood Hills. These casual onlookers probably could not quite figure out what was going on. There were readings from the Bible, the Koran, thoughts of the Dalai Lama, and various secular humanists. Then each of the six participants shared their feelings on this day. There were many sentiments reflecting on the power and place of family. There were many expressions of love and commitment.

What most captured the hearts of the onlookers were two noticeably young girls, dressed in fine new dresses but clearly from a distant land since they talked in an unknown tongue when they talked at all. Mostly they clung to the legs of Cate and Meena, who had labored so hard to get them out of the squalid refugee camps where their fate was so uncertain. The last to speak was the only male in the group of six celebrants. He spoke quietly of choices and commitment, the need to hold on to what was important and finding one's center. That was where he ended, thanking all with him that day for helping him rediscover his center. Casual onlookers enjoyed the spectacle and then left. They had their own lives to complete, unaware of the full import of what they had witnessed. For them, it was just another intriguing moment in one of America's more interesting cities.

Josh mused on the transitory nature of all that we deem essential to our individual worlds. After the ceremony, he looked across the lake for a moment toward the State Capitol building, the growing city skyline, and the buildings of a world class research university. Some four-plus decades ago, Madison had been a hotbed of protest against the war in Vietnam. Riots and tear gas were routine. Even the future long-term mayor of the city, a student then, was bludgeoned by police and thrown in jail. The escalating fury reached a peak as the 60s eased into the 70s when a large car bomb blew apart the Physics building where it was rumored that research for the military was taking place. A Ph.D. student with a wife and young child was killed while working through the night. After the bombing, four young men fled to Canada, as Josh had done. They did so after a choice was made from which there was no return. Josh made his choice just before the point of no return, but that was a close-run thing in his mind. Three of them eventually were apprehended and sent to prison. The fourth, Leo Burt, disappeared and was never heard from again. What if he had not come north that snowy day back in the 1960s, what if he had stayed and continued to struggle. Would he have become another Leo Burt?

Now, Josh thought, no one remembers those days. Madison is peaceful and prosperous, often ranked among the most desirable places to live in the U.S. Was all the agony, the angst, the endless internal conflict worth it? After all, no one cared anymore. The kids going about their studies on campus only hear about Viet Nam in their history class, if at all. It is like the Civil War to most of them, a quaint artifact of long-ago times. For those who lived through it, Josh realized, it was a defining moment of their lives. They had come of age in this cauldron of bitterness and transformation. Some perished in that moment, others slowly expired in a slow, lingering aftermath, and still others spent their lives coming to terms with it all. Each made choices in the turmoil of that era, and each lived, or died, with the choices they made.

Those who happened to pass by and witnessed this ceremony on Picnic Point that day could never understand the meaning. It was not just a celebration of love; it was much more. It was a final ending of old pains and unresolved anguish. It was a day of human connection and hope. It was a moment of renewal and new beginnings. Most important of all, it was another opportunity to discover the warmth too often buried deep within every human heart.

ABOUT THE AUTHOR

THOMAS J. CORBETT is emeritus senior scientist and a long-time affiliate of the Institute for Research on Poverty at the University of Wisconsin–Madison, where he served as associate and acting director for a decade before his retirement. He received a doctorate in social welfare from the University of Wisconsin and taught various social policy courses there for many years in the School of Social Work. During his long academic and policy career, he worked with governments at all levels including a stint in Washington, DC, where he helped develop President Clinton's welfare reform legislation. He has written scores of articles and reports on poverty, social policy, and human services issues and given hundreds of talks across the nation on these topics. In addition, Dr. Corbett has consulted with numerous local, state, and federal officials on various poverty, welfare, and human services issues both in the United States and Canada. Among many other things, he has testified before Congress, worked with the Wisconsin and other state legislatures on important social issues, consulted with many local governments, and served on an expert panel for the National Academy of Sciences. His most recent fictional works include ***Palpable Passions, Ordinary Obsessions, and Felicitous Fates.*** His sole-authored works include several non-fiction books: ***A Clueless Rebel, A Wayward Academic: Reflections from the policy trenches***, and ***Confessions of an Accidental Scholar.*** Recently, he rereleased a memoir of his India Peace Corps Service in India during the 1960s under the title of ***Our Grand Adventure: The trails and triumphs of India-44.*** He has also co-authored several works and written too many book chapters and scholarly pieces to mention. His latest academic work, the 2nd edition of ***Evidence Based Policymaking*** was coauthored with Karen Bogenschneider and released by Routledge Press in early 2021. Now retired, the author resides in Madison, Wisconsin. You can find more information at www.booksbytomcorbett.com